Baby Business

KAREN TEMPLETON

MILLS & BOON

First published in Great Britain 2012
by Mills & Boon, an imprint of Harlequin (UK) Limited,
Eton House, 18-24 Paradise Road, Richmond, Surrey TW9 1SR

BABY BUSINESS © by Harlequin Enterprises II B.V./S.à.r.l 2012

Baby Steps, The Prodigal Valentine and *Pride and Pregnancy* were first published in Great Britain by Harlequin (UK) Limited.

Baby Steps © Karen Templeton Berger 2006
The Prodigal Valentine © Karen Templeton Berger 2007
Pride and Pregnancy © Karen Templeton Berger 2007

ISBN: 978 0 263 89692 3
ebook ISBN: 978 1 408 97056 0

05-0612

Printed and bound in Spain
by Blackprint CPI, Barcelona

BABY STEPS

BY
KAREN TEMPLETON

Since 1998, two-time RITA® Award winner and bestselling author **Karen Templeton** has written more than thirty books. A transplanted Easterner, she now lives in New Mexico with two hideously spoiled cats and whichever of her five sons happens to be in residence.

To Gail

For giving this couple another chance to finally get
together (and for unfailingly knowing when I most need
a word of encouragement) and to Charles for loving
this book and wanting it to be the best it could be..
How blessed can a girl get?

The baby business is booming!
And these bachelors need to wake up and see
what they really want!

Baby Business

Three terrific, fulfilling novels from
Karen Templeton

Chapter One

"**Y**ou get back here, Cass Carter!"

Dana Malone zipped across the sales floor after her rapidly retreating partner, nearly landing on her butt when a crawling baby shot out in front of her from behind a St. Bernard-sized Elmo. Half a wobble and a shuffle later, she was back on track. "What do you mean, *I* have to do it—*ouch!*"

"Watch out for the new high chair," the long-legged, denim-skirted blonde tossed back, cradling the tiny head jutting out from a Snugli strapped to her chest.

"Thanks," Dana grumbled, rubbing her hip as she snaked her way through cribs and playpens, Little Tikes' playhouses and far too many racks of gently used baby clothes. Her two partners—and their skinny little fannies—could navigate the jumbled sales floor with ease. For Dana, the space was a minefield. As was Cass's request. "Have you lost your *mind?*

I can't pick the store's new location by myself, Cass! What on earth do I know about real estate?"

"This is Albuquerque, for heaven's sake," Cass said as she slipped into the store's pea-sized office. "Not Manhattan." She shimmied past her desk, heaped with paperwork and piles of newly consigned clothes, then swiped a trio of original Cabbage Patch Kids dolls in mint condition from the rocker wedged into one corner. "How difficult can it be to choose one strip mall store-front over another? Here, take Jason for a moment, would you?"

The weight of the month-old infant—and the ache—barely had a chance to register before Cass, now settled into the rocker, reached again for the softly fussing infant. Dana allowed herself an extra second of stolen new-baby scent before relinquishing her charge, watching Cass attach baby to breast with a neutral expression. The baby now contentedly slurping away, her partner lifted amused blue green eyes to her. "C.J.'s already got several potential locations lined up. All you have to do is weed out the ones that won't work."

A trickle of perspiration made a run for it down Dana's sternum, seeking haven in her cleavage. "I'd just assumed we'd all do this together."

"I know, sweetie. But I'm pooped. And Blake's on my case as it is about coming back to work so soon. Besides, between our lease being up next month and the store about to burst at the seams—"

"What about Mercy? Why can't she do it?"

"Why can't I do what?"

The third side of the Great Expectations triangle stood in the office doorway, sports car-red fingernails sparkling against a frilly little skirt Dana wouldn't have been able to wear when she was twelve.

"Go property scouting," Dana said. "You'd be much better at it than me."

Meredes Zamora swiped a dark curl out of her face as she squeezed into the office. "I'm also much better at juggling five customers at a time. You get rattled with two."

"I do not!"

Both ladies laughed.

"Okay, so maybe I do get a little flustered."

"Honey," Mercy said, not unkindly, "you start *stuttering*."

"And dropping things," Cass added.

"And—"

"Okay, okay! I get your point!"

It was true. Even after nearly five years, even though wall-paper books and Excel spreadsheets held no terror for her, Dana still tended to lose her composure under duress. Especially about making business decisions on her own—

"He's expecting your call," Cass said.

Dana suddenly felt like a bird being eyed by a pair of hungry cats. "Who is?"

"C.J."

She sighed in tandem with the soft jangle of the bell over the front door. In a flounce of curls and a swish of that mini-skirted fanny that had, Dana was sure, never felt the pinch of a girdle, Mercy pivoted back out to the sales floor, leaving Dana with the Duchess of Determination. She decided to ignore the feeling of dread curdling in her stomach as a slow, sly grin stretched across Cass's naturally glossed mouth. "You've never seen C.J., have you?"

Curdled dread never lied. Especially when it came to Cass, who, now that her own love life was copacetic, had made fixing Dana's woeful lack in that department her personal crusade.

Wiping her palms on the front of her skirt, Dana pivoted toward the door. "Mercy probably needs me out front—"

"No, she doesn't. Sit." Cass nodded toward the pile of clothes on her desk. "Those things need to be tagged anyway."

Scowling, Dana plopped behind the desk, snatching a tiny pink jumper off the pile. "Twelve bucks?"

"Fifteen. Macy's has them new for forty." Cass shifted in her chair, making Jason's hand fly about for a moment until his tiny fingers grasped her bunched up blouse. Envy pricked at Dana's heart as Cass continued, more to the baby than to Dana, "C.J. is…mmm, how shall I put this…?" *Zing* went those eyes. "Magnificent."

So she'd heard. Dana *phh'd* at her.

"As if it would kill you to spend the afternoon with the man with the bedroom, blue eyes." Cass tugged her skirt back over her knee. "Butt's not bad, either."

Just what Dana needed in her life. Lethal eyes and taut buns. She scribbled the price on the tag, then jabbed the point of the ticket gun into the jumper, entertaining vaguely voodoo-esque thoughts. "I think that's called sexual objectification."

"Yeah. So?"

She grabbed the next item off the pile, a fuchsia jumpsuit with enormous purple flowers. "Twenty?"

"Sure. Sweetie, I nearly drooled over the guy myself when he helped me sell the house a few months ago. And don't you dare tell Blake."

Dana's head snapped up. "Excuse me? You were seven months pregnant, recently widowed—"

Never mind that Cass's second husband had been a dirtwad of the first order, but a friend has a duty to point out these things.

"—your ex-husband was hot to get back together, and you were salivating all over your Realtor?"

"Yeah, well, it was like having a close encounter with a chocolate marble cheesecake after a ten-year diet. Fortunately, since I'm not all that crazy about chocolate marble cheese-cake, the temptation passed."

*Un*fortunately, Dana had a real thing for chocolate marble cheesecake. Which Cass knew full well. As did Dana's hips.

"This wouldn't be you trying to fix me up, by any chance?"

"Perish the thought."

Dana sighed, wrote out another price tag. "You forget. I had inside information." She plopped the last garment on the "done" pile, then folded her hands in front of her on the desk. "C. J. Turner's idea of intimacy is cozying up to his cell phone on his way to one appointment, making follow-up calls from another. The man is married to his business. Period."

A moment of skeptical silence followed. "You got this from Trish, I take it?"

"Not that I know any details," Dana said with a shrug. Her much younger cousin and she had never been close, despite Trish's having lived with Dana's parents for several years. She'd worked for C. J. Turner for six months before vanishing from the face of the earth, more than a year ago. Before the alien abduction, however, she had talked quite a bit about the apparently calendar-worthy Realtor. Professionally, she'd sung his praises, which was why Dana had recommended him to Cass when she'd needed an agent's services. Personally, however, was something else again. "But I gathered the man hasn't exactly listed himself on the Marriage Exchange."

Cass gave her a pointed look from underneath feathery bangs. "So maybe he hasn't met the right woman yet."

"Boy, you are sleep-deprived."

"Well, you never know. It could happen."

"Yeah, and someday I might lose this extra thirty pounds I've been lugging around since junior high, but I'm not holdin' my breath on that one, either."

"You know, sweetie, just because Gil—"

"And you can stop right there," Dana said softly before her partner could dredge up past history. She rose, grabbing the pile of newly marked clothes to cart out front. "I've already got one mother, Cass."

"Sorry," Cass said over the baby's noisy suckling at her breast. "It's just—"

"I *am* happy," Dana said, cutting her off. "Most of the time, anyway. I've got a good life, great friends and I actually look forward to coming to work every day, which is a lot more than most people can say. But trust me, the minute I start buyin' into all the 'maybes' and 'it could happens,' I'm screwed."

Silence hovered between them for a few seconds, until, on a sigh that said far more than Dana wanted to know, Cass said, "C.J.'s card's in my Rolodex."

"Great," Dana said, thinking, *Why me, God? Why?*

"You keep staring out the door like that, your eyeballs are gonna fall right outta your head."

C.J. smiled, relishing the blast from the lobby's overzealous air conditioner through his dress shirt, fresh out of the cleaner's plastic this morning. "Haven't you got phones to answer or something, Val?"

"You hear any ringing? I don't hear any ringing, so I guess there aren't any phones to answer." The trim, fiftysomething platinum blonde waltzed from behind the granite reception desk to peer through silver-framed glasses out the double glass door at the gathering clouds. "You giving that cloud the evil eye so it'll go away, or so it'll come here?"

One hand stashed in his pants pocket, C.J. allowed a grin for both the storm outside and the Texas tempest beside him. Out over the West Mesa, lightning periodically forked in the ominous sky; in the past ten minutes, the thunder had gone from hesitant rumbling to something with a real kick to it. If it weren't for this appointment, he'd be outside, arms raised to the sky, like some crazed prehistoric man communing with the gods. Ozone had an almost sexual effect on him, truth be told. Not that he was about to let Val in on that fact.

"Ah, c'mon, Val—can't you feel the energy humming in the air?"

"Oh, Lord. Next thing I know, you're gonna tell me you're seeing auras around people's heads—"

The phone rang, piercing the almost eerie hush cloaking the small office. Already cavelike with its thick, stone-colored carpeting and matching walls, the serene gray décor was relieved only by a series of vivid seriographs, the work of a local artist whose career C.J. had been following for years. Normally the place was hopping, especially when the three other agents he'd brought on board were around. But not only were they all out, even C.J.'s cell phone had been uncharacteristically silent for the past hour or so.

Unnerving, to say the least.

"I hear you, I hear you," Val muttered, sweeping back around the desk, assuming her sweetness-and-light voice the instant she picked up the receiver. A wave of thunder tumbled across the city, accompanied by a lightning flash bright enough to make C.J. blink. Behind him, he heard a little shriek and the clatter of plastic as Val dropped the receiver into the cradle. Some twenty-odd years ago, an uncle or somebody had apparently been struck by lightning through the phone; nobody in her family had touched a telephone during an electrical storm since. Still, the quirk was a small enough price to pay for unflagging loyalty, mind-boggling efficiency and the occasional, well-deserved kick in the butt.

She was standing beside him again, her arms crossed over a sleeveless white blouse mercilessly tucked into navy pants, warily eyeing the blackening sky.

"Looks like you're about to get your wish…oh, *Lordy!*" Another crack of thunder nearly sent her into the potted cactus

by the door, just as a white VW Jetta with a few years on it
pulled into the nearly empty lot. His three o'clock, no doubt,
he thought with a tight grin.

Not that Cass Carter hadn't given it the old college try, with
her enthusiastic recital of Dana Malone's virtues. Nor could
he deny a certain idle curiosity about the person belonging to
the warm Southern drawl on the other end of the line, when
Dana herself had called to make an appointment. Still, if it
hadn't been for all the business Cass and Blake Carter had
brought to the agency over the past few months, he would
have gladly handed off this particular transaction to one of the
other agents. He rarely handled rental deals these days, for one
thing. And for another, God save him from well-intentioned
women trying to fix him up.

His last…whatever…had been well over a year ago, a
one-night stand that should have never happened. And he
shouldered the blame for the whole fiasco, for a momentary,
but monumental, lapse of good judgment that—thank
God!—hadn't turned out any worse than it had. *By the skin
of his teeth* didn't even begin to cover it. But the affair had
brought into startlingly sharp focus exactly how pointless his
standard operating procedure with women had become.

It would be disingenuous to pretend that female companionship had ever been a problem, even if C.J. hadn't taken
advantage of every opportunity that presented itself. At twenty,
he'd considered it a gift; by thirty, somewhat of an embarrassment, albeit one he could definitely live with. Long-term relationships, however, had never been on the table. Not a problem
with the career-focused women who were no more interested
in marriage and family than he was, liaisons that inevitably self-
destructed. But it was the gals for whom becoming a trophy
wife was a career goal—the ones who saw his determination

to remain single as a challenge, yes, but hardly an insurmountable one—that were beginning to get to him.

What he had here was a mondo case of bachelor burnout, a startling revelation if ever there was one. But far easier to avoid the mess to begin with than suffer through cleaning it up later—

The phone rang again; Val didn't move. "What do you suppose is taking her so long to get out of her car?" she said, her voice knifing through his thoughts.

Twenty feet away, the car door finally opened, and out swung a pair of beautifully arched feet in a pair of strappy high-heeled sandals. C.J. watched with almost academic interest as the woman attached to the feet pulled herself out of the car, the wind catching her soft, billowing white skirt, teasing the hem up to mid-thigh. Her little shriek of alarm carried clear across the parking lot.

In spite of himself, C.J. smiled: he now knew she wore garterless stockings with white lace tops.

"Val? Would you mind checking to be sure all those property printouts for Great Expectations are on my desk?"

"Since I put them there, there's no need to check. Cute little thing, isn't she?"

She was that.

Assorted debris and crispy, yellowing cottonwood leaves whirlwinded through the parking lot, whipping at long, tea-colored hair swept up into a topknot, at long bangs softly framing a round face. He could see her grimace as she tried to yank the hair out of her eyes and mouth, hang on to her shoulder bag and hold down the recalcitrant skirt all at once. Huddled against the onslaught, she made a dash for the front door, the weightless fabric of her two-piece dress outlining a pleasant assortment of curves. She hit the sidewalk the precise moment the first fat raindrops splatted to earth; C.J. pushed open the door, only to have a gust of wind shove an armful of fragrant, soft female against his chest. His arms wrapped around her. So they wouldn't fall over.

"*Oh!*"

Wide gray-green eyes met his, her skin flushed underneath that unruly mass of shiny hair, now adorned with several leaves and a Doublemint gum wrapper. Inexplicably, he thought of freshly laundered linens and gardens and cool evening breezes at the end of a hot, sultry day.

And, because some habits are simply harder to break than others, he also thought of the pleasant things one could do on freshly laundered linens with a woman who smelled like sunshine and fresh breezes and exotic flowers—

She shot backward as if stung, a full lower lip hanging slightly slack, glistening with some natural-colored lip goo that suited her fair skin to a tee.

C.J. smiled. "Dana Malone, I presume?"

"Oh!" she said a second time, then started madly plucking things out of her hair. Her hands full, she looked frantically around, as if trying to find someplace to stash the evidence before anyone noticed. Always the gracious hostess, Val brought her a small wastebasket. Dana gave a nervous little smile, wiggling her fingers for a second until the disintegrating leaves drifted into their plastic grave. "The wind…" she began as she dusted off her hands, tugged at the hem of her tunic. "A storm's comin'…you were closer than I expected…oh."

Her blush heightened, as did her Southern drawl. Mississippi, he guessed. Maybe Alabama. Someplace that brought to mind verandas and Spanish moss and ladies who still wore white gloves to church during the summer. She wiped her hand on her hip, those glistening lips twitching around a nervous smile. "I don't usually make such spectacular entrances."

"And it's not every day lovely women throw themselves into my arms."

"Oh, *brother*," Val muttered behind him as a slightly indignant, "I did not *throw* myself anywhere, I was *blown*," popped out of Dana's mouth.

Val cackled. C.J. turned his gaze on his office manager.

"Don't you have someplace to be, Val?"

"Probably," the blonde said, her reply swallowed by a flash of lightning and a window-rattling clap of thunder, as the sky let loose with torrents of rain and marble-sized hail that bounced a foot off the ground.

Dana whipped around to face outside, her palms skimming her upper arms. "Oh, my goodness," she breathed, radiating what C.J. could only describe as pure delight. "I sometimes forget how much I miss the rain!"

Don't stare at the client, don't stare at the— "So you're not from New Mexico, either?"

She shook her head, her attention fixed on the horizon. "Alabama. But I've lived here since I was fourteen." Now her eyes cut to his. "Did you say 'either'?"

"South Carolina, here. Charleston."

"Oh, I love Charleston! I haven't been back in a while, but I remember it being such a pretty city—"

Val cleared her throat. They both turned to her.

"Those printouts are right where I said they were," she said. "On your desk. For your appointment." She paused, looking from one to the other. "Today."

"Oh! Yes! I, um…" Dana lifted a hand to her hair, her face reddening again. "Do y'all have someplace I can pull myself back together?"

"Ladies' is right around the corner," Val supplied.

C.J. watched Dana glide away, her fanny twitching ever so slightly. Then he glanced over to catch Val squinting at him.

"What?"

"Nothing," she said, her backless shoes slapping against

her heels as she finally returned to her station. But when he passed her on the way back to his office to get the printouts, he thought he heard her mumble something about there being hope for him yet, and he almost laughed.

But not because he found her comment amusing in the slightest.

Dana squelched a yelp when she flipped on the light in the mushroom-colored restroom and caught a load of her reflection. Not that her heart rate could possibly go any higher than it already was after catching her first glance of C.J.

Those eyes…

That *mouth*…

Wow.

"Cass Carter," Dana muttered, sinking onto a stool in front of the mirror, "you are *so* dead." She shook her head, which sent the last few hairpins pinging off the marble countertop, her tangled hair *whooshing* to her shoulders. Then, with a small, pitiful moan, she dropped her head into her hands.

The man went *way* beyond chocolate marble cheesecake. Heck, he went way beyond any dessert yet known to man. Or woman. He was…was…

In a class all to himself, is what. Who knew people could actually look that good without airbrushing?

Well, this musing was fun and all, but it wasn't getting her fixed up. She plucked out another leaf and a crumpled straw wrapper, then dug her brush out of her purse to beat it all back into submission again. Dana stood and bent over at the waist, brushing the dust and grit out of her hair. Maybe the blood would rush back to her head, reestablish some semblance of intelligent thought processes. Grabbing the slippery mass with both hands, she twisted it into a rope, then coiled it on top of her head, standing back up so quickly she got dizzy.

So she sat down again, clamping the coiled hair on top of her head while she rummaged through her bag for the loose hairpins she was forever finding and dropping into the leather abyss.

Wow.

So much for the blood to the head theory.

After the kind of sigh she hadn't let out since Davey Luken's clumsy kiss in the seventh grade, she jammed a half-dozen pins into the base of the topknot, finger-fluffed her bangs. Yeah, well, Dana hadn't dated as much she had, as long as she had, not to gain an insight or two along the way. Because for all C. J. Turner's Southern charm and suaveness and brain-fritzing masculinity, he also positively buzzed with I-am-so-not-into-commitment vibes. Must've driven Trish right around the bend.

Only then did Dana burst out laughing as she realized what she'd felt, on her hip, a split second before she pulled out of C.J.'s arms. Heeheehee…she'd bet her entire collection of Victoria's Secret knickers the man had not been amused by *that* little reflex reaction.

Although, come to think about it, it hadn't been all that little.

Still chuckling, Dana stood again, tugging and hitching and flicking leaf pyuck off her bazooms, only to take a long, hard, honest gander at herself in the mirror. Generally speaking, she was okay with her body. For the most part, things curved in and out where they should, even if a few of the outs were a little farther "out" than average. But she'd long since learned to work with what she had, to spend a few extra bucks to have highlights put in her hair, to use makeup to emphasize her large gray green eyes, to wear clothes that made her feel feminine and good about herself. Dowdy, she didn't do.

However, that didn't mean she wasn't a realist, or that while she knew any number of full-figured women—her mother included—in very happy relationships, neither did her father look anything like C. J. Turner. Nor had any of her former boyfriends. The odds of C.J. being interested in her in that way, even as a passing fancy, were slim.

Well, that certainly takes the pressure off, doesn't it? she thought, giving those bodacious bazooms a quick, appreciative pat. If nothing else, they'd always have Paris. Or something.

She flicked off the light to the ladies' room and walked out into the hall, chin up, chest out, feeling pretty and confident and…

"Ready to go?" C.J. said from the lobby, his model-bright smile lighting up those baby blues.

…seriously out of her depth.

"Sure am," she said, smiling back, praying for all she was worth that she didn't snag her heel on the Berber carpet and land flat on her equally bodacious fanny.

"Yes, that'll be fine, I'll see you then," C.J. said into his cell phone, clapping it shut and slipping it back into his pants pocket. Not a single call between lunch and Dana's appointment; since then, the damn thing had rung every five minutes. "Sorry about that," he said. From the other side of the vacant storefront, she waved away his concern.

"At least this way," she said, making a face at the bathroom, "I don't feel guilty about takin' up so much of your time."

"It goes with the territory," he said. "Take all the time you need."

Her back to him, she lifted both hands in the air and waggled them as she click-clacked over the cement floor toward the stockroom.

Chuckling softly, C.J. decided he wasn't quite sure what to make of Dana Malone. She exuded all the charm and femininity befitting her Southern upbringing, but none of the coyness. No eyelash fluttering, no feigned helplessness. On the contrary, her incessant fiddling with the printouts, the way she worried her bottom lip as they inspected each property, told him she was genuinely nervous about the position her partners had put her in. And becoming increasingly embarrassed—and ticked off—about being unable to make a decision.

The storm had lasted barely ten minutes, but leftover clouds prowled the sky, leaving the air muggy, the temperature still uncomfortably high. And, after a half-dozen properties, Dana was grumpy and irritable. Now, at number seven, C.J. stayed near the front, his arms folded across his chest as he leaned against a support pillar, watching her. Trying to parse the odd, undefined feeling that kicked up in his gut every time she looked at him.

"It's okay, I suppose," she finally said, her words literally and figuratively ringing hollow in the vast, unfurnished room. "It's certainly big enough. And the double doors in back are great for deliveries…."

She looked to him, almost as if afraid to say it.

"But?" he patiently supplied.

Her shoulders rose with the force of her sigh. "But…there's not much parking. And you can't really see the front of the store from the street. I mean…" Annoyance streaked across her features as she fanned herself with the sheaf of printouts. "I suppose we really don't need more than five or six spaces in frunt." She crossed to the front window, her skirt swishing softly against her legs. "And this big window is not only perfect for display, it lets in lots of outside light for the play area Mercy wants to put in. Right now, the toddlers have the run of the shop, and we're so afraid one of them is going to get hurt…."

He thought he heard her voice catch, that she turned a little too quickly toward the window. "And maybe that Mexican restaurant next door would pull in enough traffic to compensate for being on a side street…." Fingers tipped in a delicate shade of rose lifted to her temple, began a circular massage.

"So we'll keep looking," C.J. said mildly as he straightened up. "Next?"

A couple of the papers fell from her hand as she tried to shuffle them; he went to retrieve them for her, but she snatched them up before he had a chance, pointlessly pushing back a strand of hair that kept falling into her eyes. "Oh, um, this one near the Foothills might not be bad. Great square footage for the price, lots of families in the area…" Then her brow creased. "But I don't know, maybe we should stick with something more centrally located…oh, *shoot!*"

"At the end of our rope, are we?"

"There's an understatement…oh! What are you doing?" she asked as C.J. took her by the elbow, ushering her through the glass door.

"Break time. For both of us."

"I don't—"

"You're making yourself nuts. Hell, you're making *me* nuts. This is only a preliminary look-see, Dana. No one expects you to sign a contract today."

"Good thing," she said, her hand shooting up to shield her eyes from the glaring late afternoon sun as they walked back to his Mercedes, "since it's all a blur." He opened the car door for her; she didn't protest. Once he'd slid in behind the wheel, she plonked her head back on the headrest and closed her eyes. "But what a weenie-brain," she said on a sigh. "I can't even eliminate the dogs."

C.J. felt a smile tug at his mouth as he pulled out into traffic. "I can assure you I've met a fair number of people who'd qualify for that title, Dana. You're definitely not one of them."

She seemed to consider this for a moment, while her

perfume sambaed around the car's interior. Something high-end and familiar. But, on her, unique. "Thank you," she said at last, her eyes still closed. "But I sure do feel like one." Her eyes blinked open. "Why are we pulling in here?"

"Because it's at least five-hundred degrees out, you're obviously fried, and this joint makes the best ice-cream sodas in town. My treat."

A pickup festooned with yapping mutts rumbled up the street behind them as a whole bunch of questions swarmed in Dana's hazy gray-green eyes.

"You hate ice-cream sodas?" he asked.

A startled laugh burst from her throat. "No! I'm just…" She shook her head, dainty, dangly earrings bobbing on tiny earlobes that had gone a decided shade of pink. "But I think I'll stick with Diet Coke."

A four-by-four roared past, spraying soggy gravel in its wake.

"It's that woman thing, isn't it?"

Her eyebrows lowered. "Excuse me?"

"Where you won't eat in front of a guy. If at all."

Her mouth twisted, her gaze slid away. "I think it's kinda obvious I'm no anorexic."

"Good to know. Because I'm here to tell you that not-eating business annoys the hell out of me. But hey—" he popped open his car door, then loosened his tie, having already given his jacket the heave-ho three properties ago "—if you really want a Diet Coke, knock yourself out."

"Actually…" She hugged her purse to her middle, as if trying to shrink. "I can't stand the stuff."

"Then it's settled." He shoved open his door, then went around to open hers. "Maybe if you just chill for a bit, you'll be able to think more clearly. Damn," he muttered as his phone rang again. He grimaced at the number—a deal he'd been trying to close for nearly a month—then at her.

"Hey—" she said, as they both got out of the car "—you've got ice-cream sodas to pay for, far be it from me to hinder your earning capacity." She glanced up at the sky. "Wonder if it's going to rain again? It sure feels steamy, doesn't it?"

It did. But somehow, he mused as he answered the phone, he doubted the humidity had anything to do with it.

Chapter Two

Dana would lay odds the diner probably hadn't changed much in twenty years. At least. Formica soda fountain and booths, nondescript beige vinyl upholstery. It was clean, though, and light, and hummed with conversation, laughter, canned mariachi music. Despite the dearth of patrons this late in the afternoon, C.J. swore the tiny restaurant would be packed by six. Dana believed it. Although Albuquerque had more than its share of tony eateries, this was one of those unassuming little holes-in-the-wall the well-off liked to think they'd "discovered," where the menu selections were few but the serving sizes generous, the food simple but excellent and the staff treated everyone like a lifelong friend.

And, if she'd been here with Mercy or Cass, she'd definitely be more relaxed. But sitting across from C.J., she was about as relaxed as Sallymae Perkins's hair on prom night.

Plus—to make matters worse—she also had to admit that none of the places they'd looked at was going to work.

"Sorry," she said, her mouth screwed up as she poked at a lump of ice cream in the bottom of her collarbone-high glass, dolefully considering the wisdom of broiled chicken breasts and salad with lemon juice for the next three nights.

"Don't apologize." C.J. certainly seemed unfazed, slouched in the booth, the top two buttons undone on an Egyptian cotton shirt only a shade lighter than his eyes. Light brown hair sprinkled with gray shuddered in the breeze from a trio of lazily *fwomping* overhead fans, as his mouth tilted up in a half smile. A gentle smile. A tired smile, she thought, although she doubted he'd admit it. Especially since she was, in all likelihood, as least partly to blame. "That's why we're here."

"But I took up half your afternoon—"

"Would you stop it?" he said gently. "That's what the first rounds are for, to get a feel for what the client really wants."

Lazy raindrops began to slash at the window by their booth, while, in the distance, thunder rumbled halfheartedly. What she really wanted, Dana thought with a stab, had nothing to do with anything C. J. Turner had to offer. Unfortunately. She speared the chunk of ice cream, popped it into her mouth.

"So why not just ask?" she asked over the whir of the milkshake mixer behind the counter, the high-pitched chatter of a bevy of kids three booths over.

"I did. And Cass gave me the basics." One arm now snaked out along the top of the booth seat; he offered her another smile. "The rest she left to you…damn."

A salesman's smile, she told herself as he answered his phone with yet another apologetic glance across the table. Impersonal. No different from those he'd bestowed on everyone they'd met that afternoon, on everyone who'd called.

Then, out of the corner of her eye, she caught the sudden

appearance of tiny, dimpled fingers hooking the edge of their table. Seconds later a mass of fudge-colored curls bobbed into view, over a set of matching, devilish eyes. Just as quickly, eyes and curls and pudgy fingers vanished, supplanted by a howl.

Dana was out of the booth and on her knees at once, hauling the sobbing baby onto her lap. About two years old, she guessed, smelling of chocolate sauce and baby shampoo.

"Oh, now, now," she soothed as she struggled to her feet, bouncing the child on her hip, "you're not hurt, are you?" Laughing, she glanced over at C.J., whose stony expression knocked the laughter right out of her.

"Enrique, you little devil!" A pretty young woman dashed back to their booth, taking the child from Dana's arms. His wails immediately softened to lurching sniffles as he wound his plump little arms around his mother's neck.

Dana crossed her own arms over the void left in the child's wake, wondering why, after all this time, she'd yet to move past this point. In any case, the emptiness, in combination with the look on C.J.'s face, knocked her off an emotional ledge she hadn't even known she was on. "He's not hurt," she assured the baby's mother, struggling to banish from-out-of-nowhere tears.

The brunette rolled her eyes, then laughed. "He never is. But I've really got to get a leash for him! I turn my back for five seconds to wipe his brother's nose, and he's gone." She jostled the child, more to comfort herself than the baby, Dana decided. "Scared me half to death. Yes, you did, you little terror! Oh, no!" She plucked a tiny hand from around her neck and inspected chocolate-coated fingers, then groaned. "I'm so sorry! He got chocolate on your pretty white dress! I'll be happy to pay for the dry cleaning!"

Dana glanced down at the smudge over her left breast, then shrugged, figuring the young woman had better things to spend her money on than a dry-cleaning bill. Once assured a squirt of Shout would make it good as new, the woman whisked her son away, and Dana slid back into her seat across from C.J., only to realize, to her mortification, that she was still teetering on that emotional edge. Yeah, well, being surrounded by far too many reminders of all those things that were, or seemed to be, out of her reach, would do that to a person.

"Are you okay?" came the soft, genuinely concerned—for himself as well as her, Dana thought—voice across the table.

Looking at him was the last thing she wanted to do. But what choice did she have? She cleared her throat as discreetly as possible, then met his gaze. "Just tired, is all," she said, but the cant of his eyebrows told her he didn't buy it for a minute.

"That stain, though…"

She tried a smile, anything to remove the sudden wariness in his features. "Hey, you hear a kid cry, you don't even think about getting dirty, you just want to make it all better."

He watched her for a long, hard moment, during which she could practically see the gears shifting in his thought. "You follow your instincts, in other words."

"Well, yes, I suppose—"

"So why do you think your partners elected you to do the footwork?"

Nothing like a conversational right turn to obliterate self-pity. Dana blinked, then said, "I have no idea, actually. In fact, I tried to get out of it."

"Because?"

She sighed, wadding her napkin into a ball. "Let's just say decision making's not my strong suit. Which I'm sure comes as no surprise."

"And yet…" C.J. leaned forward, shoving his empty glass to one side so he could clasp his hands together, his eyes holding her fast. "Cass tells me you're not only a financial whiz, but have a real flair for decorating kids' rooms, as well."

Another blush stole up her neck. "Well, yes, I suppose, but—"

"She also said if anyone could find Great Expectations' next home, it would be you, because you wouldn't make a decision until you were absolutely positive it was the *right* decision."

He reached across the table, briefly touching her wrist. His fingers were cool, a little rough. And suddenly squarely back in front of him, leaving a mild, buzzing sensation in their place.

"Trust your instincts, Miss Malone. The same way you trust your instincts about how to handle children. It's a gift. Be…be grateful for it. So…"

His posture shifted with his train of thought, giving her a chance to anticipate the next right turn. "Now I have a better idea of what to show you next time." He shrugged. "No big deal."

No big deal, her fanny. Never in all her born days had she met a man who could put her so much at ease and keep her so off-kilter at the same time.

"So," C.J. said, "what day looks good for you to take another stab at this?"

Dana sucked on her empty spoon for a moment, squinting slightly at those lovely, keep-your-distance eyes. The spoon clanged against the inside of the glass when she dropped it in. She looked up, pasted on a smile.

"How's Friday look?"

Grateful for an excuse to look away from that far too trenchant gaze, C.J. scrolled through his Palm Pilot, then nodded. "First thing in the morning looks good. Say…nine?"

"Perfect," she said, then stood. "Is there a restroom here? I hope."

"In back. Not ritzy, but it works."

"That's all I ask," she said, then headed toward the back of the diner. No less than a half-dozen male heads turned to watch her progress.

"Hey, C.J.! How's it goin'?"

With a smile for Felix, the diner's owner, C.J. picked up the check the bulky man had dropped in front of him. "Oh, fine. This heat's a killer, though."

A chuckle rumbled from underneath Felix's heavy, salt-and-pepper mustache. "I'm surprised you haven't already *melted,* my friend. Maria's already smacked me twice for staring!" He leaned close enough for C.J. to smell twenty years' worth of *sopapillas* on his white apron. "These women who think we want them skinny, they got it all wrong, no? Give me a woman I'm not afraid is going to break, anytime."

C.J. swallowed a smile. Felix's wife certainly fit the bill there. He handed a ten to the grinning proprietor, told him to keep the change, then stood as Dana emerged from the restroom…and a vaguely familiar female voice said, "C.J.? What on earth are you doing here?" right behind him.

He turned to find himself face-to-face with an artfully streaked blonde in one of those short, shapeless dresses and a tennis visor, flanked on either side by miniature versions of herself, twin girls who could have been anywhere between three and seven.

He thought back. Five, he decided, had to be the cut-off.

"I thought that was you when I came in," the woman said, perfect teeth flashing, the ends of her straight, gleaming hair skimming her shoulders. "We don't live far, the girls love the milkshakes here." The grin widened. "My goodness, it's been way too long. How *are* you? You look terrific!"

"Um, you, too." Out of the corner of his eye, he caught Dana's approach, her raised eyebrows. "Well, well," C.J. said, glancing at the little girls. "You've certainly been busy, haven't you…?"

"Oh. Hello." The blonde offered Dana a cool smile, and C.J. thought, *I'm dead.*

"Dana Malone, this is…"

"Cybill Sparks," she mercifully supplied, assessing Dana as only a female who feels her territory threatened can. Never mind that he hadn't even seen the woman—with whom he'd had a brief (and not particularly sweet, as he recalled) affair— in years. Or that she'd clearly moved on.

A weird blend of protectiveness and irritation spiked through C.J., even as Dana, her smile as gracious as Cybill's was frozen, said, "C.J.'s my Realtor. We were just scouting out properties for my store."

Which was apparently sufficient to silence Cybill's Incoming Threat alarm. "Oh? What do you sell?" she asked, her smile more natural again. "Not women's clothing, I presume?"

A moment passed. "No, a children's store. Maybe you've heard of it?" Dana grinned for the twins, who had ducked behind their mother's legs and were both smiling up at her with wide blue eyes. "Great Expectations?"

"Ohmigod, yes! I *love* that store! We're in there all the time! With four sets of grandparents, the girls get far more clothes than they could ever wear. It's so great having someplace to unload them. Especially since I can make a few bucks on the deal." She laughed. "Although don't tell any of the grands!"

"Wouldn't dream of it," Dana muttered, but Cybill's atten- tion had already slithered back to C.J. Her hand landed on his arm, her expression downright rapacious. "I've been meaning to call you for, gosh, ages."

"To let me know you were married?" C.J. said lightly.

"No, silly, to let you know I'm divorced! My number's the same, so give me a call sometime." Another tooth flash. "With all those grandparents, it's no trouble at all finding a sitter on short notice! Nice to meet you," she tossed dismissively in Dana's direction, then steered the children toward the counter.

Dana waited until they'd gotten outside to laugh.

"What's so damned funny?" C.J. grumbled.

"You had no idea who she was, did you?"

"Of course I knew who she was," he said, giving his lungs a second to adjust to the breath-sucking heat. "It was just her name that temporarily escaped me."

"That is seriously pathetic."

"Not nearly as pathetic as the way she threw herself at me," he muttered.

"True. For a moment there I thought she was going to unhinge her jaws and swallow you whole. I take it she's an old girlfriend?" she asked over his grunt.

"She'd like to think so. But I swear, the kids aren't mine."

She chuckled again, a sound he realized he enjoyed. Very much. He stole a glance at her profile as they walked to the car, thinking what a bundle of contradictions she was—self-deprecating one minute, completely comfortable with teasing him the next. About another woman's putting the moves on him, no less.

He literally shook his head to clear it.

"So what happened?" Dana said as they got to the car and C.J. beeped it unlocked.

"Nothing, in the long run. Much to her chagrin."

Once in the car, they clicked their seat belts in place almost simultaneously. "So tell me…" Dana briefly checked her makeup in the visor mirror, then turned to him, amusement glittering in her eyes. "Do women launch themselves at you on a regular basis?"

C.J. wasn't sure which startled him more—the question itself or the ingenuousness underpinning it. He met Dana's curious, open gaze and thought, *There's something different about this one,* even as he said, "You do realize there's no way I can answer that and keep either my dignity or your respect intact?"

"My…respect?"

He twisted the key in the ignition, backed out of the lot. "A Realtor who doesn't have his clients' respect isn't going to get very far."

"I see." She faced front again, severing what he realized had been a gossamer-thin thread of connection, leaving him feeling both annoyed and relieved, which made no sense whatsoever. "Thanks," she said, her voice definitely a shade darker than moments before. "For the soda, I mean. I needed that. And I promise not to be such a worrywart on Friday."

"Don't make promises you can't keep," he said lightly, wondering why her soft laugh in response sent a chill marching up his spine.

In combat boots.

Sometime later, Dana let herself into her parents' Northeast Heights home, breathing in the pomander of swamp-cooled air, that night's fried chicken and a brief whiff of fresh roses, at once comforting and disquieting in its immutability. Her pull here tonight was equally comforting, equally disquieting. Tonight, she needed home, even though, paradoxically, this was the one place guaranteed to remind her of those areas of her life currently running on empty.

She found her father first, molded to a leather recliner in the family room, a can of diet soda clutched in one thick-fingered hand, the baseball game on the movie-theater-sized TV screen reflected in his glasses.

"Hey, Daddy. Whatcha up to?"

Gene Malone jerked up his head and grinned, his thinning hair fanned out behind his head like a limp peacock's tail.

"Hey, there, baby!" he said over the announcer's mellow drone. "What brings you around?"

Her father, a Sandia Labs retiree, was rounder, and balder, than he used to be, but the humor simmering behind his pea-soup-colored eyes was the same as always. Dana bent over to kiss his forehead, then crackled onto the plastic-armored sofa beside the chair, staring at the TV. "Nothing much. Just hadn't seen y'all in a bit." Trying to keep from frowning, she studied his face. "How're you feeling?"

"Never better." A heart "episode" the year before had scared the willies out of them; unfortunately, she strongly suspected he wasn't following his diet and exercise regimen as scrupulously as he should. Especially when he said, "You know, this eating more chicken and fish routine really seems to be helping. I haven't felt this good in ages."

Uh-huh. Somehow, she didn't think *fried* chicken was what the doctor had in mind. "Glad to hear it, Daddy. Where's Mama?"

"In the den, sewing. Leastways, that's what she said she was gonna do." The leather squeaked when he shifted. "You know Trish called?"

This was news. "No. When?"

"Day or so ago, I don't remember."

"She say where she was?"

"Have no idea. You'll have to ask your mother."

Wondering, and not for the first time, how two people could live together for so long and talk to each other so little, she left her father to cheer on whoever and headed toward the smallest bedroom—the one that had been Trish's for nearly eight years—which they generously referred to as a den. In a sleeveless blouse and cotton pants, Faye Malone sat with her back to the door, as comfortably padded as the futon beside her. As usual, she was keeping up a running conversation with the sewing machine while she worked, pins stuck in her mouth, tufts of touched-up-every-three weeks auburn hair sticking out at odd angles where she'd tugged at it while trying to figure something out.

Heaven knew, having Faye for a mother had never been exactly easy, and not only because of the woman's habit of walking out on anyone who didn't agree with her. Or her nearly obsessive protectiveness when it came to family. All her life, Dana had variously loved and feared the woman whose scowl had been known to set people to rethinking opinions held dear from the cradle. Tonight, however, Dana envied her mother her single-mindedness.

And her strength.

"What's that you're making, Mama?" she asked, once Faye had removed the pins from her mouth.

Her mother jumped and pivoted simultaneously. "Lord, honey, you gave me a start," she said, laughing, dropping the pins into an old saucer by the machine. "This? Oh, um…just a little something for Louise at church." She cleared her throat. "Her daughter's havin' her first baby next month."

Dana sat on the end of the futon that had replaced the old iron daybed, fingering the edge of the tiny royal blue and scarlet quilt. The vent over the door blasted too-cool air at the back of her neck, making her shudder. "Pretty," she managed, trying to keep her voice light, to ignore the tension vibrating between them. Not to mention the unmistakable wistfulness in her mother's voice, that she'd never get to watch *her* daughter grow big with a grandbaby.

"So…" Eager to change the subject, Dana clasped her hands, banging them against her knee. "Daddy said Trish called?"

"Oh, yes!" Her mother pulled off her glasses, tucking them into her shirt pocket. "I would've mentioned it, except there didn't seem to be much point."

"So she didn't tell you where she was, I take it?"

"Not a word."

"She say she was coming back?"

Her mother shook her head. "Although she had that funny little hitch in her voice, like when she'd done something wrong and was afraid we'd get mad at her? To this day, I don't know what my sister was thinking, marrying that…creep. Man wasn't worth the price of the marriage license. *And* cost Marla her own daughter."

An observation made many times over the past dozen years. Dana's aunt's second marriage, to a man the family fondly referred to as The Cockroach, had had a disastrous effect on her already troubled daughter. After Trish's third attempt at running away, and since Dana had been more or less on her own by then, Dana's parents had offered to let the teen come live with them in Albuquerque. And on the surface, especially after Aunt Marla's death a few years back, Trish had certainly seemed to be getting her life on track. She'd settled down enough to finish high school, gotten through community college, and had finally landed that job at Turner Realty. She'd even talked about becoming an agent herself, one day.

But threaded through Trish's marginal successes ran not only a string of rotten relationships with men, but a chronic resistance to letting either Dana or her parents get close enough to help her. Other than the occasional call during the past year to let them know she was still alive, she'd cut herself off from the only family she had.

Sad, but, since her cousin had consistently rebuffed Dana's attempts at being chummy, none of her concern. If Trish was out there somewhere, miserable and alone, she had no one to blame but herself.

"She asked about you," she heard her mother say.

Dana started. "Me? Why?"

"Beats me." Mama threaded a needle and moved to the futon, where she preferred to do her hand sewing. "I thought it was odd, too." She fell into the cushion with an *oof*. "Although she did ask how you were getting on since…"

Her mother caught herself, her lips puckered in concentration as she stared at her sewing.

At the beginning, Mama had meant well enough, Dana supposed, doing her level best to take Dana's mind off her situation. Tonight, though, Dana realized she'd lost patience with pretending. And with herself for allowing the silence to go on as long at it had.

"Go on, finish your sentence. Since I had my operation."

Faye smoothed the quilt with trembling hands. "I'm sorry, honey. It just sort of slipped out."

Dana sighed. "It's been more than a year, Mama. Way past time for us to still be sidestepping the subject, don't you think?"

"I…I just don't want to make you feel bad, baby."

Stomach wobbling, Dana snuggled up against her mother, inhaling her mingled scent of soap and sunscreen and cooking.

"I know that," she said softly, fingering the tiny quilt. "But ignoring things doesn't change them. Not that I'm not okay, most of the time, but…but there are definitely days when I feel cheated, when I get so angry I want to break something. And if I can't unload to my own mother about it, who *can* I tell?"

"Oh, honey." Faye dropped her handiwork; Dana let herself be drawn into her mother's arms, suddenly exhausted from the strain of putting on a brave face, day after day after day. Whether it had been holding Cass's baby, or the toddler in the diner, or even the strange mixture of kindness and wariness in C.J.'s eyes that had brought on the sudden and profound melancholy, she had no idea. But today, this minute, all she could see were the holes in her life. And with that thought came a great, unstoppable torrent of long held-back tears.

Why did the ordinary rites of passage that so many women took for granted—boyfriends, marriage, motherhood—seem to slip from her grasp like fine sand? In her teens and twenties, there had always been "later." But watching relationship after relationship crash and burn—if they ever got off the ground to begin with—had a way of eroding a girl's self-confidence. Not to mention her hopes.

Was it so wrong to want a family of her own, to ache for a pair of loving, strong arms around her in bed at night, to be the reason for someone's smile? Was it foolish to want a little someone to stay up late wrapping Christmas presents for, to wonder if they'd ever get potty trained or be okay on their first day of school, to embarrass the heck out of by kissing them in public, to tuck in at night and read to?

Or was she just being selfish?

And her mother listened and rocked her and told her, no, she wasn't being selfish at all, that someday she'd have her own family, a husband who'd cherish her, children to love. That she had so much to offer, she just had to be patient. Things happen for a reason, Mama said, even if we might not understand the particulars when we're in the middle of it.

So what, exactly, Dana wondered over her mother's murmurings, was the reason for C. J. Turner's appearance in her life? To torment her with eyes she had no reason to believe would ever sparkle just for her, a pair of arms she'd never feel wrapped around her shoulders, a chest she'd never be able to lay her head against?

She sucked in a breath: What on earth was she going on about? She didn't even know the man! Were nice guys so rare these days that simply being around one was enough to send her over the edge? Because even in the midst of her pityfest, she knew the meltdown had nothing to do with C.J. Not really. No, it was everything he represented.

All those things that, for whatever reason, always seemed to elude her.

But even the best crying jags eventually come to an end. Dana sat up, grabbed a tissue from the tole-painted box on the end table, and honked into it, after which her mother pulled her off the futon and led her to the kitchen. Yeah, yeah, the road to Jenny Craig was paved with comfort food, but there you are. And as she ate—fried chicken, coleslaw, potato salad—and as Amy Grant held forth from the clock radio on the counter, punctuated by the occasional war whoop from the family room, the conversation soon came back around to her cousin.

"So…" Dana wiped her fingers on a paper napkin, perking up considerably when her mother hauled a bowl of shimmering cherry Jell-O out of the fridge. "What was Trish asking about me? And is there whipped cream?"

The can of Reddi-wip plonked onto the table. "Just if you still lived alone, still worked at the store." Mama scooped out two huge, quivering blobs into custard dishes. "I gave her your number, I hope that's okay?"

"Sure. Not that she'd ever call me." The first bite of Jell-O melted soothingly against her tongue, reminding her of the last dessert she'd eaten. As well as the lazy, sexy, South Carolina accent of the man who had bought it for her.

Her mother was giving her a pained look. So Dana smiled and said, "Speaking of the store, I started looking at possible sites for the new location today."

"Well, it's about time! A body can't hardly breathe in that itty-bitty place y'all are in now. Find anything?"

Yeah. Trouble. "Not yet."

"That's okay, you will, honey. You just have to keep looking."

A twinge of either aggravation or acid reflux spurted through Dana as she stared hard at her spoon. And how long, exactly, was she supposed to *keep looking?* She thought back to how she'd spent weeks searching for the perfect prom dress, finally finding one she absolutely loved in some little shop in the mall. Except…the neckline was too low. And it was red. With a full skirt. And all those sparklies…

So she'd kept looking. And looking. Until, by the time she finally realized that was the only dress she really wanted, it was gone. So she'd had to settle for something she hadn't liked nearly as much because she'd dithered so long.

Because she'd believed herself unworthy of something so perfect.

She nearly choked on her Jell-O.

She was still doing it, wasn't she? Refusing to even try something on because of some preconceived notion that it wouldn't work. And maybe it wouldn't, once she got it on (she stifled a snort at the double entrendre). God knew she'd left plenty of clothes hanging in dressing rooms over the years. But at least she owed it to herself to *try*, for crying out loud—

"Dana, honey? Why are you frowning so hard?"

Dana blinked herself back from la-la land and smiled for her mother, even as fried chicken and potato salad tumble-dried in her stomach.

"Yes, I'm fine," she said, thinking, *Damn straight I have a lot to offer.*

And absolutely nothing to lose.

Chapter Three

C.J. clattered his keys and cell phone onto the Mexican-tiled kitchen countertop flanking a professional-grade cooktop he never used, gratefully yielding to the house's deep, benign silence. His briefcase thumped onto the stone floor as he glanced at the message machine: nada. Good. However, since his cleaning lady, Guadalupe, only came twice a week, his cereal bowl greeted him where he'd left it more than twelve hours earlier, bits of dried corn flakes plastered to the sides, a half cup of cold, murky coffee keeping it company. He tossed the dregs into the stainless steel sink, splattering his shirt in the process, aggravating the vague irritability clinging to him like seaweed.

C.J. yanked open the dishwasher and rammed the dishes inside, then grabbed a beer from the Sub-Zero fridge. Moments later, he stood on his flagstone patio, his gaze skating over the infinity pool, its mirrored surface reflecting the cloudless, almost iridescent early evening sky, then across the pristinely kept golf course dotted with fuzzy young pines and delicate ash trees beyond. And backdropping it all, the rough-cut Sandia Mountains, bloodred in the sunset's last hurrah. A light, dry breeze shivered the water's surface, soothing C.J. through his shirt. He took a pull of his beer and thought, glowering, *What more could I possibly want?*

Other than dinner magically waiting for him, maybe.

And not having to make a certain phone call this evening.

Back inside, a couple of touches to assorted wall panels instantaneously produced both cool air and even cooler jazz. Damn house was smarter than he was, C.J. thought grumpily, continuing on to the master suite at the back of the house.

From the middle of the king-size bed, a yard-long slash of gray surveyed him—upside down—through heavy-lidded yellow eyes. The cat pushed out a half-assed meow that ended in a yawn huge enough to turn the thing inside out.

"Don't let me disturb your rest," C.J. said as he tossed the day's dress duds into the leather club chair in the corner, adding to the mountain of clothes already there, waiting to be hauled to the cleaners. He'd barely tugged on a soft T-shirt, a pair of worn jeans, when he felt a grapefruit-sized head butt his shin.

"Nice try, fuzzbutt, but you've still got food in your dish, I looked. Which is more than I can say for myself. Unless you want to make this phone call for me?"

The cat flicked his tail in disgust and trotted away, and C.J. mused about how he wouldn't mind having a tail to flick in disgust himself, right about now.

He rolled his shoulders as he returned to the kitchen, his aching muscles a testament to the fact that too many years of twelve- and fourteen-hour days were beginning to take their toll. Still, work was what he did. Who he was. Besides, what was the alternative? Watching reality TV for hours on end?

He glanced at the microwave clock. Eight-thirty-two. Two hours later in Charleston. If he put this off long enough, he'd miss his father's birthday altogether. A tempting, if unrealistic, thought. "Forgetting" the occasion would only add fuel to the implacable fire of bitterness and resentment lodged between them.

The cat writhed around his ankles, startling him. The house was beginning to cool off. C.J., however, was not.

Eight-thirty-six. Frosted air teased his shoulders as he opened the freezer, yanked out a microwaveable dinner. He peeled back the corner and stuck it in the zapper. Fifteen minutes. More than enough time.

He snatched his cell off the counter, hesitated another moment, then dialed. His father answered on the first ring, his voice bombastic, irritable, condemning the caller for having interrupted whatever he'd been doing. "Turner here!"

"Dad. Happy birthday."

A moment of silence followed. Then: "That you, Cameron?"

"Who else would it be? Unless I have a half brother you forgot to mention."

Again, brittle silence stretched between them. Ah, yes—one did not joke with Cameron James Turner, Sr.

"Wondered if you were going to remember."

"Of course I remembered." Although he hadn't sent a card. Hadn't in years, since Hallmark didn't make one that said *Thanks for never being there for me.*

"Well," his father said. "It got so late."

"I just walked in the door. Long day."

That merited a grunt, but nothing more. Then, "Business good?"

"Fine."

"Growing?"

"Steadily."

"Glad to hear it," his father said, but perfunctorily, without any glow of pride. Not surprising, considering how small potatoes his father obviously considered a four-person real estate agency. In Albuquerque. C.J. glanced at the microwave and mentally groaned. How could two measly minutes seem like an eternity? "So. You do anything for your birthday?"

"Like what?"

"I don't know—go out with friends?"

"Why would I do that?"

Why, indeed? "Well. I just wanted to say…happy sixty-fifth. 'Night—"

"Not so fast, hold on a minute. You planning on coming out anytime soon?"

Shock sluiced through C.J. He and his father hadn't seen each other in more than a dozen years. "What did you say?"

Why?

"Simple enough question, Cameron. I'm getting my affairs in order, need your signature on some papers."

C.J.'s fingers strangled the phone. He should have known. "I can't get away right now. You'll have to courier the papers to me."

"But they have to be witnessed—"

"So I'll have them witnessed!"

The dial tone snarled in his ear; his father had hung up on him, shutting C.J. off, and out, as he always had. Always would.

C.J. slapped the phone shut. From two thousand miles away, he felt the burning look of disapproval etched into his father's overlarge features, the disappointment shadowing blue eyes like C.J.'s own. He'd never understood why, nor had he ever felt compelled to dig around for answers he wasn't sure he wanted, anyway. The basics were simple enough: his father had denied him nothing, except himself.

And while C.J. would never intentionally treat another human being as dismissively as his father had him, his well didn't exactly run deep, either, judging from his lack of any real connection with the women he'd dated over the years. Clearly, he'd inherited his father's factory-defective heart.

But Dana's different, came the thought, as unexpected and unwelcome as a bee sting.

Followed immediately by *Don't go there, Turner*.

Not a problem, he thought with a rueful grin. Not after all he'd gone through to reach a place where he was finally as much in control of his life as was humanly possible. And blissfully, gloriously free—free from the pressure to be someone he wasn't, free from either his own or anyone else's expectations.

At his feet, the cat meowed, a tiny interrogative *eeerk*.

Almost nobody, anyway.

The microwave beeped. In a daze, C.J. popped open the door, grabbing his dinner with his bare hand. He cursed, dropping the hot tray with a great clatter.

Free, he mused, to make a fool of himself without witnesses.

He let the cat out back, then followed, his meal and drink in tow, to sink into one of the pricey, thickly padded patio chairs the decorator had picked out. The sky had gone a deep, soothing blue; C.J. took another pull of his beer, then let his head loll back against the cushion. Overhead, the first stars had begun to twinkle. And if he wanted to sit here for the next two hours watching them, he could. If he wanted to turn the volume up all the way on the sound system, he could. If he wanted to leave the toilet seat up, or his towels on the floor, or two weeks' worth of clothes piled on his chair, he could.

It was as close to heaven as any man could wish for, he thought, forking in a bite of tasteless…something.

"Such a shame you have to go out in this heat to look at more properties today," Mercy said from her perch on the counter beside the cash register, dunking a donut into her coffee.

Squatting in front of a display of infant toys, Dana lifted her eyes, caught the smirk. "Uh, yeah. You look *real* broken up about it."

"Oh, come on," Mercy mumbled around the last bite of donut, then dusted off her hands. A geranium-pink tank top emblazoned with a rhinestone heart set off her ebony curls, today caught up in a series of clips studded with even more rhinestones. *Subtle* was not one of Mercy's strong suits. "I can think of a lot worse things than tootling around the city with a good-looking guy."

"Whom you haven't even met, so how do you know how good-looking he is?" Dana stood, moving over to a rack of toddler dresses to yank out a 3T that had gotten wedged in with the 2s. "And you have powdered sugar on your chin."

The brunette rubbed at the spot. "Did I get it?" Dana glanced at her, nodded. "And I trust Cass's taste in men. So…" Mercy slithered off the counter, tugging at the hem of her short white skirt, then knotted her hands around the top of the chrome rack, chin propped on knuckles. "How hot are we talking, exactly?"

Her just-try-it-on initiative about C.J. notwithstanding, Dana wasn't about to give her partners any ammunition toward the cause. This was one uphill battle she intended to tackle on her own, thank you. So she shrugged and said, "He's okay, I suppose. If you like that type."

"*Type* as in *gorgeous?*"

"No. Type as in 'I-don't-*do*-serious'."

"Oh, that." Mercy batted the air. "Not a problem."

Dana couldn't help the laugh. "And you're saying this because…?"

"Yeah, yeah—I know what you're getting at. But *I'm* still single not because I don't think there's a man alive who doesn't, deep down, want to come home to the same woman every night, but because I'm…particular." She flounced over to the door, peered out at the still-empty parking lot. In this heat, it was unlikely they'd get many customers. "A girl's gotta have standards, you know."

Dana eyed the leftover donuts still on the counter, forced herself to look away. "And one of mine is that the sight of children and wedding rings doesn't make the guy puke."

Mercy *pff'ed* her disdain through glossed red lips, then tented her hand over her eyes. "Speaking of standards…bad-ass vehicle at three o'clock. Yowsa."

Dana glanced over to see the familiar silver sedan glide into a parking space. "Oh, no! I was supposed to meet *him,* at the agency," she said over a pounding heart, suddenly not at all sure she was ready to put her new resolve to the test. Especially before her second cup of coffee. "What on earth…?"

Both women stood, transfixed, as C.J. got out of the car, slipped on his suit coat. Poor guy, dressed for a board meeting in this weather. Still, that first glimpse of tall, handsome man in a charcoal suit was enough to make anyone's heart stutter. Including Mercy's, apparently.

"He's *okay?*" she said, eyes wide. "Hey, you don't want him, toss him this way. I got no problem with leftovers."

"What happened to your standards?"

"Trust me, *chica.* He meets them."

The door swung open, and he was in. And smiling. "Morning, ladies," he said, his voice still holding a hint of just-out-of-bed roughness that made Dana swallow. Hard.

Then she smiled, thinking, *Okay, toots. You can do this.*

Damn.

The Dana Malone smiling broadly for C.J. from across the store was not the same Dana Malone he'd left three days ago. Where was the nervousness, the shyness, the insecurity, that had—C.J. was pained to admit—made it much easier to blow her off as any kind of a threat to his hard-won autonomy?

You are man, he reminded himself. Strong. Above temptation. Impervious to…smiles.

While he stood there, thinking about how strong and above temptation he was, the curly-haired dynamo standing beside Dana jutted out a slender, long-nailed hand. "Hi! I'm Mercedes Zamora. Partner Number Three."

"Oh! I'm sorry!" Dana said. "Mercy, this is C. J. Turner—"

"I know who the man is, honey," Mercy said with a warm—*very* warm—smile. Out of the corner of his eye, C.J. caught Dana's glare. The phone rang. Nobody moved.

"Merce?" Dana tugged one of the woman's long curls. "The phone's ringing."

"What?" she said, still grinning at C.J. like an overeager retriever. Dana tugged again, harder. "Ow!"

"The *phone?*"

"Well, why didn't you just say so?" Mercy said, rubbing her head. But as she turned away, she glanced over her shoulder at C.J., then gave Dana a look he decided was best left untranslated.

Dana rolled her eyes, shrugged in a we-love-her-anyway gesture, then said, "I'm sorry…wasn't I supposed to meet you at your office?"

"You were. Except it occurred to me I might get a better feel for what you all needed if I saw the shop first."

She laughed. "There's a thought," she said, then ducked behind the counter and held up the coffeepot, grinning. "Can I tempt you?"

Uh, boy.

It wasn't fair, the way that nearly weightless dress, barely darker than her skin, caressed her curves, skimmed her breasts, her thighs, fell in a graceful sweep to her ankles.

It wasn't fair, the way her thick hair, corralled into a braid, exposed her delicate jaw and neck, the way that same wisp drifting around her temple still eluded capture. As she swept it back, he noticed she wore simple pearls in her earlobes.

It wasn't fair, her having earlobes.

"No. Thank you."

"Your loss," she said, pouring herself a cup.

"So," C.J. said, turning to face the sales floor. And frowning. "Hmm. Now I understand why you need a bigger space."

"You don't miss a trick, do you?" he heard behind him, and he smiled. But it was true. He'd never in his life seen so much stuff crammed into one store. Not an inch of wall space had been left exposed, and you took your life in your hands navigating the floor, as well. There were even mobiles and stuffed animals and wall hangings suspended from the ceiling. Something…indefinable spread through him, gentle and warm and oddly…scary.

He grinned anyway, taking in the racks of tiny clothes, the miniature furniture, the shelves of whimsical lamps and tea sets and fancy dress dolls. The combined scent of rich coffee and her perfume as she came to stand beside him. "This reminds me of what I'd always imagined the Old Woman's shoe to look like on the inside. No wonder you nixed all the places I showed you. Which means…damn. You're probably going to hate everything I picked to show you today, too."

"Now, now…guess we won't know until we try, right?"

Tempted to peek behind the counter for the telltale pod, C.J. instead crossed to a display of christening gowns, fingering one whisper-soft garment frothed in ivory lace.

"The workmanship's incredible, isn't it?" she said. "That one's nearly seventy years old."

C.J. let the fabric fall from his fingers, stuffed his hand in his pocket. "You'd think the family would want to hang on to something like that, pass it down."

"If there's someone to pass it down *to*." Before he could decide if he'd only imagined the slight edge to her voice, she said, "Let me grab my purse and we can get going, I've got an appointment with a decorating client at twelve-thirty."

She disappeared into the forest of racks and displays, leaving her perfume in his nostrils and a decided sense of foreboding in his brain.

On the surface, Dana mused upon her return to the shop two hours later, one probably couldn't call the outing successful. Because C.J. had been right—all the new places sucked, too.

"Well?" Mercy said the instant the door *shooshed* shut behind her.

"Nothing."

"Oh. Well, did you find a place, at least?"

Dana gave her a dirty look. One that belied what she was really thinking, which was that on a personal level, things couldn't have been more successful. As in, there was a lot to be said for having spent a whole two hours in the man's company without angsting about how she looked or what she said or even what he thought about her. Not more than once or twice, anyway. "Where's Cass?"

"The baby kept her up all night with colic, so she's taking the day off. Says she'll switch one day next week with you, if that's okay."

"Yeah, sure," Dana said distractedly, leaning on the counter and leafing through the mail. "Although we really need to think about hiring another body or two. So we could, you know, have lives?" The phone rang. Without looking, she reached for the receiver.

"Great Expectations—"

"Dana?"

"Speaking. May I help you?"

"Dane…it's me. Trish."

She jerked upright, the mail forgotten. "Trish? Where are you? Mama's worried sick about you."

"I'm okay. Which I told her last week when I talked to her. Listen…I need to see you."

It took a second. "You're here? In Albuquerque?"

"Yeah, just for a couple days, though."

"Where? Give me a number where we can reach you—"

"You coming into the shop tomorrow?"

"What's tomorrow? Saturday? Yes, I'll be here all day—"

"When do you get in?"

"Around nine, I suppose. But wouldn't it be better to get together at my place? Or Mama's house—?"

Click.

Dana stared at the phone for a second, then slammed it down.

"What was that all about?" Mercy asked.

"*That* was my airhead cousin."

"The one who disappeared?"

"The very same." Dana huffed a sigh. "Says she's in town, but won't tell me where she is. Said she's coming to the shop tomorrow, although God knows why."

Swishing a lime-green feather duster over a display of ornate frames, Mercy shrugged. "She probably wants money."

"Yeah, well, she's in for a rude surprise, then, since between the medical bills from last year and our expansion, this is one dry well. If she needs help, she can jolly well haul her butt back home and go to work like the rest of us poor slobs."

Mercy laughed.

"What's so funny?"

"Anyone who didn't know you would think you were this wussy Southern belle, all sweet and helpless. But let me tell you, if I had to pick someone to be on my team against the bad guys? I'd pick you in a heartbeat."

Dana tilted her head at her friend. "Yeah?"

"Yeah."

The phone rang again the very moment a mother with four stair-step children tumbled into the shop.

"Great Expecta—"

"Hey, I'm on my way to another appointment," C.J. said, and Dana's face warmed with pleasure. Dumb. "But I just thought of a place I bet would be great for the shop. Don't know why I didn't think of it sooner. Must be the heat. In any case, I'm tied up until five, but wondered if you wanted to see it then? It only came on the market this morning, and I don't know how long it's going to last. And the great thing is the owner's willing to sell, so you could apply the rent toward the purchase price if you all want to buy eventually—"

"Slow down, slow down," she said, laughing. "Yes, five would be fine. But let me meet you there."

She wrote down the address on a scrap of paper, then hung up, deciding she was feeling all fluttery and trembly inside because of the prospect of finally finding the right location for the store. Yes, that must be it.

Mercy drifted over to the sales counter while the mother browsed and the kids wreaked havoc. Since there was little they could hurt or that could hurt them (despite the place being an obstacle course for Dana), no one paid the children any mind.

"Let me guess," she said. "That was C.J."

"Why would you think that?"

"Because your face wasn't darker than your dress five minutes ago."

"Bite me."

That merited a cackle. "He ask you out?"

"No, goofball—he has another place to show me."

"Miss?" the mother asked. "How much is this play kitchen?"

"It should be tagged," Mercy said with a smile. "Let me

see if I can find it for you." Then, over her shoulder to Dana as she edged toward her customer, "I've got a real good feeling about this one."

"Oh, for pity's sake, Merce—"

"The property, the *property*," Mercy said, saucer-eyed. "Why, what did you think I meant?"

Then she cackled again, and Dana thought, *With friends like this…*

Dana was so quiet, so expressionless. C.J. listened to her sandals tapping on the dusty wooden floor as she wordlessly walked from room to room in the quasi-Victorian, her expression telling him nothing.

"The Neighborhood Association would be thrilled to have you in the area. Plus, it's close enough to Old Town to pull in a nice chunk of the tourist traffic. And I think the other businesses around would complement yours—"

She shushed him with a swat of her hand.

It was beastly hot in the house, which smelled of musty, overheated wood and dust and that damned perfume; several strands of her hair hung in damp tendrils around her neck.

And he stared. As if he'd never seen damp necks and tendrils before. So he looked out a grimy window, thinking maybe it was time to bring the electronic little black book out of retirement. Except the thought made him slightly nauseous.

The tapping came closer, stopped. He turned; she was smiling. *Beaming.*

"It's perfect! When can the others see it?"

"Whenever you like."

She clapped her hands and let out a squeal like a little girl, her happiness contagious. And C.J. hoped to hell his inoculations were up to date.

A few minutes later, after they'd returned to their cars,

C.J. said, "See, what did I tell you? When it was right, you had no trouble at all making a decision."

Her laugh seemed to tremble in the heat. "True. In fact…" Her gaze met his over the roof of his car. She glowed, from the heat, from excitement, from what he guessed was profound relief. "I feel downright…empowered."

C.J. opened his car door, letting out the heat trapped inside. "And what," he asked without thinking, "does an empowered Dana Malone do?"

Her grin broadened. "She offers to cook her Realtor dinner."

Nothing to lose, Dana reminded herself as perspiration poured down her back in such a torrent she prayed a puddle wasn't collecting at her feet. As she watched C.J.'s smile freeze in place, the undeniable beginnings of that *Oh, crap* look in his eyes.

"But before you get the wrong idea," she said over her jittering stomach, "this is only to thank you for all your patience with me, especially since I know how busy you are and you probably eat out a lot, or stick things in the microwave—"

"Dana," he said gently, looking wretched. "I'd love to, really—"

And here it comes.

"—but I don't think…that would be a good idea."

Despite having steeled herself for the rejection, embarrassment heated her face. Still, she managed a smile and a light, "Oh. Well, it was just a thought. No harm, no foul." Except after she opened her own car door, she wheeled back around. "Although you could have at least *lied* like any other man, and told me you already had plans or something."

"And if you'd been any other woman," he said softly, "I probably would have. But you deserve better than that." He drew in a breath, letting it out on, "You deserve better than *me.* Marriage, babies…not in my future, Dana. But something tells me you very much see them in yours."

Her eyes popped wide open. "Who said anything about…? It was just *dinner,* for heaven's sake!"

Now something dangerously close to pity flooded his gaze. "Would you have extended the same invitation if I were involved with someone? Or if you were?"

"Um…well…" She blew out a breath, then shook her head.

His smile was kind to the point of patronizing. "I'm a dead end, Dana. Don't waste your effort on me."

She glanced away, then back, her mouth thinned. "I'm sorry, it was stupid, thinking that you'd…be interested. Especially after everything Trish said."

His head tilted slightly. "Trish?"

"Lovett. My cousin. She worked for you for about six months, oh, a year ago? And she said…never mind, it's moot now."

"Dana," C.J. said, a pained look on his face, "trust me, it's better this way."

Their gazes skirmished for a second or two before she finally said, "Yes, you're probably right," then got into her sweltering car and drove off, repeating "*No* isn't fatal" to herself over and over until, by the time she got home and called Cass with the good news about the store, she was almost tempted to believe it.

Way to go, dumb ass, C.J. thought as he sat at a stoplight, palming his temple. In less than a century, man had invented cell phones, the Internet and microwave pizza. And yet after fifty thousand years, give or take, no one had yet to figure out how to let a woman down without hurting her.

But what else could he have said? That, yeah, actually he would have killed for the privilege of spending a little more time in her company? To see that dimpled smile, to hear her laugh? To simply enjoy being with a woman without an agenda?

Except…she did have one, didn't she? Maybe a bit more soft-edged than most, but no less threatening. Or sincere. And how fair would it have been, to accept her offer, to give her hope, when he knew it wouldn't go any further? That selfish, he wasn't.

And then there was the little sidebar revelation about Trish being her cousin. Uh, boy…he could just imagine what would hit the fan if Dana knew everything about *that* little side trip to insanity.

C.J.'s brow knotted. So why *didn't* Dana know? Then he released a breath, realizing that whatever Trish's reasons for keeping certain things to herself, if she hadn't told Dana by now, she probably wouldn't. And there was no reason for her to ever find out, was there?

A car horn honked behind him: while he'd been on Planet Clueless, the light had changed.

And even if she did, he thought as he stepped on the gas, what difference would it make? Once this deal was finalized, he'd have no reason to see or talk to Dana Malone ever again.

Which was a good thing, right?

In a bathroom flooded with far too much morning sunshine, Dana blearily stared at herself in the mirror. She pulled down a lower lid—yeah, the bloodshot eyes were a nice touch. Not to mention the still slightly visible keyboard impression in her right cheek. Charming.

She shakily applied toothpaste to brush, only to realize she wasn't sure she had the oomph to lift the brush to her mouth. From the living room, her pair of finches chirped away, merrily greeting the new day, momentarily tempting her to go find a hungry cat. But if she'd been up until nearly 4:00 a.m., at least she hadn't spent it brooding. Much. Since here she was, still alive (sort of), she guessed her "*No* isn't fatal" mantra had worked. And anyway, she'd only have to see C.J. once, maybe twice more, right? If that. So. Over, done, let's move on.

She shoved the brush into her mouth. And naturally, right at the pinnacle of sudsiness, the phone rang.

Dimly, from some tiny, marginally awake corner of her brain, it registered how early it was. She spit and flew back into her bedroom, fumbling the phone before finally getting it to her ear.

"Hel—"

"Dana?"

A few more brain cells jerked awake. "Trish?" She glanced at the caller ID. Blocked call. Shoot. "Where are you—?"

"I just wanted to make sure you were going to be at the shop at nine. That's what you said, right? Nine? I mean, are you going to be there any earlier?"

As usual, she sounded borderline crazed, but in a controlled sort of way.

"I usually get there around ten 'til. Trish what's going on—?"

Click.

The girl *really* needed to get herself some phone manners. Sheesh.

An hour or so and a half bottle of Visine later, Dana pulled into the far side of the empty parking lot in front of the shop. It was her day to open up, a good thing since she wasn't yet ready to face humanity. Or Mercy's inevitable squinty assessment of Dana's putty-knife makeup application. She was, however, supposed to be facing Trish, who was nowhere in sight. But then, reliability had never been her cousin's strong suit.

Bracing herself, Dana took a deep breath and swung open the car door. Instant oven. Already. Yech. And it always took an hour for the store to cool off after being closed up all night. Double yech.

Her purse gathered, she slammed shut her door and crossed
the parking lot, noticing the drooping petunias in the oversized
planters by the front door. If they didn't get water soon, she
thought as she shoved her key into the lock, they'd turn into
twigs. Lord, her slip was already fused to her skin. Knowing
she had thirty seconds to deactivate the alarm before it went
off, she shoved open the door—

Behind her, something sneezed.

The key still in the lock, the door swung open as whatever
it was sneezed a second time. She turned, letting out a half-
shrieked, "Ohmigod!"

The baby peered at her from underneath the nylon hood of
the car seat, its face tinted blue from the reflection. It stared
at Dana for a long moment, then offered a big, basically toothless, drooly grin.

Dana was far too stunned to grin back. But not too stunned
to immediately scour the neighboring parking lots, her hand
shielding her eyes from the morning sun glinting off the top
of a beige sedan as it disappeared down the street. She stepped
off the sidewalk—

Brrrrannnnnnnnnnnnnnnnnnnnngggggggg!

Dana yelped and the baby started to yowl like a banshee
as the alarm blared loud enough to wake the dead. On Mars.
She grabbed the car seat and roared into the store, thunking
the seat onto the counter so she could dump out her purse to
find the key to deactivate the alarm. Ten seconds later, she'd
killed it, but not before nearly wetting her pants.

In the ensuing silence the baby's howls seemed even
louder. Dana unlatched the ridiculously complicated harness
and hauled the little thing into her arms, then paced the
jammed sales floor, almost more to calm herself than the
infant. After a bit, the wails had softened to exhausted sobs,
and Dana no longer felt as though her heart was going to

pound out of her chest. She dropped into a rocking chair, the infant clutching the front of her dress, now adorned with baby tears and drool.

"No…" she breathed. "No, God, no…this can't be happening…."

Trish surfaces out of the blue, asks when Dana's going to be at the shop; lo and behold, a blond baby appears, smelling of cheap perfume and cigarettes. As she assumed the baby didn't wear cheap perfume or smoke, it didn't take a real big leap of faith to figure out who *did.*

She got up, deposited the baby—dressed in a miniature football outfit, so she was guessing boy—into a nearby playpen and stormed back outside, startling a couple of pigeons.

"Well, Patricia Elizabeth Lovett," she muttered to the air, "you've outdone yourself this time."

Since said Patricia Elizabeth obviously wasn't going to jump out from behind a Dumpster and yell, "Surprise! Had you there for a minute, huh?" Dana's only option was to go back inside and figure out what to do next. As she turned, however, she noticed the shopping bag. A quick glance inside revealed a small stack of clothes, six or seven disposable diapers and three filled bottles.

How thoughtful.

Dana snatched up the bag so hard one of the handles broke, nearly dumping everything into the gasping petunias. That's when she noticed the note. Of course. There was always a note, wasn't there?

She dumped the bag on the counter, saw that the baby seemed happy enough gurgling to his own hands as he lay on his back, then tore open the envelope.

Her eyes flew over the one-page letter, picking up the essentials. "*…tried it on my own…knew how much you loved and wanted kids…it'll be better this way…full custody…hope* *you'll forgive me...Ethan's really a little doll, you'll love him...birth certificate enclosed..."*

It was *so* Trish. On a sigh, Dana unfolded the birth certificate, if only to find out how old this kid was.

"WHAT?"

The baby lurched at the sudden noise, then started to cry again. Nearly in tears herself, Dana threw the letter and birth certificate on the counter and went to pick him up. None of this was the baby's fault, she reminded herself as she hauled the infant out of the playpen and cuddled him in her lap. None of it. Least of all who his daddy was.

Cameron James Turner, the paper said.

Cameron James Turner, of "fatherhood isn't part of my future" fame.

"Well, guess what, buddy?" Dana hissed under her breath as she grabbed a bottle off the counter and stuck it in her new little cousin's mouth. "Fatherhood sure as hell is part of your *present.*"

Chapter Four

Dana thanked the police officer for coming so promptly, assured her she'd be in touch if she heard anything or needed her, then showed her out. Not that the visit had been exactly productive. Or even illuminating. Turned out there wasn't a whole lot anybody could do, seeing as Trish had left Ethan with family and all. Technically, it wasn't abandonment. Of course, the officer had said, if Dana really felt she couldn't take care of the baby, there was always foster care…

Uh-huh. Sharp sticks in eyes and all that.

Mercy took the baby from her as Cass—whose own son was sawing logs in a cradle in the back—slipped an arm around her shoulders.

"For crying out loud," Dana said, "how could anyone be so selfish? *Ooooh!*" Her palm slammed the counter, dislodging a teddy bear from its perch by the register. She caught it, only to squeeze the life out of the thing. "If Trish showed her

face right now—" the bear's floppy limbs flailed as she shook
it "—I swear I'd slap her silly. What an air-brained, self-
centered, addlepated little *twit.*"

"Familial love is such a wonderful thing," Cass wryly
observed.

Ignoring Cass, Dana stuffed the bear back into its chair.
"What am I supposed to do now?" She shook her head,
watching six-month-old Ethan play with Mercy's hair. Her own,
as usual, was coming undone. "How am I supposed to take care
of a baby on my own? I live in this itty-bitty apartment, and
hello? I work full time? What on *earth* was Trish thinking?"

"Maybe your parents could take over during the day,"
Mercy suggested, but Dana wagged her head emphatically.

"Neither one of them is up to full-time babysitting at this
point in their lives."

Then both of her partners went ominously silent, instantly
putting Dana on the alert. "What?"

"What about C.J.?" Mercy asked, wincing a little as she
dislodged curious little fingers from the three-inch-wide gold
loops dangling from her ears.

"Oh, right. Mr. Family Man himself." When they both
blinked at her, she sighed and 'fessed up about the day before.
Okay, she might have done a little judicious editing of the conversation—they didn't need to know about the dinner invite—
but she definitely left in the "He doesn't want kids" part.

"Be that as it may," Cass said, assuming the role of Voice
of Reason. She folded thin, bare arms over a button-front
blouse already adorned with a telltale wet spot on one
shoulder. "C.J. doesn't strike me as the kind of man who'd
blow off having a kid. So my guess is Trish left town without
telling him."

Dana hadn't thought about that. Still, she wasn't exactly
in a charitable mood. "And if she did?"

Mercy leaned against the counter, setting the baby on the edge, protectively bumpered by her arms. He yanked off her turquoise satin headband and began gnawing on it; she didn't seem to notice. "Hey, if he knew about the baby and refused to take responsibility, you better believe I'd be first in line to string him up by his gonads. But if he didn't—and remember, you're not absolutely sure Ethan *is* C.J.'s—then I think you're gonna have to wait and see. Give him a chance."

"You weren't there, you didn't see the look on his face..." Dana began, then shook her head, her mouth pulled tight. She reached for Ethan, her eyes burning for reasons she had no intention of thinking about too hard. "I think it's pretty safe to assume I got me a baby to raise."

The bell jangled over the door; with a grunt of annoyance, Mercy left to help the pregnant woman slowly picking her way through the store. Cass, however, stroked Dana's arm for a second, then grasped Ethan's chunky little hand.

"Honey, I understand what you're saying. But you really have no idea how C.J.'s going to feel once he sees his son. Look at him—he's adorable. How could he not fall in love with him?"

At that, the baby turned all-too-familiar blue eyes to Dana and grinned as if to say, "Hey! Where ya been, lady?" Amazement and terror streaked through her, so powerful, and so sudden, she could hardly breathe. Dana nestled the infant to her chest, rubbing his back and sucking in a sharp breath. *I've been given a baby,* she thought, only to then wonder...was this a dream come true?

Or the beginning of a nightmare?

She gave Cass a wan smile. "Hand me the phone, wouldja?"

Hours later, Dana watched Mercy scan the tiny one-bedroom apartment, her features a study in skepticism. Between her Firebird and Dana's Jetta, they'd managed to

haul a portacrib, playpen, baby swing, a case of powdered
formula, two jumbo packs of disposable diapers, clothes,
rattles, wipes, bedding and at least a million other "essentials" Mercy insisted Dana would probably need before
sunrise. In the middle of all this, Ethan lay on his back in the
playpen, grunting at the birds. Mercy's eyebrows knotted a
little tighter.

"You sure you're gonna be okay?"

"Uh-huh," Dana squeaked out. "Besides, I don't want any
witnesses when C.J. shows up."

"Damn. I always miss all the fun."

Dana managed a weak, but nonetheless hysterical, laugh.
All afternoon she'd ping-ponged between hope and profound
skepticism. Maybe prejudging the man wasn't in anybody's
interest, especially Ethan's, but she wasn't so naive as to expect
him to take one look at his kid and suddenly switch tracks.

"Sweetie," Mercy said gently, "why don't you call your
mom? Let her come help you out."

"I will, I will. Soon. But one does not spring potentially
life-altering news on my mother without a plan. The woman
has turned worrying into an art form."

"I hear ya there. At least let me set up the portacrib—"

Dana took her friend by the arm and steered her toward her
door. Not that it wouldn't make sense to let her stay. Most of
Mercy's sisters were spittin' out babies like popcorn. No
matter when one visited the Zamora household, it was awash
in little people. But while Mercy's presence would have been
a great help in many ways, Dana wouldn't have been able to
think. And thinking was the one thing she most needed to do.

And she really didn't want any witnesses when C.J.
arrived. Not because she was going to kill him—she didn't
think—but because Ethan's sudden appearance had turned a

nonrelationship into…well, she didn't know what, actually. But so much for never having to see the guy again.

Thirty seconds and a heartfelt hug later, Dana was finally alone.

With a baby.

She zipped to her bedroom, rummaging through her bottom drawer for a pair of old shorts, and a faded UNM T-shirt, changing into both at warp speed. The gurgling, drooling six-month-old pushed himself up on his elbows when she walked back to the living room; Dana squatted down in front of the playpen as if inspecting a new life form. Yesterday, she had no idea this child even existed. Now she was responsible for him, maybe for a few days, maybe for the rest of her life.

The thought slammed into her so hard she nearly toppled over. *One day,* she figured she'd adopt a child or two, when she was ready, both financially and emotionally. At the moment, she was neither. She'd always assumed she'd have some prep time for accepting a child into her life. As, you know, part of a couple?

So much for that idea.

A particularly ripe odor wafted to her nostrils. A by-product of the earlier grunting, no doubt.

"Let me guess. You messed your pants."

Ethan grinned and cooed at her, lifting his head at exactly the right angle for Dana to get a good gander at his eyes. Lake-blue, flecked with gold around the pupils, exactly like you-know-whose. On a sigh, she stood and hefted the smelly little dear out of his cage and over to the sofa, where she changed his diaper with surprising aplomb and less than a dozen wipies.

"Now I bet you're hungry, right?"

In answer, Ethan stuck his fist in his mouth and started

gnawing on it with the enthusiasm of a lion ripping into fresh wildebeest. Dana picked up the much sweeter smelling child and plopped him back into his car seat, which she figured was as safe a place as any to try to shovel food down his gullet. But what food, she wondered, might that be?

"Next time you dump a kid on me, Trish," she muttered, ransacking the paper bag full of little clanking jars Mercy had helped her pick out at Albertson's on their way home, "don't forget the dag-nabbed feeding instructions!"

She yanked out a jar, holding it up to the baby hunk with the killer eyes. "Carrots?"

Ethan gurgled, then let out a loud "Bababababababa" while waving his arms. Then he chortled. Not giggled. Chortled.

Dana sort of chortled back, popping open the jar. "Carrots it is, then."

Except carrots, it wasn't. It was like trying to shove a video into a malfunctioning VCR—it slid right back out.

She opened another jar, held it up. "Peaches?"

That got a slightly more forceful rejection.

"O-kaaay…maybe orange stuff isn't your thing. How about green?"

Green beans went in… and green beans oozed out, accompanied by the quintessential "*Get real, lady,*" expression.

Dana quickly discovered that baby food didn't exactly come in a wealth of colors. Or tastes. But she gamely tried creamed corn, chicken (that, she couldn't get past the baby's lips), squash, pears and beets.

Pears and beets went down. And down and down and down, until Dana wondered if babies, like puppies, would simply stuff themselves until they got so full they threw—

"Oh, *gross!*"

—up.

At least four times more food came back out as had

gone in. Krakatoa had nothing on this kid, she mused while frantically trying to catch the maroon-and-pear colored mess that kept spewing forth from those little rosebud lips.

Three saturated napkins later, Ethan chortled again. Not seeing the humor this time, Dana did not. And she was hot and getting hungry herself. Not only that, but it was beginning to sink in with alarming speed that no one was going to come take this vomiting bundle of joy away in an hour or two. And what if he didn't sleep through the night?

With a little groan, Dana let her head clunk onto the tabletop, not realizing how close she was to a pair of enterprising little hands.

"Ye-ouch!" Her own hands flew to her head, prying five tiny and amazingly strong fingers from her hair, which was now liberally infused with regurgitated Gerber 1st Foods. Well, hell. Somebody, somewhere, probably paid big bucks for this look. She got it for free.

Rubbing her scalp—man, the kid had a grip—she regarded her little charge, now in deep conversation with the Tiffany-style lamp over the table. She skootched over, out of Clutcher's way, and laid her head down again.

So many questions and thoughts swarmed in her brain, she couldn't sort them out, let alone act on any of them. For tonight, her top priority was keeping the child alive. She was off all day tomorrow, and Ethan had to sleep *sometime,* right?

Dana lifted her head far enough to prop it in her palm, reaching out to the baby with her other hand. Ethan grabbed Dana's fingers and tried to stuff them into his mouth. The two little teeth on the bottom made their presence known really fast, but she felt ridges on top, too.

"You getting yourself some new teeth, big guy?" she said with a tired smile.

Ethan chortled.

Dana's heart did a slow, careful turn in her chest. She stood and scooped the baby out of his car seat, cuddling him on her lap. Ethan settled right in, tucking his head underneath Dana's chin, and her heart flopped again, more quickly.

This was all too unpredictable for her taste. Her cousin might change her mind, C.J. might want…actually, God knew what C.J. might want.

She cursed under her breath, noting that more no-nos had slipped past her lips in the past several hours than in the entire thirty-two years that had preceded them. Insecurities and turmoil and all the unanswerables swirled and knotted together into a nebulous anger no less fierce for its vagueness. Her eyes stung as she realized how furious she was, at Trish, at C.J. (yes, even though he probably didn't know about the baby), at fate.

At herself.

All her life, she realized tiredly, she'd let people push her around. All her life, she'd been the one voted most likely to say "sure" when she really wanted to say "I don't have time" or "I'm not comfortable with that idea" or even, simply, "I don't want to." Suddenly, she was a kid again, hearing her mother's gushing to some neighbor or teacher or saleslady who'd admired Dana's impeccable manners. "Oh, Dana's never given us a single moment's worry," she'd say. "Always does what she's supposed to do, never gives us any lip. Just a perfect little angel!"

"Just ask Dana—she won't mind…"

"You can always count on Dana for a job well done and a smile to go with it…"

"You know, I've never heard Dana complain, not even once…."

"Dana won't be a problem. She'd go along with whatever we decide to do. Won't you, Dana?"

She pushed herself off the sofa, hugging Ethan, realizing there was nowhere to go. So she stood in place, jiggling the baby, fuming and muttering and cussing—but not so Ethan could really hear her—over the finches' agitated twittering.

Okay, that's it—Dana Malone's doormat days were o-*ver.* No more swallowing her anger when someone pissed her off. No more smiling when she really felt like popping someone upside the head. No more Ms. Nice Lady. She was *mad,* dammit, and God help the next person who got in her way—

The doorbell rang.

She marshaled all her newfound fury into one hopefully emasculating glare and marched to the door.

The way her topknot hung by a thread over her right ear was C.J.'s first clue that something was very, very wrong.

The baby slung on her hip was the second.

Her voice mail had been short, and not exactly sweet. *"Meet me at my place anytime after six,"* she'd said, then left her address, finishing with, *"And believe me, it's not what you think."*

"You…wanted to see me?"

Wordlessly, Dana spun around and stomped back inside the apartment, which he cautiously took as permission to enter.

His first horrified thought, when he saw the room, was that she'd been burgled. After he swallowed his heart, however, he realized the damage seemed superficial. In fact, it was all baby stuff. A swing and playpen fought for space between a peach-colored armchair, a glass-topped coffee table; diapers—both clean and dirty, from what he could tell—littered the pastel, Southwest design sofa; an infant car seat took up half the blond dining table, the rest of which was covered by no less than a dozen open jars of baby food and a mountain of dirty napkins or paper towels or something.

She'd gone into the kitchenette, where she dampened a cloth to wipe off the squirming baby's cheeks. Said child giggled, somehow snatched the wet rag out of Dana's hand and tossed it with unerring accuracy smack into her face.

A finely honed survival instinct told C.J. to proceed with extreme caution.

"Babysitting?" he asked.

"Funny you should say that." Dana caught the cloth as it fell, slapping it onto the counter. Hot little flames sparked in her eyes. "Trish breezed back into town today."

C.J. literally felt the blood drain from his face.

"Oh?"

"Yeah. She brought me a present. Now, it's a very nice present, to be sure, but heaven knows I wasn't expecting anything like this. Nor did I realize I wasn't going to be given any say in whether or not I even *wanted* this present."

He looked at the baby, who flashed him a wide, gummy smile, then back at Dana. Somehow, even her *hair* seemed redder. Okay, *Trish in town* probably equaled *Trish told Dana*. But she'd have hardly asked him to come over about that, for crying out loud. And what did the baby have to do with anything?

"I'm sorry," C.J. said, "but am I missing something?"

Her mouth set, she swept past him on her way from kitchen to living room, bending awkwardly with the child still balanced on her hip in order to pull something out of her handbag. Then she marched over to him and smacked a triple-folded sheet of paper into his palm.

Acid etched at the lining of his stomach as he unfolded the paper, burst into flame when he read it. The first word out of his mouth was particularly choice.

"Yeah. That was about my reaction, too," Dana said. "Well?"

"Well, what?"

"Did you and my cousin…"

"You mean, she didn't tell you?"

"She didn't *tell* me squat."

Still staring at the paper, C.J. pushed out a sigh. "Once, Dana. Right after she'd quit. And we both knew it was a mistake."

He couldn't quite tell if that was disappointment or flat-out, go-to-hell-and-don't-come-back hatred that was making her eyes so dark. "And does the date correspond to that *once?*"

"Yes. But…" He shook his head, as if doing so would make it all go away. "This can't be right."

"Why not?"

He lifted his eyes to Dana's. "Because I had a vasectomy. Five years ago."

Silence stretched between them, painful and suffocating. Until, on a soft little "Oh," Dana dropped onto the sofa with the baby on her lap.

The baby, C.J. thought, with eyes exactly like his.

But then, lots of babies had blue eyes. Tons of babies. Millions, even.

And somewhere, some deity or other was grinning his— or, more likely her—ass off.

"Wow," Dana said. "You weren't kidding about not seeing babies in your future."

C.J.'s mouth pulled tight. "That had been the plan. But—"

"Oh, geez, sorry to have come down so hard on you. I should have realized… Especially knowing my cousin…" She frowned. "What?"

"I think I need to sit."

"Uh…sure. Make yourself at home."

C.J. shoehorned himself into a half-blocked club chair across from the sofa and stared again at the birth certificate. At the letters that formed, of all the crazy things, his name. Yeah, as screwups went, this one was in a league of its own.

He supposed Trish could have been lying, otherwise why wouldn't she have surfaced sooner? Still, something deep in his gut told him she wasn't.

"C.J.?"

He let out a humorless laugh, then collapsed back into the chair, meeting her gaze. "You really believe me, don't you? About Ethan. Not being mine."

"Um…yeah. Shouldn't I?"

"No. I mean, yes, I'm telling you the truth. But for all you know, I could be some bastard who'd say anything just to get out of accepting responsibility."

"Are you?"

"A bastard?" he said with a weak smile.

"Trying to duck responsibility."

He shook his head.

"I didn't think so," she said, and he hauled in a huge breath.

"The thing is…I've been a bad boy."

She smirked. "I don't think you want to go there."

"No, I mean…" He exhaled. "The procedure's ninety-nine percent effective. About the same as the Pill. Which your cousin told me she was on, by the way. Why are you shaking your head?"

"Trish couldn't take the Pill, she had bad reactions to the hormones."

C.J. stared at Dana for a moment, then scrubbed the heel of his hand across his jaw. "I'll have to get back to you on *that* piece of information. But as I was saying—"

"Ninety-nine percent."

"Yes."

She was quiet for a long time. Then: "Bummer."

In spite of himself, he felt his mouth pull into a smile. "See, I'm supposed to have things checked every so often. To make sure…"

"I get the picture," she said, flushing slightly. "I take it you—"

"Oh, I did. Every six months for the first two years. No worries, they said."

"But they were wrong?"

"Well, *something* sure as hell was."

She made a funny noise, like a balloon beginning to leak air. "No wonder you look kind of sick. So you really didn't know?"

His own anger, at Trish, at circumstances, but mostly at himself, erupted. "Of course I didn't know! How could I know about something that wasn't supposed to happen, for God's sake?"

She hauled the baby up onto her shoulder, as if shielding him. "Sorry. I had to ask. Because you're right. For all I know—which isn't a whole lot, obviously—maybe you are a master at sidestepping consequences and I'm a fool for believing otherwise."

"You're not a fool, Dana. You're nobody's fool."

"Unlike some people in this room," she said, and he shut his eyes, his head on the back of the chair.

"I suppose I had that coming."

She snorted softly, then said, "Hold on a minute. Did you tell Trish you'd been…fixed?"

"It didn't come up. What I mean is," he said quickly, pushing his head forward to look at her again, "since she volunteered that she was taken care of first, there didn't seem to be any reason to mention it."

"Or to use a condom?"

"You know, I think I liked things better when I thought you were a shrinking violet." She glowered at him. "No, Dana, we didn't use anything else. Since we'd both recently had insurance physicals, there didn't seem to be any point. Especially since I thought, oddly enough, we were doubly safe."

"One chance in a hundred is still pretty slim odds," Dana said, nuzzling the baby's soft, flyaway hair, and C.J. forced himself to take a good look at this kid who may well have beaten the odds, just for the dubious honor of being his son. For a moment, the room spun, as though the earth had shifted under his feet.

"Oh, God," he said on a rush of breath. "What the hell do I know about taking care of a kid?"

Dana had wanted so badly to hold on to her anger, to not feel sorry for the obviously shattered man in front of her. Staying angry with him gave her some focus for her own turmoil, at least. But the shock contorting his features tore her apart. She'd been left with the child, true—but at least she'd always wanted children. C.J., on the other hand, had every reason to feel duped. By everybody.

Still and all, he was a big boy. A big boy who should be more than acquainted with the actions-have-consequences concept by now. Take enough swings at the ball, sooner or later you're gonna break a window.

Even, apparently, one made out of safety glass.

However, in answer to his question, she now swept one arm out, indicating the disaster-stricken apartment. And herself. "And does this look like the living space of someone who *does* know what she's doing?"

"But you're such a natural with kids."

A slightly panicked laugh burst from her mouth. "Loving them and keeping them alive are not the same thing. I'm an only child, never had any little siblings or anything to practice on. I never even babysat, because I was too busy being the nerdy straight-A student. So I don't have anything more to go on than you do."

"I somehow doubt that," C.J. said, and there was no

mistaking the bitterness edging his words. But now was not the time to pursue it. Especially when he asked, "Why do you think your cousin lied about being on the Pill? Why would she have taken that chance?"

Dana lowered Ethan onto his tummy in the playpen, then sat on the sofa in front of it, laying her cheek on her folded arms across the padded top. "Logic has never exactly been Trish's strong suit," she said, watching the baby. "Who knows? Maybe she…" She gulped down the pain. "Maybe she wanted to get pregnant."

"That's nuts."

"No, that's Trish."

"Then why didn't she tell me about the baby, for God's sake?"

She shifted to look at him. "Because this wasn't about you, it was about whatever was going on in my cousin's head at the time. Although those I'd-rather-eat-scorpions-than-become-a-father vibes you give off probably didn't help. And no, it wouldn't even occur to her to fight that. Staying power isn't exactly her strong suit. Heck, sitting through a two-hour-long movie is a strain."

C.J. pushed out a groan. "And you have no idea where she is?"

"Not a clue. I did talk to the police, however," she said, filling him in on the events leading up to her becoming Ethan's caretaker, including her chat with the officer that morning.

"You think she'll come back?"

Dana leaned to one side to see if his face gave more of a clue than his voice as to what he was really thinking, then stood up, retrieved the note. Handed it to him with a, "For what it's worth."

She watched him read it, watched his expression grow more solemn.

"C.J., until you know for sure that Ethan's yours, maybe

you shouldn't get yourself anymore tied up in knots than you already are."

Haunted eyes met hers. "And if he's not?"

"Then I'll deal," she said quietly. "Somehow."

He held her gaze in his for several seconds. "And if he is, then so will I." He handed the note back to her, his gaze drifting to Ethan. "What a crappy thing to do to a kid," he said, the steeliness underlying the softly spoken words sending a shudder up her spine. "No way am I turning my back on my own son, Dana. I'm not hurting financially, he'll have everything he'll ever need. But if she wanted you to have custody…" He shook his head, letting the sentence trail off unfinished.

Several seconds passed before she could speak. But no way in hell was she going to just sit here and nod and go, "Okay, sure, whatever." That Dana didn't live here anymore. "*Excuse me?* What happened to 'no way am I turning my back on my own son'? I didn't shove that birth certificate in your face in exchange for your checkbook, you big turkey!"

"But Trish left him with *you!*" he said, and a raw anguish she hadn't seen before blistered in those deep blue eyes. "Not me."

And with that, comprehension dawned in the deep, muddled recesses of her brain.

Dana sucked in a steadying breath and said, "C.J., my cousin is so many sandwiches short of a picnic she'd starve to death. But she certainly knew I'd recognize your name, and that I'd contact you. So in her own weird way, I don't think she deliberately meant to shut you out."

"Never mind that that's exactly what she did," C.J. said coldly, and Dana thought, *Ah-hah.*

"In any case," she said, "we'll deal with Trish later. Maybe. But right now, this is about Ethan. And if he is yours, damned if *I'm* letting you off the hook like she did."

C.J. flinched as though she'd poked him with a cattle prod. "Dammit, nobody's letting anybody 'off the hook!' Believe me," he said, his mouth contorted, "nobody, *nobody,* knows more than I do that this is about a helluva lot more than money. But pardon me for needing more than fifteen minutes to get used to the idea of being somebody's father!"

The last word came out strangled. His throat working overtime, C.J.'s head snapped toward Ethan, sprawled on his tummy in the playpen. The baby had been contentedly gumming a teething ring; now he lifted his face to them, his drooly grin infused with a trusting curiosity that twisted Dana's heart.

She shifted her own gaze to C.J., thinking, *This is not a bad man.* Screwed up, maybe, but not bad. And expecting him to turn on a dime was not only unfair, but unrealistic. Especially when she remembered how she'd felt after receiving her own life-altering news not all that long ago. It takes time to regain your balance after getting walloped by a two-by-four.

At that, Dana rammed her fingers through her hair; it finally succumbed to the inevitable and came completely undone. "Look," she began again, more gently, "this is a really bizarre situation, and I don't know any more than you do what the next step's going to be. I mean, it all hangs on what you find out, right?"

"Yeah. I suppose."

"All righty then. So. Ethan and I are good for now. And you…" she pushed herself away from the playpen to take C.J. by the arm and steer him toward her door "…need to go home."

Genuine astonishment flashed in his eyes. "You're throwing me out?"

"What I'm doing, is giving you some time to adjust. Trust me, you'll thank me later."

At her doorway—which he did a remarkable job of

filling—he twisted, his eyes grazing hers, rife with emotion. "Later, hell. I'm thanking you now."

"Whatever." Then, with a half-assed shove, she turned him back around. "But if you don't leave immediately," she said, so tired she was beginning to wobble, "I'll have to sic the birds on you."

C.J. looked over her shoulder at Ethan for a full five seconds, gave a sharp nod and left. Dana leaned back against the closed door, watching the small person happily smacking the bottom of the playpen, and thought, *Well, this has been one swell day, hasn't it?*

Back home, C.J. turned on the air-conditioning, ignored his mail, which Guadalupe had left neatly stacked on the kitchen island, and changed into a pair of holey jeans he couldn't imagine any woman putting up with. From the center of the bed, the cat did the one-eyed stare routine and it hit C.J. with the force of a tidal wave that his unencumbered bachelor days were, in all likelihood, history. Because while he'd be an idiot not to get proof that Ethan was his, he'd be a lot more surprised to find out the baby wasn't.

C.J.'s stomach growled. His bare feet softly thudding against the uneven, cool tiles, he stalked to the kitchen and threw together a sandwich without paying much attention to the contents. One set of nitrates was as deadly as another, right?

Ignoring the air-conditioning, he cranked open the kitchen window over the sink, breathing in the scent of fresh cut grass from his neighbor's yard that instantly suffused the still, stuffy room. Steve jumped up onto the sill, mashing his ears against the screen and chattering to the delectable whatever-they-weres incessantly chirping in the juniper bushes under the window. Still standing, C.J. attacked the sandwich, somehow swallowing past the grapefruit-sized lump in his throat as an image of Dana sprang to mind, barefoot in that matchbox of an apartment, her burnished, baby-food-streaked hair floating around her face.

The hard, unforgiving look in her eyes when she'd greeted him at the door, Ethan firmly parked on her hip. Now there, he thought as he took another bite of the sandwich, was someone with all her nurturing instincts firmly in place.

Unlike him. Who wouldn't know a nurturing instinct if it bit him in the butt.

A plan, he thought. He needed a plan. Plans solved problems, or at least reduced them to manageable chunks. When in doubt, just bully your life into order, was his motto. So, still chewing, C.J. marched into his office. Steve followed, complaining; C.J. tromped back to the kitchen, filled the cat's bowl, returned to the office. Sat down. Rammed both hands through his hair.

Thirst strangled him. Seconds later, ice cold beer in hand, he sat down again, yanking open desk drawers until he found a legal pad and a pen. He slapped the pad on his desk, to which Steve promptly laid claim. C.J. threw the beast off; he hopped right back up and settled on top of the phone, glaring. C.J. glared back, then picked up the pen, stared at the paper.

Nothing. Not a single, solitary, blessed thought came to him. But then, how the hell was he supposed to make a plan without all the particulars? Instead, all he saw were two sets of eyes, one blue, one glinty gray green. A child for whom he might very well be responsible, and a woman he had no business getting anywhere near. And, if he got the test results he expected, the two were inextricably linked.

As he would then be to them.

Because while he really wouldn't turn his back on his own child—no matter how unlikely the situation in which he now found himself—neither would he, could he, take the baby away from Dana if her cousin didn't come back. Not that she'd let him, he thought on a wry smile. Poleaxed as she undoubtedly was, she was also clearly already superglued to the kid.

Envy sliced through him, along with a sense of longing so sharp, so unexpected, it took his breath away.

The pen streaked across the room, dinging off the wall. What if he couldn't do this, couldn't be what both woman and child needed him to be? Not that he wouldn't give it his best shot: Even going through the motions would be better than letting a child grow up believing he was a mistake. A burden. But what if that wasn't enough? Would they both end up hating him? The boy, when he realized his father had been faking a connection he'd never really felt? And Dana. Oh, God, Dana. Could he deal with the inevitable disappointment in her eyes?

So what are you going to do about it, lamebrain?

Seconds later, C.J. found himself standing in one of the two guest bedrooms. The one he'd left empty, since guests had never been an issue.

As Steve writhed around his ankles, his questioning meow seeming to ask what the hell they were doing in here, C.J. stood frozen in the center of the room, visualizing a crib in one corner. And in that crib, a chubby little boy with blue eyes leaning over the side, smiling, arms outstretched…

…trusting in his father's unconditional love.

C.J. shut his eyes and waited until the dizziness passed.

Chapter Five

At 8:00 a.m., the phone rang. Wedged in the corner of the sofa with twenty pounds of guzzling baby in her lap, Dana could only glower from across the room as some chick with this godawful Southern accent told whoever to leave a message.

"Hey, it's C.J. I'm on my way over."

Click.

She muttered something unseemly, realizing she wouldn't be able to use the no-no words for long with a baby around. Not only did the apartment look worse than it had yesterday, but she was still unwashed and in her Mickey Mouse sleep-shirt. And despite the Glade PlugIns rammed into every available outlet, she strongly suspected the place reeked of beet-infused baby doo.

Mercy said six-month-olds generally slept through the night. Unfortunately, no one had informed His Highness of that fact. The kid not only peed like a herd of goats, but was

apparently one of those "sensitive" types who didn't tolerate
wet diapers very well, stay-dry linings be damned. Dana cal-
culated she'd had roughly three hours sleep over an eight-hour
period. Again. The last thing she needed was company.
Especially sexy male company who would probably waltz in
here looking ready for brunch at the country club. Whereas
she, on the other hand, looked like week-old roadkill.
Probably smelled like it, too.

She jiggled the bottle, determining Ethan had maybe five
minutes yet to go. It occurred to her she had no idea where
C.J. lived. With any luck, Taylor Ranch, clear on the other
side of the—

Bzzzzzzzt went her doorbell.

—city.

Cell phones, she decided, were the instrument of the devil.

"Who is it?" she yelled, as if she didn't know.

"Dana? Honey?"

Apparently, she didn't.

"Dana?" Her mother's voice came through the door, thin
and anxious. "It's just me, honey, I thought I'd drop by before
I went on to church. You okay in there? Why aren't you
opening the door?"

There was only one person she'd rather see less than C. J.
Turner at that moment, and that person was standing on the
other side of her door.

"Just a sec, Mama!" Dana heaved and grunted her way out
of the deep-cushioned sofa. Ethan never broke his rhythm.
"I'm not, um, dressed."

"Oh, for heaven's sake, honey, I've seen you undressed
before…*oh*…"

The last *oh* was the kind of *oh* people say when they think
they've caught you at an awkward moment. Which was true,
God knew, but, alas, not *that* kind of awkward moment.

"Hang on, almost there…" Swinging Ethan to one hip, she looked down into his fathomless blue eyes. "Okay, you're about to meet your great-aunt Faye." Formula dribbled out of the corner of the baby's mouth, making tracks down his chin. Dana bunched up the hem of the already baptized sleepshirt and wiped away the trickle. "Now, she really loves babies, but don't be surprised if she acts a little peculiar there for a bit. Just hang loose, and we'll all get through this. Okay?"

And exactly who was she trying to reassure here?

"Dana? It's gettin' hot out here in the sun, honey…."

She plastered a smile to her face and swung open the door. "Hey, Mama! What brings you here?"

Her mother's eyes zinged straight to the baby, then drifted over Dana's shoulder to inside the apartment. "I, uh, made coffee cake," she said, sounding a little distracted, "and figured I'd better not leave it around or your father'd eat the whole…dang thing." There was a small, anxious pause, then, "Honey?"

"Mmm?"

"Why are you holding a baby?"

"Because he can't walk yet?"

In a flash of pale rose polyester, Mama pushed her way past Dana into the apartment. "Looks to me," she said, her voice gaining altitude with each syllable, "you've got any number of places you could put him—it is a him, isn't it?—"

Dana nodded.

"—down…oh, my word!" Her hand flew to her mouth. Dana somehow caught the foil-wrapped paper plate before it landed on the carpet and set it on the dining table. She cringed as realization bloomed in her mother's eyes.

The hand fell, and words gushed forth. "Oh, sweet heaven, tell me that isn't Trish's baby! But it has to be, doesn't it? He's the spittin' image of her when she was a baby! That's why she suddenly left town, isn't it? Because she was pregnant? Why she called, wanting to know all about what you were doing and all? Because she had a baby? Well, say something, Dana, for goodness sake!"

"As a matter of fa—"

"Oh, my stars, he looks *exactly* like her! That chick-fuzz hair, and those fat little cheeks… Except for those blue eyes. Where did those blue eyes come from?"

"Anybody home?"

Both women snapped their heads around to the man of the hour, standing in the doorway. He held up a McDonald's bag, as if in explanation for his presence.

"Breakfast?"

Ethan let out a series of gleeful grunts, as if he recognized C.J., who wasn't, Dana realized, dressed for brunch in any country club she'd ever heard tell of. A gray sleeveless sweatshirt, ratty jeans, well-worn running shoes. Far cry from dress shirts and business suits. And yet, he had the nerve to still look good. Probably smelled good, too, fresh from the shower, she guessed, judging from the way his damp hair curled around his ears.

Yeah, heckuva time for the hormones to kick in.

"And who might *you* be?" Dana's mother shrieked, effectively smashing to paste all hormones foolish enough to venture forth this fine Sunday morning.

C.J. thrust out his free hand, laying on the charm thick enough to suffocate the entire Northeast Heights. "C. J. Turner, ma'am." Dana saw her mother's eyes pinch in concentration as she tried to place the name. "And you must be Dana's mother," he said, grinning. "There's no mistaking the resemblance."

Faye's eyes popped wide open, arrowing first at C.J.— "The Realtor Trish worked for"—then to Dana—"the one who's showing you places for the shop?"

Wouldn't be long now. "The very same."

"Well, what's he doing here this early on a Sunday morning? And why is he bringing you breakfast?" Her eyes zipped up and down his body, settling on his eyes. His very blue eyes. With gold flecks around the pupil. Just like Ethan's. "Dressed like tha—" The word ended in a gasp as Faye slumped against the edge of the table, clutching her chest.

The woman had truly missed her calling.

"You…and Trish…and…and…" Faye jiggled her index finger at C.J.'s face, her jaw bouncing up and down for several seconds before she got out, "Blue eyes…*your* blue eyes. The baby…you…and Trish…and…oh."

And still, he managed to give her mother the perfect smile, a little abashed, a little nervous, appropriately contrite. "Yes, Mrs. Malone," he said calmly, "there's a strong chance I'm Ethan's father."

Shock gave way to blazing indignation, of the kind peculiar to Southern women whose kin have been wronged. "Lord have mercy, boy—you must be at least ten, twelve years older than Trish! What were you thinking? She was barely more than a *child!*"

"Oh, come on, Mama." Bouncing Ethan on her hip, Dana grimaced at her mother. "You know as well as I do Trish hasn't been a child since she hit puberty. Or it hit her. And C.J. already told me how it happened, so you can't put all the blame on him—"

Sparking eyes shot to hers. "What do you mean, he already told you?" Dana's face flamed. She was eight years old again, caught sneaking off to her girlfriend's house before she'd cleaned her room. "Yesterday," she said in a somewhat steady voice. "Which is when, uh, Trish left Ethan with me."

"So you spoke with her?"

"Well, no, not exactly. You know all those old movies

where somebody finds the baby in the basket on the doorstep? It was kind of like that."

"Oh, for the love of…" Her mother shut her eyes, shaking her head, but only for a second. Presumably recovered, she said, "Wait a minute—she left him with *you?* Instead of with—" her eyes shot to C.J., then back to Dana "—him? And why didn't you tell me?"

"Because I couldn't deal with having a baby dumped in my lap *and* your overreacting, too!"

"Don't be ridiculous, I've never overreacted in my life!" Faye quit clutching herself long enough to press her fingers into shut eyelids. "But I'm so confused. Was this a secret or something? Did you know about this?" she lobbed at C.J., then to Dana, "Did *you?* I mean, what did Trish say when she dropped the baby off? And where is Trish, anyway?"

Not before a shower and breakfast, Dana decided, could she deal with this. And since C.J. looked as though he'd had the luxury of at least one of those things already—and probably more than three hours sleep, to boot—he was more than welcome to have first crack at her mother.

It was a rotten thing to do, but hey. In all likelihood, he was family now. The sooner he weathered his first Faye Malone interrogation, the better it would be for all concerned.

"Tell you what—" With a sweet smile, Dana handed the baby to a very startled C.J. "Why don't you play with Ethan while I go jump in the shower before the city slaps me with a condemned notice? And you can get acquainted with my mother, while you're at it." She grabbed the McDonald's bag out of C.J.'s hand, extracted coffee and an Egg McMuffin. "Good choice," she noted, then got her fanny, as well as her unconfined 38 D's, the hell out of there.

Holding an active six-month-old, C.J. immediately discovered, was like trying to hang on to a stack of greased phone books. Every part of the child—and there seemed to be an amazing number of those—was hell-bent on veering off in a different direction from all the other parts. After nearly dropping the kid three times in as many seconds, he settled for securing him to his hip under his left arm, his hand braced across the baby's chest. That finally settled, he dared to look up at Dana's mother, who was glowering at him with all the sympathy of a highway patrolman who's clocked you at eighty in a fifty-five-mile-per-hour zone.

Talk about curveballs. Here he'd been all revved up to discuss possible options with Dana, only to be confronted with this fire-breathing she-dragon ready to chew him up and spit him back out in itty-bitty pieces. Her daughter's quick vanishing act didn't seem to faze her. Nor did the fact that two minutes ago, they'd never laid eyes on each other.

"One question," Mrs. Malone said, crossing her arms. "Why are you doubting my niece's assertion that you're the father?"

After he explained, as obliquely and quickly as he could, she regarded him shrewdly for several seconds, then blew out a breath.

"I think I need to sit down," she said, doing just that. "And you do, too, before you drop that baby. Oh, for heaven's sake," she said, leaning over, "this isn't nuclear physics…."

After several seconds of fussing and adjusting, the child was finally seated on his lap to her satisfaction. Then she leaned back, squinting. "So if there's a good chance the baby *isn't* yours," she said, more calmly, "why are you here?"

"Because I don't feel right about leaving Dana to shoulder the burden alone."

"I see. And if it turns out he isn't?"

At that moment, the baby grabbed one of C.J.'s hands, doubling over to gnaw on his knuckle. Without thinking, C.J. shifted to keep the little guy from falling on his noggin, then lifted his eyes to Mrs. Malone's. "Guess I'll deal with that moment when it comes."

Faye gave him a strange, inscrutable look, then shook her head. "I cannot believe that girl just *left* the baby. Then again," she said on a sigh, "knowing Trish, I can. Well…" She slapped her hands on her thighs. "I guess, for once, they'll have to do without me at church."

With that, she sprang from the couch, then began picking up and straightening out as if being timed, only to stop suddenly in front of the balcony door, hugging her elbows. "I owe you an apology, Mr. Turner," she said, her voice tight with humiliation and frustration. "It's not you I'm mad at. My niece has always been headstrong. Always determined to do whatever she wanted and damn the consequences. Even her own mama finally gave up on her, when she was fourteen, sent her to Dana's daddy and me to see what we could do with her."

She turned to him, her mouth set, her eyes hidden behind the window's reflection in her glasses. "Obviously, it wasn't enough. But it's true. By this age, Trish is nobody's responsibility but her own. Whatever the outcome, it's a little late to be accusing anybody of leading my niece down the primrose path. Heaven knows, if she walked in here right now?" Her hair, darker than Dana's, tangled in her collar as she shook her head. "I'd be tempted to throttle the living daylights out of her. Dumping her baby on Dana like that, not having the decency to even tell you about the child…nobody in this family has *ever* done anything like this."

She snatched an empty baby bottle and a rolled-up diaper off the coffee table. "But this family sticks together, Mr. Turner," she said, wagging the bottle for emphasis. "That child's gonna know he belongs, that he has kin that care about him, no matter what his scatterbrained mama might have done."

"I couldn't agree more," C.J. said. "Which is why, if Ethan really is mine, I want him to come live with me."

Three feet from the living room, Dana froze in her tracks.

Her wet hair hanging in trickly little snakes down her back, soaking the fabric of her camp shirt, she cautiously peered out into the living room. Her mother's back was to her, partially blocking her view of C.J. Not that she needed to see his face to picture his expression.

"You don't exactly sound overjoyed about this," Mama said.

"It's hard to sound much of anything when you're still in shock. But it's a no-brainer, wouldn't you say?"

Dana ducked back into the shadows to lean against the wall, too stunned to think clearly, let alone join the fray. Which would probably not be a wise thing until she figured out which side she was on. Shoot, at this point, she didn't even know what the sides *were*. Her mother, however, didn't miss a beat.

"Then why d'you suppose Trish left the baby with Dana and not you?"

It got so quiet, Dana peeked around the corner to make sure everyone was still there. She could see C.J. clearly now, cradling Ethan to his chest, one strong hand cupping the fuzzy little blond head in a protective, masculine pose that set her insides to bubbling.

No instinct for fathering, her foot. Only then his quiet, "Probably because I didn't exactly give her the impression I wanted children," made Dana wince.

"And now you do?"

"Now…I'll *do* whatever I have to. If he's mine."

"Well, he *is* ours," her mother said in that tone of voice that always raised the hair on the back of Dana's neck. "So why not leave him where you know he'll be loved? Without reservation?"

Showtime, Dana thought, lurching into the living room as if pushed. "Okay, Mama, this is really none of your business—"

"Nonsense," her mother replied, completely unperturbed. "This is about *family.*"

"I realize that, but this is a bizarre enough situation without having to deal with outside interference."

"Interference?"

"Yes, interference. As in butting in, an activity at which you excel."

"Well, I never—"

"Yes, you do. Every opportunity you can get. C.J. and I haven't had two minutes to discuss our options—"

"Do you *want* him to take the child?"

She knew what her mother was really asking. And it had nothing to do with C.J. "You mean, because here's a shot at getting the grandbaby I can't give you?"

Her mother flushed. "No, of course not—"

"For goodness' sake, I didn't even know about Ethan forty-eight hours ago! How dumb would it be to start thinking about him as my own this early in the game? Besides which, we already talked about this, how I can always adopt. You'll have your grandchild, Mama," she said, tears prickling behind her eyelids. "Someday. When the time's right. But at the moment, I only want what's best for Ethan."

"And how is it best for the child to send him to live with a man who doesn't even want children?"

"Mrs. Malone," C.J. said quietly, getting to his feet, "I appreciate your concern, which is more than valid. But until I know for sure I'm Ethan's father, there's really nothing to discuss."

"And anyway," Dana said, "Trish is a completely unknown factor in all this. For all we know she might well come to her senses and want her baby back. Until then," she said with a daggered, determined look in C.J.'s direction, "the equally determined expression in his eyes making her own sting even harder, "this kid's going nowhere." She looked back at her mother. "But I wouldn't dream of keeping Ethan from his daddy, whoever that turns out to be."

A war raged in her mother's eyes: anger at being dismissed—for that was what Dana was doing—tangling with an unwavering love, that primal maternal desire to see everything work out. To keep her own child from getting hurt. And that, when all was said and done, tamped down Dana's own annoyance and frustration.

She walked over to the dining table, picked Faye's handbag off the table and handed it to her. The older woman hesitated, looking like the last guest at a party who can't decide how to make a graceful exit, then took the bag.

"If you hurry, you won't even miss the first hymn," Dana said quietly.

Defeated—though for how long, was anybody's guess—Faye simply nodded and headed to the door. Then she turned, worry brimming in her eyes. Dana touched her arm. "It's gonna be okay."

"You're sure?"

"Oddly enough, yeah. I am."

Her mother smoothed away a strand of hair from her daughter's face, squeezed her hand and left. Dana shut the door, leaning her head against it, staring at her bare feet for a moment. "Well," she said to the doorknob, "that went well, don't you think?"

"You can't have children?" C.J. said softly behind her.

Her head jerked around, her insides constricting at the kindness in his eyes. "Nope. Stork took me off his delivery route more than a year ago."

"God, Dana...I'm so sorry. Of all people for that to happen to." He released a sigh. "Talk about not being fair."

She nodded toward the now dozing infant slumped against C.J.'s chest. "You should know."

He gave her the oddest smile, and something kicked in her stomach, a premonition that she wasn't going to like what she was about to hear. She walked over to C.J. to remove the slumbering infant from his arms and lower him into the playpen. The man followed, close enough to feel his heat, for that soap-and-male scent to reach right in and yank her idiot libido to attention.

"I have no intention of taking Ethan away from you, Dana. Especially now."

Hanging on to the side of the playpen, she pressed the heel of her hand to one temple, deciding the heat was making her fuzzy-brained. "Then why did you tell my mother you were?"

"No, what I said was, I wanted him to live with me."

She twisted around. Moved over a bit. Frowned. "Is this where I point out that you're not making any sense?"

His laugh sounded…strained. "No. This is where I ask you to move in, too."

"Get *out*," Mercy and Cass both said simultaneously when Dana got to that point in the story.

After reaching a deal with the owner of the new place, the partners returned to Cass's (since the store was always closed on Mondays) to discuss the hows and whens of the relocation.

Only Dana's insane weekend was proving a much more interesting topic than floor plans and moving company selection. Go figure.

"Yeah, kinda stopped me dead in my tracks, too," Dana said, then frowned at the box of gooey, glistening, probably-still-warm glazed donuts Mercy had just plopped in the middle of the tempered glass table out on Cass's patio. "And you're blatantly setting temptation in my path why?"

Curls glistening, the tube-topped elf settled her tiny fanny on the cushioned faux wicker chair. "Not to worry, these have half the sugar of the regular ones."

Dana's frown deepened. "Oh, you're talking serious crime against nature. Donuts with half the sugar is like sex without…you know."

"And sex without 'you know'," Mercy said, delicately selecting a long john and taking a huge bite, "is better than no sex at all." She wagged the mangled treat at Dana. "He's actually making noises about you moving in before he even knows for sure Ethan's his?"

On a heavy sigh, Dana snatched one of the donuts from the box and morosely bit into it, surprised to discover it wasn't half-bad. As opposed to her life, which was rapidly going down the tubes. She took another bite before mumbling, "He even started talking schedules, believe it or not."

"And like most men," Cass said drily, "he'd no doubt decided that since he'd come up with *a* solution, it had to be *the* solution."

"Yeah, that pretty much covers it." Dana licked guilt-free glaze off her fingers, then popped the plastic top off her skinny latte. "Guy looked like he'd just bagged the mastodon single-handed." If scared out of his wits, Dana silently amended. "Because, he said, it would be the best solution for Ethan. If…well, if things work out that way. Apparently his outrage over Trish's little stunt trumps whatever issues he has about being a father. Oh, for heaven's sake!" she said when she realized they were both giving her say-it-isn't-so looks, "I didn't *agree* to move in with him. Years of dealing with my mother's unilateral decisions notwithstanding, I'm not about to blithely go along with one made by a man I barely even know. Especially when it involves sharing the kitchen at seven in the morning."

Mercy winced in sympathy, while Cass muttered something about God saving them all from men's honor complexes.

"Hah!" Mercy said. "I could name names…." She rolled her eyes.

"So can I," Cass said. "Blake pulled the same number on me, remember? My second husband hadn't even been dead a month and there my first husband was, asking me to remarry him. To *save* me."

"Yeah, except you needed saving," Dana said. "Alan had left you in debt up to your butt, you were pregnant, you had like a million people dependent on you—"

"Hardly a million, Dana."

"Okay, so three. Four, counting the baby. Plus, you and Blake did still have a son together. A teenaged son at that. Oh, and another thing…" She selected a second donut, because she could. "Blake really, really wanted you back. I don't think honor had a lot to do with it, frankly."

"Chick's got a point," Mercy said.

"Still," Cass said with a daggered looked toward Mercy, "why do they insist on equating 'rescuing us' with 'doing something'?"

"Because they're hardwired that way," Mercy said. "The good ones, anyway. Protecting their womenfolk and children is what they do. And sometimes," she went on before Cass, who Dana knew had suffered from her father's obsessive overprotectiveness, could object, "we rescue *them*. Even if they don't know it." The brunette shrugged tawny shoulders. "Basically, I don't see the harm in a little well-placed macho protectiveness, but that's just me."

"In any case," Dana interjected, "that's not what's going on here. This isn't about rescuing *me*, it's about doing right by a six-month-old. And it's not as if I'd be giving up my apartment or anything." Wide-eyed, she looked from one to the other. "Oh, God…I really said that, didn't I?"

"Hey," Mercy said, taking a sip of her rudely unskinny latte with gobs of whipped cream, "if it were me, I'd be over there so fast it'd make his head spin." When both Cass and Dana gawked at her, she shrugged. "The guy's loaded, right? So we're probably not talking some crumbling old adobe in the South Valley. And let's face it, sweetie…" She leaned over and patted Dana's hand. "You live in a shoebox. Besides, if the man wants to help take care of the kid, why not?"

"Because nothing's settled yet?" Dana said.

"And the longer he has to mull things over before the paternity issue *is* settled, the more chances he has to change his mind. Trust me, honey. Giving a man time to think is never a good idea."

Dana's gaze swung to Cass, who lifted her shoulders. "I'm afraid I have to cede that point to her. And you do live in a shoebox. Of course," she said, swirling the remains of her coffee around in her cup, "you could always move back in with your parents."

"Like hell," Dana said, and Cass smiled.

"So when will C.J. know for sure whether he's the father?" she asked.

"In a few days, depending on the lab's turnaround. He had an appointment for first thing this morning. He, uh, decided to go ahead and submit…samples for both tests now, rather than wait on the…you know, before initiating the paternity test. As a matter of fact, I have to take Ethan when we finish here to let them swab the inside of his cheek for the DNA sample. What?" she said at Mercy's head shake.

"I think the word you're looking for is *semen?*"

Cass choked on her coffee while Dana blushed. "We're practically strangers," she said in a whisper. "Talking about his…"

"Swimmers?" Mercy supplied.

"…just seems a little…personal at this point."

"And yet, somehow, you're not still a virgin. Amazing."

"So still no word from Trish?" Cass asked. Bless her.

"Nope. But C.J.'s got her social security number from her employee records, he said he might have someone see if they can find her that way. He wants some answers. So do I." Her eyes burned. "I never realized how much I hated being taken advantage of before this happened. And you know what's most annoying about this whole thing? The unsettledness of it. So what happens if I take care of Ethan for a few months, or a year? Or more? And then Trish waltzes back and decides she's changed her mind? Not only have I put my own life on hold during the interim, but how is this good for Ethan? It kills me to think that right when everybody starts thinking in terms of permanent, Trish'll have a change of heart and we'll all the get rug yanked out from under us."

Dana caught herself, flushing with embarrassment. Because her outburst hadn't been only about Ethan, although it was true—withholding part of herself from the child, in case she lost him, wasn't even an option. She simply wasn't made that way. Withholding part of herself from C.J., however, was another issue entirely. Yes, falling for him would be beyond stupid, but, like every other woman in the known universe, *stupid* was not as alien a concept as she might have wished.

And if she did end up moving in with him, maybe sharing living space would knock those stars right out of her eyes. With any luck, he put on all that charm and suaveness like one of his thousand-dollar suits, shucking them the minute he got back home, revealing the real throwback lurking underneath the public persona. Maybe C.J.'s living alone was actually a blessing to womankind the world over.

Okay, so it was a long shot. But you never knew, right?

Then Lucille, Cass's former mother-in-law, tottered out

onto the patio in platform sandals, clutching a squirmy, Onesie-clad Jason to her nonexistent bosom. "Somebody wants his mommy," the blazing redhead said as Cass quickly took her infant son from his grandmother. "And yours," she said to Dana, "is still sacked out in the middle of my bed like somebody slipped him a mickey. Hey, donuts! Don't anybody tell Wanda," she said, reaching over and snagging one, "or my tuchus is in a sling for sure."

But Ethan *wasn't* hers, Dana thought with a prick to her heart, only half listening as her partners finally got the business discussion back on track. Because for all Trish's tenuous grasp on reality, she'd still clearly taken good care of her baby. Yeah, she'd freaked, as Trish was wont to do, but still, that it had taken her six months to reach her breaking point said a lot.

Namely, that in all likelihood she would change her mind. Maybe tomorrow, maybe months from now. But eventually she'd come back for her child, leaving Dana with nothing but memories…and an ever-widening hole in her heart. And then, to make matters ten times worse, there was C.J.'s offer to consider.

If he turned out to be Ethan's father.

If Trish didn't return.

If Dana decided there was no better way to handle the bizarre situation. For Ethan's sake.

If, if, if…the tiny words pelted her like hyper BBs.

One day, she thought, it'll be for real.

One day, she thought, scarfing down another donut, *maybe I'll finally get to live my own life, instead of being a place-holder in everybody else's.*

If. If.

If.

Chapter Six

C.J. stared through his office window at the mottled Sandias on the other side of the city, backlit by masses of foamy, billowing white thunderheads. He checked his watch for the hundredth time, but it was still too early.

Today. Today, he'd know for sure.

The first lab result—which showed that, yep, his little guys had indeed, against all odds, found their way back into the game—had left the door open for the second. He'd been reasonably able to concentrate up till now, but the closer he got to D-Day, the more toastlike his brain became. Every time his phone rang, his stomach jolted. He'd even spaced on an appointment with a new client earlier, something he *never* did.

Not since his MBA days, when he'd sweated out that last, excruciating final in Statistics, had he gone through this kind of wait-and-see hell. Only a damn sight more was hanging on the outcome of *this* test.

Worst of all, C.J. still had no idea how he felt about any of it. Or was supposed to feel. Not that the idea of being responsible for this innocent little dude still didn't make his stomach knot, but the initial constant howl of outrage had at least throttled down to the odd, intermittent burst of irritation. After all, he'd been warned this could happen, that he needed to be diligent about checking. That he hadn't was nobody's fault but his. So if he'd dodged the bullet, by rights he should be profoundly relieved.

Except…

C.J. glared at the cloud-shaped shadows scudding across the face of the mountains. So what was up with the kick to his gut every time he saw the baby—which had only been a couple of times, given both his and Dana's impossible schedules and Dana's justified resistance to getting too cozy before the results came back? Never in a million years would C.J. have guessed that, in the end, some idiotic biological imperative could override more than twenty years of what he'd been completely convinced he'd wanted. Or, in this case, not wanted.

But there it was, jeering at him from the sidelines: an unwarranted, and completely illogical, anxiety that Ethan might *not* be his.

Val appeared in his doorway, hands parked on hips. "Okay. You want to tell me what in tarnation is up with you today?"

C.J. swiveled his gaze to her don't-even-think-about-messin'-with-me one. And part of him wanted nothing more than to come clean to this woman who'd become far more than an office manager over the past few years. But until he knew for sure, he wasn't keen on letting any more people into the loop than absolutely necessary. Even Val, increasingly difficult though it was to keep her out.

"Sleepless night," he said. Which was true. And not only because of the whole tenterhooks thing about his possible paternity, but because every time he'd start to drift off, Dana's horrified reaction to his suggestion that they live together would romp through his thoughts. Not that he blamed her. Why in God's name he'd thought it made perfect sense at the time, he had no idea. Why he still thought so, he understood even less.

Especially considering the serious train wreck potential of having Dana Malone living under his roof.

"Never affected your work before," Val said, her power-saw twang slicing through his musings. "Sleepless nights, I mean."

He glowered at her. "And how would you know whether I've had sleepless nights or not? I don't exactly advertise it."

"Other than the fact that on those mornings you grunt instead of talk, you guzzle coffee like somebody declared a shortage, and your ties never go with the rest of your clothes? I've seen subtler billboards. Still and all, I've never known you to let your private life—if you even have one, which I sometimes doubt— affect your work. So I repeat…what's going on?"

C.J. gave his office manager a long, steady look. "First off, there's a reason it's called *private,* Val." She gave an unrepentant snort. "And secondly, *I* repeat, nothing's going on. So sorry to blow your theory."

"You haven't blown anything. Because sure as I'm standing here you're lying through those movie star teeth of yours. And you do know there will be hell to pay when I find out the truth."

Refusing to rise to the bait, he said instead, "Thanks for covering with the Jaramillos, by the way."

"No problem. Just remember it when it's time for my salary review. And when you come out of that fog you're not in, that market analysis you're gonna ask for is already on the computer. As are the month-end sales figures. We're up ten percent over last year, by the way, so you shouldn't have any trouble finding money for that raise you're gonna give me. You want more coffee?"

"God, yes. But you don't have to—" Her raised eyebrows over her glasses cut him off. "Thank you," he said on a rush of air.

"You're welcome," Val said, turning to leave.

"Don't know how I'd live without you," he called to her retreating back, chuckling at her fading, "That makes two of us," from down the hall. A half minute later, she appeared with a huge mug of steaming coffee, his mail and a pink While You Were Out Slip, all of which he took from her.

"You took this message five minutes ago," he said, frowning at her scrawled time notation beside the unfamiliar name and number. "Why didn't you put it through?"

"Because I'm screening your calls today, that's why. Said she's got a house up in High Desert to go on the market, some friend of hers recommended you."

He handed her back the slip. "I've got more listings than I can handle, pass her on to Bill. What?" he said after a moment when he realized Val was still standing there, gaping at him.

"Since when do you pass up a listing for a million-dollar house? She gave me the address and the square footage, I checked the comps," Val said to his unanswered question. "Maybe even a million-two." She firmly put the slip back on his desk. C.J. picked it up again, held it in front of her.

"And the whole reason I took on the other agents was to give me at least half a shot of seeing forty. And Bill could use the finessing practice. *What?*" he said again at the twin lasers piercing him from those beady eyes of hers.

"*Nothin's goin' on,* my fanny," she muttered, snatching the slip and once again hotfooting it out of his office. A few minutes later, she buzzed him to announce she was going to lunch and that all the calls were being forwarded to his office, and to ask, did he need anything before she left?

"No, I'm good," he said, although he wouldn't mind

putting in an order for an auxiliary brain right about now. He cursorily checked his mail, which included an invitation to yet another charity function, then forced himself out of his chair and down the hall to the small room where they kept employee records, finally addressing a task he'd been putting off for days.

Minutes later, he was back at his desk, Trish's social security number scrawled on a Post-it note, making a phone call he'd never in his wildest dreams envisioned himself making. And not only because he'd once dated the P.I., years ago when she'd been a rookie cop who'd pulled him over for speeding.

"You say this chick left the baby with a friend of yours?" Elena Morales now said, clearly unable to suppress the curiosity in her voice.

"Yeah. The mother's cousin, actually."

"I see. And you're worried this gal won't come back?"

"No, actually, I'm worried she will. That is to say…" C.J. rubbed the space between his brows, realizing he must sound like a primo nutcase. "It's complicated. And I'd like to see as few people hurt as possible."

"The baby's yours, C.J., isn't he?" Elena said quietly.

"Very possibly," he admitted. "I'll know soon."

"Wow," Elena said, the single word positively drenched in amused irony. "Sounds like somebody's finally grown up."

C.J. grimaced. Even in her early twenties, Elena had wanted more than C.J. had been willing, or able, to give her. From what he understood, she'd found it, with someone else, shortly after they'd split. "I was twenty-five when we dated, Lena. Thinking back, I probably shouldn't have been allowed out in public, let alone anywhere near another human being."

She laughed. "Oh, don't be so hard on yourself. It's over, it's done, and I seem to recall we had a lot of fun. For a while, anyway." He could hear the smile in her voice. "Besides, regrets are a waste of energy. I'm just saying, I'm hearing something now I never heard then."

"And what might that be?"

"I'm not sure. Like maybe you actually give a damn? That you're *involved.* Anyway. I'll get on this, and I'll let you know as soon as I find something. Or the woman herself."

But instead of feeling more settled now that he'd taken at least some control of the situation, he felt more discombobulated than ever. Involved? Try trapped. In a situation not of his choosing, and yet undeniably a result of his own idiocy. If he'd only listened to his urologist…if he hadn't given in to Trish's entreaties…

If, if, if.

The phone rang; without checking the display, he punched the line button.

"Turner Realty—"

"Mr. Turner? It's Melanie from Foothills Lab. We have the results of your DNA test…."

This, there was no keeping from her mother. Not that she hadn't been tempted.

"But why, Dana? Why do you have to go *live* with the man?"

As she was saying.

"Because, Mama," Dana said, mindlessly tossing enough clothes into a suitcase to get her through the week, "now that there's no question that C.J.'s the father, his custodial rights far outrank mine. No matter what Trish wants," she added, cutting her mother off. "And, you know, considering his initial aversion to fatherhood, maybe everybody should see his willingness to do right by his kid as, you know, a *good* thing?"

"What's this?"

Dana turned to find her mother fingering through one of the many spiral notebooks Dana kept around the house, confusion etched in her features when she glanced up. "You're still writing?"

"Yes, Mama, I'm still writing," Dana muttered, practically grabbing the book from her mother and tossing it on top of the clothes. She'd started scribbling down ideas for a story as a way to dodge the depression that had threatened to take her under a year ago, only to find the outlet far more fulfilling than she would have ever expected. And increasingly habit-forming, despite all the other demands on her time. She'd only mentioned it to her mother once, however.

"Oh. I thought you'd given up on that. I mean, isn't it kind of pointless?"

"Ma? Hello?" She zipped up the bag. "Bigger fish to fry right now?"

Her mother huffed and seamlessly shifted gears again. "So why can't you share custody? Ethan could go to his father's house one night, yours the next—"

"Because C.J. knows less about taking care of a baby than I do? Because it's going to be hard enough for him to bond with his son without shunting him back and forth between our houses? Because my place is too small? Because Trish left him with *me*."

Dana headed to the living room, her mother's, "You could move back in with us, you know," following in her wake. Grabbing the birdcage cover, she tossed her mother a brief, but pointed, *not-in-this-lifetime* glare in response. "It's an option, honey," her mother said, wilting slightly.

"One which I entertained for about two seconds and immediately rejected." Dana tossed the cover over the cage, earning her a squawk from Ethan, who'd been holding a lengthy conversation with the finches from his playpen. When she caught the *just-kill-me-now* set to her mother's mouth, however, she let out a long breath, then put her hands on the older woman's arms. "Look, I know this isn't ideal. But what can I tell you, crazy circumstances call for inventive solutions. And this is the only way I can figure out how to do what's right by everybody. Including not violating Trish's wishes."

Worry still crowding her mother's eyes, she reached across to lay her hand on top of Dana's. "But you don't even know what she's gonna do, honey. And I hate the idea of you gettin' in over your head. It's happened before, you know, more than once. Now, don't be put out with me," she added when Dana pulled away to gather up the rest of her writing journals and laptop from her desk, tucking them into a canvas totebag. "The way you always see the good in people is a wonderful thing, it truly is. But while I'm sure C.J. intends to do his best by his child, that doesn't mean—"

"—that he's even remotely interested in taking us as a package," Dana finished over the sting of her mother's words.

"Well. It's just that you're so tender-hearted, you know—"

"That doesn't mean I'm blind," Dana said, reeling on her mother, her arms clamped over her midsection. "Or stupid." Faye's eyebrows lifted. "Okay, fine. To put an end to your pussyfooting around the subject, I don't suppose there's any point in pretending I'm not attracted to the man."

"See, that's what worries me—"

"Well, stop it. Right now. Because I am also very well aware that C. J. Turner isn't interested in me that way. Besides, even if he was looking to settle down, which he's made plain he isn't, I can't see that we have anything in common other than Ethan. So see, Mama, I have thought this through. Long and hard. So you're going to have to trust that I'm made of sterner stuff than you're apparently giving me credit for."

"And if your heart gets broken? Again?"

"Not gonna happen." Dana looked steadily at her mother, knowing full well it wasn't only Dana's potential attachment to

C.J. she was worried about. She tapped down the twinge of apprehension that echoed through her and said, "Now if you want to be helpful, you could pack up Ethan's diaper bag for me."

A request that, amazingly enough, derailed the conversation.

Two hours later, however, standing in the stone-floored entryway to C.J.'s more than spacious house, holding a babbling Ethan and gawking through the living room's bank of floor-to-ceiling windows at the mountain vista scraping the periwinkle sky, her only thought was, *I am so screwed.*

And only partly because of the excruciating awkwardness of the situation, the way C.J. and she were suddenly acting with each other like a couple on a forced blind date. Nor was it—she told herself—because she was in any danger of falling for the guy. His house, however…

Slowly, she pivoted, taking in the twelve-foot ceilings, the stone floors, the archways leading in a half-dozen directions. Not that her parents' three-bedroom, brick-and-stucco ranch house was exactly a shack. But compared with *this*…

This, she could get used to. Unfortunately.

"You hate it," she heard behind her.

She turned to see C.J., in jeans and a faded Grateful Dead T-shirt, carefully setting the birdcage into a small niche right inside the living room. "Not at all. Why would you think that?"

"There's not exactly a lot of furniture."

True, other than the floor-to-ceiling bookshelves crammed to the gills, the decor was a bit on the spartan side. But the oversized taupe leather sofa and chairs, the boldly patterned geometric rug in reds and blacks and neutrals underneath, got the job done. "It's okay, I like it like this."

"Really?"

"Really."

His eyes swung to hers. Tonight, an odd whiff of vulnerability overlaid the cool confidence, that aura of success he normally exuded. In fact, if she weren't mistaken, there was the slightest shimmer of a need for approval in his expression. Although she imagined he'd chop off a limb rather than admit it.

"I'm here so seldom, I never got around to…" He made a rolling motion with his hand. "You know. The stuff."

She smiled, his obvious discomfiture settling her own nerves a hair or two. "Accessories, you mean?"

"Yeah. All those little touches that make a house a real home. Like your apartment."

What a funny guy, she mused, then said gently, "It's not the stuff that make a house a home, C.J. It's the people who live there."

He nodded, then apparently noticed she was about to drop the baby. "Um…well, I suppose I should show you where you and Ethan are going to sleep."

"Good idea. Although…" She hefted the baby toward him. "Here, he's gettin' heavier by the second."

"Oh…sure." After only a moment's hesitation while he apparently tried to figure out the best way to make the transfer, C.J. gingerly slipped his hands under the baby's armpits, giving her a relieved smile once the baby was securely settled against his chest, rubbing his nose into the soft gray fabric of his daddy's shirt. C.J.'s eyes shot to Dana's. "Does he need a tissue or something?"

Dana laughed, even as her insides did a little hop-skip at the mixture of tenderness and panic on C.J.'s face. "No, I think that means he's sleepy. We'd better get the crib set up pretty soon so we can put him down."

"Crib. Right. Follow me."

C.J. loped down the hall leading off the foyer, Ethan clearly enjoying the view from this new, and much higher, vantage point. Dana trotted dutifully along behind, catching glimpses of a simply furnished dining room, a massive kitchen given to heavy use of granite and brushed steel and a family room with a billboard-sized, flat-panel TV.

"I thought we could put the baby in here," he said, as she followed him into a large, completely empty bedroom with plush, wheat-colored carpeting and a view of the golf course…and the pool. Of course. "And then *this* room," C.J. said, barely giving Dana the chance to register that he'd already bought a beautiful wooden changing table and matching chest of drawers, "is yours." She double-stepped to catch up.

"Oh!"

Not at all what she'd expected, given the masculine minimalism in the rest of the house. And certainly the cinnabar-hued walls were a shock after the inoffensive real-estate neutrals in her own apartment. But the rich color, the honeyed pine headboard on the high double bed, the poufy, snowy-white comforter and masses of pillows, immediately brought a grin to her lips.

"Blame the decorator," he said behind her.

"*Thank* the decorator, you mean," she said, unable to resist skimming a hand across the cool, smooth surface of the comforter. She could sense him watching her; she didn't allow herself the luxury of contemplating what he might be thinking. That he'd been invaded, most likely.

"Well," he said. "That's good, then. Okay. Well. Here," he said, handing back the baby. "I'll go bring in the rest of the stuff."

Jiggling Ethan, she stuck her head into the adjoining bathroom, shaking her head at the expanse of marble and the multiheaded shower stall that looked far grander than anything that utilitarian had a right to look. "Heck, you can even see the entire city from the john," she murmured to the baby, who had decided prying off her nose would be amusing. "Is that weird or what?"

But then, so was this whole setup. Moving in with a man

she barely knew wasn't exactly something she did on a regular basis. Heck, moving in with *any* man wasn't something she did on *any* kind of basis. But still. As weird setups went, this was about as classy as they came.

Once back in the bedroom, she stopped dead at the sight of the gargantuan, charcoal-gray cat sitting smack dab in the middle of the bed. Pale green eyes—curious, bored—assessed her with unnerving calm. C.J. had a cat? A cat who undoubtedly made walls tremble when he walked through the house. A cat who— the thing yawned, sucking up half the air in the room—probably lived for catching and eating things. Like mice. Chihuahuas. Tasty little finches.

With another yawn, the beast fell over on his side and began to clean one paw. "You are so not sleeping with me," Dana said, then carted the baby out of the cat-infested room and back to his own, where C.J. had set up the portacrib in a corner close to one window.

"Do we need to change him or something?" C.J. asked.

"Nope. Already did that before we left the apartment, so he's good. Okay, sweetie," she whispered to the tiny boy, nuzzling his corn-silk head before lowering him into the crib. "It's night-night time. Get that white blanket out of the diaper bag, would you? Yes, that's it," she said to C.J. Except instead of reaching for it, she said, "On second thought, why don't you give it to him?"

"Me? Why?"

"Because it's his 'lovey.' It makes him feel secure. So he'll start associating feeling safe with you."

"Uh, gee, Dana. I don't know...."

"C.J." she said firmly. "The idea's to make *him* feel safe. Not you."

Those blue eyes, gone a soft gray in the twilight, grazed hers for a moment before he nodded, then lowered the blanket into the crib. The baby grabbed it and keeled over, his eyes shutting almost immediately. C.J. stood as though paralyzed, gripping the railing.

"Good God," he breathed, his voice littered with the shrapnel of confusion, amazement, shock. "There's a *baby* sleeping in my house."

"Now you know how I felt the past two nights. Except he didn't do a whole lot of sleeping. Come on, we can finish up in here later."

But when she got to the door, she turned to find C.J. still rooted to the spot, his gaze glued to the now-sleeping infant.

She opened her mouth to call him again, only to tiptoe away instead.

Hours later, C.J. lay in bed, his hands linked behind his head, staring at the ceiling. Had he ever had—what had Dana called it? A "lovey?"—when he'd been a baby? Somehow, he doubted it. Although, from what she'd said when he asked her about it over pizza a little later, most babies had something they use to soothe themselves when they were by themselves—a blanket, a stuffed toy, a small pillow.

Actually, she was a font of information, especially for someone who insisted she knew nothing, really, about taking care of babies. With a pang of sympathy, he wondered how long she'd been studying up, in anticipation of being a mother herself someday. How cheated she must have felt to have had that particular opportunity ripped from her. And yet, when he'd questioned her about it, there'd been no bitterness in her voice that he could tell. Just acceptance.

Grace, he thought it was called.

C.J. hauled himself upright, his abs having plenty to say about how long it had been since he'd even set foot inside the state-of-the-art exercise room next to his bedroom. Still, there was no denying the wonder in Dana's eyes when she looked at Ethan. Or the longing. And watching the two of them, the way they seemed to mold themselves to each other, he'd felt…ashamed. Inadequate.

And, again, envious.

He forked his hand through his hair three times in rapid succession, it finally registering that the cat had abandoned him sometime during the night. At the same time, a tiny sound came from the baby monitor next to his bed—his nod to gallantry, since Dana had been clearly dead on her feet. In the dark, C.J. stared at it, not breathing.

There it was again. Not exactly distressed, he didn't think, but definitely a call for attention. Sort of a questioning gurgle. On a sigh, C.J. got up, adjusted the tie on his sleep pants and plodded to the other end of the house, flicking on the hall light to peer into Ethan's room. The wide-awake baby inside turned his head toward the light, then flipped over onto his tummy, giving C.J. a broad grin through the mesh of the portable crib. A second later, C.J. caught wind of the reason behind the baby's wakefulness.

Uh…

He scooted down the hall toward Dana's room, both surprised and relieved to find her door open. A shaft of light from the hall sliced across the bed, where she lay sprawled in a tangle of sheets and nightgown, making cute little snuffling sounds. With an unmistakable "What the hell?" expression, the cat's head popped up from behind the crook of her knees.

From the other room, Ethan made a noise that sounded like "Da?"

"Dana?" C.J. whispered.

Nothing. Out like a light. Although the cat *prrrped* at him. And Ethan let out another, more insistent, "Da?" Or maybe it was "Ba?" Hard to tell.

Resigning himself to the inevitable, C.J. released another breath and returned to the baby, who was now lying on his back, thoughtfully examining his toes with a scrunched-up expression that made C.J. chuckle in spite of…everything. Ethan swung his head around, his entire face lighting up in a huge, nearly toothless smile of welcome. Or maybe gratitude.

And way deep inside C.J.'s gut, something twinged. Like unexpectedly pulling a previously unused muscle.

"I suppose you need your diaper changed," he said, turning on the light. Ethan, now beside himself with anticipation, started madly flapping his arms and kicking his legs, which wasn't doing a whole lot for the smell factor.

Okay, he could do this. Just as soon as he figured out what the hell half the things in the diaper bag were for. C.J. rummaged around in the bag for a few seconds, pulling out some kind of pad thing that looked reasonable to spread underneath the kid on the changing table, followed by a diaper, powder, wipes and lotions. There. That should do it. Then he sucked in a huge breath, hauled Mr. Stinky out of the crib and over to the table, and got to it, trying to picture his own father doing this for him. Somehow, he wasn't seeing it.

A minute or so and roughly half a container of wipes later, he heard Dana's huge yawn behind him.

"Now you show up," C.J. muttered, stashing the last of the wipes inside the gross diaper and cramming the whole mess into what he hoped was a bag for that purpose. But, judging from Ethan's kicks and little squeals, the kid was clearly enjoying being sprung from the nastiness so much C.J. hadn't had the heart to put the clean diaper on him yet.

"Sorry," she said on another yawn. "I was really out. Uh, C.J.?"

He twisted around and thought, simply, *Uh, boy.* Heavy-lidded eyes. Masses of sleep-tangled hair in a thousand shades of red, brown, gold. Pale shoulders, nearly bare save for the skinny little straps holding up that nightgown. A plain thing, nothing but yards of thin white fabric skimming her unconfined breasts, falling in deeply shadowed folds to the tops of her naked feet, revealing toenails like ten little rubies. Except for where it clung just enough, here and there, to stir all sorts of unrepentantly male thoughts and musings and such. C.J. mentally shook his head. "What on earth have you been feeding this kid?"

"Food. C.J., really, this isn't a criticism, but you might want to—"

"Oh, crap!" he yelled as a warm stream hit him square in the chest.

"—not let the air get to his…him like that."

C.J. yanked one of the wipes from the container and started swabbing himself off. "Don't you dare laugh."

He heard her clear her throat. "Wouldn't dream of it." The gown billowed at her feet as she crossed the room. "Go get cleaned up," she said, laughter bubbling at the edges of her words. "I'll finish up here."

When C.J. returned a minute later, she was bent over the crib, babbling at the baby, her voice soft and warm as a summer breeze, radiating enough femininity to drown a man in all things good and bad and everything in between. When she smiled up at him, he frowned. She misinterpreted.

"Oh, don't be such a grump," she gently chided. "It's just a little baby pee. Isn't it, sweetie?" she cooed to Ethan. "You were just doin' what comes naturally, weren't you?"

C.J. grunted, appreciating the irony of his son, the by-product of *his* doing "what comes naturally," returning the favor. "Glad you're having such fun at my expense."

Dana handed Ethan's blanket back to him, then padded back toward the door, signaling to C.J. to follow. "They say," she whispered, "if you don't play with them when they wake up in the middle of the night, they're more likely to go back to sleep. Otherwise they'll think it's party time. And if it makes you feel any better, he got me good the first night I had him, too."

"Yeah?"

"Oh, yeah." She started down the hall as C.J. flicked off the light. "I looked like I'd been in a wet T-shirt contest—" Her eyes squeezed shut for a moment, and one hand shoved her hair back from her face. Which probably wasn't the brightest move in the world on her part in that lightweight gown. "Wow, I'm suddenly *starved.* What I mean to say is…how about I meet you in the kitchen and we can see what you've got. In your refrigerator, I mean."

C.J. folded his arms over his bare chest, thoroughly enjoying the moment. Especially the part involving the play of the hall light over all those folds and things. Dear God, the woman had more curves than a mountain road. And C.J. wouldn't have been human—let alone alive—had he not entertained at least a brief thought involving the words *test drive.*

"Oh, I can tell you what I've got," he said evenly, even as *You are so screwed* blasted through his skull. Because if they kept meeting up at night like this, with her dressed like that, he was gonna have a helluva time remembering she was here strictly for the baby's sake. And only temporarily, at that.

Ah, hell. Not the doe eyes. Anything but the doe eyes.

"Leftover pizza," he said, and she flinched slightly and said, "What?"

"What I've got. In the refrigerator. Leftover pizza."

"Oh," she said, then smiled brightly. "Fine. Let me grab my robe and I'll be right there."

"You want it hot?" C.J. said to her back as she scurried away. When she spun around, those eyes ever wider (how *did* she do that?), he grinned. Because, dammit, he was having fun. And okay, because he wanted another glimpse of her before she covered everything up with a robe. "The pizza," he said.

Their gazes sparred for a moment or two before she said, in a voice that managed to be sweet and sultry at the same time (and he really wanted to know how she did *that*), "Don't put yourself out on my account. I'm perfectly capable of…taking care of myself." Then *she* grinned. With her head tilted just…so.

A doe-eyed, sweet-sultry voiced smart ass. Yeah, he was in trouble, all right.

Chapter Seven

"Okay," Dana said, peering into C.J.'s destroyer-sized refrigerator at the box of leftover pizza, three cans of beer and quart of milk staring balefully back at her. "Somebody's gotta do some serious shopping tomorrow. This is pitiful. And so—" she hauled out the box of pizza "—clichéd."

Speaking of pitiful. And clichéd. What was up with that little do-si-do between them out in the hallway a few minutes ago? Not to mention her reaction to it? Okay, so it had been a while, but…yeesh.

She stuck a piece of mushroom-and-olive pizza in the microwave, stole a surreptitious glance at the beard-hazed, bed-headed hunk somehow sprawled on a barstool, his elbows propped behind him on the bar, and thought, *This will never do.* Well, actually, he'd do quite nicely, she imagined, but *there,* she was definitely not going. Unfortunately, *here,* she already was, which was why she was having all these wayward, albeit intriguing, thoughts at two-thirty in the morning.

"So we'll go shopping," C.J. said on a yawn, then gave a lazy, not-quite-focused grin. "There you are, you rotten beast," he said to the cat, who had wandered into the kitchen and was now sitting in the middle of the floor like the world's largest dust bunny. "So what's with throwing me over for the first beautiful woman to cross your path?"

Dana's gaze hopped from the cat back to C.J. Such a simple sentence to produce so many questions. And, as if sensing the most profound of those questions, C.J. shrugged and said, "You and Ethan are our first overnight guests."

"And how long have you been here?"

"In this house? Two years, give or take. I was previewing it for a client and decided to buy it myself."

"I don't blame you, it's really spectacular."

"What it is, is an investment. In five years, it'll be worth twice what I paid for it, easily." The muscles in his face eased, though, when he said, "Funny, though, how I wasn't even looking for a house." He tore off a tiny piece of cheese and threw it either to or at the cat, Dana couldn't tell "Anymore than I was looking for a cat. But I opened the door one stormy night, just to smell the rain, and this soaking wet *thing*—" another piece of cheese rocketed through the air "—ran inside. And never left. Right, Steve?"

"Steve?"

C.J. shrugged. "It seemed to fit, what can I say?"

The microwave dinged. She retrieved her pizza and leaned against the counter to eat it standing up. "You don't strike me as a cat person."

"I'm not." He tossed Steve a piece of pepperoni. Dana could hear the cat's purr from clear across the kitchen.

"You could have taken him to the pound, you know."

"Not once I'd named him."

"Of course."

He chuckled. "You—" he stabbed the air with his pizza crust for emphasis "—don't like cats."

She smirked. "I think it's more that they don't like me."

"Why would you think that?"

"I've had, at various times in my life, three cats. They've all run away."

"Don't take it personally. Cats are just like that sometimes."

"My point exactly. At least with birds you put them in a cage, and there they stay."

"Unless they get out. And birds aren't real good at coming when you call."

"Oh, and cats *are?*"

"When it suits their purpose, sure. But Steve's the perfect roomie. Food, water, a patch of sunlight, access to my bed," he said with a slanted grin, "and he's good. And best of all, there's none of that messy emotional stuff to weigh us down."

"Ah. One of those no-strings, you-just-sleep-together relationships."

"Like I said. Perfect."

"Are you deliberately trying to annoy me or what?"

"Nope. Just tellin' it like it is. Although, as I said, Steve dumped me for you tonight."

She blinked, his earlier words finally sinking in. "What?"

"You didn't notice? When I peeked in on you—"

"When you what?"

"I thought the baby might've awakened you, so I looked in to check. Anyway, there the cat was, plastered right up against you, happy as a clam. Not that I blame him." He grinned, heat lazily flickering in half-hooded eyes.

Dana huffed. "You're doing it again, aren't you?"

"What can I tell you, it's late, my defenses are down."

Even if other things aren't.

Bad enough that the unsaid words practically rang out in the cavernous room without Dana's having no idea whose unsaid words they were.

Brother.

"So, shopping," he said, scattering the unsaid words to the four winds. "What time do you have to be at work?"

And so it began. The great baby-and-work shuffle. Because their momentary sharing of living space notwithstanding, it wasn't as if either of them could drop everything to stay home with a baby. The situation was still more expedient than living separately, perhaps, but far from ideal.

"Nine. Or thereabouts. I have to drop the baby off at my mother's first."

"Yeah, I'll be gone by eight, so I guess the morning's out." Then his forehead knotted. "I thought you said your parents couldn't take care of him?"

"What I said was, I didn't think they *should* be saddled with taking care of a child at their ages. Especially since they've finally gotten to the point where they can load up the RV and hit the road whenever the mood strikes. As hard as they've both worked all their lives, they deserve time to themselves. When I suggested looking into day care, however, my mother had a hissy and a half."

"I bet she did. Your mother's a real—"

"Piece of work?" Dana said around a mouth full of blissfully gooey cheese.

"I was going to say, a real she-wolf when it comes to her family."

"Same thing," Dana muttered, and C.J. chuckled. But she'd caught, before the chuckle, a slight wistfulness that had her mentally narrowing her eyes.

"I take it, then," C.J. said, his hands now folded behind his head, "a nanny or an au pair wouldn't be an easy sell, either?"

"Let a *stranger* look after her own great-nephew? Not in this lifetime. Trust me, you do not want to get her started on the evil that is day care."

His gaze was steady in hers. Too steady. "But sometimes there's no alternative."

"Yeah, well, you know that and I know that, and God knows millions of children have come out the other side unscathed, but this is my mother we're talking about. As far as she's concerned—" she finished off the slice of pizza and crossed to the sink for a glass of water, only to find herself completely bamboozled by the water purifier thingy on the faucet "—a child raised by anybody but family is doomed to become warped and dysfunctional. Okay, I give up—how the heck do you get water out of this thing?"

She heard C.J. get up, sensed his moving closer. He took the glass from her hand, flipped a lever and behold, water rushed into it. Amazing.

"Thanks," she muttered, taking a sip as he returned to his seat.

"Maybe she has a point," he said softly, and Dana started.

"Who?"

"Your mother. After all, I was raised by nannies and look at me."

As if she could do anything else. He'd donned a T-shirt to go with his sleep pants, but for some reason it only added to the whole blatantly male aura he had going on. And while she was looking at him, she set the glass on the counter and crossed her arms. "Your mother worked?"

A small smile touched his lips. "No. She died in a crash when I was a baby."

"Oh, God, I'm so sorry—"

"Don't you dare go all 'oh, poor C.J.' on me. I never knew

her, so it's not as if I ever missed her. We're not talking some great void in my life, here. Okay?"

She nodded, thinking, *Uh-huh, whatever you say,* then said, "What about your father?"

The pause was so slight, another person might have missed the stumble altogether. "He made sure I had the best caregivers money could buy," he said. "All fifteen of them. You want another slice of pizza?"

"Fifteen?"

"Yep. Pizza?"

"Uh, no, I'm good," she said, and he rose to put the rest back in the fridge. Somehow, she surmised the fifteen-caretakers subject was not on the discussion list. For now, at least. "Still," she said to his back, "I've known warped people in my time. Trust me, you don't even make the team."

"Thanks for the vote of confidence," he said, shutting the door, then shifting his gaze to hers. "But I'm hardly normal, am I?"

"And is there some reason you waited until *after* I'm living in your house to mention this?"

He smiled, then said, "You do have to admit, reaching my late thirties without ever having been in a serious relationship is pushing it."

"So what?" she said with a lot more bravado than she felt. "Lots of people are slow starters. Or…or prefer their own company. That doesn't make you weird."

Even if it did make him off-limits, she reminded herself. Especially when he leaned against the refrigerator, his arms crossed over his chest and said, "I'm not a slow starter, Dana," he said quietly. "I'm a nonstarter. A dead end. Remember?"

The occasional rapacious glance aside. Yes, he might be willing to take responsibility for his own child, or a nondemanding stray cat, but that was it.

Which she knew. Had known all along. *Remember?*

"And just to set your mind at ease," she said, "I learned a long time ago it's easier to grow orchids in the Antarctic than to convert a die-hard bachelor into husband material. And lost causes ain't my thang. Because, someday? You better believe I want 'all that messy emotional stuff.' And the strings. Oh, God, I want strings so bad I can taste them. But only from somebody who wants them as badly as I do. So you can quit with the don't-get-any-ideas signals, okay? Message received, C.J. Loud and clear."

His eyes bore into hers for a long moment, then he said, "So we'll go shopping after we get off work tomorrow night?"

"Sure," she said, then left the kitchen, Steve trotting after her, hopping up onto her bed as though he owned it. She and the cat faced off for several seconds, she daring him to stay, he daring her to make him get down. Finally she crawled into bed, yanking up the cover. "Mess with my birds and you're toast."

The cat gave a strained little *eerk* in reponse, then settled in by her thighs, absolutely radiating smugness.

No wonder C.J. hadn't taken the thing to the pound.

Sunlight slapped Dana awake the next morning, along with the alarm clock's *blat...blat...blat*. Like a sheep with a hangover. Groaning, she opened one eye to discover that she'd apparently hit the snooze button.

Three times.

Covers, and a very pissed cat, went flying as she catapulted from the bed and hurtled toward Ethan's room, not even bothering with her robe since C.J. had said he'd be gone by eight, and—sad to say—eight had long since passed.

"Hey, sugar," she sang, sailing through the door, "you ready to get up…?"

No baby.

She scurried across the room to check the crib more

closely, because that's what you do when you're not firing on all jets yet and the baby entrusted to your care isn't where you last left him, only to spin around and make tracks toward the kitchen, hoping against hope C.J. had lied about leaving at eight and/or that wherever he was, Ethan was with him.

But no. Oh, she found Ethan, who greeted her from his high-chair with a joyful "Ba!" But instead of a tall, good-looking man in his prime, there, beside the baby, stood (at least, Dana thought she was standing, she wasn't quite sure) a short, squat, black-haired woman whose prime, Dana was guessing, had predated color television. But before she could get the words, "And you are?" out of her mouth, the phone rang. Whoever-she-was picked it up, said, "*Sì*, Mr. C.J., she is right here," and held it out to Dana with what could only be called a beatific, if curious, smile.

"Hey," C.J. said, "did I happen to mention Guadalupe?"

Dana's gaze slid over to the smiling woman. "I take it that's who answered the phone?"

"That would be her. She comes in to clean for me twice a week. It completely slipped my mind that today was her day. I briefly explained things to her when she came in this morning. I would have awakened you before I left, but Steve looked like he'd remove a limb if I tried."

With a flickering smile at Guadalupe, whose steady stream of Spanish Ethan was apparently eating up as enthusiastically as his rice cereal, Dana carted the portable phone out of earshot. "Never mind that I nearly had a heart attack when I went to get Ethan out of his crib and he *wasn't there*," she whispered into the phone. "A little warning might've been nice. And how the heck does one *briefly* explain the sudden appearance of a baby and a strange woman in your house?" She put up a hand, even though he couldn't see her. "Unfamiliar, I mean."

After a barely perceptible pause, she heard, "You have no idea how tempting it is to say, no, you were right the first time."

"And where I come from, bantering before coffee is a hanging offense."

A soft laugh preceded, "In any case, I simply told her the truth, that Ethan's my son and you're his cousin, that neither of us knew of his existence two weeks ago, and that we're trying to figure out the best way to handle a very complicated situation. She seemed to take it in stride. But then, taking things in stride is what Guadalupe does. You'll see." He paused, as though catching his breath. "I really do apologize for the brain cramp. Are you okay?"

"Yeah, *now*. Five minutes ago was something else again. Look, thanks for calling, but I'm running seriously late—"

"Right, me, too, I've got an appointment in ten. See you tonight, then."

And he was gone. Dana told herself the sense of watching an un-subtitled foreign movie was due to the combination of severe caffeine deprivation and leftover heart arrhythmia from the earlier shock.

She returned to the kitchen, where Guadalupe was busy wiping down a squealing Ethan, who wasn't taking kindly to having his attempts at pulverizing a blob of cereal on his high chair tray thwarted whenever Guadalupe grabbed his little hand to clean it. The older woman flicked a brief, but chillingly astute, glance in Dana's direction.

"So," she said. "Mr. C.J. says you are not the mother?"

Dana shook her head. "No. His mother's my cousin."

"She as pretty as you?"

Warmth flooded Dana's face at the out-of-left-field compliment. She sidled over to the coffemaker and poured herself a huge cup. "Trish is…very different from me," she said, dumping in three packets of artificial sweetener, some half-and-half. "Lighter hair. Tallish. Skinny."

One eyebrow lifted, Guadalupe went for the other little hand. "So how well do you and Mr. C.J. know each other?"

"Not very, really. Oh, let me take the baby, I need to get him dressed to go to my mother's."

"I can get him dressed, just leave out what you would like him to wear. And while you shower, I fix breakfast, no? I bring eggs, chorizo, the green chile for Mr. C.J.," she said when Dana opened her mouth. "There is plenty extra for you. Is *muy bueno,* you will like. So, go," she said, shooing.

Fifteen minutes later, Dana returned, face done, hair up, body clothed in a silky loose top and a drapey, ankle-length skirt in jewel tones that coordinated with the plastic fruit gracing her high-heeled, Lucite mules. The baby was dressed and in his car seat, ready to go; from the tempered glass breakfast table, a plate of steaming, fragrant eggs and sausage beckoned. Her brain said, "*Stick with the coffee,*" but her stomach said, "*Who are you kidding?*"

After depositing her purse on the island, she clicked across the stone floor, sat at the table. Lifted fork to mouth. Groaned in ecstasy.

"Is good, no?" Guadalupe said, smiling, from the sink.

"Delicious. Thank you."

"*De nada.* You cook?"

"I love to cook. But I've never gotten the hang of Mexican."

"I teach you, if you like. I teach all my daughters, now my grandchildren. Twenty-seven," she said with a grin, and Dana nearly choked on her eggs.

"Goodness. Y'all must have some Thanksgivings."

The old woman threw back her head and laughed, her bosoms shaking. "*Sì,* last year we had three turkeys and two hams, and enough enchiladas to feed half of Albuquerque. Done?" she asked, when Dana stood, whisking away her empty plate before she had a chance to carry it to the sink.

"Well, this little guy and I better hit the road," she said, moving toward the seat, which Guadalupe had set by the patio door in a patch of filtered sunshine. But the old woman touched her arm.

"I know I am a stranger to you, but I have worked for Mr. C.J. for many years, I am good with children, you could leave *el poco* angel with me…."

"Oh…I'm sorry, I can't. Not because I don't trust you," she hastily added at the woman's hurt expression, "but my mother would kill me. Because it's very possible that Ethan's as close as she's going to get to a grandchild. At least for the foreseeable future."

Confusion clouded the dark eyes for a moment, replaced by an understanding sympathy so strong Dana was glad for the excuse to squat in front of the baby's seat. Steve shoved himself against her calves, mewing for attention.

"Hey, guy," Dana said softly, crouching in front of Ethan, who gave her a wide, trembly smile when she came into focus. "Ready to go? You are?" she said, laughing, when the baby started pumping his arms. "Well, come on then, your Auntie Faye's waitin' on you…."

Just like that, the unfairness of it all squeezed her heart so tightly, she could barely breathe. Clutching the sides of the seat, waiting for her lungs to get with the program, she heard behind her, very gently, "What will you do when your cousin comes back for her *niño?*"

Dana stood, hefting seat and baby into her arms. "There's no guarantee that she will."

"But if she does?"

"Then I suppose we'll cross that bridge when we get to it."

"And if the bridge is one you do not wish to cross?"

Balancing the seat against one hip, Dana grabbed her purse off the counter and slung it over her shoulder. "Thanks again for breakfast, it was great," she said, making herself smile. "Will you be here this evening when we get home?"

Heat flooded Dana's cheeks at the slip. *We* and *home* in the same sentence? After one day?

A little presumptuous, yes?

Guadalupe's eyes narrowed, but all she said was, "I usually leave at three, there is not much to clean in a house where only one person lives. But anytime you need me to take care of this precious child," she hastily added, "I will be more than happy to stay. You have a good day, Miss Dana, okay?"

Yeah, well, Dana thought as she lugged His Highness out to her car, she'd do her best.

During a lull between appointments, C.J. brought Val into his office, shut the door and told her about Ethan. Not surprisingly, the further into the story he got, the higher went her eyebrows, until he half thought they'd crawl off her face altogether.

"The Trish who worked *here?*" she said at the appropriate point in the narrative. "What the hell were you thinking, boy?"

"Could we please not go there, Val? The past is past."

"Actually, it looks to me like the past just came up and bit you on the butt, if you don't mind my sayin' so."

"If I did, I wouldn't have told you. But wait. There's more."

There went the eyebrows again. "You mean, you can top a six-month-old son you didn't know about?"

"I don't know about topping, but…" His desk chair creaked when he leaned back in it. "You remember Dana Malone? The woman who was in here a couple of weeks ago?"

"Sure do. Cute little thing. Big eyes. What about her?"

"Trish is her cousin. And she kind of…left the baby with her. Granted her guardianship, actually. In writing. So she's kind of…living with me. Well, they are. Dana and the baby."

Three, four seconds later, Val blinked at him, then lifted her hands in an I-don't-even-want-to-know gesture. Then she sighed. "I *knew* there was somethin' goin' on, I just knew it, the way you were acting mush-brained all last week. And didn't I tell you I'd find out?" When he didn't answer—because, really, what could he say?—she finally sank into the chair across from his desk, her eyes brimming with concern. "So what are you going to do?"

"Find Trish. Solidify custody arrangements. After that…" He shrugged. "Take it day by day, I guess. Although I guess I'll be cutting back my hours, so I can spend time with…with my son."

"Boy, those are two words I never thought I'd hear come out of your mouth."

His mouth stretched. "You and me both."

"Couldn't you get one of those au pairs or something?"

C.J.'s stomach turned, even as he grimaced. "I suppose I'll have to look into it eventually. But it has to be the right person. And I have to get the idea past Dana's mother first.

"And what about the gal? Dana? How's she fit into all of this? Long-range, I mean?"

"Hell, Val. Right now, I'm doing well to plan out the next ten minutes. I can't even begin to wrap my head around 'long range'."

Any more than he'd been able to wrap his head around that bantering business this morning. Because bantering was not something he did, as a general rule. Oh, he could hold his own in a serious discussion with the best of 'em, as long as the conversation stayed on safe topics. Like politics or religion. And as long as it was conducted from behind nice, thick impersonal walls.

But Dana had no walls. Dana, in fact, was the antiwall.

Dana not only made him banter, she made him want to banter. To indulge in playful, affectionate exchanges, like some happy couple on a sitcom.

And all this after less than twenty-four hours in his house.

He started at Val's touch on his arm. "There anything I can do?" she asked gently.

"Other than promise me you won't start sending out your résumé?" He shook his head. "Nope. Not a damn thing. I'm all on my own with this one."

For the rest of the day, work crowded his thoughts, albeit with an occasional detour into the personal when he spoke with Elena (no, she hadn't found anything yet, but it had only been a day, after all), and when the papers his father had promised finally arrived, prompting C.J. to realize he should probably tell the old man he was a grandfather, at some point. Not yet, though. Not until he'd come to terms with the whole thing himself. And one by one, he told the other agents he'd be turning over more clients to them. And why. If they were shocked, none of them let on. Not too much, anyway.

At six, he left. Just like that. Packed his briefcase and walked out the door. Not to see a property, or a client, but his own child.

And Dana, he thought with a tingle of anticipation that made him frown. It was okay to like her, he reassured himself as he steered the Mercedes across town, thinking how strange it was to be heading home while it was still this light, this early. But was it okay to look forward quite so much to being with her, to hearing her laughter, to being the brunt of her gentle teasing? Wasn't it cheating, the one-sidedness of it?

It had been wrong, and selfish, to bring her here, he thought as he parked his car beside hers, already in the driveway. Even more wrong to have put her in such a tenuous position, he chided himself as he walked into the house, heard those silly birds of hers, then her laughter, blending with the baby's from several rooms away.

He found them in Ethan's room, where she was changing the

baby's diaper, still dressed from work, he assumed, in some floaty skirt and top, a pair of crazy shoes that made him smile. Made him…other things. She looked up at his entrance, her smile dimming slightly, and a brief, bright spark of annoyance flashed in his brain, that she should feel wary of him. That she needed to continue being wary, for her own good.

As if sensing C.J.'s entrance, Ethan twisted himself around, grinning. Trusting. After a moment of stillness, all four limbs struck out simultaneously, pumping the air in pure, joyful abandon.

"Somebody's sure glad to see his daddy," Dana said

Oh, God. This was what it was like, having someone to come home to.

Having someone giddy with happiness that you'd *come* home.

Giddy. Not wary.

"Oh, shoot," Dana said. "I brought home a whole bag of clothes for him from the shop, but I left them in the other room."

"Stay there, I'll get them."

Grateful for a moment to regroup, C.J. sprinted down the hall and into Dana's room, glancing around for the telltale bright blue Great Expectations bag, at last spotting it on a chair beside a little writing desk the decorator had called "too, too precious for words." In grabbing the bag, however, he bumped the desk, startling the open laptop on top of it awake.

To a word processing program she hadn't shut down.

Chapter Eight

He hadn't meant to read the text that appeared on the screen, but eyes will do what eyes will do, and before he knew it, he'd scrolled through five or six pages of some of the driest, funniest stuff he'd read in ages—

"Ohmigod…no!" He turned to see Dana striding across the carpet, a diapered Ethan clinging to her hip. "Nobody's supposed to see that," she said, slapping closed the computer, her cheeks flushed.

"You wrote this?" he asked.

"Yes, but—"

"But, nothing. It's good, Dana. No, I'm serious," he said when she snorted. "The old Southern lady going on and on about her ailments…" He chuckled. "Priceless. You should be published."

Her blush deepened. "Yeah, well, it's not that easy."

C.J. took the baby from her, a little surprised to see how

quickly he'd grown used to the squirmy, solid weight in his arms. How quickly, and completely, the instinct to protect this tiny person had swamped the initial shock and panic and anger. "Have you even tried?" he said, laying the baby on the bed, then holding out his hand, indicating to Dana she needed to give him something to put on the kid.

"Um…well, no. I mean, I can't, it's not finished yet."

"Then finish it," he said, taking the little blue sailor outfit from her and popping it over the baby's head. Getting arms and legs into corresponding openings was a bit trickier, however, so it took a while for him to realize Dana had gone silent behind him. When he turned, her eyes were shiny. And, yes, wide.

"You really think it's good?" she asked.

"I really do. And for what it's worth, I'm not a total philistine. I minored in contemporary American lit in college. So I know my stuff."

"Oh. Wow. I'm…"

"…extremely talented. Really."

She blinked at him for another few seconds, then said, "So. Are you ready to storm Smith's?"

Ah. He'd embarrassed her. She'd get over it. What *he* wouldn't get over, he realized as they all trooped out to his car, in which he'd installed the Cadillac of baby seats in the back, was that he'd never championed anyone before. Had never met anyone he'd wanted to champion.

What a rush. A breath-stealing, heart-stopping, panic-inducing rush.

Once in the store, he gave her free rein, offering little comment as she filled the cart with vegetables and fruits and roasts and fish and whole grain breads, with things he had no idea what to do with, other than to consume them once they'd been cooked. A perk he hadn't even thought about, when he'd asked her to move in. And one he couldn't help feeling a pang of guilt about now. Not a huge pang—he couldn't remember the last time he'd had roast pork—but a twinge nonetheless.

"Your cooking for me wasn't part of the arrangement."

After a smile for the baby when he grabbed for C.J.'s hand with the obvious intention of gnawing on his onyx ring, she said, "I'm not cooking for you. I'm cooking for myself." She snagged several boxes of Jell-O off the shelf, tossing them into the cart. "May as well toss in a little extra while I'm at it."

"So I take it you know your way around a kitchen?"

"People who love to eat generally love to cook." She held up a small jar. "How do you feel about capers?"

"Just don't put them in the Jell-O."

"Deal."

And so it went, their conversation. Careful. Circumspect. He talked about work, she intermittently grilled him about his food preferences. He'd have had to be blind to not notice that she didn't look his way unless she absolutely had to, that her smiles were fleeting, rationed. Strike what he'd thought before about her not having any walls, because there was definitely one up between them now, transparent and flimsy though it may have been. Not that she was a whiner. In fact, it was the way she seemed to curl around her obvious bad mood, swallowing her true feelings, that annoyed him so much. He didn't like this Dana, he wanted the other Dana back, the one who'd tease and flash that dimpled smile for him.

Periodically piercing the annoyance, however, was the swell of pride whenever someone stopped to admire Ethan. Which happened approximately every twenty feet. And Ethan took to his role as the charmer with equanimity, bequeathing wrinkle-nosed, two-toothed grins on everyone who spoke to him. After one gushing elderly couple continued on their way,

C.J. looked at the baby and said, "How could anyone walk away from such a perfect kid?"

That was enough to earn him a sideways glance, at least. And a smirk. "Says the man who's lived with the child for one night. Believe me, he has his moments—"

"Ohmigosh, aren't you just the cutest little thing?" yet another admirer said, cooing at the baby as though she'd never seen one. "Oh, would you look at those two little teeth! How old?" she asked Dana.

"Six and a half months."

"Aw, that's such a wonderful age. Enjoy it, honey—it goes so fast. I had four, they're all parents of teenagers themselves now, but it still seems like yesterday. And look at you, expecting again already, bless your heart! Well, bye-bye, sweetie," she said to Ethan with a fluttery wave, then trotted off.

The whooshing in C.J.'s ears nearly obliterated the piped-in seventies oldie bouncing off the freezer cases. At last he turned to Dana, his heart cracking at the stoic expression on her face.

"You want me to go beat her up?"

"That's very sweet," she said with a fleeting smile, "but I think I'll pass. And anyway, better she think I'm pregnant than I'm nothing but a lazy slob without the willpower to starve myself down to a size eight."

"One isn't better than the other, Dana."

"Maybe not. But I'm used to it. Come on," she said quietly, nudging the cart toward the checkout. "It's getting close to Ethan's bedtime."

If she'd been subdued before, she was downright uncommunicative on the ride back to the house, his every attempt to draw her out meeting with little more than a monosyllabic reply.

Oh, man, not since he was a kid had he felt this…this extraneous. Not that he hadn't been well aware of his inability to connect with another human being except on the most basic of levels, but if this didn't drive it home, boy, he didn't know what did. Because, whether he understood it or not, whether he liked it or not, he did genuinely care about this woman, about what she was feeling. He hated seeing her hurt. But even more, he hated not knowing what to do to make it better.

When they got back to the house, he offered to get Ethan ready for bed while Dana started their dinner. He wondered, as he carted his sleepy son down the hall, how he thought some biological connection was going to make him any more able to fix the inevitable hurts for his child than for Dana. With that, the resentment demons roared back out onto the field from where he'd tried desperately to keep them benched, fangs and claws glinting in the harsh light of C.J.'s own fear.

Ethan lay quietly on the changing table during the diaper-changing process, gnawing like mad on his fist, watching C.J. with those damn trusting eyes, and hot tears bit at the backs of C.J.'s. He hadn't wanted this, he thought bitterly, stuffing plump little legs into a pair of lightweight pajama bottoms. Hadn't asked for it—

The baby clung to him like a little koala when he picked him up, and C.J. clung right back, his hand cradling his son's head, his cheek pressed against one tiny shell of a little ear.

How the hell was he supposed to be something he didn't know how to be?

He lowered Ethan into his crib, unable to resist the tug to his emotions when the kid grabbed his blanket, his eyelids drooping almost immediately. "'Night, Scooter," he whispered, slightly startled when the nickname popped out of its own accord. Then he stepped into Dana's room to grab the baby monitor off her nightstand, his emotions assailing him a second time at the basic here-ness of her—a pair of shoes, carelessly kicked underneath the chair, her lingering scent. The laptop, firmly closed, like an old woman with secrets.

* * *

Standing barefoot at the island, tossing a salad, Dana glanced up when C.J. entered the kitchen. Her forehead creased in concern. "Everything okay?"

"What? Oh…sure. I just…" He smiled, shook his head. "It's nothing," he said, setting the monitor on the counter. "Work stuff."

Her expression said she didn't believe him for a minute, but all she said was, "I fake-baked a potato in the microwave for you, but I thought we could do the steaks out on the grill?"

C.J. grabbed a beer from the fridge, then allowed a rueful smile. "Guess this is as good a time as any to tell you I've never used the damn thing."

"Get out! What kind of red-blooded American male are you?"

"One who eats out a lot."

Dana huffed a little sigh that eased his mind somewhat—at least his ineptitude as a backyard chef was giving her something to focus on besides herself. Undeterred, she picked up the salad bowl and the monitor, commanding him to bring the steaks, adding it was high time he learned this basic suburban survival skill. When they got outside, she shook her head in amazement at the built-in grill tucked into a low wall on one side of the patio.

"Heck, compared with my daddy's little old barbecue, this is like going from a motorboat to a yacht. So maybe you should go sit way over there, so you won't see me make a fool out of myself, trying to figure this thing out."

But for all her concern, the steaks turned out fine. And as the sun set, the temperature dropped and a light breeze picked up, there they were, just two people enjoying dinner out by the pool.

Yeah, right.

"So if you can't cook," she said, dangling a tiny piece of steak for Steve, whose purr C.J. could hear from five feet away, "what *can* you do?"

"Well, I make a great deal of money. Does that count?"

"Maybe," she said, her eyes sparkling for the first time that evening. "Of course, it depends on what you do with all that money."

"Meaning, do I horde it like Scrooge? No. Although I do have quite a bit socked away in various retirement funds. The thought of ending my life living in a cardboard box does not appeal."

"No," she said softly. "It doesn't."

"But then, the thought of anybody else living in a cardboard box doesn't appeal, either. So I support a lot of local charities. For the homeless, the food bank, things like that. In fact…" He took a pull of his beer, thought *What the hell.* "I've got a fund-raiser to go to a week from Saturday, and—"

"Oh, I can stay with Ethan, no problem."

"—*and* I was wondering if you'd like to go with me."

She stared at him for a second or two, then jumped up and began clearing their dishes.

"Dana? What the—? It wasn't a trick question!"

Plates balanced in both hands, she turned. "Wasn't it? I mean, why ask me now? Tonight?"

He stood, as well, taking the plates from her. "Look, if you don't want to go, just say so."

"It has nothing to do with whether or not I'd like to go."

"Then what is it?" When she didn't answer, he sighed. "This wouldn't have anything to do with that woman in the store, would it?"

She snatched up their water glasses and headed inside. "You tell me."

"You think I'm inviting you because…what? I feel sorry for you? Dana, for God's sake." He followed, setting the plates by the dishwasher. "It was a simple invitation, no ulterior motives behind it."

"C.J., get real. Nothing's *simple* between us."

"Point taken. But I swear, I only asked you because I hate going to these things alone, and I thought you might enjoy getting out…and I'm just digging myself in deeper, aren't I?"

She emitted a desiccated little sound that might have been a laugh, then looked at him. "You're not exactly winning any major points," she said, but without a lot of steam behind it. "What happened to the charmer who's supposed to know exactly the right thing to say?"

"Is that what you think I am? A charmer?" When she shrugged, he reached out, taking her hand. "Fine, so maybe playing the game is what's gotten me through so far. You say what people want to hear, they generally do what you want them to do."

"And you're proud of this?"

"I've never deliberately misled anyone, Dana. Or used anyone for my own purposes. There are ways of working it without hurting people. Still, to answer your question…no. I don't suppose I am particularly proud of how I've lived my life. But what I'm trying to say is…the baby…" He stopped, shutting his eyes for a moment, trying to make the words line up, make sense. When he opened them again, it was to meet that cautious, careful gaze. "I look at Ethan, and I realize a large part of who I was won't cut it anymore. I don't really know yet what that means, what I'm supposed to do, or who I'm supposed to be. But I do know you're somehow part of that revelation."

She flinched. "Me? How?"

"Because when I'm with you, I don't want to be who I was before, either. I mean, before tonight, I can't remember ever being angry enough on someone else's behalf that I wanted to hurt another human being. Not that I'm going to go off the deep end and start beating up little old ladies—"

"Good to know."

"—but my point is, since Ethan came into my life, I suddenly…care. About how someone else might feel."

She tilted her head. "Empathy?"

"Yes! That's it! I mean, yeah, I've always felt I needed to help people who were down on their luck, or who'd gotten a raw deal, but never on a personal level before. And tonight, the more I realized how hurt you were, the angrier I got."

Her eyes narrowed. "And yet you weren't inviting me to this charity thing because you felt sorry for me."

"No, dammit, I invited you because I *like* you! Because I want to beat people up for you! And that's not all!"

"It…isn't?" she said, looking slightly alarmed.

"No! Because I grew up in a house where nobody talks to anybody, and it sucks. Which is why I've always preferred to live alone. But Ethan's here, and you're here, and if you need to vent, I'm not going anywhere. In the meantime, get out of here, go write or whatever you want to do while I clean up."

"Lord have mercy," she said after a long moment, "but you are one strange man."

"Yeah, well, if you felt like somebody'd just removed your brain, rearranged all the parts and crammed it back inside your skull, you'd be strange, too."

She blinked. "Maybe…I'll go sit out by the pool for a while, then."

"Fine."

She walked to the door, hesitated a second, then turned back around. "Okay, I'll go with you. To the charity thing."

"Taking pity on the *strange* man, are we? Hey, don't do me any favors."

"I'm not. Like you said, it's been a while since I've been out."

And she left. Fifteen minutes later, however, he was finishing the washing up when he heard the muffled double-shushing of the patio door opening, then closing. C.J. watched as she padded over to the fridge, pulling out a jug of orange juice. After pouring herself a small glass, she slid up onto one of the barstools.

"See," she began quietly, "the skinny people of the world look at people like me and think, What's wrong with her? Why can't she control her weight? They never stop to think that, you know, maybe I have tried every diet known to man, maybe I've even gone to doctors about it, maybe I do exercise and eat right ninety-five percent of the time." Her mouth pulled into a tight smile. "That maybe I would have done anything to stop the other kids from calling me Fatty when I was a kid. Except it doesn't always work that way. For some of us, it's not just a matter of eating less, or exercising more, or having willpower."

"You're not fat, Dana," he said, meaning it.

"Oh, but according to every chart out there, I am. I weigh thirty pounds more than I 'should' for my height. Which, by the way, is thirty pounds less than I weighed about five years ago, when I finally realized scarfing down a pint of Ben & Jerry's every time I got stressed was a bad idea. Then again, the thought of never again eating real ice cream, or a piece of cheesecake, or mashed potatoes with gravy, or a cheese en-chilada…" She shook her head. "Now *that's* depressing. But God forbid I go into a restaurant and order something besides a piece of broiled fish and a salad, hold the dressing. People look at me like I'm a criminal."

"That's their problem, honey. Not yours."

"And most of the time I do know that. But every once in a while it gets to me, what can I say? Just like the other thing. Not being able to have kids. And with all this about Ethan…you happened to catch me at a bad time."

"Lucky me," he said, and she smiled. Not a big one, but enough to see the dimples. God, he loved those dimples.

"Okay, your turn," she said, her expression brightening. "If

I have to open up, so do you. So what's your story…oh, shoot," she said as Ethan's reedy cry came through the monitor. Her gaze touched his. "Coin toss?"

"No, that's okay, I'll go," C.J. said, barely managing to keep from jumping off the stool. "And anyway, it's late, and I've got a seven-thirty breakfast meeting tomorrow, so maybe we should call it a night, anyway."

Still smiling, Dana shook her head. "You are so transparent, C. J. Turner," she said quietly. "But you know something? You can run, but you can't hide. Maybe from me, but not from yourself. And one day, you're gonna have to face whatever you don't want to face. And deal with it, too."

But as C.J. tromped down the hall to see what was up with his son, it occurred to him that "one day" was already there.

"Sorry I'm late," Dana shouted to Mercy over the Friday-night crowd chatter in the little bistro by the university. "Traffic tie-up on the freeway."

"It's okay, there's a fifteen-minute wait." Mercy held up a small pager. "They'll call us when the table's ready. Outside or bar?"

"Your call."

"This was a great idea, by the way," Mercy yelled over her shoulder as they pushed their way through the throng. "If a surprise."

"Yeah, well, it occurred to me that C.J. needed some one-on-one time with Ethan," Dana yelled back. "And I needed the night off."

"So naturally you decided to spend it with someone you already see five days a week," Mercy said, slithering up onto a bar stool. "Makes total sense."

"Says the woman who pounced on the idea like a cat on a grasshopper."

Shortly thereafter, as Dana reluctantly sipped a glass of white wine and Mercy tackled a margarita larger than her head, her partner nodded appreciatively at Dana's outfit, a low-cut blousy top tucked into a long, tiered skirt. "The cleavage is seriously hot."

Dana glanced down. "Not too much?"

"No such thing, *chica*. Really, you should take the girls out more often, they look like they could use the air. Well, look at *you*, Ms. Techno Babe," she said as Dana set her cell phone on the bar. "Welcome to the twenty-first century."

"C.J. insisted I needed one. Because of the baby."

"And you love it already."

Dana smirked. "And I love it already."

After a chuckle into her drink, Mercy poked Dana's wrist with one long fingernail. "So. Have you slept with the guy yet?"

"Honestly, Merce. You really do have a one-track mind, don't you?"

That got an unrepentant grin. "I live to yank your chain, you know that. But seriously. How's it going? It's been, what? Nearly a week, right?"

Dana took a small sip of her wine, flinching when some man brushed against her as he got up onto his bar stool. "Not quite. Five days. Seems longer."

"Is that good or bad?"

"I'm not sure. In some ways it's a lot easier than I thought it would be. I mean, we've worked out a pretty good routine, C.J.'s been a real trouper about taking care of the baby…"

"But?"

"But…" Dana frowned at the slightly trembling liquid in her glass. "No matter how gracious C.J. is, I'm still a guest." She lifted her eyes to Mercy's dark, sympathetic gaze. "And the question is, for how long?"

"Because of Trish, you mean?" Dana nodded. Mercy fingered the rim of her sombrero-sized vessel. "So you haven't heard anything yet?"

"The investigator C.J. hired keeps running into dead ends, apparently. As though Trish dropped off the baby, then the planet—"

"Hey," said a reasonably good-looking suit who'd popped up out of nowhere. His gaze bounced off Dana's breasts, then zeroed in on Mercy in her bright red spaghetti strap top and matching, flippy skirt. "Can I buy you ladies a drink?"

"Thanks," Mercy said, "but we're fine."

"Hey, you know, maybe it'd speed things up if we shared a table—?"

One French-manicured hand shot up. "No. Thank you." She faced Dana again, pointedly turning her back to the guy. "So. You were saying?"

As the poor schlep trundled off, his wounded ego trailing behind like a strip of toilet paper, Dana smiled and said, "We don't *have* to hang out tonight. I mean, if something better comes along…"

"Better than you? Never happen. Besides, when have you known me to pick up a strange guy in some bar?" At Dana's raised brow, she huffed out, "Recently?"

Dana chuckled, then sighed. "But what does it say about us that, here we are, two women in our thirties, spending our Saturday night with each other?"

"That we're comfortable enough with who we are to do that?"

"Or bored out of our skulls."

"Yeah, that, too…oh! I'm blinking!" Mercy said, snatching the pager off the bar, then her drink. "Although you know," she said as the hostess signaled them over, "at least *you* had an option. *You* could have stayed home with Mr. Gorgeous, flashing your girls at him instead of me. But no… Thanks," she said with a bright smile for the hostess as they slid into their booth. Then she leaned across the table. "You're here. With me. Instead of there. With him."

And Dana leaned over and said back, "And maybe there's a reason for that."

"One can hope."

Dana rolled her eyes, then told her about the whole "You make me want to beat people up" speech, which didn't exactly elicit the reaction Dana had hoped.

"*Dios mio,* you little idiot!" Mercy's dark eyes glittered in the dim light from the puny little votive in the center of the table. "This is *huge,* like something right out of a movie, when the guy suddenly realizes he can't live without the girl! We're talking *When Harry Met Sally,* or *As Good as It Gets.*"

"Oh, this is definitely as good as it gets, all right."

Mercy's eyebrows collided over her cute little nose. "Not following."

"Merce, all this is, is C.J.'s coming to terms with being responsible for another human being. Meaning Ethan. I watch him, and I can tell being with his son is opening him up to all sorts of emotions he's never dealt with before. Never *let* himself deal with before. And it's as if…" She glanced away, trying to find the words, then looked back at her friend. "You know what it's like, when you first fall in love, how the whole world seems brighter? And suddenly you love everybody, because what you're feeling is too overwhelming to focus on a single person? That's all that's going on here, trust me. Only it's with Ethan, not me."

After a couple of seconds of introspective frowning, Mercy said, "So you think he said all that because, what? You happened to be in the vicinity? Like the victim of a gas cloud?"

"Basically, yeah. Nothing's going to come of this, Merce," she said firmly when the brunette pushed out a sigh.

"Well, it sure as hell won't as long as you go out with me, or spend the night in your own apartment."

"But that's what it's going to come down to eventually, anyway. Or did you think I was going to live with C.J. until Ethan graduates from high school? It was only ever supposed to be temporary, so the last thing either of us needs is to get too used to the other's company."

"I see. And you're not just saying this because you're afraid of getting hurt?"

Dana's eyes snapped to Mercy's, irritatingly astute under those perfectly arched brows. "I'm saying this because I'm a realist."

"And?"

"And…I'd be a fool to believe the man's done a complete about-face in less than three weeks, baby or no baby. Accepting his responsibilities as a parent doesn't mean he's changed his mind about anything else."

"So this *is* about protecting yourself."

She snorted. "Can you blame me?"

"No," Mercy said gently. "But people do change, honey."

"I know they do," Dana said. "Because I have. Or at least, I'm trying to. And it's going to take a lot more than a single impassioned declaration for me to let my guard down—"

She clamped shut her mouth, focusing on the flickering little flame between them. And Mercy, bless her, did nothing more than reach across the table to quickly squeeze Dana's trembling fingers.

Somehow, though—probably because of the mutual, unspoken moratorium imposed on the subject of C.J. and/or anyone's love life—she actually enjoyed the rest of the evening. For the most part they talked business, since the move into the new space was imminent, so by the time they went their separate ways a little after nine, Dana was beginning to feel at least a little less crazed.

In fact, she even thought she might get some writing done before she went to bed, only to remember she'd left her laptop and all her notebooks at C.J.'s. She was half tempted to forget it, except it seemed a shame to blow off her muse simply because she didn't feel like trekking all the way back to C.J.'s.

Praying he wouldn't notice her return, Dana let herself in and started toward "her" room, only to be waylaid by Steve, plaintively meowing and head-butting her shins as though he hadn't seen her in three years. Or been fed, more likely. Honestly. She followed the cat into the kitchen, where, as she suspected, Iams abounded in his food dish.

Which is when she heard C.J.'s voice coming in low, angry bursts through the slightly open patio door.

Chapter Nine

Dana froze, knowing she should hotfoot it out of there, and yet…she couldn't. Not that she could really hear what C.J. was saying—or wanted to!—but simply because it was such a shock, hearing those sounds come out of that man.

The sounds of a man having his heart shredded, basically.

Then suddenly the door slid open and he was there, barely ten feet in front of her, his cell phone clamped to his ear, a hundred emotions roiling in his eyes. Not the least of which was irritation at her unexpected presence.

Blushing furiously, Dana pointed toward her room and hurried away, even more hurriedly stuffing her laptop and notebooks into a canvas tote. Although if her muse hadn't run for the hills by now, she'd be very surprised.

Naturally, she had to peek in on the baby on her way back down the hall. In the charcoal light, she saw him lift his head, heard him burble at her.

"Hey, little guy." She set down the tote by the door and crossed the room, fighting the urge to pick him up. Bad enough she'd come in instead of walking away, letting him get back to sleep. Still, since she was here anyway, she bent over and sniffed. Nope, nothing but baby powder and tear-free shampoo.

"'Night-night, sugar,'" she whispered, handing him back his blanket, which earned her a quavering, sleepy smile. Oh, heck, how could she not touch him? So she cupped the silky head, only to practically jerk back her hand, as though she'd been tempted to take something that didn't belong to her.

On a sigh, she crept back out, snatching her tote bag along the way, hoping against hope to make her escape without running into C.J.

"Dana?"

So much for that.

His voice drained of its earlier fury, her name floated out from the darkness in the living room. Then, like an apparition, the man himself appeared. Wrecked was the only word for his expression. Exhaustion, and something else Dana couldn't quite identify, slumped his shoulders, fettered his smile. "What are you doing here? I thought you weren't coming back tonight."

She lifted the bag. "Left my writing stuff here. I'm sorry, I didn't mean to—"

"It's okay. You just surprised me, that's all."

"Sorry," she repeated. "So…how'd it go with Ethan?"

The smile relaxed, a little. "I gave him a bath. Or he gave me one, I wasn't quite sure which. He asked where you were."

"He…? Oh. You almost had me there for a second."

C.J. slid his hands into his khaki pockets, his eyes fixed on hers. "You aren't going to ask who I was arguing with?"

"Why would I do that?" she said, slightly confused. "It's none of my business."

"It's not an old girlfriend, if that's what you're thinking."

"I'm not thinking anything. Really."

Actually, her brain was processing so many possibilities she half expected it to short out. But if he was hinting that maybe he was ready to talk…well. He'd have to do more than hint. Because almost every time she'd handed him an opening the past few days, he'd clammed up. So, tough.

Never mind that everything inside her was screaming to give him one more chance, one more opening. To be the sounding board she suspected he'd never had, or at least not for a long time. But torn as she was, the new Dana—the older, wiser Dana—had finally learned there were some roads best left unexplored.

At least, until she was sure she'd come out okay on the other end.

C.J. closed the space between them, taking her bag. "I'll carry this out to the car for you."

"You don't have to—"

"Hush, woman, and let me be the man."

The cat barreled past her when the door opened, streaking into the night. They walked to her car in silence; C.J. opened her door, setting the bag in back.

"Thanks."

"*De nada.*" Was she hallucinating, or was he focusing entirely too much on her mouth? Then he lifted his hand, and she held her breath…

…and he swatted away a tiny night critter fluttering around her face.

Then, with what sounded like a frustrated sigh, he gently fingered a loose curl hovering at her temple.

"I'm a mess, Dana."

"So I noticed."

He dropped his hand. And laughed, although the sound was pained. "And here I always thought Southern women bent over backward to be diplomatic."

"Clearly you've been hanging out with the wrong Southern women."

"Clearly," he said, his expression unreadable in the harsh security light. Then, gently: "Go, Dana. For both our sakes…go."

Only, after she slid behind the wheel, he caught the door before she could close it. "That was my father," he said. "On the phone."

Her breath caught. "Oh? Um…I'm sorry?"

"Don't be. I finally got some things off my chest. Someday, I'll tell you the whole sordid story. If you really want to hear it, I mean."

Afraid to speak, she simply nodded. He pushed her door shut; her throat clogged, Dana backed into the street, put the car into Drive, drove away. Noticed, when she glanced into her rearview mirror, C.J. still standing in the driveway, hands in his pockets, watching her until she got all the way to the end of the street.

"Oh, Merce," Dana whispered to herself. "Now *this* is huge."

"No news yet?" Val asked from the doorway to C.J.'s office.

He swiveled in her direction. "What? You're bugging the phones now?"

"No, I was on my way to the kitchen and your voice carries. And when you're the youngest of seven you get real good at deducing what's going on from only one side of the conversation." She waltzed in and plopped down across from him. "So what'd she say? That private investigator gal?"

"Not much. But if Trish is working off the books somewhere, or hasn't used a credit card recently, it might be harder to track her down."

"Well, the child couldn't have just vanished. She's bound to turn up, sooner or later."

"That's what worries me."

"I don't understand, I thought you wanted to get things settled. Legally. So there'd be no question."

On a weighty sigh, C.J. leaned back in his chair, tossing his pen on his desk. Frankly, he doubted things would ever feel settled again. With Trish, with Dana...

Oh, God, Dana. The more he was around her, the less he could figure out if she was the best thing, or the worst thing, to happen to him. If she'd had any idea how close he'd come to kissing her the other night...

And then what? Take her to bed? Lead her to believe things were headed in a direction he couldn't, wouldn't go? That much of an idiot, he wasn't.

At least, he hoped not.

He stuffed his thoughts back into some dark, dank corner of his brain and once again met Val's quizzical, and far too discerning, gaze. "If Trish doesn't reappear soon," he said, "the law's on my side. I'd get custody free and clear. It's the limbo that's killing us."

"Us? Oh. You and Dana?"

He let his gaze drift out the window. "Until we know what Trish is really up to, we can't make any permanent arrangements. Which we very much want to do. Need to do. For Ethan's sake."

The older woman eyed him for several seconds, then rose. "Well, I truly hope it all works out. For everybody. And soon. So...subject change—you ever decide who to take to the charity dinner Saturday night?"

Despite the permanent knot in his chest these days, C.J. chuckled. "It's not the prom, Val. And I'm taking Dana."

"'Bout time you did *something* right," she said, and waltzed back out.

Big whoop, he thought. One measly thing out of, what? A hundred? A thousand? Not that he didn't want to do the right thing, or *things*, it was just that he still wasn't sure what, exactly, that was.

Two showings, an office meeting and a closing later, he walked through the garage entrance into his house to be assailed by the mouth-watering aroma of roast pork, the pulse-quickening beat of bluegrass fiddle. Tugging off his tie, he followed his nose to the kitchen, where Dana—oblivious to his arrival—was stirring something in a pot on the stove, her white-shorted fanny wiggling in time to the music. In one corner, safely out of harm's way, Ethan sat up in his playpen, gnawing on a set of plastic keys. The instant he caught sight of C.J., though, the keys went flying. With a huge grin, the baby lifted his arms, yelling "Ba!"

Dana whipped around, her hand splayed across her stomach. As usual, several pieces of her hair had escaped her topknot, curling lazily alongside her neck, the ends teasing her collarbone and the neckline of her loose tank top. She laughed. "Somebody needs to put a bell on you, mister! You're home early!"

Home. The word vibrated between them, like a single note plucked on a violin, clear and pure and destined to fade into nothingness. A word C.J. had never associated with this house. Or any other place he'd ever lived, for that matter. A concept he'd never associated with *himself,* he realized as he set down his briefcase and scooped up his baby son, who began to excitedly babble about his day.

C.J. stood there, literally soaking up his baby's slobbery smile. At that moment, he felt as though he'd stepped into some family sitcom, where no matter what tried to rip apart the characters during the course of the episode, family ties always triumphed in the end. Except real life wasn't a sitcom, and the habit of a lifetime wasn't going to be fixed in twenty-two minutes.

"What's all this?" he asked, deliberately derailing his own train of thought.

"Nothing 'all this' about it. Business was slow so I took off early, figured I might as well throw the pork in the oven. We're eating in the dining room, by the way."

He glanced toward the room in question, saw the table set with place mats, cloth napkins, candlesticks. A *centerpiece,* for God's sake.

"I never eat in the dining room," he said.

"Then it's high time you did," she said.

Honest to Pete, she'd had no agenda behind dinner beyond feeding everybody. Roasts were no-brainers, for heaven's sake. As were boiled potatoes and steamed asparagus. Okay, so maybe the gravy was a little tricky, but not if you'd been making it since you were twelve.

And really, she hadn't been trying to impress him or anything with the table setting, she'd just thought it seemed a shame, never using the dining room. The man needed to start appreciating his own house, that's all.

So the look on his face when he'd walked in, smelled the cooking, seen the table, taken that first bite of pork…was icing on the cake. Seriously.

His chuckle when she handed him a dessert dish of Jell-O topped with a fluffy mountain of whipped cream, however… priceless.

They'd progressed to the family room, ostensibly to watch a film. She'd raided her parents' stash of DVDs, hauling back everything from old Hepburn-Tracy flicks to Clint Eastwood westerns, vintage Woody Allen to *Indiana Jones,* eighties-era chick flicks to over-the-top disaster movies. But the slim, colorful cases lay fanned out on the coffee table, temporarily forsaken. Instead, C.J. sat cross-legged on the floor in front of the fireplace with Ethan in his lap, halfheartedly fending off the baby's attempts to steal his whipped cream, and Dana thought, *Yeah, it's like that.*

Or could be, anyway.

"I'd forgotten how good this is," he said.

"Isn't it crazy?" she said, spooning a big glob into her own mouth. "Mama always used to make Jell-O for me when I was feeling down in the dumps."

He lifted one eyebrow. "So it's a comfort food, then?"

"Well, the whipped cream is the comfort food, actually. But squirting whipped cream directly into your mouth is really pathetic."

"Or efficient," he said with a grin. "Go away, cat," he said to Steve, who kept trying to bat at the whipped cream. C.J. held the dish up out of the cat's reach. "Mine. Mine, mine, mine." Ethan's eyes followed the dish, followed by a squawk. C.J. gave her a helpless look, and she giggled.

"Oh, go on, let him have some."

C.J. blew out a sigh, but lowered the dish anyway. Only the poor cat couldn't figure out how to attack something that wouldn't stay still, his head bobbing along with the quivering whipped cream. C.J. laughed, and Ethan chortled, and the cat finally stalked off, thoroughly put out.

"So how's the writing coming?" C.J. asked. Then frowned. "What?"

"Oh, nothing. It's just that I hate that question."

"Oh. Sorry. Why?"

"Because I never know how to answer it. I know you mean well, but—"

"It's okay, I understand. Well, actually, I don't, but if you don't want to talk about it, you don't want to talk about it." He fed another bite of Jell-O to the baby, then said, "One question, though—does anyone else know you're writing?"

"Not really. Well, my parents do," she said on an exhaled breath. "My mother thinks it's silly."

His forehead creased. "Has she read any of it?"

"I doubt that would make a difference. It's all a little too pie in the sky for her. Offends her practical sensibilities."

"Because it's a risk, you mean?"

"I suppose. She had enough trouble dealing with me going into business with Mercy and Cass, instead of getting a nice, secure accounting job with some well-established firm." A smile flickered over her lips. "She worries."

His dessert finished, C.J. set the dish up on the coffee table, then turned Ethan around to face him. Laughing, the baby dug his feet into the carpet and pushed up, clutching the front of C.J.'s shirt.

"Hey, look at you, hot stuff!" he said, clearly delighted, only to immediately suck in a breath. "Oh, God—when do they start walking?"

"Whenever they're ready. Around a year, maybe later. He has to crawl first, though. At least, so I gather."

And will I even be in the picture when that happens?

The thought pricked the haze of contentment she'd let herself be lulled into, propelling her to her feet to gather dessert dishes, which she carted back into the kitchen. C.J. followed, the baby in his arms.

"Hey. What's wrong?"

"Nothing. Really," she said with a forced smile when he frowned at her. "Just one of my moods again." Then, because melancholy always led to masochism, she said, "So how exactly did you end up with my cousin, anyway?"

Clearly startled, C.J. pushed out a short laugh. "Where on earth did that come from?"

"I'm a chronic scab-picker, what can I tell you?"

He held her gaze in his for several seconds, then sighed.

"Trish had quit, maybe a week before, I don't really remember. I was the only one in the office when she came in to pick up her last paycheck, except I had a little trouble finding it since Val had put it someplace 'safe.' Anyway, by the time I did, your cousin seemed very distraught. So…I asked her if she wanted to go get a drink." His mouth pulled flat. "And things…took their course."

She opened the dishwasher, started loading their dinner plates. "I see."

"I'm not proud of it, Dana," he finished softly. "It shouldn't have happened. But I didn't take advantage of her, if that's what you're thinking. Even if I did take advantage of…the situation. Just so you know, however," he said, shifting the baby in his arms, "I don't do that anymore. Start something I have no intention of finishing, I mean." He smiled tiredly. "It gets old."

"Yes," Dana said carefully, once again all too aware of the warning in his words, no matter how mildly they'd been delivered. "I can see how it would. Well. Thanks. For being honest with me."

"It's the least I can do," he said, and she thought, *Geez, story of my life or what?*

"Like hell you can wear that," Mercy said, her face a study in horror.

Dana looked down at the black charmeuse tunic and ankle-length skirt, still in its transparent shroud from the cleaners, she was holding up to her front. They'd just locked up for the night, leaving only a couple of spotlights on in the front of the store, and Dana had—in a clearly misdirected moment—decided to show her partners what she was wearing. "What's wrong with it?"

"You'll look like a leech?"

"Don't be ridiculous. It's even got sparklies. See?" She wiggled the bag in front of Mercy, who recoiled.

"Okay, a leech with a Cher fixation."

Dana looked to Cass, who was also going to the shindig. Under duress, apparently. Blake had insisted it would "do her good" to get out and mingle, although, according to Cass, all she really wanted to do was stay home and sleep.

"What are you wearing?" Dana now asked the blonde.

"Some red jersey number I've had forever."

Mercy blinked. "As in, the slinky little thing you wore to my sister's wedding? The one with no back? And not a whole lot of front, either, as I recall?"

"That would be the one."

Mercy gave Dana a pointed look.

"These hips don't do slinky, Merce," she said. "They do…softly draped."

"Yeah, well, your hips need to break out of their rut. Hold on." Mercy vanished into the back to return a second later with something…*not* softly draped. Or black. But not, at least, slinky, either. "Which is why I brought this. The color will go great with your hair, don't you think?"

"Where did you get that?" Dana asked. "And why is it here?"

"From Anita, and because I consider it both an honor and my duty to save you from yourself. Anyway, 'Nita's more or less your size. But instead of hiding her body, she *celebrates* it." She thrust the dress at Dana hard enough to make her lose her balance. "If that doesn't work, there are others. And ditch the bra, there's one built right into the dress."

"You might as well humor her," Cass said at Dana's glare. "You know she'll only make your life miserable otherwise."

On a sigh, Dana snatched the dress out of Mercy's hand and tromped to the bathroom to change. Five minutes later, upon glimpsing herself in the narrow, full-length mirror on the back of the bathroom door, she let out a shriek.

"Let us see, let us see!" she heard from the other side of the door.

"No way! For God's sake, I'd put somebody's eye out in this thing! No! Don't open the door!"

Too late. There stood her partners, one grinning like a loon, the other gasping.

"Get your butt out here," Mercy said, grabbing Dana's wrist and yanking her through the door, "so we can get the full effect."

"Yeah, *full* is right," Dana mumbled, then swung a pleading glance in Cass's direction. "Tell her I can't possibly wear this."

After a pause, during which Dana assumed Cass was working to get back her voice, the blonde said, "Honey, don't take this the wrong way, but I have never, ever seen you look better."

"See, Merce, what did I tell y—" Dana's eyes cut back to Cass. "*What* did you say?"

"You look unbelievably gorgeous. I swear."

"These go with it," Mercy said, handing Dana—who was too busy gawking open-mouthed at Cass—a small silver box, already open. Inside lay a pair of outrageously ornate chandelier earrings that, sad to say, immediately made Dana's mouth water.

"Ohhhh," she said on a soft sigh, almost not caring when she caught Mercy conspiratorially poking Cass in the arm.

He couldn't take his eyes off of her in that dress.

Neither could any other straight man in the room. Including Cass's husband Blake, who'd been trying so hard all through dinner *not* to stare at Dana's breasts. C.J. almost felt sorry for the poor bastard. But who could blame him? Dear God, they were magnificent.

She was magnificent. And if C.J. found himself occasionally battling the urge to deck every guy whose eyes lingered a little longer over that magnificence than he would have preferred…

Man, this protective business really packed a wallop.

Not that Dana needed protecting. Except, perhaps, from him.

His reaction, when she'd come out of her room, knocked him clear into next week. The dress, in some shiny fabric the same lush, deep blue of the sky just before nightfall, was truly a marvel of engineering, both lovingly and aggressively displaying Dana's no-holds-barred curves to perfection. But it was the woman inside the dress who'd set his pulse rate off the charts, the tilt of her chin that said *Yes, I know* exactly *how I look in this dress,* warring with the remnants of insecurity in her eyes, that made him want to do things to her, *for* her, he had no right to do. That he'd told her as considerately as he could he *wouldn't* do.

So, yes, he'd given her an appreciative whistle, but he'd otherwise played it cool. Careful. Not letting on how much he ached to trail his fingertips along the line of her jaw, down her neck, across the swells of those flawless, oh-God-just-kill-me-now breasts.

He tore his gaze away to scan the ballroom, recognizing probably half the people there. Including more than one woman he'd dated over the past decade. All of them beautiful, stylish, classy. Some of them at least momentarily intriguing. Or so he'd thought at the time. And yet, he couldn't remember ever anticipating being with any of them the way he did with Dana, simply preparing a meal together, or giving Ethan a bath, or just sitting out by the pool, shooting the breeze.

As if hearing his thoughts, she glanced over, a quizzical smile playing over her lips, and the thought of her leaving nearly made him dizzy.

Dinner over, the band started to play a run-of-the-mill pop

standard that got people up and moving, but not too fast. C.J. suddenly felt, if not old, at least close enough to middle age to give him pause. The other couples at their table, including Cass and Blake, all headed toward the dance floor; C.J. smiled over at Dana.

"Shall we?"

"Uh, thanks, but no. I am, without a doubt, the world's worst dancer."

"I don't believe that. I've seen your moves in the kitchen."

She laughed. "Sorry, you'll have to take my word for it…. What are you doing?" she said on a tiny squeal when he stood, took her by the hand, and led her out on the dance floor anyway. "I told you—"

"Hush," he said, settling one hand at the small of her back, tucking one of hers against his chest. Stupid move, but whatcha gonna do? "It's a slow dance, all we have to do is stand here and sway. Even you can sway, can't you?"

"And you're not afraid people will get the wrong idea?"

"Because we're swaying?"

"Because of the position we're in while we're swaying."

"Can't sway without touching," he said, pulling her closer to avoid colliding with another couple. "It's in the rulebook."

"And what rulebook would that be—?"

"C.J.! My goodness, I've been trying to catch your eye all night!"

Damn. And he'd been doing everything in his power to avoid hers.

"Cybill," he said smoothly, even as Dana jerked out of his arms, bumping into the person behind her. Grabbing her hand to keep her from bolting (which earned him a brief but potent glare), C.J. turned, meeting the other woman's glossy, predatory smile with a cool one of his own. Her nipples blatantly on display in a shimmery, silvery gown that looked more like something she'd wear to bed than a charity function, she was a mere illusion of womanhood, he realized, reeking of designer perfume and desperation.

"You are *such* a bad man," Cybill said on a breathy laugh, completely ignoring Dana. "Pawning me off on that Bill person when I called your office and specifically asked for you."

C.J. frowned. "I'm sorry, I don't remember getting a message."

"Oh, this was a couple of weeks ago. Silly me, I should have used my maiden name, I forgot you wouldn't have known my married one, which I only use for the children's sake." A cool, spindly hand landed on his arm. "Bill said you'd been really tied up, but I said I'd be more than willing to wait—" a brief glance speared in Dana's direction "—until things had, um, calmed down." Her smile veered back to C.J. "I'm in no hurry."

He wondered now how he'd ever found Cybill and her ilk even momentarily appealing. Women who, for whatever reason, felt they were somehow entitled to whatever they wanted.

"I'm very flattered," he said, "but unfortunately I don't see my schedule easing anytime in the foreseeable future. And I can assure you, you're in excellent hands with Bill." He placed his hand at the base of Dana's spine, gently tugging her to him. "You remember Dana Malone, don't you?"

Recovering quickly from C.J.'s less-than-subtle brush-off, the woman blinked once, then turned her puppetlike smile on Dana. "Of course I do. A *client* of C.J.'s, isn't that right? Did you two happen to run into each other here?"

Offended for Dana at the presumption, he casually roped one arm around her shoulders, knowing he'd pay dearly for the unspoken *What the heck are you doing?* practically vibrating from her as a result. "No, actually. We came together."

Her smile frozen in place, Cybill said, "Well, isn't that

nice?" Then, to Dana, "And don't you look absolutely adorable in that dress! I'd never have the nerve to wear something that…revealing."

"I suppose it helps to have something to reveal," Dana said sweetly.

C.J. managed, barely, to choke down the laugh. "Well, point to you," Cybill said with a watery laugh of her own, the twin spots of color on her thin-skinned cheekbones completely ruining the makeup he guessed she'd spent hours perfecting. She lifted her hand, as though to touch him again, only to apparently think better of it. "I'll call you," she said.

Unbelievable. "You'd only be wasting your time," he said, as kindly, but as firmly, as he knew how. Something like defeat flickered in her eyes for a moment before, on a tiny nod, she spun around and took off across the dance floor.

Just as Dana did the same thing in the opposite direction.

She heard his "Dana! Dana, wait…!" behind her as she slalomed around a half dozen couples toward Cass and Blake, who were standing at their table, checking the room with concerned looks on their faces. But suddenly, she'd had it. With the evening, with C.J., with…everything.

"Oh, good," Cass said when Dana got to the table, "we didn't want to disappear without telling you we were leaving, but I've got to get back and feed Jason. So much for my wild partying days—"

"Could I get a ride with you guys?"

"What? I mean, of course, but—"

Dana let out a small, startled yelp when C.J. grabbed her hand, pulling her around to face him. "Honey, I apologize, I know that was rude—"

"Yeah, it was." She yanked her hand from his, snatched her evening bag off the table. Despite his crowding her, she managed to face him, holding the bag up between them like a tiny, jeweled shield. "I'm leaving with Cass and Blake."

"If you want to go, I can take you home."

"And where exactly is that, C.J.? No—*what* is that?"

For several painfully awkward seconds, C.J.'s gaze swam in hers. Until he finally said, on a clearly frustrated breath, "Damned if I know." Only then he narrowed his gaze at her, throwing her completely off guard with, "But that's not what this is about, is it?"

Dana started when Cass touched her arm. "How about we meet you out front in five minutes?" she said, then left without giving Dana a chance to protest. Taking his cue, C.J. cupped Dana's elbow and led her outside. *Don't touch me,* she wanted to scream, but she'd already caused enough of a kerfuffle for one night. Despite their attempts at keeping their voices low and civilized, people had begun to stare.

Once outside, a valet who barely looked old enough to drive pounced on them; C.J. waved him away. Dana vaguely wondered where her ride was, deciding they must have gone for a short, discreet drive to give C.J. and her time to talk.

Except she didn't want to talk, she wanted to stew. She wanted to be left alone to berate herself for being the wussiest of the wusses, for not even having enough willpower to resist falling for someone she knew—knew!—would never fall for her. Hell, would never even be *attracted* to her.

But alas, being alone was not meant to be. At least, not until she got through the next five minutes. Or maybe four, if she was lucky.

"I take it this means you're going back to your place?" C.J. asked.

She nodded. They'd left Ethan with her parents; her mother had said it made no sense for them to disturb the baby by picking him up late, that they might as well let him stay until morning.

"Dana," C.J. said softly, "look at me. Please."

The last thing she wanted to do. But God forbid she came across as childish and petulant. When she finally twisted her head, he said, "Look, you can spend the night wherever you want. As long as you tell me what the hell is going on."

She looked away again. "I'm not sure I can."

"You? At a loss for words?"

"It's not the words, it's…" She walked over and sat on a low wall flanking the entrance, farther away from the clutch of valets, laughing and talking under a drooping old cottonwood. Even now, she was still more than half-tempted to keep her feelings to herself, to at least hang on to some semblance of dignity. But what was the point? Heaven knew how long their lives would be entwined because of Ethan. Did she really want to spend the next, oh, twenty years or more pretending?

The very thought made her queasy. So she looked up and said, "I thought I could do this, but I can't."

"Do what?"

"Whatever it is we're doing. Trying to figure out where the boundaries are, mostly."

"I'm sorry…I thought…" C.J.'s pricey loafers scuffed the mica-glittery pavement as he came closer. "I thought we were doing okay," he said on a sigh, sitting beside her.

"Yeah. I did, too."

She could feel his gaze on the side of her face. "So what happened?"

There she stood, on the very edge of the cliff. But instead of jumping, she backed up and said, "Good Lord…what on earth did you ever see in that woman? She has all the substance of a saltine."

"Hey, don't knock saltines. There may not be much to them, but at least you always know what you're getting."

Dana snorted. "Is that what's bothering you? Cybill? Because I thought it was pretty obvious it was all one-sided."

"No, not her, precisely. What she represents."

"I don't understand."

"The kind of woman you're used to being with. To…" *Just spit it out, sister.* "To taking to bed."

C.J.'s brows shot up. "They weren't all like Cybill, believe me—" He shut his eyes, a look of extreme consternation flattening his mouth. "That didn't come out quite the way I intended. Okay, yeah, I've dated more than a few women along the way. But I didn't sleep with all of them. Hell, I didn't sleep with *most* of them."

"And yet you did with my cousin," she said, earning her a flash of guilt in response. "Dammit, C.J.," she said softly. "Even Trish had one night with you. Which is more than I'll ever get, isn't it?"

The silence that followed told her everything she needed to know. Thank God, then, the Carters' SUV glided to the curb just at that moment. Dana stood up and walked over to the car, cringing when C.J. opened the back door for her, claiming her hand before she could duck into the backseat. He was close enough for her to smell his cologne, the fruity tang of wine on his breath. Close enough for her to see the *"I'm sorry"* in his eyes. A brief, tortured smile flickered on his lips. "You're not a saltine, Dana. You're more like…"

"Cracked wheat?"

He blew out a breath, looking away, then met her gaze again, shaking his head slightly as if not quite able to decide what to make of her. "I'll pick Ethan up from your parents' place tomorrow morning," he said. "You might want to warn them."

Then he walked away, handing his ticket to one of the valets. He glanced over, his eyes touching hers once more, but this time she couldn't even begin to decipher what was going on behind them.

"Sweetie? Are you okay?" Cass asked the moment Dana sank into the butter-soft backseat.

"I'm fine."

Two beats. Maybe three. Then, "Wanna spend the night with us?"

The mere thought of all those people in residence at the Carters was enough to pull out a tiny smile. "Maybe another time. But thanks for the offer."

Ten minutes later she was in her own apartment, prying off a spike-heeled sandal and thinking, irritably, *Now what?*

Get some air in here, that's what. The sandals dangling from one finger, she padded from room to room, opening windows, turning on fans. Not allowing herself to think. Because, really, what was there to think about? She'd said her piece, C.J. had clearly been appalled, and now she'd made more of a mess of things than they already were.

Good going, babe.

Much to her chagrin, there was absolutely nothing even remotely comforting in the fridge. Or in any of the cupboards. She couldn't even make quickie Jell-O because she'd forgotten to refill the ice cube trays. Besides which there was no whipped cream. And, sorry, but as a means of solace, sugar-free fake lemonade wasn't gonna cut it.

The air shuddered around her as she slammed shut the refrigerator door, then stomped to her bedroom, only to discover, after contorting herself into several Kama Sutra–worthy positions, that getting into the dress had been a whole heck of a lot easier than getting out of it. Finally, though, the thing lay on the carpet, like the shucked shell of some large blue insect, as everything that had been confined or hoisted or cinched in spread gratefully back to normal. Really, she thought as she massaged the welts on her ribs, if God had meant her breasts to sit up around her chin, He would have put them there to begin with—

The doorbell rang.

The doorbell rang?

Dana grabbed an old Victoria's Secret kimono out of her closet, still trying to arrange it around her newly freed body when she heard C.J.'s "It's me, open up."

She yanked open the door, the bizarre Hawaiian shirt barely registering before he'd grabbed her by the shoulders so hard she gasped.

"Dammit, Dana! Don't you get it?" Anguish contorted his mouth, choked his words. "I *like* you! I… Oh, *hell!*"

Then he planted one on her she'd remember until her dying day.

He almost groaned in relief when their mouths met, as he poured every ounce of the frustration and need that had built up over the past few weeks into that single, albeit noteworthy kiss. And she kissed him right back, boy, just as hard, just as eager, her fingers curling inside his waistband, tugging him closer…

She teetered for a second when he jerked away, her shoulders soft and slippery beneath his grip. Teetered again when he gently shook her, her hair shuddering around her shoulders.

"How in the hell could you have thought I wasn't attracted to you?"

Slowly, those soft gray-green eyes came into focus, followed by twin creases setting up camp between her brows. "Where would you like me to start?"

With something like a stifled howl, C.J. released her and stumbled over to her sofa in the nearly dark room. He dropped like a stone, his head in his hands, hoping against hope to put his brain back in charge before it shorted out completely.

Talking was all he'd intended to do. Everything he'd wanted to say had been right on the tip of his tongue.

Which had then gone and gotten real cozy with hers. Damn.

He looked up. Oh, God. She was naked under that flimsy little robe, wasn't she? "And if I had come on to you, what would you have thought?"

"Excuse me, but isn't that what you just did?"

"I mean, before."

"Oh, I don't know…." She crossed her arms under her breasts. "That maybe I wasn't chopped liver?"

"Try again," he said wearily, and after a moment he heard a soft "Ohhh," followed by the sofa sinking when she sat beside him.

He heard the release of her breath. "Okay, I guess I would have wondered if you were just, you know. Being kind."

"Or a bastard."

"That, too." Several beats passed. Then, "I take it you weren't being *kind* just then."

He laughed. "No."

"And the other?"

They sat in silence for several seconds, both staring into the darkness, before C.J. finally said, "You want strings, honey. And I don't."

"Oh, for God's sake, C.J.—this isn't about *strings!*"

After a second's recovery from the blast, he said, "Then what *is* this about?"

Dana twisted to face him, folding one leg up underneath her. The robe gapped open, most of one breast softly illuminated in the faint light coming from her bedroom. He didn't even try not to look, and she smiled.

"You really want me?"

"Like you wouldn't believe. But—"

"Geez, I got it, okay?" She hiked her elbow up onto the back of the sofa, her head cradled in her hand. "But you know what? If I can't get Godiva, I'm perfectly happy with Ghirardelli."

"You don't know what you're saying. Hell, *I* don't know what you're saying."

Her gaze was disconcertingly steady for several seconds. Then she brought both hands to her waist, hesitating for barely a moment before deftly undoing the loose knot in her robe sash. A slight shrug and it slithered off her shoulders, a pale blue puddle of silk in the crook of her arms, her lap.

"Is this clearer?"

"Uh…yeah," C.J. said, hoping to hell he didn't look like one of those cartoon characters with his eyeballs out on stalks.

"The point is," she said, leaning forward to cup his jaw in her soft palm, "I know what *you're* saying. So if you're all done being noble, here's where I remind you that I'm a big girl. In more ways than one," she added with a small smile.

"This…is wrong," he said miserably.

"Says who?"

"Me."

"Too bad, you're outvoted," she said, starting to unbutton his shirt.

"And why, exactly, does your vote count more than mine?"

"'Cause I'm the girl," she said, wrinkling her nose at him, and from somewhere deep, deep inside the tangled mess of cells called his brain came the thought, *This could be yours forever,* she *could be yours forever,* and he mentally stuck his fingers in his ears and shouted, *No! Can't hear you, can't hear—*

"Hey," she whispered, apparently misinterpreting his silence as her fingers spread across his chest. "What happens, happens, okay? And with any luck, it'll be lousy and we'll never want to do this again."

"With any luck," he echoed, and gave up the good fight,

easing her back into the cushions, his fingers tangling in her hair as he joined their mouths in a kiss that he'd fully intended to keep tender, gentle. Sweet, almost. Except the cute little she devil in his arms had other ideas, apparently.

Man, could this woman kiss or what?

Man, could he get himself in *deep* or what?

Speaking of getting himself in *deep,* which was looking good for his immediate future... C.J. hauled in a long breath, grateful for her breasts, milk-pale in the scant light, the weightless robe slippery in his fingers as he brushed it away. "You are so damn gorgeous, I can't stand it."

"Okay, C.J.?" she said, nibbling at his neck. "You're already going to get lucky, no need to overdo it."

He lifted himself up, frowning down at her, only to avert his eyes from what sure as hell looked like forgiveness in hers. As if she knew. And understood.

But he didn't want her to be understanding. Or good. Or kind. Or all the things that had brought him to this point to begin with, God help him.

"You think I'm just blowing air up your skirt?" he asked.

"Well, no." She giggled softly. "Since I'm not wearing one."

Actually, the only thing she was wearing at the moment was her perfume, and him, which should have made this one of life's damn-near-perfect moments if it hadn't been for the not-being-able-to-look-in-her-eyes thing. So he moved smartly along to those aspects of the activity that didn't involve locked gazes, thinking, *Okay,* this *I can do.* This *I can give her.* Which, judging from all those sighs and murmurs and clutched fingers in his hair, seemed to be fine with Dana. Except, after some serious breast worship that had her writhing nicely underneath him and had him so hard he thought he'd pass out, he stumbled across a series of angry red marks on her ribcage, visible even in the low light.

"What are these?" he whispered, trying to soothe them with his fingertips, his eyes darting to hers—for only a second—when she winced.

"From that torture device I was wearing tonight."

"Damn. Want me to make it better?"

"Knock yourself out. Um…C.J.?"

"Hmm?"

"There aren't any welts…there…"

"No?" He moved farther down, pressing kiss after soft, lingering kiss in her soft, yielding flesh, as *bastard… bastard…bastard…*played on a continuous loop inside his brain. "My mistake…"

It was hard to tell, what with her crying out and all, when the phone had started to ring. But even after they both froze, listening, hearts pounding, it took another two rings before C.J. finally propelled himself off all that glorious, giving softness and over to the phone, blaring evilly at them from across the room.

He glanced at the lit display, then blew out a breath.

"It's your mother."

Dana instantly sat up, grabbing the phone and trying to shrug back into her robe at the same time. "Mama?…Is Ethan okay?…I know, I'm sorry, I had my cell phone ringer turned off, I forgot to turn it back on. But it's nearly 1:00 a.m., why on earth—?" Right as she'd been about to rake her fingers through her hair, she stilled. "Oh. I see." Her hand dropped. "Uh, yeah, of course. I'll be right over." Then she grimaced, her eyes slanting to his. "Sure. I'll tell him."

She punched the end call button, then sat there, her expression blank, the phone clutched to her chest.

"Dana?" C.J. said softly over the feeling of his chest caving in.

As if coming out of a trance, Dana blinked up at him, then

released a shuddering sigh. "Trish is back," she said, then added, with a rueful grin, "And Mama says to tell you that you may as well come, too."

Chapter Ten

It was like being caught in a hurricane's path, Dana thought as she stood in the doorway to her mother's sewing room, watching her cousin watch Ethan sleep: knowing what was coming didn't make the actual event any less devastating.

"Trish?" she whispered into the half light. The young woman jerked at Dana's voice, her hands tightening around the crib's rails. Anguish radiated from her in palpable waves; in the unforgiving shaft of light seeping into the room from the hallway, Dana could see how thin she'd gotten, the way each vertebrae stood out in relief underneath her cropped top, the jut of a hipbone over the waistband of her low-riding jeans.

"What are you doing here, Dana?"

"Mama called me. She was worried."

"About me?"

"About everything. Come on back to the living room. We need to talk."

Nodding, Trish glanced back at the baby once more, then followed Dana down the narrow, carpeted hallway. Dana's father sat in a wing chair by the picture window in his summer robe and slippers, looking extremely disgruntled; her mother, her hair in curlers and wearing a floral housecoat Dana didn't recognize, stood nearby, arms crossed, frown in place. And in the center of the room, scowling mightily, stood the man she'd been naked with not a half hour before.

Maybe this wasn't the best time to remember that.

"C.J.!" Trish gasped behind her. "Why are *you* here?"

"Because I'm Ethan's father?"

"Trish…" Dana's mother interjected, but C.J. lifted one hand.

"This is between Trish and me, Mrs. Malone," he said softly, the slight curve of his lips doing little to ease the ferocity hard-edging his features. "And Dana."

Clearly befuddled, Trish's distressed eyes darted from Dana to C.J. and back again, before she sank onto the edge of the sofa and began to quietly weep, her face in her hands. If she'd hoped to generate sympathy, it wasn't working, judging from the decided lack of people rushing to her side to offer comfort. Only then she lifted her soggy face and said to C.J., "Except…except he's *not* yours."

Well, that got everyone's attention. Lord, Dana thought her poor father would have another heart attack. If not her mother. As for C.J., he was obviously struggling to check his anger. "Actually, he is."

Trish blanched. "But that's not possible. I mean, I was already…I thought I was…" She swallowed. "Are you sure?"

"Positive. Funny, but when a woman names me as the father of her baby—especially a woman who *abandons* her baby—you better believe I'm going to get proof."

"I didn't abandon him!" Trish's brown eyes took up nearly half her gaunt face. "God, you make it sound like…like I'm some mental case who leaves her baby in the bathroom, or in a trash can somewhere! I made absolutely sure Dana saw him before I drove away!"

"Maybe you didn't endanger him," C.J. said with a lethal softness that made Dana's hair stand up on the back of her neck, "but you still dumped him on Dana and vanished, leaving no way to get in touch with you. And now you say you didn't think I was Ethan's father? Exactly what kind of con were you trying to pull?"

Wedged as far into the sofa cushions as she could possibly go, Trish shook her head, her long, dishwater blond hair gleaming dully. "I wasn't...I didn't mean..." Apology glittered in her eyes when she scanned the room, looking at each of them in turn, before the whole story came tumbling out in semicoherent chunks—that she'd thought she was pregnant by someone else, how she'd been so bummed out that night she ended up with C.J., how she didn't think of putting his name on the birth certificate until after the baby was born and she was already involved with this other dude who really wasn't into kids, you know?

"And then everything completely fell apart. Randall left me, too, and I wasn't making enough to pay for day care, and..." She shrugged with great effort, as though her shoulders were weighted with sandbags. Her eyes at last landed on Dana. "I'm sorry, Dana, I know I took the coward's way out, but I knew how much you'd always wanted kids, and it seemed so ironic that here I was with a kid I couldn't take care of, while you wanted one so badly and couldn't have any. I was worn out and scared and desperate to make sure Ethan would be taken care of better than I could. And I knew you'd never put him in foster care."

"Then why on earth didn't you just *ask* for help?" Dana's mother said.

"Because…because I couldn't stand to see that look in y'all's eyes. Yes, that look right there, Aunt Faye," she said, waggling her finger in a move so much like her aunt's that, under other circumstances, Dana might have laughed.

Instead, she said, keeping her voice as steady as she could manage, "And now you want him back?"

After a long moment, Trish nodded, her eyes glittering. Only everybody jumped when C.J. said, "For how long, Trish? Until you freak out a second time, or a third or fourth?"

"C.J." Dana closed both her hands around his rigid fist, hoping to deflate his anger. But when his gaze jerked to hers, she saw, way past the immediate fury, a raw pain that she realized in an instant had nothing to do with Trish and Ethan.

"No!" Trish said, as Dana caught her mother's all-too-perceptive frown, her glance in Dana's father's direction. "That's not gonna happen! Not this time, I swear! I…I found a pretty good job in Vegas, I've got a nice place and can afford to pay somebody to watch him for me while I work. Look, I'm really sorry for putting everybody through this, but…but I didn't realize how much I'd miss my baby."

"Except you've obviously forgotten something," C.J. said. When she turned perplexed eyes to his, he said, "I *am* his father. And no way in hell am I giving you custody. Not after the stunt you pulled."

Confusion wrinkled her forehead. "But you don't even want kids."

"So why in the name of God did you set me up?"

Leaning forward, her hands tucked around her knees, Trish stared at the coffee table for several seconds before saying, "I was scared. And you were the only decent guy I knew. I guess I figured, if nothing else, you'd provide for Ethan."

Her gaze shifted to Dana. "That was one of the reasons I thought it wouldn't be so bad, if I left him with you, because

I knew you'd contact C.J. Only then I started to feel bad about tricking you," she said to C.J. "Especially now that I want him back." Her hands shoved into her hair, she collapsed back into the cushions. "Oh, man…I've really screwed things up, haven't I?"

"Yes, you have," C.J. said. Then he sighed. "But you haven't screwed things up entirely on your own. And no, that doesn't mean you're off the hook," he said when hope sprang to life in her eyes. "Maybe I *didn't* want kids, but I want this one. And damned if I'd ever do to him what you did. How do you think a judge would feel about that, Trish?"

At that, a determination such as Dana had never seen in her cousin's expression hardened her features. "No matter what, I'm his mama. Yes, I freaked, I'll admit that. And I made mistakes. But nobody can say I neglected him. I love that little boy to death, I swear. How I thought I could just walk away from him—"

"But you did," Dana's mother put in, showing remarkable restraint in having held out this long, Dana thought. And indeed, now she planted herself on the sofa, taking Trish's hand and giving her that now-you-will-listen-to-*me* look that could still make Dana quake in her boots.

"Patricia Elizabeth, all the time you lived here your uncle and I watched you dig yourself into more holes than a prairie dog. But even you have to admit this one's bigger and deeper than all the rest put together. Seems to me it's going to take longer than a couple of weeks and a few promises to dig yourself out."

"I know, but—"

"Honey, I don't doubt you love this baby. Anybody could see you'd taken good care of him. And God knows, I've been waiting for you to turn over a new leaf for a long, long time. But right now, this isn't about you. It's about what's best for your little boy."

"I know that, Aunt Faye," Trish said, defiance edging her words. "Why do you think I came back for him?"

"To appease your own conscience, most likely."

"That's not true!"

"Maybe not. But neither is anything going to be decided tonight. It's late," the older woman said, taking in everyone in the room. "We all need to get to bed. Or back to it, as the case may be. You can stay here, Trish, if you like—"

"If she stays here," C.J. said, "Ethan comes with me.'"

Trish swung around, her face scarlet. "I'm not gonna run off with him, C.J.!"

"No, you're not. Because I'm not giving you the chance."

"You don't trust me?"

"I'm sorry, Trish," he said. "At some point, maybe I'll feel more in a forgiving mood. But not tonight."

Trembling, her eyes sheened with tears, Trish grabbed her purse, muttered something about getting out of everybody's hair, and stormed out of the house.

And nobody—not even Dana's mother, amazingly enough—tried to stop her.

When Dana looked around afterward, however, C.J. had disappeared.

"He went to check on the baby," her mother said, snagging her hand to keep her from going after him. Giving her one of her looks. "You've done it, haven't you? Gone and lost your heart to that man, just like I was afraid you would."

"Actually, last time I checked, my heart was still safely inside my own chest." When the corners of her mother's mouth turned down, she added, "It's okay, Mama. Trust me," then pulled away before the woman could work up a full head of steam.

Of course, she thought as she found C.J. in almost the same position as she had Trish earlier, holding on to the rails of her old crib, staring down at the sleeping baby, that all depended on how one defined *okay*. For sure, things weren't the same between her and C.J. than they had been an orgasm ago. Some lines, you just couldn't cross back over. Nor did she want to. Still and all, they were talking a whole new ballgame, with all new rules.

Only she doubted she and C.J. were playing by the same ones now anymore than they had been.

He glanced up at her entrance, that same tight, weary smile stretched across his mouth, before returning his gaze to the baby. He reached into the crib, carefully rubbing Ethan's back between his tiny shoulder blades.

"It's not that I don't sympathize with how Trish feels…."

"C.J., really, you don't have to explain. Besides, maybe—hopefully—this was a corner-turning moment for her. All her life she's done whatever pops into her head at the moment, screw the consequences. It had to stop sometime."

He nodded, moving his hand up to cup his son's head. "After my mother died, my father…" He took a breath, his voice so low Dana could barely hear him. "My father withdrew into his own world. And didn't bother to take me with him. Nothing mattered but his business. No matter what I did, how hard I tried to please him…" One trembling thumb stroked the baby's temple, over and over. "He gave me everything I wanted—cars, ski trips with classmates, you name it—except the one thing I needed most. Eventually I stopped trying."

Dana leaned against the crib, almost but not quite touching him. "Want me to go beat him up for you?" At his low chuckle, she ventured, "You're not your father, C.J. In case you haven't figured that out."

"No. I can't imagine ever doing to Ethan what my father did to me. But there's still something missing. Although…" He hauled in a huge breath, let it slowly out. "When you heard me on the phone the other night? I was basically reading him the riot act, for all those years he basically ignored me."

"What did he say?" she asked gently.

"Nothing. No apology, no explanation." He shook his head, then pushed away from the crib. "Come on, let's get out of here, let your folks get back to bed."

Except, as they left the room, something nagged at her, that she had a very strong feeling she hadn't heard the whole story. Could C.J.'s inability to forge a lasting relationship really stem simply from his father's neglect, as painful as that must have been? Except what did it matter, in the long run? By now, his resistance was so ingrained, so intractable, the actual cause probably no longer even played into it.

And yet he clearly adored his son.

Hmm. Maybe orchids *could* grow in Antarctica, if given the right conditions.

If they didn't know it was forty below outside the greenhouse.

If someone had the guts to build a greenhouse in Antarctica to begin with.

Not that she could come right out and say any of this to the poor guy's face. That really would send him screaming in the opposite direction. No, this was going to take a little finessing, a bit of good old Southern gal subterfuge. But if *she* didn't believe C.J. capable of change, who would?

Saying she'd meet him at the car, Dana begged off to use the bathroom. Only C.J. had barely gotten to the end of the hall when she heard her father say, "Got a moment, son?"

Man, it had been a long time since he'd been on the receiving end of a father's take-no-prisoners glare. Didn't like it when he'd been seventeen, liked it even less now. Especially since Gene Malone didn't look any more comfortable about the prospective conversation than C.J.

"Let's go on outside," he said. "So the women can't hear us."

"You planning on whupping my butt?"

A brief smile flashed over the man's droopy features, but the look in his eyes said C.J. was treading on very thin ice. "If this had been twenty years ago, I just might." He opened the front door and gestured for C.J. to precede him outside.

The house had no porch to speak of, only a narrow slab of concrete underneath a three-foot overhang. But Gene led C.J. out farther into the small front yard, a circle of grass bordered by crushed rock, sage, a Spanish broom still in flower, its spicy fragrance skating on the cool, feathery breeze. "Lookit that," the older man said. "Even with all the city lights, you can still see the stars. Back home it'd be so hazy with humidity, the sky would be nothing but a big, blank slate." Then he glanced over, his mouth tilted up on one side. "*Whup,* huh?" he said over the incessant chirp of a nearby cricket. "Didn't figure you for a country boy."

"Not exactly. But growing up in the South, you're bound to pick up an expression or two."

A heavy silence preceded, "Seems to me maybe there's one or two other things you should've picked up while you were at it. I don't know what the term is now, but back in my day we called what you're doing tomcatting."

Yeah, he'd known this was coming, ever since he'd caught Dana's parents' exchanged glances when he and Dana had arrived. Together. "Look, I know this looks bad—"

"*Bad* doesn't even begin to cover it. Correct me if I'm wrong, but you spend one night with my niece, get her pregnant, and now you're getting cozy with my daughter? And there's no sense in denying it, it's pretty obvious something's goin' on between you. Now I know you and Dana are both adults, and in theory I've got no right sticking my nose into your business, but…"

His hands rammed into his robe pockets, Dana's father looked across the street. "Dana might be just another woman to you, but she's Faye's and my only child. The one thing they don't tell you, when you become a parent, is that there's no statute of limitation on worrying about your kid."

A concept his own father wouldn't have understood, C.J. thought bitterly, if the words had been branded across his chest. "Your daughter's anything but 'just another woman' to me, Mr. Malone," he said quietly.

Gene looked over. "So you're serious about her?"

"I'm serious about...not wanting to hurt her."

A moment passed. Then, "She tell you about Gil?"

"Gil? No, I don't think so."

"Oh, you'd know if she'd mentioned him. She and Gil had gone together, I don't know, more than two years. She was crazy about him. And we thought he was crazy about her. They were knee-deep in wedding plans when Dana found out she wouldn't be able to have children. And that was that."

"He broke it off?"

"Guess you'd call it that. When he didn't come see Dana in the hospital, or even send her flowers, she got the message." Gene paused. "Had her wedding dress all picked out and everything." The older man's eyes cut to C.J.'s. "Far as her mother and I know, she hasn't dated anybody since—"

"For heaven's sake, Daddy!" Dana said in a hushed voice from the doorway, bustling in their direction. "The Flannigans' bedroom isn't even twenty feet away!"

"They're out of town," her father said, protectiveness once again flashing across his features. Still, how much was too much? God knew C.J. had no intention of tossing his son to the wolves to fend for himself, as his own father had more or less done to him, but neither was it realistic—or even wise— to try protecting a child from ever getting hurt.

Exhaustion suddenly swamped him. As it obviously had Dana, who looked ready to drop, bracing her hand on her father's arm before stretching up on wobbly tiptoe to kiss him on his cheek. "I'll call you guys in the morning," she said, then let C.J. steer her to his car.

Once there, silence jangled between them, until they reached the end of the block and C.J. signaled to turn right. To return to her apartment.

"No," she said softly. "Left."

Not looking at her, he tapped the steering wheel with his thumbs. "You sure?"

"If it's what I want? Yes. Unless *you're* not—"

He changed the turn signal, headed west. A few seconds later, she said, "I'm sure you're right. That no judge in his or her right mind would let Trish take Ethan away from you. Not with her history of instability."

While he appreciated Dana's support, her words didn't comfort him as much as he would have thought. Now the silence was his to break. "So you're really okay with what happened between your cousin and me?" When she didn't answer, he glanced over to see her frowning. He returned his gaze to the nearly empty street as the car glided through pools of viscous, peach-colored light from the overhead halogens. "Or at least dealing with it?"

She laughed faintly. "For the most part. And by the way, whatever we're doing *is* nobody's business but ours."

"Your parents might take exception to that."

After a noisy yawn, she slumped down into her seat, watching him. "My father told you about Gil, didn't he?"

There was no point dissembling. "How'd you know?"

"Intuition?"

It clicked. "You overheard."

"Enough."

"So why didn't *you* tell me about him?"

She shrugged. "Because I didn't want to play the pity card? Because it's past history? Because it has nothing to do with…" She stopped herself.

"Us?"

"Anything."

"He really left you because you couldn't have children?"

"He really did."

"The creep never heard of adoption?"

"And waste all those sperm?" He could feel more than see her smile. "Let me guess. Your fists are itching."

"You have no idea."

"C.J.?" she said after a moment. When he cut his eyes to hers, she said, "I'm not gonna lie, I was devastated when Gil dumped me. He hurt me worse than I've ever been hurt by another human being, and I was very tender for a long, long time. Because I'd trusted him, because he'd made promises to me. Promises that went right out the window when I no longer fit his image of what a perfect wife should be. Here I'd thought for sure I'd finally found someone who'd accept me for who I was…" She faced front again. "He was a liar, basically. You're not."

"Still—"

"Yes, you have issues. But at least you're honest. And since you haven't made any promises, there aren't any to break. I know exactly where I stand. Or more to the point, where you do. No surprises, no curveballs, no—" she yawned "—pain."

"And you don't think you're deluding yourself?"

Her laugh startled him. "No, *deluding* myself would be pretending there's more between us than there is." Her fingertips landed on his wrist. "I may not be the most experienced gal in the land, but I haven't been a starry-eyed virgin for some time. I do know when a man's in it just for the sex. And that's okay, as long as everybody's—" another yawn "—on the same page."

C.J.'s hand tightened around the steering wheel. "I'm not in it 'just for the sex,' Dana. There is more to this than… that."

But when he looked over, she was down for the count, her head tilted to one side against the seat, her breathing slowing, deepening.

God help him, he was drowning here.

It was nuts. On the surface, could this be any more perfect? The company, the companionship, the luscious body of a warm, generous, undemanding woman who expected nothing more than his respect and honesty? By rights, he should feel like the luckiest SOB on the face of the planet.

So the "feeling lucky" thing could kick in anytime now. *Any*time.

His heart punishing his ribs, C.J. drove on, steadily, smoothly, navigating the nearly empty streets a helluva lot easier than he was navigating his own life these days. All those years of striving for an uncomplicated, undemanding existence…

"Oh, shut up," he muttered to that rotten little whoever, or whatever, still laughing his/her/its butt off, even weeks after his discovery that his vasectomy had gone kaflooey.

Minutes later, he pulled into his garage and cut the engine. "Hey," he whispered, stroking Dana's cheek. "We're ho…here."

"Hmm?" She blinked awake, yawning again as she stared blankly out the window. "Oh. Right. Don't even tell me what time it is," she said, pushing open her door. "I don't want to know."

His arm securely around her waist, C.J. guided her inside, amazed to realize how much he'd grown accustomed to Ethan's presence in the house, how off-kilter it already felt not having him there. And he knew, with a sudden clarity that stole his breath, exactly how shattered he'd feel if some judge decided the baby *was* better off with his mother, if Trish took him away.

Who'da thunk it?

"No, this way," he said when Dana leaned toward "her," room, instead steering her toward his.

She came to a dead, if wobbly, halt, looking up at him. "I hog the bed."

"It's a big bed."

"And so it is," she said, even though he wasn't so much of a fool as to think she hadn't at least peeked in here at *some* point during the past two weeks. He caught her head shake at the clothes still piled in the chair before she crashed like a felled tree, fully clothed, on top of the comforter. She curled up on her side, wadding one of the down pillows under her cheek.

"Mmm..." she breathed, and passed out again.

He stood there, watching her sleep, this bundle of contradictions whose very presence made his chest constrict, with joy, longing, regret...this unassuming woman who'd inexplicably goosed his inner white knight into action. And yet, he thought as he eased off her sandals, sending Steve rocketing from the room when he tossed them onto the carpet by the bed, instead of a great, roaring gush of emotion when he looked at her, C.J. still felt only a frustrating trickle, as though his heart was a rusted faucet that turned only so far. Okay, so, yeah, he was crazy about his little boy. He'd admit that. But Ethan was *his*. And a baby. A baby who needed his father to *be* his father. Dana, however...

He fetched a lightweight blanket from the chest at the foot of the bed, carefully draping it over her before curving his body to spoon hers from behind—a slightly unsettling impulse, considering he'd never been much of a cuddler. If only he could strong-arm that faucet open all the way, he thought as his breathing slowed to match hers, then maybe

Dana wouldn't feel compelled to keep hers to a trickle, too, to withhold the one thing he didn't deserve…the one thing, he now realized—selfishly, irrationally—he wanted more than anything in the world. Because what, he wondered, would it be like to bask in the full force of Dana Malone's love?

There was a pointless thought. But if *this* was all there was between them—Dana stirred in her sleep when C.J. kissed her shoulder—then, come morning, he'd just have to make damn sure this was the best *this* she'd ever had.

Chapter Eleven

Dana woke to far, far too much sunlight, the sound of the shower running in the master bath on the other side of the wall, and fish-scented purring in her face. Slowly, she hauled herself upright, raking her fingers through her matted hair as she grimaced at her wrinkled T-shirt and capris.

Only she could wake up in C.J.'s bed with all her clothes still on.

Although "wake up" was probably a stretch, since—she squinted at the clock—she'd only been asleep for five hours. If that. With a sound that was more growl than groan, she crashed back into the C.J.-scented pillows. Who the heck gets up at seven on a Sunday morning? Besides her mother?

Her mother. Who would be here at nine to drop Ethan off before she went on to church. Ethan, yay. Mama…

Dana shut her eyes, as if that would stop…everything. Except Steve was back in her face, rumbling like a '67 Chevy.

An odd, strained *airp* punctuated the purring every now and then, as though he couldn't work up the energy to push out a real meow. A huge yawn—from Dana, not Steve—roused a few more brain cells. And a memory or two of that conversation on the ride home.

She'd felt like one of the characters in her own stories, her words carefully scripted. Except she'd only had one shot at getting it right, no editing allowed. Strangely enough, she'd actually been more sincere about accepting things the way they were between her and C.J. than she might have expected. Hey, getting screwed over by a man you'd completely trusted tends to make a girl *real* cautious. With her heart, at least.

Still, either because she was very brave or very stupid, she still nurtured her precious little hope with all the ferocity and single-mindedness of that crackpot gardener in Antarctica with his orchids. The difference was, she now fully understood the risks involved. She could hope and pray until the cows came home that C.J. would come around, but that didn't mean it would happen—

"Mornin'."

She actually shuddered at the sound of his voice, all low and sexy and silky, only to chuckle when she looked over at him. "Love the hair."

"Yeah?" he said, roughing it up a little more with a small beige towel, the big brother of which was wrapped around his hips. Hmm. Apparently his hair wasn't the only thing at attention.

His gaze followed hers, then slid back up, unmistakable yearning in his eyes, and the room seemed to close around them, an impenetrable fortress shielding them from all that pesky ambivalence.

Well, some of it, anyway.

Eyes crinkling to beat the band, he moved toward the bed. With definite purpose. "Sleep well?" he asked, one knee on the edge of the mattress, his mouth suddenly inches away from hers—

"No!" she shrieked, springing from the bed. "I mean, yes, I slept okay, but um…I need to…" *Floss. Pee. Close the blinds.* "…take care of…things."

"Sure," he said. And ditched the towel. "We'll wait."

Oh, my. Amazing how…*there* things looked in broad daylight. Which meant…oh, dear God. Getting nekkid with the guy in her nearly dark living room was one thing. Doing it here would be like having sex in an operating theater.

"Dana?" he said quietly, jerking her back to attention. A resigned half smile curved his lips. "Look, if you've changed your mind…"

"No, it's not that, it's…" *Weenie, weenie, weenie.* "Hold that thought."

Never had a man looked more relieved. And oddly enough, suddenly the idea of getting it on in the middle of an operating theater sounded…not so bad. Scary as all get-out, yes. But doable.

Five minutes later, brushed and flossed and perfumed and whatnot, and swaddled in the largest towel she could find, she returned to the (still) brightly lit bedroom to find C.J. (still) waiting for her on the bed, his back to the headboard, one pale beige sheet discretely covering his lap. Stretched out beside him, Steve kneaded the air with a goony look on his face (and one eye trained on her) as C.J. idly scratched the thing's belly.

She'd expected…well, she wasn't sure what. An offhand remark, maybe. Instead he rose from the bed, his whole expression softening as he approached her.

And tugged off her towel.

The sunlight slashed across her bare breasts, her belly, her thighs, as the plush cotton sighed to the carpet at her feet…as C.J. gently, softly, sweetly kissed her mouth, tugging her lower lip oh so tenderly between his teeth before gathering her in his arms, hot skin to hot skin, to tongue the hollow of her throat, and it didn't take long for the filmy haze of sun and sex to soft-edge any lingering reservations about things sagging and swaying and jiggling.

He lowered himself to his knees in front of her to suckle her breasts, and she smiled, bending forward to shield him with her long hair, the room's deep silence swallowing her sighs, the sounds of a lover's worship, her own soft cries of sharp, achy pleasure when he pulled her deeper, deeper into his mouth, as though he couldn't get enough of her, give enough to her…

She braced her hands on shoulders like rock, eyes closed, savoring, reveling…trusting, that he wouldn't hurt her, wouldn't take her anyplace she didn't want to go, wouldn't let her fall…as his hot, moist breath heralded a hundred lazy, lingering kisses across her breasts, her ribs, her belly, lower…

Dana whimpered, her fingers tangled in C.J.'s hair, as he spread her, loved her, brought her to climax, once…twice…

"Oh! *Oh!*"

She cried out, in amazement, in gratitude, as the pulsing peaked a third time, as she felt more glad to be a woman than she ever, ever had in her life.

"Your skin…" Sounding slightly amazed himself, C.J.'s voice cut through her après-climax haze. "It's the color of the light."

"W-what?"

"Your skin. Look."

He got to his feet, pulling her over to face the huge mirror over his dresser, and the "No!" of surprise, of embarrassment, escaped before she could catch it. Acute self-awareness surged through her, a furious blush following in its wake. Not a second before, she'd felt beautiful, almost ethereal, and now he'd ruined the moment, *destroyed* it, by making her see herself as she really was.

"Damn you!" she cried, struggling to get free, but C.J. only chuckled, wrapping one strong, darker arm, around her waist, pulling her back against him. When she dropped her eyes, he tightened his hold, making her gasp again.

"Look at yourself, dammit!" he hissed, his breath hot in her ear. "See what I see. Yes, like that," he said when she forced herself to look at her reflection, watching his splayed hand track across her stomach, cup her full breasts, his thumb rhythmically circling her rosy nipples.

"Don't you see?" he said, pressing his temple against hers, and she met his gaze in the mirror, saw something in it she'd never seen in another man's eyes. "You're *real*, Dana," he said, touching her, stroking her wherever he pleased without an ounce of compunction, one finger tracing the faint, silvery pink scar from her operation. "You're so…damn…real, you make my mouth go dry."

Her skin flushed anew, this time with arousal, as the sharp, delicious sting of anticipation bloomed once more between her legs. "How on earth could you not know how beautiful you are?" he said, and tears threatened.

"Because I never saw myself through your eyes," she whispered.

"Oh, Dana…" he said on a rush of air, ribbons of fire streaking her hair when he sifted it through his fingers, then let those fingers skim her neck, shoulders, down her goose-bumped arms to claim her hands, pull her toward the bed. And he started all over, his exploration thorough, unhurried, making her blush again and again when he'd pause for a moment in the proceedings to extol, in explicit detail, her many—as he put it—charms.

"C.J.…" she said, laughing, when things had gone on in

this manner for far longer than most men would even consider, especially since it was patently clear that he wasn't doing all this to buy time for himself "…you must be about to explode!"

"Now that you mention it…" Wicked amusement danced in his eyes. "Yeah. I am. But, oh, what a mind-blowing explosion it's going to be."

"Wow. You sound pretty sure of yourself."

"Call it—" he said, kneeing apart her legs, his eyes darkening "—an educated guess."

"Prove it," she said, sighing in pure *okay-I-can-die-now* happiness as one very ready Tab A plunged effortlessly into one even more ready Slot B, as he tormented her with tantalizingly, agonizingly slow thrusts, each one deeper than the last, filling her more…and more…and more, until their bodies finally said to their brains, *Move over, our turn,* and then there was nothing but heat and friction and lots of heavy breathing and the mad, frantic pumping that if you thought about too hard, you'd laugh, and then there were moans and cries and just before that final, glorious burst of stars and white lights (because, yes, sometimes it really is like that), Dana opened her eyes to see the barely concealed terror in C.J.'s.

Then it was over, their hearts the only things left pumping, their cries already faded into the silence. Only before she could catch C.J.'s eyes a second time he wrapped her so tightly in his arms she could hardly breathe.

And she thought, *Damn you, C.J., what am I going to do with you?*

"I still haven't decided whether I should thank you or smack you."

At Dana's teasing words, C.J. looked up from his three-cheese omelet. As he watched Dana spoon applesauce into Ethan's baby-bird-wide mouth, it struck him that he couldn't even remember the afterglow hanging around for more than ten minutes, let alone two hours. But not even the baby's return—accompanied by the noxious cloud of disapproval radiating from Dana's mother—or the mundane tasks of feeding him his lunch and preparing their own breakfast, could fully eradicate the lingering vestiges of a hunger not nearly as sated as one might have expected.

The edge to Dana's voice brought him back to earth with a resounding *thud*.

"For what?"

With a rubber-tipped spoon, she scraped leaked sauce off Ethan's chin and shoved it back into his mouth. "For raising the bar. Because, really…" She glanced over, her ponytail—still damp from their second shower, finished mere minutes before Faye's arrival—falling over one tank-topped breast. "I'm not sure how the next guy is ever going to be able to top your…talent."

His fingers tightened around his fork. "The next guy?"

"Sure," Dana said lightly, softly dinging the spoon against the bottom of the jar. "Since this is only for the moment and all. I was just thinking ahead, you know. Oh, for heaven's sake—why the long face?" She stood, screwing the top back on the jar. "I would think your ego would be puffed up like the Pillsbury Doughboy after that compliment," she said, grabbing the container of wipes off the counter to clean Ethan's hands, earning her a squeal of protest. "And I was taught—oh, now, quit squirming, sugarpie, I'll be all done in a sec—to always give credit where it's due."

"I wasn't alone in the bed, Dana," C.J. grumbled. But she'd turned the water on at the sink and hadn't heard him. And what was with his nose getting out of joint, anyway? It wasn't as if he had any claim on her future affections, after all. Still, at least she could have had the good grace not to bring up the subject now.

Since *now* was all they had.

"Hey," he said, "why don't we take Ethan to the zoo today? My client cancelled his open house, so—"

"Oh…I'm sorry, C.J., I can't." Wiping her hands on a dish-towel, Dana faced him. "The workers are coming tomorrow to start on the new place, so Cass and Merce and I already made plans to meet there this afternoon to prepare. But there's no reason why *you* couldn't take him to the zoo. By yourself."

"Well…no, I suppose not. Except…I just thought it would be fun. All of us going together."

"Yes, it would," she said softly. "But…"

"What?"

"With Trish back in the equation, maybe we shouldn't get too carried away with acting like a family. For Ethan's sake, if nothing else. It would only confuse him."

C.J. frowned. "She's not getting custody, Dana."

"You don't know that. And even if you two get joint custody, that kinda removes me from the equation, doesn't it?"

His chest felt as though it would cave in. "It doesn't have to."

"Of course it does," she said gently, patiently, waiting for him to connect the dots. Which he finally did.

"You're going to leave already?"

"Not until things are settled about Ethan, obviously. But since it appears that's going to happen sooner than later… Oh, come on, C.J.—you know as well as I do that if it weren't for Ethan, I wouldn't even be here. Let alone that we'd've gotten naked. Our lives just happened to bump up against each other, and we both took…advantage of the opportunity."

She came up behind him to slip her arms around his neck, laying her cheek against his temple. "You're an incredible lover," she said, giving him a squeeze. "You're incredible, period. But even you have to admit that the longer I hang around, the harder it's going to be to keep things casual. And

I know that's the last thing you want. So I'm just saying…
maybe Trish's return is a blessing in disguise. Oh, shoot," she
said, her gaze glancing off the microwave clock, "it's later
than I thought, I need to get my butt in gear—"

"Dana?" he said, catching her before she got all the way
out of the kitchen.

"For the life of me, I can't figure you out. And it's beginning to seriously piss me off."

She lifted her hands in a *that's-the-way-it-goes* gesture,
then walked away.

"Okay." Mercy swept her hair back with her wrist,
adorning her forehead with blobs of cobalt-blue paint.
"Explain to me again why we didn't hire painters?"

"Because we're cheap," Cass yelled from the other side of
the room over the constant hum of floor fans, the pounding
of hammers, the continuous stream of Spanish—off-color
jokes (according to Mercy) from the other side of the house.

Mercy slammed her roller against the wall. "No, I think it's
because we're stupid."

"And who said the more sweat equity we put into the place,
the bigger stake we have in its success?"

"Yeah, well, *there* was a delusional moment."

Curled up apart from the fray in a window seat with her
laptop, Dana allowed herself a wry smile as she put the finishing touches on the print ad to run in the paper the following Sunday, Monday being the grand opening for the new
location. Insanity, is what this was, allowing only a week to
get everything up and running. She'd hardly seen either Ethan
or C.J. the past several days, one of those good news/bad
news kind of things.

But she couldn't dump everything in her partners' laps,
and closing the store for longer would wreak havoc with

their cash flow, already stretched to the max as it was. Even with Mercy's father's construction company doing the lion's share of the work, it was still costing a fortune to retrofit the old house. God alone knew how they were going to afford an elevator, an absolute must if they wanted parents with strollers to even consider going up to the second floor.

At least—she hit the Send button to e-mail the ad to the paper—the craziness here distracted her (somewhat) from the craziness that was the rest of her life. Who would've guessed she'd have the guts to toss that little gauntlet down between her and C.J. the other morning, putting him on notice that she was already thinking about the future? The one in which sex wasn't on the menu?

Not that she'd expected C.J. to pick it up. Not then, anyway. Even if he had looked slightly ill. But nothing strained the old ego more than an ignored gauntlet, lying there collecting dust as everybody stepped over it, day after day.

Dana slipped the laptop back into its case, resisting the temptation to sneak a peek at the last few pages of her book, finally written in the wee hours the night before. At least she had that. Now all she had to do was work up the gumption to actually ask editors and agents if they wanted to read it.

Thinking about it made her heart beat so hard, it actually hurt.

"Hey!" Mercy barked. "You over there in a fog. Got a roller here with your name on it. And did you call the sign people?"

"I did," Dana said, unfolding herself from the seat and wending her way through ladders and paint buckets and drop-clothed display cases, her hands sunk into the pockets of a pair of ancient denim overalls she'd unearthed from the bowels of her old closet. "They'll be here tomorrow. Hey, you missed a spot—"

"Dana?"

She spun around to see Trish silhouetted in the open doorway, a vision in a belly-baring tank top and short-shorts, the ends of her twisted-up hair fanned around the top of her head like a worn-out paintbrush. By some unspoken mutual agreement, they hadn't seen or spoken with each other since that night at her parents' house. Despite Trish's having left Ethan with Dana, whatever happened about the baby now was between Trish and C.J., a realization which produced a little burst of anger in Dana's chest.

"Trish! What are you—?"

"Aunt Faye told me y'all were over here," she said, side-stepping a stack of lumber, her eyes darting between Cass and Mercy, who were assiduously pretending not to listen, before meeting Dana's again. "I need to talk to you."

"Why?" The word came out hard enough to make her cousin flinch.

"Dana, please don't be like this. I know I put you in an awkward situation and all but—"

"Not me, Trish. Ethan. And C.J. I'm just…" She waved her hands. "A bystander."

"Is…is there someplace we can talk?" Trish whispered. "In private?"

"I've got a million things to do—"

"This won't take long, I promise."

"Outside, then. And make it snappy."

And indeed, they'd barely gotten out onto the porch before Trish said, "I've changed my mind. About wanting custody of Ethan."

"Oh, for the love of God, Trish! *Again?*"

Her cousin's eyebrows slammed together over her nose. "Don't you dare go gettin' mad at me when you know good and well this is what you wanted all along!"

"And I repeat, this isn't about *me*. It's about you not being able to stick with a decision for longer than five minutes! So how long is this one going to last? Until you get back to Vegas and miss Ethan again?"

A couple of seconds passed before Trish pushed out a sigh, then clomped over to the steps in her platform shoes, plunking her butt down on the top one. "I'm not goin' back to Vegas. I'm stayin' here."

"What do you mean, staying here? What about your job? Your apartment?"

Trish seemed to take a sudden interest in the mail carrier across the street. "The job was only temporary, some under-the-table thing in one of the casinos. And I was living with an old friend from school who'd moved out there."

"So you lied."

"Yeah. Well, sorta. Becky does have a pretty nice place."

Dana exhaled. "Why?"

"I don't know, I just… All I wanted was to see Ethan again, make sure he was okay and stuff. Not that I thought he wouldn't be. Except then I saw him and…I kinda went a little crazy. And then C.J. was there, and I guess I freaked, and then I heard myself telling C.J. that Ethan that wasn't his."

"Wait a minute. So the story you told C.J., about thinking you were already pregnant…?"

Bony, bare shoulders shrugged.

"Oh, Trish." This was the problem with Trish—how could you stay mad at somebody that screwed up? Shaking her head, Dana joined her cousin on the steps. "Honey, don't take this the wrong way, but you really, really need help."

"Yeah," the girl said on a sigh. "I know. But…"

"You know we'd all help with the expense, if that's what's holding you back. As long as you're willing to try to make it work this time."

After a moment, her cousin nodded, not looking at her.

"God, Dana," she said in a small voice, "you have no idea how much I hate my life. Sometimes I even hate myself, for making such a mess of things." She twisted around, tears glittering in her eyes. "But I do love Ethan, you've gotta believe that. I always have. And if things'd been different, I wouldn't've left him with you to begin with. But now that I've been back for a while and had a chance to think things through, I know I really can't take care of a baby right now. And probably not for a very long time. So whatever you and C.J. want to do about custody's fine with me. Although I'd still like to be part of my baby's life. I mean, if that's okay?"

After a moment, Dana took her cousin's hand in hers. "I'm sure we can work something out."

"Really? Because I'd like him to know who his mama is, that she loves him. That way, maybe he won't hate me so much for giving him up."

"He won't," Dana said over the lump in her throat. "I won't let him."

"Swear?"

"Swear."

"What about C.J.?"

Ah, yes, C.J. C.J. with the parent-abandonment issues. Still… "I can't see C.J. letting that happen, either. Although you need to talk to him yourself."

"Already did, earlier today. But I needed to tell you in person. It's part of my new resolve, facing things head-on instead of runnin' from 'em, or hidin' behind a lie. Or six," she added with a small smile. Trish glanced back at the house, then faced Dana again, rubbing her palm over her bare knee. "You suppose maybe y'all might need some extra help, once you open again?"

Dana started. "You mean here? At the store?"

"I can run a register like nobody's business. And I've always liked kids, you know that." The girl's face fell at

Dana's apparently poleaxed expression. "But if you don't think it's a good idea, I totally understand."

"No, it's not that." Dana pushed out a breath. "I'll have to discuss it with Mercy and Cass. And if—*if*—we do hire you, you cannot flake out on us. Is that understood? Because I've worked too hard for this business to put it in jeopardy."

Trish grinned, then saluted. "Got it. And I *swear* you won't be sorry—" Dana held up a hand to cut her off; Trish giggled, then angled her head. "And…d'you think I could stay with Aunt Faye and Uncle Gene until I save up enough to get my own place?"

Honestly. If the girl ever got the common sense to go with the cojones, there'd be no stopping her. "Knowing Mama?" Dana said. "What do you think?" Then she pushed herself to her feet. "And now I've really got to get back in there, or Mercy's gonna have my hide."

"You do believe there wasn't ever anything between C.J. and me, don't you?" Trish said, standing, as well. "Well, apart from the one night, I mean."

Dana thought of her previous jealousy—because that's what it was, no sense pretending otherwise—about that "one night." Not an issue any longer, she thought with a flush. "Yes, actually. Although…did you want there to be more?"

"Oh, heck, no. He's not my type at all. Not for the long haul. I mean, it was fun and all—"

"Trish? TMI, okay? And anyway, I'm not sure what that has to do with anything."

At that, her cousin reared back to look at her, incredulity swimming in her eyes. "You're not serious? Anybody with two eyes in their head can see how crazy you are about the guy. The way you looked at him that night at Aunt Faye's?" She shook her head. "Shoot, I'll bet nobody's ever loved him like you do."

An embarrassed, nervous laugh popped out of Dana's mouth. "How on earth would you know that? You worked for him for, what? Six months?"

"Hey. Maybe I've got problems, but I can read people a lot better than you might think. And besides, that office manager of his is a gold mine of information," Trish added with a grin. Then she sobered. "And from what Val told me, I'm gathering not many women liked C.J. for just himself, if you get my drift. Either they were after his money, or because he was arm candy, or both. You're not like that, Dana."

"Maybe not, but—"

"Oh, for pity's sake, do I have to spell it out for you? One of the reasons I don't feel as bad as I might about giving Ethan up is because I can see he's got a shot of havin' two parents. Obviously I didn't even consider that when I left him with you, because I honestly didn't think C.J. would step up to bat the way he did. And of course I had no idea you and C.J. would hook up, so that part's a total fluke, but now…well, it couldn't be more perfect, could it—? Ohmi*god!*"

"What?"

"You're playin' hard to get, aren't you? Instead of puttin' yourself on the line and goin' after the man, you're gonna let him get away." Trish laughed, shaking her head. "And you think *I'm* the dumb one?"

Her cousin was halfway back to the front door by the time Dana found her voice again. "What are you doing?"

"I think it's called *going for it,*" her cousin said from the open doorway. "A concept apparently some of us on this porch are currently havin' a little trouble with?" When Dana rolled her eyes, Trish giggled and said, "Heck, I need a job. And if slapping paint on the walls is what it takes to get in y'all's good graces, then that's what I'll do."

After Trish disappeared inside, Dana collapsed onto the top

step, a million thoughts pinging around inside her head like drunken moths. Well. Trish's change of heart about Ethan pretty much annihilated her "out" with C.J., didn't it? Stay or not, whatever decision she made, using Ethan and/or Trish as a reason was no longer an option. Ball was in her court and all that.

But what really chapped her hide was the mortifying realization that her spacey cousin had read her a heckuva lot better than she'd read herself. Because what kind of risk *was* she taking, really? As long as she kept her heart locked up in its safe little cage, how on earth could she expect C.J. to trust her enough to reciprocate? Or even try? At the very least— she sucked in a steadying breath—he deserved to know how she really felt. That she did love him.

What he did with that information was completely up to him.

Chapter Twelve

Stretched out on a chaise by the pool, C.J. jerked out of his doze when he heard the patio door open behind him. He twisted his head as Dana sank into a nearby chair, her breath leaving her lungs in a long, obviously exhausted whoosh. Odd how, these days, he could never fully relax until she was once again where he could see her, hear her. Touch her. Reassure himself that she was safe.

Stupid.

"What time is it?" he asked, sitting up.

"After nine. Ethan go down okay?"

"Not really, no." He paused. "I think he misses you."

"I doubt it." She plucked something off her knee. "Trish came by."

"Yeah, she said she was going to. So you know."

"Yes. Congratulations, by the way," she said, leaning her head back against the cushion, ruffling Steve's fur when he jumped up onto her lap and began to knead that awful, baggy, paint-spattered thing she was wearing. "That must be a huge load off your mind. Or will be, once it's all on paper."

"Frankly, I think it's a huge load off Trish's, too," C.J. said cautiously, trying to gauge Dana's obviously strange mood. Fraught with danger though that might be. "Knowing she never has to worry about Ethan being taken care of. I suppose you and I need to work out something official now. I'll make an appointment with my lawyer sometime next week."

In the darkness, he sensed the slight smile she offered in lieu of a response. Then she got to her feet, jettisoning the cat. "Is there anything to eat? I'm starved."

C.J. stood, as well, opening the patio door for her. "Guadalupe brought homemade tamales, will that do?"

"God bless Guadalupe," she said, moving past him to the kitchen. Keeping her gaze trained straight ahead.

"You look beat."

"Twelve hours straight of manual labor will do that to you."

"Sit," he said, pointing to the table in the breakfast alcove. "Nuking, I can do. How many do you want? Two or three?"

"How about a dozen?" she said, dropping like a stone into one of the chairs. "Although I'll settle for three." She'd pulled her hair back into a ponytail, but great hunks of it hung around her face as though they were too pooped to stay up in the clip. But it was the look in her eyes that sent shockwaves coursing through his veins. Shuttered, cautious. Guilty, although what Dana would have to feel guilty about, he had no idea.

He put three tamales on a plate and shoved them in the microwave.

"Tea?"

"Please."

He poured her a large glass, handed it to her, then said, "Talk, Dana."

She took a long sip of her tea, carefully setting the glass back on the table. Then she wiggled her mouth from side to side before saying, "Well, it's like this, see…" Her eyes met his. "I'm in love with you."

C.J.'s ears rang for several seconds. Then, on a groan, he leaned heavily against the edge of the island, eyes squeezed shut, shaking his head. "Oh, Dana…" He looked over at her. "Honey…no."

She shrugged. "Sorry. Can't be helped. Oh, yay," she said when the microwave beeped. "Food."

In a daze, C.J. removed the tamales and put them in front of her, followed by a container of sour cream. She pried off the top, slathered both tamales with the cream. "But you said—"

"That I knew where I stood with you, that I didn't expect anything more. And I still don't. I just left out a salient fact or two."

"Why?"

She smiled the smile of someone who knows things can't get any worse. "Why do I love you, or why didn't I tell you?"

"Why didn't you tell me? Everything we said, about being honest with each other—"

"You don't want honesty, C.J.," she said, chewing. "Not really. You want…I don't know." She swallowed. "Absolution?"

"Absolution? For what?"

"For whatever it was I saw in your eyes when we made love. For that tiny, but oh so crucial part of yourself you just can't let go of."

He felt every muscle in his body stiffen. "Dana, I told you—"

"You know," she said softly, pressing the side of her fork into the next tamale, "if you didn't want me to fall in love with you, maybe you should have rethought that whole knight in shining armor routine." She tilted her head. "Nobody's ever made me believe in myself the way you have. Or pushed me to trust my instincts. Pretty powerful stuff for a gal who's always been surrounded by people hell-bent on protecting her."

Whether she would have brought the subject up on her own without his prodding, he had no idea. What difference did it make? It didn't make the pain any less excruciating, knowing whatever he said was only going to hurt her. Knowing he already had.

"I was just being a friend."

A tiny smile touched her lips. "I don't believe that. Hey," she added when he flinched. "You said you wanted honesty."

"I know, but…" He frowned. "What do you mean, you don't believe me?"

"I didn't say I didn't believe *you*. There's a difference. C.J.…. Over the past several weeks, I watched a man so rattled by the idea of being a father he initially didn't even want to hold his own baby, turn into this big old softie who can't hold his baby enough. So it's not your *capacity* to love that's in question."

"It's different with Ethan."

"Because he's yours? Because you had no choice?"

"Well…yes."

Dana got up from the table, carrying her now empty plate to the dishwasher. "You didn't have to take him into your home," she said, putting her dish inside. "You didn't have to fight his own mother for him. You didn't have to fall in love with him." She turned. "But you did. Every step of the way, you made choices. Just like you've been making choices all your life, about where you'd live, your career…your relationships."

He smirked. "If you could call them that."

"My point exactly. Still, having me live here was your idea. And heaven knows, nothing compelled you to sleep with me. You could have turned me down," she said when he opened his mouth to protest. Then her hand was on his cheek, warm and slightly trembly, and his heart nearly cracked in two. "You knew full well what you were getting into," she whispered. Her hand dropped. "And so did I."

"Oh, God, Dana…" C.J. said on an exhaled breath, then gathered her in his arms, tucking her head under his chin, stroking her hair. "Okay, so you're more than a friend," he said, and she chuckled into his shirt. "But if you're implying that I'm somehow making a choice about loving you or not…I'm sorry. Your intuition's let you down with that one." He held her slightly apart, his hands framing her face. "Because believe me, I'd kill to be able to feel what you're feeling."

She looked at him steadily for a long moment, then said, "Actually, I think you'd kill not to be feeling what you are right now."

He flinched. "What?"

"You remember how I said I knew the difference between when a guy's in it just for the sex, and when he isn't? Well, you're not. Oh, you can deny it up one side and down the other, but you're dangling off the precipice, aren't you? And you're absolutely petrified. If you're looking for honesty, C.J.," she said gently, "you have to start with yourself. And until then…" With a shrug, she pulled out of his arms. "Things are going to be crazy for the next week or so, but I'll be completely out of here right after that, if it's okay with you."

"You don't have to—"

"Yes. I do." Steve rubbed up against her shins; she bent over to pick him up. "Look, this is probably a stretch—and God knows none of my business, really—but have you ever tried to fix things with your father?"

"What's my father got to do with anything?"

"Don't be disingenuous, C.J.," she said with a slight smile. "It doesn't suit you. And frankly, I think your father has everything to do with this. And you know something else? If I ever meet the guy, I just might deck him, for doing whatever he did to you to make you so afraid to accept somebody's love."

"Dammit, Dana, do you honestly believe I *like* being like this?"

"Honestly?" she said. "Yes. I do. In some ways, anyway. Oh, come on, C.J., keeping things simple is what you do. And that's not a criticism—exactly—simply an observation. Except, I'm wondering where you get off telling *me* to take risks, to put myself on the line, when you don't take your own advice?"

She released the cat. "Now if you'll excuse me, I'm half-asleep on my feet. And joy of joys, I get to do it all over again tomorrow—"

"What about Ethan?"

When she met his gaze, he saw tears flooding her eyes. "You're his father, C.J.," she said, her softly spoken words pummeling him like hailstones. "Whatever you decide about how we should divide our time with the baby is fine with me."

He watched her leave the room, knowing better than to ask where she'd be sleeping tonight.

Steve meowed at the patio door, asking to go outside again. C.J. opened the door, followed him out into the cool, still night. The water's surface grabbed the moonlight, shredding it into thousands of shimmering strands. Once Ethan became mobile, he realized, he'd have to keep the pool covered when they weren't actually using it. A high fence around it probably wouldn't hurt, either. With a good lock.

With a jolt, he realized he was thinking, for the first time in his life, about a house, *this* house, in terms of permanent. The house where his son would grow up, learn to walk, learn to swim, bring buddies over after school, return to during college breaks.

The house where he'd finally, fully understood what "making love" really meant.

C.J. dropped into one of the chairs, staring bleakly at the glittering water. When was the last time a woman's exit from his life had provoked much feeling one way or the other, with the occasional exception of relief? This time, however…

He let his head fall back, his gaze sweeping the vast, star-studded sky. This time, he felt hollow. No, worse—gouged out, a fragile shell of BS that protected the horrible, aching emptiness.

Except Dana hadn't caused the void. She'd only exposed it.

Because she was right, about his making choices. Careful choices, choices guaranteed—or so he'd hoped—not to bite him in the butt. Until a baby entered his life, not by choice, but by…what? Happenstance? Stupidity? And suddenly, he found himself faced with a whole new set of the suckers.

Not to mention a woman with the courage to call him on his sorry-assed excuse for a life.

Regret spasmed through him, as palpable as any physical pain. But with the regret—for things he couldn't change, perhaps—came, at last, a resolve. To face the past he'd spent twenty or more years avoiding, with those "choices."

To face himself. Or at least, the himself he'd never let anyone see.

A long shot, at best. But he owed it to his son.

And to the woman who'd honored him with her love.

Even if he couldn't return it.

Her cursor hovered over the Print icon, Dana listened to the *whoompa, whoompa, whoompa* of her heartbeat in her ears. One little click, and her baby would soon be ready to send out into the world.

To be judged. And most likely rejected. She knew the odds,

and they didn't exactly make a girl's heart sing. Of course, there was always option number two, which was to cop out altogether.

"Cowabunga," she whispered. And clicked.

The laser printer in C.J.'s home office whirred awake. From the playpen, Ethan looked up at the sound, a bland curiosity filling his big, blue eyes. Steve, however, who'd been curled up in a splotch of sunlight on the desk, leaped onto the printer, all the better to attack the pages as the printer spit them out. Yeah, toothmarks would add a nice touch, huh?

"Hey!" Dana squawked, swatting the cat on the rump. He went flying, his indignant expression when he landed butt-first on the carpet making her laugh in spite of the heaviness inside her chest.

Oh, the grand opening two days ago had gone over like gangbusters. And a two-bedroom had opened up in her complex, one with better views and more light than her old apartment. Not to mention brand new carpeting and a new fridge. C.J. had insisted on making up the difference between her old and new rent, and she'd decided it was stupid to argue, especially since it wasn't as if he couldn't afford it. Down-right gallant of him, in fact. So now she'd have a lovely extra bedroom for Ethan, when it was "her turn." But—

As if reading her mind, the baby screeched to get her attention, grinning hugely when she picked him up. On a sigh, she sank back into the leather desk chair, imagining it smelled like the man whose bed she'd hadn't even seen in more than a week, let alone shared.

And she'd thought giving up Doritos had been hard.

Her car was already packed; as soon as this was printed and C.J. got home, she'd be outta here. Odd to think that by this time tomorrow living here would be only a memory. No more chats by the pool, no more sharing a bowl of Jell-O in the middle of the night, no more—she hugged the baby closer—grocery trips together, or watching a movie together, or doing anything else together. That particular gamble, she'd lost. And annoyingly, it stung a lot more than it should have, considering she'd been well aware of the odds against that, too.

Still, even though hope whimpered in its sleep inside her, she had no real regrets. Not about sleeping with C.J., or telling him how she really felt. Had she let the opportunity slip by she would have regretted it for the rest of her life.

You could guard your heart, or you could give it, but you couldn't do both. *Safe risk* was an oxymoron.

Which is why she now watched the printer spew out page after page of the novel she could have started sending out feelers for months ago, if she hadn't been such a scaredy-cat. If she'd had the guts to trust her instincts instead of listening to the nasty little voice demanding to know who the hell she thought she was, to think someone might actually want to even read what she'd written, let alone buy it. At this point, it wasn't about whether it sold or not, it was about having the guts to take chances.

"I take it that's your book?" C.J. said from the doorway.

Dana turned awkwardly with the baby in her lap, ignoring her overeager-beagle heart leaping in her chest. Funny how that same little—actually, brass-band-huge—voice had also asked her who the hell she thought she was, expecting to attract someone like C.J. There was one worry, at least, that could be put to rest. So she could take some comfort in knowing—really knowing, not just telling herself—that this wasn't about her. And that if she hadn't taken a chance, she *wouldn't* know that.

"It sure is," she said with a smile. "I already printed out the query letters, and I'm sending them out tomorrow."

"You promise?"

"Cross my heart."

"Excellent." His smile was tender. Damn him. He hadn't

changed out of his work clothes yet, although he'd ditched his suit coat, loosened his tie. The babbling-idiot effect of his handsomeness on her brain had more or less worn off by now, although she still suffered the odd weak knee now and then. "I'm proud of you, Dana. This is a huge step."

And if it hadn't been for his cheerleading, his pushing her past her fear, she wouldn't be taking this step. For that, if nothing else, she'd always be grateful.

"We should celebrate," he said.

"We definitely should," she said, although she knew they wouldn't. Not now. "Thanks for letting me use your printer, by the way. I'll be more than happy to contribute toward the cartridge replacement—"

"It's a laser," C.J. said patiently. "Your manuscript will barely make a dent. Forget it."

"Well. Thanks. Because my printer sucks."

"So you said."

Jerks, she was used to. Jerks, she could deal with. Jerks, she could get over. But this…

This would all be so much easier if they hated each other.

Go away, she thought when he simply stood there, as though *basking* in the awkward silence. Just a few more minutes, though, and it would all be over—

"I have something to tell you," he said, the edge to his voice making her head snap up.

"What?"

He took the baby from her, smiling when Ethan squealed and batted at his face. Then he looked at her again, a mixture of apprehension and resolve in his eyes.

"I've decided to take Ethan back to Charleston to meet his grandfather."

Her breath caught. "Oh, C.J.…are you sure you want to do this?"

"I'm sure I *have* to do this." His gaze rested on the top of Ethan's head for a moment, then swung back to her. "I find I don't much like being a hypocrite."

She got up to straighten out the already printed pages before the printer choked. "Imagine that," she said, as lightly as she could considering how loudly her brain was screaming. Which in turn woke hope up all over again. And here the poor thing had been having *such* a nice snooze. "When do you leave?"

"Late tomorrow morning."

"Wow. Nothing like striking while the iron is hot."

A smile touched his lips. "I think this falls into the 'before I chicken out' category. But I'll be back in a couple of days. Sooner, if things don't go well. But at least this will give you some time to get settled into your new apartment without worrying about taking care of the baby, right?"

And hope said, *You woke me up for that?,* yanked the covers back up over its head and went back to sleep. Grumbling.

C.J.'s cell rang at the same time the printer spit out the last page and whined to a stop. He fished the phone out of his pocket, laughing when Ethan tried to grab it away from him. But instead of handing the baby back to her, he moseyed on out of the office, contentedly—at least, so it seemed—balancing phone and baby. Her stomach churning, Dana quickly smacked the sides of the manuscript pages against the desk to even them out, then stuffed them into a Tyvek envelope.

Then, a minute later, she quietly left the house she'd grown a lot more fond of than she should have, knowing full well that C.J. would be ticked at her for not saying goodbye.

C.J. idly wondered, as he maneuvered a child, a stroller, a car seat, a diaper bag the size of Texas and his own carry-on through the Charleston airport, how someone a tenth of his size could generate five times more *stuff*. He also wondered, not so idly, whether he'd ever be able to show his face again on a Delta flight. Oh, Ethan had outdone himself in the cute department, charming the flight attendants and making everyone in first class swoon. Until they were airborne. Apparently his son was not a natural-born flyer.

"Oh, poor thing," the flight attendant—a motherly type somewhere in her fifties—said. At first. "Try giving him a bottle, the sucking will make his ears pop."

"Hmm," the same attendant said ten minutes later over the screaming. "As soon as the Fasten Seat Belt sign goes off, why don't you walk him? I'm sure that'll do the trick."

Forty-five minutes later—and right about the time C.J. was getting some strong *"Who wants to shove them both out the emergency exit?"* vibes from the other passengers—Ethan passed out in midshriek.

Only to do a number in his diaper C.J. was sure could be detected back on the ground. Or at least in the seat across the aisle, if the prune-faced expression of the woman sitting there was any indication. Well, let's see…change the diaper of a baby who'd been screaming his head off the past hour, thereby risking waking him, or pass out clothespins? Fortunately, they only had another half hour before the plane landed in Dallas.

Unfortunately, their layover was only twenty minutes.

And their first plane was five minutes late.

To say that C.J. wasn't exactly in the best of moods by the time they touched down in Charlestown was a vast understatement. Exhaustion and ringing ears will do that to a person. Ethan, however—changed, fed and back on terra firma—was happy as a little towheaded clam, grinning at everybody they passed in the airport, and generally getting a head start on his 2044 Presidential bid. Then C.J. went to put his son in the car seat in the back of the rented Lexus, and the baby gave him a huge *"Hey, how's it goin'?"* grin, and his heart felt close to bursting, and he thought, *How could a father not want to have anything to do with his own son?*

Well, that's what he was going to find out. Come hell, high water or stinky diapers.

By the time they left the airport, it was already close enough to rush hour for traffic into town to be a pain. But eventually C.J. pulled up in front of the three-story, wrought-iron-trimmed redbrick that had been in the family for three generations. As someone who appreciated fine architecture, C.J. should have loved the stately house, infused with both charm and provenance as it was. Instead, memories flooded his thoughts like raw sewage, years of hurt suffocating him more than the oppressive humidity, obliterating whatever affection he might have, should have, felt for his childhood home.

He parked in the driveway alongside the shallow front yard, underneath a massive live oak twice as large as he re-membered. Dense foliage—ten-foot-tall hydrangeas, azaleas, rhododendron—hugged the side of the house, nearly con-cealing from view what had once been the carriage house in the back, where a lonely little boy had spent far too much time playing make-believe.

Pretending he was "away on business," like his father so often was. Only when *he* returned home, it would be to a large, loving family who'd missed him terribly and were thrilled to have him back.

"Hey, guy," C.J. whispered to the baby, who'd conked out again. He stroked one down-soft cheek with his fingertip until Ethan squirmed, his golden eyelashes fluttering. With a start, C.J. noticed for the first time the slightest hint of Dana in the boy's coloring, the same dimples when he smiled, even the directness of his gaze. Then again, he could be full of it, seeing a resemblance that only existed in his head. "Time to meet your grandfather. Just remember," he said, hauling the solid little body out of the car seat, "I've got your back."

As expected, the maid, or housekeeper, or whoever the woman was who opened the pristinely white, multipaneled door at the top of the steps, was deferential and black, and—except for the brief conversation he'd exchanged with the woman a few days before, to make sure his father would be around—completely unfamiliar. C.J. idly wondered how many there had been between her and Jessie, the last one he remembered.

A broad, but somewhat cautious, smile rounded cheeks nearly the same warm, rich color of the polished banister sweeping behind her to the second floor. "Oh, you just *have* to be Mr. Cameron," she said, bright green eyes sparkling underneath a meringue of white hair. "I recognize you from your graduation photo, the one Mr. James keeps on the living room mantle. I'm Carmela, I don't usually stay this late, but no way was I gonna miss meeting *you*." Trim gray eyebrows rose behind oversized, eighties-vintage eyeglass frames. "And would you *look* at this handsome boy? And don't you know it?" she said, laughing softly when the baby opened his eyes and flashed his two teeth at her. "What's his name?"

C.J. grabbed the baby's hand before his chubby little fingers latched on to all that irresistible fluffy hair. "Ethan."

"Ethan Turner," she said, tumbling the sounds around in her mouth as though tasting wine. Then she nodded. "I like it. A good, solid name. I put one of those little mesh folding cribs in the closet in your old room for the baby. My daughter just moved her youngest into a bed so she wasn't usin' it."

"Thank you, you're a lifesaver."

"Yes, I am," she said with a low laugh, "and don't you forget it. Well, I best be gettin' on home, before my husband calls out the dogs."

"Before you go, may I ask you something?"

"Yes?"

"How long have you been working for my father?"

"Long enough to know it's been at least six years since you came to see him."

Letting the gentle chiding pass, C.J. said, "That's three times longer than any of your predecessors was able to hold out."

She chuckled. "Oh, yes, I know all about the revolving door in this place. Knew it before I was hired, since word does gets out. Your daddy still can't keep a cook to save him. Either finds some half-baked reason to let 'em go, or else drives 'em so crazy they leave of their own accord."

"Then how have you managed to stay on so long?"

"Lord only knows," she said with a smile. "Wasn't anything I did or didn't do, I don't think. Except maybe… seems to me like he just got *tired* of all the changes. Gettin' old'll do that to a person. You'll be here in the morning, I take it?"

C.J. breathed out, "That's the plan."

"Well…" Carmela gathered her things from the hall table. "Whatever your reasons for showin' up now," she said softly, laying her hand on his arm, "just remember, he's probably more scared of you than you are of him."

The front door had barely clicked shut behind her when C.J. heard behind him, "Cameron?"

C.J. turned, meeting the clearly stunned, ice-chip-blue gaze with a steady one of his own. The old man commanded his space as completely as he ever did, no pot belly straining the waistband of his Dockers or marring the smooth fit of his light blue knit shirt. In fact, if it weren't for the white hair, the less sharply defined jaw, this could have easily been twenty years ago.

Except twenty years ago, C.J.'s father had the power to hurt him, to intimidate him, a mental stranglehold broken only by C.J.'s leaving. And by never looking back. Now, however, they stood as equals. Not in terms of wealth or social status, but simply as grown men.

Neither of whom was about to take any crap from the other.

C.J. shifted Ethan in his arms, protectively cuddling his son against his chest.

"Hello, Dad," he said quietly, gathering strength from his baby's smile before again facing his father's incredulous expression. "Meet your grandson."

Chapter Thirteen

"This might come as a surprise," Dana's mother said, wrapping Dana's largest casserole dish in a towel, "but I'm not the enemy."

A pile of books in her arms, Dana glanced up from the cardboard box at her knees. From her bedroom came much grunting and cussing as her father tried to take apart her bed frame. The books clunked into the box, raising an embarrassing cloud of dust. "Why would I think that, Mama?" she said mildly.

"Oh, I don't know. Maybe because you rarely tell me what's going on in your life anymore."

Dana struggled to her feet, swiping a lose strand of hair out of her eyes, catching sight of the time as she did. A little after two-thirty. Two hours later in South Carolina. C.J.'s plane would have landed a half hour ago; he might even be at his father's by now.

"I am over thirty, Mama," she said, yanking her thoughts

back to the here-and-now. "I kinda caught on to the concept of taking care of my own problems a while back."

"And what problems might those be?"

She smiled. "Nice try."

"I'm just saying—" Faye reached up on her tiptoes to snag a serving platter from the cupboard, letting out a huff when she had the thing firmly in her grip "—there's nothing says you outgrow needing your mother."

"Never said there was. Would you toss me the packing tape doohickey, I left it by the sink."

Instead of tossing it, however, her mother brought it to her and slapped it into her hand. "So are you ever going to tell me what really happened between you and C.J., or do I have to keep guessing for rest of my life?"

"I pick option *B,*" Dana said, *wrrrratching* the tape across the box.

Faye let out a sigh. "It was your father's talking to him, wasn't it? He scared him off."

Said father chose that moment to wander back into the living room, wiping his forehead with his handkerchief. "I did not scare him off, Faye. I *warned* him. And anyway, it was your idea to talk to him, so don't you lay all this on me."

"Hey, guys?" Dana said, hands up. "There is no 'all this' to lay on anybody. Okay," she said on a rush of air when they both frowned at her. "Maybe I was sort of hoping things would get off the ground. They didn't, case closed, let's move on. Some men simply aren't the marrying type." A gross oversimplification of the situation, true, but hey, life was short.

Her mother snorted. "That's what your father said. I changed his mind."

"You did not," Gene said. "I was just...puttin' up barriers until I was sure you were 'the one.'"

"And if that isn't the most ridiculous thing I've ever heard—"

"No, Mama, he's right. Some men say they're not the marrying kind when what they really mean is they're waiting for the right woman. Others really don't want to get married." *Or face their fears.*

"I take it back," Faye said after a moment. "*That's* the most ridiculous thing I've ever heard."

On a shrug, Dana went back to her book packing—a far more productive endeavor than arguing with her mother—while her father, grumbling about crazy women, went back to wrestling with Dana's bed. She flinched, though, when she felt a soft hand land on her shoulder, a move that—dammit!—threatened to jar loose the tears Dana had been holding in for the past week.

"When I first saw C.J. with Ethan," her mother said, revealing a sadistic side to her character Dana had never quite noticed before, "I had serious doubts. But eventually…well. I think he's going to make a fine daddy, don't you?"

"Absolutely."

"I think being around this family helped him, don't you?"

Dana swallowed her laugh. "I'm sure it did."

Faye patted her back and moved away. Thank God. Then Dana heard, "What's this?"

Her hands full of old paperbacks, Dana turned to see her mother flipping through the pages of her manuscript. Which she'd deliberately left out.

"My book," she said quietly. "I finally finished it. In fact—" she took a deep breath "—I've already starting sending out query letters to agents."

Her mother's eyes shot to hers. "Oh, honey, do you really think you want to set yourself up for more disappointment? Especially so soon after…you know."

Irritation—no, outrage—flashed inside her. The books

clattered onto the carpet as she dropped them, then stomped over and around boxes and piles of crap to snatch the manuscript off the dining table, clutching it to her. "*This* is why I don't share things with you anymore, Mama," she said, her voice shaking. "Because instead of encouraging me, supporting me, all you ever see are the pitfalls."

"But the odds of actually getting published—"

"Are a thousand to one. *Ten* thousand to one. I know, Mama. Dammit, I *know*. But if I don't ever try, the odds are zip."

"I just don't want to see you get hurt."

"So what are you saying? You'd rather I never put myself out there, never see what I'm capable of? Yeah, rejection hurts," she said, her eyes watering. "Like a b-bitch. But…" She stopped, willing herself not to lose control. It didn't entirely work. "But it's not fatal," she finished in a small voice.

"Oh, honey." Her mother lifted one hand, wiping a stray tear from her cheek. "You really love him, don't you?"

One tear, then another, trickled down her cheek. "You have no idea."

"His loss," her father said from the doorway. Dana looked up, offering him a shaky smile.

"Yeah, that's what I'm thinking."

The birds' twittering filled the silence for several seconds, a silence broken when her mother cleared her throat, then asked, "Do you…think I could read it? Your book?"

The pages actually seemed to squeak when Dana increased her stranglehold on them. "I don't know." She leaned closer, whispering, "It's got s-e-x in it."

"I should hope so," her mother said, and they both laughed. Then the older woman frowned.

"If you don't like it, that's okay," Dana said. "I can take it."

"Yes," Faye said, understanding dawning in her eyes. "I suppose you can."

* * *

Judging from the maître d's somewhat disdainful expression, the restaurant—a favorite of Charleston's old guard—wasn't exactly family friendly. However, the staff graciously rose to the occasion, even rustling up a high chair for Ethan. Who seemed to be settling quite nicely into his new role as a grandchild of the Southern aristocracy, calmly taking in his surroundings while gumming an oyster cracker. And occasionally flirting with the carefully coiffed matron at the next table.

Ostensibly perusing the menu, C.J. stole a glance at his father from across the linen-shrouded table. Ethan, apparently bored with both the cracker and the matron, began batting the high chair table and gurgling. After thirty seconds or so, the old man's gaze at last veered toward his grandson, eyes glowering underneath dark, formidable eyebrows. He'd already expressed his bewilderment at C.J.'s not having an au pair or nanny to "keep the kid out of his hair," as he put it.

"This is why babies don't belong in restaurants," he grumbled.

Ethan went completely still, eyes huge. Then he laughed, a great big belly laugh that made heads turn and lips curve upward within a ten-foot radius. His father grunted, returning his attention to his menu. Ethan looked over at C.J., who palmed the baby's head in reassurance.

"You keep coddlin' the boy like that," his father said, not looking up, "you'll turn him into a sissy for sure."

The waiter appeared to take their order, giving C.J. a chance to tamp down the flash of anger. Once the man was gone, however, C.J. selected a warm roll from the basket in the center of the table, buttering half of it before he said, "And there we have it, friends…" He leaned back in his chair, giving Ethan a tiny piece of the roll, which the child crammed into his mouth. "The core philosophy behind my father's child-rearing method."

They'd said very little to each other up to this point, other than C.J.'s bare bones explanation of the hows and whys of his having a son. But C.J. had no doubt that his father knew as well as he did that this was showdown time. And if only one of them was left standing when it was over, C.J. had no intention of it not being him.

After a moment, his father also chose a roll, separating it with excruciatingly deliberate slowness. "In more than forty years," he said quietly, not looking at C.J., "I never made a single bad investment. Goes to a man's head, thinking he's infallible. That he's somehow incapable of making a mistake." He lifted his gaze to C.J.'s. "But I sure as hell screwed it up with you, didn't I?"

Well, hell. Instead of a shootout, his father had laid his gun down in the dirt, backing away with his hands raised. If the old man thought, however, that was his ticket to freedom, he was sorely mistaken.

"Yes, Dad. You did."

The waiter brought their salads, offered the peppermill, which both men passed up, disappeared. His father stabbed his fork into the sea of romaine, then lanced C.J. with his gaze. "So, why are you here? The real reason."

It shouldn't have been a surprise, his father's scramble to regain the upper hand. But C.J. doubted the sudden acid taste in his mouth had anything to do with the tart vinaigrette dressing on his salad. "Ethan's not enough?"

"My guess is he's an excuse. Not the reason. Not after the way you reamed me out over the phone."

"Fine." C.J. set down his fork, lifted his wineglass. "Now I want to know *why* you couldn't stand the sight of me."

His father waited out a burst of laughter from the next table, then said, "If I died tomorrow, you wouldn't feel much one way or the other, would you?"

C.J. refused to let the out-of-the-blue question knock him off balance. Neither was he about to buy into whatever guilt trip the old man was trying to lay on him. "Can't say that I would."

His father seemed neither taken aback nor disappointed by his answer. Instead, he nodded, almost in approval, before spearing a cherry tomato with his fork. "Ever been in love?"

C.J.'s stomach twisted. "No."

Liar, something whispered inside him.

"So you've never had your heart broken?"

He rammed his fork into a chunk of lettuce. "No."

Liar. Liar, liar, liar.

"Then I guess my plan worked, after all," his father said.

"Your…plan?"

The waiter returned to clear their salads, replacing them with their entrees—halibut for C.J., filet mignon for his father. The older man picked up his utensils, seeming to weigh them in his hands before cutting into his steak.

"Your mother didn't die in a car crash," he said softly, not looking at C.J. "She killed herself."

C.J.'s fingers vised the stem of his water goblet. "What did you say?"

Almost irritably, his father hacked off another slice of steak. "Took her own life. Pills. I found her. I…" The knife and fork clattered to his plate as he reached for his own water glass with a shaking hand.

"Why on earth didn't you tell me?"

His father's eyes snapped to his. "To *protect* you, why the hell do you think?"

"From *what,* for God's sake? Especially after I was grown?"

"And what difference would it have made?"

"I don't know! But I would have at least appreciated the gesture."

Once again, his father picked up his utensils, although

with little enthusiasm. "Sheila was my life," he said, his words barely audible. "I'd never met anyone like her. The way she could see straight through me…" C.J. was startled to see tears in his father's eyes when he looked up. "The pain afterward…it was unimaginable."

"I'm sure," C.J. said, trying to reconcile the obviously crushed man in front of him with the cold, imperious figure from his youth. Another bite of steak disappeared into his father's mouth, but he chewed it with great difficulty, as though the tender meat had somehow turned to rubber.

"So tell me, Cameron," he said after he'd finally swallowed. "What kind of father would I have been if I'd left *you* that vulnerable?"

"Vulnerable? To what?"

"To having your heart ripped out of your chest." His father leaned forward, his dinner forgotten. As was C.J.'s. "I didn't keep my distance because I couldn't stand the sight of you, I did it because I wanted to spare you that kind of pain. No attachment, no risk of getting hurt."

And at last, understanding shuddered through him.

"Spare me, hell," C.J. said in a low voice. "You *robbed* me."

"For your own good, dammit!"

"Bull." His even voice belied the inferno raging in his gut. "You cut yourself off from me—your only child—so *you* wouldn't get too attached, so *you* couldn't be hurt again. And how twisted is that? Especially considering that under your *plan*—" he spat out the word "—instead of occasionally suffering the normal, human pain of loss, I ached with it constantly. *Constantly,* Dad. Every…single…damn day of my childhood. I could never figure out what I'd done to make you hate me so much."

"I never hated you, Cameron."

"Yeah, well, you had a pretty bizarre way of showing it."

Obviously picking up on the tension, Ethan started to whimper. C.J. grabbed his napkin off his knee, throwing it down on the table before rescuing the baby from his high chair. He sat back down with the child on his lap, giving him a very messy sip of water, tiny teeth clinking on the glass. "You at least knew what it felt like to be loved. Where did you get off denying me that right?"

"It's not all it's cracked up to be," his father said wearily.

"That wasn't your decision to make for me, dammit. What you did was wrong, Dad. Not misguided, *wrong*. But you want to hear something really ironic? I thought I'd *escaped* your poison, by leaving. By not coming back. Now I'm sitting here, realizing every choice I've made over the past twenty years has only increased its potency. No, wait, that's not entirely true." C.J. set down his glass, then pointlessly tried to smooth down Ethan's flyaway hair. "Because, your fine example notwithstanding, I *choose* to be everything for this little boy you never were for me. If I screw up, I screw up, but at least I'll have *tried—*"

C.J. sagged back in his chair. "Oh, God," he whispered. "That's it, that's…" After a second, his eyes found his father's confused ones again. "You're wrong, Dad. Getting attached, making that connection, *love*…it *is* all it's cracked up to be. Hey, you want to live in your cold, empty little world, you go right ahead. But despite your best efforts…" He leaned forward, the white-hot light of epiphany melting his anger. "In the end, your plan didn't work."

His father's eyebrows took a dive. "Thought you said you'd never been in love."

"Apparently I was wrong," C.J. said in wonder, then let out a startled, high laugh as that old, rusty faucet finally, and completely, gave way. "Hell, I was still trying to deal with what it felt like to just be on the receiving end. And to think I very nearly…"

"Where the hell are you going?" he said when C.J. popped up out of his chair.

"I'm not sure. To make a phone call, I think—"

"Sit down, Cameron," his father said under his breath. "People are beginning to stare."

"So let them stare! I'm in love! *I'm in love!*" he announced to the room at large, earning him a smattering of applause, a titter of laughter.

"For crying out loud," James said, "sit *down!*"

C.J. sat, and Ethan gave one of his belly laughs, and C.J. released a huge breath, and with it more than three decades of misery and mistakes and misapprehensions. And man, that felt good. Then, holding Ethan sideways (a position perfect for batting his eyes at the lady at the next table), C.J. said, "And you know the craziest part of all this?"

"What?"

"That maybe I could have helped get you through your pain. Only you never gave me the chance."

They stared each other down for a long moment, until his father finally pushed out a sigh. "You're a lot like her, you know."

"Like my mother?"

He nodded. "Bright. Passionate." His father's throat worked for several seconds before he whispered, "*Kind.* God, she was a far better person than I'll ever be. And, oh, my, how she loved *you.* I see…I see the same thing in your eyes, when you look at Ethan. I just didn't…I had no idea she was so sick."

"It wasn't your fault," C.J. said over the knot in his chest. "Not that, anyway."

His father actually chuckled, then signaled the waiter for the check. "What do you say," he said, tugging his credit card out of his wallet, "we blow this joint. Then you can tell me about this obviously extraordinary woman who somehow managed to undo all my damage." He glanced up. "Or is it too late?"

"Well, I need to get Ethan to bed pretty soon—"

"I don't mean that," his father said, with something very much like hope in his eyes. And regret.

C.J.'s mouth pulled into a half smile. "Why don't we just take it one step at a time?"

"Fair enough," his father said.

Dana pulled into her parking space, only to shut her eyes, letting out a long, *well*-you're-*an-idiot* sigh. Because this wasn't her parking space. Not anymore. *Her* parking space—the tires squealed when she backed out, clearly startling the old guy from R building walking his stiff-legged poodle—was over…*here*.

She got out, slammed shut her door and stomped up the steps to her apartment. Her larger, lighter, closer-to-the-laundry room/playground/pool apartment that she absolutely, positively despised with every fiber of her being.

Huh. Guess she'd moved into the angry phase of her grief.

Because, she'd realized this morning—right about the time she moved from *numb* to *sad*—grieving was exactly what she was doing. No, she and C.J. hadn't exactly broken up—it being kinda hard to break up when you were never really a couple to begin with—but apparently her heart hadn't gotten that particular memo.

Because *okay* was the one thing she did not feel right now. What she felt right now, she thought as she kicked—yes, kicked!—her door open was—

"Ohmigod!"

Clearly, a band of marauding six-year-olds had broken in and thrown the mother of all birthday parties. It was every-where, in pinks and purples and oranges and a hideous Day-Glo green, hanging from the ceiling fan and draped over her furniture and all the unpacked boxes, even dangling from the bottom of the birdcage, a veritable spider web of—

"Strings," C.J. said, sending her back into her door with a shriek.

"Wh-what?"

His teeth flashed in the semidarkness of the hallway. In his arms, wearing a blue-and-red T-shirt, green shorts and an orange hat, Ethan bobbed and babbled, reaching out for her.

"You want strings," C.J. said, moving out of the shadows. The mini fashion disaster lurched for Dana; she caught him before he landed on his nose, as C.J. calmly surveyed his handiwork. His gaze—hopeful, pleading and almost frighteningly sure all at once—returned to hers. "So strings, you shall have."

Their gazes tangoed for another couple of seconds until her brain caught up. Then she sucked in a breath. Hard.

"No..." she said, coughing, waving her hands, the movement sending the nearest veil of Silly String into a gentle hula.

"It's not enough? Because I've still got a can or two left, I can certainly do more." While she stood there, rabbit-eyed, he wrapped his hand around the back of her neck, touching his forehead to hers. "In case you missed it," he whispered, "I love you, too."

Her heart went *ka-thud.* Birds twittered and baby babbled while she took a few more seconds to bask in his smile. Then she burst into tears. Great, honking, *somebody-pinch-me* sobs, sobs that a second later were buried in C.J.'s soft knit shirt as he wrapped both of them up in those long, solid arms. Sobs that, a second after that, turned to a yelp when Ethan grabbed a handful of her hair and called it lunch.

They group-hug-shuffled over to her sofa, where she sort of melted into C.J.'s side, thinking, *Ohmigod, ohmigod, ohmigod,* while Ethan, sitting in her lap in his little baby world, happily chattered away to the birds.

"You're sure about this?" she finally whispered, leaning

against C.J. "This isn't just jet lag talking? Or—" she waved one hand, making a face "—Silly String fumes?"

"Yeah," he said, his chuckle vibrating in her ear. "I'm sure. You and Ethan…you're the most important things in the world to me. And if I can't spend the rest of my life with you, then what's the point?"

"None that I can see," Dana said, smiling like a goof. Then she frowned. "But how did you get in?"

"Your mother," C.J. murmured into what was left of her hair. "She gave me her key. Apparently she likes me."

"Because clearly you didn't let her in on the Silly String scheme." Not moving—which she didn't intend to do until she had to eat, pee or change a diaper—she surveyed her living room. "How many cans are we talking, anyway?"

"Have no idea. I just told the kid at Party Barn to give me all he had."

A fresh round of tears threatened. She swallowed, twice, then said to the baby, "Daddy made a big mess."

"I know," C.J. said softly, his breath warm on her temple. "So I figured I'd better do something to fix it."

"You didn't—"

"I did. So shut up and let me grovel."

Dana twisted around, frowning up into his eyes. "Wow. That must've been *some* trip."

C.J. kissed the top of her head, then stood, pulling the baby up with him and carrying him to stand in a shaft of sunlight in the dining area, his gaze fixed outside. "Turns out my mother wasn't killed in a car crash. She committed suicide."

"Oh, C.J.…how awful. But why didn't your father tell you?"

"I suppose because he saw it as a personal failure when she took her own life." He jiggled the baby, making him laugh. "He was obviously crazy about her. I wouldn't have believed it possible, until I saw the look in his eyes when he finally told me the truth. I honestly believe he was devastated. Frankly, I think he still is."

As much as she already loved this man, hearing the obvious forgiveness—or at least, the *desire* to forgive—in his voice melted her heart even more. She got up from the sofa and walked over to thread her hands through C.J.'s arm, laying her head against it. "And that's why he shut you out?"

"If only it had been that simple," he said on a sigh. "In some sort of bizarre, misguided attempt to spare me that kind of pain, he decided to never let me become attached to anything. Pets, nannies, house servants…the minute I'd start to get close, he'd get rid of them. Needless to say, by the time I reached adolescence, I'd learned to never let down my guard, never trust anyone to stick around."

She squeezed his arm, in part to quell the outrage threatening to choke her. "But what about friends?"

"Oh, I had them. After a fashion. But I'd learned my lesson well," he said softly, sadly, brushing his lips over the baby's head. "So when I started to date, it was the same thing. Pick someone you know from the outset won't last, and you're safe." He angled his head to look into her eyes. "Then you and Ethan happened into my life. And suddenly I was being pulled in two, between all those years of habit and self-protection and everything I was convinced I could never have. Could never be. And yet…deep down, wanted so damn much. You had no idea, how right you were. About the precipice thing. I *was* scared. Hell, I was terrified."

"Then what changed your mind?"

He smiled. "Other than the obvious remorse in my father's eyes? Finally realizing that the only power he'd ever really had over me is what I'd given him." He tilted her face up to kiss her softly on the lips. "That the choice is, always has been, mine. Even if I didn't know it. I can either stay in my safe, but empty, excuse for a life. Or I can have a *real* life. With you. And my son." His expression gentled. "And maybe someday we'll find Ethan a little brother. Or sister. Or both," he finished on a laugh.

Dana's breath caught. "Ohmigosh, C.J.—are you sure?"

A funny smile on his face, he reached into his shirt pocket and pulled out a small, silver ring. "It's the best I could do on short notice. But it seemed appropriate."

With trembling hands, Dana took the delicately crafted Celtic knot ring from his fingers and slipped it on. "It's perfect," she said, tears making her voice wobble.

"Let's go home, honey," C.J. whispered, and all she could think was…

Wow.

Epilogue

Being put to bed when it's still light out gives a guy a lot of time to think. To reflect on his purpose in life. Oh, please— you don't really think all we do is babble at those stupid mobiles dangling over our cribs, do you? Trust me, that gets old real fast. And this one has these creepy clowns, for Pete's sake—I'll be lucky if I'm not scarred for life.

So now you know. When we give you those funny looks? It's not gas. We really do know a heckuva lot more about things than we let on. Or can verbalize. But the thing is, from everything I've heard, by the time our facility for coherent speech catches up with our brains, a lot of the inside info we were born with has pretty much faded. By my second birthday I won't remember any of this. So take notes.

Common wisdom says I shouldn't even have happened. Slim odds and all that. Well, here's a newsflash—you can hereby forget everything you've ever believed about things happening for no good reason. Trust me, there's a plan. Trish, my birth mother, didn't just *happen* to cozy up to my dad. I mean, yeah, I was skeptical, too, when they told me who my father was going to be. "Him?" I said. "The guy who doesn't want kids? What kind of sick joke is that?"

"Trust me," the Big Guy said.

Not that I had any choice. We just go where we're assigned, it's not like we have any input or anything. "They need you," He said. Implying lives were at stake, the fate of civilization was in my itty-bitty hands, the whole enchilada. Man, that's an awful lot to put on a little dude's shoulders. But hey, when the Big Guy gives an order, you do what you can.

Although, if Trish sounded a little Looney Tunes about the whole should-she-keep-me-or-not thing, or even whether my dad was my dad, that's understandable, when you think about it. You know, that whole "mysterious ways" thing and all. Hard for some people to swallow. Please don't feel bad for her, though, because I've got some pretty heavy-duty inside info that she's going to come out of this on top. That having me actually *was* the wake-up call she needed to get her act together. Don't quote me on this, but I think I heard something about a hottie cop and more babies down the road? And a career? I might be fuzzy on the details—like I said, it's all fading pretty fast now—but I do know it's good.

Uh-oh, I hear Dana and my dad coming down the hall to check on me. If I'm not asleep there will be *H-E*-double hockey sticks to pay. Where's that rag I sleep with? Got it. Thumb in place, check. Eyes shut, check. Butt up in air (that gets 'em every time), check.

I crack open one eye to notice Dad's got his arm around Dana's waist. Again. Sheesh, those two cannot keep their hands off each other, it's disgusting. Not that I mind all the hugs and kisses *I* get from them, but please, people—a little decorum, okay?

"You think he has any idea how much he's changed our lives?" my dad says, and Dana laughs. It's a nice laugh. Good thing, considering how often she does it.

"Of course not, he's just a baby. All he knows is that he's loved."

Well, not exactly. But, yeah, I know I'm loved. Every single second of my life. It's a nice feeling, what can I say?

"'Night, sweetie," she whispers, even though she's already told me that once tonight. Not that I mind hearing it again. Then my father's hand lands on my back, and I feel…safe. Wanted. And very, very glad to be here.

"'Night, Scooter," he says softly, and I give him one of those precious fluttery smiles. In my sleep, of course.

They both tiptoe out, but I keep smiling.

Mission accomplished.

* * * * *

THE PRODIGAL
VALENTINE

BY
KAREN TEMPLETON

Acknowledgements

With many thanks to Mary Jaramillo,
whose contributions to this book have
hopefully kept this *gringa* from sounding like
a complete *pendeja* (dumb-ass)

As always, to Jack, my Valentine
for twenty-eight years and counting

Chapter One

"How hard can it be," Mercedes Zamora muttered through chattering teeth as she elbowed her way into the mammoth juniper bush bordering her sidewalk to retrieve her Sunday paper, "to hit the frickin' *driveway? Crap!*" A flattened branch slapped her in the face; on a growl, she dove back in, thinking she had maybe three seconds before her bare feet fused to the frosty driveway, only to let out a shriek when something furry streaked past her calves and up to the house.

The cat plastered himself to her front door, meowing piteously.

"Hey. Nobody told you to stay out last night," she said as she yanked the paper out of the greenery, swearing again when she discovered her long, morning-ravaged curls and the bush had bonded. She grabbed her hair and tugged. "I feel for you but I can't…quite…*reach you!*"

The bush let go, sending her stumbling backwards onto the cement, at which point a low, male, far-too-full-of-himself chuckle from across the street brought the blood chugging through her veins to a grinding halt. Frozen tootsies forgotten, Mercy spun around, wincing from the retina-searing glare of thousands of icicle lights sparkling in the legendary New Mexican sunshine.

Oh, no. No, no, no…this was not happening.

Ten years it had been since she'd laid eyes on Benicio Vargas. And seared retinas notwithstanding, it was way too easy to see that those ten years had taken the shoulders, the grin, the cockiness that had been the twenty-five-year-old Ben to a whole 'nother level.

Well, hell.

What effect those years might have had Mercy, however—stunning, she was sure, in her rattiest robe, her hair all juniper-mangled—she wasn't sure she wanted to contemplate too hard. Not that she was ready to be put down just yet—her skin was still wrinkle-free, her hair the same dark, gleaming brown it had always been, and she could still get into her size five jeans, thanks for asking. But the last time Ben had seen these breasts, they hadn't had their thirtieth birthday yet. Quite.

Not that he'd be seeing them now. She was just sayin'.

Ben flashed a smile at her, immediately putting her father's glittering Christmas display to shame. Not to mention his own parents', right next door.

Mercy wasn't sure which was worse—that once upon a time she'd had a brief, ill-advised, but otherwise highly satisfactory fling with the boy next door, or that here she was, rapidly closing in on forty and still living across the street from the lot of them in one of her folks' rental houses. But hey—as long as she was leading her own life, on her own terms, what was the harm in keeping the old nest firmly in her sights?

As opposed to Mr. Hunky across the street, who'd booked it out of the nest and never looked back. Until, apparently, now.

"Lookin' good over there, Mercy," Ben called out, hauling a duffle out of his truck bed, making all sorts of muscles ripple and such. Aiyiyi, could the man fill out a pair of blue jeans or what?

"Thanks," she said, hugging the plastic-wrapped paper to the afore-mentioned breasts. "So. Where the hell have you been all this time?"

Okay, so nuance wasn't her strong suit.

"Yeah, about that," Ben said, doing more of the smile-flashing thing. If she'd rattled him, he wasn't letting on. Behind her, the cat launched into an aria about how he was starving to death. "I don't suppose this is a good time to apologize for just up and leaving the way I did, huh?"

Huh. Somebody had been spending time in cowboy country. Texas, maybe. Or Oklahoma. "Actually," she called back, "considering you've just confirmed what half the neighborhood probably suspected anyway…" She shrugged. "Go ahead, knock yourself out."

His expression suddenly turned serious. Not what she'd expected. Especially since the seriousness completely vanquished the happy-go-lucky Ben she remembered, leaving in its place this…this I-can-take-anything-you-dish-out specimen of masculinity that made her think, *Yeah, I need this like I need Lyme disease.*

"Then I'm sorry, Mercy," he said, the words rumbling over to her on the winter breeze. "I truly am."

She shivered, and he waved, and he turned and went inside his parents' house, and she drifted back up to her own front door, her head ringing as though she'd been clobbered with a cast-iron skillet. And, she realized, in her zeal to get her digs in first, she had no idea why he was back.

Not that she cared.

The cat, who couldn't have cared less, shoved his way inside before she got the door all the way open. Her phone was ringing. Of course. She squinted outside to see her mother standing at the two-story house's kitchen window, her own phone clamped to her ear, gesticulating for Mercy to pick up. There was something seriously wrong with this picture, but she'd have to amass a few more brain cells before she could figure it out.

"Yes, Ma," she said as soon as she picked up her phone. "I know. He's back. Opening a can of cat food right now, in fact. Sliced grill, yum, yum."

After an appropriate pause, Mary Zamora sighed loudly into the phone. "Not your stupid cat, Mercy. *Ben.*"

"Oh, *Ben.* Yeah, I saw him just now, in fact. Talk about a shock. Got any idea why he's here?"

"To help his father, why else? Because his brother broke his foot the day after Christmas on that skiing trip?" she added, rather than waiting for Mercy to connect the dots. "Yes, I know Tony's not exactly your favorite person—"

"Did I say anything?"

"—but since the man is married to your sister, I really wish you'd try a little harder to like him. For 'Nita's sake, at least. Did she tell you, they're adding to the back of the house? And that new wide-screen TV they bought themselves for Christmas…not bad, huh?"

Mercy rolled her eyes. Tony did okay, she supposed, but her mother knew damn well that if it weren't for Anita's second income as a labor and delivery nurse, most of that extra "stuff" wouldn't happen.

"But anyway," Mary Zamora said, "now that Tony can't drive for at least a month, and God knows Luis couldn't possibly handle all those contracts on his own, Ben's come home to fill in."

Something about this wasn't adding up. Three or four years back, Tony had been down with mono for nearly six weeks, and Ben hadn't come home then. So why now? However, having developed a highly tuned survival skill where her mother was concerned, Mercy knew better than to mention her suspicions.

Just as she knew better than to mention her hunch that all was not well in Tony-and-Anita land. Seriously not well. But her parents would be crushed if Anita's marriage went pffft, especially since they hadn't completely recovered from Mercy's oldest sister Carmen's divorce two years ago. The two families had been tighter'n'ticks for more than thirty-five years, from practically the moment the Zamoras had moved next door. Two of their children marrying had only further cemented an already insoluble bond.

Since Anita hadn't confided in Mercy, all she had was that hunch. Still, the Zamora women, of which there were many, all shared a finely-honed instinct for zeroing in on problems of the heart. And right now, Mercy's instinct was saying yet another fairy-tale ending bites the dust.

"He looks pretty good, don't you think?"

Mercy jerked. Okay, so one check mark in the why-living-across-from-the-parentals-is-a-bad-idea box. Clearly, four weddings (and one messy, nasty divorce) hadn't been enough to put her mother off the scent. Until Mercy was married as well, the world—and all the unattached, straight males who roamed its surface in blissful ignorance that they were marked men—was not a safe place.

"Don't suppose there's much point in denying it."

"No, there isn't. And you're not seeing anyone at the moment, are you?"

"Ma, I've been working nearly nonstop at the store, you know that. I've barely seen myself in the past two years. But to head you off at the pass—fuggedaboutit. Me and Ben…not gonna happen."

No need to mention that she and Ben had already happened. Not that she had any complaints on that score. In fact, if she remembered correctly…

And she would open the rusty gate to that path, why?

"Mercedes," her mother said. "You may have been able to stave off the ravages of time up until now—"

"Gee, thanks."

"—but it's all going to catch up with you, believe me. A woman your age…how can I put this? You can't afford to be too particular."

Because obviously a woman of Mercy's advanced years should be rapidly approaching desperate. Brother.

"Actually," Mercy said, "I can't afford not to be. And believe me, some thirty-five-year-old guy who's still blowing where the breeze takes him, who hasn't even been home since the last millennium, doesn't even make the running." The odd stirring of the old blood notwithstanding.

"So what are you saying? You're just going to give up, be an old maid?"

Mercy laughed. "Honestly, Ma—that term went out with poodle skirts. Besides, you know I'm happy with things the way they are. Business is great, a dozen nieces and nephews more than feed my kid fix, and I actually like living alone. Well, as alone as I can be with you guys across the street and Anita and them two blocks away. There's no big empty hole in my life I need to fill up."

"But think how much more financially stable you'd be, married."

Mercy pinched the bridge of her nose. "Which I suppose is your way of saying you could be getting twice as much for this house as I'm paying you."

"Now you know your father and I are only too happy to help out where we can. But, honey, it has been six years...."

Yeah, Mercy's teeter on the edge of poverty while she and her two partners got their business up and running hadn't exactly left her parents feeling too secure about her ability to take care of herself.

"I know it's been a struggle," she said quietly. "But we're doing okay now. In fact, I can start paying you more for the house, if you want. So I'm over the worst. And it was *my* struggle. You should be proud, you know?"

"I am, *mija*. I am. 'Nita with her nursing degree, and Carmen getting that good job with the state. And now you, with your own business... No mother could be prouder of her girls, believe me. It's just that it kills me seeing you alone. And

I worry that…well, you know. That if you wait too long, you'll lose out."

"Geez, Ma…did Papito sneak something into your coffee this morning? Look, for the last time—" Although she seriously doubted it would be "—I like being alone. And I'm not lonely. Okay?" At her mother's obviously uncomprehending silence, she added, more gently, "So, yes, maybe back in the day, when everybody else was falling in love and getting married and having babies, I felt a little left out that it wasn't happening for me. But I'm not that person anymore. And at this point, if I were to consider marriage, it would have to be to somebody who's going to bring something pretty major to the table, you know? Somebody…well, perfect."

"Nobody's perfect, Mercy," her mother said shortly. "God knows your father's not. But I love him anyway. And I thank God every day for sending him to me."

"But don't you see, Ma? Pa *is* perfect. For *you*. Okay, so maybe you had to whip him into shape a bit," she said with a laugh, and her mother snorted, "but the basics were already all in place. And besides, you were both so young, you had the time and energy and patience on your side. I don't. I'd rather stay single than expend all that energy on either ignoring a man's faults or trying to fix them. So the older I get, the less I'm willing to settle for anything less than the best. And I can tell you right now, Ben Vargas doesn't even make the short list."

And at that moment, the man himself came back outside to get something out of his truck, and Mercy let out a heartfelt sigh at the unfairness of it all.

"Well," her mother said, clearly watching Ben as well, "when you put it that way…no, I don't suppose he does."

"*Thank* you. So does that mean you're off my case?"

"For now. But damn, the man's got a great backside."

Mercy hooted with laughter. "No arguments there," she said as the clear winter sun highlighted a jawline much more defined than she remembered. And since when did she have a thing for wind-scrambled hair? And—she leaned over to get a better look—beard haze? "But butt or no butt," she said, still staring, "as soon as Tony's back in the saddle, so's Ben. Riding off into the sunset."

Her mother chuckled.

"What?"

"You're watching him, too, aren't you?"

Mercy jerked back upright. "Of course not, don't be silly."

"Uh-huh. So maybe you're the one who needs to remember he's not going to be around long."

With her luck, Mercy thought after she hung up, her mother would live to a hundred. Which meant she had another forty years of this to go.

And wasn't that a comforting thought?

Seated at the tiny table wedged into one corner of his parents' kitchen, Ben tried to drum up the requisite enthusiasm for the heavy ceramic plate heaped with spicy chorizo, golden hash browns and steaming scrambled eggs laced with green chile his mother clunked in front of him.

"If you've been driving most of the night," Juanita Vargas said over the whimpering of a trio of overfed, quivering Chihuahuas at her feet, "you should take a nap after you eat. I'll make sure your father keeps the volume down on the TV when he gets back from his golf game."

Still trying to wrap his head around the odd sensation of having never left—he could swear even the orange, red and yellow rooster-patterned potholders were the same ones he remembered—Ben smiled, picked up his fork. "That's okay, I'm fine."

"You don't look fine. You look like somebody who hasn't had a decent meal in far too long. Did I give you enough eggs? Because I've got plenty more in the pan…here," his mother said, reaching for his plate, "I might as well give them to you now, save me the trouble later—"

"No, Mama, really, this is plenty," he said, shoving a huge bite of eggs into his mouth. "Thanks."

The phone mercifully rang. The minute the wisp of a woman and her canine entourage shuffled and clickety-clicked to the other side of the kitchen, Ben quickly wrapped half of his breakfast in his paper napkin to sneak into the garbage later. He'd die before he hurt her feelings, but he'd also die if he ate all this food.

Why, again, had he expected this trip home to provide him with the peace he so sorely needed? Not only was his mother fussing over him like he was a kindergartner, but the minute he got out of his truck he could feel all the old issues between him and his father rush out to greet him, as bug-eyed and overeager as the damn dogs. And then, to top it all off, there was Mercy.

Oh, boy, was there Mercy.

Ben took a swallow of his coffee, wondering how a ten-second interaction could instantly erase an entire decade. For one brief, shining moment, as he'd watched her battling that bush—he chuckled, remembering—he was twenty-whatever and about to combust with need for the hottest tamale of a woman he'd ever known. Who, physically at least, seemed to be in the same time warp as his mother's house. Except he was glad, and surprised, to see she'd finally given up on trying to tame her insanely curly hair. Not much bigger than one of the Chihuahuas—although a helluva lot cuter, thank God, he thought as the biggest one of the lot returned to cautiously sniff his ankles—Mercedes packed a whole lot of punch in that thimble-sized body of hers.

Except, her appearance aside, he doubted she was the same woman she'd been then. God knows, he wasn't the same man. Why he'd thought—

Stupid.

Yeah, his mother had wasted no time in telling him Mercy was still single, but Ben somehow doubted his abrupt departure all those years ago had anything to do with that. Mercy as a torch-carrier? No damn way. A grudge-nurser, however…now that, he could see.

Not that he'd broken any promises. After all, she'd been the one who'd made it clear right from the start that it had only been about itch-scratching. Because he knew she wanted what her sisters had—marriage, babies, stability. And she knew the very thought made him ill. So there'd never been any illusions about permanent. Still, that didn't excuse Ben's taking off without giving her at least a heads-up. She'd deserved better than that.

She'd also deserved better than a pointless affair with some *pendejo* who'd been convinced that running away was the only way to solve a problem he didn't fully understand.

Too long it had taken him to realize what a dumb move that had been.

"You're finished already?" his mother said at his side, going for his plate again. "You want some more—?"

"No! Really," Ben said with a smile, carefully tucking the full napkin by his plate. "I'm fine. It was delicious, thank you."

She beamed. "You want more coffee?"

"I can get it—"

"No, sit, I'm already up."

After handing Ben his coffee, Juanita sat at a right angle to him, briefly touching his hand. Although her stiff, still-black hair did nothing to soften the hard angles of her face, her wide smile shaved years off her appearance. "It means a lot to your father," she said softly in Spanish, "that you came back. He's missed you so much."

Ben lifted the mug to his lips, not daring to meet his mother's gaze. He'd known how much his leaving would hurt Luis, but staying simply hadn't been an option. Now, however…

"Just doing my duty," he said, only to nearly choke when his mother spit out a Spanish curse word. Now he looked up, not sure what to make of the combined amusement and concern in her ripe-olive eyes.

"For ten years, you stay away," she said, still in Spanish. "As if to return would contaminate you, suck you back into something bad—"

"That's not true," he said, except it was. In a way, at least.

"Then why didn't you even come home for holidays, Benicio? To go off and live your life somewhere else is one thing, but to never come home…" Her face crumpled, she shook her head. "What did we do, *mijo?*" she said softly. "Your father adored you, would have done anything for you—"

"I know that, Mama," Ben said, ignoring his now churning stomach. He reached across the table and took his mother's tiny hand in his, taking care not to squeeze the delicate bones. "I was just…restless."

Not the entire truth, but not a lie, either. In fact, at the time he might even have believed that *was* the reason he'd left. Because he'd never been able to figure out why, after he'd been discharged from the army, he couldn't seem to settle back into his old life here. But time blurs memory, and motivations, and reasons, and now, sitting in his mother's kitchen, he really couldn't have said when he'd finally realized the real reason for his leaving.

But for damn sure he'd always known exactly what he'd left behind.

His mother smiled and said in English, "Considering how much you moved around inside me before you were born, this is not a surprise." Then her smile dimmed. "But now I think that restlessness has taken a new form, yes? Something tells me you are not here because of Tony, or your father, but for *you.*"

A second or two of warring gazes followed, during which Ben braced himself for the inevitable, "*So what have you really been doing all this time?*"

Except the question didn't come. Not then, at least. Instead, his mother stood once more, startling the dogs. She took his empty mug, looking down at it for a moment before saying, "Whatever your reason for coming back, it's good to have you home—"

"Ben!"

At the sound of his father's voice, Ben swiveled toward the

door leading to the garage, where Luis Vargas, his thick, dark hair now heavily webbed with silver, was attempting to haul in a state-of-the-art set of golf clubs without taking out assorted wriggling, excited dogs. Ben quickly stood, tossing his "napkin" into the garbage can under the sink as his father dropped the clubs and extended his arms. A heartbeat later, the slightly shorter man had hauled Ben against his chest in an unabashedly emotional hug.

"I didn't expect you for another couple of hours, otherwise I would've stayed home!" The strong, builder's hands clamped around Ben's arms, Luis held him back, moisture glistening in dark brown eyes. Slightly crooked teeth flashed underneath a bristly mustache. "You look good. Doesn't he look good, Juanita? *Dios,*" he said, shaking Ben and grinning, "I've waited so *long* for this moment! Did you eat? Juanita, did you feed the kid?"

"Yes, Pop," Ben said, chuckling. "She fed me."

His father let go, tucking his hands into his pockets, shaking his head and grinning. A potbelly peeked through the opening of his down vest, stretching the plaid shirt farther than it probably should. "I see you, and now I'm thinking, finally, everything's back the way it should be, eh?" He slapped Ben's arm, then pulled him into another hug while his mother fussed a few feet away about how he shouldn't do that, the boy had just eaten, for heaven's sake.

Now the house shuddered slightly as the front door opened, followed by "For God's sake, woman! I'm okay, I don't need your help!"

Ben stiffened. Damn. Would another hour or two to prepare have been too much to ask?

Apparently not, he thought as, in a cloud of cold that briefly soothed Ben's heated face, his brother and sister-in-law, along with their two kids, straggled into the kitchen.

"Look, Tony!" Luis swung one arm around Ben's shoulders, crushing him to his side. "Your brother's finally come home! Isn't that great?"

His brother's answering glare immediately confirmed that nothing had changed on that front, either.

Chapter Two

"So…" Tony banged his crutches up against one wall and collapsed into the nearest kitchen chair, stretching out his casted foot in front of him and glowering. Shorter and stockier than Ben, Tony resembled their father more than ever these days. A neat beard outlined his full jaw, obliterating the baby face Tony had detested all through high school. "You made it."

His mother was too busy fussing over the kids to notice the vinegar in her oldest son's voice, but Ben definitely caught his sister-in-law's irritated frown.

"Don't start, Tony," she said softly, and his brother turned his glower on her.

"Yeah, I made it," Ben said, taking the coward's way out by turning his attention to his niece and nephew. A sliver of regret pierced his gut: Although his mother had e-mailed photos of the kids to him, he'd never seen them in person before this. His chest tightened at the energy pulsing from lanky, ten-year-old Jacob, at little Matilda's shy, holey half-smile from behind her mother's broad hips.

"Come here, you," Anita said, shucking her Broncos jacket and holding out her arms, her fitted, scoop-necked sweater brazenly accentuating her curves. Ben couldn't remember Mercy's next youngest sister as ever having a hard angle anywhere on her body, even when they'd been kids. A biological hand Anita had not only accepted with grace, but played to full advantage. Her embrace was brief and hard and obviously sincere. "Welcome home," she whispered before letting him go.

"You haven't changed a bit," Ben said, grinning. "Still as much of a knockout as ever."

Her laugh did little to mask either her flush of pleasure or the slight narrowing of her thick-lashed, coffee brown eyes as she gave him the once-over. Masses of warm brown curls trembled on either side of her full cheeks. "And you're still full of it! Anyway…little Miss Peek-a-Boo behind me is Matilda, we call her Mattie. And this is Jacob. Jake. Kids, meet your Uncle Ben."

Since Mattie was still hanging back, Ben extended his hand to Jake, gratified to see the wariness begin to retreat in his nephew's dark eyes. "I hear you play baseball."

A look of surprise preceded a huge grin. "Since third grade, yeah. Short stop. Do you?"

"After a fashion. Enough to play catch, if you want."

"Sweet! Dad's like, always too tired and stuff."

"That's crap, Jake," Tony said, and Anita shot him a look that would have felled a lesser man.

"And when's the last time you played with him, huh?"

"For God's sake, 'Nita, my leg's broken!"

"I meant, before that—"

"Are you the same Uncle Ben that makes the rice?"

In response to his niece's perfectly timed distraction, Ben turned to smile into a pair of wide, chocolate M&M eyes. Twin ponytails framed a heart-shaped face, the ends feathered over a fancy purple sweater with a big collar, as the little girl's delicate arms squashed a much-loved, stuffed something to her chest. Ben was instantly smitten. "No, honey, I'm afraid not."

"Oh." Mattie hugged the whatever-it-was more tightly. The ponytails swished when she tilted her head, her soft little brows drawn together. Curiosity—and a deep, unquestioning trust that makes a man take stock of his soul—flared in her eyes. "Papi talks about you all the time," she said with a quick grin for her grandfather. "He says you usta play with Aunt Rosie and Livvy a lot when you were little."

"I sure did." Ben nodded toward the thing in her arms. "Who's your friend?"

"Sammy. He's a cat. I want a real kitty, but Mama says I can't have one until I'm six. Which is only a few weeks away, you know," she said to Anita, who rolled her eyes.

"You must take after your mom," he said, with a wink at Anita, "'cause you're very pretty."

"Yeah, that's what everybody says," Mattie said with a very serious nod as her mother snorted in the background. "I'm in kindergarten, but I can already read, so that's how come I know about the rice." She leaned sideways against the table, one sneakered foot resting atop its mate, then closed the space between them until their foreheads were only inches apart. "My daddy broke his leg," she whispered, like Tony wasn't sitting right there.

"I know," Ben whispered back. "That's why I'm here, to help your grandpa until your dad can go back to work."

"Never mind that it's totally unnecessary," Tony said to his father, not even trying to mask his irritation. "For a few weeks, one of the guys could drive me around. Or you could," he directed at Anita, who crossed her arms underneath her impressive bust, glaring.

"And I already told you, I don't have any vacation time coming up—"

"And maybe," Ben's mother said, clearly trying to keep her kitchen from becoming a war zone, "you should be grateful your brother is back home, yes?"

"Yeah, about that," Mattie said, startling Ben and eliciting a muttered, "God help us when she hits puberty," from Anita. "If you're my uncle, how come I've never seen you before? And are you gonna stay or what?"

Ignoring the first question—because how on earth was he supposed to explain something to a five-year-old he didn't fully comprehend himself?—Ben gently tugged one of those irresistible ponytails and said, "I don't know, bumblebee," which was the best he could do, at the moment.

An answer which elicited a soft, hopeful "Oh!" from his mother, even as his brother grabbed his crutches, standing so quickly he knocked over his chair.

"We need to get goin'," he said. "'Nita, kids, come on."

"But you just got here!" Ben's mother said as his father laid a hand on his arm.

"Antonio. Don't be like this."

"Like what, Pop?" Tony said, halting his awkward progress toward the door. "Like *myself?* But then, I guess it doesn't matter anyway now. Because it's all good, isn't it, now that *Ben's* back. Kids…*now.*"

Both Jake and Mattie gave Ben a quick, confused backwards glance—Mattie adding a small wave—before Anita, apology brimming in her eyes, ushered them all out. In the dulled silence that followed, Ben's mother scooped up one of the whimpering little mutts, stroking it between its big batlike ears. "It's Tony's leg, he's not himself, you know how he hates feeling helpless."

Ben stood as well, swinging his leather jacket off the back of his chair. At the moment, it took everything he had not to walk out the door, get in his truck and head right back to Dallas. Why on earth had he thought that time in and of itself would have been sufficient to heal this mess, that everyone would have readjusted if he took himself out of the equation…?

"Where are you going?" his father demanded.

"Just out for a walk. Get reacquainted with the neighborhood."

"Oh." His father's heavy brows pushed together. "I thought maybe we could watch a game or something together later."

"I know. But…" Ben avoided his father's troubled gaze, tamping down the familiar annoyance before his mouth got away from his brain. Knowing something needed to be fixed didn't mean he had a clue how to fix it. Not then, and not, unfortunately, now. He smiled for his mother, dropped a kiss on the top of her head. "I'm not going far. And I'll be back for that game, I promise," he said to his father.

"Benicio—"

"Let him go, Luis," his mother said softly. "He has to do this his own way."

Ben sent silent thanks across the kitchen, then left before his father's confusion tore at him more than it already had.

For maybe an hour, he walked around the neighborhood, his hands stuffed in his pockets, until the crisp, dry air began to clear his head, until the sun—serene and sure in a vast blue sky broken only by the stark, bare branches of winter trees—burned off enough of the fumes from the morning's disastrous reunion for him to remember why'd he come home. That he'd made the decision to do so long before he'd gotten the call from his father, asking for his help.

So even if everything he'd seen and faced and overcome during his absence paled next to the challenge of trying to piece together the real Ben out of the mess he'd left behind, he still felt marginally better by the time he turned back on to his parents' block…just as Mercy's garage door groaned open.

From across the street, he watched her drag a small step stool outside, wrench it open. Now dressed in jeans and a bright red sweater small enough to fit one of his mother's dogs, she plunked the stool down in the grass in front of her house. She jiggled it for a few seconds to make sure it was steady, then climbed and started to take down the single strand of large colored Christmas lights at the edge of the roof. In a nearby bald spot in the lawn, that Hummer-sized cat of hers plopped down, writhing in the dirt until Mercy yelled at it to cut it out already, she'd just vacuumed. Chastened, the beast flipped to its stomach, its huge, fluffy tail twitching laconically as it glared at Ben.

Speaking of a mess he'd left behind. If he knew what was good for him, he'd keep walking.

Clearly, he didn't.

* * *

"Need any help?"

Mercy grabbed the gutter to keep from toppling off the step stool, then twisted around, trying her best to keep the *And who are you again?* look in place. But one glance at that goofy grin and her irritation vaporized. Right along with her determination to pretend he didn't exist. That he'd never existed. That there hadn't been a time—

"No, I'm good," she said, returning to her task, hoping he'd go away. As if. All too aware of his continued scrutiny, she got down, moved the step stool over, got back up, removed the next few feet of lights, got down, moved the step stool over, got back up—

"Here."

Ben stood at her elbow, the rest of the lights loosely coiled in his hand. A breeze shivered through his thick hair, a shade darker than hers; the reflected beam of light from his own truck window delineated ridges and shadows in a face barely reminiscent of the outrageous flirt she remembered. Instead, his smile—not even that, really, barely a tilt of lips at once full and unapologetically masculine—barely masked an unfamiliar weightiness in those burnt wood eyes. An unsettling discovery, to say the least, stirring frighteningly familiar, and most definitely unwanted, feelings of tenderness inside her.

She climbed down from the stool. "You started at the other end."

"Seemed like a good plan to me."

"Creep."

That damned smile still toying with his mouth, he handed the lights to her.

On a huffed sigh, she folded up the stool and tromped back to the garage. The cat, wearing a fine coating of dirt and dead grass, followed. As did Ben.

She turned. "If I told you to go away, would you?"

He shrugged, then said, "How come you're taking down your lights already? It's not even New Year's yet."

Mercy and the cat exchanged a glance, then she shrugged as well. "I have to help Ma take her stuff down on New Year's day, I figured I'd get a jumpstart on my own, since the weather's nice and all. And they're saying we might have snow tomorrow. Although I'll believe that when I see it. Not that there's much. Which you can see. I still have my tree up, though—"

Shut up, she heard inside her head. *Shut up, shut up, shut up.* Her mouth stretched tight, she crossed her arms over her ribs.

"And why are you over here again?"

"I'm not really over here, I'm out for a walk. But you looked like you could use some help, so I took a little detour. Damn, that's a big cat," he said as she finally gave up—since Ben was obviously sticking to her like dryer lint—and dragged a plastic bin down off a shelf, dumping the lights into it.

"That's no cat, that's my bodyguard."

"I can see that."

Mercy glanced over to see the thing rubbing against Ben's shins, getting dirt all over his jeans, doing that little quivering thing with his big, bushy tail. Ben squatted to scratch the top of his head; she could hear the purring from ten feet away. "What's his name?"

"Depends on the day and my mood. On good days, it's

Homer. Sometimes Big Red. Today I'm leaning toward Dumbbutt."

The cat shot her a death glare and gave her one of his broken meows. Chuckling, Ben stood and wiped his hands, sending enough peachy fur floating into the garage to cover another whole cat.

"Because?"

"Because he's too stupid to know when he's got it good. If he sticks around, he's got heat, my bed to sleep in and all the food he can scarf down. But no, that would apparently cramp his style. Even though the vet swore once I had him fixed, he wouldn't do that. She was wrong. Or didn't take enough off, I haven't decided. In any case, he periodically vanishes, sometimes overnight, sometimes for days at a time. Then he has the nerve to drag his carcass back here, all matted and hungry, and beg for my forgiveness."

Silence.

"You wouldn't be trying to make a point there, would you?"

Mercy smiled sweetly. "Not at all."

"At least I'm not matted," he said, his intense gaze making her oddly grateful the garage was unheated. "Or hungry. My mother made sure of that."

"How about fixed?"

He winced.

"Yeah, that's what I figured." She turned to heft the lights bin back up onto the shelf. "But you're not getting back in my bed, either."

Funny, she would have expected to hear a lot more conviction behind those words. Especially the *not* part of that sentence.

"I lost out to the cat?"

There being nothing for it, Mercy faced him again, palms on butt, chest out, chin raised. As defiant as a Pomeranian facing a Rotty. "You lost out, period."

They stared at each other for several seconds. Until Ben said, "You know, I could really use a cup of coffee."

"I thought you were out for a walk?"

"Turned out to be a short walk."

More gaze-tangling, while she weighed the plusses (none that she could see) with the minuses (legion) about letting him in, finally deciding, *Oh, what the hell?* He'd come in, she'd give him coffee, he'd go away (finally), and that would be that. She led man and cat into her kitchen, hitting the garage door opener switch on the way. Over the grinding of the door closing, she said, "I'm guessing you needed a break?"

The corner of his mouth twitched. "You could say."

"I don't envy you. God knows I couldn't live with *my* parents again. What are you doing?"

He'd picked up her remote, turned on the TV. "Just wanted to check the news, I haven't seen any in days. You get CNN?"

"Yeah, I get it. And you're gonna get it if you turn it on."

On a sigh, he clicked off the TV, moseyed back over to the breakfast bar. "You still don't watch the news?"

"Not if I can help it. Feeling overwhelmed and helpless ain't my thang." She pointed to one of the bar stools. "Sit. And don't let the cat up—" Homer jumped onto the counter in front of Ben "—on the bar."

Long, immensely capable fingers plunged into the cat's ruff, as a pair of whatchagonnadoaboutit? grins slid her way. On a sigh, Mercy said, "Regular or decaf?"

"What do you think?"

No, the question was, what was she *thinking,* letting the man into her house? Again. When no good would come of it, she was sure. And yet, despite those legion reasons why this was a seriously bad idea, the lack of gosh-it's-been-a-long-time awkwardness between them was worth noting. Oh, sure, the atmosphere was charged enough to crackle—surprising in itself, considering her normal reaction (or lack thereof) to running into old lovers and such. *That was fun...next?* had been her motto for, gee, years. So who'd'athunk, that in spite of the unexpectedness of Ben's reappearance, the sexual hum nearly making her deaf, in the end it would be a completely different bond holding sway over the moment, lending an *Oh, yeah, okay* feeling to the whole thing that made her feel almost...comfortable. If it hadn't been for that sexual hum business.

Which led to a second question: If yesterday—shoot, this morning—she'd been totally over him, what had happened since then to change that?

Digging the coffee out of the fridge, she glanced over, noticed him looking around. Then those eyes swung back to hers, calling a whole bunch of memories out of retirement, and she thought, *Oh. Right.*

"Cool tree," he said.

Grateful for the distraction, Mercy allowed a fond smile for the vintage silver aluminum number she'd found at a garage sale. Some of the "needles" had cracked off, but with all the hot pink marabou garland, it was barely noticeable. Well, that, and the several dozen bejeweled angels, miniature shoe ornaments and crosses vying for space amongst the feathers. This was one seriously tarted up Christmas tree, and Mercy adored it. "That's Annabelle. You should see her at night when I've got the color wheel going. She's something else."

Ben shook his head, laughing softly, and yet more memories reported for duty. Including several that fearlessly headed straight for the hot zones.

"I just met Mattie and Jake," he said.

Whew. "Yeah? Aren't they great? That Mattie's a pistol, isn't she?"

"She is that." He sounded a little awestruck. "Took to me right away."

"Don't take it personally, the child doesn't know the meaning of 'stranger.' A second's glance in her direction and you're doomed. Drives my sister nuts."

"She wouldn't…Mattie knows better than to go off with someone she doesn't know, I hope."

"With Anita for her mother? What do you think?"

Ben's shoulders seemed to relax a little after that, before he said, "I can't believe you're still here. In this house, I mean."

A shrug preceded, "Why not? It's home." She spooned coffee into the basket; took her three tries to ram it home. "It's just me, I don't need a huge house. And the landlord gives me a good deal on the rent."

"You've made some changes, though."

"Not really," she said, wondering why she was flushing. "Oh, yeah, those lamps by the sofa are new—Hobby Lobby specials, half off. And I did paint, about three years ago. During my faux-finishing phase. That lacquered finish was a bitch, let me tell you."

"Huh." He paused. "The walls are certainly…red."

"Yeah, I almost went with orange, but thought it would be a bit much with the sofa."

"Good point." Another pause. "Never saw a sofa the color of antifreeze before."

"Do I detect a hint of derision in that comment?"

Ben's mouth twitched again. "Not at all. But the walls… your father must've nearly had a coronary."

"To put it mildly. Until I pointed out that since I'll have to be blasted out of here, painting over the walls is moot."

He chuckled, then asked, "How are your folks?"

"Fine," she said, even though what she really wanted to do was scream *Stop looking at me like that!* "Dad's finally retired, driving Ma nuts. Her arthritis has been acting up more these past couple of years, which is why I have to help her take down her decorations."

"She still turn the place into the North Pole?"

"You have no idea. And every year she buys *more* stuff. For the grandbabies, she says."

"How many are there?"

"Twelve. Although Rosie's pregnant with her fourth. A fact my mother never tires of shoving down my throat. That I'm the only one without kids. Oh, and a husband."

His expression softened. "Guess there's no accounting for some men's stupidity."

Uh…

Mercy spun back to the gurgling coffeemaker. "No matter. What can I say, that ship has sailed."

After a silence thick enough to slice and serve with butter and jam, Ben said, "So what are you up to these days?"

The coffeemaker finally spit out its last drop; Mercy pulled a pair of mugs down from a cabinet, filled them both with the steaming brew. She handed him his coffee, then retreated to lean against the far counter, huddling her own mug to her chest. "Actually, I finally got my business degree, opened a children's gently used clothing store with two of my class-mates, about six or seven years ago. Except it grew, so now we carry some furniture and educational toys, too."

He held aloft his mug in a silent toast. "And you're doing well?"

"Fingers crossed, so far, so good. We were even able to hire an assistant last summer. A damn good thing since both of my partners have babies now. Had to find a larger place, too. One of those old Victorians near Old Town? Your father's company did the remodel, actually."

"No kidding? I'll have to drop by, check it out."

"You, in a kid's store?"

"Why not? Hey, I've got a niece and nephew to spoil. Es-pecially…" His eyes lowered, he thumbed the rim of his cup, then looked back up at her. "Especially since I've got a lot of lost time to make up for."

"And whose fault is that?"

"You know, you could at least pretend to be diplomatic."

"I could. But why? And since we're on the subject…so what exactly *have* you been doing for the past ten years?"

His eyes narrowed, a move that instantly provoked a tiny *Hmm* in the dimly lit recesses of her mind. "This and that," he finally said. "Going where the work was."

"Whatever that's supposed to mean."

He looked at her steadily for a long moment, then said quietly, "I didn't vanish without a trace, Merce. My family's always known where I was, that I was okay. And I'm here now, aren't I?"

"But *why,* is the question? And don't give me some song-and-dance about your father needing you. Because I'm not buying it."

Ben leaned back on the bar stool, gently drumming his fingers on the counter, as he seemed to be contemplating how much to tell her. "Let's just say events provided a much needed kick in the butt and let it go at that."

"A kick in the butt to do what?"

One side of his mouth kicked up. "Thought I said to let it go?"

"Not gonna happen. So?"

He slid off the stool, moseying out into the living room and picking up a family photo of her youngest sister Olivia and her family, including four little boys under the age of nine. "I needed some time to…reassess a few things, that's all." He set the photo back down and turned to her, his hand in his back pocket, and something in his eyes made her stomach drop.

"Ben…? What's wrong? Did something happen?"

"You always could see through me, Merce," he said softly, a rueful grin tugging at that wonderful, wonderful mouth. "Even when we were kids. But this isn't about something happening nearly as much as…well, I find myself wondering a lot these days how I got to be thirty-five with still no idea how I fit in the grand scheme of things."

Yep, she knew that feeling. All too well. Only, up until a few minutes ago, she could have sworn she'd left that "Who the hell am I?" phase of her life far behind her. Apparently, she'd been wrong.

Not only because the grinning, cocky, nobody-can-tell-me-nuthin' dude of yore had morphed into this man with the haunted eyes who'd clearly been knocked around a time or two and, she was guessing, had come out all the stronger, and perhaps wiser, for it. But because, in the time it took to drink a single cup of coffee, whoever this was had turned everything she'd thought she'd known about herself on its head.

On a soft but heartfelt, "Dammit," Mercy sidestepped the breakfast bar and crossed the small room, where she grabbed Ben's shoulders and yanked him into a liplock neither of them would ever forget.

Chapter Three

He'd been as powerless to stop their mouths' colliding as he would have been a meteor falling on his head.

But nothing said he'd had to wrap his arms tight around her and kiss her back, with a good deal of enthusiasm and no small amount of tongue. Or lower her onto that hideous green sofa—except his back, which wouldn't have taken kindly to bending over like that for longer than a second or so. Damn, she was short. Even so, he could still stop, no sweat, any time he wanted to, still pull away from that warm, wicked mouth and the warm, wicked woman that came with it.

Which eventually he did, if for no other reason than they both needed air, bracing his hands on either side of her shoulders and searching her eyes before once again lowering his mouth to hers, this time going slow, so slow, so mind-druggingly slow, pulling back whenever she tried to cozy up to his tongue, gently nipping her lower lip, her chin, her neck…remembering how it had been between them.

How good.

She made a sound that was both growl and whimper as her long, pale fingernails dug into his arms, as one leg snaked around his waist, trapping him, claiming him, even as his body completely ignored his brain's strident protests, that this was stupid and wrong and what the hell was he thinking?

Breathing hard, she pushed him slightly away, even as she clutched his shirt. "So, how long are you here again?"

Right.

His heart pounding, Ben waited, silently swearing, for the testosterone haze to clear. Then he pushed himself up, and away, walking back into the kitchen to get his coat.

"Four weeks," he said, flatly. Because damned if he was going to hold out the same bone to Mercy he never should have to his family. Because he had no idea what his plans were. What came next. "Maybe six."

She sat up, her hair as knotted as her forehead, and need and regret and a whole mess of pointless, inappropriate feelings got all tangled up in his head. He'd missed that bizarre mixture of vulnerability and toughness that was Mercedes Zamora. Missed it way too much to risk screwing things up now.

"What are you doing?" she asked.

"I think it's called coming to my senses."

"Uh-huh." Laughing, she shoved her hair out her face with both hands. Her swollen lips canted in a crooked smile, she slumped against the cushions, propping one foot on the brightly painted wooden trunk she used for a coffee table. The shiny red walls made the air seem molten, flooding his consciousness with possibilities he had no business considering. "And just what do you think," she said, "the odds are of our keeping our hands off each other while you're here?"

"That's not the point." His hands shot up by his shoulders. "I can't do this, Mercy."

"Yeah? Could've fooled me."

"No. I mean, I can't do this again. Mess around. With you."

"Because…?"

"Because it wouldn't be right."

"Yeah, well, it wasn't right the first time. Don't recall that stopping us."

He squeezed shut his eyes against the onslaught of memories. "God, Merce," he said, opening them again, "what is it about you that makes me so hot my brain shorts out?"

She shrugged, then grabbed a bright blue throw pillow, hugging it to her, looking uncannily like a very grown-up version of their niece. "I'm easy?"

This time, he laughed out loud. "Oh, babe, one thing you're not is easy."

"Fun, then. And by the way, that thing where you said I made you hot?" She gave him a thumbs up.

"Like men don't say that to you all the time."

"Ooh, somebody's just racking up the brownie points right and left today." Two heartbeats later she stood in front of him again, her thumbs hooked in his belt loop, tugging him close. "No, really, that's a very sweet thing to say, considering I'm not exactly the nubile young thing I used to be. But what other men might or might not say to me isn't the point. The point is…" Her gaze never leaving his, she let go to skim a fingernail down his chest, smiling when he involuntarily flinched. "The point is, it's been a long, long time since anyone made me hot enough to short out my brain, too."

"Oh, yeah? How long?"

The fingernail slid underneath the front of his shirt, gently scraping across his skin. "Guess."

He pulled away.

"Would it put your mind at ease," she said behind him, "to know I'm not looking for the same things I was ten years ago?" When he turned, she added, "Not with you, not with anybody else. I'm not looking for forever, Ben." Her mouth stretched into an almost-smile. "Not anymore."

He frowned. "You don't *want* marriage? Kids?"

She walked over to the same photos he'd been looking at earlier, straightening out the one he'd apparently not put back correctly. "It's like when you're a teenager, and you just *know* if you don't get that album, or dress, or pair of shoes, you'll expire. Then one day you realize you never did get whatever it was you thought you couldn't live without, and not only did you survive, you don't miss it, either."

And clearly she'd forgotten just how well he'd always been able to see through her, too. Her reluctance to make eye contact was a dead giveaway that she was skirting the truth. But this wasn't the time to call her on it, especially since he was hardly in a place where he could be entirely truthful with her, either.

So all he said was, "You're one weird chick, Mercy," and she laughed.

"Not exactly breaking news," she said, facing him again. "Look, whether we should have let things get out of hand or not back then, I can't say. But I've never regretted it. Have you? No, wait," she said, holding up one hand. "Maybe I don't want to know the answer to that."

Ben realized he was grinding his teeth to keep from going to her. "Not hardly," he said, and she smiled.

"Well, then. Ben, I knew from the moment you came home after the army that you'd never stick around. Yeah, I was supremely annoyed that you took off without saying anything, but I always knew you'd leave." She did that thing where she planted her palms on her butt, and Ben's mouth went dry. "Just like I know you'll leave this time. But while you're here, we could either drive ourselves nuts pretending we're not interested, or we could enjoy each other." Her shoulders bumped. "Your call." When he shook his head, she said, "Why not?"

"*Porque nadie tropieza dos veces con la misma piedra,*" he said softly, repeating an old Mexican proverb he'd heard a thousand times as a kid. *Because nobody trips over the same stone twice.*

They eyed each other for a long moment, then she returned to the kitchen, collecting their mugs.

"You're angry."

"Don't be ridiculous." The dishwasher shuddered when she banged it open. "It was just a thought."

"Merce. A half hour ago you gave the very distinct impression you'd rather eat live snakes than start something up again with me. So why the sudden change of heart?"

She slammed the dishwasher shut, turned around. "That was my wounded pride talking. So good news—guess I'm a faster healer than I realized."

"And I'm just getting started," he said, and her brows

plunged. "Honey, I'm not rejecting you. I'm rejecting the past. Because I *don't* want to pick up where we left off. Because, yeah, I want you so much I can't think straight, but it's more than that with you." His throat ached when he swallowed. "It was always more than that with you."

In the space of a heartbeat, her expression changed from confusion to stunned comprehension to bemusement. The cat jumped up on the counter beside her, bumping her elbow to be petted. Being obviously well-trained, she obeyed, then said, "You remember the scene early in *It's a Wonderful Life* where Jimmy Stewart finds himself in Donna Reed's living room, and her mother hollers down the stairs, asking her what he wants, and Donna Reed says, 'I don't know,' then turns to Jimmy Stewart and says, 'What *do* you want?' and he gets all mad because he doesn't really know?" She cocked her head. "Well?"

"I don't know," Ben ground out, stuffing his arms into his jacket. "But I can tell you I'm not looking for the same things I was before, either."

Then he strode to her door and let himself out, not even trying to keep from slamming the door.

The forecast had called for a slight chance of snow on New Year's Eve—pretty much an empty threat in Albuquerque, which, Ben mused as he listened to his mother fuss at his father at their bedroom door, rarely had weather in the usual sense of the word. Muttering in Spanish, his mother trooped down the hall, all dressed up for her night on the town.

"You sure you're going to be okay?" Juanita said, wrapping a soft, fuzzy shawl around her shoulders, half concealing the glittery long-sleeved dress underneath. Her eyes sparkled as brightly as the diamond studs in her ears—his parents and Mercy's were spending the night at one of the fancy casino resorts on a nearby Indian reservation, and she'd spent most of the day primping in preparation. When he'd been a kid and money had been tight for both families, "doing something for New Year's" meant getting together to play cards, or, later, watch videos. Apparently, though, their parents had been celebrating in grand style for some years now, and seeing how excited they were tickled Ben to death.

"I imagine I'll muddle through somehow," he said with a smile.

The doorbell rang; his mother opened it to let Mary and Manny Zamora inside. "Luis!" she tossed over her shoulder as Ben and the Zamoras shook hands, exchanged hugs and small talk. "They're here!" She minced to the end of the hallway in high heels she wasn't used to wearing. "What *are* you doing?"

Grumbling under his breath, his father appeared, still adjusting the ostentatious silver-and-turquoise bolo on his string tie. After a burst of chatter, the Zamoras and his father headed back out, but his mother lagged behind.

"Now there's plenty of food in the refrigerator," she said, "and you know how to use the microwave—"

"Juanita! *Per Dios!*"

"I'm coming, I'm coming!"

Ben stood in the doorway, watching them drive off, the headlight beams from his father's brand new Escalade glancing off a handful of tiny, valiantly swirling snowflakes. As he was about to close the door, he noticed Mercy's Firebird in her driveway, its lightly frosted roof glistening in the light from the street lamp several houses over. Ben frowned—the quintessential party girl, alone on New Year's? Now that was just wrong.

Close the door, Ben. None of your business, Ben. Stay out of it, Ben…

A minute's raid on the family room bar produced a bottle of Baileys he hoped didn't predate Nixon. If nothing else, they could spike their coffee.

Or, he considered as he stood on her doorstep, ringing her doorbell, she could—justifiably—tell him to take his Baileys and stick it someplace the sun don't shine—

"No!" he heard Mercy say on the other side. "Never, ever answer the door without first making sure you know who's on the other side!"

The door swung open (because clearly Mercy didn't take her own advice, which provoked a flash of irritation behind Ben's eyes). From inside floated the mouthwatering scents of baked chocolate and popcorn. "Ben! What are you doing here?"

Her hair sprouting from the top of her head in a fountain of ringlets, the party girl was dressed to kill in a three-sizes-too-big purple sweatshirt that hung to midthigh, a pair of clingy, sparkly pants, and blindingly bright, striped fuzzy socks. Not surprisingly, considering the way they'd left things the day before, her eyes bugged with total astonishment, which pleased Ben in some way he couldn't begin to define.

"I, um, didn't like the idea of you being by yourself on New Year's?" he said as Mattie, swallowed up in a nearly identical outfit and crying, "Uncle Ben! Uncle Ben!" launched herself at his knees, adhering to him like plastic wrap. Then she leaned back, giving him her most adoring, gap-toothed smile.

"Aunt Mercy an' me're watching *Finding Nemo* but Jake doesn't wanna, he says it's a sissy movie." The squirt latched onto his hand and dragged him across the threshold. "Wanna come watch with us?"

Ben's gaze shifted to Mercy, who shrugged. The sweatshirt didn't budge. "Welcome to Mercy's Rockin' New Year's Eve. I'm babysitting," she said, standing aside to keep from getting trampled as Jacob yelled from the back of the house, "I'm not a baby!"

"Get a job and we'll talk," Mercy called back as they all returned to the living room.

No reply except for the muffled pings and zaps of some video game.

"Popcorn's ready," she yelled again, plopping a plastic bowl as large as a bathtub in the middle of that trunk with identity issues. Over in her corner, Annabelle shimmered red...blue...green...red as the color wheel did its thing, while a small fire crackled lazily in a kiva fireplace in the opposite corner, and Ben felt a chuckle of pure delight rumble up from his chest.

Mercy reached up to adjust her hair, her hands landing on her hips when she was done. Her nails were as red as her walls, with what looked like little rhinestones or something imbedded in each tip. Amazing. Ben's gaze shifted to her face; she looked more befuddled than ticked, he decided. "We've already had the first course—brownies—but I think there's still a few left in the kitchen."

"Thanks, but I think I'll pass. Um…" Ben slipped off his jacket, flinging it across the back of a chair. "Are you okay with this?"

One eyebrow hitched, just slightly. "That you crashed my party? Yeah, I should've had the dude at the door check the guest list more carefully. But hey, no problem, we've got chaperones and everything."

"What's a chaperone?" Mattie asked.

"Somebody who makes sure nobody does something they shouldn't," Mercy said, never taking her eyes off Ben's, the eyebrow hiking another millimeter. Okay, definitely not ticked. Not that having the kids here meant a whole lot in the tempering-the-sexual-tension department. Apparently.

"What's that?" the little girl said, latching on to the Baileys. "C'n I have some?"

"Not if you want your mother to ever, ever let you come here again," Mercy said, taking the bottle from Ben and nodding in approval. "Later," she said, holding it up, then setting it on top of the fashionably distressed armoire housing a regular old TV and DVD player. She walked the few steps to the hall, pushing up the sleeves of the sweatshirt. They fell right back down. "Jacob Manuel Vargas! If you don't get out here *right now* and get yourself some popcorn, your uncle Ben's gonna eat it all up!"

"Uncle Ben's here? All *right!*" he heard from down the hall, followed by pounding footsteps and a grinning kid in a hoodie and jeans. He high-fived Ben; Mercy stuck another plastic bowl in his hands with the warning that if he got a single piece on her bed his butt was going to be in a major sling.

"Wanna play games with me later?" he asked Ben around a mouthful of popcorn, looking less than terrorized by his aunt's threat. "I got this really cool racing game for Christmas, I'm already at the third level."

"Sure thing," Ben said, feeling a little like the new kid at school getting picked for the best team. "But in a sec, okay? So," he said to Mercy, imbuing his words with as much meaning as he dared. "Tony and Anita went out?" He settled on the sofa, swiping the bowl of popcorn off the coffee table. Mattie wriggled into place beside him, grabbing a far-too-large handful that promptly exploded all over her, the sofa and the floor.

"Sorry, Aunt Mercy!"

"Don't worry about it, cutie-pie, it happens." Mercy bent over to pick up the scattered kernels, her hair and face glimmering red…blue…green…red. "Yeah," she said. Deliberately avoiding his eyes? "They'd already made reservations at the Hilton, so it seemed a shame to give them up just because Tony broke his leg. But the real party's here—right, munchkin?" she said to Mattie, lightly tapping her niece on the nose with a piece of popcorn. The child giggled, snuggling closer to Ben and swiping a piece of popcorn out of his hand.

"We get to stay up until midnight—" she yawned "—and watch the ball drop in Tom's hair."

"*Times Square,* stupid," Jacob said, prompting an immediate "Don't call your sister stupid," from Mercy.

Apparently unfazed, the little girl twisted around to look up at Ben with big, solemn, slightly sleepy eyes. "It's funner over here. Mama 'n' Daddy've been fighting a lot. I don't like it when they do that."

Mercy's eyes flashed to Ben's as Jacob, instantly turning beet red, muttered, "Shut up, Mattie."

"Well, they have. An' you're not supposed to say 'shut up,' Mama says it's rude."

"Guys!" Mercy said. "Enough. But you know what? Your mama and I used to fight like crazy when we were kids, and it didn't mean anything."

"Really?" Mattie said.

Mercy laughed. "Oh, yeah. Yelling, screaming…ask your grandma, she used to swear it sounded like we were killing each other. And then it would blow over and we'd be best buddies again—"

"C'n I have a Coke?" the boy said, bouncing up out of the chair.

"Sure, sweetie," Mercy said. "You know where they are. And by the way," she said to his back as he walked away, "what happens here, stays here, got it?"

That got a fleeting grin and a nod. Only Ben wasn't sure if Mercy was talking about the questionable menu or the even more questionable conversation. He stuffed another handful of popcorn into his mouth, staring at the slightly trembling image of a red-and-white fish on the screen in front of him. As Jake traipsed back to Mercy's bedroom with his popcorn and soda, Mattie dug the remote out from under Ben's hip, punched the Play button and the red fish started talking to a blue fish that sounded oddly like Ellen deGeneres.

"So you really think that's all this is?" he said softly over Mattie's giggles as Mercy sank into the cushion on the other side of her niece, tucking her feet up under her.

Her silence spoke volumes as she reached across their niece to pluck several kernels from the bowl. "No," she said, her eyes on the screen. "Unfortunately."

"You think somebody should go talk to Jake?"

"I've tried, but…" She shrugged, her forehead puckered.

"Guys, shh," Mattie said, poking Ben with her elbow. "This is the best part, when Dory pretends she's a whale."

Out of deference to Mattie, they stopped talking. But Ben wasn't paying the slightest attention to the movie, and he somehow doubted Mercy—whose mouth was still pulled down at the corners—was, either. Under other circumstances, he would have been perfectly fine with staying right where he was, with this goofy little girl cuddled next to him and her goofy aunt not much farther away, munching popcorn and watching a kid flick.

But sometimes, life has other ideas.

So he gently extricated himself from the soft, trusting warmth curled into his side, shifting the child to lean against her aunt instead, then followed the sound of engines roaring and tires screeching until he reached Mercy's bedroom. Sitting cross-legged on the end of Mercy's double bed, Jake was intently focused on the game flashing across the smaller TV sitting on the dresser in front of him, his thumbs a blur on the controller as he leaned from side to side.

Ben leaned against the door frame, his thumbs hooked in his jeans pockets. "Hey," he said softly, acutely aware that, as far as Jake was concerned, Ben was a stranger. Not to mention he was venturing into potentially explosive-ridden territory. No doubt Tony would see Ben's attempt to help as blatant, and extremely unwelcome, interference.

Attention riveted to the car zooming and swerving wildly on the screen, Jake bumped one shoulder in acknowledgment. "Soon as I'm done—" he hunched forward, pounded one button a dozen times in rapid succession, then whispered "*Yes!* I can set it up…for two players…"

"No hurry."

The room was dark except for a single bedside lamp, but he could see she'd gone with the orange in here, Ben noted with a wry smile. Sort of the same color as that clownfish, actually. But for a woman as unabashedly female as Mercedes Zamora, her bedroom was almost eerily frou-frou free. Even more than he remembered. No lace, no filmy stuff at the windows, no mounds of pillows or—God bless her—stuffed animals on the unadorned platform bed, covered with a plain white comforter. Nothing but clean lines as far as the eye could see.

And all that color, drenching the room in a perpetual sunset.

Ben turned his attention to his nephew, then eased over to sit next to him. The cat, who'd been God knew where up to that point, jumped up and butted his arm, then tramped across his lap to sniff Jake's hand.

"Go away, Homer," he said, giggling. "Your whiskers tickle."

Yeah, that's how kids are supposed to sound. "Wow," Ben said, sincerely impressed. "You really rock at this."

A quick grin bloomed across the kid's face. "Thanks. Okay," he said a minute later, his fingers again flying over the buttons as the image changed to a split screen. "The other controller's in my backpack, if you want to get it?"

"Sure." Ben dug through a wad of rumpled, detergent-scented clothes, pulled it out, plugged it into the console. "You have to promise to go easy on me, though," he said. "I think the last video game I played was Mario on Nintendo."

"You mean, like Game Cube?"

"No, I mean the *original* Nintendo. Way before your time."

"Oh, yeah…my dad still drags that out every once in a while. But mostly he likes my PlayStation, 'cause it's way cooler."

Ben chose his car—a red Porsche, what else?—and they were off. Twenty seconds in, Ben realized his reaction time needed some serious retooling. The kid was beating the crap out of him. "Your dad play games with you?"

"Yeah, sometimes. Mom doesn't like it much, though."

"Oh?" Ben said carefully.

"She keeps saying…he needs to…grow up." Apparently realizing his gaffe, the kid flicked a glance in Ben's direction, only to then say, "Why's Dad mad at you?"

Ben stiffened, tempted to pretend he had no idea what the kid was talking about. But what would be the point? "I'm not sure I can explain." He glanced at the boy. "Why?" he asked, smiling. "Was he bad-mouthing me?"

Jake flushed. "Kind of. Papi though, he like couldn't stop talkin' about you when they were over at our house last night. He's really, really happy you came home."

"So am I," Ben said. Then he bumped the boy's shoulder with his own, earning him a quick, slightly embarrassed grin.

After another couple of seconds, though, Jake said quietly, "Mattie's right, Mom an' Dad really have been yelling a lot at each other lately."

"That must suck," Ben said after a short pause.

"Totally. Especially since it really scares Mattie, she's just a little kid. And I know what Aunt Mercy said, about how she and my mom used to fight when they were kids, but this is different."

"Why do you think that?"

"I dunno. It just is. Me 'n' Mattie fight all the time, too, but…" Jake shook his head.

Ben's game car crashed into a wall, bounced back onto the

road, righted itself and kept going. Which is exactly what this conversation was going to do if he wasn't careful. Except for the keep going part, maybe. "I don't know, maybe it's not as bad as it looks. After all, do you think they would have gone out tonight if they really weren't getting along?"

Beside him, the kid shrugged. "Dunno. Maybe."

After another few seconds—and another wipeout—Ben ventured, "Have you told your mom and dad how you feel?"

When several moments passed with no reply, Ben looked over to see the boy's jaw set much too tightly for such a small person, and his heart cramped. "Jake?" he said gently.

His breathing suddenly labored, his nephew tossed down the controller. "This game is dumb, I don't want to play anymore, okay?"

"Sure, no problem." Ben tried to lay a hand on the kid's shoulder, but he jerked away. So he lowered his head to look up into his face. "I know we only just met, but you can tell me how you feel, it's okay—"

Huge, scared eyes met his. "You're gonna tell, aren't you?"

"Is anybody actually getting hurt?"

Jake looked away. Shook his head.

"Then I swear, dude, this is strictly between you and me. So are we cool?"

After a moment, the boy nodded.

Ben thought for a moment, then said, "When your mom and dad get mad, do they yell at you? Or Mattie?"

"Uh-uh."

"You're sure?"

"Yeah, 'course. Well, Mom gets kinda crazy when I forget to clean my room an' stuff, but that's different."

Ben smiled. "Yes, it is." He sucked in a breath, then asked, "And you're sure it's only yelling? No hitting?"

Jake's head popped up at that, his entire face contorting with his incredulous, "No! Geez, why would you think that? They just argue, is all." He smacked at a tear that had trickled down his cheek. "Sometimes it's not even loud or anything. It's just like…I dunno. Like they forgot how to talk to each other an' stuff."

"Maybe this night out will be good for them, then," Ben said. "Give them a chance to be alone, just with each other. So maybe they can figure out how to talk to each other again."

"Yeah, maybe," the kid said, but he didn't exactly sound hopeful.

"Sometimes it's tough, being a parent," Ben said, and the kid frowned up at him.

"How would you know? You don't have any kids, right?"

Right to the gut. "No, I don't. But I've been around. And besides your Mami and Papi Vargas always swore your dad and I drove them crazy."

A tremulous smile flickered across the child's face. "For real?"

"Oh, yeah. And they used to argue, too, now and then. Nobody's going to get along all the time, no matter how much they love each other. Sometimes, they're going to disagree about stuff. Loudly. Like your aunt said, it usually blows over—"

From the doorway, Mercy softly cleared her throat. Both Ben and Jacob twisted around. "I thought I'd make root beer floats—how does that sound?"

"Cool," Jacob said, grabbing his controller again. "Call me when they're ready, 'kay?"

"Sure thing, your highness," Mercy said on a soft laugh,

her expression sobering when she shifted her gaze to Ben. "Come help me in the kitchen?"

Uh, boy.

"What happened to your sidekick?" Ben asked easily, warily, as he followed Mercy down the hall.

"She passed out long before they found Nemo," Mercy said in a low voice. "No, leave her, I'll put her to bed in a bit."

"Brownies, popcorn, root beer floats…" Shaking his head, Ben leaned against the front of the sink, lowering his voice as well so as to not wake Mattie. "You trying to poison these kids or what?"

"It's a party, I'm hardly going to serve them Brussels sprouts. And I overheard a lot of what you said to Jake."

Yeah, he figured this was coming. "You're not going to even apologize for eavesdropping, are you?"

The refrigerator's compressor jerked awake when she opened the freezer to get out the ice cream, then the fridge itself for the bottle of root beer. "Nope."

"And do I detect an edge to your words I should worry about?"

"It's not that I don't appreciate you trying to make the kid feel better, but…" She plunked both soda and ice cream onto the counter, frowning at him. "But giving him false hope when you don't really know the situation seems a little, I don't know. Presumptuous?"

"Because who the hell am I to come waltzing back into everyone's life and try to fix things I know nothing about?"

"Something like that, yeah."

"I was only following your lead."

"I know, I know," she said on an exhaled breath. "Reach

me those goblets over the sink, would you? Only three, Mattie's down for the count, I'm sure." As he retrieved a trio of heavy, short stemmed glasses, she said, "Somehow, hearing the BS coming out of your mouth made me realize how ridiculous it must have sounded coming out of mine."

Ben frowned, only half watching Mercy pour the root beer into the glasses. "What little I was around Tony and Anita the other day…things definitely seemed tense. But do you think their marriage is in that much trouble?"

"Honestly? I don't know. I've tried to bring up the subject with my sister, but she won't bite."

"Which isn't a good sign."

Obvious worry deepened the faint lines already bracketing her mouth. "No. It isn't."

Ben released a breath. "I guess I assumed the tension was due to Tony's breaking his leg and they hadn't quite adjusted to how they were going to get through the next few weeks." Not to mention how Tony was going to deal with Ben's taking over for him during that time. That, Ben understood. Whatever was going on between his brother and Mercy's sister though…not a clue. "Tony's being a jerk, isn't he?"

"*Oh*, no," Mercy said, vigorously shaking her head. "There's no way I'm taking sides in this. For Jake's and Mattie's sakes, if nothing else."

"It's okay, I do remember what Tony can be like. Especially around women. To tell you the truth…well, I was kind of surprised that 'Nita and he even got together. I always thought she was smarter than that."

"Tell me that didn't come out the way you meant it."

He laughed a little. "Apparently not. And anyway, I guess I hoped either Tony'd gotten his head screwed on straight, or that 'Nita would be able to screw it on for him. But he's always had this weird attitude where women were concerned."

"I think the word you're looking for is *throwback*."

"Not that you're putting yourself in the middle or anything." When she smirked, he added, "And our folks have no clue, do they?"

"Are you kidding? God knows, Anita wouldn't say anything, she'd feel like a failure. Especially considering how thrilled they all were that the two of them got together. You'd have thought they'd made the perfect royal match. And in any case, I'm sure she really loves your brother."

"And you have no idea why."

"Please. I'm the last person to try explaining the workings of the human heart. Although, to give credit where it's due, he's definitely not a slacker—your father wouldn't get half the jobs he does if it weren't for Tony's getting out there and beating the bushes. And he loves his kids. Even if he does seem to think it's mainly 'Nita's job to keep them alive. Still…" Her brow furrowed. "I'm not sure which is worse— having our parents watch the slow, painful death of their kids' marriage, or getting blindsided by a possible divorce announcement."

Mercy scooped out the ice cream, carefully dropping it into the first glass of root beer. "Can I ask you something?" she asked softly.

"Like my saying 'no' would stop you."

"True," she said, a smile making a brief appearance. Another scoop of ice cream tumbled into the second glass.

"Given everything you said yesterday…" Her gaze veered to his. "Why'd you come over tonight? Assuming you didn't know the kids were here, I mean."

She had him there. "I'm not sure. It just seemed like the thing to do."

Again, she dipped the scoop into the carton. A glob caught on her knuckle when she drew it out; she licked it off and said, "Should I leave it at that?"

"I'd be immensely grateful if you would."

A low laugh rumbled from her throat. "Oh, admit it—" Her eyes sparkling with laughter, she leaned close and whispered, "I'm the flame and you're nothin' but a big old horny moth."

He met her gaze steadily, fearlessly. "You're dripping."

She flinched. "What?"

"The ice cream. It's dripping."

Swearing under her breath, she finished off the last float, then asked him to call Jacob.

A few minutes later, they woke a very drowsy Mattie to welcome in the New Year, after which Ben scooped the boneless little girl off the sofa and carried her to the twin-bedded room next to Mercy's. A dead weight against his chest, she smelled of popcorn, chocolate, girly shampoo and Mercy's perfume.

Mercy peeled back the covers so Ben could lay her down; she grabbed that disreputable stuffed kitty and curled onto her side, mumbling, "Love you, Uncle Ben," and almost instantly drifted back to sleep. With a squeaked meow, Homer hopped onto the bed, forming a tight, furry knot at the small of her back.

Ben straightened, his throat constricting as he watched Mercy draw the covers up over those defenseless little shoulders, reveling in a sense of belonging he'd deliberately ignored for far too long in the name of the "bigger" picture.

Jake begged to stay up a little longer to finish his game. "Fifteen minutes," Mercy said at her bedroom door, then continued to the living room, where she collapsed on the sofa, her toes curled on the edge of the trunk, her eyes closed.

"I should go," Ben said. "Let you get to sleep."

"We never got to the Baileys," she mumbled, her eyes still shut, then yawned.

"Maybe we should save it for another time."

Slowly—reluctantly—her eyes opened. "*Another* time?"

"You know what I mean."

She laughed. "Not only do I not know what you mean, I seriously doubt you do, either. No, it's okay," she said, vaguely waving one hand. "No explanation necessary." Her forehead crimped. "Bet you hadn't banked on walking into the middle of a domestic crisis."

"Can't say that I did. But—" he shrugged "—that's just part of being a family, right?"

"Ain't that the truth." Her eyes lowered to her knee; she stretched forward to pick off a piece of popcorn stuck to the glittery fabric, then looked back up at him. "Actually, I'm glad you came over. I didn't realize how much I needed to talk to somebody about all this stuff until there was somebody to talk to. Somebody not totally crazy, anyway. Okay, a different brand of crazy, maybe," she said when he chuckled. Again, she leaned back, her expression speculative. "It's good to have you home."

"Even if we don't…you know."

"Yeah," she said drowsily. "Because it was always more than that with you, too."

Over the sudden buzzing inside his skull, Ben quickly leaned over to kiss her on the forehead. "It's good to be here," he whispered, then let himself out.

And it *was* good to be back, he thought later, as he lay in the far-too-small twin bed in his old room, scratching a snoring rat-dog's upturned belly. Even though, if it had been sanctuary he'd sought, the joke was on him. Between leftover issues from the past and a heap of fresh ones from the present, he hadn't exactly walked back into a fifties sitcom.

Nor would he have ever believed how quickly a couple of kisses, and a conversation or two could bring the past rear-ending into the present. But apparently he'd carried Mercy's scent and feel and offbeat sense of humor with him, inside him, all these years like an old photograph. And worn and faded and cracked though it might be, all it took was a single glance to turn memories back into reality.

To turn "What if?" into "What now?"

Chapter Four

The week following New Year's passed uneventfully enough, Mercy supposed. Decorations came down and got put away, and life returned to its usual post-holiday stuttering, sluggish semblance of normalcy. Mercy sometimes saw Ben coming out of his parents' house, and they'd wave and say "How's it going?" and the other one would say, "Fine, you?" but that was pretty much the extent of their interaction.

All things considered, probably a good thing, she mused as she leaned heavily against one of the shop's glass counters, her head braced in one palm, morosely leafing through a display catalog. Since Ben—despite his showing up on her doorstep on New Year's Eve in a cloud of super-saturated testosterone—still clearly wasn't interested in starting something nobody had any intention of finishing. Nor, apparently, in a friends-with-benefits scenario.

She slapped to the next page. So why, exactly, was she morose again?

Other than the fact that it had been far too long since she'd gotten naked with anybody, that is. Or that, now that she'd done the kissy-face thing with Ben, Ben was the only "anybody" she cared to get naked with.

Sometimes, life was just plain cruel.

The bell over the door jingled. Mercy glanced up as a young mother with two very small boys in tow pushed her way inside. "Timmy, stay with me," the mother said to the older boy, an adorable curly-headed blond, then smiled her thanks when their part-timer, Trish, helped the mother settle her youngest into a collapsible stroller before leading them back to the baby and toddler section.

"So what do you think?" said Cass, one of Mercy's partners, leaning her tall, Eddie Bauer-ified frame against the case. Cotton sweater, cord skirt, shades of beige. Her feathery blond hair swept over her shoulders when she pointed to one of the photos. "Those heart-shaped balloons would look great tied in bunches in the centers of the displays, wouldn't they? We could give them away to the kids when they came in."

"Valentine's Day sucks," Mercy muttered, slapping down the next page.

"Hey. You've been grumpy all week. What gives?"

"PMS?" Mercy said without looking up.

"Nope, your chocolate binge was two weeks ago. Try again."

"Yeesh, you keeping track of my cycles now or what? So I'm just in a weird, rotten mood, okay? And sure, the balloons are fine." She flipped another page, keeping half an eye out for the little blond dude, who'd wandered back out to the front and was now holding a low, intense conversation with a panda bear in the stuffed animal display.

"And how about," Cass said, "a bunch of large foil hearts on the wall behind the cash register—"

"Don't press your luck. I'm having enough trouble with the balloons. *What?*" she said when the blonde poked her arm.

"What's his name?"

"Who?"

"Whoever's brought on this sudden, rabid hatred for Valentine's Day."

Mercy slammed shut the catalog, folding her arms over her white fur-blend sweater. "Nobody. It's just…" Her mouth thinned, she met Cass's amused—or maybe that was be-mused—blue-green gaze. "You know the last time somebody gave me a Valentine's card? Not counting my nieces and nephews? When I was *sixteen.* Is that pathetic or what?"

"Well, join the club, honey," came a chipper Southern accent from a few feet away.

Mercy glowered at Dana Turner, Great Expectations' third partner. Her happily married, undoubtedly-getting-it-and-she-didn't-mean-a-card-regularly partner. "Where the hell did you come from?"

"My, my, aren't we the cheery one this morning?" said the chestnut-haired beauty, her full cheeks adorably dimpled. "And the parking lot, actually." A long, soft cardigan skimmed a figure not dissimilar to Anita's, a thought which, seeing as Anita was married to Ben's brother, led right back to Ben. She was doomed.

They'd all three been single when they started up their little business. But in the past year both Cass and Dana had fallen in love—or in Cass's case, fallen back in love, with her first husband—gotten married, become mothers. Or close enough to count, Mercy thought as Dana whipped out the latest photo of Ethan, her husband's toddler son.

"Oooh," Trish—who happened to be not only Dana's cousin, but Ethan's biological mother—said, "Let me see."

An unorthodox arrangement, to say the least. But as long as it seemed to be working for all parties concerned, who was she to say? In any case, Mercy had been genuinely thrilled for both of her partners that they'd found something so precious. So this ridiculous and unexpected stab of…of *envy* made no sense. None. Because how could she be envious of something she didn't even want?

So what the hell, she was blaming Valentine's Day. And all the stupid, unrealistic romantic notions it engendered. Hearts, flowers, candy…piffle. She didn't need no stinkin' Valentine's Day—

"May I help you?" Mercy heard Trish say, and Mercy looked up to find herself caught in Ben's slightly lost gaze.

Heart, meet throat.

She practically mowed Trish down as she zipped out from behind the counter, but letting some twenty-something, big-eyed, sweet l'il ole Southern gal get her hooks in was not on her to-do list this morning. "Ben! What are you doing here?" Was it her, or did she seem to be asking that a lot these days?

And yes, those were three sets of eyes glued to the scene. He smiled. Behind her, somebody gulped. "I'm working on a site close by, and since it's Mattie's birthday next week, I figured this was as good a place as any to find a present."

"Oh! Right! And as it happens, she's got her eye on this really cool craft set, right over here…"

She glared at Dana's hand-waggle as she passed, ignored the *Ah…now I get it* look in Cass's eyes. Thankfully, the game and toy area was down the hall in another room entirely, and Mercy doubted whether even Dana and Cass would stoop so low as to follow. But then, you never knew.

She skimmed her fingertips along a long, wooden shelf. "Ah. Here it is."

Ben pulled it off the shelf, frowning at the box, and she stood there, inhaling him, not even caring if her brain exploded from pheromone overload. Any sane person would have moved out of range. Yeah, well…

"You sure this isn't too old? She's only going to be six."

"I know how old my niece is, Ben. Especially since I'm hosting the birthday bash. And no, it's fine. See?" She pointed to the age recommendation at the bottom of the box. "Ages four to ten. Trust me, she'll love it."

She saw Ben's head snap up as the little boy, the panda now clutched in his arms, wandered past the archway. "Is anybody keeping an eye on that kid?"

"We all are. And anyway, there's no place he can go. We keep the stairs and back hall gated. He's fine."

Still, Ben watched for another second or two until the boy's mother popped into view, taking him by the hand and steering him back into the clothing area. Ben breathed an audible sigh of relief, then distractedly put back the kit.

"About the other night…" His eyes slanted to hers, and her

heart wriggled loose from her throat to bounce back into her chest. Oh, goody—junior high flashback. "I had a great time."

"Playing video games and watching a kid's movie?"

"What can I say? I'm easily amused."

"Obviously." Their gazes wrestled for an interesting second or two before she looked away, straightening out a shelf that didn't need straightening. "And is there some reason it took you a week to tell me this?"

"Not really. I've just been busy." He picked the kit back up off the shelf. "So you really think this is good?"

Oh. Well. So much for that. Dredging up her most disarming smile, Mercy said, "Give her this and you'll be her best friend for life. Want it gift wrapped?"

"That'd be great."

She led him toward the counter, becoming increasingly annoyed with herself the longer the silence stretched between them without his asking her if she'd like to go to lunch. Or something. Gee, the you're-all-grown-up-now bolt could strike anytime now. Praise be, Dana and Cass were both in the office and thus not present to witness her humiliating regression to adolescence.

"Trish, would you please wrap this in the birthday paper? *Trish!*"

The young woman jumped, making the little crest of light brown hair fanning from the top of her head—not to mention assorted dangly earrings—frantically quiver. At least it was too cold to flash the belly button ring. "Oh, yeah, Mercy, right away. So…I take it you two know each other?"

"Our families have been neighbors forever," Mercy supplied shortly, ringing up Ben's purchase. Not looking at him. Ignoring the heat flooding her cheeks. She swiped his credit card, handed it back to him. "And my sister's married to his brother."

Behind her, Trish cut off a hunk of paper from one of the supersized rolls.

"Yeah? That's so cool, being friends that long. I don't have any friends left from when I was a kid, since I haven't been back home in, gosh, like ten years or something…."

Once again, the little boy tootled past, still hanging on to the bear, his thumb plugged into his mouth. Leaning casually against the counter, Ben said, "Hey, kiddo…where's your mama?"

Not about to let go of that thumb, the child spun around, then swung the panda in the direction of the back room.

"You think we should go find her?"

Out came the thumb with a soft pop. "I'm not s'posed ta go anywhere wif somebody I don't know, 'less Mommy says it's okay."

"Good boy," he said, and the baby grinned. Ben crouched to his level. "How old are you?"

Three fingers shot up.

"Wow. What a big kid!"

Another enthusiastic nod. "I know! I'm the big brover!" he said proudly, thumping his own chest.

Ben smiled and held out his hand, palm up. "Gimme five, big stuff." After they did the guy thing, Ben said, "But you know, it's probably a good idea not to go where you can't see Mommy, either. So tell you what—why don't you stand right here with these nice ladies, and I'll go tell her you're here, how's that?"

"'Kay."

Before Ben could straighten up, however, the mother appeared, annoyance flattening her mouth as she pushed her snoozing youngest one-handed in the stroller, a bunch of clothes draped over her other arm. "There you are! Honestly, Timmy—how many times do I have to tell you to stay with me?" She grabbed his hand and tugged him to her side, dispensing apologetic looks all around. "I hope he wasn't being a bother!"

"No, of course not," Mercy started, but one brief glance from Ben squelched her reassurance. And sprouted more than a few questions inside Data Processing Central.

"With all due respect, ma'am," he said levelly, "your son's only three. You're lucky this is a small place, and all these ladies are good at watching out for the customers' kids. But what if this had been Wal-Mart or someplace like that?"

Mercy could see the woman bristling. "Then he would have been in the cart," she snapped. "Are you implying I can't take care of my own child?"

"Not at all. But since he seems to wander so much, you might want to consider one of these…" He reached past Mercy to unhook a child's harness and tether from a display by the register.

The mother let out a gasp and visibly recoiled. "No way am I putting my child on a *leash!*" She threw the items in her hand at Trish and hustled both her children toward the door. On a gasp, Mercy hustled right after her.

"I'm so sorry, ma'am, I'm sure he didn't mean anything by it—"

Too late. She was gone.

Mercy wheeled around, flapping her hands at Trish to put everything back. "Gee, thanks, Ben," she said. "Anytime I need to clear customers out of the store, I'll know who to call."

He gave her a funny look. "Better you lose a sale than she lose her child," he said, picking up his wrapped package and sweeping past her. When he hit the door, though, he said, "And you might want to think about installing some security cameras, or at least mirrors. This setup you've got here is a nightmare waiting to happen."

Mercy was still gawking at the door when Trish returned. "Geez," she said, "what was up with the testosterone tsunami?"

Indeed.

Like sporadic bursts of gunfire, Tony and Anita's raised voices assaulted Ben's ears the minute he got out of his truck. He walked up to the front door anyway, one hand propped on the stucco wall while he waited for someone to answer the doorbell. His cell rang; he unclipped it from his belt, checked the number, his mouth pulling flat as he deliberately ignored it. For now.

Mercy's sister did the honors, greeting him with a smile as bright as the teddy bears adorning her wrinkled scrubs, one that warred with both the weariness and annoyance flooding her dark eyes.

"Just came to give Tony an update," he said as a squealing Mattie, still in her little plaid jumper and white blouse from school, zoomed over to him. Ben flew her up into his arms, grinning when she planted a big, sloppy kiss on his cheek.

"Yuck!" she said, the bridge of her nose wrinkled as she swiped the back of her hand across her mouth. "You're all scratchy!"

"Mattie, honestly," Anita said, swatting her daughter lightly on her bottom before chuckling, Ben returned her to terra firma. With a wave, the little girl scampered off. "Yeah, he said you might drop by. Come on in, but enter at your own risk. The place is a holy mess. Tony!" she hollered over the sounds of dueling televisions, their German Shepherd alternately whining and barking his head off at the patio door. "Ben's here!"

"'Nita…" He waited until he had her attention, then asked in a low voice, "Is everything…okay?"

He didn't miss the flinch. "Sure, everything's fine. Why do you ask?"

"No reason. You look beat, that's all."

She seemed to relax. "It's just been totally nuts at work. We had ten mothers give birth yesterday, and only three of us on duty. That was rough. Then I get home, and there's homework to see to and laundry and…well. I'm sure you don't want to hear about any of that, Mr. Bachelor."

"Doesn't Tony help with the homework?" Ben asked mildly. "Pop always did with us."

Wariness peered out from her eyes before she shrugged. "Yeah, well, half the time he comes to me, anyway, moaning that he doesn't get it, so he ends up confusing the kids more than helping. It's easier on everybody if I do it. Hey—wanna stay for dinner? I brought home enough KFC for an army."

"Thanks, but I think Mom said something about green chile stew. Which she apparently hasn't made in years, so my butt would be in a major sling if I don't show up."

"Hell, maybe we should *all* show up—"

"Mom!" boomed from down the hall. "Mattie's bugging me!"

"Oh, for the love of…Mattie!" Anita yelled, her voice trailing off as she disappeared down the hall, the hem of her top twitching with each movement of her round hips. "Leave your brother alone, baby, so he can do his homework!"

Ben shook his head, relieved in a strange sort of way. Maybe yelling was just the way people communicated with each other around here.

"I'm telling you," Tony said as he hobbled into the living room on his crutches. "These things are a bitch." He fell into a recliner, levering it back to prop his feet up on the rest as the crutches dropped with a clatter onto the carpet beside him. After his initial blowup that first day, Tony had apparently decided to bury his personal feelings about Ben's return at least enough for them to work together. Tension still bubbled just beneath the surface, even if everyone was choosing to ignore it. For the moment. "Did I hear something about Mom making green chile stew?"

"That's what she said."

"Man…" Tony shook his head, the very picture of sorrowfulness. "I can't remember the last time 'Nita put something on the supper table that didn't come in a foam takeout box or outta the microwave."

Ben shoved aside the Sunday paper, Jake's backpack, and a pair of skinny, big-haired dolls with abnormally large chests—he frowned at that one—to perch on the edge of the tan leather sofa, his hands linked between his knees. "I imagine she's pretty worn out by the time she gets home from work."

"Which she wouldn't be if she quit." When Ben frowned, Tony pushed out a frustrated breath. "I keep telling her, we don't need her salary, I can take care of all of us just fine on what I bring home. But no. She's got this thing about 'keeping her hand in,' or something, says she'd go bananas if she had to stay home all day. So instead the house always looks like crap and I haven't had a decent meal in years. And why are you looking at me like that?"

"I'm trying to see the marks left from the rock you clearly crawled out from under. Where do you get these ideas? Certainly not from our parents. Mama worked, too, remember?"

"Part-time. And not until we were in middle school. And she still kept up the house and all that."

"'Nita's not Mama," Ben said, walking right into the line of fire with his eyes wide open. A character trait he was obviously never going to shake. "Which you knew when you married her. She always wanted to be a nurse, you know that. And she loves her work. So why should she give it up for the privilege of cleaning your house and cooking your meals?"

His brother's face collapsed into a glower. No surprise there.

"And where do you get off, *hermanito,* handing out family advice when you haven't even been around for the past ten years? At least I stuck around. *I* went into the business with Pop instead of drifting all over the place like a damn tumbleweed. You broke their hearts, Benny. Bet you didn't know that, did you? Hell, I bet you didn't even give them a second thought when you took off."

"That's not true, Tony." Ben pushed out through the hot, hard knot at the base of his throat. But his brother was on a tear and didn't hear him.

"An' hey—at least I *got* a family. And a home. What've you got to show for your thirty-five years, huh? *Nada.* Not a damn thing. So maybe you should stop and think about that before you go spouting off at the mouth about stuff you don't know jack about."

"Okay, you two, enough," Anita said tiredly from the entry, walking over to halfheartedly shuffle the stacks of magazines and newspapers on the glass-topped coffee table into some semblance of order. "God, I would've thought you'd both be past all this sibling rivalry crap by now."

"I'm jus' saying…" Tony started, but Anita shut him up with a glare.

"How Ben chooses to live his life is nobody's business but his," she said. Then she straightened up, her hands on her hips, as the glare veered in Ben's direction, giving him a pretty good idea of exactly how much of the conversation she'd overheard. "But Tony's right. Seems to me you're in no position to be doling out domestic advice. Now. You two got work stuff to talk about, I suggest you get on with it. 'Cause KFC is gross when it gets cold."

Which they did, because neither of them was about to let this thing between them jeopardize the business their father had spent thirty years building from scratch. Still, Tony's words had sliced a lot more deeply than Ben was about to let on, especially in the light of all those feelings that being with Mercy and the kids on New Year's had brought to the surface.

But then, wasn't this why he'd come home? To face everything he'd been ignoring for far too long?

The question plagued him all through dinner with his parents, as he talked new construction methods with his father, listened to his parents' good-natured Spanglish bickering while his mother's dogs pranced on their hind legs, begging.

"No, no, I'll get that," his mother said when they were done and Ben tried to help her clear the table as the Chihuahuas went bonkers, scurrying around like bug-eyed, big-eared bumper cars. "You go on into the family room, spend some time with your father."

Ben gathered up their plates and silverware anyway, carting it all over to the counter. "I will. I need to make a quick call first, though." Then, impulsively, he gave his mother a one-armed hug. "Thanks for dinner. It was great."

Her eyes sparkled. "If I didn't know better, I'd think you missed my cooking."

"Now why would you think that?"

"Could be the three bowls of stew you put away."

"Could be," he said, and she gently swatted his head.

He didn't bother putting on his jacket before slipping outside, ambling toward the street. The afternoon had felt almost springlike, but par for the course in the high desert, when the sun went down the temperature plummeted right with it. Within seconds, the cold seeped through Ben's flannel shirt; his nose tickled with the pungent, hot-dog-roast scent of fireplace smoke. He breathed it in, letting it settle him. Ground him. Across the street, Mercy's house was dark. Huh. It was after seven and she wasn't home yet?

Not that it was any of his business. Except for his visit to the store earlier, they hadn't seen or talked to each other since New Year's. Because, he realized after a good night's sleep—as good as could be expected, at least—how could he even begin to do something about that until he figured out what to do about *this*. He dug his cell out of his shirt pocket.

"Hey, Roy," he said softly when the man on the other end picked up.

"So. You are listening to your messages. Have you decided yet?"

Ben was silent for a moment, watching Mercy's car pull up into her driveway. "And I told you before I left, this was open-ended."

"Oh, come on, Ben—broken legs don't take that long to heal. Six, eight weeks, tops—"

"Roy. Don't."

On the other end, a huge sigh preceded, "You not coming back—you and I both know that's hogwash. This isn't about what you do, Ben. It's who you are."

"And somebody's been watching way too much daytime TV."

"I'm serious. You're one of the best. And you know it." When Ben didn't respond, Roy said, "What happened wasn't your fault. You know nobody's blaming you."

"Maybe not. But it definitely cut things a little too close for my comfort."

"Yeah," the other man said quietly. "It's hell findin' out you're not infallible."

Ben massaged the space between his eyes, then let his hand drop. "This isn't about me being infallible. Or not. It's about me realizing maybe I don't want to check out before I've had a chance to explore a few more options."

Across the street, Mercy killed her car lights, swung open her door. She climbed out of her Firebird, doing a double take when she noticed him standing there. She slammed shut her door and started in his direction, a breeze tugging at all those shiny curls.

"I've gotta go," Ben said.

"Fine. But stay in touch, you hear me?"

"Sure thing."

Ben clapped his phone shut and slipped it back into his

pocket, watching Mercy's deliberate, measured approach as she crossed the street, one hand stuffed in the pocket of her open, ankle-length red coat, the other tightly clutching the strap of one of those metallic, fish-scaly purses he saw all over the place these days. Loosely wrapped around her neck, a flimsy, pale green scarf fluttered around her, like limp bug wings. His eyes traveled down, past the tight jeans to those pointy-toed, sky-high-heeled boots.

Just looking at her, his pulse kicked up a notch.

She came to a stop a few feet in front of him; the air stirred, disseminating her musky, heady perfume, and he took a deep breath, both to drink in her scent and keep his head from exploding.

"Don't cut your conversation short on my account," she said.

"I didn't. In fact, you showing up gave me a good excuse to end it."

Curiosity flickered briefly across her features before she said, "So. Care to explain why you overreacted in the store this morning? About the little boy?"

"I didn't—"

"Uh, yeah. You did. I told you we were all keeping an eye on him. In fact, the parents who come into the store know they *don't* have to worry about anything happening to their kids while they're shopping. But I'd like to think they don't have to worry about some yahoo embarrassing the hell out of them, either."

Ben's jaw tightened. "Look, I'm sorry if I cost you a sale—"

"Oh, screw the sale, Ben. And it's not as if I don't understand how that mother's attitude might have seemed a little cavalier to you. Or ours. Just because I don't like thinking about the scary stuff doesn't mean I don't know it happens.

Or that I—we—shouldn't be on our toes. Why do you think we *sell* the harnesses, for cripe's sake? But she wasn't in Wal-Mart, she was the only customer in a small store with only one way in or out. The chances of somebody making off with her kid were virtually nil. Which you can't tell me you didn't know, your macho man act notwithstanding."

They stared each other down for several moments before, on a sharp exhale, Ben said, "I didn't mean to upset that mother. I swear. I just…" He dug through his brain for an explanation he figured she'd buy. Yeah, telling her the truth would be the obvious choice, but he wasn't ready for the fallout that would inevitably cause. "You remember the one time when we were kids, and our parents took us all to the fair? And I got separated from the rest of you?"

"I don't…oh, wait a minute! We were on the midway, right? And Carmen and 'Nita and I were arguing with our folks that we were too old for the dumb kiddy rides, and we turned around and you were gone." She laughed. "My sisters and I were already miffed at being stuck with the stupid *boys.* Then you ran off and all we could think was how much time we were losing while our fathers had to go look for you."

"And here all these years I'd envisioned tears streaming down your little faces, because you were all worried about me."

She snorted. "Oh, there were tears, all right. Tears of profound annoyance. I believe Carmen called you a doo-doo head." Another laugh bubbled out of her throat. "And Livvy started singing *Doo-doo head, doo-doo head* from her stroller, which shattered our poor mothers' last nerves. Carmen was so busted." Still chuckling, Mercy shook her head. "God,

Ben, I can't believe you remember that. You couldn't've been more than what? Four?"

"Five. And for years I had nightmares about wandering around by myself…" He shuddered. "All those legs, and the bright lights, and those weird, scary dudes in the booths with all the stuffed animals…"

"Yeah, I've had a nightmare or two about those weird, scary dudes myself. But for heaven's sake, Ben, you weren't gone for more than five minutes."

"Believe me, it seemed like a lifetime. Anyway, whenever I see a little kid wandering off on his own like that, I guess I flash back a little."

After several seconds, Mercy shook her head.

"What?"

"Not a half-bad attempt at covering your butt. Except you forget—" she smiled "—I know exactly what that butt looks like. But if it makes you feel better—and yes, that would be me giving you an out—I talked it over with Cass and Dana, and they agree it wouldn't hurt to at least put in security mirrors until we can afford something more sophisticated. We probably should have done it months ago, anyway, just to mitigate the shoplifting factor if nothing else."

"Sounds like a plan to me."

"We thought so." The purse slipped, sparkling and flashing like mad in the security light; Mercy hiked it back up on her shoulder. "Well. 'Night." Then she stepped off the curb, and Ben found himself wrestling with the idiotic sensation that she was taking his breath with her.

"Hey, uh…wanna go get a cup of coffee or something?"

Already to the middle of the street, she turned. "Why?"

Ben pushed out a weary laugh. "You know, it amazes me how women can split a simple question into a thousand layers. All I'm asking is, would you like to go have coffee with me? Because it's cold out here and in there—" his head jerked back toward his parents' house "—is a minefield. And over there—" he nodded toward hers "—is even worse."

A sly smile snaked across her mouth. "Without our little chaperones, you mean?"

Damn. "They do come in handy," he said.

"I see. Don't trust yourself? Or don't trust me?"

"I don't trust…us."

Her brows shot up. "Wow. I wasn't expecting *honest.* But you see…" She walked back to stand right in front of him, her eyes deep and dark and far too discerning. "There *were* layers, weren't there? Not a thousand, maybe. But enough. Because I figured out some time ago that that whole 'simple' schtick you guys have going? It's just a ruse to get us to quit trying to dig below the surface. Because, according to male lore, this isn't anything below the surface. The surface is all there is. Well, guess what, bud?" She shoved her hair out of her face, leaned close enough for him to feel her breath, a warm, weightless caress across his jaw, and whispered, "*I don't buy it.*"

Her keys jangled loudly in the stillness when she fished them out of her pocket. "But in any case, thanks but no. I've been on my feet all day, and frankly all I want to do is take a long bath and hit the hay. Besides, I need to see if Homer's around."

Ben frowned. "He run away again?"

"Yeah," she said with a sigh. "Couple nights ago. I know he's okay, but…I miss the big lug, y'know? So, I assume I'll see you at Mattie's party on Sunday?"

"Wouldn't miss it. Hey," he called to her back as she again started across the street. "Is it just me, or was that the world's most convoluted blow-off?"

Her laughter drifted back to him on the breeze.

Doofus-brain was indeed whining piteously at the back patio door when Mercy walked into the house. Ignoring the stupid surge of relief she felt every time the thing returned, she clunked her purse and keys onto the breakfast bar and wrenched open the door. Rumbling like a power saw, the cat launched himself at her shins, peering up at her from time to time with those big, soulful, amber eyes as he pushed out yet another strained little cry. Because, you know, he was about to keel over from hunger and all.

And because Mercy was a total pushover, the instant she dumped her coat she clicked across the tiled floor to the cupboard for a can of Fancy Feast. Homer's dish filled, she hunkered down beside him, her chin resting on her knees as she stroked his smoked turkey-scented fur. Unlike some cats who didn't like to be messed with while they ate, Homer's philosophy ran along the lines of as long as the food was going in, she could do anything she wanted to him.

Come to think of it, she'd known a few guys like that in her time, too.

She sighed, twice, then slid down onto her butt on the not-as-clean-as-it-should-be kitchen floor to lean her back against the cabinet. If she were smart, she'd just grit her teeth until Ben left. Put him right out of her pretty little head. Unfortunately, he didn't seem terribly interested in vacating the premises.

"The thing is, cat," she said, plucking pieces of God-knows-what out of his fur, "I can't figure out what Ben and I are to each other. Is he an old friend or an ex-lover?" The cat looked up at her and meowed. "Oh, don't give me that scandalized look. Like you couldn't figure that out? Then again, what do you know, you're a eunuch." Homer *brrped* indignantly, then promptly hauled himself onto her lap to regale her with cat-food breath. Mercy sank both hands into his ruff and started to scratch. "But then, there's not much point in thinking about any of it, is there? Well, there was that whole 'wanna go have coffee' thing. Oh, right, you weren't around for that. Yeah, he asked me out for coffee."

Homer reared back, his eyes narrowed.

"I know, I know, usually that's manspeak for 'let's have sex.' But not this time. At least, I don't think so." On yet another sigh, she clunked her head back against the whitewashed wood. "Dammit, Home—why don't men come with user manuals—"

The doorbell sent the cat flying off her lap, leaving many little perforations on her thighs. Swearing, Mercy hauled herself to her feet and hobbled to the door, massaging her butt to get the blood flowing again. Her mind tore through the short—or in her case, fairly long—list of possibilities: Ben, her mother, any of her sisters, your friendly neighborhood psychopath…

Clutching her down jacket at her neck but still shivering in the cold, Anita gave her a weak smile. "Got anything stronger than Kool-Aid?"

Chapter Five

Uh-oh. In fact, Mercy guessed this was the Mother of All Uh-Ohs.

"A cheap California red from two Christmases ago?" she said.

"Hell, at this point I'd take nail polish remover," her next youngest sister said, coming inside and following Mercy to the kitchen. As Mercy climbed onto her kitchen stool to retrieve the hitherto-forsaken bottle of wine from a top cupboard, her sister regaled her with bits and pieces of a conversation she'd overheard between Tony and Ben earlier that evening.

"Wow," Mercy said, dusting the bottle off with a dish towel. "Ben really stuck up for you like that?"

"Yeah, but that's not the point. The point is, Tony's still

being a butt about me working. And I've pretty much given up on his ever *not* being a butt about me working."

"I take it you've talked it over with him."

"Only until I'm blue in the face. Thanks," she said when Mercy handed her a glass of wine, downing half of it before coming up for air. "Only it wasn't until tonight that it hit me—I think he's deliberately refusing to help around the house, waiting for me to crack."

"If you haven't cracked in ten years, what makes him think you will now?"

"Yeah, well, you keep dripping water on the rock long enough, eventually it wears down. And how come you don't look surprised?"

"Sweetie, I hate to break it to you, but you and Tony…" Mercy took a sip of her own wine, made a face. Maybe nail polish remover would be better. "It's pretty obvious the two of you aren't exactly lovey-dovey these days."

"But that's the weird thing. The sex is almost as good as it ever was." At Mercy's raised brows—half of her didn't want to know, but it was that train-wreck thing—Anita sighed. "After ten years, sure, things slow down. The kids, our work…they take a toll. At least on the frequency. But when they do happen, they really happen."

"So…your night out on New Year's…?"

"What can I say?" she said acerbically. "Get us away from the house and our issues, pour a few drinks in us, and it's twelve years and fifty pounds ago." She took another slug of her wine, grimacing this time. "God, this stuff really *is* awful. Whoever brought it to you should be shot. But the point is—" she swished the wine around in her glass, as if maybe that would improve it "—great sex every couple of weeks isn't enough. Not for me, anyway. And I'm tired of fighting, of trying to change things that aren't going to change. Of trying to change a *man* who's never going to change. So, as soon as Mattie's birthday's over…" Tears swam in her eyes. "I'm seriously thinking of separating."

"Oh, honey…" Mercy's glass clinked onto the counter; Anita held hers out. Mercy refilled it, waiting until Anita'd knocked it back before tucking her hand in her sister's on top of the bar. "Isn't that a little drastic? I mean, maybe you should try, I don't know, counseling or something first?"

"Already did. Tony refused to go after the second session."

"Oh. Wow. I didn't know."

"Nobody did. I'd hoped…" Anita drew in a deep breath, letting it out on a shuddering, "I'd hoped we could fix things without anybody finding out. Because you don't have to say it, I know this is going to kill Ma."

Mercy squeezed her sister's hand. "No, it won't. If she survived raising five girls, I think she'll survive this."

"But Carmen—"

"Was the first. It probably gets easier with practice?"

That got a tiny, soft laugh.

"What about the kids, though?" Mercy asked.

Anita shrugged sadly. "Part of me thinks it's better to stick it out for their sakes. At least until they're older. But I know they're picking up on the tension."

They're doing a helluva lot more than that, Mercy wanted to say. But her sister had enough to deal with without adding that to the pile. At least, not now.

"Do you still love him?" Mercy asked softly.

Her sister's eyes cut to hers, her mouth pulled tight. "Are you asking that because you hope I do, or hope I don't?"

"What *I* think has nothing to do with it—"

"C'mon, Merce—you've never liked Tony."

"Well, I wouldn't have wanted to marry him. Which, considering, I would have thought was a good thing."

Another little laugh. "I know Tony was—is—a little rough around the edges. But underneath all that…there's a good man in there, somewhere. Pig-headed, yes. But good." Then she sighed. "But this business with Ben…" She shook her head, then lifted her glass to her lips again.

"What business with Ben?"

"What do you think?" she said, gesturing with her nearly empty glass. "The way Luis always favored Ben over Tony. You never noticed?" Mercy shook her head. "Yeah. Ben could do no wrong in his father's eyes. Even after he left, even though every time Juanita or Luis talked about Ben, it was with all this disappointment in their voices, like they couldn't figure out where they'd gone wrong. Tony, on the other hand…"

Her brows knit, she ran one short-nailed finger around the rim of her wineglass. "Once Ben was out of the picture, Tony thought maybe *finally* Luis would start giving him some credit, you know? Because Tony was the good one, see, the one who stayed, the one who did follow his dad into the business. But it's been ten *years,* Merce," she said, tears crested on her lower lashes, "and Luis still won't acknowledge everything Tony's done."

Mercy reached for a tissue box by the kitchen phone, handed it to her sister. "Do you hear yourself?" she said gently. "Hate to tell you this, honey, but this does not sound like a woman ready to leave her husband."

Anita honked into a tissue. "Just because I wish Luis would see Tony for who he is doesn't mean I don't wish Tony would see me for who *I* am, too. But on that score…" One hand came up, pointing unsteadily in Mercy's direction. "You mark my words, when this hits the fan, it's not my side they're going to take."

"Why would you think that? Juanita and Luis love you."

"They love that I gave them grandkids. But Luis actually took me aside one day and said—get this—that me working keeps Tony from feeling like *the man*."

"That's insane."

"Not to mention prehistoric. Although they do love to throw Ma's never working outside the house in my face."

"Yeah, because she had five kids in like as many minutes. And she never *wanted* an outside job. But you know damn well Ma was thrilled when you got your nursing degree."

Anita pinned her with a now slightly bleary gaze. "And from seeds such as these are family feuds grown…crap," she muttered, nearly falling from the stool to grab her coat off the end of the counter, digging into the pocket for her cell phone. "Yeah, baby," she said after she answered. "I'll be home soon, I'm just over at Aunt Mercy's… Sure, you pick out two books you want me to read, we'll do it as soon as you've had your bath, okay?… A few more minutes. See you soon, baby."

She clapped shut the phone, holding it to her chest, staring out into space as if she'd forgotten Mercy's presence. Mercy reached up and smoothed a curl off her sister's face, smiling a little when the conflicted eyes veered in her direction. "You look exhausted," she said. *And slightly drunk,* which she didn't. How the woman thought she was going to read to the kids, she had no idea.

"There's an understatement," Anita said on a sigh, then frowned. "Did I ever thank you properly for taking the kids on New Year's?"

"*De nada.* They tell you that Ben came over, too?"

"Did they ever. I think Mattie's in love. Aiyiyi, every five minutes, it's 'Uncle Ben' this or 'Uncle Ben' that. You can imagine how well *that's* going over with Tony." Anita shifted on the stool, propping her chin in her palm. "And…is that interest I see in *your* eyes?"

Okay, maybe not so drunk. Unfortunately. "What that is," Mercy said, "is cheap wine shorting out my neurons."

Her sister laughed, then slid off the bar stool to stand on wobbly legs. "You do realize we all know you and Ben had a thing before he went away."

Mercy stilled. "Excuse me?"

"Mercedes. Please. We weren't blind."

After several seconds of sparring gazes, Mercy sighed. "You *all* knew?"

"Are you kidding? Miss Nobody's-Good-Enough-For-Me gets it on with the bad-boy-next-door? That's seriously hot stuff, *chica*. We were *so* scandalized." She grinned. "And envious as hell. So…are things heating up again?"

Mercy stared her down. "Do I *look* like someone with a death wish?"

"Yeah, but what a way to go," Anita said, slipping her coat back on. At Mercy's front door, she turned and said, "By the way, I cannot tell you how grateful I am you're doing this birthday party for Mattie. At this point I think it would take me under."

"I'm sure. And hey, anytime I'm around, you want to send the kids over, feel free. I'm serious," she said when Anita made protesting noises. "I'm crazy about the little rug rats, and you need the break." Mercy hesitated, then said, "Look, God knows I'm no expert here, but maybe you and Tony just need more time alone to hash out a few things. And don't shake your head at me, I heard what you said. I also heard what you didn't say. It's not Tony you want to divorce, it's his attitude."

Again, her sister's eyes filled with tears. "Am I crazy for still loving him?"

"*Love* is crazy," Mercy said, then smiled. "Or so I've heard. So you need to fight for him, sweetie. You've got one helluva arsenal there," she said, nodding toward her sister's ample bosom. "Might as well use it."

Anita choked on a laugh, then opened Mercy's door, wiping her eyes on her sleeve. "I don't suppose I have to tell you not to say anything. To the folks."

"Last time I checked, I didn't have the word *idiot* stamped on my forehead, so I think we're good." She drew her sister into her arms, rubbing her back. "It'll work out, you'll see." Then she let go, saying, "Let me get my keys, I'll drive you home—"

"No, it's okay, I walked." Anita dug in her pocket for a stick of gum, shoving the unwrapped piece into her mouth. "The air will sober me up."

"Fine. But you call me when you get there!" Mercy called out to her sister's retreating form.

Afterwards, though, Mercy wondered where she got off reassuring her sister about something she'd become more cynical about with every passing year. At the moment, the success-in-romance ratio for the Vargas sisters wasn't looking so good—one divorce, one marriage on the rocks, and one sister with a remarkable propensity for picking losers—

Okay, run that by her again?

But it was true. Because despite her oft-sung I'm-good-with-being-single refrain, choice hadn't been the sole deciding factor in Mercy's lone wolfette lifestyle. In fact, her contentment probably spoke more to an adapt-or-die philosophy that had guided her since birth. A good philosophy to have, she thought wryly as she threw together a chef's salad, when life seems determined to toss you its dregs.

Or, when something good finally washes up on your shores, and the tide carries it right back out again.

Mercy lit a pair of candles, then sat at her dinette table, Homer stretching to hook his claws on the table's edge beside her, begging. She tossed him a pinch of ham, which he inhaled. Yeah, old Benny-boy was just like this dumb cat. A chronic wanderer, the type who skirted the edges of anything resembling a real relationship. Sure, the sparks were still there between them, which was why she definitely wouldn't have minded a reprise of their affair. And the friendship, which, she now realized, probably did complicate things too much to once again trip over that particular stone. Still, she doubted his refusal to mess around a second time stemmed as much from nobility as it did sheer self-preservation.

Mercy's land line rang; a moment later she heard, "*Just me, I'm home, don't bother answering.*" She got up anyway, forking in dressing-soaked greens as she walked across the room to close her blinds. One hand on the wand, she peered outside to catch a glimpse of Ben inside his parents' open, lit garage. He was on his phone again. Evidence, she supposed, of his life away from here. His real life, she reminded herself.

A life that had nothing to do with her.

The dozen balloons tethered to Mercy's mailbox, eye-popping bright against the grays and beiges of the winter day, brought it all back in an instant. Oh, yeah, Ben thought as he crossed the street, his present for Mattie buried in the towering stack he carried from the pair of indulgent grandparents walking beside him, these people knew how to *celebrate*.

Teeth-rattling salsa pulsed from inside when Rosie, Mercy's very pregnant next-to-youngest sister, opened the door. "Benicio!" she cried, dragging him across the threshold to strangle him in a brief hug. Shiny red lips erupted into a smile; with her short, spiked hair and funky makeup and earrings, she could have easily passed for a teenager instead of a thirty-something mother of three. And eight-ninths. "Abby!" she then called to her daughter, a skinny girl of about nine or ten who emerged from the crowd and noise, giving him a smile. "Show Uncle Luis where to put the presents, then take Aunt Juanita's food to the kitchen," Rosie said with a quick smile for Ben's mother, who'd helped raise the Zamora girls as much as Mercy's mother had helped keep Ben and Tony from running amok, more than earning her the honorary title.

"You look great," Ben said after the crowd swallowed up the girl and his parents. "When's this one due?"

"Not soon enough, unfortunately. And no, I don't know whether it's a boy or a girl, so don't ask. It's not like it matters, right? Anyway, food's on the dining table, help yourself. Mingle. Get reacquainted. The men are all huddled together somewhere, probably in Mercy's bedroom watching a game." And with a little wave, she was gone.

The tiny house was jammed to the gills with bodies, laughter, music, food. As expected, the living area had been birthdayfied within an inch of its life, balloons and twisted streamers in every color imaginable hugging the walls, the ceiling. Ben chuckled though, when he caught sight of Annabelle, still standing proudly in the corner, now adorned with tootie horns and leis, a purple foil birthday hat in the place of honor on top.

"Hey there," he heard beside him.

He looked down into Mercy's laughing eyes and it was like seeing the warm, beckoning light in the window after hours of trudging through a blizzard. Odd, considering the way they'd left things. Then again, this was Mercy. Not your gal if you liked things tidy and logical. As apparently Ben didn't, since, as the emotional dust stirred up by his return had begun to settle, it was becoming increasingly clear that his memories of her, of their time together, had been far more than the musings of a lonely man obsessing about his first really hot relationship.

The hot pink cousin of Annabelle's tree-topper nestled crookedly in her curls; a trio of leis practically hid—and clashed with—a lacy top nearly the same green as her sofa. A dozen kids of various ages streaked through the room behind them, their shrieks of laughter knifing through the din. In retaliation, somebody turned the music up louder. Forget peace and quiet—it was more like being dropped into the middle of Mardi Gras.

On impulse, he reached for Mercy's hand. One eyebrow

arched, but she didn't try to pull away. Instead, she leaned closer so he could hear her over the roar of music, children's laughter and conversation.

"You need introductions?"

"What I need is a beer."

"Follow me. But hang on tight, the undertow around here is vicious."

"These aren't *all* your nieces and nephews, are they?" he asked as she tugged him through the throng.

"No, at least ten of 'em are Mattie's friends from school. But you know us, any excuse for a party."

It seemed to take forever to navigate the twenty or so feet to her kitchen, where Vargas females of assorted ages vied for counter space and bragging rights. All conversation ceased, however, when Ben arrived, the expressions before him ranging from mild interest to rampant speculation to borderline hostility.

"Well, well, well," Carmen, Mercy's older sister, said with a slanted smile and a smoky voice. A dozen silver bangles clattered as she lifted her drink to Ben. "The prodigal has returned, in all his glory." Her dark, streaked waves tumbled across the sharp angles of her face as she set her drink on the counter, then looked up, crossing her arms over a black sweater. "And I do mean glory. My God, honey…where *did* you get those shoulders?"

"Didn't I tell you he filled out real nice?" Anita said, tossing him a grin as she uncovered his mother's dish.

"You guys have been talking about me?"

"Well, duh," Olivia, the baby sister, said from a chair by the kitchen table, spooning baby food into a little dark-haired boy's mouth, while another curly-haired imp leaned on her lap, regarding Ben with a soulful gaze. Still skinny even after four kids, Livvie flicked her long, straight hair behind one shoulder. "It's a lot more fun than clipping coupons."

"You know how it is," Mercy said, finally handing him that beer. "Handsome hunk, poor, bored housewives…"

"Hey!" Rosie said, smacking Mercy in the shoulder. "Take that back!"

"Yeah," Livvie said, peeling the older child off her lap so she could get up to yank a paper towel off the roller under the cabinet. "With four kids, who has time to be bored?"

"And may I remind you," Carmen said in her husky voice, adjusting the big collar on her sweater, "that some of us aren't wives at all, bored or otherwise."

Ben saw Anita and Mercy exchange a quick glance before his brother's wife carried the casserole from the room. "She okay?" Carmen said in a low voice to Mercy, who shrugged, at which point Carmen's gaze cut to Ben's.

"Hey," he said, lifting his hands. "I just got here. Don't look to me for answers. Or expect me to take sides."

"Yeah, easy for you to say," Carmen said, shoving her hair behind one ear to reveal a hula-hoop sized earring, "since you'll be outta here again in a few weeks, anyway."

And because there is a God, somebody's husband picked that moment to wander into the kitchen, said, "What the hell are you doing in here, man?" and dragged him away before he suffocated in all the girl-cooties.

But for all Ben willingly let himself be sucked into the football-and-food frenzy of Mercy's brothers-in-law, she was rarely far from his line of vision as she shepherded kids and adults through the various stages of a party only marginally less elaborate than an embassy dinner, often with some little niece or nephew hanging off her hip. She was totally in her element, with that silly little hat perched on her head, her long tiered skirt gracefully swishing around her legs as she zipped from room to room in a pair of high-heeled boots that wreaked havoc on his breathing.

He realized how easily he could pick out her laugh from the crowd.

How he kept one ear cocked for it, even in the midst of a conversation with someone else. On the other side of the house. And over the next two hours, new images accumulated in his head, as clear as any saved on a digital camera: Mercy crouched in front of a pair of toddlers, her skirt billowed around her, quietly diffusing a squabble; Mercy helping Mattie cut her birthday cake, hugging the little girl from behind as she held her tiny hand steady; Mercy rolling her eyes in ecstasy on her first bite of his mother's cheese enchiladas.

Mercy listening to Anita, head tilted, forehead creased in concentration as she held her sister's hand.

Regret pierced his otherwise mellow mood, that he'd been a fool for leaving her.

Only if he hadn't, he wouldn't be the man he was now.

And now was all that mattered. That, and the future. What he'd done, who he'd been, was irrelevant. As was whatever she'd been doing during that gap. Was her still being single a sign? Did it mean that, just maybe, there was a chance? That *he* had a chance at something he hadn't even known he'd wanted until he'd seen her locked in mortal combat with her juniper bush?

But want, he did, he realized on a rush so profound he almost shook with it.

He wanted…this, he thought as the party began to wind down. The family, the craziness, the sense of being part of something.

And most of all, he wanted Mercy.

Which was where things got hairy.

Because she'd made it pretty damn clear, hadn't she, that she wasn't looking for anything serious? Oh, sure, she'd come on to him like gangbusters that first day. But that was like…like channel-surfing and running across an old movie you'd thought was so great when you first saw it, so you watch it again just see if it's as good as you remember.

Doesn't mean you want to go out and buy a copy.

His mood suddenly souring, Ben grabbed one of the few remaining beers from the cooler in the kitchen and slipped out into Mercy's small, winter-drab backyard. Typical of the neighborhood, Mercy's patio was little more than a cement slab with a corrugated metal cover over it. But pots of assorted sizes lined the edges; Ben imagined them filled with all kinds of flowers during the summer. At least a dozen wind chimes hung from the eaves, pinging and bonging in the unseasonably warm breeze. Brew in hand, Ben leaned against one of the wrought-iron support posts, listening to a hundred finches twittering their heads off, way up in one of the tall, slender cypresses bordering the back cement wall.

He took a long swallow of his beer, only half aware of the dwindling, muffled party sounds behind him, when he heard the patio door open. The jangle of bracelets alerted him to Carmen's presence a second before he heard a gravelly, "God. Can't a girl sneak a smoke anywhere around here?"

Ben looked over, allowing a grin for Mercy's older sister. "Your secret's safe with me."

"Not that it's much of a secret," she said, lighting up and taking a deep drag, the breeze whisking away the smoke the moment it left her mouth. "But Ma getting on my case is more than I can deal with. Especially since I'd actually quit. Three years, not a single cigarette. Then the rat bastard cheats on me and drives me right back to it."

Ben weighed his words for a long moment, then said quietly, "Then he's won, hasn't he?"

Carmen's eyes cut to his before she shrugged, propping her back against another post. She lifted the cigarette to her lips again, blew out the smoke. "I would've thought you'd be long gone by now."

"Haven't figured out a way to break the gravitational pull."

"Yeah, I know how that goes." She flicked her ash into an empty plastic glass, then pinned him with her gaze. "Although in your case I'm guessing 'pull' is due primarily to my sister? And don't you dare ask 'which one?'. Speaking of not exactly a secret. Before you left, I mean."

Ben squinted out over the yard. "Ten years is a long time."

"Yeah, well, the older you get, the faster time zips by." Carmen tapped the cigarette against the edge of her glass, her earrings flashing through her waves as earnestly as all those wind chimes dangling from the overhang. "Bet you anything she remembers you taking off like it was yesterday."

He frowned. "She talked to you about it?"

"She didn't have to. Not that she moped around or took to her bed or anything. Unfortunately. The world would have been far better off if she had. Instead, we were treated to weeks of Mercedes at her crankiest. Since she couldn't get to you, she took out her extreme annoyance on all of us."

"I'm sorry."

"Heh. *You're* sorry."

"She says she got over it."

"Of course she *got over it.* You didn't break her heart, you just pissed her off. But that was then. This is now. And here's a word of warning, pal—I'm already dealing with one sister with Vargas man troubles, I sure as hell don't need another one. You mess with Mercy's head—or worse, her heart—and there will be hell to pay."

Ben did his best to control the grin trying its damnedest to hijack his mouth. As the oldest, Carmen had always been fiercely protective of her younger sisters, and both he and his brother—not to mention every other male their age in the neighborhood—had the scars to prove it. That she hadn't changed on that score was weirdly reassuring, in a God's-in-His-heaven kind of way. In this instance, unfortunately, he couldn't possibly assuage her concerns without divulging a thing or two he hadn't yet shared with Mercy.

Who, judging from her sister's out-for-blood stance on the issue, maybe wasn't quite so adamant about staying single as she let on?

Ben shifted against the post, giving the grin its head. "Carm?"

"What?"

"I hate to break this to you—but you don't scare me anymore."

"Honey," she said, stubbing out her cigarette in the bottom of the glass. "You do not want to cross a perimenopausal woman with the nasty taste of divorce still in her mouth." Her smile was clearly intended to shrivel certain parts of a man's anatomy. "Trust me, you do not know from scary. But you hurt my sister, and believe me, you will."

She stuffed the glass into a metal trash can by the back door and went back inside, as Ben considered the very real possibility that, if his plan backfired, *Mercy* wouldn't be the one who ended up getting hurt. But if he didn't put his butt on the line now, take that risk, he'd regret it for the rest of his life.

Then he pulled a plastic chair out from the wall, plunked that butt into it, and waited.

Chapter Six

"No, no, you don't have to do that," Mercy heard behind her when she went to load Juanita's empty casserole dish into the dishwasher. Everyone else, including Luis, had taken off ages ago, leaving Mercy with the uneasy feeling that Ben's mother had an ulterior motive for hanging around. "I can take it home," Juanita said. "Clean it myself."

Smiling, Mercy firmly shut the dishwasher and turned it on. "Too late. I'm only sorry there weren't any leftovers," she said as she hauled a half-full garbage bag out to the living room. "I was hoping to score lunch tomorrow. I've always been crazy about your enchiladas," she said, dumping a stack of frosting-smeared paper plates into the bag.

"And maybe that's not the only thing of mine you're crazy about?"

"Oh. Well, I sure wouldn't complain if some of your tamales found their way over here, either—"

"I'm not talking about my cooking, *querida.*"

Okay. She could play dumb, or cut to the chase. Either way, she was screwed, but playing dumb would only prolong the agony.

Another bunch of plates met their fate. "I take it you mean Ben?"

"*Si.*"

Mercy wasn't sure what she'd expected to see in Juanita's eyes when she finally looked over, but *misgiving* hadn't been in her top ten. "There's nothing going on between Ben and me. Well, except for being old friends."

Juanita gave an annoying if-that's-what-you-choose-to-believe shrug before saying, "Then I don't suppose you noticed how he couldn't tear his eyes away from you all afternoon?"

"What? Oh, um, well…no." Flushing, Mercy spun around to swipe a small herd of paper cups off the coffee table into the bag. "I've been kind of busy. And anyway, I really doubt that."

"You're calling me a liar?" Juanita said softly, the smile evident in her voice.

"No, of course not…" On a huff, Mercy plunked down on the trunk, the bag squished between her knees. "So are you trying to push us together, or warning me off? Because you can save your breath either way. You know Ben, he doesn't stay in one place long enough to gather dust. And I took myself off the market a long time ago."

Ben's mother slowly walked around the breakfast bar, laying one hand on Mercy's shoulder and looking deep in her eyes. "I have always loved you and your sisters like you were my own, you know that. And I see that look on Ben's face and part of me thinks…" Sighing, Juanita gently tugged at a wayward curl dangling by Mercy's temple. "Perhaps he *would* stay, if he had a good enough reason. Unfortunately, the other part of me worries that he's in danger of giving his heart to someone who doesn't really want it."

Mercy blanched. "Juanita! I—"

"Shush, little one, I'm only telling you how things look from where I'm standing. I only want what's right for both of you. But Ben—"

"—is your son. I get it."

After patting Mercy's shoulder, Juanita headed for the front door. "I need to get back, Luis wants to go see some new action movie." She rolled her eyes. "So would you tell Ben we won't be home until after nine?"

Mercy frowned. "What do you mean, *tell Ben*?"

One hand on Mercy's door, Juanita smiled. "What is it they say about 'right in your own backyard'…?"

The patio door ground across its track when she pushed it open. And yep, there he was, sprawled in one of her plastic lawn chairs, eyes shut, legs extended, feet crossed at the ankle.

"Dude. Didn't you get the memo that the party's over?"

Ben swung that hazy, lazy gaze to hers, one corner of his mouth slowly tilting. "Did you think I'd leave without saying goodbye?"

"You? Leave without saying goodbye? Can't imagine why I'd think that."

He grimaced. "Nothing like setting myself up," he muttered, then shifted forward, as if to rise. "I'll be on my way, then…"

"No, no, it's okay, I just—"

Some bizarre centrifugal force spun his mother's words faster and faster inside her head, splattering them against the back of her skull. Why was he here? Why *had* he been fixated on her for most of the afternoon (because, yeah, she'd noticed), especially since he'd made it more than clear that down and dirty, they were not going to get?

Half curious, half wary and frankly too tired to worry overmuch about anything, Mercy came all the way outside, collapsing into somebody's left-behind folding chair. The cold, hard top of the chair dug into her neck when she leaned back, letting her own eyes rest for a second.

"Pooped?"

"Heck, I passed 'pooped' an hour ago. And I didn't even do any of the cooking. What are you doing?" she said, her eyes popping open when she felt her foot swing up onto his knee, her boot being unzipped.

"Giving you a foot rub."

She snatched her foot back, hiked the zipper up again. "You can't do that, I've got a huge hole in my sock."

"You're wearing *socks* inside these?"

"I hadn't exactly planned on anybody seeing them."

Chuckling, he reclaimed her foot, slowly undid the zipper. Her fingers tightened around the arms of the chair. So did her nipples. Although thankfully not around the arms of the chair.

"W-why?"

"There you go again," he said, rolling off the white cotton sock before settling her foot on his lap, gently shoving the pads of his thumbs into the ball. Uh-boy. "Anybody ever tell you that you overthink things way too much?"

"Other than you?"

He smiled. "How's this feel?"

"Like it's a shame you don't want to have sex with me, 'cause what you're doing right there would be a surefire way to get lucky."

His eyes lifted to hers. His thumbs kept up their magic. And that damn crooked smile never wavered. Mercy sucked in a breath.

"You *do* want to have sex with me?"

"Oh, *wanting* to was never in doubt." He carefully lowered the first foot, lifted the other one. Stripped it bare. Ravaged it with his thumbs. Ye gods. Somehow, Mercy didn't think his mother had considered this particular possibility. Then again, maybe she had. Ugh, now she was creeping herself out—

"Whether I should was something else again."

What? Oh, right. Ben. Sex. As in, looking good. "And...now?"

Those shoulders shrugged. "Now...let's just say I'm...reconsidering things."

Okay, *very* good.

"Um, not to be pushy or anything...but you got any idea when you might reach some kind of conclusion? Because what you're doing there is kinda getting me worked up."

"You mean, this?"

"That would be it."

"And here I was so proud of myself for finally figuring out how to extend foreplay."

She swallowed as his fingers inched up to stroke the area right above her ankle. New erogenous zone, *hel*-lo.

"Okay, remember back? How getting me warmed up was never a problem?"

He stilled. Thought. Smiled. "Oh, yeah…"

"Well, I got news for ya, toots. Things haven't slowed down on that score. So unless you want me to, uh…" She shifted in the chair. Bad idea. "…scandalize the neighbors, I suggest we move this inside."

"Now?"

"Now would be good."

Her foot dropped like a stone when he stood, grabbed her hand and hauled her to her feet. And before you could say *Who's got the condom?* they were on her bed, very naked and very cozy.

Very cozy.

Oh, my, she'd forgotten how nicely he fit in there, how extraordinarily good he was at multitasking. In fact, she idly mused as they slowed down for a second to savor their reunion, her hands tightly captured in his, above her head, as he tongued and nuzzled and nipped at her jaw, her neck, her breasts, that he was the only man she'd ever done this with who could telescope the preliminaries and the main event with such panache. She couldn't help it, she'd never been one to tarry, whether the guy could keep up or not. Especially the first time.

And bless him, Ben had no trouble keeping up. In more ways than one.

Those first, delicious stirrings of warmth flared, consuming every reservation, every *This really isn't a good idea* that tried to crop up in her thoughts. She was woman, hear her roar.

Quite literally.

Oh, no, Mercy had never been one to keep things locked up inside. Especially when, with one last, amazingly wonderful thrust, Ben set off an orgasm that might have made her brain explode if she hadn't been able to release the pressure vocally.

Damn, he was good.

They were good.

And then it was over—for the moment, she had no doubt there'd be an encore or two—and he pulled her into his arms, and she thought, *This is pretty nice, actually.*

If a little weird. Because this felt very different from the last time they'd done this. More…real. Or something.

"Why?" she finally asked.

He laughed, the sound rich and warm. "You'll never learn, will you?"

That he hadn't asked for clarification was both reassuring and unsettling. She wasn't all that sure she liked the idea of a man accessing her brain that easily. Even if the guy was Ben. "So sue me," she finally said. "You must have had some reason for changing your mind."

His fingers traced lazy circles between her shoulder blades. Also apparently an erogenous zone, sheesh. "What can I tell you? Being here today put me in the mood."

"Five thousand kids and all their nosy parents turns you on?"

"Being part of something turns me on." He stopped stroking to tighten his hold, rubbing his lips over her hair. Rubbing other things over…other things. "Finally admitting I've missed all this turns me on." He paused, grinning, watching her expression as his jolly sidekick sprang to life again. God, he was such a man. "Watching you with your family turns me on."

"You are one strange dude, you know that?"

Ben chuckled. "I'm sure. Of course, if you've changed *your* mind, I'd completely understand."

"I'm here, aren't I?"

"But for how long?"

Mercy pulled back to look at Ben, her chin resting on her palm, leaving the jolly sidekick to its own devices for a moment. "It's my bed, where would I go? But let's go back for a sec to the 'being part of something' comment. Are you saying… Hell, what *are* you saying?"

He stilled, his eyes steady in hers. "That I hadn't fully realized how tired I was of being alone until I came home."

Her blood came to a complete standstill in her veins. Ohmigod—his mother hadn't been imagining things. "Ohmigod," she said. "You're ready to settle down."

One deftly executed maneuver, and she was on her back once more, pinned underneath him. He kissed one nipple, circled it with his tongue. Gently tugged it with his teeth. Blew on it for good measure. "At the very least," he said over her whimper, "I'm more ready to consider it than I ever thought I would be. What are you doing?"

"Trying to sit up," she said, wriggling out from under him to sit on the edge of the bed, her hands forked through her now-matted hair. "Oh, God, Ben…this…this isn't at all what I'd expected. I mean, really, I thought it would be fun to have sex with you again, but…"

"But what?"

She twisted around, shivering at the take-no-prisoners look in his eyes. "You know what."

"Why not?"

"Because while you were gone, doing whatever it was you were doing, I was back here making a life for myself. Becoming something, *someone,* I didn't even know existed ten years ago. If being around all these kids has got your pro-creative juices going, then maybe you need to go find some little honey who'd love nothing more than to give you a batch of baby Bens, who wants nothing more than to play the devoted wifey. Because I seriously doubt I can fill the bill on that score."

Ben sat up, skimming one warm palm down her arm, kissing her shoulder. Sending up shouts of joy from every skin cell. "But you're terrific with kids, Merce. You always have been. You adore your nieces and nephews—"

"And at this point," she said, not listening, "who knows if I could even *have* kids, what with the fertility factor taking a dive after thirty-five and all? And I can't think when you're doing that," she said, swatting his hand away from her breast.

"For heaven's sake, Merce, older women have babies all the time—"

"Yeah, except it's harder for us geriatric types to conceive a *first* baby. And here's a head's up—reproductive hoop-jumping isn't my thing."

Seemingly unfazed by her outburst, Ben moved behind her, wrapping her up in his arms and resting his chin in the crook of her neck. For a good minute or so, he simply held her until her heart stopped trying to claw its way out of her chest.

"Can I say something?" he said quietly, his breath warm against her ear. She nodded. He hugged her a little tighter. "Okay, first off, for the record? I'm not looking for a brood mare. And secondly…I hate to point this out, but for somebody so set on nothing coming of this, you sure do have an awful lot to say about things that wouldn't even be an issue."

"I'm just—"

"Covering *your* butt. I know. And in some ways, I can't blame you. But honestly, Merce, does it really make things easier, worrying about every eventuality at once, right from the get-go?"

"Yes," she mumbled, stubbornly, and he chuckled, kissing her temple. And her neck. Then her shoulder, as he palmed her breasts from behind, thumbing what had to be the most sensitive nipples in the lower forty-eight, damn them. She bit her lip but the whimper escaped anyway, betraying her, and he laughed again, slipping one hand down her belly, between her legs, two fingers sliding into the wetness that would have betrayed her, anyway.

"You want me to go?" he murmured, stroking her, and she said, "Uh, no, *going* isn't the word I had in mind," and she let him roll her back onto the bed, arching her back as he loved her with his mouth, his tongue, and then she heard the rip of foil, the snap of latex, her own unhurried sigh as he entered her again.

Filled her as only Ben could.

"Damn you," she whispered, tears gathering at the corners of her eyes, and he cradled her face in his hands, thumbing away the moisture.

"I don't know what the future will bring, Merce," he said, softly, "but for sure I'm not the least bit interested in going out and looking for some little 'honey,' as you put it." He partially withdrew (no!), then plunged (yes!), then stilled, his breathing labored served him right. "If that's all I'd wanted," he gritted out, "I could have had that a long time ago."

An odd combination of jealousy and pleasure made her skin tingle. "You were…holding out for me?"

A slightly startled look crossed his features before he grinned. "Who knew?"

He lifted her knees to sink more deeply inside her, and a shower of the most beautiful glitter burst behind her eyes, and she cried "Oh!" and he chuckled, even though she sank her fingers into his shoulders and said, "You do realize this has disaster written all over it?"

Again, he retreated, his arms braced on either side of her head, a trickle of sweat meandering through the black hair in the center of his chest. "Because it's a risk? Because it might not work out?"

"Yeah."

"Then how about we don't think about anything more than *this*," he said, pushing into her so hard, she gasped, then sighed, relishing the shiver of delight. "Think you can handle that?"

Her eyes caught his, held it fast.

"Bring it on, big boy."

"Hmm," Cass said the next morning when a brisk, bone-chilling wind blew Mercy through the front door to the shop. "You look different. New coat?"

Fighting a blush, Mercy shrugged out of her leather jacket and made her way back to the office, flinching from the heat of those big turquoise eyes squinting at her through shaggy bangs. "Nope, had it for years. Boots are, though." She lifted one foot, admiring the luscious expanse of black suede stretching out below the hem of her leather miniskirt, the pointed toe, the killer heel. Her heart pitty-patted. "Sixty percent off at Dillard's."

"Can't beat that. But that's not it...ohmigosh! You had sex!"

"Who had sex?" Dana said, popping up in the doorway. "Wow. You're actually *glowing*."

Oh, God, not before coffee. Already ruing whosever bright idea it was to open the store on Mondays, Mercy poured herself a cup from the maker behind the desk, then split her glare evenly between the two of them. "And *how* old are we, exactly? You know, I could've just had a good night's sleep. Or run for three miles this morning. Or maybe I overdid the blusher. Not that it's any of your business."

Cass grinned. "It was that hottie who was here last week, wasn't it?"

"What hottie?" Dana said, then sucked in a breath. "You did it with your *brother-in-law?*"

"Man, what is it with you two today? You don't hear me grilling you two about your sex life, do you?"

"Only because we made the preemptive strike," Cass said. Mercy stuck her tongue out at the blonde.

Standing in front of the three-quarter-length mirror next to the door, Dana pulled a comb from her purse to run it through her long hair, plucking a stray off her bright green sweater. "You may as well fess up now, sugar," she said, dimpling at Mercy in the reflection, "and save yourself a whole lot of grief."

"You're ruthless."

"We learned from the best."

They had her there. Since she might have tormented the two of them about their love lives a time or six in the past. "Fine," she said on a sharp breath. "You're right. On both counts," she added with an eye-roll at their fist bump. "Although this isn't really breaking news." At their frowns, she added, "Because Ben and I sort of had a…thing once before. Ten years ago."

"Wow," Dana breathed, her green eyes the size of kiwis. "Y'all must've had *some* catching up to do." Then she giggled. Fortunately, her cell phone rang, her sappy grin at seeing—Mercy assumed—her husband C.J.'s number on the display giving Mercy an excuse to leave the office. Unfortunately, that still left Cass.

"So. Is this serious?"

"What it was," Mercy said, straightening out a jumbled rack they'd been too tired to deal with on Saturday, "was sex."

"Yes, I got that part. And?"

She met her partner's concerned gaze. "This is the first time the man's been home in a decade, Cass. I'm not exactly seeing a future here. And I'm fine with that. Really…Dana?" she said when the redhead appeared, dragging her poncho and purse and looking slightly dazed. "What is it, sweetie?"

After a couple of blinks, Dana shook her head as if to clear it. She slipped the poncho over her head, yanked her hair out from the neckline. "D'you think you could hold the fort for a couple of hours? Something's come up, I need to meet C.J.…."

She was gone before either of them could answer her one way or the other. But if nothing else, Dana's sudden disappearance—not to mention one of the busiest mornings they'd had since Christmas—took the heat off Mercy.

Until, a little after noon, she looked up when the bell over the door jingled and there was Ben, all big and bad-looking in solid black—jeans, Henley, pea coat, cowboy boots.

The three dozen or so yellow roses, however, kinda killed the Bad Bart effect.

"Damn," Cass whispered behind her. "You must be really, *really* good."

Judging from her wide eyes, Ben guessed he'd knocked her right off those adorable pins of hers.

Point to him.

He watched her struggle to regain control of the moment—the slow, deep breath, the deliberate toss of her curls. The breath-stealing, blood-heating direct gaze. "Subtle," she said.

His eyes lowered to the flowers. "Overkill?" he asked, frowning slightly as he twisted them in his hand.

She laughed. "Just a touch. But very sweet." *Sweet?* "Here, let's get them in water. I think we've got an old vase around here somewhere…." He followed her past the sales rooms and down the hall, admiring the view. The butt, the curls, those boots…how she could be so damn cute and so damn sexy at the same time, he had no idea. It was a gift.

He leaned one forearm against the bathroom doorjamb, surveying the room as she crouched down to rummage in the storage space underneath the sink. The aqua sink. Against gold-and-green flocked wallpaper.

"Charming."

"I think the word you're looking for is *retro,*" she said, plunking a pot of some kind into the sink and filling it with water. "Kinder owners would have put it out of its misery. But it amuses us, so we left it." She carted the filled pot back out front, relieving him of the flowers to plop them into the water.

"They're really gorgeous," she said softly, fingering one blossom. "Thank you."

"Huh." Ben folded his arms. "I half expected you to give me grief. Or do that whole 'you didn't have to' crap."

"Uh, no. This is the chick who spent the first ten years of her life convinced that somewhere, a small but very wealthy principality was missing its princess." She buried her face in the blooms, then grinned up at him. "I was born to be spoiled, but apparently nobody else seemed cognizant of that fact."

"Well, then…can you get away for lunch?"

"Yes, she can," Cass called from the other end of the room.

"Not that you're eavesdropping or anything," Mercy said as her partner snaked back to the register through the circular racks.

"Are you kidding?" she said. "I'm the mother of a teenager. I have hearing like a bat. Anyway, Dana called, she'll be back in a half hour or so. And Trish only has classes this morning, so she'll be in soon, too. So go." The blonde smiled at Ben, before her gaze slid back to Mercy. "Enjoy."

Why did he get the feeling Mercy was fighting the urge to smack the woman?

"So…" Ben said once they were safely out on the sidewalk. "I take it she knows we…?"

"Trust me, it's not like I announced it or anything. We're walking?"

"It's only three blocks, it's not worth driving."

She shrugged, then said, "Do I look like I'm glowing to you?"

He reached out to capture her chin in his fingers, pretending to angle her head to get a better look. "Now that you mention it, you do, kind of."

"I rest my case."

"I made you glow?"

"Oh, for God's sake, wipe that smug look off your face. After five orgasms, I could probably guide ships into harbor."

"Yes, but who gave you those five orgasms?"

She smacked his arm, and he laughed. Then Mercy glanced up at him, skepticism oozing from every square inch of that terrific little body of hers. "So, is this, like, a date?"

"Considering the five orgasms and all, I didn't think I was exactly rushing things."

"Well, no, but…" She hiked her purse up on her shoulder as they walked. "We don't date." Her eyes angled to his. "Do we?"

"We do now."

They walked in silence for a few seconds. He could practically feel her struggle to keep her mouth shut. But this was Mercy they were talking about. And sure enough, ten seconds later, out it came.

"Okay, I can't stand it…why?"

He commandeered her hand, lifting it to his lips and kissing her knuckles. "Because it's lunchtime and I'm hungry and I don't want to eat alone. *And* the only person I wanted to eat with is you. So deal."

"And that's it?"

He chuckled. "If I say 'no,' I'm screwed. If I say 'yes,' you'll run. So since I can't win, I'm saying nothing."

"Coward."

"No, smart. I like what you're wearing, by the way."

"Yeah? You don't think it's too…"

"What?"

"I'm not sure. I mean, I've always dressed like this. But sometimes these days I look in the mirror and I think maybe I should take it down a notch."

He frowned. "Why would you do that?"

"Because maybe I'm getting a little old to pull off the Latina pop tart look?"

"So what are you saying? You're ready for orthopedic shoes and those awful print blouses like our grandmothers wore?"

"Wash your mouth out. But maybe something a bit more…subdued. Grown up."

He let go of her hand to wrap his arm around her shoulders, tugging her close. "Honey, all I see when I look at you is a sexy, beautiful woman. Not old, not young, just…you. Subdued is for everybody else. And what the hell is mature, anyway?"

She shrugged under his arm. But he could tell she was pleased. "Beats me." After a second, she said, "I color my hair, by the way. In the interest of full disclosure."

"Yeah, I know."

Her head snapped around. "What do you mean, *you know?*"

"Because…" He tugged her closer, kissed the top of her head. "I found a couple of grays."

"Ohmigod, you're kidding!" She grabbed a handful of her hair, yanking it in front of her face. "I certainly didn't notice any when I did my hair this morning!"

"They weren't on your head," he said quietly.

She squawked, turned bright red and tried to pull away. Laughing, Ben caught her and twisted her around, holding her firmly by the shoulders. "Mercy, honey…I don't give a damn what you wear. Or whether you color your hair, or use makeup or not. None of that means squat. All I know is, I like being with you. I'm *happy* when I'm with you. And that's because of who you are, not what you look like. Because you're open and honest and generous and I don't have to drive myself nuts trying to figure out what you're really saying."

Then he took advantage of her apparently thunderstruckedness to add, "That you happen to be one of the hottest things going is just a bonus."

She gave him one of those pitying looks women were born knowing how to do. Then her forehead knotted. "You haven't been happy in all the time you've been away?"

Damn. She was too smart for her own good. And certainly for his.

"I'm not sure *happy* is the right word," he said with a tight smile, lifting her hair away from her face. "Not unhappy, certainly. It's not like I feel I've *wasted* the last ten years of my life." He waited out the swirl of memories, good and bad, then said, "Just that it's time for a change."

Their gazes tangoed for several seconds before, without comment, she pulled away, stuffing both her hands in her own pockets as they walked. "So where are we going, anyway?"

That she hadn't bolted was a good sign. He thought. "Little Chinese joint in the next block. Not much to look at, but great food."

"Huh," she said when they reached the place, which Ben had to admit looked a little seedier than he remembered. Still, the rich aroma of fried rice and stir-fry swirled around them, seductive and tantalizing.

"I take it you're not exactly dazzled."

"It takes a lot to dazzle a princess," she said, and he thought he'd do well to remember that.

Chapter Seven

Upscale the place wasn't, the decor running mostly to gaudy posters and paper umbrellas. In one corner, a large, fake dumb cane plant indifferently shielded the listless broom, mop and vacuum cleaner behind. But Ben was right, the food *was* good. In fact, the food was fabulous. A "secret" that had gotten out, judging from the dearth of empty tables in the shoe-box-sized restaurant. The two little waitresses were about to run themselves ragged, trying to keep up.

"You," Mercy said, jabbing chopsticks in his direction, "are brilliant."

"Not really," he said, not even trying to hide his smile. "I've just gotten really good at pegging the best cheap places to eat within a half hour of setting foot in a new town."

Mercy picked up her nearly empty water glass, the ice

rattling when she drained the last few drops of water it . "A highly prized survival skill, to be sure."

"You betcha… You need water?"

"Um, yes," she said, chewing. "But they're so busy, I don't have the heart to bug them."

Ben glanced over at the water pitcher, sitting on a table by the kitchen door, then shrugged and rose, striding to the table. "Anybody else need water?" he asked, holding up the pitcher, then proceeded to top at least a dozen glasses before he finally got to Mercy and filled hers, too.

"No, no…you don't have to do that!" Half laughing, but clearly embarrassed, one of the waitresses scurried over, taking the pitcher from him and filling his glass.

"It's okay," Ben said, grinning as he sat back down. "You guys looked like you had enough to do. By the way, this is the best garlic chicken I've ever had."

She flushed, nodding and smiling, nodding and smiling. "Thank you, thank you so much. I get you more noodles, yes?" And off she went.

"That," Mercy said, "was way cool."

Ben looked over at her from underneath his thick, dark lashes, his mouth slanted. "Yeah?"

"Oh, yeah."

And this could be yours.

The ice jittered in her glass when she picked it up, downing half of it at once. How had this happened? *When* had this happened? Before, the sex had been just sex, and the friendship had been just friendship, but now…

Oh, God. This was bad. Really, really bad.

"Hey," Ben said softly from across the table. Grudgingly,

she met his gaze. "Call me crazy, but I worry when you get quiet." He made a rolling motion by his ear with his chopsticks. "You're thinking again, aren't you?"

"One of the hazards of a functioning brain," Mercy muttered, spooning the last of the lemon chicken onto her plate. She hesitated, then leaned forward. "Look, Ben, taking me to bed is one thing. But this…uh…"

"Is what people do when they want to see where things lead."

"Well…yeah."

Dark eyes flashed to hers. "Funny, I thought I'd been pretty clear about that. So if you're so dead set against this, why'd you come to lunch?"

"Because Cass made me?"

One side of his mouth kicked up. "Like anybody can *make* you do anything." When Mercy lowered her eyes to her plate, he reached across the table, snagging her wrist in his fingers. "So is the obvious terror on your face because you don't believe that I'm tired of drifting, or because I'm pushing you in directions you don't want to go?"

"I'm not terrified, Ben, I'm being practical. After being alone for so long, I *can't* see me doing the cozy family thing, frankly. Which I also made clear. But even if I did, can you blame me for being a little…skeptical? Oh, come on," she said when he dropped his chopsticks on his plate and pushed away, his jaw set. "You enlisted in the army like five seconds after you graduated. You hardly ever came home on leave. After, what? A year working with your father after your discharge, you took off again. For ten *years.* Why would I, or anybody else for that matter, believe you'd want to stick around this time?"

"And I told you," he said darkly, "it's time for a change."

"Oh, for God's sake," she said gently. "How many places have you lived in over the past decade? How many different jobs have you had? *It's time for a change* is your motto! It's more than my not believing you're ready to put down roots. I don't think you're *capable* of putting down roots. But I do think you're running from something, seeking some kind of, I don't know, sanctuary—"

The word caught in her throat. Dear God—where had that come from? But if the startled, cornered look in Ben's eyes was any indication, she'd just hit a bull's-eye she hadn't even known she was aiming for. Without warning, a host of sharp, achy feelings burst to life inside of her, prompting her to reach for his hand. But he jerked away before she could make contact.

"Ben…?"

"Are you finished?" he said. Too quietly. Too calmly.

"Oh. Uh, sure, I guess." Mercy twisted around to unhook her purse off the back of her chair, feeling unaccountably sad. And extremely confused. "I should have been back to the store twenty minutes ago, anyway."

The waitress had already left their check and fortune cookies; Ben tossed one of the cookies toward her, then stood, swiping the check off the table and striding toward the cashier. He paid, held open the door for her, insisted on seeing her back to the store, even though they walked the three blocks or so in painful silence. When they reached the shop, however, he grabbed her shoulders again and jerked her around to face him, not roughly enough to hurt or frighten her, but definitely enough to get her attention. Every muscle in his face had gone rigid, his eyes glittering like polished onyx.

"I don't know how to make you believe something you

don't want to believe. But trust me, I'd *never* expect you to change your life for me, or give up what's important to you. But dammit, Merce…"

His shoulders heaved with the force of his breath. "If *you've* changed, why can't you give me the benefit of the doubt that I've changed, too? That I want different things now? And that maybe, just maybe—" she wobbled when he gently shook her "—one of those things is the shot at a life with *you?*"

He let her go, his eyes fixed on hers for a heart-stopping moment, then strode away, a menacing slash of black in the blindingly bright midday sun.

Mercy stood, frozen, staring, her brain buzzing with static. No man had ever spoken to her like that before. Looked at her like that before. Made her so weak in the knees she didn't dare move for fear of falling flat on her can.

And if that didn't scream WATCH OUT! she didn't know what did.

Finally, she forced herself to turn around, clutching the handrail for dear life as she hauled herself up onto the store's porch, through the door to the shop, back to the office, like an extra from *Night of the Living Dead*.

She barely noticed Cass's glance in her direction as she passed, although she was dimly aware of her partner's here's-your-hat, what's-your-hurry? act with her customer immediately afterwards. Yeah, talking about this was real high on her priority list. But after all these years of working with each other, *privacy* was a pipe dream.

"I hope to God that's food poisoning making you look so wretched," Cass said when she found Mercy a few minutes later, desultorily rearranging items in the game and toy room.

"Now that you mention it, I do feel like puking. So close enough. Dana's not back yet?"

"Uh, no. She called and apologized, said she'd be in as soon as she could make it." After a moment of silence, Cass plunged her hands into the pockets of her droopy, oversize cardigan and said, "Okay, Tinkerbell, what's wrong with this one? And don't give me that 'I have no idea what you're talking about' face, you find fault with every single guy you go out with. Not that I haven't agreed with you most of the time, but still. You do have a bit of a rep for being…picky."

"Gee, thanks, *Mom*. And this has nothing to do with being picky, it's…"

"It's what?" Cass said gently when the words bottlenecked at the base of Mercy's throat.

She picked up a craft set like the one Ben had given Mattie, then sank onto a nearby ottoman, unconsciously picking at one corner of the cellophane wrapping. "The whole time I was growing up," she began, "Ben was just the obnoxious boy next door. Since he's four years younger than I am, we might as well have come from different planets. Our mothers regularly traded off, so we were always at each other's houses, but we didn't exactly hang out together. Not by choice, anyway. I mean, really, when I was a seventh grader, he was still watching Saturday morning cartoons. And by the time I was a teenager, I sure as hell wanted nothing to do with some squeaky-voiced adolescent."

She got up, replacing the craft set, then folded her arms across her middle. "Then, one day my second year of community college, I came home to find Ben in my parents' living room with Rosie and two other girls, working on some project for their English class. He was sixteen by then, nearly a foot taller than I was, and cocky as only a really, really cute sixteen-year-old boy can be, and I remember thinking *Whoa, when did that happen?* Except then he realized I was there, and… This is going to sound stupid."

"Oh, you can *not* quit now," Cass said. "Not when it's just getting good."

Mercy glowered at her, then said, "Okay. So he looked at me, right? And his whole expression changed."

"He came on to you at sixteen?"

"No!" Mercy said, giggling. "In fact, just the opposite. Somewhere along the way, he'd turned into…a real human being. *Totally* full of himself, and God knows he'd flirt with anything with breasts, but even then he positively radiated integrity." She shook her head. "And somehow after that, we each become someone the other one could talk to. About all sorts of stuff. He had girlfriends, I had boyfriends, but Ben…"

She blew out a sigh. "Ben knew me better than anybody. I don't know how it happened, it just did."

"So you were friends?"

"Like this," she said, tightly crossing her middle and index fingers. "At that point, I figured that's all we'd ever be. And that was okay. Then he went into the army, and for six years we hardly saw each other. But whenever he'd come home on leave, we'd fall right back into the same comfortable pattern. We even double-dated once, me with whoever I was going with at the time and Ben with an old high school girlfriend. That was a trip, let me tell you. And then," she said on a pushed breath, "he got out of the army, and came home 'for good'—" Mercy drew quotation marks in the air "—and suddenly…things shifted. Neither of us were kids anymore, or in a relationship, and…" She shrugged.

"It wasn't good?" Cass said softly.

"Oooh, it was a helluva lot better than *good.* What it was, was mind-blowing. But weird. Very, very weird. For both of us. But before we had a chance to figure out what to do about that, he was gone again." She looked at Cass, the ache reasserting itself like a long-healed broken bone bitching in damp weather. "No goodbye, no warning, nothing. He just left."

"And somehow, he still lives."

"Only because jailhouse orange is hideous with my skin tone."

Cass laughed, then said, "And now he's back, and let me guess—he's playing the Serious Card."

Mercy blinked. "God, you're scary. But how did you know?"

"Because I know that look *very* well. Remember?"

Blake, Cass's husband, had walked out on her and their now sixteen-year-old son when the kid had been a toddler, only to pop back into her life a dozen years later, asking for a second chance. Which, eventually, he got. Mercy sighed. "I half expected him to pull a golden retriever out of his back pocket."

"Wow," Cass said. "Forget *good.* You must be downright *phenomenal.*" At Mercy's halfhearted smirk in her direction, the blonde smiled sympathetically. "Sorry. So. You don't trust him."

"It's not a matter of trust."

"Of course it is. He betrayed your friendship, Merce. In your shoes, I'd be leery, too. Hell, I *was* in your shoes. And leery doesn't even begin to describe it."

"But it's different with you and Blake. He left you because of a misunderstanding. Ben took off because he's incapable of staying in one place for more than ten minutes. That he'd come home and suddenly decide he wants the very thing that gave him hives before… It doesn't make sense. *This* doesn't make sense."

After a moment, Cass said, "So you're not falling for him."

"Of course I'm not falling for him! What do you take me for? I mean, sure, he's funny and kind and sexy as hell, but…minivans and retrievers? Get real!"

Several seconds of intense scrutiny later, Cass said, "So tell the guy to take a hike and put both of you out of your misery. I mean, if you're not falling for him, what's the big deal?"

"Besides the sex? Not a thing."

"You could get sex anywhere."

"Not this sex, I couldn't," Mercy said on a mildly despondent sigh.

"And, as an added bonus," Cass said dryly, "Ben seems like a really nice guy."

"What are you, the little devil on my shoulder? Besides, you've met him exactly twice. And what the hell happened to 'I'd be leery, too'?"

"I got over it," Cass said. "And you of all people should know the farther past thirty you get, the quicker you can size 'em up. Besides, if Ben's into you, he obviously has excellent taste."

"Yeah, for crazy people."

"Oh, please," her partner said as the bell over the door jingled, announcing a customer. "The world would be a far better place with more crazy people like you." Then she shrugged. "Well, it's up to you, baby cakes. Just remember, though, if you do decide to play along and he screws up again, Blake and C.J. would be delighted to take him out, no problem."

Mercy laughed. "Yeah, I'm sure your husbands would love to know they've been volunteered for goon duty. Thanks, honey, but that's Carmen's province."

A fact which Ben knew all too well, she thought as they both went out front to help customers. So she could add courageous to the rapidly growing list in Ben's plus column.

Too bad she couldn't add it to her own.

Because, frankly, this whole thing had her rattled out of her wits, like expecting to land in Cleveland and finding yourself in Rio. Or in this case, maybe the other way around. A fling, she could handle. In fact, she'd become the Queen of the Flingers in the past few years. In her world, men were like shoes—pick something flashy and trendy that catches your eye at the moment, wear 'em constantly until you get bored, then toss 'em in the Goodwill bag at season's end without a second's regret. Because who wants to wear the same boring old pumps year after year?

Never mind that her feet were constantly blistered from breaking in new shoes.

Thankfully, a steady stream of customers for the rest of the afternoon kept her reasonably distracted. Then Dana finally returned, with a funny look on her face that Mercy immediately surmised would be far more than a distraction.

"Dana? Sweetie—what is it?"

"Okay, y'all…" Her dimples playing a nervous game of peekaboo, the redhead shooed Cass and Mercy back toward the office. "We need to talk."

Cass and Dana exchanged glances, but it was obvious from the blonde's shrug that she had no more clue than Mercy what was going on. Since it was near closing, anyway, Cass killed the front lights, except for the display windows, then trailed Mercy back to the office. Dana was sitting at her desk, her face buried in her hands.

"Dana! Ohmigod, honey…" Cass perched on the end of an old chair, her voice choked with worry. "Is something wrong?"

"No, no…" Her laugh sounded almost frantic. "I'm sorry, guys, I didn't mean to scare you. But…Oh, God, there's no easy way to say this." She looked from one to the other, her mossy green eyes riddled with apology. "I want out."

Cass clicked in first. "Of the *business?*"

Tears pooled on the redhead's lower lids, one dribbling overboard when she nodded. "You know how C.J. and I went to an open adoption agency a couple of months ago, to get the ball rolling to give Ethan a little brother or sister? Well, we figured it would take months, probably, before we found a match." She pressed both hands to her mouth, then said, "Turns out we're going to be parents again in about three *weeks.*" She gave a wobbly smile. "To a little girl."

"Oh, my God," Mercy said softly, then both women lunged for Dana, wrapping her up in a group hug. "Ohmigod, sweetie…that's *fantastic!*"

After the hugging and squealing died down, Dana said, "I'm so excited I can hardly stand it. I mean, yeah, I know the mom might still change her mind, but we met her today— that's why I was gone so long, we took her to lunch and we all really clicked—and I don't think she will. She's a real sweetheart, but she's only sixteen, she's just not ready to be a mama yet. Anyway, we're going to have a newborn and a toddler, and as much as I love bein' here—especially with the two of you—" she got all teary again "—I've waited too long for this. I want to be home with my babies, at least for a couple of years. I could still handle the decorating service, probably, since that's only part-time, but…if y'all want to buy me out, or find another partner, I'd completely understand."

"Well, I can only speak for myself," Cass said, her gaze flicking to Mercy, then back to Dana. "But as long as you want to keep a hand in, I see no reason why you'd have to bow out completely."

"I agree," Mercy said immediately. "I'm sure we can work around this, honey." A couple of years ago, a devastated Dana had lost not only her ability to have a baby of her own, but a jerk of a fiancé who apparently only wanted a wife with a working uterus. Now she was happily married to a guy who scored off the Richter scale in the "good" department, had already been having a blast raising her cousin's little boy with his father, and soon would have the infant nature had seemed determined to steal from her. Not every woman's definition of paradise, certainly, but definitely Dana's. And Mercy was delighted for her. "This is such great news! You must be floating!"

"You have no idea," Dana said. Then she laughed. "Ohmigosh—I've got three weeks to get a nursery ready!" And with that, she bounced up out the chair and flew into the small room they'd set aside for furniture catalogs and wallpaper books.

"You think there's any point in even trying to steer her away from pink?" Cass asked Mercy.

"Not a chance in hell," she said.

Yeah, she thought as she slipped back into her jacket and gathered up her purse, nice girls not only finished first, but way, way ahead. Which is how it should be. Both her partners, in fact, had seen their lives do a serious one-eighty in the past year, a thought which produced the strangest little twinge in the center of her chest. Like mild heartburn.

But as oddly as both their happy endings had come about—Cass remarrying her ex-husband, Dana and C.J.'s shared custody of Trish's son leading to their falling in love—there'd at least been compelling reasons for them to be together to begin with. Not so with Mercy and Ben. All they had in common was sex, history and family ties. Right?

Mercy hollered her good-nights and went out to her car, thinking Cass was right. Not about playing things by ear, but about cutting this thing with Ben off at the knees.

Because, really, what was the freaking point in pursuing something that was doomed, anyway?

"We have to talk."

Amazing, how such quietly spoken words could cut right through the whine of the power saw.

Releasing the power button, Ben looked up from the two-by-four straddling a pair of sawhorses to see Mercy standing at the foot of his father's driveway. The harsh, unforgiving beam from the security light did nothing to soften that obstinate set to her mouth he remembered all too well from their childhood. While Carmen had been protective and Anita nurturing, Mercy's nickname had been *La Cabezudita,* Little Miss Stubborn, hell-bent on controlling everything—and everyone—in her path.

"What about?"

"Maybe we should go someplace where the entire neighborhood can't hear us?"

The one thing Mercy underestimated, though, was how transparent her show of toughness had always been. In fact, the more that chin jutted out and her eyes flashed, the more flustered she really was. And the protective part of him hated forcing her hand, disconcerting her like this. But Ben knew making her mad was the only way to lure her out from behind that steel wall he suspected she kept up to keep anyone from hurting her.

And God help him, Ben was not above savoring the thrill of power that came from understanding that about her. Of knowing he could allow her that little illusion of control when he was actually the one calling the shots.

Only this time, he wasn't yielding an inch.

"Whatever you've got to say, you can say right here," he said, revving the saw once more.

"Fine. Oh, for God's sake—turn that damn thing off!"

So he did. In fact, he even set it down on the metal table he'd dragged out from the garage. Then he waited, thumbs hooked in pockets. He'd gotten real good at waiting over the years.

"We can't do this," she said.

Just what he'd figured she'd say. Would have been disappointed, in fact, if they'd skipped this step. Since after all, challenges were right up his alley.

"Can't do what?"

She gestured back and forth between them. "*This*. And not because I'm scared, before you play that particular card. Because it's…pointless."

He caught her eyes in his, saw exactly what he'd hoped to see. And it wasn't at all what she probably thought was there. "Says who?"

Now her lips pressed together so tight her mouth disappeared altogether. A breeze ruffled all those curls. "Dammit, Ben," she said in something close to a snarl. "You can't bully me into a relationship!"

"Is that what I'm doing?" he said quietly.

Her chest rose once, twice, three times before she finally said, "This isn't going to work, it's over, end of story."

Then she spun around on those spiky heels of hers and started off, and he watched, giving her time to get almost all the way across the street before he called out her name. And, yep, she turned around. One day he'd have to give her a lesson in following through on her convictions, but not today. Today, it was all about following through on *his*.

"You're wrong, Merce. Because it's not over. Not by a long shot."

They stood there, staring each other down from across the street. As he imagined, he could see the steam coming out of her ears from thirty feet away. Then she spun around again and trounced into her house, because it was either that or stand out there in the middle of the street and argue with him, and he knew she wasn't about to do that.

Still, he thought on a satisfied chuckle as he picked up the saw and cut off the next marked piece for the built-in shelves in the family room his father had been promising his mother since before he'd gone into the Army, for godssake, he'd given her due notice of his intentions now, both in private and in public. In fact, he imagined her mother was probably already on the phone with her, asking her what on earth was that all about.

Not that he expected Mercy to give in without a fight. And

he would lay odds that she was chalking up whatever had gone on between them to nothing more than chemistry.

Oh, they had chemistry, all right. The kind of chemistry that blew up stuff, brought about cataclysmic changes. They always had, although he doubted even Mercy would argue that things were ten times more combustible now that everybody had a better handle on what they were doing and all. Yeah, there was a lot to be said for being with a woman who knew exactly what she wanted and wasn't afraid to ask for it.

Who wasn't shy about returning the favor, either, he thought with a very sly grin.

But if she thought this was only about sex, she was crazy. And while Mercy was definitely crazy, she wasn't *that* kind of crazy.

And if she thought Ben was going to simply give up and walk away because she was having doubts, or running scared, or whatever the hell it was she was doing, she was dead wrong about that, too. Because, yeah, he was *real* good at waiting, a thought which sent a twinge of guilt sliding through him, that he was keeping such a large part of who he'd been from the woman he now knew he wanted to spend the rest of his life with. Some folks would undoubtedly say he wasn't playing fair. And, in many ways, they'd be right.

But to tell her now would only muddy the waters. Shake her up more than she already was. When the time was right, when he felt she could deal with it without going ballistic on him, he'd tell her. Until then, this was about being patient. In fact, you might say patience was one of his strongest attributes.

What he wasn't good at, however, was failing.

Especially when it wasn't only *his* welfare at stake.

* * *

Over the incessant pounding reverberating inside the half-built walls, the deafening Mariachi music blaring from the boom box in the middle of the concrete slab, Ben had no idea his father had arrived at the job site. That is, until he felt the familiar, slightly harder than necessary slap between his shoulder blades as he hunched over the working drawings—heavily annotated with Tony's nearly illegible scrawl—spread out on a makeshift table in the middle of what would be the house's family room.

"Checking up on me?" Ben asked, straightening as he rerolled the plans.

"Your mother sent lunch," Luis said, his mustache curving into a smile as he held up a metal box and a large thermos. "But that, too." He looked around, nodding in approval. "After thirty years," he said, "I still get a kick out of seeing drawings turn into a real house. Of knowing it'll probably still be standing long after I'm dead and buried."

"I know what you mean," Ben said, earning him an under-standably quizzical—and hopeful—look. But his father only set the lunchbox and thermos on the table, then walked over to inspect the framing where a pocket door would go, bracing one callused, ugly hand against a pine two-by-four.

"You used to build little houses when you were this high," his father said, holding out a hand at knee level. Then he chuckled. "I taught you how to use a saw when you were four, I thought your mother would kill me for sure."

"I remember," Ben said, smiling. "That was around the time I added a few choice words to my Spanish vocabulary, as I recall."

Now his father laughed out loud. "Your mother has a real mouth on her when she gets mad, that's for sure." He angled his head at Ben. "I'm thinking that hasn't changed, no? How you love building things?"

A truth that had occupied Ben's thought almost constantly the past few weeks, although not the way his father meant it. Yes, he loved the orderliness, the satisfaction of watching a building take shape, morph from idea to drawing to reality. Nor could he deny that the fresh, living scent of lumber, the reassuring tattoo of hammers and whines of saws, both soothed his blood and made it tingle with possibilities. But even after a couple of weeks, he'd begun to realize that the thought of doing this day-in, day-out would drive him slowly insane.

Not that he was about to admit this to his father, not when the old man was counting on him to keep his business from collapsing while Tony was indisposed. "It's been fun," he said, which got the expected grin.

Luis picked up the food again, nodding that they find someplace to eat, the workers having broken for lunch a few minutes before. Ben led his father out onto what would eventually be the house's porch, overlooking a long drive and already partially terraced front yard, half thinking how ironic it was that Luis had spent the better part of his life building houses far grander than his own modest brick-facade ranch. And that he was every bit as content—probably more so—in that unassuming little house than half the people who lived in these overblown, overdone monstrosities that had sprouted like steroidized mushrooms all over Albuquerque's far Northeast Heights in the past twenty years.

Luis handed him a sub sandwich piled with enough lunch

meat and cheese to open a deli counter, then twisted the top off the thermos of coffee. They ate in silence for a minute or so until his father finally asked, "Not that I'm pressuring you or anything…but have you given any more thought to hanging around? Because I'd like to retire one of these days. I'd hate to see everything I'd worked so hard for fall apart."

This was it, then. The chance to ease into the subject Ben hadn't been sure how to bring up before this. He took a bite of his sandwich and said, "Tony wouldn't let that happen."

"Not intentionally, no. Oh, he does his best, but…" His father blew out a breath. "Half the time I think he's only doing this because he's sucking up." Dark, penetrating eyes swerved to Ben's. "Because he thinks it's a good way to rack up points. To be the 'good son' because you left. But I don't think his heart's really in the construction business."

Ben stifled the impulse to contradict his father, at least until the old man shed more light on the subject. From everything Ben had seen since his return, his father had nothing to complain about as far as Tony's work was concerned. That he was finding fault now only confirmed Ben's original gut instinct that he hadn't been wrong in staying away. Staying out of something he hadn't understood at the time, still didn't understand now.

Something that would have to be sorted out, one way or the other, if he was to reestablish his life here. With or without Mercy.

The crew's laughter drifted over to them on the breeze. "What makes you think I'd be any better at this than Tony?" Ben asked.

His father's gaze warred with his for several seconds before he said, "Because if you did stay, if you decided to come into the business with me, I'd know it would be because you *wanted* to. Not because you felt you *had* to. It's not huge, by some standards, but it's solid. And yours for the asking."

"I hope to God you haven't said any of this to Tony."

His father shook his head. "No. But if you stayed, maybe that would give him an out. A chance to do what he really wants to do. Whatever that is."

Ben sighed, thinking what bizarre, complicated creatures humans were. He knew his father loved his brother, but he also knew full well Tony would still see Ben's coming on board—an inevitability, whether it drove him crazy or not, since what else would he do if he stayed?—as the first step to push him out. As a flare-up of the competitiveness that had always marked their relationship, despite Ben's best efforts to avoid it.

"And I think you're wrong, Pop," he said. "Tony's completely devoted to the business. And he's damn good at it. Certainly better than I would be. Hell, all I'm doing is carrying out his orders. Without him, I'd be screwed."

"Don't sell yourself short, *mijo*. Yeah, I know you've got some catching up to do, but once you did…" A smile trembled underneath Luis's moustache before he looked away, took another bite of his sub.

"Dammit, Pop," Ben said softly, rubbing the heel of one hand over his thigh. "By rights you should hate me."

"For what? Leaving?" His father shook his head. "Your mother, now *she* didn't understand, that sometimes a man has to leave home in order to find it. But I do. Hell, I did the same thing, when I was eighteen. Maybe it didn't take me as long to find my way back," he said, "but I always understood what was going on. Just as I think maybe I understand what's going on now. Why you're finally ready to sink those dusty, dry roots you've been dragging behind you all over the country. You want some of this coffee? It's still hot."

Ben took the thermos from his father, staring at it for a long moment before finally lifting it to his lips. He couldn't ever remember talking to the old man like this. But then, he hadn't exactly provided many opportunities for long conversations, had he? Even when he'd called home, he'd kept the exchanges deliberately short, sidestepping any chance of questions he didn't feel were in anybody's best interest for him to answer.

"I didn't know you'd done the wandering thing, too," he now said, handing back the thermos.

"Yeah. Five or six years. Just like you, I went where the jobs were. Of course, even then there was plenty of work right here, but the thought of spending my entire life where I was born…it gave me the willies, you know?"

Ben nodded. "Why'd you come back?"

His father bit off a chunk of his own sandwich, chewing for some time before saying, "I didn't like it much. It gets lonely, drifting like that."

Ben waited out the zing of recognition before he said, "Did you know Mama before you left?"

"No, that happened afterwards. And it wasn't like there weren't girls I could have married before I met your mother. But I didn't feel like I had anything to offer anybody, you know what I mean? Not that I did when I met your mother, either," he said with a soft chuckle, "but she wasn't taking 'no' for an answer."

He stuffed the last bite of sandwich in his mouth, then wiped his fingers on a napkin. "You know, everybody always talks about how women are so anxious to get married and have a family, that it's the men who fight it. But you know something? I think women are a lot better at being alone than men are. We need them a lot more than they need us."

Ben grinned. "I think you may be on to something there."

"It's true! And anyway, if it weren't for women, we'd probably all still be running aroun' in animal skins, clubbing things over the head for our suppers." When Ben chuckled, his father glanced over, then averted his gaze again, his hands linked between his knees as they sat on the steps.

"Family's everything. *Everything*," he said with a vehemence that made Ben frown. "Something your brother seems to have forgotten somewhere along the way. And yes, I know all about him and Anita having problems, so you don't have to preten' you have no idea what I'm talking about." He sighed. "First rule of marriage, you learn to compromise. Otherwise known as agreeing with your wife," he said with a grin, then sobered. "Tony has no idea what a good deal he's got going there. Anita's a good woman. A good mother. So what if she works? If you ask me, sometimes I think Tony's just jealous because his wife has a job she loves, an' he doesn't."

It was all Ben could do not to slam his hand into his forehead. Had his father not heard a thing he'd said? Why did the old man have such a blind spot about this?

"Anyway," Luis said, "if Tony screws up his marriage, I will never forgive him. Maybe you could talk to him?"

Ben nearly choked. "No way. My toe still smarts from sticking it in that particular tub of scalding water. In case you missed it, Tony and I aren't exactly buddy-buddy. Not to mention the fact that I'm the last person to be advising anybody about marriage."

"It's not a buddy he needs," his father said, ignoring the marriage comment. "It's someone with the *cojones* to knock some sense into him."

"Maybe. But I'm not that person. Sorry."

"Even though Mattie and Jake are suffering?"

The one comment guaranteed to make Ben's stomach roil. Because it killed him, watching his niece and nephew unwittingly stuck in the middle of Tony and Anita's crisis. If Tony even had a clue…

Still, he shook his head. "I feel awful for the kids, I really do. But you know if I intervene it's only going to make things worse. For everybody."

Luis shrugged, then dragged a hand through his thick salt-and-pepper hair. "You never answered my question. You gonna stay or not?"

His lunch finished, Ben leaned back on his elbows, one knee bent. The noonday sun made it feel as warm as spring, the few puny clouds overhead barely breaking the expanse of clear blue sky. "Depends," he said. "Maybe."

Without looking, his father reached around and briefly squeezed Ben's knee. "You know, Anita's not the only Zamora girl I've got a soft spot for." When Ben remained silent, Luis twisted around. "Or did you think I hadn't figured that one out, either? She's why you're thinking of sticking around, yes?"

Ben sat forward again, his brows drawn. "Not much point in denying it."

"Yeah, that's what I thought. But you don't think she's been sitting in that little house of hers, never dating anybody while you've been gone, do you?"

Despite the odd, unexpected surge of jealousy, Ben laughed softly. "Hardly. Although you could spare me the details."

"Details, I don't have. But I'm not blind—or deaf, although your mother and Mercy's mother seem to think I am, considering the things they talk about when I'm aroun'—and I can see that as the years go by, she goes out less and less. All I'm saying is, maybe you've come home at the right time."

"I'm not sure she'd agree with you." When his father lifted one brow, Ben said, "She's not exactly making things easy."

"Which only makes the victory all the sweeter. Or so your mother tells me," Luis added with a grin that almost immediately softened. He looked out over the front yard. "She doesn't trust you, does she? That you'll stay?"

"That's certainly part of it. But she also keeps saying it's too late, that she's past wanting to get married, have a family."

"You believe her?"

"Some women don't, you know."

"We're not talking about some women, we're talking about Mercedes."

Ben laughed, then said, "She said I can't bully her into a relationship. And I can't. Wouldn't want to. But for damn sure I'm not going down without a fight."

"Good for you." Luis paused. "The part about her thinking she doesn't wanna get married—you're on your own with that. But the other thing, about you sticking around…"

He reached into his jacket pocket, pulling out a long envelope which he handed to Ben. "Maybe this will help convince her, no?"

Chapter Eight

Mercy felt like a mouse in its hole, knowing the cat was just outside, waiting, biding his time. Not that she was into stalking fantasies, but…

Four days had passed since she'd told Ben it was a no-go. Four days during which she'd decided it was not in her best interest to mention to anybody exactly how gratifying—not to mention stimulating—she'd found his adamant refusal of same. Four days during which his compelling voice repeatedly sauntered through her head, sending wickedly delicious chills over her skin.

Some feminista she was.

Logically, she knew she'd made the right decision. Emotionally—and heaven help her, physically—turning away from Ben was like vowing never to eat chocolate again. And by chocolate, she was talking the good stuff, not that lethicin-laden crap they sold at the checkout.

But by her reckoning, she only had to hold out for a few more weeks, since Tony would be out of his cast by mid-February and thus able to resume his full workload. Once that happened, Ben would go back to wherever he'd come from, and she could resume her normal life, and all would be well.

At least, that was the plan, she thought as she pulled forward into the pick-up lane at Mattie and Jake's school, in answer to a frantic call from Anita who'd been roped into starting the second shift when her replacement didn't show and neither grandma had been available. Since Mercy had taken the day off herself, she'd won the coin toss. Not that she minded, she thought, grinning, as her niece and nephew spotted her car and raced toward her, visions of all sorts of auntie-indulgences undoubtedly dancing in their little heads.

"Cool!" Jake announced as he clambered into the front seat, ramming home his seat belt. Even under his open jacket, Mercy could see his uniform shirt untucked from his black pants, his tie completely askew. Mattie, by contrast, still looked as though she'd just left the house. Even her hair was combed. Ah, yes, this was Mercy's niece, all right. "Where's Mom?"

"Still at work," Mercy said, her forehead crinkled as she carefully maneuvered the car out of the lot. Last thing she needed was to cream some little kid. "So you're stuck with me."

She had no idea what was going on with Anita and Tony—since Anita's surprise visit the other night, she'd been oddly quiet about the subject. Mercy glanced at the kids, but judging from their smiling faces she was guessing their world was still fairly intact. "But don't think this is all fun and games. I've been given strict orders to make sure you get your homework done. And don't tell me you don't have any," she said, cutting her eyes at Jake, who already had his mouth open. "Your mother said this teacher *always* gives you homework."

Jake clamped his lips together and slumped down in the seat, clearly annoyed at being thwarted. Then he brightened. "C'n we go to McDonald's?"

Mercy glanced over at the kid. Since a stiff wind would blow him into the next county, she decided fast-food-induced obesity probably wasn't an issue. At least not within the next three hours. Still, since she knew Anita was making a concerted effort to cut down on the junk food, she had to make it look good.

"What did they serve for lunch?"

"S'ghetti an' salad an' peaches," Little Bit piped from the back seat.

"Did you actually *eat* it?"

"Uh-huh," both kids said. And indeed, that would appear to be tomato sauce stains on Jake's shirt.

"Okay, I suppose. But don't you *dare* tell your mother."

"That's lying." Again from the back seat.

Jake swiveled around as much as his seat belt would allow. "No, s'not. It's only lying if, like, Mom asks us if we went to McDonald's and we tell her no."

"I *know* that," Mattie said with clearly exhausted patience. "But what if she does? Then what?"

Jake's eyes popped back to Mercy. "I'll handle your mother," she said, figuring she'd deal with it when she had to. And not a moment before.

Fifteen minutes, two Happy Meals, a Spicy Chicken

sandwich and three chocolate shakes later, they all tumbled into her house, their nonstop chatter instantly banishing the heavy silence that normally cloaked the space. Jake threw himself down on the sofa in front of the TV and Mattie trailed after her into the dining nook, thunking her glittery Hillary Duff backpack onto the table and wriggling out of her puffy pink coat, letting it land on the tile floor.

"Where's Homer?"

Mercy stopped sucking on her milkshake long enough to mutter, "Off on one of his jaunts. And pick up your coat, peanut. This floor isn't exactly clean." Damn cat had been gone since Monday. And it had been below freezing every night. She told herself he was fine, that he was smart enough to get out of the cold. But then, he clearly wasn't smart enough to stick around, so there you were. "So," she said, "do you have homework?"

That got an eye roll. "Aunt Mercy."

"What?"

Little hands flew up in the air. "Hello? I'm in kindergarten? We don't *do* homework."

"Boy, Catholic school's certainly different than it was in my day. *We* had homework in kindergarten."

"Yeah, well, that was then and this is now," the kid said, and Mercy gawked at her. "I got my Valentines, though," Mattie said, ratching open the zipper and digging around inside the backpack. "We could do those, if you want."

Mercy stopped short of saying "Blech." Bad enough she'd been railroaded into the whole Valentine's decorating thing at the store. If she never saw a heart-shaped anything again, it would be too soon.

"Isn't it kind of early? Valentine's is ages away yet. And why do you have them with you, anyway?"

"I know, I'm not s'posedta, but they're so pretty I didn't want to leave them at home. See?"

Ah, yes. Princess Barbie. What was up with this kid and blondes?

Mercy settled at the table with what was left of her sandwich and the shake, feeling all warm and filled up inside. Yeah, grease and chocolate'll do it every time. "Wow. What are you going to do with forty-eight cards?"

Another eye roll. "Aunt Mercy."

"What?" she said again, her mouth twitching.

"The *family?*"

"Of course. I forgot," she said, then turned away so Mattie wouldn't see her smile when the little girl shook her head at her aunt's obvious cluelessness.

"An' maybe we could put some of the extras on Annabelle," Mattie said, pointing toward the tree, standing naked and forlorn in her corner, waiting patiently for Mercy to get off her duff and put her away already.

"Sure," Mercy choked out, then yelled to Jake, "Need any help with your homework?"

"Nope, I'm good," floated back. Along with assorted TV-land voices. Mattie spread all her cards out on the table.

"Mama said Valentine's Day is for telling people you love them. Except I don't get it—what if I *don't* love them?"

"Then you just avoid the issue." When the little girl frowned at her, Mercy said, "You don't have to give a Valentine's to someone you don't like."

"That's not true. Mrs. Miller says we gotta give one to

everybody in class, so we don't hurt anybody's feelings. Even the dumb boys."

"Well, that's a little different. When you get older, it's okay to be more selective."

"What's that mean?"

"That you don't have to give Valentines to anyone you don't want to."

"No dumb boys?"

"Nope. You can scratch the dumb boys right off your list."

The child looked immensely relieved. After a few minutes of painstaking copying, complete with tongue sticking out of her mouth, Mattie said, "Should I give one to Uncle Ben?"

"Don't see why not. He's part of the family, after all."

"*And* he's not a dumb boy."

"No," Mercy said, telling herself now the grease and chocolate was making her feel all trembly inside. "He's definitely not a dumb boy." Just a dumb bunny.

Mattie frowned, pencil poised, then looked up at her with a wrinkled nose. "How do you spell it?"

"U-N-C-L-E B-E-N."

When she was done, the kid held up the envelope with a satisfied sigh, admiring her handiwork, backwards B and Es notwithstanding. Then she stuffed the card and envelope in with the others, got down off the chair and climbed into Mercy's lap, and Mercy felt the strangest *sproing* inside her chest. "How come grown-ups don't give out Valentine's cards?"

"They do. Just not to half the free world."

"Huh?"

"Never mind. Your grandma used to give me and my sisters

Valentines when we were little, just like your mama does to you. But when we got bigger, she stopped doing that."

"That sucks."

Mercy chuckled. "We survived. Now Grandma only gives a card to Grandpa. Because he's her *real* sweetie."

"Do I have a sweetie?"

"I have no idea," she said, rubbing her cheek against the little girl's soft, silky hair. "Is there a boy at school you like better than any of the others?"

Mattie seemed to ponder this for a second, then shook her head. "No. They're *all* dumb. They keep chasing me and pullin' my hair and stuff."

"Ah. That's because they like you."

"Then they should give me candy or somethin' instead of pulling my hair."

"You might have a point there."

"Aunt Mercy?" she said after a moment.

"Hmm?"

"How come you don't have kids?"

"Because I never got married, I suppose."

Mattie twisted around to look up at her. "Jake says a lady doesn't have to be married to have babies."

Thank you, Jake. "Well, that's true. But it's harder that way. To be a mommy. Besides, not every lady has kids, you know."

"You should be a mommy, though," she said, very seriously. "You're real good at taking care of Jake and me."

Mercy laughed. "Thanks for the vote of confidence. But being a good auntie doesn't necessarily mean I'd be a good mommy."

Mattie shimmied off Mercy's lap to dig around again in her backpack. "Here," she said, handing Mercy a blank card.

"What's this for?"

"It's for you to give to Uncle Ben."

Mercy froze, looking at the card as if expecting it to strike. "Why would I do that?"

"Because maybe then he'd marry you and you could have babies."

She burst out laughing, only to pull the little girl to her again when her face crumpled. "I'm sorry, sweetie, I didn't mean to laugh. But…it doesn't work that way." Although, she thought with a squirrelly sensation in her midsection, considering the way Ben had looked at her the other night, she half wondered if giving him a Princess Barbie Valentine would be enough to elicit a proposal from him. And wasn't *that* a scary thought?

"But you like him, right?"

"Well, yeah, but—"

"Aunt Livvie says you two make a cute couple. So does Aunt Rosie."

Somehow, Mercy refrained from suggesting the child tell her other aunties to mind their own damn business, just as Mattie added, "But Aunt Carmen said once a badass, always a badass, and you should stay away from him."

On a bark of laughter, Mercy said, "Um…maybe you shouldn't let your mother hear you say that word."

"'Kay." Mattie gathered up the remaining cards and headed for the living room, where she randomly stuck them amongst Annabelle's branches, then said, "C'n I go outside to play? Maybe Homer'll come back if he sees me outside."

"Sure, knock yourself out."

Because far be it from her to disillusion the child by telling her that wanderers don't come home simply because you want them to.

Ben no sooner alighted from his truck when his niece and nephew yelled out to him, standing at Mercy's chain-link fence and waving their arms, which left him no choice but to cross the street to see them.

Laughing, he hauled Mattie up into his arms from the other side of the fence, hugging her back when she threw her arms around his neck and buried her sweet-smelling little self in his neck, all the while listening to Jake's nonstop litany about everything that had gone down in his life since they'd last seen each other.

Then Mercy came out of her house to see what all the commotion was about, her smile going a little stiff when she saw him. Ben set Mattie back down in the yard and stuffed his hands in his jacket pockets, aiming to look as relaxed and cocksure as he knew how. Because to tell the truth, after his ultimatum or whatever that had been the other evening, he'd realized there was a big difference between resolve and having a clue about how to carry through on that resolve.

Until his father had handed him that envelope.

"You draw the short straw?" he asked, grinning.

"Two of them," she said, not exactly grinning back. But not exactly not grinning, either. He guessed he'd be pretty wary, too, if he were her. They hadn't spoken since the night she'd tried to break things off and he'd said *no,* so she was probably a trifle perplexed about what, exactly, their relationship was at the moment. Other than being related through their siblings' marriage, that is.

"Where's Tony?" she asked.

"With Pop, working out some kinks on that job out in Placitas. He probably won't be home for another couple of hours." He got an idea—a probably stupid one since he hadn't thought it through, but what the hell. "You guys up for going for a short ride up into the mountains?" he said to the kids, and of course they both jumped up and down like he'd offered to take them to Disneyland. "With dinner at Dion's after?" he added, which made them jump up and down even more.

"How about you?" he said to Mercy, smiling. "You look like you could use some pizza."

"Oh, I don't know…they already had Mickey D's," she said, which immediately set off a chorus of "*Pleeeease, Aunt Mercy?*" and she made the requisite feeble protesting noises because she had to at least *try* to sound adult and responsible and all. Except Ben knew from the moment he'd said *Dion's* she was a goner. She'd once said, when they'd done this dance the first time, that if she were stranded on a desert island with all the Swiss chocolate and Dion's pizza she could eat, she'd never even miss civilization. Although unless that island had a mall and cable, Ben sincerely doubted she'd last a week.

"I'll just call your dad and make sure it's okay," Ben said, pulling out his phone, which his niece and nephew took as a signal to take off for his truck, zipping around and tripping over each other like his mother's dogs.

"Look…why don't you go ahead and take the kids?" Mercy said after he'd gotten Tony, who'd sounded relieved as much as anything. "I've got, um, stuff to do here."

Ben slipped his phone back into his shirt pocket. "What kind of stuff?"

She made a lame gesture with her hand. "Just…*stuff.*"

He held her gaze in his for several seconds, considering his options. He could cajole her into going, or shame her, or even trick her, if it came down to it. Or he could cut the crap and go the direct route.

"You know I'm crazy about the kids," he said, "but it's your company I want right now. Besides, I've got something to show you."

Curiosity flared in her eyes. "What?"

Gotcha. "Guess you'll have to go with us to find out."

Several seconds passed. Then she said, "No funny stuff?"

"With the kids around?"

"Okay, fine," she said on a sigh like she was making the sacrifice of the century. "I'll go. But only because pizza's included in the deal."

Mercy told herself this was only about going for a ride with the kids, and pizza. She was thinking in terms of chicken, jalapeños, black olives. There was a lot to be said for having a cast-iron stomach. But the minute Ben pulled onto the vacant lot with the view of the mountains to the east and the entire city below to the west, she knew this was about far more than dinner.

At a little after five, the sun was just beginning to kiss the Sandias with the watermelony light that had given the mountain range its name so many years before, as the sky stretched benignly, limitlessly overhead. Although the surrounding area was littered with huge, sometimes pretentiously Southwest-style homes, this particular parcel was situated so that nobody could ever build behind it, impeding the incredible view.

"Wow," Mercy said as a chilly breeze messed with her hair. The kids had taken off, infected with the instant exuberance that comes from feeling boundary-less. "This is really something. Is it one of your father's building sites?"

"No," Ben said after a moment. "It's mine."

Her head whipped around. "You *own* this?"

"Yep. My grandfather left it to me when he died. Tony's got one, too, about a mile away. The old guy had bought them up probably forty, fifty years ago for practically nothing, then never did anything with them." His hands shoved in his pockets, he walked to the edge of the property, the wind rustling his hair, looking more relaxed than she'd seen him since he'd gotten back. As if he'd finally come to terms with whatever it was he'd needed to come to terms with. "I hadn't thought about the lot in years."

Mercy overlapped her jacket closed, hugging herself against the breeze. Against the internal trembling making her voice shake. "It must be worth a small fortune."

"So Dad tells me. Amazing what some people will pay for a bunch of lizard-infested rocks and sagebrush."

She looked away. Swallowed. "I know a great R-Realtor if you want to sell. He'd make sure you got the b-best price for it."

"You cold?" he said behind her, and she shook her head. His boots crunched the uneven ground when he came up to stand at her back, close enough for every one of her skin cells to vibrate from his proximity. "Or I could build on it."

"Oh. Well, yeah, that makes sense," she said, the trembling getting worse. "Because you could make a killing, developing the property and *then* putting it on the market…why are you laughing?"

"Because I've never known anyone who could be as deliberately obtuse as you, Mercy." Now he took her by the shoulders, turning her to face him, the heat from the gentle pressure of his fingers searing her through the jacket, the heat in his eyes searing her far more. "I think it's about time I had a home of my own. Don't you?"

Oh, God. She ached for the sincerity behind his words, the earnestness in his eyes. And had this been ten years ago, she might have been sorely tempted to take those words at face value. For a brief moment, however, she saw an earlier Ben, the one she used to be able to pour her heart out to, knowing he'd listen, and even commiserate, but never judge her. And in that flash of recognition bloomed a revelation, that her trust had never been fully reciprocated, had it?

Because when all was said and done, she honestly didn't know who this man was…because he'd never let her far enough in to find out.

What really drove you back here? she asked him with her eyes. *To me?*

And when his own eyes flickered, then shadowed, she knew she'd hit her mark. Damn.

"You haven't even been home a month, Ben," she said quietly. "It's like somebody who goes on vacation and falls in love with Tuscany or Mexico or the Outer Banks and decides on the spur of the moment to move there. No, listen to me," she said when he tried to interrupt her. "It's not that I don't believe *you* think you're really ready for this. And maybe you are, I don't know. But odds are, you're going to change your mind in six weeks, or six months, or maybe even a year, and where would that leave me? So I'd be an idiot to believe you'd had a complete change of heart—that basically you'd become someone else—in such a short time."

There, she thought. *There's your opening. Go for it.*

Instead he said, "So this has nothing to do with whether you want to get married or not, does it?"

Well, one of them should be honest, Mercy thought even as annoyance shot through her. Never mind that she'd nearly bought into it herself. She pulled out of his grasp, walking away, the wind whistling mournfully in her ears. "Not really, no."

"You never used to be so cynical," he said softly from a few feet away. But she knew he wouldn't argue with her. That he wouldn't dare.

"Not cynical. Realistic. One of the hazards of growing up. It's getting cold," she said, turning toward the children. Away from Ben. "Maybe we should go get that pizza, huh?"

An hour later, after Ben took the kids back to their house, Mercy let herself into hers. This time, the cus-tomary, and usually welcome, silence seemed to heckle her. Her already unsettled mood darkening by the second, she draped her jacket over the back of one of the bar stools, then unlocked and shoved open the patio door, calling Homer, just in case. But no tank-sized kitty barreled across the yard, roared past her into the kitchen, begged for food and attention.

Disappointment settled over her like a fog.

Well, get over it, sister, she thought as she rammed the door closed again and relocked it, then yanked the drapes over the cold glass. Homer was just like that. Always had been, always would be. Why get her panties in a twist about it now? After all, it wasn't as if he was the greatest conversationalist in the world, anyway.

She grabbed the remote off the coffee table and jabbed the On button, surfing through fifty channels in less than thirty seconds, only to realize the boxed voices were making her grind her teeth more than the quiet. Except the minute she turned off the TV, all the thoughts she'd refused to entertain for the past hour crowded into her head like crazed shoppers into stores the day after Thanksgiving.

Strangling a pillow to her stomach, Mercy wondered—and not for the first time in her life—if something was seriously wrong with her. Because what woman in her right mind would keep pushing away this superb specimen of masculinity as hard as she was? So she'd gotten used to being single. So she even liked it. Where was it written that she couldn't get used to being *un*single? After all, she'd been all for it at one point in her life. So why not now?

Then she remembered that shuttered look in his eyes and had her answer.

On a groan, she keeled over onto her side, still hugging the pillow, only to jump when her land line rang. She was up and off the sofa in a flash, pouncing on the poor hapless instrument faster than Homer on a lizard. Didn't even bother to check the caller ID first.

"Hey, there," Dana said, sounding nearly as desperate as Mercy. "You busy? 'Cause for the life of me I cannot decide between a carousel or fairies theme for this nursery, and C.J. is no help whatsoever."

Hmm. She loved Dana and all, but… "I don't blame him. Those are your only two choices?"

She heard a frustrated breath on the other end of the line. "Better than some cartoon character that'll be out of style before the baby's first birthday."

Marginally. "Then again," Mercy said, "you *could* ditch the whole 'theme' idea altogether. Just paint the room pink and be done with it."

"How'd you know I was goin' with pink? Never mind— d'you think you could come over? I'm about at my wits' end."

"I'll be there in fifteen minutes," Mercy said, hoping that, if nothing else, the effort of keeping a straight face whilst considering the relative merits of fairies over horses in drag would keep her from thinking about other things.

Like the six-foot-tall hunk of temptation across the street who had taken the concept of "bad for you" to a whole nother level.

Chapter Nine

C.J. Turner, Dana's hubba-hubba hubby, opened their massive, carved front door when Mercy rang the bell. On his face, a killer smile. In his arms, a sleepy, pajama'd toddler, clinging to his side like a blue-eyed, towheaded koala bear.

"Cavalry's here," she said, stepping inside the marble-floored vestibule.

"Thank God. Two more minutes," he said, his bourbony Southern accent swirling around her as she came in, "And I'd've lost it for sure."

"I heard that!" came from down the hall a second before Dana appeared, her round figure sausaged in skintight jeans and a low-cut apple green sweater that made her mossy eyes sparkle like gemstones underneath her bangs. Long auburn tendrils snaked around her pale neck and collarbone, escapees from what was left of the topknot listing off-center at the top of her head. "Although it's true," she said, cupping Ethan's head. "Five minutes was all it took to do up this guy's room. Why this one's bein' such a bear, I do not know."

Mercy grinned as she unwound her scarf, dumping both it and her purse on a small wrought-iron table by the front door. "Of course you do. Males could care less about their surroundings. Girls, however…" She laughed. "You're probably afraid she's going to wake up one morning and wonder what on earth you were thinking."

"Yeah, that'd be it," Dana said, and burst into tears, clearly overwhelmed with happiness.

"Ohmigosh…sweetie!" Mercy put her arms around her friend, blinking pretty rapidly herself.

"She's been doing this a lot," C.J. said with that half sympathetic, half panicked edge to his voice common to men in the presence of a weeping woman. Except then Mercy glanced up and saw that C.J.'s deep blue eyes seemed brighter than normal, too.

Brother. At this rate she'd be lucky to get out of here alive.

"I'm okay, really," Dana said, swiping at her eyes and giving an embarrassed giggle. "It's just all happenin' so fast, I've hardly had a moment to catch my breath!"

C.J. leaned over to give his soggy wife a quick kiss, then disappeared with Ethan, leaving Mercy and Dana to trot off the mile or so to the other side of the house, where C.J.'s old office was being converted into a very frilly, girly nursery. Heaven help them all if the kid turned out to be a tomboy.

"So where are these wallpaper swatches?" Mercy said.

Still sniffling, Dana dragged over two sample books the size of the Ten Commandments plaques, plopping them open on the floor at their feet. Yep, fairies and carousel horses, all right.

"Of course, if I go with the fairies," she said, producing a catalog out of nowhere and flipping to a dog-eared page, "I could do this with her bed later on."

Mercy blinked at the picture of some gauzy, flower-littered, tentlike thing floating evilly over a twin bed. "You're not serious."

Dana bit her lip. "A bit much?"

"Uh, yeah. But you know," she added gently when Dana's forehead puckered, "maybe you should wait and ask your daughter if she'd like it. Because I'm not the one sleeping in here, she is… Honey? What is it now?"

Two more tears tracked down the redhead's cheeks. "That's the first time anybody's said 'daughter.' I just wasn't expectin' it, is all."

Mercy tamped down a sigh, then pointed. "Fairies."

"You're sure?"

Heh. "Absolutely."

Like the sun coming out from behind a cloud, a huge grin burst across Dana's face. "That's what I thought, too! In fact, I've already talked to a faux painter about havin' a big old white castle painted on that wall!"

Just shoot her now. But, you know, the only thing that mattered was that her friend was happy. And yeah, that the kid shared her tastes or Dana and C.J. would be footing wonker therapy bills down the road, but hey—not her problem.

"So. Is that it?" Mercy asked.

"Actually…" Dana threaded an arm through hers and led her back out into the hall. "No."

"Tell me you're planning the kid's first birthday and I'm outta here."

Dana laughed, then shook her head. "No, I'm savin' that for next week. Actually...I didn't really need your help pickin' out the nursery wallpaper. But Cass and I are worried about you and—"

Mercy dug her boots into the stone floor. "You got me here under false pretenses? I will so get you for this."

"Oh, come on," Dana said, tugging Mercy toward the kitchen, a granite-and-cherrywood masterpiece straight out of a decorating magazine. "My mother brought pineapple-upside-down cake, you have to help me eat it."

"And plying me with baked goods doesn't change anything," she said, hauling herself up onto a bar stool in front of a kitchen island the size of Maui. "You and Cass can stop worrying. I'm fine."

"Yeah. Like I was 'fine' before C.J. and I finally stopped runnin' from each other. Like Cass was 'fine' when Blake waltzed back into her life after all that time, suddenly lookin' to get back together." She cut them both huge pieces of cake, dumped forks on the plates and slid one across to Dana. "Trust me, sugar. We know the look."

"And what 'look' might that be?"

"The 'what the hell do I do now?' look."

Mercy rammed a forkful of blissfully moist, sweet cake into her mouth. Dana's mother could be hell-on-wheels, but *day*-um, the woman could cook. She chewed, swallowed, took another bite, then finally said, "Actually, I took Cass's advice and broke it off. She didn't tell you?"

Dana looked at her from underneath her lashes. "Why do you think we're worried? So? What happened?"

Mercy sighed. And forked in more cake. Dana held up one finger—the universal signal for *Hold on a sec, I don't want to miss anything*—and poured them both glasses of skim milk. "Go on, I'm listening," she said.

"Ben didn't seem real interested in taking 'no' for an answer. And then," Mercy said, chewing, "he takes me up into the mountains to show me this piece of land he's apparently had since birth or something, tells me he's going to build on it." She waved her fork. "As, you know, proof that he's not going anywhere."

"And?"

Edging closer to despondent by the second, Mercy shrugged one shoulder. This time, Dana sighed.

"And I can tell from that hangdog look on your face that all that hooey you gave Cass about you not being the domestic type is just that. Hooey."

"Actually, I—"

"Well, let me tell you something, missy. You're just sayin' that because it's the only way you can figure out how to save your skinny little butt. And anyway, there's all kinds of 'domestic.' Making a home for somebody doesn't mean havin' to stand behind the stove all day or make sure people could eat off your kitchen floor. Obviously, Ben looks at you, just the way you are, and sees exactly what he needs. And wants. And there's a lot to be said for that, you know."

A point that was hard to argue against, considering everything Dana had gone through before she'd met C.J. Still, Mercy wagged her head. "Yeah. *Now.*"

Dana frowned. "So maybe the timing wasn't right before.

And if y'all had tried to make it work back then, before he'd gotten whatever this was out of his system, you probably *would* have had a holy mess on your hands."

Mercy stabbed at the last piece of cake on her plate, trying to keep her breathing even. She knew Dana meant well, but *damn,* the woman was getting on her last nerve. "You really don't know anything about this, Dane. Anything about us."

"I know this sad-sack routine isn't like you. At all. And it's only gotten worse since you supposedly 'broke up' with the guy."

She couldn't argue with that, either. With a groan, Mercy propped her head in her hands, her fingers tangled in her hair. "You're right, this isn't like me." She peered up at her friend through her eyelashes. "I've never been this ambivalent about a man in my life. I don't get it—why can't I just make a decision about Ben and stick with it? Why do I keep feeling, no matter which path I take, I'm making a huge mistake?"

On the other side of the island, Dana set down her own fork to lean both hands against the granite's smooth edge. "If this were ten years ago," she said softly, "would you be this cautious?"

"Moot point. He left, remember?"

"And it hurt more than you wanted to admit."

Her mouth twisted, Mercy picked up the fork again, pulverizing the remaining crumbs on her plate. Then, finally, she nodded.

"So what this really boils down to," Dana said, "is that you're afraid to risk it again. Because this time, there's more on the line than there was before. And don't tell me I'm talkin' outta my bee-hind, because I wouldn't believe you. Any more than I believe this story you keep feedin' everybody about how

you don't want a family of your own anymore, that you're perfectly happy living by yourself."

Dana sliced off another sliver of cake, plopped it onto
Mercy's plate, then did the same for herself. "Trust me, I
know all too well how easy it is to convince yourself of something you think's never going to happen. So what are you
gonna do, Merce? Take a chance on getting what you've
always wanted, or take the easy way out now and maybe
regret it for the rest of your life?"

"I hate you," she muttered around a mouthful of cake, and
Dana grinned.

"Long as you make me godmother to your first baby,"
she said, "I'll forgive you. Except…" She leaned back, her
eyes narrowed. "How come you *didn't* tell me I was talkin'
outta my butt? Don't tell me you'd already figured this out,
all by yourself?"

Mercy snorted. "It does happen, you know. And anyway,
you didn't exactly give me a chance, did you?"

"Oh. I guess not, huh?"

They ate in silence for a minute or two while Mercy contemplated how much her world seemed to be tumbling upside
down all around her, with Dana's leaving the business and
whatever was going on with her sister and Tony and now this
thing with Ben. Ben, who was the last person on earth she'd
ever expect to be promising stability. Permanence. Solidity.
The very things she'd never thought mattered to her, the very
things she now realized she couldn't live without.

There was irony for you.

"It's funny," she said, "how everybody's always thought of
me as the free spirit of the family. The one who wasn't afraid

to put myself out there, who did everything the hard way." Frowning, she looked up at Dana. "When did I become such a stick-in-the-mud?"

"Oh, honey, it happens to the best of us," her friend said, smiling, then collected both their plates, carrying them to the state-of-the-art dishwasher on the other side of the kitchen. "So you just have to ask yourself, would you be more unhappy with Ben, or without him? Once you figure that out, the rest is—" she grinned "—a piece of cake."

Mercy groaned. Then frowned. "The thing is…I can't help feeling there's something he's not telling me. Something that has to do with his time away. Something that's at least partly responsible for why he wants to stay."

"So ask him. If he's so hot to work this out with you, he'll tell you."

"And if he isn't?"

"Then at least it will make your decision easier."

"Thank you for being no help whatsoever."

"Anytime. Although…" The redhead swallowed the last bit of milk in her glass, then said, "If he is keeping something from you, maybe there's a good reason. Men aren't real good at coming right out and saying what's on their minds, in case you haven't noticed. Sometimes you just gotta be patient. Trust you'll find out whatever you need to know, when you need to know it."

And on that comforting note, Mercy drove home again, where, as it happened, Ben was sitting on the tiny slab of concrete that passed for her porch, his long legs stretched out in front of him. Long legs that Homer hurdled gracefully in his zeal to reach her, meowing nonstop as he told her all about his latest escapades.

Ben got to his feet. "He was meowing at your door so loudly I decided to come over here to keep him company until you got back."

Mercy slammed shut her car door. "Really?"

"Okay, I'd already decided to wait until you came back and the minute I sat down, Homer showed up."

Hands in his pockets, Ben stayed right where he was. Waiting for her to make the next move. Still, he couldn't have known what she'd been thinking, all the way back from Dana's, that she'd already figured out what she needed to do. Sort of. Mostly. She swallowed.

"It's cold out here," she said, rubbing her arms. "How long have you been waiting?"

"Ten minutes." His smile was gentle. Wistful. "Ten years."

Her eyes stung. "You're like a pesky fly, aren't you?"

Ben glanced down at the ground, shaking his head, then back at her, his expression downright rueful. "I keep thinking, stay out of the woman's way. Give her whatever space she needs. And then I think…how else can I prove that I *want to be with you?*"

Mercy hugged her jacket closed a little more tightly as Homer writhed around her ankles, complaining. "The first time somebody broke my heart," she said, "I thought I'd die—"

"Ricky Gonzalez," Ben said, startling her. "I remember. You were sixteen. When you hadn't shown your face in almost a week," he said at her stymied expression, "I asked Rosie if you were sick."

"And she told you about Ricky?" Mercy squeaked. "I'll kill her."

That got another chuckle. "Rosie and I were both twelve,

your boy troubles were all the excitement we could dredge up that summer. She thought you were being a drama queen."

Mercy rolled her eyes, then shook her head. "Anyway. My point is, after that, I thought it would get easier. Why I thought that, I don't know, but I did. I was wrong." She took a step closer, her heartbeat thundering in her ears. "I'm not as tough as I look, Ben."

"Neither am I," he said softly. "Honey, I would never, ever knowingly hurt you. Especially not now. All I'm asking for is a chance."

She could barely swallow past the knot in her throat. "It's just that, after all these years…" She shook her head. "It all seems to be happening so fast."

"Call it making up for lost time."

So confront him already, rang in her head. *Right here. Right now.* Only she opened her mouth and the words refused to budge. Because maybe he needed her to trust him. To be patient with him. Because maybe he thought she was the only person who could really do that, which was pretty amazing, when you thought about it.

Then again, maybe she should shove him out of the way, run inside and lock the door.

Only then she'd be by herself on the other side, wouldn't she?

"Oh, what the hell," she said, moving into his arms.

Sometime around midnight, the grating crash of a closing minivan door jarred Mercy awake, propelling her instantly from the bed.

"What is it?" Ben rumbled behind her, yawning, as she wrestled her robe out from the underneath the cat, stumbling the short distance between bed and window as she clumsily put it on, yanking the tie closed. A quick twist of her mini-blinds revealed Anita's sandy-beige Voyager in her mother's driveway, her sister marching Jake up to her mother's front door with a sacked-out Mattie slumped against her chest.

"Crap," Mercy muttered, leaving the blinds open to ransack the chair by the closet for the jeans and sweater she'd been wearing, sparing a brief glance for Ben propped up on one elbow in the bed. "Anita's brought the kids to Mom's."

"You're kidding?"

"Nope." Mercy grabbed clean underwear out of her dresser drawer and rushed into her bathroom. "That can't be good," she called out through the open door, only to jerk slightly when she turned to find Ben in the doorway, already dressed, clearly furious.

She knew what he was thinking, that everyone had hoped the relative quiet from that front had meant Anita and Tony had somehow patched things up. Wishful thinking, obviously. For her sister to disrupt the kids' sleep on a school night meant something was seriously wrong.

"I assume you're going over there?"

"What do you think?" she said, wincing as she rammed a brush through her guess-what-I've-been-doing? hair. "In fact, wanna bet my phone rings before I finish up in here?"

Right on cue, her land line rang. Ben snatched the portable out of its charger by the bed and tossed it to her, then wrapped his arms around her waist from behind as she answered. Just to hold her, absorbing her trembling. She glanced up at their reflection in the mirror, at his strong, serious eyes looking back at her, and relaxed. A little.

"Anita's over here with the kids!" her mother's agitated voice came through the line. "She says she's left Tony!"

"Yeah, Ma, I know. About her being over there, I mean. I heard the van."

"You don't sound surprised."

Uh, boy. "Actually, 'Nita and Tony have been having problems for a while. And before you jump down my throat, I didn't say anything because 'Nita asked me not to. She didn't want to worry you and Papi."

Her mother muttered something in Spanish, then said, "He's not…" She lowered her voice to a whisper. "He's not hurting her, is he?"

"No! God! At least, I don't think so, she never said anything. I just think he…doesn't get who she is," she added over her mother's whoosh of relief. "He never really has. Are the kids okay?"

"Mattie's still half asleep, 'Nita's putting her down in your old room. But Jake…Jake's a mess. He's in the family room, he won't talk to anybody. Poor little thing…so much to put on those small shoulders." Then she heard a tiny intake of air as her mother started to cry, as if this was somehow her fault.

"Oh, God, Ma…hang on, I'll be there in a minute."

Ben took the phone from her, putting it back while Mercy sat on the edge of the rumpled bed to stuff her bare feet into a pair of shearling boots she'd grabbed from the floor of her closet.

"This is what you do, isn't it?"

At the wonder in his voice, Mercy looked up, shoving her hair behind her shoulders. "What do you mean?"

"Give the parties, watch the kids, keep everyone from losing it in a crisis."

Breathing a little harder than she'd like, Mercy sat upright, her hands curled around the edge of the mattress. "Is that a criticism?"

"Hardly. I just think it's ironic that you can't watch the news because it depresses you so much, yet you're the one everybody else relies on."

She stood, shoving her arms into a down vest. "Maybe because my family's across the street, not halfway around the world. So I feel like I can actually be of some use, you know?"

In the half light, she saw Ben's mouth curve into a smile. Then he peered out the window, slipping his corduroy shirt back on. "Huh. My mother's on her way to your folks' house." His eyes touched hers. "You really ready for this?"

"No. But I suppose it was bound to come to a head sooner or later. You going to stay here?"

He stared out the window another few seconds, apparently considering his options, before turning away to pocket his cell phone and wallet. "Tempting as that is," he said with a half smile, "I've dodged my family responsibilities long enough. Maybe I can talk to Jake while you help the women sort things out. Then we'll see. If my mother's at your house, odds are my father will head to Tony's. An impartial third party might come in handy."

Suddenly Mercy remembered, or at least half remembered, Anita's comment about Ben and his father—something about Luis favoring Ben? Tony's feeling left out? In all the backings-and-forthings of the past little while, she'd forgotten. Now, seeing the pained look on Ben's face, she wondered if there was more to her sister's words than she'd realized.

"Impartial?" she said.

"Compared with my father? Or Tony? Yes. Not that I have any idea what I'm supposed to do, but…" He shoved his hand through his hair, and Mercy thought, *Yeah, definitely something going on there.* She doubted, however, if this was the time to get into it. "Sometimes," he said, "I guess all you can do is play it by ear. Whoa," he said when she threaded her arms around his waist and nestled up against him. "What's this for?"

"You're really not the same Ben as before, are you?"

"Finally," he said, dropping a kiss in her hair. "The light dawns."

Seconds later, they stepped outside, the brisk, clean high-desert air banishing the last vestiges of sleep. The door clicked closed behind her, but before she could head down the walk, Ben grabbed her, turning her around to kiss her quickly, softly, his lips warm, solid, reassuring. "Just remember, this has nothing to do with us," he said, and she nodded.

Then he took her by the hand and they crossed the street, and she had to admit there was something to be said for not going into battle all by her lonesome.

Chapter Ten

By the time Ben reached his brother's house a half hour later, he was loaded for bear.

Not that he'd let on before this how angry he was, although he guessed from Mercy's solicitous frown that she pretty much figured his blood was boiling. Two people taking their frustrations out on each other was one thing. But to put their children in the middle of it…

Idiots, he thought as his truck door thundered shut, setting off a chorus of dogs. Over their crazed barking, his footsteps ricocheted into the night as he trudged past his father's SUV. The raised voices inside came to an abrupt halt when he rang the bell; his father opened the door, eliciting a bitter "What the hell are *you* doing here?" from Tony on the other side of the living room.

"Seeing if I can knock some sense into that thick head of yours, that's what," Ben said, sidling past Luis and jabbing one hand toward the east. "I've just spent nearly a half hour trying to calm down your son, who has no idea what the hell is going on, or why his parents can't see past their differences long enough to see how much their fighting is upsetting their kids!"

Tony recoiled like he'd been sucker-punched, only to immediately lurch in Ben's direction on his crutches. "This is none of your business! And don't you worry about me taking care of my own kids! I managed just fine without your help up until now, I sure as hell don't need it now!"

"Well, you sure as hell need *somebody's* help!" Ben yelled, half tempted to grab one of his brother's crutches and smack him upside the head with it. "You and Anita, both! Because she's not exactly on my list right now, either, dragging the kids out into the middle of the night!" He muttered a choice swear word, then leveled his gaze at his brother again. "You're supposed to be the older brother, dammit! So maybe it would be nice if you acted like it, you know?"

"Benicio, please…" Luis had slumped down onto the edge of Tony's sofa, his stubby-fingered hands limp on his knees. "Everybody's on edge, maybe this isn't the best way to go about fixing things—"

"You want me to stick around, to be part of the family again?" Ben said, reeling on his father. "Then you can't dictate how that plays out. And you," he said, turning again on his brother, "have no idea how good you have it! When you asked me what I had to show for my life, did it occur to you to take five seconds to appreciate your *own?* That you found a woman who put up with you for all these years, and who would continue to put up with you if you'd get your head out of your butt long enough to figure out that her wanting her own life isn't some kind of threat to *you*. And your kids," he said, his throat clogging on the word. "God, Tony—is this what you want for them? To put them in the middle, to make *them* suffer for their parents' hardheadedness?"

His words echoed in the resulting silence. Until Tony, his face purpled with rage, stamped one crutch ineffectually into the carpeted floor…and lit into their father.

"Dammit to hell, Pop—Ben's home for, what, five minutes? And you *ask* him to stick his nose in my business?"

As angry as Ben still was with his brother and sister-in-law, the chronic pain in Tony's voice tore him up inside. The pain that had made him less than enthusiastic about getting in the middle to begin with…the pain that had been a large part of his leaving all those years ago.

"*Why,* Pop?" Tony said, the word wrung from his throat. "Why was Ben always the good one, even though I was the one who stayed, who worked my butt off for you? *With* you? Why was he *always* the better son?"

His expression ravaged, Luis pushed himself to his feet and reached out to Tony, who rebuffed him. "I never thought Ben was better than you, Tony—"

"No, only that he would have done a better job than me," Tony hurled at the old man.

"Which was wrong," Ben said, purposely drawing fire. "Why *did* you always seem to favor me?" he asked his father. "Especially when it was completely unwarranted."

"I told you," his father said, "I wasn't put out with you for leaving—"

"I'm not talking about that. Tony's got five times more on the ball about the construction business than I ever did. Or ever would have. And maybe if you'd start appreciating *him* more, he'd stop taking out his frustrations on his wife." He shifted his gaze to Tony, who stood there openmouthed. "Part of the reason I left was because of you. Not the only reason, God knows. But getting out of the way so maybe you and Pop could work things out between you definitely had a lot to do with it."

Somewhat recovered, Tony smirked. "Nice try, little brother. The fact was, you couldn't wait to get out, to leave the family. There was nothing for you here, and you know it."

A tight smile pulled at Ben's mouth. "You have no idea how much there was here for me. What I gave up in some obviously misguided attempt to save this family, even if I didn't fully understand it at the time. What I gave up for *you,* Tony." His gaze veered back to Luis. "Because as long as I stuck around, you refused to see Tony for who he was. And I hated it, Pop. *Hated* it."

He spun around and headed toward the door, tossing a glance in his brother's direction. "So you'll have to forgive me if I seem a little put out that you seem determined to destroy the very thing I sacrificed for you. Now if you'll excuse me, I've got a life to get back."

Before Ben had stormed off into the night, presumably to knock some sense into his brother, Mercy had slipped him the spare key to her house from the hook by her mother's back door. She hadn't even thought about it, it simply seemed like the logical thing to do. Even though she'd neither hoped nor expected him to return. She'd just thought he should have the option, that was all.

And giving him a key avoided all that messy having-to-wait-up business.

Not that she wasn't awake when he let himself in, sometime around two. Or if she hadn't been, she would have awakened anyway, when he undressed again and slipped into her bed to spoon up against her. When his arm snaked around her waist, she automatically skootched into his warmth. This wasn't about sex, however, but about something far more precious and real and heart-stopping. What they'd had so long ago, multiplied by a hundred. A thousand.

Or could be, if he'd ever let that little—maybe not so little?—piece of him he was holding back out to play.

"So?" she murmured, and he nuzzled her hair. "Is everyone still alive?"

He chuckled tiredly, tightened his hold. "Barely."

A moment passed. "You okay?" she whispered.

"I'm fine," he said after a beat. "Go back to sleep."

As if. Mercy skimmed her fingers up and down his arm. "What is up with you and your brother, anyway?" When he didn't respond, she said, "Anita seems to think your father always pitted the two of you against each other. That he favored you, at Tony's expense."

Ben went very still. "It would seem that way."

"Why would he do that?"

"No idea. Can we go to sleep now?"

Resisting the temptation to pluck out one of his arm hairs, she said, "You do realize that everyone now knows we're sleeping together?"

"Mm-hmm," he said, his breathing slowing. "They can deal. They're grown-ups, we're grown-ups…" She felt him shrug. "No more lies, babe," he mumbled. "No more secrets…"

Oh?

A nanosecond later, he was sound asleep, while Mercy lay there, eyes wide open, thinking, *Be careful what you wish for…*

Except two days later, she still had no clue what Ben had been talking about. And whenever she brought up the subject, he frowned, like he had no idea what *she* was talking about. Which, come to think of it, sounded pretty much like every married couple she knew, so maybe they were on the right track with this relationship thing, after all.

Anyway. So here it was, Morning *Numero Dos* since she and Ben had officially Become a Couple, and there her sister was, in bright pink scrubs and her down jacket, standing at the counter and looking about as forlorn as a girl could, pouring herself a cup of the lovely, strong coffee Ben had put on when he'd gotten up a half hour before. On the other side of the breakfast bar, Mercy sat alternately guzzling said coffee and yawning, listening to the shower running from down the hall and wishing there was some way to politely tell her sister the sounding board wasn't on duty for at least another hour. Or two.

"What I don't get," Mercy said after another yawn, "is why you just don't call Tony already, if you're so bummed."

"Can't do that." The coffee sloshed over the edge of the blurred carafe when Anita shakily set it back on the warming plate. "He's the one who has to come to his senses," she said over the sizzling.

"But the kids—"

"The kids are fine. Really. Ma and Papi are overcompensating like mad, and Tony talks to them twice a day. And they went over there last night for a little while…" Her voice trailed off, then she pulled her shoulders back, shoving her hair behind one ear. Oh, hell, her bottom lip was trembling. "So…" She sucked in a steadying breath. "How are things going between you and Ben?"

And a deaf person could have heard the "I hope to hell you know what you're doing" in her sister's voice. Not that Mercy needed the warning. Or the meddling, well-meaning though it might have been.

"Not bad, actually. Although maybe you shouldn't be here when he gets out of the shower."

"He's still pissed with me?"

"He's pissed with everybody. Why do you think he's been staying over here? He and his father aren't even talking."

Anita gave her a hard look. "Like I'm gonna believe Ben's staying with you has anything to do with his father."

Mercy sighed. "You know, if you'd asked me six weeks ago how I would have felt about sharing my house and my bed and my life with another human being—especially this particular human being—I would have broken out in hives."

"And now?" When Mercy only shrugged, her sister leaned across the breakfast bar, laying a hand on her wrist. "*Chica,* take it from someone who knows…do not get yourself into anything you're not one hundred percent sure about. When I think back about how young I was when I got married…" Her hair grazed her shoulders when she shook her head. "Love really is blind, you know?"

"Yes, I do. I also know there's no such thing as one hundred percent. Or are you saying I don't get to take the same chances the rest of you did?"

Anita's mouth fell open, but at the sound of the shower being turned off she hurriedly finished her coffee, then grabbed her purse off the counter. "Just be careful," she said, then hustled around the bar, through the living room and out the front door.

A minute or so later, Ben had replaced her sister in the kitchen, all damp-haired and yummy-smelling in a corduroy shirt and jeans, chatting away to the cat while leaning against the counter waiting for his toast to pop up. Like he belonged there or something.

Unbelievable.

"I take it Anita was here?"

"How'd you know?"

He held up her empty mug.

"She misses your brother," Mercy said, holding out her own mug for Ben to refill while he had the coffeepot in his hand. "I told her you're staying over here because of all the stuff between you and your dad."

A smile played around his mouth. "What other reason would there be?"

She threw her spoon at him, which, laughing, he dodged only to laugh harder at Homer's double axle when it clattered to the floor. "Anyway," she said as he bent over to pick up the spoon, "I get the feeling she thinks we're being a trifle impetuous."

His gaze never leaving her face, Ben took a long sip of his coffee, then set his mug on the counter. "Do *you?*"

Aside from than the occasional spurt of anxiety about whatever it was he wasn't telling her?

"No," she said, deciding not to let on that, actually, his being around felt a lot like, after years without a sofa, she'd been sure the room would feel cramped once she finally decided to live like a grown-up and get one. And yet, amazingly, the minute the delivery guys set it down it was as if it had always been there.

Except having Ben around was much nicer, since sofas don't ask how your day was or make coffee in the mornings or listen to you bitch or give you orgasms.

Of course, they also stay where you put them, which was a big point in their favor.

His toast shot out of the toaster; he caught it midair and plunked it onto a plate. "So did you tell her to mind her own business?" he asked while he buttered it, giving her one of those skin-prickling, tummy-fluttering looks that immediately brought on the Naughty Thoughts. Even at this hellacious hour.

"She's probably a little vulnerable right now for the direct approach. But yes, basically."

Ben set a piece of harmless, glistening toast on a plate in front of her; this early, it might as well have been something from Fear Factor. Still, to show she appreciated the thought, she picked it up and nibbled on one corner. Carrying his own toast into the living room, Ben reached over to reinsert one of Mattie's Valentines that had fallen out of Annabelle's branches.

"Are we sending our parents to early graves?" he asked.

"Hey. If they've survived everything the seven of us have put them through thus far, they'll live through this, too." She lowered the toast to the plate, flicking crumbs from her fingers. "Why? Have yours said something to you?"

Ben walked back into the kitchen, shoving the rest of his toast into his mouth. "They're a little preoccupied with the Tony-and-Anita Show at the moment, so no," he said, chewing. "Yours?"

"Oh, we had an agreement," she said lightly, waving one hand. "If they wanted me to live across the street, they had to stay out of my private life."

Ben's eyes crinkled at the corners. "Yeah, I can see your mother agreeing to that."

She blinked at him, then slapped one hand on her cheek in mock astonishment. "Ohmigod—you don't think Anita was a *spy,* do you?"

Chuckling, he checked his watch, then grabbed his jacket off the back of the chair, leaning across the bar to give her a soft, lingering see-you-later kiss as he slipped it on, and she sat there for twenty minutes after he'd gone feeling as dreamy and mush-brained as a fourteen-year-old with her first crush.

And almost as willing to believe in happily-ever-afters.

Go figure.

If it hadn't been for Mercy, Ben thought as he shuffled through a stack of invoices in his father's office, he'd've lost it by now for sure. Nearly a week after Tony and Anita's split, Tony and Ben and Luis only spoke with each other about business, and then as briefly as possible. Even so, the hurt in his father's eyes, and the confusion in Tony's, nearly took him under. But what else could he do? At least he'd dragged the problem out into the open, half-decayed though it may have been after having been buried for so long. Getting past the layers of grime and identifying it, however…that was up to them. Especially his father.

So Mercy had been his bulwark through the whole ordeal. Except, despite her repeated assurances that she was fine with the way things were going between them, Ben could practically smell her lingering insecurities. Willing to give this a shot though she might be, only a fool would believe she completely trusted him. And he could hardly blame her, could he? Especially since—

His cell rang, derailing his thoughts. Ben glanced at the display, frowning when he saw Tony's number.

"You about to knock off?" his brother said.

"Soon. Why?"

"It's okay," Tony said on what sounded like a defeated sigh. "I'm not gonna bite your head off or anything. It's just that it's taken me this long for a lot of what you said to sink in. An' now I'm thinking maybe it's time you and I talk. Finally. So you wanna pick me up when you get off, we could go to Applebee's or something? I'd say here but there's nothing in the house except cereal and yogurt, and I can't face another pizza."

Deciding he didn't detect murderous undertones in his brother's voice, Ben agreed to pick Tony up shortly, then called Mercy to tell her his plans.

"O…kay…" she said. "And you're telling me this why?"

"In case you were counting on me being there for dinner, why else?"

"Actually, Rosie strong-armed me into helping her with a Pampered Chef party tonight, which I'd totally forgotten about until she called me a little bit ago. So I wasn't going to be home, anyway."

"A Pampered what?"

"Never mind. Girl thing. So…does this mean we're officially living together now, or what?"

The cell reception wasn't the best down in the Valley, but even so, Ben couldn't tell if Mercy was surprised, annoyed or strangely pleased. Nor was he about to jump in with an answer guaranteed to elicit the wrong result.

"Call it anything you like. I was only giving you a heads-up. In case you were expecting me."

"I wasn't *expecting* anything," she said, a little shortly, he thought. "It's a lot safer that way."

"In other words, you still don't think you can count on me."

"How about I'm good with taking this day by day."

"Then how about I make it clear, so there's no misunderstanding," he said, leaning heavily on the desk, the phone tightly gripped in his hand. "We're *together,* Mercy. Which by my definition means we share our meals and we share a bed, unless something comes up on either end, in which case we let the other one know what's going on. You got a problem with that?"

Finally, he heard her chuckle. "And if I did?"

"Then tell me to back off, and I'm gone."

"Yeah. Like that worked so well before."

"Only because I didn't think you really meant it."

"God, you are such a man."

"You complaining?" he said, leaning back in his chair, a grin sliding across his face. "In fact, being as I'm the guy and all, guess what I'm thinking about right now…?"

"And maybe you should hold that thought, since I'm here at the store and all?"

His smile broadened. "Thought I was gonna talk dirty, didn't you?"

"You weren't?" she said, sounding slightly disappointed.

"Guess you'll never know," he said, disconnecting the call.

"I take it that was Ben?" Cass said, wrapping up a vintage christening gown in tissue paper while the customer—a pint-size, white-haired thing who had to be in her seventies, her blue eyes positively radiant over the birth of her first granddaughter—floated amongst the racks, seeing what else she could add to her already prodigious stack of goodies for her seven grand*sons*.

Mercy rolled her eyes. There'd been little point in pretending to her partners that she and Ben weren't back together. Although she could have done without the smug expressions on both their faces when she'd fessed up. "Get this—he called to tell me he wouldn't be available for dinner. Because he didn't want me to feel, I don't know, stood up or something."

The tissue paper stopped rustling. Mercy glanced over to see Cass frowning at her. "I don't suppose I have to tell you how much a considerate man goes for on the open market these days?" At Mercy's weak laugh, Cass tilted her head. "So…is this a good thing or no?"

"I'm not sure," Mercy said on a sigh. "Although he did indicate if I felt crowded, he'd back off."

Cass resumed her rustling. "Not that I was listening or anything, but I don't recall hearing anything that sounded like telling him to go jump in a lake."

Mercy thought about that for the next few minutes, while the grandmother toted more stuff up to the counter and finally pulled out her credit card, which Mercy swiped for her. Once the woman, gleefully laden down with a half-dozen multicolored Great Expectations shopping bags—and a bilious pink heart-shaped balloon for good measure—bounced off, Mercy looked at her partner and said, "Actually, what I feel is…hold on to your hat—happy."

"It's okay, you'll get used to it," Cass said.

Yeah. That's what worried her.

For the past thirty minutes, Ben and Tony had been sitting at the Applebee's bar, watching some college hoops game on the closest TV and nursing a pair of beers. Since his brother had initiated the contact, Ben was more than willing to let him initiate the conversation as well. Although at the rate they were going, they'd be into a new administration before that ever happened.

They'd been close when they'd been kids, Ben supposed, being only two years apart. But by the time Tony started middle school, they had little to do with each other, a gap that only widened after they moved into separate bedrooms when Ben turned nine or ten.

Now, though, despite the awkwardness of the moment, Ben felt as though the impenetrable wall of animosity that had been wedged between them for as long as he could remember had finally begun to dissolve. A little, anyway. Especially, when—at long last—his brother slid a glance in his direction and said, "I called 'Nita this morning. Said if she wanted to go to counseling or something, that would be okay with me."

"Miss her, do you?"

"Worse than *ESPN* that time I forgot to pay the cable bill."

Ben smiled. "You can't back out this time, you know."

"I won't. I *swear,*" Tony repeated at Ben's skeptical expression. "I love that woman, Ben. Yeah, we make each other crazy, but the thought of life without her…" He shook his head. "I would die, man. Just curl up in a ball and freakin' *die*. I guess it took her actually walking out for me to realize that maybe I've been a little…stubborn. That maybe I could be a little more, you know, supportive. Show her how much I appreciate her."

Ben hid his smile behind his glass as he swallowed his beer, then said, "You do know, don't you, if you so much as think of backsliding—"

"Not gonna happen. I know people think I'm dumb as a rock, but I'm not *that* dumb."

Ben clunked down his glass. "You're not dumb, Tony. Shortsighted, yes—a quality you share with me, for what that's worth—but not dumb."

"Thanks," Tony said, and Ben nodded, then Tony said, "I think maybe I owe you an apology, too."

"What for?"

"For blaming the wrong person all these years. For not realizing it wasn't you who was the problem, it was Pop."

Ben stared blankly at the TV screen, fingering the condensation dripping down the side of the glass. "I don't think it's that simple."

"Like I don't know that? But at least now I've got some idea what I'm really dealing with. After you left the other night, I came right out an' asked Pop why he never thought I was good enough, and he looked like I'd slapped him in the face. Of course, he was already shaken up pretty good, after what you'd said, but…" Tony wagged his head back and forth. "It was like he'd suddenly woken up or something. And he apologized."

"Did it sound sincere?"

Tony seemed to mull that over for a moment, then shrugged. "I think he's really sorry for everything that's happened. Whether or not he would've, or could've, changed the way he felt, I don't know. But when you stood up for me like that…" His dark gaze swung to Ben's. "That meant a lot. Especially since I didn't get the feeling you were just blowing smoke up my ass."

Ben smiled. "No. I wasn't." He released a breath. "I have no idea why Pop's always thought I'd be better at running the business than you. From everything I've seen since I've been home, there's absolutely no reason for him to think that. Although…" He pushed the beer away, leaning back to cross his arms over his chest. "*Are* you happy? Working for Pop, I mean?"

One side of Tony's mouth quirked up. "I'd be a lot happier if he'd get off my case an' trust me every once in a while, you know? I mean, sure, I screwed up a couple of times when I started out. But that was years ago. An' even then, it wasn't anything serious. Just stupid stuff." Again, Tony's eyes cut to Ben's. "You really left because of me?"

"In a roundabout way, at least. Because Pop was driving me nuts, too, putting me up on some damn pedestal that I didn't deserve. And for sure didn't want. I despised what he was doing to you, but I couldn't figure out any other way to solve the problem except by removing myself from the picture."

Tony got very quiet. "All that you were saying, about me having no idea what you'd had here…you were talking about Mercy, huh?"

After a moment, Ben nodded. "Yeah."

"And you really gave her up because of me?"

"That's how it played out."

"And people think *I'm* stupid." When Ben started to protest, Tony raised a hand. "Okay, fine, I'm not stupid. But, damn— what were you thinking?"

"It's okay, it wasn't that serious between us, anyway."

That got a narrow-eyed look. "On your part? Or hers?"

Smiling, Ben shook his head. No, if it was one thing Tony wasn't, it was dumb. "Far as Mercy was concerned, it was just a passing thing. If not an outright mistake. I don't think it ever even occurred to her to associate the word *permanent* with what we were doing." He twisted his glass of beer around by its base. "And I figured I might as well make my move before it did."

"Man," Tony said on a rush of air. "I mean, I hear what you're saying, but it's not registering. That you'd do something like that. For me." He took a long swallow of his beer. "It didn't work, you know."

"Yeah. I can see that. I'm really sorry."

"Me, too," Tony said on a short laugh, then added, "But it's not your fault. Apparently, it never was."

"I've never been in any kind of competition with you, Tony. I swear."

"I know. At least, I know *now*." His brother lifted his beer to his lips, taking several swallows before saying, "So. You hoping to start over or win her back or what?"

"That's the plan, yep."

"Is it working?"

"I'll let you know."

Tony chuckled, then said, more seriously than Ben could ever remember hearing him before, "For sure, you are definitely not the same person you were when you left."

"Is that good or bad?"

After a noncommittal shrug, his brother said, "I'll say one thing, though—I think maybe I could learn to like the dude sitting beside me right now." He hesitated. "If you'd be interested, I mean."

"I'll take it under advisement," Ben said, and they both smiled.

Only then Tony came up with, "Does that mean you might consider telling me what you really been doing all this time you've been away?"

Startled, Ben frowned in his direction. Tony misunderstood and immediately started backpedaling. "Not that it's any of my business, so if you don't want to tell me, that's cool—"

"No, it's not that, it's…" Ben shook his head. "I just don't—"

"—get how I figure that? For one thing, for somebody's who's supposedly been working in construction all along, you're practically clueless about the newest materials and techniques. For another, I've run into too many guys over the years with stuff in their backgrounds they don't want me to know about not to recognize the signs." When Ben looked away, Tony said, "So am I right?"

"Yeah," Ben said on a sigh. "You're right." Their waiter brought their steaks; Ben picked up the salt shaker, staring at the sizzling meat for several seconds before looking over to run smack into a combination of curiosity and expectancy in his brother's eyes.

And he realized it was time to come clean.

So, as they ate, Ben filled Tony in on what had really kept him away from home for so long, and Tony's eyes got wider and wider until eventually he said, very quietly, "Wow." Then, in a rare demonstration of understanding, he said, "I can sure see why you kept this to yourself," only to then add, with a fork jab for emphasis, "but if you don't tell Mercy, like, yesterday, you can kiss any chance you have of winning her back *adios*. 'Cause keeping something like this from her…" Tony shook his head.

"I know, I'm working up to it," Ben said, grabbing the dessert menu, reasonably sure his stomach's churning had nothing to do with his dinner. He'd left that life behind, of his own accord; there was no reason, none, for the sudden surge of ambivalence his conversation with his brother had provoked. He'd stuck it out longer than most, for God's sake. Didn't he deserve a life of his own now? "Although you do realize if you breathe a word of this to anybody—"

Tony's laugh cut him off. "Are you kidding? An' spoil the joy of for once being the only one in the family that knows something the others don't? Not on your life," he said, turning the small laminated menu over. "I can't decide between the apple pie and this brownie thing, whaddya think?"

Ben smiled halfheartedly, wishing with all his heart for just *some* of his decisions to be that uncomplicated.

Chapter Eleven

When Mercy returned from the Pampered Chef party, Ben was sprawled on the sofa watching TV, hands behind his head, his crossed, socked feet propped on her coffee table. He'd turned Annabelle's color wheel on, the goof. And speaking of goofs, Homer was stretched out on the sofa beside Ben, flat on his back, looking positively filleted. Mercy shook her head.

"How was your thing?"

"It wasn't *my* thing," she said with a yawn, sinking into the cushions beside him, melting into his side when he put his arm around her and drew her close. "And please, shoot me if I ever even suggest doing a home party. But it was fine. I bought one of those pizza stone dealies for the oven."

"Does that mean homemade pizza in our near future?"

"Probably not. But Rosie kept giving me the evil eye so I

caved." She laid a hand on his stomach, toying with a shirt button. "How was dinner with your brother?"

"Okay," he said, and she thought, *Sheesh, men,* only then he said, "More than okay. We talked, really talked, more than we ever have before." He gave her a little squeeze. "Speaking of caving…he's going nuts without your sister."

"Yeah?"

"Oh, yeah. I think we can all strike that particular crisis off our list. Until the next time, at least."

The furnace kicked on with a whoosh, then a rumble; seconds later, heat murmured through the vent. Outside, some old truck rattled by. She could hear a dog barking on the next street over. All sounds Mercy normally wouldn't have even noticed, if it hadn't been for the profound silence that had suddenly taken her living room hostage. Anxiety sparked inside her; before it had time to flare, she twisted around to find Ben staring blankly at nothing, his forehead bunched.

"Hey," she whispered, dragging a knuckle down his rough cheek. "What's going on in there?"

He sucked in a quick, sharp breath, as if to clear his head, then took her hand in his, stroking his thumb over one fingernail. "I haven't exactly been honest with you," he said quietly. "About the time we've been apart."

Finally, Mercy thought, even as she wondered why, instead of feeling relieved, she felt like a character in a Japanese horror movie, waiting for the oogly-woogly to git 'er.

She pushed herself up. Looked him straight in the eye. "Tell me you have a wife and four kids in Boise and you are so dead."

"No," he said on a dry chuckle. "No wife. No kids. Never been to Boise."

"Then what?"

Ben lowered his feet to the floor, leaned forward. "For the past eight years, I've been working with this P.I. based in Dallas, helping to rescue lost and abducted kids."

For who-knows-how-long, she just sat there, staring at his profile, his words clanging in her head. Then she shifted to sit on the trunk so she could face him. So he'd have to face her. "You're telling me you haven't been drifting from place to place all this time, working construction?"

"Not after the first couple of years, no."

After that, she only heard bits and snatches of his explanation, about how he'd gotten to talking to this P.I. who'd specialized in rescuing kids when they'd both ended up in the E.R. one afternoon, the "click" when he realized that maybe this was something that would give him a sense of purpose.

"I was a real mess at that point, Merce," he said. "I had no idea what I was supposed to be doing, I was getting real tired of the freelance construction routine, and I couldn't come home. Not then, at any rate. Roy took me under his wing, showed me the ropes, helped me to get my own license a few years ago." He shrugged, then pushed out another breath. "And that's it. The truth."

"So all this time…you've been a private investigator? And nobody knew?"

"No."

Her eyes burned. "You bring babies back to their parents?"

"That's pretty much the job description, yeah."

Mercy released a huge breath of her own. Well, that explained a whole lot, didn't it? Why he'd been so concerned about the little boy at the store, why he'd questioned her about

Mattie's friendliness with strangers…just his connection with kids in general. Then, even as the first stirrings of anger began to bubble inside her, she said, *"Why?* Why on earth did you keep it a secret?"

"Think about it, honey—can you imagine my mother's reaction if she'd known what I'd really been up to? Yeah, for the most part it's a lot of Internet searching and talking to the authorities and sitting on your butt behind the wheel, watching and waiting for hours on end. But sometimes…" He scrubbed a hand down his face. "Let's just say things can get kind of hairy."

The inside of her head felt like a presidential news conference with a hundred questions being shouted at once. Only in her case, it was which one to ask first, not answer, that had her stymied. "But…isn't that what the police and the FBI are for?"

"You'd think," Ben said with a tired, tight smile. "But there are far more cases than the authorities can handle. And frankly, in many jurisdictions, if it's a parent who's taken the kid, they still don't treat it as a kidnapping. The parents left behind…they're desperate. Beyond desperate."

Just the thought sent a wave of nausea through her. "So, what? You did the commando thing and went in and rescued the kids?"

"Not unless we absolutely have to," he said. "It's dangerous, borderline illegal and a Rambo number can definitely traumatize the kids more than they already are. If we're lucky, the abducting parent gives up without a struggle, once they're discovered."

"And if you're not?"

His eyes searched hers for a long moment. "The kid's welfare is always, always the first priority. But the longer a child's kept in essentially a hostage situation, hiding out, not allowed contact with his or her other parent or friends or family, the harder it is on them."

"In other words, you did what you had to do."

When he looked away, the muscle in his jaw working overtime, she felt like a kid playing that searching game where somebody tells you if you're getting warmer or colder, the closer or farther you get to whatever it is you're looking for. Even if you don't know what that is. And right now, she guessed she was pretty damn warm.

"Sometimes, yes," he said, and she thought, *Warmer...*

"And...?" she prodded.

Several beats passed before he met her gaze again, the haunted look she'd seen that first day back in spades. "Last fall I had a very close call—no, the kid's fine," he said at her swift intake of breath. "Back home with his mother in Oklahoma. It was my partner. Who's fine, too. Now." When he paused, she realized he had no intention of elaborating, at least not then. "But it shook me. Not because I might have gotten hurt, but..." He swiped a hand over his mouth. "I've never lost a kid, Merce. But what happened, it really drove home..." She saw his throat work. "For the first time, I found myself wondering how long my lucky streak could hold out."

Almost soundlessly, his fear crept out of the shadows to stand before her, awaiting her judgment. Mercy reached out to wrap her hand around his as snapshots flashed in her mind's eye, of an obnoxious ten-year-old, reduced to helpless laughter over farting noises; a charming teenager, too full of himself for his own good; the easygoing young man who'd somehow become her friend, sitting across from her at her mother's kitchen table the night before he left for boot camp, his eyes brimming with a cocktail of excitement, anticipation and sheer terror.

The passionate young lover she'd catch watching her as though he couldn't believe his good fortune.

All gone now, leaving in their place a man of conviction, compassion and quiet courage. A man who she realized she loved so much it hurt. The last man she'd have never thought would meet all her requirements for a perfect mate.

Except for one, she thought as the anger she'd been holding back erupted to the surface, propelling her off the trunk and into the middle of the room.

Ben knew the instant realization hit. Now all he could do was batten down the hatches and weather the storm.

Her arms tightly crossed over her ribs, Mercy paced the small patch of empty carpet in front of the TV, her curls bobbing nonstop as she shook her head. "I knew something was up," she muttered. "I *knew* it." She stopped long enough to shoot daggers in his direction. "But did it occur to you to *tell* me what was going on in your head? What you'd been doing all this time? To tell me the *real* reason you'd come home? Dammit, Ben—you *lied* to me!"

He shot to his feet. "I didn't lie to you! I would *never* lie to you!"

"Well, you sure as hell sucked me into this relationship under false pretenses, didn't you? My God, Ben, how could you keep something that important from me? How can I possibly think about a future with you if I don't even know who the hell you *are?*"

"Because I'm *telling* you who I am, Merce," Ben said quietly, standing his ground. "Who I *was*."

"So glad you finally got around to it."

"I never intended on keeping it a secret forever."

"Then why keep it a secret at all?"

"Because I didn't dare tell anybody with the way things were between my father and me!"

Her brows crashed together. "What does your father have to do with it?"

"How about everything? He's always had this crazy idea that I'm supposed to take over the business. Not Tony, me. He's always…favored me—and I know how that sounds, but I don't know how else to say it. God knows, I've never done or said anything to encourage him, especially when I could see how much it hurt Tony. I mean, yeah, if I have to go into the business with them, that's one thing. But taking it away from my brother was never part of my game plan."

Her arms still crossed, Mercy stood absolutely still, apparently trying to absorb what he'd said. Then something shifted in her face. "Ohmigod. That's why you left, isn't it? To save your brother's butt?"

The cat hopped off the sofa to rub up against Ben's calf, doing his little broken meow thing. "Mainly, yeah."

Finally, though, she shook her head, hurt and distrust littering her eyes. "And what does that have to do with me? With us? Okay, keeping this from your father—maybe I can understand that. To a point. But not from me. Oh, wait a minute…this is some macho don't-worry-the-lady's-pretty-little-head-about-it thing, isn't it?"

"No! Okay, maybe a little," he said, when she blew a disbelieving breath through her nose. "Hey, you're the woman who still can't watch the news because it upsets her too much! So yeah, every time I thought about telling you, you'd say or do something and I'd think…not yet. But it wasn't just that. It's…"

One hand hooked on his waist, he began some pacing of his own. "The people I help, they act like…like I'm this big hero or something. But I'm not, I'm just a guy doing what needs to be done, and it makes me real uncomfortable when people make more out of it than it is. Maybe this only makes sense to me, I don't know. But the last thing I want to do is come across like some fatheaded jerk who thinks he's hot stuff."

"So you decided it was better not to say anything at all?"

He stopped. "Basically," he said on a rush of air.

She glared at him for another several seconds, then stomped into the kitchen and yanked open the fridge door, pulling out a bottle of fruit juice.

"Well, *that* was stupid," she said, wrenching off the top.

"I'm sorry, Merce," he said softly. "And you're right, it was stupid, not telling you. But since that part of my life is over, I honestly didn't think it mattered."

"You were wrong," she said. "And anyway, what, if I may ask, is so terrible about being a hero?"

"Because it's not me. I don't know, maybe Pop wouldn't've blown things out of proportion, but I wasn't about to take that chance. To give him anything he could use as another wedge between Tony and me. And yes," he said to her eye roll, "I know, I know—that has nothing to do with us. Bad call, okay?"

"*Really* bad call." Mercy tilted the bottle to her lips, then lowered it, saying, "And I think you've gotta accept the fact that to those parents, to the kids, you're definitely Super Ben.

Yeah, yeah, yeah," she said, cutting off his protest. "Just a guy doing his job, I got it." Another sip. Another dead-aim look in the eyes. "But it's over? You're really giving it up?"

"Yes," he said, shoving aside the niggling doubt that had been plaguing him more and more over the past few weeks. He cocked his head. "This mean you're not mad at me anymore?"

"Don't kid yourself. I'd smack you silly if I didn't have to get up on something to reach that big fat head you're so worried about. But I don't understand." Her gaze was steady. And far too discerning, like it had always been. "Why would you give it up? I mean, yeah, I can understand having to take a break, I can't imagine how rough it could be to keep putting yourself on the line like that. But to just…walk away and not look back?" Her brow creased, she shook her head.

Ben sighed. "Because working with all those families drove home what was really important. The more parents I reunited with their kids, the more I realized what I'd really given up. What I really wanted. And being ready to go wherever, whenever, not to mention the constant stress— that's hell on a family. I can do one or the other, but not both. And I've made my choice."

He watched her chest rise and fall, rise and fall, under-neath her soft sweater. "So Tony's broken leg had nothing to do with it?"

Ben smiled slightly. "I wouldn't say that. It provided the kick in the butt I needed to get back here and fix some stuff that sorely needed fixing. To see if…"

"What?"

"To see if my memory had been playing tricks on me all these years."

"And?"

"It hadn't."

Mercy set down the juice bottle, then propped her elbows on the breakfast bar, sinking her face into her hands. When she looked up, hope peered cautiously from her eyes. "Honest to God, you're here to stay?"

Even though Ben could hardly blame her for asking him virtually the same question three times in as many minutes, her obvious skepticism and uncertainty cut him to the quick. Helluva lot to fix, here.

Helluva bridge to burn behind him. But for crying out loud—he'd devoted a good chunk of his life to taking care of other people. Was it so wrong to want to grab a little happiness for himself?

Even if that meant, once again, giving up one thing for another, Ben thought as he looked deep into the eyes of the woman he hadn't fully realized how much he needed until he'd thought he'd lost her.

No. The woman he hadn't realized how much he'd needed until the promise of actually *having* her shimmered like El Dorado in front of him.

The cat scooted out of his way as he crossed to the breakfast bar in three strides, leaning across it to thread his fingers through Mercy's thick, lush hair. He pressed his lips to her forehead, then eased back, taking her hands in both of his, kissing her fingers. "You're as much a part of me as my own heart, Mercy," he said, banishing those niggling doubts to a galaxy far, far away. "I *love* you, you crazy woman. So I swear, as long as you want me in your life, I'm not going anywhere."

In the space of a second, a hundred emotions played over

her features. Then she pulled away to put the half-drunk juice back in the fridge. Well aware that she hadn't returned his declaration—and trying his best to be a man about it—Ben straightened, wondering what was coming next.

She suddenly whirled around, her eyes huge.

"You almost died," she said.

"What? No, I didn't, it was my partner—"

"No, not then. When you were a baby. Maybe around two, because I think I was in first grade. You got really, really sick, spent something like a month in the hospital. I remember Tony was at our house a lot because your parents were with you. Your mother…ohmigod."

She pressed a hand to her mouth; he could practically see the memory shuddering into focus. "Carmen and I had come home from school, we'd walked, nobody knew we were there, and our mothers were together in the kitchen. Yours was crying. Sobbing, actually, so hard I could hardly understand her. But I got the gist of it. And I…I ran into the kitchen, yelling, 'The baby can't die! Babies don't die, only old people die!' I can still see the horrified look on my mother's face. I thought she was going to knock me clear into the next week."

Ben frowned. "You're sure of this?"

"Yes."

He blew out a breath, shaking his head. "But I didn't die."

"No," Mercy said, smiling weakly. "You didn't. In fact, I think they brought you home a few days later. But I was only a little kid, I'm probably not the most reliable source." She tilted her head. "They never told you?"

"No. Oh, when I went into the army, there was some stuff in my files about having had a bad case of the flu when I was two, but I certainly never knew it was that serious." He felt his forehead cramp.

"Not that I'm any expert," Mercy said, "but if your father thought he'd nearly lost you…"

"That might have accounted for the preferential treatment."

"It's a thought," she said, lapsing into silence, during which Ben felt far more anxious than he ever had during any of his operations. All he wanted was to wrap her up in his arms and promise her the moon. But one did not promise Mercy the moon. One either delivered it, or shut the hell up.

Finally, she said, "Okay, this isn't about you leaving to save your brother's butt, or any of the other stuff you've been doing while you were away, because I don't want you to think I'm all blinded—" she waggled her hands by her shoulders "—by the glory or anything stupid like that. And it's going to take me a while to get over being ticked with you for not telling me the truth sooner than you did. That was so wrong, buddy, and if you *ever* do anything like that again, I swear I'll sic Carmen on you without a moment's hesitation. But…"

She propped her hands on her butt. Stuck out her chin. Looked him right in the eye. "But in the interest of full disclosure, I guess I should tell you this is it for me, too." When he frowned at her, she rolled her eyes. "I'm in love with you, too, you big turkey."

His ears heard her words, but his brain had clearly stepped out for a moment. Then it hit. Hard enough to knock the breath out of him. Finally he got back his breath and said, "Then what the *hell* are you doing over there?" and next thing he knew, *whoomph!* She'd launched herself at him like a linebacker, and they fell onto her sofa, laughing, the stupid cat frantically meowing at them from the trunk as Ben kissed Mercy over, and over, and over, determined to banish the lingering doubt lurking at the edges of her words.

However, it wasn't until a long time later, after they'd made love until neither of them could move and she was tucked safely, securely against his chest, that he remembered that thing about promising her the moon, and he smiled.

One moon, he thought, *coming right up.*

Her hand tucked underneath her pillow, Mercy lay in bed, staring blankly at the digital readout inches from her nose, waiting for seven-thirty, only dimly remembering Ben's goodbye kiss before he'd left a half hour before. Sunlight bled through the blinds; with her orange walls, it was like waking up inside a fat, juicy orange. Through the closed window, she could hear a lone, overachieving dove hoo-hooing its head off outside.

He loves me.

She stretched and rolled over, not even trying to resist the pubescent impulse to gather Ben's pillow to her, inhale his scent. Anything to jumpstart the contentment that by rights she should be freaking *drowning* in by now.

But no.

Because even two days later, it still hadn't fully registered. That he loved her and she loved him and that they'd both actually said the words, so that must make it real.

On a groan, she tossed the pillow aside and sat up, vaguely aware that no pushy orange cat was bugging her to feed him. Ben must have done the honors, let him outside.

Ben. Ben, Ben, Ben, Ben, *Ben.*

Grimacing, Mercy shook her head.

Had she been too rash, admitting how far gone she was? Except the look on his face afterwards…well. Some things a girl just can't dismiss out of hand. Especially when those things had been *so* long in coming. And anyway, it wasn't as if he'd asked her to marry him or anything. Gosh, it might be months…years before the subject even came up. If ever.

*In…out…*she breathed, her heart rate slowing. *In…out…* There. Much better.

Stealing a glance at the clock—two minutes to go—she wrapped her arms around her knees. Life was never perfect, God knew. But Anita and Tony seemed to be on the mend ("Ay, you should have seen his face, Mercy," Anita had said, laughing. "I've never seen a man so scared!") And Danas and C.J.'s new little girl had arrived yesterday, two weeks earlier than expected, and they were both disgustingly happy, if poleaxed. Ben and his father were still on the outs, but Rome wasn't built in a day, either—

"*Dios!*" Mercy yelped when the alarm finally blatted. She slammed it off, then dragged herself out of bed. Yawning and exaggeratedly hoisting her eyelids open as she tugged her robe tie closed, she shuffled down the hall toward the aroma of coffee, thinking that Ben's having repeatedly witnessed her in all her first-thing-in-the-morning glory—and not bolting— spoke volumes about his character. In fact, when she'd gotten up the other morning and cried out in alarm at her reflection, he'd only shrugged and said, "So?"

So, indeed, she thought, yawning again…

Then she blinked.

What the…?

Stumbling closer to the breakfast bar, Mercy rubbed her eyes and looked again, in case it had been a mirage the first time.

It hadn't.

"Holy…" she murmured, picking up the tiny velvet box with trembling hands. Popped it open. Then, on a whimper, she sagged against the countertop, her free hand pressed to her mouth.

The emerald-cut stone, and its companion baguettes on either side, winked up at her. The ring wasn't huge, but then, neither was her hand. It was, however, perfect and exquisite and perfectly exquisite and exquisitely perfect and…

She clamped shut the box and grabbed her phone. Ben answered on the first ring.

"Made it out to the kitchen, did you?" he said, sounding both so tickled and so nervous, her outrage shrugged and left the building.

"You're asking me to *marry you?*" she squeaked. Or, more accurately, croaked.

"Just letting you know where I stand. I'm not expecting an answer."

This was far too much for the caffeine-deprived to process.

"You're insane," she said.

"True. Anyway, I was going to wait until Valentine's Day, but it seemed so…"

"Tacky? Clichéd?"

"Far away."

Mercy realized she was sniffling. But really, she'd've been happy with a box of Godiva and a card. She'd've been *thrilled* with a box of Godiva and a card. She grabbed a napkin and swiped at her nose. "It's in less than two weeks."

"Like I said."

She crumpled up the napkin, tucking it against her ribs when she crossed her arm over her waist. "Um, you do realize that most guys do this in person?"

"I know," he said, so gently her insides hurt. "But I didn't want to put you on the spot."

"Huh?"

He laughed softly. "I know you're probably not ready for this. And that's okay, that's fine. I just wanted you to know, to *really* know, that I am. But I thought if I sprang this on you—"

"Which you just did."

"—in person, you might…well, I didn't want you to feel pressured to, I don't know, put on a show or something."

She opened the box again. Again, the diamonds winked at her. The box sounded like a firecracker when she snapped it shut. "Since when have you ever known me to BS you—or anybody else—about anything?"

"True. Okay," he said on a sigh, "so I was afraid you'd say no. Or, worse, hate the ring."

"Uh, no. The ring…" She blinked. "The ring is gorgeous."

"Really?"

"Really. And if you had help picking it out, I don't want to know."

Another laugh—but no volunteering of information, she couldn't help but notice—before he said, "I'm serious, Merce."

"Yeah, I got that—"

"No, I mean about not pressuring you. I know what I want, but I don't know what you want. If and when you're ready, you put the ring on. But if you don't, I'll completely understand. I swear."

Then he said he had to run, and he loved her, and after he hung up Mercy stared at the little blue box for a long, long time, as though it was going to explode in her face or something. Finally, however—because she was female and breathing—she opened it. Pulled the ring out of its cozy little nest. Wriggled it a bit, just to see how the light played over all the darling little facets in the stones.

Slipped it on.

And let out a long, trembly breath.

It couldn't have been a more perfect fit.

Chapter Twelve

"Okay," Mercy's mother said, handing her a stack of the "good" dishes to put back up on the top shelf of the freshly-scrubbed and repapered kitchen cupboard, "you going to tell me what's going on with you and Ben or do I have to beat it out of you?"

From her precarious perch atop the step stool, Mercy now remembered why the prospect of helping her mother with her annual scourge-and-purge of the kitchen hadn't exactly filled her with gleeful anticipation. But everybody else was busy either minding babies or having babies or mending their marriages or fixing their lives or—in her father's case—out playing golf, so that left her. As it always did. Normally she didn't mind—the job went much more quickly with two people, she usually got a good lunch out of the deal, and when you're one of five it never hurt to suck up a little—but she'd known this conversation was coming.

Funny thing, though, how the older you get, the more you realize you don't have all the answers. Which meant that, instead of her standard knee-jerk "Stay out of my life, Ma!" response, all she said now was, "As if you don't know."

"I'm not talking about sex," Mary Zamora huffed, signaling for Mercy to return to terra firma. In more ways than one, most likely. Hmm…had her mother's honey-colored hair always been nearly the same color as the cabinets? "I know how things work these days. Okay, how they've always worked, for some people. But this is *Ben,*" she said, worry crowding her eyes. "Doesn't that make things more…complicated?"

Braced though she may have been for the conversation, actually knowing what to say was something else entirely. Trying to order her thoughts, Mercy poured herself a cup of coffee from the never-empty pot on the counter. "You don't know from complicated," she muttered into her cup.

Taking the carafe out of Mercy's hands and filling her own cup, her mother barked out a laugh. "With you five? Believe me, I'm no stranger to 'complicated.'" She glanced over. "So…it's not only about sex?"

"Geez, Ma, would you quit saying that?"

"Hey. I didn't find you five in the cabbage patch, you know."

The oversize castered kitchen chair wobbled when Mercy pulled it away from the table, sank into the vinyl-covered cushion. A second later, her mother joined her, waiting. Mercy took two, then three swallows of coffee before she grabbed her purse off the table, searching through the depths until her fingers closed around the little velvet box. After a week, her heart still bumped whenever she touched it or saw it or thought about it.

She opened the box, set it on the table between them. Her mother let out a little "Oh…" Then a more forceful, more understanding, "Ohhhh…" Her eyes lifted to Mercy's. "You're not wearing it."

"Boy, nothin' gets past you, does it?"

"Don't be a smarty-pants." Then her mother's expression softened. "You don't like it?"

A half laugh climbed out of her throat. "Liking the ring—" which glittered at her when she scooped the box back up "—isn't the issue. Liking *Ben* isn't the issue. But that's the thing—half of me wants to jump up and down like a sixteen-year-old who got asked to the prom by the cutest guy in school. But the other half… Oh, Ma," she said on a long breath. "I feel like somebody's split my brain in two. I'd honestly thought I'd be single for the rest of my life. And frankly, when I looked at my future, I liked what I saw—complete autonomy, being able to make my own decisions, the whole nine yards. So what happens? Here comes Ben, offering me something I'd pretty much thought I'd never have, and…"

"It scares you?" her mother said gently.

"You have no idea. Except then I look at Dana and Cass…and I envy them," she said, literally jumping at her own words. "I want what they have." Her mouth stretched tight. "Sometimes so badly I think I can't stand it."

Her mother chuckled. "Wondered how long it would take."

"But is that really *me* talking, or am I just feeling…left behind? Just because Cass and Dana got their happy-ever-afters, so, what? It's my turn now?"

"And what's wrong with that?"

"Because I'm not a lemming?"

Smiling, her mother rested her chin in her palm. "Do you really love Ben?"

Tears pricking at her eyes, Mercy nodded. "Yeah. Go figure."

"So screw all the other stuff," her mother said, and Dana choked on her coffee. "I'm serious. So maybe it is your turn now."

"But with *Ben?*"

"Why not? That spacey kid he used to be doesn't exist anymore," she said, and Mercy thought, *And you don't know the half of it.* "*Querida,* this is a good man. Grab him before he changes his mind. Because I don't care what you say, the face I see before me is not the face of a woman who really wants to spend the rest of her life alone." Her mother leaned forward to cup Mercy's cheek in her warm hand. "Just scared to death of having her heart broken."

Mercy pulled away, shaking her head. "That's crazy. At my age—"

"—it's harder to take a chance."

"That's not what I was going to say."

"I know it wasn't. But it's true. You're afraid he'll leave again, aren't you?"

"He swears he won't."

"But you don't entirely believe him." When Mercy shook her head, Mary said, "Why? Has he done or said anything to make you doubt him?"

Mercy got up to refill her coffee cup, trying desperately to pinpoint the source of the anxiety that only seemed to increase with every promise Ben made. Considering everything she now knew, how could she even think of questioning the man's integrity?

Because, she realized, it was that very integrity that kept keeping her from taking him completely at his word.

She turned, holding her coffee close. "Okay, this is going to sound completely out of left field, but bear with me. When we were kids, did you ever notice Ben's father playing favorites with him?"

Her mother smirked. "Baby doll, when you were kids, I had my hands full keeping you and your four sisters alive. I can't say I was all that aware of what was going on between Ben and his father. Why do you ask?"

"Because Ben told me the real reason he took off, especially the second time, was because his father was making him crazy, always building him up and making a fuss over him. And unfortunately Tony got the short end of that stick."

"That's crazy, Luis would never have done that—"

"Yeah, he did. I didn't remember it, either, until Ben brought it up and then a whole lot of pieces I hadn't even thought about until then started to fall into place. Anyway, Ben finally decided things were never going to get better as long as he stuck around. That if he left, maybe his father would finally start appreciating Tony."

"And it took him nearly ten years to realize what a dumb idea that was? Especially considering he'd already been in the army, for heaven's sake."

Mercy smiled. "This is the male brain we're talking about. But that was only why he *left*. There was another reason that kept Ben from coming home," she said, then filled her mother in on Ben's activities in the intervening years. The more she talked, the larger her mother's eyes got behind her glasses until Mercy thought they'd pop out of her head altogether.

"*Madre de Dios,*" her mother breathed when Mercy was done. "I knew he'd changed, but…my goodness. And Juanita and Luis don't know?"

"No. And don't you *dare* tell them. That's up to Ben, when he's ready."

Her mother's mouth tightened. "Not to worry. Since that whole mess with Tony and Anita, we're barely speaking."

Mercy frowned. "Even though 'Nita and Tony are back together?"

Her mother's round, capable shoulders shrugged. "I may have said some things to Juanita…about Tony…" Contriteness pinched her mother's features. "I was angry and hurt for Anita's sake, I wasn't thinking. I apologized, but…"

"Ma. You guys have been friends for a million years." The old dishwasher's door whined when Mercy opened it. "She'll get over it."

"You're probably right, it's just…all these changes…"

"Yeah," Mercy said, staring out the kitchen window with her arms crossed. The middle of February and her mother's Japanese cherry was already budded out, honestly. "I know." Then she turned, sinking into her mother's embrace. "I hate this feeling," she mumbled into her mother's shoulder. "Like I'm seeing spooks in every shadow. And it's not that I don't believe Ben, when he says he's missed family, that he wants one of his own. With me." She lifted her head, seeking—and knowing she wouldn't find—answers in her mother's eyes. "But I still can't shake the feeling that it's too soon for him to really know what he wants. To be sure."

"Which is why you won't wear the ring."

"Right."

"But you haven't given it back, either."

When Mercy only shrugged, her mother laughed softly, then said, "Ever since you were a little girl, you've always worried yourself half to death about what *might* happen. Maybe it's time you stopped doing that?"

Heh. Easy for her to say.

Now this was the way to spend Valentine's, Ben thought as he lay on his side in Mercy's bed, his head propped in his hand. Streaming through the partially open miniblinds, the Sunday afternoon sunshine lapped at Mercy's golden skin as she crossed to the closet to get a robe, something weightless and red and shimmery. The same color as her toenails, as it happened.

"No," he said as she started to slip it on. "Wait."

The robe dangling from one hand, she cocked her head, then shifted, uninhibited, to let the pulsating light, like a hundred white-gold butterflies, dance over her breasts, her dimpled hips, tease the shadowed thatch between her legs. In this, she withheld nothing from him. Ever.

He signaled with his other hand for her to turn around.

"Is this about to get kinky?" she asked.

"With any luck," he said.

Mercy replied, "In your dreams," only to yelp when he sprang out of the bed and started to chase her around the room, eventually catching her and tossing her back onto the bed, both of them laughing and breathless. Now pinned underneath him, her smile flickered when he swept her insane hair away from her face, and he ached with loving her so much.

And with the constant knowledge that, after nearly two weeks, she still hadn't worn the ring. A one-and-a-half carat symbol of her chronic ambivalence.

"What?" she whispered, touching his face, and he smiled.

"Just reminding myself how lucky I am."

"Damn straight," she said, laughter reigniting in her eyes, and he claimed her mouth in a kiss that was tender and hot and sweet and crazy all at the same time, prodding Ben to remind himself that he was a patient man, an understanding man. The kind of man who could tell a woman he was crazy about her, give her a ring to show her how crazy he was about her, and then get out of her way while she made up her mind what she was going to do about that.

Well. Maybe not that out of her way, he thought as she slid her calf along his, tempting. Inviting.

They had all the time in the world, he thought as he came up for air, looked deep into her eyes. "And to think, I don't even need Internet access."

She tried to slug him but he pinned her hands up by her head and kissed her until her indignation melted and his cell rang again.

"Go ahead, answer it." She wriggled out from underneath him, snatching her robe up off the end of the bed. "I need food, anyway. Want some popcorn?" she said as she stood, tugging the end of the belt out of his hand so she could tie it.

"Sounds great," he said, watching her pad away with no little regret.

Not nearly as much regret, however, as he felt when he noticed Roy's cell number on the display. As promised, Roy had left him alone, given *Ben* the space to make up *his* mind.

That it hadn't worked, at least not as well as Ben had hoped, wasn't Roy's fault. Or Ben's. Or anybody's.

Oh, yeah. He understood all about ambivalence. Just as he understood exactly what answering this call would likely mean.

He flipped open the phone. "Yeah?"

After a long moment, Roy said, "I'm gonna take the fact that you answered as a positive sign."

"Don't be so sure of yourself."

"Hell, Ben, I'm not sure of anything, you know that." He hesitated. "Except that, after all these years, I think I know you pretty well."

"I told you, Roy—"

"The father's got the kid right there in Albuquerque. Mother's a Mexican national, doesn't speak much English. We need to move fast."

Ben's chest tightened. Through the open door, he heard Mercy singing along with some pop star over the rapid-gunfire sounds of exploding popcorn in the microwave. He imagined her bopping along in time to the music in her bare feet, that flimsy little robe gliding over her body. How warm and soft and willing she'd be when she came back to bed.

Grinding his palm into his forehead, Ben forced in a deep breath. Then another. "You got a positive ID…?"

He was already dressed when she returned, sitting on her chair and tugging on one of his boots.

Her stomach plummeted like a 747 hitting an air pocket. The popcorn bowl rattled against the dresser when she set it down; sucking in a steadying breath, she met one very troubled gaze.

"That was Roy," he said.

"Oh?"

He stood, shoving his hands in his pockets. "It's a one-off, Merce. The last time. Roy only called me because the case is right here." His jaw worked. "The kid's four. Holed up with his dad in some motel over on Central." A pause. "All you have to do is say 'no,' Merce, and I'll call him back right now, tell him—"

"No," she said, cutting him off. "I mean, no, don't call him back."

"You're sure?"

Despite feeling like the mother of all exposed nerves, she nodded. "I'm sure," she said, clenching her fist behind her back when a combination of relief and eagerness flooded Ben's face.

"Since the boy's mom's Mexican," he said, visibly pulsating as he moved around the room, collecting his watch, his keys, shoving his phone into his pocket, "the police aren't all that motivated to help her. Dad didn't return the little boy after his weekend visit, three weeks ago. According to the day clerk at the front desk, he's already been there for a week. But God knows how long he'll stay—"

She touched his arm; he jerked to a stop, frowning into her eyes. "How can I help?" she asked.

"Merce…"

"Later," was all she said, even though she would've had to be dead not to not feel the cataclysmic shift in the status quo during the last fifteen minutes. But right now, all that mattered was a little boy who'd been taken from his mother.

Searching her eyes, Ben lifted one hand, stroking her hair

away from her temple. "I can't go in to get the boy myself," he said. "Or it's kidnapping. If his mother gets him, it's not. But it probably wouldn't hurt to have another woman along, to support her. Help keep her centered."

"I'm in," Mercy said, and Ben smiled.

"Get dressed. And then listen very carefully to everything I say…."

"What if tonight is the night he does not go out?" Flora Rivas, the little boy's mother, asked in Spanish from the middle seat of Mercy's parents' SUV.

For the past hour Ben, Mercy and Flora had been waiting in the parking lot of the Buena Vista motel, one of the many, mangy, fifties hangers-on sharing this stretch of the old Route 66 with the seedy bars and the mobile home sales lots. The young woman was barely in her twenties and scared out of her wits, her dark eyes huge with worry in Ben's rearview mirror. Mercy, her expression calmer than Ben would have expected, sat beside her, tightly holding the girl's trembling hand in hers. Flora had begged a family friend to drive her to Albuquerque from El Paso, but the friend couldn't hang around. How she and her son were going to get back, she had no idea.

Ben twisted around to give her as encouraging a smile as he dared. This was one courageous young woman, one who'd found the *cojones* to leave an abusive husband, despite her family's berating her for having a serious screw loose. After all, what woman in her right mind would walk away from a man living legally in the States, someone who'd been regularly sending money to her impoverished family back in some flyspeck of a town in Mexico? That he'd been also regularly beating the tar out of her was beside the point.

"The desk clerk said he's brought the boy for her to watch every night for the past week," Ben said in Spanish. "Chances are he will tonight, as well." Because clearly, they weren't dealing with the sharpest knife in the drawer. Yes, the jerk had taken his kid, but staying in one spot made him a pathetically easy target. "And even if he doesn't," Ben said, "we will simply return tomorrow, yes?"

A smile flickered across the young mother's mouth, followed by a little nod…and then a frown. "But what if he decides to leave?"

A very valid worry. Although not one Ben was going to entertain tonight.

"The clerk told me your former husband said he'd found work, so he probably isn't going anywhere too soon."

Flora shook her head. "He thinks I am not smart enough, or do not have the courage, to try to find my baby. That I would just let him take Rico from me without a fight. *Atrasado.*"

A dimwit, indeed, Ben thought as Mercy choked back a laugh, prompting the young woman to say in broken English, "You are very *considerada,* to let me stay with you."

"*De nada—*"

"*Dios mio!*" Flora said on a gasp, grabbing Mercy's arm and practically lunging through the car's window. "*Ay,* Rico…*nino…*" Her voice lowered to a growl. "*Que pasa* to your *hair?*"

Ben felt the familiar thrum of adrenaline as they watched a short, wiry young man in baggy jeans and a tatty leather jacket close the door to one of the upstairs units, then lead a practically bald little boy by the hand slowly down the stairs…across the lot…into the office. Through the large, bare window, they could see the man talking with the clerk, laughing, looking down at the child.

Ben held his breath. *C'mon, dirtwad, just leave the kid and go….*

The door to the office opened. Both man and boy emerged.

"No," Flora whimpered, rocking back and forth. "Noooo…"

Then she bolted from the SUV.

Spitting out an obscenity and tersely ordering Mercy to stay put, Ben scrambled out from behind the wheel, as Flora's shrieked "*Rico!*" knifed through his skull. Both man and boy wheeled at Flora's cry, the man bellowing "*Cabrona!*" as he clumsily grabbed the child, tried to stuff him into a beat-up sedan.

"No! *No!*"

Flora flew toward them, still screaming her son's name, when suddenly her ex let out a scream of his own, clutching one hand with the other as Rico, his tiny legs a blur, sped across the parking lot and launched himself into his mother's arms.

"In the car, Flora!" Ben yelled in Spanish, hustling the pair toward the SUV. *"Get him in the car!"*

"Ben!" Mercy cried as she hauled Rico into her arms. "Watch *out!*"

Unfortunately, she was a split second too late.

Chapter Thirteen

"Hey," Mercy said softly, one hand on the dividing curtain in the E.R. exam room. Fear melted into relief when Ben looked over and smiled. "You're sitting up. Good sign."

Smirking despite the fierce pain barely dulled by the meds they'd given him, Ben made a half-assed attempt at buttoning up his shirt over the bandage cushioning his ribs.

With a gentle "Here, let me," Mercy stepped closer to do the job for him, even though her hands were shaking. One long red nail was gone, a victim of the scuffle at the end. Ben stroked the naked finger, smiling.

"I dunno…dyed hair, fake nails. And to think the whole reason I fell for you was because of your honesty."

She made a tiny choking sound. Ben slipped one hand underneath her hair to grip her neck and pull her closer, shutting his eyes as he inhaled the scent of her shampoo. "It's okay, babe," he whispered. "Rico's fine, I'm fine…all's well that ends well, right?"

"Heh," she said.

"So I suppose you want to kill me, too," he said, nuzzling all that soft, silky craziness.

"Too?" she said, focusing on a particularly stubborn button.

"First words out of my mother's mouth."

Her task accomplished, she patted his chest, then lifted her eyes. "I can't believe you still hadn't told them. They're out in the waiting room, by the way. Basket cases, the pair of them."

"Yeah," Ben said on a released breath. "I know. Not exactly how I'd envisioned their finding out about my 'secret' life. For a moment, I really did think my mother was gonna kill me."

"And your dad?"

"I think he understood. Why I had to keep this to myself. Didn't make him any less pissed, though."

"I don't imagine so."

"How are Flora and Rico?"

"Fine, considering." Mercy stepped back, her arms crossed, looking extremely grateful to have something else to talk about besides the obvious. "They're with my folks. Immensely grateful and obscenely guilt-ridden. Well, Flora's guilt-ridden. Rico's just happy to be back with his mom." She paused. "He said his father told him his mother was dead."

"Sick SOB."

"To put it mildly. But if it's any consolation, the sick SOB's a guest tonight in one of APD's four-star facilities, thanks to the desk clerk's calling 911 as soon as she saw Flora jump out of the car. You talked to the police, I take it?"

"Yeah. A little while ago."

Mercy was quiet for a moment, then slipped her hand into his. "The clerk said the sleazebag had settled his bill. He was leaving, Ben," she said quietly. "If Flora hadn't gone for it, she might not have her son tonight."

"None of which changes what happened," he said, watching her face.

Frowning, she gently touched the bandage through his shirt. "Are you in a lot of pain?"

"At the moment? Not too much. The minute the happy pills wear off, though, I'm not making any promises."

"But the doctor said it's not serious?"

"Only because I moved when I did. The bullet sideswiped a rib and kept on going. An inch or two further over, though…"

Mercy's troubled eyes met his the same moment a round, cheerful lady in scrubs swished through the curtain, handing him his chart. "You're good to go, Mr. Vargas. There're instructions here on how to care for the wound, but feel free to give us a call if there's any problem. The P.A. wants to see you next week, you can make an appointment at the desk."

After the nurse left, Mercy moved to help him off the exam table. Ben tried to laugh. "Forget it. You weigh like ten pounds."

Hands lifted, she stood back, only to shake her head and mutter something about *stubborn man* as he wobbled for a second on his feet. She moved closer again; he decided maybe bracing his hand on her shoulder, at least, wasn't such a bad idea, after all.

"Man," he said as they started out of the room. "This is good stuff. I can't even feel the floor."

Chuckling, she slipped one arm around his waist to guide

him down the hall and back to the waiting room. His parents stood at his entrance, leftover panic etched into their faces.

"You're coming back to our house so I can look after you," his mother said, flashing Mercy a look that was equal parts defiance and plea.

To his surprise, though, Mercy said, "That's a good idea, actually. Since now that Dana's new baby's here, I can't really be away from work too much."

"I'm not in traction, for God's sake," Ben growled. "I think I can take care of myself—"

"Benicio." His father laid a hand on his arm. "This has nothing to do with being able to take care of yourself." Ben caught the look in his mother's eyes, and he understood.

The look in Mercy's eyes, however, would have freaked him out if the pain meds hadn't dulled the freak-out center in his brain. Still, he insisted on riding with her, instead of his parents, because the longer one waited to exercise damage control, the less effective it was.

After they'd been driving for a minute or two, he said, "Don't think I'm not well aware that somebody else might have gotten hurt. Flora, Rico…" He swallowed. "You."

"Well, we weren't. So let's move on, shall we?"

"Still, it wasn't exactly one of my finer moments—"

"Ben? Shut up."

His brows crunched together. "Okay. Out with it."

Her hands gripped the steering wheel more tightly. "God, this sucks," she whispered. "This totally, completely sucks."

"That I got hurt?"

"That, too. I mean, yeah, that scared the crud out of me. But that's not what…" They slowed for a stop light. Shaking her head, she stared straight ahead at the traffic streaming across the intersection.

"Did you realize, that night you finally came clean about what you'd been doing, that you never once talked about it past tense? You might have thought you'd put it all behind you, when actually you'd lugged the whole shebang right back to Albuquerque." She paused, then said quietly, "Rescuing Rico *wasn't* a one-off, was it?" When he didn't answer, she looked at him again, long enough for the driver behind them to beep his horn when the light changed. Mercy pulled ahead, muttering, "Yeah. That's what I thought."

"If I say it was," Ben said at last, "will you stop looking like your dog just died?"

"Yeah, lying to me will make me feel a whole lot better. No, hear me out. I'd frankly given up on falling in love, did you know that? On ever finding someone to really love *me*. Nobody, ever, has even come close to making me feel the way you do. But at this point in my life, I'm not naive enough to believe that people can be happy together by pretending. By burying who they really are in the name of *the relationship*. And from the moment I saw your game face after you got that phone call…"

She checked her side mirror, pulled into the next lane. "You didn't put off telling me because of your father, or me, or anybody else. You put it off because you weren't sure what you really wanted to do." A glance, then, "I think it's safe to say your down time is over."

Ben would have slumped down in his seat if his wound would have let him. As it was, though, her words—and the pain behind them—roared through him like floodwaters after a summer storm, washing away every objection in their path.

"Do you think I was…" He fought for the right words. "Using you, *us,* to avoid dealing with what had happened?"

"Intentionally? No. Not sure what difference that makes, though."

"Baby," he said over the knot in his throat, "everything, *everything,* I've said or done over the past six weeks, I meant. You've got to believe that. I did come back for you, Merce. Whether you'd have me, I had no idea. But when I walked away ten years ago, I was already falling for you. Harder than I had any idea how to handle."

Silence stretched between them for several seconds before she said, "Then what was all that about your brother?"

"Having more than one account to settle doesn't in any way lessen the one I had to settle with you. The difference was, if my *brother* and I had stayed on the outs, it wouldn't have killed me."

"I see."

"I seriously doubt that," he said bitterly, "since I sure as hell didn't. Still don't, not entirely. So let me just take a stab at explaining, and hopefully when I'm done it'll all make at least enough sense that you don't take out a contract on my life, okay?"

When her only reply was a grunt, Ben shifted, trying in vain to find a more comfortable position before continuing. "No matter how you slice it, the timing was all wrong back then. For me, at least. Not only were there all those issues with my family, but it's true, I *was* restless."

"Aha," she said, and he glared at her.

"I never denied it. I did feel like I'd suffocate, if I stuck around. I watched my brother and your sisters settle into their lives, and it gave me the willies. Definitely not for me. Then you and I got involved, and I freaked, because I felt like I was getting sucked into something I wasn't ready for. Because I would have only ended up feeling trapped. And then we would have both been miserable."

"Yeah," she said. "I knew that. That's why…"

"Why you didn't let on how you really felt, either?"

He could see her mouth pull to one side. "Okay, so maybe you're not the only person in this car who sidesteps the truth now and then. Not that I took to my bed or anything," she quickly added, and Ben smiled in spite of the heaviness in his chest.

"So I heard," he said, and a frown shot in his direction. "Carmen. Those exact words, in fact." She snorted. "So I'm glad, because even then, I never wanted to hurt you. In any case, when I took off, I really was as aimless as everybody thought. My only goal at that point was to get away from here."

"And from me?"

"Especially from you. From everything I thought you represented, anyway. I just couldn't see myself settling into family life when my own seemed to be such a mess. Only the ironic thing was that the longer I stayed away, the more I began to see what family really meant. Especially when something threatens to tear it apart. And somewhere along the line, standing on the outside looking in wasn't cutting it anymore."

Ignoring the pain, he reached over to trace her jaw with his knuckle. "I guess I finally got it through my thick head that I'm nothing on my own. And that I'm never going to feel complete without something to *call* my own. I also honestly believed that chapter of my life was closed. I wasn't lying to you."

"Even if you were lying to yourself."

They'd pulled up in front of his parents' house. Mercy left the engine running, a clear signal that she wasn't coming inside with him. Ben held out his hand. She glanced over, then let go of the steering wheel to link their fingers. "I don't want to lose you, Merce," he whispered. "Not a second time. Not after I've finally found the one thing that finally plugs me up inside. So I'm telling you again—just say the word and the subject's closed forever."

Her eyes shot to his, twin creases between her brows. "You don't honestly think I'd actually ask you to quit, do you?"

"And you don't honestly think I'd put you through that kind of hell?" He lifted her hand to his lips, snagging her tortured gaze in his. "The way you take everything so hard? And how much I'd have to be away? What kind of relationship would that be?"

"I don't want to lose you either, Ben," Mercy said, a tear trickling down her cheek. "But I was right all along, wasn't I? That staying here, doing the 'burbs thing…it's not you. Not the whole you, at least. In which case I'd lose you anyway. And besides…" She smiled sadly. "How could you possibly turn your back on the children? Not to mention all those desperate parents?"

He'd rather get shot a hundred times over than feel his gut being torn out like this. "So you're saying it's not going to work?"

After a long moment, she shook her head. "I don't see how. Do you?"

Ben kept her gaze in his for another second or two, then got out of the car, slamming the door shut behind him.

* * *

She had to say, she held it together pretty damn well, all through returning her father's truck and checking up on Flora and Rico, who—thanks to her parents' generosity—were flying home to El Paso later that evening. But the minute Mercy literally stumbled into her house, she doubled over, gripping her stomach as though a huge, nasty vacuum cleaner had sucked out her insides.

To come *that* close…

Her gaze landed on Annabelle. Poor hapless Annabelle, still bedecked with Mattie's little Barbie Valentines. And underneath, a two-pound box of Godiva and the biggest, tackiest, gaudiest, mushiest Valentine's card ever created. Mercy stormed over to the tree and plucked it clean in five seconds flat, grabbed the candy and card and carted the whole stinkin' lot to the kitchen. She hesitated, then, with a cry bordering on anguished, she shoved the candy into the trash. The cards, however, she dumped into the sink and turned on the water, ramming the bleeding, pulpy remains down the garbage disposal with the back end of a wooden spoon, a multilingual array of swear words blending with the demonized grinding.

Panting, Mercy leaned against the sink, until the pounding in her head stopped long enough for her to think she heard Homer, scratching to be let in.

She whirled around to the patio door, slid it open, the sharp wind instantly freezing the tear tracks she hadn't even known were there.

No cat.

"Homer!" she yelled into the wind, holding her stinging hair off her face with one hand. "Ho-*mer!* Where the hell *are* you?"

Her eyes burning, Mercy stomped out onto the patio to kick the metal food dish she left out whenever he disappeared, sending week-old kitty kibble flying all over creation.

This time, the wind seemed to whine, *he's not coming back.*

Mercy sank to her knees on the cold, hard cement and cried herself sick.

Chapter Fourteen

"**H**ey," Luis said softly from the doorway to Ben's old bedroom, where he stood in front of his unmade bed, stuffing the last of his clothes into a duffel bag that had long since seen better days. "You leaving already?"

"Tony's out of his cast," Ben said, zipping the bag, "so my work here is done. Besides, I've got a meeting with Roy back in Dallas."

"But your injury—"

"It's been a week, they said it's healing up fine. As long as I don't strain it," he said, hefting the bag to the floor. His father's mouth tightened, but he only shook his head.

"You'll be back?"

"Yeah, I've got unfinished business here to take care of."

"So you talked to that Realtor?"

"C.J.? I did. We went up to the property yesterday, in fact. He figures he can move it for me pretty quickly." And Ben had literally dropped his jaw at what C.J. said he could probably get for the land, even undeveloped.

His father came into the room, sat on the edge of the bed. "I know I should've talked things out with you before this. About what you said that night. When Anita left Tony. But I couldn't ever figure out how to go about it. I'm not real good with words." A brief smile pulled at his mouth. "In either language. But you were right, about how I treated you. And Tony. I mean, I didn't really understand that's what I was doing, but that's no excuse. It was wrong, and I'm sorry."

Ben's gaze drifted to his father, the constant tightness in his chest easing a little at the obvious contrition in his father's eyes. "Why didn't you or Mama ever tell me about how sick I'd been as a baby?"

Tears brightened his father's eyes. "Some things hurt too much to remember, *mijo*. Let alone to talk about."

It would have to do, Ben supposed. Only then his father added, "Speaking of keeping secrets…your mother and I, we were mad as hell at first that you hadn't told us what you were doing. But we're proud of you. The path you've chosen…that's not something just anybody would do, you know."

Ben felt blood rush to his cheeks. "It's no big deal, Pop. Please don't make more of this than it is."

"*Que chinga,* it *is* a big deal! Anyone who's nearly lost a child…" The older man's eyes got all shiny; uncomfortable with the rare display of emotion, Ben looked away. "Well," his father finally said, "You're a godsend to a lot of people,

Benicio. And there's nothing you can say to diminish that. But I've gotta say…you make one helluva lousy contractor."

It took a second. Then Ben's eyes snapped back to his father's, creased in amusement. "What?"

"You heard me. It's a damn good thing Tony was still doing the paperwork, otherwise we'd've been screwed to the wall. *Dios mio,* you suck at this."

Ben stared at his father for several seconds, then let out a loud laugh. "I think those are the sweetest words I've ever heard come out of your mouth," he said, grinning. "I just hope to hell you let Tony in on your little revelation."

"You bet I did." Luis rubbed his mouth, looking sheepish. "I've got some major making up to do where your brother's concerned. I don't know where my head's been all these years, but it's way past time I let Tony know how much…I love him, too. And it wasn't like I didn't, you know, it's just…"

"Don't tell me, Pop," Ben said, swinging his duffle up onto his shoulder. "Tell Tony."

His father nodded, then stood, his fingers jammed in his pockets. "Well. I guess…"

With one arm, Ben pulled the old man into a hug. "Tell Mattie and Jake I'll see 'em soon," he said, then walked away before he could change his mind.

About anything.

With an annoyingly anxious glance at Mercy, Anita set out the Chinese food and bottle of wine on Mercy's table.

"If you ask me one more time if I'm okay," Mercy said, already seated, "I swear to God I'll impale you on this chopstick."

"Sorry. It's just—"

Scooping fried rice onto her plate, Mercy glared at her sister, then said, "So Tony's really taking care of the kids tonight?"

"Not only is he taking care of them, it was his idea." Anita shoveled garlic shrimp onto a mound of steaming white rice, leaning forward with her eyes closed to inhale the fragrant aroma. Peeking out from her Grand Canyon-esque cleavage, the diamond pendant Tony had given her for Valentine's Day sparkled like it was lit from inside. As did Anita.

"He's really trying, Merce," she said, sitting up straight again and digging in. "Even if half the time he looks like he's having one of those dreams where you're back in math class, having no idea what's going on."

Mercy smiled, grateful that the sensation of having gone through a car wash—without the car—had begun to subside enough to at least be happy for other people.

"Of course," Anita continued, "I don't suppose it hurt that I cut back to three days a week at the hospital. Which I'm now wondering why I didn't do years ago. I take that back, I do know why." She twisted lo mein noodles onto her chopsticks, poking the slippery mass into her mouth before saying, "Because the worse things got at home, the less I wanted to be there."

"So you didn't need the money?"

"Not *that* much. Or the 'fulfillment.' Oh, I definitely like working, but once the kids came along?" She shook her head. "I've been exhausted for the past ten years, Merce. Only I was too damn stubborn, or proud, or whatever to admit it." Frowning, she twisted up more lo mein. "Talk about cutting off my nose to spite my face. Stupid."

Her words made Mercy's shrimp boogie in her stomach. More and more over the past two weeks she'd begun to wonder if that's what she was doing—refusing to see past the obvious, digging in her heels because she'd made up her mind that her way was the only way things could work.

"Anyway, it also doesn't hurt that Luis is finally acknowledging all the good work Tony's done over the years. Definitely a huge stress reliever right there."

"So everyone's happy at your house?"

Anita grinned. "Getting there, getting there. And since I've got some time to myself, I've even started an exercise program. I've lost four pounds!"

"Well, here's to you," Mercy said, lifting her wineglass toward her sister.

"Yeah, it's all about compromise, you know?" Anita said on a sigh. "Figuring out how to make all the pieces fit so that nobody feels neglected or put-upon or whatever. Because when you come right down to it, no relationship is perfect, right?" Mercy glanced up to find her gaze caught in her sister's. "So if you love somebody, you *make* it work."

From the greasy bag between them on the table, Mercy fished out an egg roll, tore it in half. "And your point is?"

"You know damn well what my point is, *chica.*"

"It's over, 'Nita," Mercy said, dunking the egg roll in a puddle of soy sauce on her plate. "He sold the property and everything. That *hombre* is *gone.*"

"Shows how much you know."

Mercy's eyes shot to her sister's. "What are you talking about?"

"Ben got back last night. He's camped out in our family room." She grabbed the fried rice box and shoveled more onto her plate. "I'm not supposed to tell you."

"Then why did you?"

A smile twitching around her mouth, her sister met her gaze. "Because he said you never gave him back the ring."

Mercy squirmed in her chair. "He didn't exactly give me a chance, did he?"

"Bull. He was here for a good week before he left, you could have given it back to him anytime."

"Still. I'm not wearing it, am I?"

"Only because it would be tacky to keep wearing it once you'd broken up. And if it's one thing you're not, it's tacky. An idiot, maybe, but not tacky."

"Hey!"

Anita lifted her wine glass, giving Mercy the evil eye over it. "He's back, honey. And believe me, there's only one reason for that." She tilted the nearly empty glass in Mercy's direction. "*You.*"

Feeling as though she had a hornet's nest in her stomach, Mercy got up from the table and returned to her kitchen, although she had no idea what she was supposed to be doing once she got there. Her arms spread, she gripped the edge of the sink, staring out into the half darkness in her backyard, as hope and fear and rampant confusion made mincemeat of what was left of her wits. A second later, she felt her sister's arm wrap around her shoulders, the gentle pressure of her hug.

"I only told you because I didn't want you to be blind-sided," Anita said quietly. "And because I was afraid you'd blow it. If you didn't have a chance to pull yourself together beforehand."

"Thanks. I think."

"*De nada.* Honey, nothing's ideal. And I have no idea what

he's thinking, really. But he's clearly miserable without you. And you're clearly miserable without him."

Mercy's face screwed up. "It's that obvious, huh?"

Anita let out a sharp laugh. "Let's see…you've been dating since you were, what, fifteen? So that's nearly a quarter century I've been witnessing your breakups—"

"And thank you *so* much for pointing that out."

"—and every time, you bounced back like Silly Putty. Except twice. And Ben was the culprit both times."

"And if you'd seen Flora's face, after she was reunited with Rico…" Mercy shook her head. "It's no good, 'Nita. There's no way I could have asked him to give that up. I wouldn't be able to live with myself. I mean, if I ever had kids, I'd sure want to know there was someone like Ben, willing to go the extra mile if God forbid something like that happened to me."

"And next time," Anita said softly, "maybe it would be more than a cracked rib. Right?" When Mercy didn't—couldn't—say anything, her sister said, "So are you going to worry any less if you never see the man again?"

"You didn't have to point that out, either," Mercy muttered.

Just then Anita jumped and said, "Good grief—what on earth is that awful noise?"

"*Homer!*" Mercy cried, rushing to the patio door, fumbling with the lock in her haste to get it open. Filthy, matted and several pounds thinner, the cat rushed inside before the door was even completely open, writhing around Mercy's shins and cussing her up one side and down the other. Mercy dropped onto her butt on the kitchen floor, hugging the rotten thing, soaking up his purr. "You came back, you big dope! You came back!"

"And apparently not alone," Anita said, bemused.

"What?" Homer still on her lap, Mercy looked over to see a very pretty white kitty with gingery splotches, sitting primly just inside the door.

Mercy looked at Homer. "You brought home a friend?"

"A girlfriend, from the looks of things. Hate to tell you this," Anita said, squatting by the visitor, who was arching up to bump her sister's outstretched hand, "but I think you need a new vet."

Now Mercy looked at the other kitty. *"You're pregnant?"*

She blinked her big blue eyes and gave an apologetic mew.

Eventually, Anita headed home and Mercy put away the leftover Chinese food, fed the cats (*Cats.* She still couldn't believe it. And yes, Marge—what else?—was indeed very pregnant. Oh, joy.) and finally got around to mulling over this new turn of events. Ben's return and all. And what that meant to her life.

If anything.

Because, yeah, so he was back. But his being "back" didn't necessarily mean he was back for *her,* no matter what Anita said. Heck, her sister had just patched up her marriage, she and Tony were probably having the best sex of their lives. At this point, Anita's brain was so hormone-drenched she'd probably try to fix up the Pope. So how would it look if Mercy marched herself over there and offered herself up and a re-conciliation hadn't been part of Ben's plan at all?

And yet…if—*if*—there was a chance he really wasn't ready to give up…

Then again, what if he was hoping *she'd* make the first move so he wouldn't look like a loser? And when, *when,* did the freaking statute of limitations run out on this high school does-he-or-doesn't-he crap?

Bookended on her sofa between two loudly purring cats, Mercy laid her head back and groaned. *Could* she compromise? Could she live with Ben's being away, being in danger?

No, the real question was...could she live without him *at all?*

On a little cry, she shimmied out from between the cats (much to their annoyance) and tromped back to her bedroom to look for the hottest, highest-heeled pair of boots she owned.

If she was going down, at least she'd look good.

Don't think about it, just do it, Ben told himself as he got into his truck, he'd be screwed. Not that he hadn't done exactly that for the past week. In fact, he'd mulled over every possibility, every contingency, every objection she might come up with (and boy, there were plenty of those) until his head hurt. Nothing left now but to throw himself on Mercy's mercy and hope for the best.

At this point, he had nothing to lose. Except, maybe, his sanity. But that was already shredded past recognition, so what the hell, right?

He backed out of his brother's driveway, telling himself this wasn't his last shot, that if she couldn't see her way clear to go along with his plan there were still other options.

Like hurtling himself off Sandia Peak.

Stop that, a voice—the same voice that had talked him through all the phone calls and the discussions and the planning over the past seven days—yelled in his ear. She still had the ring. And Anita swore she'd softened her up, that she—Mercy, not Anita—was ripe for him to make his move.

Ben sucked in a sharp breath, his hands tensing on the steering wheel as some dumb cluck turned onto the street ahead of him, blinding him with his brights—

Huh?

The Firebird streaked past him. Screeched to a stop the same time he did. And then Mercy was out of her car, running—if you could call it that, in those ridiculous high heels—toward him, waving her arms and yelling, "Wait! Wait!"

Ben angled the truck into the curb, setting off a security light worthy of Leavenworth. He'd barely gotten out of the truck before Mercy threw herself into his arms.

Okay, this was looking good.

"Mercy, I—"

"It doesn't matter," she said into his chest, clinging to him like a limpet. "I don't care how much you have to be away, a part-time *you* is worth a hundred times more than a hundred percent of all the other men I've ever known, all put together." Still clinging, she lifted her eyes to his, sparkling in the glare of that damn security bulb. "Because who says we have to have a typical marriage, or that I need a husband who's underfoot all the time? It's not as if I don't have my own life or anything. And so, yeah, I'd probably worry, but I'm gonna do that, anyway, so we might as well be together, right? And by supporting *your* work, I'd actually feel like I was contributing something to the solution, for once, instead of doing the ostrich thing and not thinking about it at all."

People were beginning to come out of their houses, but apparently she didn't notice. And God knew Ben couldn't have cared less. Smiling so wide his face hurt, he bracketed her face in his hands. Her wild hair tickled his fingers, tickled his soul, making him want to laugh.

"You really think we could make this work?" he said, and she rested her forehead against his chest.

"It sure as heck beats the alternative," she said, still clinging. "If you have to stay based in Texas, then I'll just suck it up, I suppose."

Ben tucked his fingers underneath her chin, lifting her face to lap up the love in her eyes. "And I told you, I'm home for good."

She frowned. "And I told *you,* I don't want you to give up your work."

"I'm not. But Roy and I agreed it was time I struck out on my own. Right here in Albuquerque. I'd still be part of the same network, but I'd be based here. And hopefully, if I get enough funding, I can bring other people on board so I could stick around more. That's why I sold the property. Because I need the funds to start up my own operation."

Her gaze danced in his for several seconds before, finally, a soft "Oh" fell from her lips, followed by a sharp intake of breath…and a smile five times brighter than the stupid security lamp. Except then she let go to rummage in her jacket pocket, at last extricating the ring box. A frown bit into Ben's forehead— was his mind playing tricks on him? Hadn't she just said—

"Do it right, this time," she said, tossing her hair over her shoulder. "I haven't waited this long to get some half-assed proposal. Not having the *cojones* to give it to me in person…" She shook her head. "Lame."

"And my proposing to you in the middle of the street isn't?"

"With all these witnesses?" she said. So she had noticed.

"Oh, for God's sake, Ben…we've never done anything the 'normal' way. And I doubt we ever will. Why should this be any different?"

"Does that mean I don't have to get down on one knee?"

"It does not."

He sighed. "Can we at least go over onto the sidewalk?"

"Fine," she said on a pushed breath, leading him by the hand up onto the curb, where, in front of somebody's stinky juniper bush, Ben lowered himself to one knee, took Mercy's hand in his and kissed her knuckles. Then he looked up at her—at the woman who'd make his life a living hell, but in the best possible way—and said, "Marry me, Mercy," and she said, in a choked voice, "Okay," and then a whole bunch of people they didn't even know cheered and applauded, and then she shrieked when Ben yanked her down onto the sidewalk with him. Laughing, she threw her arms around his neck.

"I love you, Mr. Macho," she whispered, and he kissed her, and kissed her, and kissed her some more, feeling whole for the first time in his life.

Epilogue

Mercy sat cross-legged on her bedroom floor, her lap full of three-week-old kittens—one calico, one black-and-white and one gray tabby. No gingers. Mercy was guessing that Miss Marge had gotten around some before Homer'd come along and made her an honest woman. Especially since the vet confirmed that, yes, old Homer was shooting blanks.

Ben, however, was not, she mused as she nearly trampled the little furballs in her haste to get to the bathroom. You'd think, what with all the hoo-hah about fertility rates rapidly declining the closer a woman got to forty, it would have taken longer than five minutes without birth control for her to get pregnant. But no.

One day, she would find this amusing.

Mercy emerged to find her husband-to-be waiting for her on the edge of their bed, his face a study in cocky solicitousness, an expression only Ben could pull off and live to tell the tale.

"You okay?"

She had the feeling she was going to hear that a lot over the next eight months. A thought that, inexplicably—now that the woozies had passed—produced a sparkly, giddy feeling inside her, like champagne drunk too fast. She slid onto Ben's lap, sighing as his arms wrapped around her.

"You have no idea how okay I am. Even if I still can't believe this little monkey is on his or her way already."

"What can I tell you? When you're good, you're good."

"And you are so gonna get it. You sure we should wait to tell our parents until the wedding?"

"I think they can hang on for another month," Ben said, kissing her temple.

"Yeah, but can I? And anyway, the minute one of my sisters or either of our mothers figures it out—which, knowing them, is gonna take, like, a second—it's all over. Ma's already giving me funny looks."

His chuckle rumbled through her, as the unbridled joy and love in his eyes nearly brought tears to hers. "Never mind that it was your idea to wait until you were through the first three months." When she made a face, he laughed again and said, "Okay. We'll tell 'em tonight." His grin widened. "I'll bring earplugs."

Mercy lightly smacked his shoulder, then reached down

to scoop up the little black-and-white kitty, who was attacking her shoe.

"That's Mattie's, right?"

"Yep. Did I tell you I named him Bart?"

Ben groaned, then said, "You're nuts, you know that?"

"Too late to back out now, you knocked me up…what are you doing?"

"What do you think?" Ben said, nibbling her neck. And unbuttoning her shirt.

"Not in front of the babies, for goodness sake!"

"We're up here on the bed," he said, gently putting Bart back on the carpet, then deftly lifting her off his lap and onto the mattress, nuzzling her magically-growing breasts over the edge of her push-up bra. "They're down there. Besides…" He unhooked the waistband of her jeans. "They're cats, they're born knowing how this stuff works—"

His cell rang. Ben ignored it. Mercy braced her hands on his shoulders, pushed him back. Their gazes tangled for a second or two, until, on a sigh, he levered himself up and off, grabbing the phone from the nightstand.

Mercy sat up, listening. And watching, as compassion and resolve supplanted the tenderness and desire of moments before.

He clapped shut the phone; she laid a hand on his arm.

"It's okay, Ben. Go."

"But we were going to tell our parents—"

"They'll be here when you get back." She smiled. "So will we."

And two days later, when Mercy welcomed Ben's tired,

disheveled, exhilarated, wonderful self back home, it wasn't with relief, but the profound gratitude of an equally exhilarated woman who had only this to say to all those people who'd given her grief for being picky: *Thppppt.*

* * * * *

PRIDE
AND PREGNANCY

BY
KAREN TEMPLETON

To Gail, for trusting me

To Jack, for believing in me

To Jane Austen, for inspiring me (and every other
romance writer who's ever trod the globe!)

Chapter One

By the time she was thirty, Karleen Almquist had signed three sets of divorce papers, at which point she decided to make things easier on herself and just get a hamster.

After all, hamsters didn't leave their clothes scattered all over kingdom come, watch endless football or stay out till all hours. And their itty-bitty paws were too small to mess with the remote. True, they weren't of much use in the sack, but then the same could be said of most of her husbands.

Unfortunately, also like her husbands, hamsters didn't exactly have a long shelf life. Which was why Karleen was burying yet another of the critters underneath the huge, gnarled cottonwood at the back of the large yard of the aging Corrales adobe she'd kept after her last divorce, seven years ago. Each tiny grave was marked by a minia-ture cast-stone marker engraved with the rodent's name, ordered from this place online that promised a two-day turnaround, if you were willing to pay extra for FedEx overnight service.

Karleen sank the marker into the soft soil, praying the neighborhood cats wouldn't disturb Mel's rest, although he was probably fairly scavenger-proof in the little metal floral can from Hobby Lobby. Then she stood, making a face as she peeled off her gardening gloves. Fond of Melvin as she'd been, it had taken the better part of an hour to glue on these nails and damned if she was going to ruin them for a dead hamster.

A cool, dry breeze shuddered through the veritable orchard of apple trees lining the far wall, sending a shower of white blossoms drifting across her dusty pool cover. The peaches, apricots and cherries would bloom in a few weeks. By mid-summer, the ground would be a holy mess with rotting fruit. But right now, her heart lifted a little at the sight of all those blossoms glowing against the brilliant New Mexico sky, the twittering of dozens of redheaded finches scouting out the assortment of brightly colored birdhouses suspended from the branches—

What was that?

At the giggling, she swung around in time to see a pair of pale blond heads vanish behind the low wooden fence separating her yard from the one next door.

"Boys!" boomed an off-stage male voice. "Get over here!"

Karleen zipped as fast as her beaded slides would carry her back to the house, dumping the gloves on a tempered-glass table on her flagstone patio as she went. Once inside, she scurried across the brick floor through the house, twisting open the slightly warped verticals in her living-room window to get a better view. And indeed, through the assortment of glittery, spinning porch ornaments hanging from the eaves, she saw a great big old U-Haul van backed in the next driveway.

The house was the largest of the four on their little dead-end road, a two-story territorial/adobe mutt centered in a huge pie-shaped lot crammed with a forest's worth of trees—cottonwoods, willows, pines, silver maples. The property hadn't been on the market more than a few weeks (the old owners had gone to live with one of their kids in Oregon or Idaho or someplace), so the new owners must've paid cash for it, for closing to have gone through that quickly.

The little boys—twins, it looked like—raced around the side of the van, roaring in slightly off-sync unison (and loud enough to be heard through a closed window), "Daddy, Daddy! The house next door has a *pool!*"

Just shoot her now.

Karleen thought maybe they were a little older than her best friend Joanna's youngest, around four or so. Jumping up and down like that, it was hard to tell. God bless their mother, was all she had to say.

Then a Nordic god walked out from behind the truck, sunlight glinting off short golden hair, caressing massive shoulders effortlessly hefting a giant cardboard box, and her brain shorted out.

Not so much, however, that she couldn't paw for the pair of long-neglected binoculars on the bookshelf crammed with paperbacks and doodads behind her. She blew off the dust, then held them up to her eyes, fiddling with the focusing thingy for a second or two before letting out a soft yelp when The God's face suddenly filled up the lens.

Lord, it was like trying to pick a single item off the dessert cart. The jaw…the cheekbones…the heavy-lidded eyes…the mouth.

Oh, dear God, the mouth.

She licked her own, it having been a long, long time since she'd had a close encounter with one of those. Although this mouth was in a class by itself. Not too thin, but not one of those girlie mouths, either. *Just right, Goldilocks,* she thought with a snort.

Karleen lowered the binoculars, shaking her head and thinking, *Well, doesn't this suck toads?* only to brighten considerably when she remembered there was, in all likelihood, a Mrs. God. So he was somebody else's problem, praise be.

While she stood there, trying to hang on to her newfound cheer, an SUV rumbled past, parking behind the van and disgorging a pair of dark-haired hunks. Or rather one hunk and one hunk-in-progress, a teenager not yet grown into his long arms and legs. The two men did the buddy-palm-slapping thing, then got to work unloading the van while the little boys concentrated on staying underfoot as much as possible and being cute enough to get away with it.

For the next, um, twenty minutes or so, she watched as plaid Early American wing chairs and sofas and brass lamps and sections of a dark wood four-poster bed and one of those bland landscape paintings people hung over their sofas marched from van to house. Occasionally she caught snatches of flat, midwestern speech and thought, *Yeah, that figures.* And as the minutes passed, she wondered…so where was this wife, already? Shouldn't she be flitting about, directing the men where to put everything?

About this time Karleen noticed the mail truck shudder to a stop in front of her mailbox at the edge of her yard. The carrier got out, took stuff out of the box, slammed down the painted gecko flag, stuffed stuff into the box, then walked around to the back of the truck and retrieved a package. Which, instead of carrying up the walk to Karleen's front door, she tucked into a nest of weeds at the base of the post. Oh, for pity's sake.

Karleen yanked open her front door and headed toward her mailbox, blinking at the dozen or so jewel-toned pin-wheels bordering her walk, happily spinning in the breeze. Halfway down, however, she realized that all movement had ceased next door. While she had to admit she felt a little spurt of pride that, at thirty-seven, she still had what it took to render men immobile, there was also a ping of annoyance that she couldn't go to her damn mailbox without being gawked at. However, if she didn't say anything, she would be forever branded as The Stuck-Up Bitch Who Lived Next Door.

And that would just be wrong.

So she fished her mail out of the box and the box out of the weeds, then wound her way over to the fence through her ever-growing collection of lawn ornamenta-tion.

"Hey," she said, smiling. "I'm Karleen. You guys my new neighbors?"

She might even have pulled it off, too, if it hadn't been for *the eyes.*

Bimbo.

The word smacked Troy between the eyes like a kamikaze bee. Followed in quick succession by *blonde, stacked* and *oh, crap.*

It wasn't just the eighties retro hair. Or the Vegas makeup. Or even that she was dressed provocatively, because she wasn't. Exactly. The stretchy pants rode low and the top rode high (and the belly button sparkled like the North Star), but the essentials were more than adequately covered. No cleavage, even. A delicate gold chain hugged her ankle, but that was pretty much it. She was just one of those women that fabric liked to snuggle up to.

Men, too, no doubt.

Beside him, Blake cleared his throat. Troy came to and extended his hand; Karleen shifted everything to one arm to reciprocate, an assortment of fake gemstone rings flashing in the sunlight. Jeez, those fingernails could gut and fillet a fish in five seconds flat, a thought that got a bit tangled up with the one where Troy realized that her breasts seemed a little...still.

"And I'm Troy. Lindquist." Her handshake was firm and brief and he suddenly got the feeling that she wished this was happening even less than he did, which irked him for some reason he couldn't begin to explain.

"You're kidding?" She hugged her mail with both arms again, her deep blue eyes snaring him like Chinese finger traps. "My maiden name's Almquist."

"Swedish," they both said at once, and everybody else looked at them as though they'd totally lost it, while Troy noticed that Karleen's mouth said *friendly* and her eyes said *pay no attention to the mouth.*

"Anyway," Troy said. "These are my boys Grady and Scott, and this is Blake Carter, my business partner, and his son Shaun."

She said all her hello-nice-to-meet-yous, very polite, very careful...and then she turned that glistening smile on the boys, and Definite Interest roared onto the scene, huffing and puffing. Because people tended to have one of two reactions when confronted with his sons: They either went all squealy and stupid, or got a look on their faces like they'd stumbled across a pair of rattlesnakes. Karleen did neither. Instead, Karleen's expression said, *Anything you can dish out, I can take and give back ten times over,* which Troy found disturbingly attractive and scary as hell at the same time.

"Hey, guys," she said in a perfectly normal voice, with a perfectly normal smile, which was when he realized she was around his age and that she hadn't had any work done that he could tell. Not on her face, at least. "Let me guess— y'all are twins, right?"

Scotty, slightly smaller than his brother, stuck close to Troy's leg while the more outgoing Grady clung like a curious little monkey to the post-and-rail fence separating the yards. Still, clearly awestruck—and dumbstruck—they both nodded so hard Troy was surprised their heads didn't fall off. Out of the corner of his eye, he caught Blake elbowing Shaun. *"Breathe,"* he said, and the sixteen-year-old turned the color of cranberry juice.

"How old are you guys?" Karleen asked, not looking at Shaun.

"Four!" they chorused. Then Grady leaned closer and asked, "You got any kids?"

Karleen shook her head, tugging a straw-colored hair out of her lipstick. "No, sugar, I sure don't."

"Then how come you gots all that stuff?" Grady said, jabbing one finger toward her yard. Which looked like an annex for Wal-Mart's lawn-and-garden department. And no, he did not mean that in a good way. Surely all those whirligigs and stone raccoons and such hadn't been there before? Was that a *gnome* over in the far corner?

"'Cause it's fun," Karleen said with a shrug. "I like sparkly stuff, don't you?"

More nodding. Then Scotty piped up. "You got a pool, huh?"

"Yeah," she said, wrinkling her nose. Disconcertingly cute, that. "But I haven't used it in years."

"How come?"

"*Okay*," Troy said, slipping a warning hand on the boy's shoulders. "Too many questions, bud."

"It's all right," Karleen said, meeting his gaze, apparently forgetting to switch from kid-smile to I'm-only-doing-this-because-that's-how-I-was-raised smile, and his lungs stopped working, painfully reminding him how long it had been since he'd done the hokeypokey with anyone. Then, thankfully, she returned her attention to the child. "It just got to be too much of a bother, that's all."

"Oh. Daddy said we couldn't have a pool 'cause we're too little an' he didn't wanna hafta to worry 'bout us. But if we learned to swim, then he wouldn't *hafta* worry 'bout us."

"Yeah," Grady put in with another enthusiastic head nod, after which, as one, both blond heads swiveled to Troy with the attendant you-have-ruined-my-life-forever glare. But then Troy pulled his head out of his butt long enough to realize that that was the most Scotty had ever said to anyone, ever, at one time.

Karleen laughed. A low, from-the-gut laugh. Not a ditzy, tinkly, bimbo laugh. Definitely not a laugh Troy needed to hear right now, not with this many neglected hormones standing at the ready to do what hormones do. He glanced over to see Blake looking at him with a funny, irritating smirk, and he shot back a *What?* look. Chuckling, Blake poked Shaun—twice, this time—to help him unload the leather sofa for the family room, as Karleen said, "Your mama must sure have her hands full with you two," and Troy thought, *Oh, hell.*

"We don't got a mama, either," Scotty said, but with less regret than about the pool. "She died."

Karleen's eyes shot to Troy's, even as her cheeks pinked way beyond the makeup. "I am *so* sorry—"

"It's okay," he mumbled. "They've never known her."

"But you did," she said, then seemed to catch herself, the flush deepening.

"Hey, Troy," Blake called from the house. "You wanna come check out the sofa, make sure it's exactly where you want it?"

"Yeah, sure, be right there." He turned again to Karleen, who was already edging back toward her house. "Really, it's okay," he felt compelled to say, and she nodded, said, "Well. It was nice to meet you, welcome to the neighborhood," and hotfooted it back across her yard.

"I like Karleen," Grady said, still hanging over the fence. "She's pretty."

"Yeah," Scotty said. "She's nice, too."

But Troy didn't miss that she hadn't said to feel free to ask if he needed to know anything about garbage pickup and the like.

He also didn't miss the lack of panty lines underneath all that soft, smooth, snuggly fabric.

A couple of hours later, he and Blake sat on Troy's redwood deck, legs stretched out in front of them, nursing a couple of Cokes as well as their sore muscles. The twins and Shaun were gone, off on an exploratory hike of the new neighborhood. If it hadn't been for the Sandia Mountains on the other side of Albuquerque peeking through the just-budded-out trees, he could almost imagine he was a kid again, on vacation at the Wisconsin lake where his parents would drag him and his brothers every summer. Letting his eyes drift closed, Troy took advantage of the moment to sink into the padded patio chair, soaking up the spring air, and the peace.

"That neighbor of yours is something to behold,"

Blake began in his Oklahoma drawl, and Troy thought, *So much for peace.*

He scrunched farther down in the chair, his Coke resting on his stomach. "I suppose. If you like that type."

"Not talking about me. Obviously. I got me my woman," his partner said with a noisy, satisfied stretch. "Now we need to start thinking about plugging up the gap in your life. And don't even think about giving me some crap about how you're just fine, the boys are all you need, it's not time yet, blah-blah-blah."

"I wasn't going to," Troy said quietly, his eyes still closed.

He could tell he'd caught Blake off guard. After more than ten years of working together, a rare occurrence.

"You saying you're ready to move on?" Blake finally said.

"You sound surprised."

"Try flabbergasted."

"Why? It's been four years." Giving up on dozing, Troy sat forward, his Coke clasped in both hands between his spread knees. "I loved Amy. I'll always love Amy. But I'm tired of being alone."

"And you miss sex."

Troy's mouth pulled tight. "Like you wouldn't believe."

Blake was quiet for a moment. Understandable, considering how wrecked Troy had been after his wife's death, how adamant he'd been that there'd never be anyone else. Even now, the pain still lurked, even if these days it tended to stay curled up in its corner, like an old, weary dog. But for every inch the grief receded, emptiness rushed in to take its place.

"Sounds like you've been chewing this over for a while," Blake said.

Troy held up his soda can, squinting at the shiny metal in the late afternoon light. "A year or so. Ever since we started talking about relocating the business down here." He lowered the can. "I don't know, I guess the change finally rattled something loose. That maybe I'd like to think about another relationship while my working parts are all still in order."

The dark-haired man crossed his arms, fixing Troy with a far-too-astute gaze. "Any idea what you intend to do about that?"

Troy released a weighty sigh. "None whatsoever. Amy and I were together for thirteen years. And she's been gone for four." He shook his head. "Saying I'm a little out of practice is a gross understatement."

"It'll come back to you, I'm sure," Blake said dryly.

"I'm not talking about that, dirtwad. I'm talking about dating. Starting a new relationship. It was bad enough in my teens when at least I had youth to hide behind. Now I'm supposed to know what I'm doing."

One side of Blake's mouth tilted up. "You're not exactly indigent and you still have all your teeth. My advice? Leave it up to the women. They're born knowing what to do."

Both men jumped when overloud country music knifed the silence; just as suddenly, the volume receded. Not, however, fast enough for Troy.

"Like that one, for instance," Blake said when Karleen appeared in her yard, practically hidden by an umbrella-sized straw hat. A minute later, she was walking back and forth, head down, pushing something—a spreader, maybe?—singing enthusiastic backup with the female vocalist. Her cell phone rang; she stopped, answered it, that damned low, warm laugh carrying over the fence on the slightly chilly breeze.

Staring, borderline miserable, Troy shook his head.

"Why the hell not?"

"Her front yard?"

"At least there's no junkers on cement blocks. Or toilets."

"That we can see. Anyway, then there's the hair. And the nails. And the…" He rolled his hand. "Attributes."

Blake frowned. "I'm not following."

Her call finished, Troy waited until he heard the rhythmic groan and squeak of the spreader before he said, "The woman's not *real,* Blake, she's a hallucination brought on by sexual deprivation. And I'm not looking for a hook-up. Which is all that would be. If anything."

"Oh, believe me, buddy, *anything* it would be." Blake took a swig of his soda, chuckling. "*Something* is what that would be. I half expected the grass between the two of you to ignite."

"That's crazy. And do *not*—" he jabbed his soda can in Blake's direction "—shake your heading pityingly at me."

"I'll shake my head any damn way I want. I'm beginning to wonder if maybe I should go back and double check the van, make sure you didn't leave your brain inside it. The woman's pretty, likes kids, seems reasonably conversant in the English language and looked like she had her tongue stuck to the roof of her mouth for a while there. No, wait—that was you." Blake pushed himself back on the chair, grinning. "Not real sure I see what the problem is."

"Just because she doesn't have kids doesn't mean she's single," Troy said before he caught himself.

Blake tapped his own wedding ring. "No ring."

"So she could still have a boyfriend, you know. But it doesn't matter, because I'm not interested. Oh, come on, Blake…you know as well as I do that 'opposites attract' stuff is a crock. Yes, she strikes me as a nice enough woman, but I'm looking for something with some sub-stance to it."

"Like you had with Amy."

"Exactly. What?" he said when Blake shook his head again.

Dark-brown eyes met his. "They call it *starting over* for a reason, dumb-ass. There's never gonna be another Amy, and thinking that's even possible isn't fair to anybody. Especially you. But aren't you jumping the gun a little here? Thinking you're gonna find the next Mrs. Lindquist right off the bat without taking a couple of test drives first? Why limit your options by automatically tossing out any woman who doesn't immediately make you think wedding bells?"

"Because it's a waste of time? Because…" He glanced toward Karleen's house, then lowered his voice even further. "Because the enhanced look has never done it for me?"

"Must've been one helluva trick of the light, then, that poleaxed look on your face. And anyway, what makes you so sure they're not the genuine article?"

"Educated guess."

"Huh. Never realized MBA stood for Master of Boob Authenticity. Hey!" Laughing, he ducked when Troy threw his empty soda can at him, the crushed aluminum making one hell of a racket as it bounced across the wooden deck. Karleen jerked her head in their direction. They both waved. She waved back. A little reluctantly, Troy thought.

"And anyway," Blake said, "haven't you always wondered what fake ones feel like?" only to laugh again as he dodged Troy's smack upside the head. Then, hearing the boys' voices as they trooped around the side of the house toward the backyard, Blake stood, checking his watch. "I need to get back, I told Cass I'd be home by five. You ready to drop off the truck and pick up your car?"

"Might as well."

Which Troy had fervently hoped signaled the end of the discussion. Except, after the U-Haul had been returned and Blake dropped Troy and the twins back by their old apartment to pick up the Volvo, Blake called Troy back to his car.

"So, you gonna put out feelers with Karleen or not?" Blake said quietly over Shaun's hip-hop on the stereo, and Troy glared at him.

"This is payback for all the grief I gave you when you were trying to get back with Cass, isn't it?"

Chuckling, Blake put the SUV in reverse, then gave Troy one final, concerned glance. "No. But I am wondering how you think looking for another Amy is being open to possibilities. Just something to think about," he said, then backed out of the driveway.

Twenty minutes later, Troy pulled up in front of his new house, the boys springing themselves from their car seats the instant he cut the engine. "Stay in the backyard!" he yelled out the window, a moment before they vanished in a cloud of dust and giggles. Then he sagged into the leather seat, his head lolling against the rest as he looked at his new home, waiting for the dust storm of memories to settle inside his head.

Several years before, when Troy had finally felt confident enough that the business wasn't going to disintegrate out from under him, that he and Amy could actually apply for a mortgage with a straight face, they'd driven the poor Realtor in Denver nuts, looking at house after house after house. But it had been their first and it had to be perfect. Especially since they'd start raising their family there.

Meaning, the minute they'd walked inside, it had to say *home*. And the way his and Amy's tastes had dovetailed so perfectly had almost been spooky. They'd both craved clean lines, openness, light woods and walls—a house nothing like their parents' slightly disheveled, suburban two-story pseudo Colonials. The house they'd finally fallen in love with had smelled of fresh plaster, new wood, new beginnings, even if they'd filled it with the comforting, muted colors and traditional styles of their childhood.

After Amy's death, Troy had assumed he wouldn't be able to bear staying there. He'd been wrong. Instead, the familiar, the routine, had succored him in those first terrible weeks, months, after the unthinkable had happened. The house, and their beautiful, precious babies, had saved his butt. And his sanity. Leaving it hadn't been easy.

So after the move, he'd again taken his time, driving another Realtor crazy, looking for a new home for him and his boys. Another new start. He could have bought pretty much any house he wanted in Albuquerque. But he hadn't wanted any house; he'd wanted the *right* house. Only, who knew "right" would be this quirky, lopsided grandmother of a house, mottled with the patina of mold and memories? That his new definition of *home* would include bowed wooden floors and a wisteria-and-honeysuckle choked *portal,* weathered corbels and windows checkered by crumbling mullions and pockmarked wooden vigas ribbing the high ceilings?

Damn thing was twice as big as they really needed, even after getting everything out of storage. And he'd have to buy one of those John Deere monsters to mow the lawn. Still, he thought as he finally climbed out of the car, hearing the boys' clear, pure laughter on the nippy breeze, this was a house that exuded serenity, the kind that comes from having seen it all and surviving. A house that begged for large dogs and swing sets and basketball hoops and loud, boisterous boys.

Troy walked over to inspect what turned out to be a loose, six-inch thick post on the porch, shaking his head. And, because he'd clearly lost his mind, smiling. The house needed him. Right now, a good thing.

A flimsy wooden screen door whined when he opened it, the floorboards creaking underfoot as he walked through the family room to check on the boys in the backyard. The French doors leading outside were suffocated underneath God-knew-how-many coats of white enamel paint; Troy dug his trusty Swiss Army knife out of his pocket and scratched through to the wood: maple. Maybe cherry. Pocketing the knife, he pushed the doors open, his lips curving at the sight of the kids chasing each other around and around the trees, their yells competing with doves' coos, the occasional trill of a robin.

"You guys want pizza?" His voice echoed in the half-empty house, the emptiness inside him.

"Yeah!" they both hollered, running over, their faces flushed under messy, dirty hair. *Find towels,* he thought. *Wash kids.*

"C'n Karleen eat wif us?" Grady said, five times louder than necessary, and Troy thought, *What?* even as he stole a please-don't-be-there glance at her yard.

"She probably has other plans, guys. You go back and play, I'll call you when it gets here."

God, kids, Troy thought as he tromped back into the house, thumbing through the phone book for the nearest pizza delivery. After ordering two larges—one cheese, one with everything—a salad and breadsticks, he soldiered on upstairs to the boys' new room. Since it faced the back, he could work and still keep an ear out. Blake and Shaun had helped him set up the bunk bed, but the boxes of toys and clothes and heaven knew what else had clearly multiplied in the last two hours.

Shaking his head, he got to it, only to discover a couple boxes of his junk among the kids. After another glance out the window at the boys—huddled together underneath a nearby cottonwood, deep in some kind of twin conspiracy, no doubt—he stacked the boxes and carted them to his bedroom across the hall, no sooner dumping them on the floor at the foot of his (unmade) bed when his cell rang.

"Just called to see if you were settled in yet," his mother said in his ear.

"In, yes," he said, shoving one of the boxes into a corner with his foot. "Settled?" He glowered at the pile of boxes sitting in front of him, silently jeering. "By the time the boys graduate from high school, if I'm lucky."

"Which is where a woman comes in handy. Although listen to me," Eleanor Lindquist hurriedly added, as if realizing her gaffe, "I've still got unpacked boxes in the garage from when we moved in here when you were five! At this point, I think we're just going to leave them for you and your brothers to 'discover' after we're dead."

"Can't wait."

Eleanor laughed softly, then said, "I'm sorry, Troy. About the woman comment—"

"It's okay. Forget it."

A brief pause preceded "Anyway. Your father and I are thinking about coming down there for a visit. In a couple of months, we thought."

Troy stilled. "Oh?"

"We've always wanted to see the Southwest, you know—" News to him. "But we thought we might as well wait until you got your housing situation straightened out.

Of course, we can certainly stay in a hotel if it's inconvenient—"

"No! No, of course not, there's plenty of room here."
Good one, Mom. "But…how's Dad? Is he up to the trip?"

"Of course he's up to the trip, it's been more than five years, for goodness sake!"

The doorbell rang. Wow. Domino's must be having a slow night. "Pizza guy's at the door, I've got to run," he said, digging his wallet out of his back pocket as he thundered down the stairs. "My best to Dad." He clapped shut his phone and swung open the door, only to jump a foot at the sight of Karleen on his doorstep.

Bookended by a pair of slightly smudged, grinning, yellow-haired boys.

"Lose something?" she said.

Chapter Two

Troy allowed himself a quarter second's worth of sexual awareness—the perfume alone was enough to make him light-headed—before the hindsight terror thing kicked in nicely and he grabbed two skinny little arms, yanking the bodies attached thereto across his threshold.

"What's the big idea, leaving the yard? You *know* you're not supposed to go *anywhere* without a grown-up! *Ever*," he added before Scotty could snow him with the pouty lower lip.

"We didn't cross the street or nothin'," Grady said, his defiance trembling at the edges. "We only went to Karleen's.'"

"Why on earth did you do that?"

"'Cause we wanted her to come over, only you said she prob'ly had plans. 'Cept she doesn't. Huh?" Grady said, twisting around to look up at her.

"I am *so* sorry," Troy said, following his son's gaze, which was when it registered that Karleen was wearing one of those painted-on exercise outfits that left little to the imagination, and that her skin was flushed—From exercise? From being pissed?—and her lipstick was eaten off and she'd pulled her hair back into a ponytail, leaving all these soft little bits hanging around her face and her eyes huge underneath her bangs and—

"We were coming right back," Scotty said softly, cruelly derailing Troy's train of thought.

Kids. Right.

Troy straightened up, forking a hand through his hair. Giving them the Dad-is-not-amused face. "That's not the point. You're too little to be by yourselves, even for a minute."

Grady's little forehead crumpled. "Then how come you always tell us what big boys we are?"

"Yeah," Scotty said, nodding, looking impossibly tiny and vulnerable. Not for the first time, responsibility walloped Troy square in the chest.

So he pointed a hopefully stern finger in their faces. "You're not *that* big," he said, just as a compact sedan with a Domino's sign clamped to the roof screeched up in front of the house, and the kids started hopping around like grasshoppers, chanting, "Piz-za! Piz-za! Piz-za!"

"No, wait," he said to Karleen as she made her getaway (he couldn't imagine why), breathing an oddly relieved sigh when she stopped, biding her time while Troy paid the pizza guy. After the very well-tipped teen loped back toward his car, Troy focused again on Karleen. Her arms were crossed underneath her breasts, her lips curved in a Mona Lisa smile as she watched the boys. The sun had begun to go down in earnest, soft-edging the shadows, leaving a chill in its wake. He wondered if she was cold…

"Good Lord, honey…how long has it been?"

Troy's head snapped up. "What?"

Bemusement danced in her eyes. "If you stare at my chest any harder, my bra's gonna catch fire."

"I—I'm sorry, I don't usually…" He blew out a breath, his face hotter than the pizza. "I didn't mean…" She laughed. Troy sighed again. "Okay, so maybe I did. But I'm not a letch, I swear."

"Oh, don't go gettin' your boxers in a bunch. You're just bein' a man, is all. No harm, no foul. It's kinda cute, actually."

Cute. Not exactly the image he was going for.

Oh, God. He was staring. Again. Not at her breasts, at least, but still.

"Uh…thanks for bringing the guys back," he said, shifting the pizzas.

One eyebrow lifted. "I hadn't exactly planned on keepin' 'em."

"More's the pity," Troy muttered, then shook his head. "Honestly, I have no idea what got into them, they've never gone off like that before. But you really are welcome to stay. If you haven't eaten, I mean." He hefted the two boxes, which he now realized were slowly melting his palms. And probably the salad on top. "There's plenty. I'll even promise to behave," he said, remembering to smile.

Now it was apparently her turn to stare, in that thoroughly assessing way women had that made men feel about six. "So the boys really came all on their own? You didn't send them over?"

Troy jerked. "*What?* No! Why would you think that?"

"Sorry. I just…" For one small moment, wisps of regret floated between them, only to spiral off into nothingness when she said, "Thanks for the offer, anyway. But I can't."

She pivoted and again started back toward her house.

Let her go, let her go…

"Another time?"

Karleen turned. "You're not serious?"

"Well, yeah, actually I am." *What?* "Was. I mean, we're neighbors and everything…" He shrugged. Lamely.

"Yeah, well, it's the *and everything* part of that sentence that worries me."

"Figure of speech," Troy muttered, fighting another blush. *Bad at this* didn't even begin to cover it. "I promise, Karleen, I'm not coming on to you."

"Well, no, you haven't reached salivatin' stage yet, maybe. But you are definitely coming on to me."

Troy snagged the *Really?* before it got past his lips, then thought, *Hey, maybe this is easier than I thought. Or maybe she is.*

Then he remembered she was the one walking away.

"And…that would be inappropriate because you probably have a boyfriend or something."

"Or maybe I'm not interested."

"Or that."

That got a head shake, which made the ponytail, if not the breasts, bounce. "You know, you really are sweet," she said, and again those wistful wisps cavorted in the chilly early evening air, more visible this time, although no less phantasmagorical. "As it happens, I haven't had a *boy-friend* since I was…" She cleared her throat. "A long time."

"You're into other women?"

She burst out laughing. The kind of laugh that made him smile, even around the size thirteen in his mouth. "Oh, God, you are too much! No, honey, I just meant *boyfriend* sounds kinda…juvenile or something. I've had lovers, and I've had husbands—"

"Husbands?"

"Three, if you must know. And three is definitely this girl's limit. Anyway. I'm trying to make a point, here—no, there's nobody in my life right now. By choice. Because if you ask me, it's all far more trouble than it's worth. Which is why I'm turnin' down your invitation. For tonight or any other time. Because you are sweet and there's no use pretending we're not attracted to each other, but some things just aren't meant to be."

She nodded toward the boxes. "Your pizza's gettin' cold, sugar," she said, then spun around, this time making it all the way across his yard.

Troy stared after her for several seconds as it all came flooding back. The part about how much it sucked to get rejected. Even when the woman wasn't someone you really wanted to get tangled up with, anyway.

He went inside, slamming the door shut with his foot, and called the boys to dinner.

"What's his name again?"

"Troy Lindquist," Karleen tossed in the direction of the speakerphone while she pedaled her butt off on her exercise bike. It had been two days since Troy and his Tiny Tots had moved in next door. Two days since Karleen had walked away from an invitation that she'd known full well had included a lot more than pizza, Troy's insistence otherwise notwithstanding.

Two days since she'd answered her doorbell to find a plastic-wrapped Chinet plate on her doorstep, heaped with two slices of pizza—one cheese, one supreme—a breadstick and salad. And taped to the top, a note:

It'll only go to waste. Enjoy. T.

And in those two days, she'd put in enough miles on this bike to give Lance Armstrong a run for his money. If nothing else, she was gonna have thighs you could bounce a rock off.

Slightly crackly, fuzzy clicking filled the room as Joanna tapped away at her computer keyboard, the rhythmic sound occasionally punctuated by her dog Chester's barking, the occasional squawk, scream or "Mo-om!" from one of her four kids. Clearly ignoring them all, Joanna said, "Huh."

"*Huh,* what?" Karleen said, panting and daubing sweat from her neck and chest with the towel around her neck. Of course, she could have Googled the guy herself, but Joanna beat her to it.

"Blond, you said? Late thirties? Blindingly gorgeous?"

"That would be him. Why? You find something?"

"Well," Jo's voice croaked over the speaker, "there's a photo of some blond hottie named Troy Lindquist, with a dark-haired hottie named Blake Carter—"

"Yes! He was there, too!"

"Yeesh, I'm surprised your retinas didn't melt. Anyway, there's a caption under the photo—oh, for God's sake, Matt, let the baby have the ball, already! And put the dog back outside, his feet are all muddy!—about their company. Ain't It Sweet."

"I don't know. Is it?"

"No, Ain't It Sweet. The frozen desserts people?"

Karleen stopped pedaling, her heart beating so hard she could hardly hear herself talk. "As in, The Devil Made Me Do It Fudge Cake?"

"The very same."

"Troy *owns* it?"

"Apparently so. Well, he and this Blake person are partners. It says here…" Karleen waited while Joanna apparently scrolled. "They recently moved their headquarters from Denver to Albuquerque…. Main ice-cream plant still in Denver…holy moly."

"What?"

"'Analysts say, with its steadily increasing sales figures and healthy profit margins, as well as a huge projected franchise growth within the next three to five years, Ain't It Sweet is poised to bolster its North American market share by as much as fifty percent, with plans to increase its overseas distribution in the works. Already, this upstart company is routinely among the top five high-quality frozen confections brands Americans name when polled in market surveys.'"

"It sure as hell's the brand I think of when I think of…whatever you said."

"Yeah," Jo said. "Me, too. Their Yo-Ho-Ho Mocha Rum Truffle cheesecake…"

"Oh! And their Everlasting Latte Cinnamon Swirl sorbet…"

Stupid names. Fabulous stuff. Holy moly was right.

"Hot *and* filthy rich," Joanna cackled. "And single, you say?"

"Don't go there."

"*I'm* not going anywhere. You, on the other hand, have an unattached, lonely, rich hottie living on the other side of your west wall. A single, lonely, rich hottie with a direct link to the best ice cream in the entire freaking *world.*"

Rolling her eyes, Karleen climbed off the bike and grabbed the phone from its stand, walking out to her kitchen for some water. "Why do you assume he's lonely?"

"I can see it in his eyes in the photo." Which, coming from anybody else, would have sounded weird as hell. But Jo was like that. And besides, much as it pained Karleen to admit it, she'd seen it, too. Up close and personal. "For God's sake, Karleen, pay attention! Ice cream! Sex! Money! *Ice cream!*"

She had to laugh. "I got it, Jo. I'm not interested."

"Are you *insane? I'm* interested, and if I were any more happily married my brain would explode. Maybe you better check your pulse, make sure you're still alive."

Karleen released a long, weary breath. "And you do know you are beating a very dead horse, right?"

After a pause, Jo said, "You never used to be like this."

"I think that's the point, honey," she said softly. "And yes, I'm very aware of how attractive he is. And nice. *And* he's got two adorable little boys. But his expression when he first saw me far outweighed whatever hormones were playing dodgeball between us—"

"There were hormones playing dodgeball?" Jo said on a squeak, and Karleen rolled her eyes.

"Jo. Even if I was thinking about followin' through, these lashes do not flutter at someone who looks at me the way Troy Lindquist did. You could practically see the 'trailer trash' lightbulb go on over his head."

"Karleen. Blond hair and a Texas accent do not trailer trash make."

"The boob job comes pretty damn close."

"Then half of L.A.'s trailer trash, too. And would you stop beating yourself up over that? You were thrilled when Nate gave them to you for your birthday."

"Uh-huh. Until I realized what's gonna happen at some point when they'll have to come out and I'm gonna end up with a pair of deflated balloons on my chest. I'll be regretting them for the rest of my life. Just like my marriages."

"Okay, that's enough," Jo said in a voice Karleen had heard far too often since the first day in seventh grade when they'd sat next to each other in Social Studies, and for some bizarre reason the daughter of a hotshot attorney and one of Albuquerque's most successful car dealers had taken a liking to a little hick from Flyspeck, Texas. "Dammit, Kar—you're smart, you've got your own business, you don't owe anybody anything. So your marriages didn't work out. It happens."

"Three times?"

"So you've had more practice than most people. Big whoop. But if being alone is what you really want, hey…go for it—"

Karleen's call waiting beeped in her ear. "Sorry, I'm waiting on a client's call, I need to take this. I'll talk to you later, honey, okay?"

At that point, she almost didn't care who was calling. That is, until she heard "Leenie? Is that you?" on the other end of the line.

A fireball exploded in the pit of Karleen's stomach. The phone pressed against her ear, she wobbled out to the family room, dropping onto the worn Southwest pastel sofa. Well-meaning friends, rich hunky neighbors, all forgotten in an instant. Not even the glass menagerie sparkling on the windowsill—usually a surefire defense against the doldrums—could withstand the all-too-familiar tsunami of irritation and guilt.

"Aunt Inky?"

"Well, who else would it be, baby? Shew, what a relief, I was afraid you might've changed your phone number or somethin'!"

Definitely an oversight on her part. Karleen resisted the impulse to ask her mother's younger sister what she wanted. Because she only ever surfaced when she did want something. "Well. This is a surprise."

"I know, I've been real bad about keepin' in touch. And

it would've been hard for you to contact me, since I've been doing so much, um, traveling and all."

"Uh-huh." Inky didn't sound drunk, for once. But then, it was only ten o'clock in the morning. The slurring wasn't usually noticeable until mid-afternoon. "So where are you now?"

"Lubbock. Been here for a couple months now. It's okay, I guess. God knows I've lived in worse places." A pause. "You take up with anybody new yet?"

Karleen shut her eyes. "No, Aunt Inky. I told you, I prefer being alone."

"What fun is that?"

"It's not fun I'm after, it's peace. You should try it sometime."

"Well, each to his own, I suppose," her aunt said. "You doing okay, then? Money-wise, I mean?"

Ah. Karleen had wondered how long it would take. "I get by."

"Well, that's good. You always were a smart little thing, though—sure as heck a lot smarter than your mama or me—so I guess I shouldn't be surprised. You still livin' in the same place, that house with all the trees around it?"

Ice immediately doused the fire in her belly. And oh, she was tempted to lie. If not to pack her bags and make a run for it. Except Inky was the only family she had left, for one thing. And for another, Karleen was done running, done believing that whatever she needed was always right over the horizon.

"Yes, I'm still here." She hesitated, then added, "It's all I've got, really," even if that *was* stretching the truth a little.

Sure enough, Inky came back with a soft "Then I don't suppose you could spare a couple hundred dollars? Just a loan, you understand. To tide me over until I get back on my feet."

Karleen nearly laughed, even as she again resisted temptation, this time to point out to her aunt that if she spent less time in a horizontal position—either in the company of men of dubious character or out cold from cheap booze—she might actually stay on her feet for more than five minutes. But it wasn't like Karleen had a whole lot of room to talk, so who was she to judge? And anyway, it had been nearly a year this time, so maybe this really was an emergency.

"I guess I can manage a couple hundred. As long as you pay it back," she added, because she wanted her aunt to at least think about it.

"Of course, baby! Let me give you my address, I'm stayin' with a friend right now—" *oh, brother* "—but I should be here for a while...."

Karleen scribbled the address on a notepad lying on the coffee table. "Okay, I'll send a check for two hundred dollars in the next mail—"

"Could you make that a money order, baby? And if you could see clear to maybe make that two-fifty, or even three, I'd really appreciate it."

Karleen sighed. But, she thought after she hung up, at least her aunt hadn't asked to come stay with her.

A thought that made her feel prickly all over, like the time she'd lifted up a piece of wood in the backyard after a rainstorm and a million great big old waterbugs had scurried out from under it. Even though it had been probably twenty years since she'd spent any significant time with her aunt, just talking to the woman disturbed a swollen, never-quite-forgotten nest of skin-crawling memories.

Karleen sucked in a lungful of air, then glanced over at

the big mirrored clock by the entertainment center. Plenty of time before her afternoon appointment to do some digging in the garden, work off some of this negative energy.

She traded her bicycle shorts for jeans, shoved her feet into a pair of disreputable sneakers, plopped her silly straw hat on her head and went outside, where she was greeted by that brain-numbing music Troy liked so much. She half thought about going back inside, only to decide she couldn't become a recluse simply because her new neighbor made her uncomfortable in ways she didn't want to think about too hard. The music, though, might well drive her right over the edge.

So she rammed a Garth Brooks CD into the boom box on the deck, hit the play button and tromped over to her shed. Honestly, she thought as the metal doors clanged open, she doubted Troy was even forty yet. How he could like music that reminded Karleen of meat loaf and black-and-white television, she had no idea. Eighties rock, she could have understood. She wouldn't've liked it any better, but at least it would've made sense.

But then, there was a lot about Troy Lindquist that didn't make sense. Like why, if he was so well off, he'd bought a fixer-upper out in Corrales when he could've easily bought one of those flashy McMansions up in the foothills. Why there didn't seem to be a nanny or housekeeper in the picture.

Not that any of it was her business, but it was curious.

After shaking out her thickest gardening gloves in case somebody with too many legs had set up housekeeping inside, she yanked them on, then batted through a maze of cobwebs to find her shovel, which she carted over to a small plot that, unfortunately, was next to Troy's fence. But that was the only spot in the yard that wasn't in shade half the day, or plagued with cottonwood roots.

The pointed steel bit into the soft soil with a satisfying crunch. By the third thonk, two little pairs of sneakered feet suddenly appeared on the lower rail, followed by two little faces hanging over the top. Two little eat-'em-up faces that she bet looked exactly like father's when he'd been that age.

"Whatcha doing?" the shorter-haired twin, clearly the appointed spokesperson of the duo, now said. The babies reminded her of leaves fluttering in the breeze, never completely still.

"I'm gettin' the soil ready so I can plant a garden."

"Whatcha gonna plant?"

"Tomatoes," she said, breathing a little hard as she jabbed the shovel into the soil. Most people would use a rototiller and be done with the chore in no time flat, but Karleen liked doing it the old-fashioned way. "Cucumbers. Squash. Maybe cantaloupe." For some reason, she couldn't grow flowers to save her soul, but vegetables, she could handle.

"C'n we help?"

"Yeah," the second, smaller one said, his voice like a butterfly's kiss. "C'n we?"

"Oh, I'm not planting anything today," she said, secure in the knowledge that by the time she did, they would have in all likelihood forgotten this conversation. "It still gets too cold at night. So not for weeks yet."

"Oh," the first one said again. "But when you do, c'n we help?"

Then again, maybe she'd have to plant by moonlight this year.

Then the littler one said, his eyes like jumbo blue marbles in a face that was all delicate angles, "Yeah, we never, *ever* had a garden before."

Oh, Lord.

"Tell you what," she said, straightening up and shoving her hair out of her face with the back of her wrist, which was when she noticed Troy, his damp T-shirt molded to his torso, standing on his deck, watching her as intently as a cat stalking a bird. "When it's time, you can ask your father, and we'll see," which of course sent both boys streaking away shouting, "Daddy! Daddy! C'n we help Karleen plant her garden?"

Troy swung the first child to reach him up into his arms, making the little boy break into uncontrollable giggles as he blew a big, slurpy kiss into his neck. Chuckling, he squeezed a few more giggles out of the kid before setting him down to scoop up his brother and repeat the process. "You two are going to be the death of me yet," he said, the top notes of amusement and exasperation in his voice in perfect harmony with the deep, almost unbearably tender melody line of unconditional love.

The ache that bloomed inside her was so sweet it clogged her throat, even as, from thirty feet away, she caught the apology in his eyes. "It's okay," she pushed out, but he shook his head. He said something to the boys, who scampered off to the other side of the yard, before he stepped inside his house. A second later he reappeared and headed her way, a bottle clenched in each fist.

Karleen jerked her head back down and plunged the shovel into the soil again like she was inches away from striking oil.

Chapter Three

Troy'd been watching Karleen off and on for ten minutes or so, going after that poor plot of dirt as though it had offended her deeply. Especially after the boys had accosted her. Not that he could hear the conversation over that god-awful country caterwauling. But after more than a decade of dealing with bank managers, suppliers, advertising agencies and potential investors, he was no slouch at deciphering body language.

A dialect in which his new neighbor was particularly fluent.

The cold, wet bottles soothed his heated palms as he crossed the fifty feet or so. A good thing, since the closer he got, the more agitated her digging became. Well, tough. She still wasn't his type, but he wasn't the bogeyman, either. And it bugged him no end that she seemed to think he was. So, okay, maybe he wasn't exactly racking up the bonus points by invading her space, but considering she'd come out of her house looking ready to bite somebody's head off, he sincerely doubted he was more than a fly on an already festering wound.

The brim of her hat quivering, she glanced up at his approach. And sure enough, worry peeked out from behind the aggravation simmering in her expression, and he thought, *See? Told ya,* followed by the inevitable pang of empathy whenever confronted by someone in trouble. Amy used to tease him unmercifully about it, about his always getting far more personally involved in other people's messes than he should. Some things, he thought as he held out one of the bottles, can't be helped.

"It's hotter than it looks. You'll get dehydrated."

"Thanks, but I'm good," she said, stabbing the dirt again. Her jeans sat intriguingly low on her hips, allowing an occasional glimpse of that sparkly belly-button stud, companioned by one of those stretchy tops that were basically just big, blah bras. Although on her, not so blah. In fact, the way the sun licked at the moisture sheening her skin…

Nope. Not blah at all.

"It's a bottle of water, Karleen. Not my fraternity pin."

Panting slightly, she shifted her gaze toward him again; fireflies of sunlight danced over her face through the straw brim. He wiggled the bottle. She reached over and snatched it out of his hand. "Fine," she said, twisting off the top and taking a swallow. "*Now* will you go away?"

"Not until you tell me what's wrong."

Surprise flickered across her features, followed by a head shake. "Nothing's wrong."

"Bull."

Now her brows lifted, as well as one corner of her mouth. "You don't know me from Eve. Why would you care?"

"Consider it a character flaw."

She met his gaze with a startling intensity that jolted his sex drive awake like a fire alarm. Underneath her T-shirt, her sigh took her breasts for a little ride.

"It's not you," she said after a moment, breaking the spell before his tongue started dragging in the dirt. Jeez. "I got a phone call that rattled me, is all." She shrugged, then set the bottle down by the fence before she went back to work. "Family stuff, nothin' too serious, and not to put too fine a point on it—" she attacked a particularly obtuse dirt clod "—but it's none of your business."

The haze nicely cleared now, Troy took a sip of his own water, then propped the bottle on the top rung of the fence. "Okay, so I didn't come over here soley to make sure you wouldn't die of thirst."

A tiny smile made a brief appearance. "No?"

"No. You were right the other night, when you made that comment about it having been a long time for me. I haven't even gone out with another woman since my wife died."

The dirt clod exploded like a supernova; her gaze touched his. "You're kidding?"

"Nope."

She stilled, clearly on the alert. "And what does this have to do with me?"

"Well…Blake—the guy who helped me move in?—suggested that maybe I needed someone—a woman, I mean—to practice on before I plunged back into the dating scene." He lifted the bottle in her direction. "And since you live right next door, he thought maybe you might be that woman."

Karleen barked out a laugh, then said, "And I can't believe you're dumb enough to say that to a woman with a shovel in her hands."

"I mean to *talk* to, what did you think I—? Oh." His

mouth flatlined. Maybe the haze hadn't cleared as much as he'd thought. Good to know the hormones were still flowing, but the perpetual leaky faucet sucked. "Sorry. That didn't come out exactly the way I heard it in my head."

She stabbed the shovel into a hard section of ground, balancing on it like a pogo stick until it sank. "Well, if that boneheaded attempt you just made is any indication, your conversational skills could definitely use some fine-tuning. But why me, exactly? Besides the convenience factor, that is."

"Because I figure if I can handle a conversation with you, I can handle one with anybody."

That got another laugh, this one a little less scary, and the faucet started dripping harder. After living with a woman for nearly ten years, not to mention four years of celibacy since, Troy knew damn well he wasn't one of those men who thought about sex 24/7. But as he watched Karleen bend over to snag the water bottle and his eyes went right to her soft, round backside, he realized that it definitely hummed in the background like a computer operating system—unseen but always on.

Her lips glistened from her sip of water. Yeah, that was helping. "You mean to tell me," she said, "that you haven't so much as talked to another woman in all this time."

"Not in the man-woman sense, no."

"And what's really pathetic," she said with a smile that only underscored her words, "is that I actually believe you."

"Thanks. I think."

"Although…you're not doing so bad right now."

"Yeah?"

"Yeah. Got off to a bit of a bumpy start, but you recovered nicely enough." She took another swallow of the water, then made a face. Troy frowned.

"It's bottled water, how bad can it be?"

"It's not the water, it's that wussy music you're listening to."

"What's wrong with it?"

"Other than I keep thinkin' somebody's about to say, 'The doctor will see you now'? Not a thing. Music's supposed to get your juices flowin', sugar, not put you to sleep."

Troy let out a slightly pained laugh. "Trust me, between my work and keeping track of my sons and...other things—" *uh, boy* "—my juices flow just fine, thank you. I want something to calm my nerves," he said with a pointed glance over at the loud country music issuing from her patio, "not frazzle them more than they already are."

She'd picked up her shovel again; now she leaned both hands on the end of the handle, striking a pose that could only be described as *sassy.* Troy didn't do sassy.

He didn't think.

"You got somethin' against country?" she said.

"When it's loud enough to rattle windows in Phoenix? Yeah."

Karleen looked back over her shoulder, considering. "I suppose I could turn it down. But..." Then she glanced up at him, the sassiness half melted into something that, once again, sent all those crazy hormones running for cover. "The CD's almost done, you mind if I let it run out?"

"No, of course not."

"Thanks. But tell you what...how about we agree not to play music outside at all? Unless the other one's not around, I mean?"

"Deal. Oh, and sorry about the kids earlier." When she frowned, he prompted, "About the garden?

The shovel stabbed at the dirt, but she glanced up from under the hat's brim. "They're just bein' little kids, it's no big deal. And anyway, since it's not even an issue for at least another month, I'm not worried."

"You should be. Trust me, those two take bugging to a whole new level. They work as a team—one stops to take a breath, the other one effortlessly fills the gap."

She laughed, then straightened up, looking in the boys' direction. "Which one's which?"

Troy studied her face for several seconds, as if to commit what he saw there to memory. Deciphering could come later. Then he followed her gaze. "Grady's the bigger, more outgoing one. The instigator. Scotty's always been more cautious. Unlike his brother, he tends to at least think about things before getting in trouble."

"Aww…they sound a lot like my friend Joanna's twins. Real different personalities." She twisted around, one hand clamped around the handle, the other pointing to a spot a few feet away. "How about we give them their own garden, over there? They could plant a pumpkin vine, kids always get a kick out of that."

Troy frowned. "You don't have to do that. I mean, it's a great idea, but I could easily do a garden for them, too. It looks like the former owners had a plot over against the back wall."

"Forget it. That soil's crap, they could never get anything to grow. And I don't mind. Really. It'll be fun."

The conversation stalled. She kept digging. Troy picked up his water bottle. "Well, I guess I'll be going," he said, turning away.

"You tryin' to dig up those old roses along the back?"

He wheeled around far more eagerly than he should have. "*Trying* being the operative word." The ancient bush had sent out dozens of treacherous, thorn-smothered runners into the yard. "I'm beginning to think nothing short of napalm's going to work. But things growing wild bug me. And I want to get as much done around here before I have to go back to work next week."

She tossed him a funny look, then said, "I was wondering how somebody in your position was able to take so much time off." When he frowned, she shrugged and said, "Google. And a nosy best friend."

"Ah," he said, then responded, "state-of-the-art home office. And besides, I can take so much time off now because I had basically no life for the first five years we were trying to get the business off the ground." Then boldness struck and he asked, "And what do you do?"

One shoulder hitched. "I'm a personal shopper."

"Really?" He looked at her house, which while much smaller than his, still wasn't exactly a mud hut. The over-zealous outdoor kitsch notwithstanding. "You must do pretty well yourself."

Her eyes followed his. "I do okay." Her brows knitted together for a moment, then she said, pain faintly pin-pricking her words, "Ex Number Three apparently decided letting me stay after the divorce was worth bein' rid of me."

"He didn't like country music, either?"

A laugh burbled from her throat, producing a small glow of triumph in the center of Troy's chest. A second later, the boys popped up on either side of his hips, positively caked with dirt and looking damned pleased with themselves about it.

A grin, this time. "You sure those're your kids?"

"Heck, I'm not sure they're *kids* at all," Troy said, using the hem of his T-shirt to wipe the top layer of dirt from

Scotty's forehead. "Mud puppies, maybe. Hard to tell until I hose them down."

The boys giggled; then, hanging onto his hands, they launched into the we're-gonna-starve-to-*death* moans, and Troy looked down into two sets of trusting blue eyes, and his chest twinged, as it did at least a dozen times a day. When he met Karleen's gaze again, however, the clouds had rolled back across her expression. Heavy, leaden things that promised days and days of unrelentingly miserable weather.

"I think Nate and I had more issues than differing musical tastes," she said, and her eyes touched his, and a great, big *whoa* went off in his brain.

A *whoa* he'd only heard once before, when a certain sleek-haired brunette had glided across his path in front of Northwestern's library, nearly two decades before.

A certain sleek-haired brunette who wouldn't have been caught dead with bleached hair, or her midriff exposed, or a belly-button stud, or listening to country music.

"Go feed your babies," Karleen said softly, jerking Troy back to Planet Earth.

"Uh…yeah. Would you like to—?"

"We'll talk about the garden when it gets warmer," she said, then turned her back on him, ramming the shovel into the dirt so hard he could have sworn the ground vibrated underneath his feet.

At 6:00 a.m. three days later, Karleen had stumbled out of bed, slammed shut the window against the din of birdsong and stumbled back to bed. Where now, at eight, daylight sat on her face like an obnoxious cat, prodding her to get up.

Then she remembered that Troy still lived next door and she grabbed her pillow and crammed it over her head, only to realize it was impossible to suffocate yourself.

She tossed the pillow overboard, frowning at her beamed ceiling. Of all the houses for sale in Albuquerque, Troy Lindquist had to buy the one next door to hers. Was that unfair or what? Good-looking, she could ignore. Sweet, she could ignore. Sexy…she could ignore. But all three rolled into one? Lord, she felt like she was running to stay ahead of a raging wildfire—one trip, and she'd be barbecue.

Oh, sure, she could go on about her resolve to stay unattached until her tongue fell out, but neither history nor biology were on her side. Because the whole reason Karleen had ended up with the three husbands—not to mention an appalling number of "gap guys" in between—was her complete and total inability to resist a handsome, sweet-talking, testosterone-drenched male. Especially considering her very healthy sex drive. Which had been sorely neglected for far longer than she'd thought was even possible.

Yeah, it was definitely easier to keep replacing the hamsters. But now she wondered if her singlehood had less to do with any resolve on her part and more to a lack of any real temptation.

And that, she decided as the sun continued its relentless ascent, must've been why Mr. My-Mouth-Says-One-Thing-but-My-Eyes-Are-Saying-Something-Else-Entirely had moved in next door. You know, to test her. See if all her talk about reforming was only so much hot air. Still, maybe she couldn't undo the past, but she sure as heck could learn from it. Although the neglected-sex-drive thing could be a problem.

Especially if it got too close to Troy's neglected-sex-drive thing.

Karleen kicked off the wadded-up floral sheets and

dragged herself out of bed, tugging at her boxer pj bottoms as she padded to the bathroom. Her cheek was creased, her eyes were puffy and her hair stuck up around her head like it'd been goosed. Lovely. She grabbed her toothbrush and squeezed out enough toothpaste for an elephant—

Wait. Was that a knock? She stepped out of the bathroom, toothbrush in mouth.

Rap, rap, rap.

Karleen quickly spit and grabbed her robe, yelling, "Who is it?" as she stomped down the hall, pulling the sash tight. One of these days she was really going to have to do something about fixing the doorbell—

"It's Troy," came from outside.

She made a silent Lucille Ball face, rammed her hands through her nutso hair and opened the door. And yep, there he was, even taller and more solid and—dammit—cuter than she remembered. And here she was, looking like a half-molted canary with overachieving hooters. The Volvo was parked in her driveway, full of twins. Who both waved to her, the little buggers. She waved back.

"Oh, hell," the father of the twins said, "did I wake you?"

"Uh-uh," she said, yawning, searching his face for signs of revulsion. Revulsion would be good. Revulsion had a way of dampening libidos. And things.

"Sorry to bother you," Troy said, not looking terribly revulsed, "but I've got a huge favor to ask…no! Not to take the kids," he said when her eyes darted back to his car. "But I've got an appointment to check out the Bosque View Pre-school and the Home Depot guys were supposed to deliver the new washer/dryer this afternoon, only they called about five minutes ago and said they were coming this morning instead, and I don't know if I'll be back by the time they get here. So I wondering if you could possibly let them in…?"

Then a breeze made her shiver, and two layers of thin jersey were no match for the Twin Peaks on her chest, and Troy didn't even try to avert his gaze and Karleen didn't even try to pretend not to notice, and his eyes lifted to hers and things got real quiet for several seconds while everybody contemplated what was going on here.

"It's—" She cleared the dozen or so frogs out of her throat. "It's okay, scandalizing the Home Depot deliverymen isn't on my list this morning," she said, and he said, "Their loss," and she said, "I don't have any appointments until after lunch, so it shouldn't be a problem."

Silence. Then: "You're a lifesaver."

"So I've been told," she said, and they stared at each other until one of the kids yelled, "Dad-*deeee!*" and Troy seemed to shudder back from wherever men go when their blood has shifted south and said, "I just didn't want to rush things. Checking out the school, I mean."

He glanced back at the boys, totally reverted to Daddymode. The mixture of worry and adoration in his expression made her tummy flutter. Or maybe that was hunger. Then his gaze returned to hers. Nope. Not hunger. Not that kind, anyway. "This will be their third day-care situation in six months," he said, reeking of guilt. "I'm hoping this one will be the last until they start kindergarten. They've been real troupers, but I know it's been rough on them, constantly having their routine disrupted."

A philosophy to which Karleen's mother had obviously not subscribed, she thought bitterly.

"Did you say Bosque View?" she now said. "Joanna's got her youngest there, he loves it. If that makes you feel any better."

"It does. It sucks, being the new guy in town."

Tell me about it, she thought as Troy dug a house key

out of his pocket and handed it over. "I've left a note on the door that you'll let them in," he said, backing away. "The machines go in the garage," he called out, then ducked behind the wheel, and she waved, and then they were gone and she stared at the Troy-warmed key in her hand and felt that wildfire about to singe her pj bottoms right off her butt.

The Home Depot truck was still in Troy's driveway when he returned, sans children, around ten. Meaning that, he presumed, Karleen was still there, as well.

One of those good news, bad news kind of things.

Troy sat in the car for a good ten seconds, his chin crunched in his palm, mentally ticking off all the reasons why he needed to get over this idiotic attraction to the woman. Why acting on some chemically induced urging was pointless. If not downright stupid.

He glanced back at her pinwheel-and-stone-critter-infested front yard. The plastic roses stuck incongruously along the base of the front porch. The birdhouses. The five million sparkly, twirly things dangling from her porch. And he shuddered. Mightily.

Then he remembered the sight of her fresh out of bed this morning, all rumple-haired and makeup-free, her sleep-graveled voice, and he shuddered again. Even more mightily.

Okay, he thought, getting out of the car and slamming shut the door, so she was cute and sexy and helpful, and she wasn't holding silver crosses up in front of the kids, but he didn't know anything about her, except for her penchant for excessive lawn ornamentation and that caution muddied her eyes. And besides, she wasn't interested, he wasn't interested (okay, so he was interested, just not that interested), end of discussion, case closed.

He could do this, he thought as he walked inside his open garage and through the maze of boxes and crap he'd yet to figure out what to do with, and there was Karleen, in some kind of flippy little skirt and a soft, hip-grazing sweater practically the color of her skin, and she was wearing a pair of backless, high-heeled shoes that were like sex on a stick, pink ones, with glittery, poufy stuff across the toes, and his mouth went dry. She looked about as substantial as cotton candy.

Only five times tastier.

And she was clearly driving the poor, mountainesque delivery guy insane as she made him put both machines through their paces.

"Okay," she said as she took the clipboard from him, "I just wanted to be sure, because the last time I got a new washer—not from y'all, but I'm just saying—they didn't hook it up right and I ended up with a lake on my garage floor.… Oh! Troy! You're back! Sign," she said, thrusting the clipboard at him. And that first, full impact of her perfume, the vulnerability trembling at the edges of her self-confidence, nearly shorted out his brain.

He gave the machines a cursory glance to make sure they were indeed the ones he'd bought before scribbling his signature on the bottom of the form. The delivery guy tore off his receipt, said, "Have a good one," and lumbered off, leaving Troy staring at a pair of control panels clearly modeled after the space shuttle.

Karleen stepped up beside him, her arms crossed. Her perfume nanny-boo-boo'd him. Her still hanging around confused the hell out of him. Way too many whys and whatchagonnadoaboutits floating around for his comfort. Then she reached out and—there was no other word for it—caressed the front of the washer, sliding two fingers along the smooth, cool porcelain edge, and Troy's mind went blank.

"I hate to admit this," she said on a soft rush of air, "but I am having serious appliance envy. My washer's one step up from a rock in the river."

"Right now," Troy said, forcing his attention to the gleaming white appliances in front of him and away from the fragrant blonde at his elbow, "a rock in the river isn't looking half-bad."

He could feel her bemused, incredulous stare. "Please don't tell me you've never used a washer before."

"Only three times a week for the past four years," he muttered. "But believe me, my expertise begins and ends with shove clothes in, dump in detergent, turn machine on, take clothes out." He squinted at the panel. "I'm guessing I'll never have to use the delicate cycle."

"Not unless you've got silk boxers."

"Uh…no."

She giggled, and his insides flipped. "Stick with normal and you'll probably be okay."

"Always been my motto," he said, and turned, and she was far too close, and it had been far too long, and it was far, *far* too soon to be feeling this far gone.

"How come you're still here?" he asked softly, and her gaze flicked to his before she shrugged. Just one shoulder. Sadness radiated from her like sound waves.

"Where're the kids?" she asked.

"Still at the school." Troy leaned one hip against the dryer, his arms folded over his chest. Watching her not looking at him. Trying like hell to figure out what was going on here. "They wanted to stay for a little while, so I'm picking them up after lunch. If all goes well, they'll start full-time on Monday. It seems like a great place."

Another quick glance. A small smile. "Feel better now?"

"A bit. It's a challenge, doing this on my own. I worry constantly about whether I'm making the right choice."

Her silence enfolded him, half soothing, half unnerving. "At least you *do* worry about them."

"That's what parents do."

"Not all parents," she said, the sadness turning more acidic. Without thinking, he slipped his hand around hers. Her head jerked up, her eyes wide. But not, he thought, particularly surprised.

"Thanks," he whispered, frozen, staring at her mouth. "For, you know. Being here."

"No problem," she said, equally frozen, staring at him staring at her mouth. "Um...don't take this the wrong way, but are you thinkin' about kissing me?"

"Don't take this the wrong way, but I'm thinking about doing a lot more than kissing."

Outside, birds twittered, breezes blew, gas prices continued to yo-yo. Inside, life-altering decisions hovered on the brink of being made.

"What happened to just wanting to *talk?*" Karleen finally said.

"Apparently, I've moved on."

The planet hurtled another few thousand miles through space before Karleen at last lifted her hand to trace one long, pale fingernail down his shirt placket.

"So I guess this means we're gonna have sex."

Somewhere, way in the back of his buzzing brain, Troy heard a resignation in her voice that, under other circumstances, might have tripped his sympathy trigger. At the moment, however, the safety on that particular trigger was firmly in place.

As opposed to other triggers, which were cocked and very, very ready.

"That's bad, isn't it?" he said. Still not moving. Away, at any rate.

"It sure as heck isn't good."

"Because…of everything you said." He lifted one hand, cupping her neck. Her breathing went all shaky. So did his.

"Uh-huh." She made a funny little sound in her throat when he touched his lips to her forehead.

"One of us should walk away," he whispered into her hair, which was a lot softer than he'd expected.

"I know," she said, and tilted her head back, and he lowered his mouth to hers, and his entire body sighed in relief, as though he'd been waiting for this moment for five years instead of five days. He knew it was wrong and foolish and pointless and he didn't care, didn't give a damn about anything except that brief shudder of surrender when their mouths met, the soft heat of her tongue against his, the softer, hotter press of her breasts against his chest. And, of course, the ever-popular collision of her pelvis against the aforementioned good-to-go trigger.

In fact, he was enjoying the whole kissing-pressing-colliding thing so much, it took a while before it sank in exactly where all this kissing and pressing and colliding was going on.

"For the record," he said, "I don't generally go around seducing women in my garage. Especially ones I've only known for less than a week."

"Somehow," she said, trickling her fingers down his arms, "I knew that."

His pulse thudding nicely in several crucial pressure points in his body, he took her face in his hands. "So how come you're *not* walking away?"

"Because…" Six inches from his face, her breasts rose as she sighed. "I guess I figure, since you have moved on, you may as well do that moving on with me."

"O-kay…" Troy shook his head, but the ringing was still there. "But why?"

Karleen linked her hands around his neck, toying with the bristly hair at the nape, and little flickers of happiness erupted all over his skin. "Because I can handle this for what it is—a man who's gone without for too long who needs…an outlet. Somebody to take the edge off, to ease you back into things." She shrugged, and the little flickers flickered more earnestly. "The way I see it, I'm actually doing the women of Albuquerque a favor. So when you go out there for real, you'll be able to see what you're actually looking for without sex cloudin' your brain."

She had a point. Except that, as murky as things definitely were in the old gray matter, he wasn't so far gone that he didn't catch the *tiniest* hint of self-deprecation in her voice. "How…altruistic of you," he said, letting his hands slide down to cup her sweet little backside.

She snorted. "Not exactly. Because it's been a while for me, too, so I'm not gonna lie, I want this as bad as you do. But, see, I'm not lookin' for anything serious, and you're not lookin' for somebody like me—and don't deny it, you know it's true—so this way, we both get what we need out of the deal. And anyway, we could both tiptoe around this thing for God knows how long until one or the other of us combusts…" Her gaze lowered to his neck, which she stood on tiptoe to—oh, *man*—lick. "Or," she murmured, her breath cooling the moist spot, "we could get this out of the way and be done with it."

He gripped her ribs, bringing her startled gaze up to his.

"I'm overdue. Not desperate. Trust me, there's not going to be anything *quick* about this."

One eyebrow arched before, slowly, her mouth stretched into a smile that was pure challenge.

"Guess we'll have to see about that," she said, then took him by the hand and led him back to her house, as his garage door groaned closed behind them.

Chapter Four

If nothing else, nobody could accuse Karleen of not being able to think fast on her feet.

Because, even after Troy'd kissed her, and her blood had gone all syrupy in her veins, she'd realized she was in far more control of the situation than she'd expected to be. Or that she'd ever been before. That she could have walked away, if she'd wanted to. And that her *not* wanting to had nothing to do with her being powerless, or weak, or over-sexed; it had to do with realizing she had a duty to pry open this guy's eyes before things got out of hand.

Because, she thought as clothes flew about her bedroom, once they got over the momentary sex crazies, he'd remember his mission, which was all about finding someone to share the rest of his life with. And Lord knew, that wasn't gonna be her—

Mouths crashed, tongues tangled, bedsprings creaked

as they fell backward onto the unmade bed she'd pulled together only an hour before.

—because, see, she'd taken a little peek into his house while she'd waited for the Home Depot guys. Not that she'd gone upstairs or done any serious snooping or anything, only enough to confirm what she'd pretty much figured, which was that Troy Lindquist liked things safe and predictable and traditional to the point of mind-numbing. Lots of browns and beiges and tans, relieved by the occasional splash of navy-blue. She wouldn't last five minutes. So she figured—

"Condoms, top drawer," she murmured when he unhooked the front clasp to her bra, but he said, "Thanks, but I'm in no hurry."

—she, uh, figured…where was she? Oh, right. She figured one good look at her place would pretty much wipe the goony look right off his face. Although it might take a while before he noticed much of anything except what was going on between them right at the moment, men not being generally known for their ability to multitask. In fact, right now, all he was getting a good look at were her breasts. With, it pained her to notice, an expression not dissimilar to the one he'd been giving the washer control panel a little while ago.

Oh, hell. He knows.

Karleen straddled him, still in her pale pink embroidered silk high-cuts. Then she leaned over (shyness in these situations having not been an issue for a very long time), knowing the hazy sunlight filtered through the lace curtains showed the darlings off to perfection. "I got the good ones," she said. "Trust me, they won't leak, deflate or pop."

Troy frowned. "Are you sure?"

"Oh, for pity's sake—" She grabbed his hand, planting it on her boob. His mouth pulled into a *not bad* expression before he tentatively gave it a little squeeze, and she went slightly cross-eyed.

"So…I'm guessing you can feel that?"

"Of course I can feel that, I'm not a blow-up doll. Think of this like…booster seats for breasts. The same, just taller. So could we please get on with it?"

He laughed. And cupped the other breast, flicking his thumbs over her nipples, and it was like first sinking into a warm bath. With candlelight. And Elvis crooning "Love Me Tender" in the background. "What's the rush? I'm having fun—" clearly getting into things now, he moved on to light plucking "—right here." He grinned. "Aren't you?"

"Mmm, yeah." Hissed breath. "But we only have an hour."

"Oh, honey," he said, flipping her onto her back, "you'd be amazed what I can accomplish in an hour."

"You bragging?"

"No. Warning." Troy shifted to lean his head in his hand, circling one nipple with his knuckle. "I have to admit, they're very pretty."

Karleen started to look down again, only to remember she got a terrible double chin when she did that. "They should be, considering how much they set Nate back," she said, and he laughed and tugged her in for another kiss. And oh, my, the man could kiss, like he wanted to get to know each nerve ending one at a time…and then he started on a lazy, meandering journey, nibbling and kissing and licking and sucking his way up…and down…first one rarely explored back road…then another…and another…

And she thought, *Hmm, not what I expected,* and from somewhere down by her knees, he said, "Why are you so tense?" which of course tensed her, even as she said, "I am not!" and he chuckled and moved up, stroking the insides of her thighs, cupping her bottom, lowering his mouth, and she was gone.

"Not tense now," she said a minute later, and he said, "Where are those condoms again?" and she limply flailed one arm toward her nightstand, vaguely considering when she'd last restocked. Although she didn't suppose it was that big a deal, since she seriously doubted disease was an issue and she'd just finished her period a week ago and besides, nothing had ever happened before....

Then Troy grinned, and she thought, *What now?* and he sat up, settling her in his lap, filling her to somewhere around her eyeballs, and she gasped, startled, even though by rights she should have been way past being startled. But the skin-to-skin was good, *he* was so good, his gentleness breaking her heart, bringing unexpected tears to her eyes.

And they stilled, him inside her, her surrounding him, each reflected in the other's eyes, and she thought, *I don't even know this man,* and he wrapped her up tight, and she felt safe, and thought, *Damn.*

He moved, still gently, still pushing, and she pushed back, not so gently, and they didn't so much find their rhythm as it swallowed them alive, swallowed up everything, everyone, that had come before. She hung on like she was almost afraid of being thrown, as the sweetness built and built and built and *built*....

Karleen arched, cried out, collapsed...and he tangled his fingers in her hair and brought their mouths together in a hard, fierce kiss, all the nerve cells colliding in a victory rumble, and another shudder of need ghosted through her, like the gradually diminishing thunder from a finished storm. Then she carefully lifted herself off, and after he got up to take care of business, she wrapped the sheet around herself, oddly self-conscious, although she could not have said why.

Well, that was different, she thought, although she couldn't pinpoint that, either.

And for sure there was nothing even remotely Muzak about the way the man made love, a thought that sent a shiny, tender green garden snake of regret slithering through her, that they wouldn't be doing this again.

Sitting tangled up in her sheets, she watched Troy—not a drop of self-consciousness in his veins, obviously—stroll back to the bed, naked as the day he was born and with a look on his face like he was half contemplating jumping up on something and beating his chest. Brother.

He sat beside her, slinging one arm around her shoulders and tugging her close to rest his cheek in her hair. "Thank you," he whispered, and Karleen heard herself ask, "What was your wife's name?"

Being sensitive was one thing. Clairvoyance was something else entirely. So while Troy had pretty much figured out that Karleen's tough-girl persona was so much BS, he had no clue what was behind it. So he'd watched, in the reflection from her bathroom mirror, as she'd pulled that sheet around herself, seen an almost pained confusion crumple her features, thinking, *What the hell?*

Then she'd asked about Amy and he thought, *Ah.* He planted a kiss in her messed-up hair. "I'm not comparing you."

"I didn't think you were," she said, predictably stiffening. Then, also predictably, she got up, mincing across the room like a character from *The Mikado* to perch on the end of a wicker chair covered in a leopard-print cushion.

In front of a window crowned in a poofy, purple valance.

Beside a small table on which crystal teardrops winked below the fluffy feather edging on the ugliest lampshade on the tackiest lamp in the known universe.

Sun catchers of every variety dotted her windows; on every surface, crystal figurines shared space with cutsy, overdecorated…stuff. And as the postcoital fog lifted, it began to register than the inside of Karleen's house was no less insane than the outside. The woman's penchant for tchotchkes knew no bounds.

"And I'm not asking because of what we just did," she said, tucking her feet up under her, hugging her pride close, and Troy's bric-a-bracaphobia eased off. Slightly. "I'm asking because in all likelihood we'll be living next door to each other for a while, and it would seem weird *not* to know her name. That's all."

Troy glanced at the clock by her bed. Only twenty minutes before he had to go pick up the boys. "Amy," he said, grabbing his boxers off the floor.

"You two had a good marriage?"

As annoyed as he was for her dragging his dead wife's ghost into their afterglow, Troy's chest still clenched at the wistfulness bleeding through the weak spots of her nonchalance. He pulled on the boxers, then his jeans. "Yeah. We did."

"How long were you married?"

He glared at her. "Is this your way of pushing me away?"

A slight smile curved her mouth. "How long?"

"Nine years," he said, shrugging into his shirt. Trying to shrug off oddly hurt feelings.

"Wow," Karleen said, bracing her feet on the edge of the chair to hug her knees. "That's longer than all three of my marriages put together. So," she continued before he could comment, "you must've been pretty young when you met?"

"Junior year of college. We didn't get married until we were twenty-five, though."

"How come you waited so long?"

Troy focused on his shirt buttons, his hands not as steady as he'd like. "According to Amy, she was ready by the time we graduated. Took me a little longer to catch up. Or catch on."

"What was she like?"

"Karleen—"

"Please?"

He jammed the tails of his shirt into his pants. "Tall. Light-brown hair. Blue eyes—"

"I'm not talking about what she looked like."

No, he didn't think so. "Four years, I've struggled to forget. And now you—"

"I know what I'm doing," she said, a hard-edged intelligence standing firm in her eyes, and Troy blew out a breath, then thought, his brow crumpled.

"She was…incredibly calm. Very little ruffled her. Probably because she was about the most together, organized person I've ever known. She didn't like leaving anything to chance, if she could help it. And she hated clutter. A dish left in the sink drove her nuts."

"But in a calm way."

His lips twitched. "Yes. In a calm way."

Karleen's expression didn't change. "What was her favorite color?"

Weird question, but what the hell. "Blue," he said. "But not just any blue, this kind of gray-blue. Like…" He looked around the room, but there was nothing in here even remotely close. So he shrugged.

"She get along with your folks?"

"They adored her. And they were wrecked when…"

"She died?"

"Yeah."

"What happened?"

Although as gentle as what he'd always imagined an angel's touch would feel like, her words knocked the stuffing out of him. And the resistance. Because most people were far too uncomfortable asking about things such as how a person's wife died, so if they didn't already know, they never asked. Troy sat on the edge of her bed— whoever thought foot-wide lavender roses were attractive should be shot—to tie his shoes, but by now his hands were full-out shaking.

"Something went wrong when the boys were born," he said, amazed that he could say the words without feeling as though his chest would cave in. "During the C-section." He took a deep breath and looked across the room at the first woman he'd made love to since his wife's death, trying to wrap his head around the significance of that milestone. "Amy died barely a week later."

He saw Karleen's eyes fill with tears, felt his own sting in response. "How on earth did you get through that?"

"For a long time, I wasn't sure I would. Forget day by day, it was all I could do to get through one minute at a time. But I had two babies who needed me. They wouldn't let me give up. Neither would my family. Or my friends." He looked up at her. "A lot of people thought I should sue."

"But you didn't."

"What would have been the point? To drag an already wrecked doctor—someone we'd known for years, one of the best in her field—through the mud? Yeah, I was a mess, and I was angry, too angry to understand anything they were saying at first. And hurting way too much to be even remotely objective about any of it. There I was, caught in the middle between the hospital needing to cover its butt and everybody insisting somebody needed to 'pay.' Hell, during those first few days, *I* wanted somebody to pay, too. Out of the blue, my wife was dead. You just don't accept something like that, something that makes no sense whatsoever."

Troy yanked the second lace tight, then dropped his foot to the floor. "But the fact is, life doesn't always make sense. And sometimes things go wrong. Even during a supposedly 'routine' procedure." He lifted his eyes to her. "Was I nuts, not going forward with the suit?"

Why had he asked that? Why had he asked *her?*

After a long, assessing moment, she said, "I doubt most people would've have been that noble."

"Believe me, this wasn't about being noble, it was about preserving what little sanity I had left. Money wasn't going to turn back the clock, and I couldn't see wallowing in all that negativity and bitterness for God knows how many years when I had two little boys to raise and a business to keep going. Speaking of whom…" He stood, feeling hideously awkward. "I need to go get them."

"Right." Karleen struggled to her feet as well, where they stood half a room apart, eyeing each other. Until Karleen broke the silence. "Please don't feel you have to say anything. This was what it was, nothing more."

"A one-time thing, you mean."

"That's what we agreed on."

After a moment of careful weighing, Troy said, "That was before," but she shook her head.

"Nothing's changed," she said softly. "Neither one of us is interested in going down some dead-end road. Which is what this would be. Not that I didn't thoroughly enjoy being the one to get you back in the saddle, but that's it."

"You're sure?"

"Positive. I still don't want to get involved. And you know full well you don't really want to get involved with *me*. Be honest, Troy. Because that's all we've got going for us. Bein' honest with each other."

The honesty of their recent lovemaking still imprinted in his memory, his reawakened libido, Troy glanced around, at the animal prints, the bilious floral sheets, the atrocious lamp. "We could—"

"No. We couldn't."

Troy watched her for a long moment, standing there all flushed and cocooned in her sheet, her sparkly toes peeking out from the folds puddled around her feet, and he knew she was right, that he wasn't interested in some dead-end road, and that continuing the affair—as tempting as the idea was—would only interrupt his quest to find someone who would fit in with his life, not agitate the hell out of it.

He walked over to her, though, clasping her bare, warm shoulders in his palms, leaning over to kiss her open-mouthed, long enough to—hopefully—get the point across exactly how much the morning's activities had meant to him. How much he genuinely appreciated—no, *liked*—her, even if he knew it would never work out.

Then he walked away before he could change his mind.

Hours later, however, as Troy hacked the heck out of the rangy lilac bush at the corner of the house and the boys *vroomed-vroomed* their Tonkas in a patch of dirt on the other side of the yard, he found himself in a very sour mood, indeed. Physically, he was feeling no pain. Emotionally was something else again.

Why, *why,* couldn't he have been born a callous bastard who could simply get his jollies and then walk away without a backward glance?

True, he hadn't put that chronic wariness in her eyes. Nor was it up to him to remove it. But it went against his nature, turning his back on something broken.

Even if he didn't have the right tools to get the job done.

He glanced up at the hum of a sleek, sand-colored minivan pulling into Karleen's driveway; a minute later, a redheaded, hippie elf climbed out, her wooden-soled clogs crunching into the gravel, her body lost in her billowy denim dress. As she bent over to spring an equally red-headed little boy from his car seat in the back, Troy caught a glimpse of crazily patterned socks.

Baby elf in hand, Mama Elf headed toward Karleen's front door. Like magic, the twins appeared at his side.

"Who's that?" Grady asked.

"Have no idea," Troy said, yanking a clipped branch out from the tangle. "They weren't exactly wearing name tags."

"They're coming over," Scotty said, as the woman yelled, "Hello?"

Troy looked over to see her standing and waving on the other side of the post-and-rail fence. "Damn." Both boys scowled at him. "Sorry," Troy mumbled, grabbing his T-shirt off the grass and wiping his face and chest with it so he wouldn't gross out the poor woman.

Underneath a thousand crazy curls, green eyes flicked over his torso before veering back up to his face. Not an elf, he decided: a Raggedy Ann doll. "Hi, I'm Joanna, Karleen's friend? She asked me to come over, only she isn't home. You wouldn't know where she is, by any chance?"

"'Fraid not." *Joanna, Joanna...* Why did that name sound familiar? "I, um, saw her drive off earlier, but that's all I know."

"Oh." The redhead flashed him a quick smile. A smile, Troy thought (hoped?), devoid of suspicion and/or curiosity. "Okay, guess I'll have to wait for a bit. What is it, honey?" she said to the little boy, who was tugging at her skirt.

"They gots trucks." He pointed. "C'n I play wif 'em?"

Grady immediately ran down to a wide spot in the fence and beckoned. "You can crawl through here!"

"Oh, Chance, honey—"

"It's okay," Troy said, smiling. "You can wait here, too, if you like. I'm Troy, by the way."

"Yes, I know. Karleen mentioned you. And your boys." Clutching fistfuls of fabric, she climbed over the fence with the grace of a woman used to chasing small boys, losing a clog in the process. As she wriggled her foot back into it, the light dawned.

"You're the Joanna whose boy is at Bosque, right?"

"That would be me." She tromped over the grass beside him. "Are you sending yours there?"

"Probably. They had a test run this morning." *While I was shagging your best friend.* "It seems like a really nice place," he said, hoping she'd think his flush was due to exertion and sun.

"It is. Chance loves it. Your two must be around the same age?"

"They turned four right before Christmas. Yours?"

"Three and a half." They'd reached the portal, where Joanna plopped down on the edge, yanking the dress to her ankles before turning a very warm, but completely un-threatening, smile on him. "My other kids are all much older, and they're usually with their father on the weekends. So other than when he's at school, Chance doesn't get much opportunity to play with kids his own age. Especially boys." She chuckled, nodding toward the three, all shoving around trucks in the dirt. When she linked her hands over her knees, a very impressive diamond and wedding band flashed on a short-nailed, sort-of chewed-up-looking left hand. "He's in heaven."

Troy smiled back, then remembered his manners. "Can I get you something to drink…?"

"Oh, no, I'm fine. And don't let me keep you from whatever you were doing, I'm sure Kar will be along soon." Troy picked up the clippers as Joanna said, "Her appointments sometimes go longer than she expects them to."

"She said she was a personal shopper?"

"Do I detect a note of incredulity in your question?"

"Not a bit of it."

That got a laugh. A shaft of sunlight caught in her wild red hair, slashed across her angular, makeup-free face. A pleasant-looking woman, but not what you'd call beautiful. "Kar's personal style might be a little out there, but she's got an uncanny knack for zeroing in on her clients' preferences. But then, that's just Kar," she said with a shrug. "She might come across as a bit on the prickly side from time to time, but deep down she's one of the most selfless people I know."

Troy grunted an acknowledgment, whacked another branch out of the lilac. Joanna went on.

"She started the business a few years ago. On a whim, really, shopping for my mother. An attorney. Loves clothes, hates to shop. Anyway, before Kar knew it, the whole thing mushroomed and now she has as much work as she can handle." From the other side of the yard, all three boys got to giggling about something; Joanna laughed softly. "I've got twin boys, too. I feel your pain."

Troy dropped the clippers, leaning over to grab a rake off the ground. "Same here," he said, smiling. Searching for something to say, he came up with "You've known Karleen for a while, I take it?"

"Since we were kids, actually. One of those strange things."

"Strange?"

"How we've remained so close, even though we're so different. I gave up trying to figure it out a long time ago." She paused, then said, "Kar's a good person. You could do a lot worse." When Troy's gaze darted to hers, she smiled and said, "For a neighbor, I mean."

Uh-huh. "She strikes me as the kind of person who doesn't take any crap off of anybody."

Joanna's brows lifted. "So you've talked to her?"

You should only know. "A couple of times." He shook the bush to loosen any stray pieces, then fixed his gaze on Karleen's *friend.* "Enough to know you're treading on very dangerous ground."

Joanna twinkled. "And from where I'm sitting, the risk is more than worth it. Oh! There she is!" she said as Karleen pulled up alongside the minivan in a valiantly shiny Toyota 4Runner that had been new three administrations ago. Joanna stood, brushing the back of her dress as she called her little boy.

All three kids ran over. "Does he hafta go?" Grady said, slinging a possessive, grubby arm around his new friend's shoulders.

"Yeah," Scotty piped up. "We're havin' fun!"

"I'm so sorry, sweeties, maybe another time—"

"Oh, let him stay for a while," Troy heard himself say. "We're not going anywhere, why not?"

"You sure?" she said as Karleen got out of her car, a small

pet-store box dangling from one hand. She was dressed in the same outfit he'd helped her remove earlier. Yeah, like he needed *that* particular memory prod. She probably would have walked straight into her house without acknowledging him, except she'd gotten distracted with glaring at Joanna. Troy instinctively took a step back from the redhead. Because, like riding a bike, some things you never forget.

Even if *somebody,* he thought, willing her gaze in his direction, seemed determined to keep that particular bike locked up good and tight from now on.

"Positive," he finally said, returning his attention to Joanna, who was doing the tennis-match head-swing thing between him and Karleen. "The boys could use some fresh blood. That is to say," he added, "somebody besides each other to play with."

On a yell, the boys took off again across the yard. Joanna grinned. "I knew what you meant. If he gets to be a pain, though," she said as she backed away, "just bring him over."

"Can I bring mine, too?" he said, and she glanced over her shoulder, laughing.

Karleen, however, was not laughing. In fact, Karleen looked ready to eviscerate anyone dumb enough to come within range of those claws of hers.

The very claws that had left marks on his back.

Damn. Instant recall was a bitch.

"Don't even give me that look," Joanna tossed at Karleen the minute they got inside her house. "What the hell was all that about?"

"What was what all about?" Marching straight back to her kitchen, Karleen set the PetSmart box on the counter. A tiny quivering nose peeked out from first one airhole, then another.

"The zippity-zap stuff between you and Troy. Outside. A second ago."

"Yeah, about that." Karleen batted that particular birdie right back over the net. "Getting a little chummy with my neighbor, weren't you?"

Since Joanna was blissfully married to her hunky baseball player, this wasn't about one woman encroaching on another's territory, and they both knew it. It was, however, about one woman sticking her cute little nose in where it most definitely did not belong.

"Oh, lighten up," Jo said, hitching herself up onto a bar stool. "You were late, and the boys took to Chance, so Troy invited me over to wait for you."

"No, you were early, since I'm right on time. *And* you have a key to my house!"

"Okay, so maybe I did get here a little early. They were out in the yard. I put out a few feelers. So sue me. You got any tea?"

"In the fridge. And you are so dead."

"Better dead than stupid," Jo said, sliding back off the stool to haul out the jug of sun tea from Karleen's twenty-year-old, the-icemaker-in-the-door's-just-for-looks refrigerator. "Holy catfish, that picture does not do the man justice. Besides which, he seems like a real sweetheart." Jo grabbed a glass out of the drainer and filled it. "One of those big, strong, protective Saint Bernard types. But less hairy. And I cannot believe you got another hamster."

Karleen took the pitcher of tea from her "friend"— at the moment, she wasn't so sure—and poured herself a glass. "Seeing as I've got all this hamster crap, it seemed a shame to not use it. And you're right, Troy's very nice."

"So I repeat, what was up between the two of you a minute ago?" Jo said, taking a sip of her tea.

Only to nearly choke on it when Karleen looked up at her, not even trying to keep the misery out of her eyes.

"Already?" Jo squeaked out. When Karleen nodded, Jo slammed her chin into the palm of her hand. "Jeez, Kar— that has to be some kind of record, even for you."

"Hey, you were the one who wanted me to get to know the guy."

"I was thinking more along the lines of, I don't know, inviting him and the kids over for lunch or something. At least *first.*"

Karleen knocked back half her glass of tea, then picked up the hamster box, carrying it over to an elaborate series of tubes and chutes and multicolored plastic "rooms" in one corner of the breakfast nook. She popped open the box and lifted the soft, squirmy little critter out. She was blond and plump and Karleen was calling her Britney.

"It was a one-shot deal," she said, lowering Britney into her new home. The little animal speed-waddled from spot to spot, nose blurred in frantic excitement.

"Which you called, no doubt," Jo said.

Karleen latched the top to the cage. "It was mutual. Although I may have encouraged things to go in that direction. Or not, in this case."

"Because it was one of those sizzle-without-the-steak kind of things?"

One side of Karleen's mouth pulled up. "No."

"So let me get this straight," Jo said. "The guy's cute, nice, rich *and,* we now know, good in the sack." She frowned. "Am I missing something?"

Karleen walked over to her sink to finger the soil of the Philodendron That Ate Albuquerque threatening to take over the entire east wall of the room. From the sun catcher in the window, distorted rainbows danced over the striped leaves.

"Yeah. That it would never work."

"A conclusion you've come to after five days and one apparently noteworthy toss in the hay. Yeah, that makes perfect sense."

"And you, Joanna McConnaughy, are gettin' to be a real pain in the can."

"Only because I don't like what's happening to you. At all."

Karleen's head whipped around. "What's that supposed to mean?"

Jo stared at her tea glass so long Karleen briefly wondered if she'd imagined the comment. Until her friend finally hauled in a huge breath, then again lifted her eyes to Karleen. "Okay, when things fizzled between you and Nate, I understood why it took you a little longer to get your feet underneath you again. Still, I've never known you not to bounce back. Eventually. You'd take some time to lick your wounds, sure, but…" Jo's curls shuddered when she shook her head. "But over the past few years, it's like…you're losing altitude. Yeah, you're doing fine, with your job and everything, but…"

She glanced down, then back up. "When did the hope die, honey? When did you give up?"

Jo's words nearly knocked Karleen over. But not for long.

"The only thing I've *given up,*" she said, her arms tightly folded over her quaking stomach, "is the idiotic notion that I can't function without a man. Took me long enough, but I finally got it through this thick head that it didn't work for my mother, and it didn't work for me, and the sooner I accepted that and got on with my life, the happier I'd be."

Not surprisingly, Jo didn't back down one iota. "Not needing a man…" She gave her a thumbs-up. "Turning your back on something potentially terrific…" The thumb emphatically jabbed toward the floor.

"Screw *potential,* Jo!" Karleen said, slamming down her glass. "This was sex! That's all! Just two adults relievin' a little pent-up tension. When I saw his house, heard him talk about his wife…" She shook her head. "Troy and I have absolutely nothin' in common. *Nothing.* And you of all people should know that being good together in bed does not a solid relationship make."

Jo made a face, but Karleen knew she couldn't argue, considering how her friend's first marriage, to a charming, sexy man who was still struggling with the concept of adulthood, had fared. Not that Troy was anything like Bobby, but the upshot was the same. Then Jo cocked her head, her brows drawn.

"He talked about his wife? While you two were…?"

"No! After. And I brought it up."

"God help me, but I have to ask…why?"

"Because my going-in-blind days are over. And besides, once we did that, it made it a lot easier for him to face facts. I know what you're thinking, that I cut this thing off at the knees before it even had a chance. But I prefer to think of it as, for once, avoiding the trap *before* getting caught. I'd call that progress, wouldn't you?"

Their gazes warred for several seconds before Jo slid off her stool, mumbling something about needing to get Chance.

Her arms crossed, her stomach churning, Karleen trailed her down the hall. But when Joanna reached the door, she turned and said, "It's only progress if you're moving forward, Kar. Treading water doesn't count."

Karleen yanked open the door. "And you know damn

well how long it's take me to feel like I'm actually in control of my life, and my choices. If you can't be happy for me about that, I'm sorry."

Worry crowding Joanna's eyes, she shook her head, then left.

Alone again, Karleen went to check on Britney, who was still snuffling around her new digs. At the sound of her cage being unlatched, the little furball sat up on her haunches, whiskers twitching. She didn't even try to get away when Karleen reached in to scoop her up, nestling her against her collarbone.

Yeah, she thought, stroking the tiny, trusting body with one finger, it really was better this way.

Chapter Five

"Daddy, how come we never see Karleen anymore?"

Troy wrestled the visor down to block out the overly cheerful early morning sun, glancing as he did into the rearview mirror at Scotty's screwed-up expression. "No real reason," he said levelly, returning his attention to the road. "Everybody got busy, I suppose."

"We're not," Grady said, which got an echoed, "Yeah, we're not," from his brother.

Waiting for the light to change, Troy rubbed his scratchy eyes—between still being half-asleep and a through-the-roof pollen count, he was surprised he could see at all—then let his wrist bang back onto the steering wheel. Two weeks since he'd slept with Karleen. Two weeks in which, between work and the house and the boys, he'd barely had five seconds to collect his thoughts. But in those five seconds, guess where those thoughts had wandered?

The light turned green; Troy pulled out onto the main drag. "Maybe. But you've both conked out right after dinner every night. And you went to play with Chance last weekend, remember? And we went to the zoo on Sunday?"

Silence ensued while they apparently pondered this. Four-year-olds' memories were bizarre things: Despite a million reminders, the boys couldn't remember to flush the toilet to save themselves, but they could call up details from their third birthday that Troy had long since expunged from the old data bank. So where the play date and field trip fit in, he had no idea. And where Karleen fit in, he had even less.

Ha. There was an understatement.

"When're we gonna get a dog?" Grady now asked.

Troy pulled up into the preschool's nearly full parking lot. "Soon," he said over the sound of slamming doors, harried parents' urging their kids to hurry up, the occasional wail of dissent. "Next couple of weeks, I promise."

"How long's that?"

"As long as…well, it's the same amount of time that we've been in the new house."

"*That* long?" Scotty said as Troy got out of the car, opened the back door. Both boys had already unhooked their car-seat latches; Troy had nearly had a cow when he'd discovered they knew how to spring themselves a couple of months ago (what one figured out, he was only too happy to share with his brother), but at least they didn't seem interested in performing their new trick when they were going seventy-five on the interstate.

"Okay, maybe this week," he said, which got dual squeals of glee from the two little boys, one dangling from each of Troy's hands as he guided them toward the school's door. Thank God *this* had worked out, was all he had to say.

As opposed to Karleen, who now avoided him like Ebola.

So he should be glad. That she'd let him go. Off the hook. Given him her blessing to go forth and date other women, put out an APB for the next Mrs. Lindquist.

So why wasn't he? Glad, dating, whatever.

He was still chewing this one over when, a half hour later, Blake knocked on Troy's half-open office door. Troy looked up from his computer.

"You're back."

"In all my glory," his partner said, sinking into the black, glove-leather chair in front of Troy's gleaming glass-topped desk. He squinted slightly from the glare coming from the giant picture window that framed sky, sprawl and the shadowed mountains at the city's eastern edge. Even though it was only eight-thirty in the morning, Blake was already loosening his tie. Still, compared with Troy's chamois shirt and jeans, his partner was dressed to the nines.

"Good trip?" Troy now asked, referring to Blake's two-week-long jaunt to personally check on their West Coast franchises. While they had eyes and ears aplenty to keep tabs on things, both men liked to keep a personal hand in the business they'd built up from a single little store selling handmade ice cream, back when they'd had no clue how high the odds had been stacked against them.

"Yep." His mouth stretched, Blake crossed his ankle over his knee and leaned back in the chair, his cheek propped on his knuckles. "Gave some of 'em a real thrill. Although not nearly as much of one as I get every time I pull up in front of one of the stores and realize, hey—that's *us*—"

Troy's direct line rang. Holding up one finger, he answered, only to feel his forehead knot. "No, Ray, I told you, I want to see the sketch for the new packaging before you go forward with the prototype…. I know, I know…just humor me, okay?"

He hung up, frowning at the phone for a moment.

"Ray's been designing our packaging since the beginning," Blake said mildly. "He hasn't steered us wrong yet."

"And it's our names behind the product. So since when did our input become optional?" Then he sighed and said, "You were saying?"

Blake eyed him for a moment, then said, "That it's good to be back. Although now I'm not so sure," he added, and Troy grunted. "I did miss the kids, though." He grinned. "And my wife."

Troy grunted again. As happy as he was that Blake and Cass had worked out their problems, right now Blake could take his domestic bliss and shove it. So naturally Blake asked, "Everything okay on the home front?"

Pretending he thought Blake meant the business, Troy said, "More or less. You see the new Web site?"

"I did. Looks real good."

"Yeah? I still think it's too cutsy, but I was overruled."

His partner flicked something off the heel of his boot, then looked at Troy again. "Marketing knows what it's doing, big guy," he said, then crossed his arms high on his chest. "But I wasn't talking about work."

And here Troy had been grateful that Blake hadn't brought up the subject—meaning, Karleen—since that first day. Actually, there'd been a time when neither one would have dared pry into the other's personal life beyond what was absolutely essential. Boundaries that, by some unspoken mutual consent, were fading more and more as time passed. Still, both men knew when to push, and when to let things ride. Judging from Blake's expression, he was in pushing mode.

Too bad for him.

"Things are fine," Troy said, returning his gaze to his computer screen, hoping Blake would get the hint.

"So you get cozy with your pretty new neighbor or what?"

So much for that. "I—or rather, the boys—invited her to have dinner with us the night we moved in," Troy said, not looking at Blake. Jocks in a locker room, they weren't. "She turned it—me, us, whatever—down."

"And that's it?"

Troy glanced over, then focused once more on the computer screen. "Well, let's see…she let in the delivery guys for my washer/dryer. And we had a chat over the back fence one morning, about maybe letting the boys have a little garden at one end of hers."

"Wow. Exciting stuff."

"We're neighbors, Blake. *Exciting* isn't part of the contract."

And you actually said that with a straight face.

Blake tapped his fingers on the desk. "She know you're rich?"

Troy shot him a look. "Excuse me?"

"You heard me." At Troy's snort of disgust, Blake said, "It's bait, that's all I'm saying—"

"And I hope to hell things haven't degenerated to the point where I have to wear a sandwich board advertising my net worth to get a woman to go out with me. But to answer your question…yes. She knows. Although not from me."

"Then how'd she find out?"

"Apparently we're plastered all over the Internet. Not our actual income, although I wouldn't be surprised if someone with sufficient know-how couldn't find that out, too. But I imagine once she saw I was CEO of AIS, it was a pretty short leap from there."

"And she *still* turned you down?"

"Yeah. Go figure."

More finger tapping. Then he said: "I'm disappointed in you, buddy."

"Hey. You said I should give it a shot. I shot. The target's out of range. End of story."

He could feel Blake's gaze on the side of his face for several seconds before the other man finally unfolded himself from the chair. "If you say so, buddy," he said, then zipped out of Troy's office before he could throw something at him.

The target, however, made a beeline for Troy the minute he pulled into his driveway that evening. Despite her agitated movement, her breasts remained immobile underneath a tight black tank top with—he could see as she got closer— "Grumpy Chick" spelled out in rhinestones. Judging from her expression, the shirt did not lie. Judging from how tight his jeans suddenly were—an unfortunate reaction to her also wearing short shorts—staying out of each other's paths had done nothing to dull the roughly five thousand extremely X-rated images that had instantly popped into his head.

And yes, at this point it was still mostly about the sex. Somewhere in the neighborhood of eight-five, ninety percent, he was guessing. Because he was male and not dead and he didn't know her well enough to override the hormones on a regular basis. Which was not to say the not-about-sex ten to fifteen percent wasn't making its voice heard, too. Her laugh, her wacky sense of humor, even her highly personal sense of style…he wasn't immune to those, by any means.

But mainly, it was about the sex.

Eventually, Troy realized her hands were full of mail.

His mail, apparently, if he read her gesticulations correctly. The second he turned off the engine, the boys were unlatched, out of the car and swarming the poor woman, yammering about the dog they did not yet own, their new school, was it time to plant the garden yet, and—oh, yes—how come she never came out in her yard anymore?

"I've haven't been around much, sweeties," she said, smiling but not touching them, he noticed (as far as Troy was concerned, they were like little magnets, but then, they were his kids). Then she tilted her head at Troy, now out of the car and standing in the driveway and looking down into her pretty, if grumpified, face. Her mouth, specifically. Speaking of magnets.

She held out the mail. "Yours," she said, then crossed her arms over the "Chick." "It was mixed up with mine. How on earth the carrier can screw up a street with four houses is beyond me."

"Thanks," he said, then yelled out to the boys to stay where he could see them as he strode back down the driveway to his mailbox. Which, yes, was empty.

"And what's this about a dog?" Karleen said as he walked back toward her, flipping through his mail. Nothing but the usual suspects, he mused, her words taking a second to penetrate. He glanced up, frowning.

"Is that a problem?"

"Not for me. Might be for the dog, though. Because the fence isn't secure?"

"Yeah, I'd thought about that. I'll probably build a large dog run along the other side of the yard."

She nodded. "What'd you have in mind? Kind of dog, I mean?"

"Something big the boys can't hurt."

That got a laugh, and Troy thought, *Oh, hell,* and

without thinking reached for her hand. "We need to figure this out," he said, and her eyes widened.

"There's no *this* to figure out. Which I thought we'd already discussed."

"I don't mean *that*," he said, nodding toward her house and all it represented. "I mean—" he dropped her hand, held up the mail "—*this*."

The space between her brows knotted. "Me bringin' over your mail?"

"Us being neighbors. Sharing a fence."

"Seems to me we're already doing that."

"No, what we're doing is avoiding each other."

"Not going out of my way to run into you's not the same as avoiding you."

On what planet? he thought, but all he said was, "Then why didn't you simply leave the mail in the box?"

"I—" Her gaze skittered away, as pink washed over her cheeks. "It didn't occur to me, okay? So don't go readin' more into it than there is."

"I'm not. Believe it or not, a repeat performance isn't my objective."

"Uh-huh."

"Well, okay, it's not like I'd turn it down. That strong, I'm not. But pretending each other doesn't exist…how is that a good thing?"

Karleen tucked a strand of hair behind her ear, making a face at the tops of her glittery, rope-soled shoes. Then, frowning, she looked back up at him. "Thought you were supposed to be lookin' for a wife?"

"Right now," he said, "I've got all I can handle looking for a dog. And anyway," he said when she chuckled again, "it shouldn't be a hunting expedition, you know? I mean, Amy…" He rubbed his mouth. "She was just *there,* and it felt right, so we ran with it. If it happened once, why couldn't it happen again?"

Two, three beats passed before she said, "I can't decide if that makes you real trusting, or lazier than all get out."

A smile stretched across his face, as he deliberately let his gaze meander from her mouth to her breasts, over the sliver of midriff peeking out above the waistband of her shorts, then back up. Behind her, her personal, miniature amusement park gyrated and twirled and sparkled in the breeze. "Oh," he said quietly, "I don't think anybody can accuse me of being *lazy*."

To her immense credit—and his profound relief—she laughed again. "Lord, you are something else."

And in that moment, tenderness once again nudged aside lust, evening out the sex-to-other-stuff ratio a little more. "Karleen…obviously we don't know each other very well. And you have no reason to trust me. But you're safe with me. I swear."

One brow slid up underneath her bangs. "Exactly how do you figure that?"

"Because I miss more than sex."

She crossed her arms again, her mouth pulled down at the corners. "So what're you saying? That you want to be friends?"

"It's not unheard of."

A few feet away, the boys squealed at a lizard darting across the driveway. Karleen looked over, amusement and pain colliding in her eyes. "And if they start thinking of me in terms of Mama?" Her gaze touched his. "Then what?"

"Then I'll tell them how things stand, and they'll deal."

"And what if it's not *them* I'm worried about?" She waited until her words registered, then added, "Now do you understand?"

Troy watched her walk back to her house. Oddly, not even the sight of her adorable, taunting little rear end was enough to cheer him up.

Karleen peeked in on Britney, snoozing peacefully in a magenta tube, then took a last, mortifying check in the hall mirror before heading out for her morning appointments. Okay, that's it—the minute she got back home she was chucking all the chips and cookies and Little Debbie snacks in the trash before her butt qualified for its own zip code. Yeesh.

Once out the door, force of habit prompted her to glance over at Troy's driveway. It had been a week since his "What I really need is a friend" nonsense, but still. A girl couldn't be too cautious.

No car, no man, no kids, she thought on a relieved breath as a little voice whispered, *Um, isn't it a little late for* cautious?

She slid in behind the wheel and checked her mirrors, as she always did, then rearranged her boobs inside her too-tight push-up bra, which she'd been doing an awful lot lately. Maybe she should cut back on the Triscuits and cheese before bed, too.

Windows down, music blaring, she backed out of the driveway, wondering why she didn't feel more relaxed. Because clearly, Troy had gotten the message. Finally. Not that they were being stupid about it—they'd chat for a minute if they happened to pull up into the driveway at the same time, or wave to each other if they were both out in their backyards. And God knew she didn't have it in her to shut out the boys, who'd helped her plant the pumpkin garden over the weekend. Little Scotty, especially, who followed her around like a puppy, chattering nonstop. God, he was cute. But even with the baby Troys, she kept things light and casual, never mind that she itched so badly to hug the stuffing out of both of them, her heart hurt.

It was the giggling that most got her, though. She'd hear them going at it with Troy, out in his yard, and she'd well right up.

And what was with that, anyway? For heaven's sake, she'd practically helped raise Joanna's babies, but being around *them* never got the waterworks going. All she could figure was she was feeling extra tetchy these days on account of being so tired all the time. Which made no sense, because she was sleeping like the dead for nine or ten hours every night, and half the time needed a nap in the afternoon.

Anyway, whatever caused what, she'd been in no mood to listen to Aunt Inky's most recent sob story when she'd called earlier, ending with—big surprise—another plea for Karleen to "help her out," which would make the second time in less than a month and consequently set off every alarm Karleen possessed.

"Just until I get on my feet," Inky had sniffled into the line.

Only this time, Karleen somehow found the gumption to say, "Help you out, my fanny. *Bail* you out, is more like it. For pity's sake, you are fifty-three years old, it's high time you learn how to take care of *yourself!*"

And she would have slammed down the phone, if her aunt hadn't called Karleen on her cell. Slamming down a cell was generally not a good idea. Of course, Karleen knew by nightfall she'd be feeling all remorseful about being so mean to her aunt, who wasn't a bad person, only a weak one. And although on one level Karleen figured if *she'd* gotten over her dependency on men and found a way to support herself, in theory there was hope for pretty much anybody, she also knew everybody had to find their own path to salvation.

Except before a person can go down that path, their eyes have to be open to see it to begin with. And unfortunately, you couldn't pry another person's eyes open for them. Sad, but true.

From time to time, Karleen wondered what Troy's reaction would be to Aunt Inky. Not that this was something she needed to worry about, their ever meeting being highly unlikely. But somehow, Troy didn't strike her as the type of person to have an Aunt Inky in his family.

Halfway to her first appointment, she suddenly got so hungry she thought her stomach was going to turn inside out. Strange, because she'd had a good breakfast—eggs and fruit and toast—not two hours before. Up the road, a Blake's Lotaburger sign caught her eye, and her stomach started growling even louder. Even a Mickey D's would be better; at least they had salads. Although she knew this was one of those times when a salad wasn't gonna cut it, her spreading butt be damned.

"Lotaburger with green chili, large seasoned fries, chocolate shake," she called into the drive-through mike, then sagged back against the car cushion and thought, *What are you* doing?, only to jerk when the garbled voice told her to pull around to the window. She paid, then sat, chewing on a hangnail, at the window (at 10:30 in the morning, there was nobody behind her) practically snatching the white, heavenly scented bag out of the woman's hands and shoving a half-dozen hot, spicy fries into her mouth before she'd even pulled away. Five minutes later— if that—there was nothing left but a few shreds of lettuce and a couple of grease spots. She'd even eaten the onions, and she *hated* onions.

Unreal.

* * *

She'd coordinated the day's appointments so that all the morning ones were in the same large, downtown law firm where Glynnie Swann, Joanna's mother, worked. At the beginning, she wasn't sure who'd been more skeptical of her talents—the women or Karleen herself. But in the past seven years, her client list had grown to rather impressive proportions. By Albuquerque standards, at least, where "dressing up" like as not meant tossing on your Navajo silver with your denim and calling it a day.

Still, even here there were occasions where denim wouldn't work, and women with more money than time. Women who'd gladly pay somebody like Karleen to do their dirty work for them. God knows, being a personal shopper would never put her in the same league with Bill Gates or Oprah. But it was the perfect job for somebody who'd always envisioned heaven as a giant, never-ending mall where they always had "it" in your size and every store had a Half Off sign out in front. And the best thing was, all she'd needed to get started was a keen eye, common sense and a genuine ability to get along with almost anybody. Especially if the anybody was paying you a helluva lot more per hour than you'd ever make peddling burgers and fries.

So, most days she was pretty much convinced she was the luckiest woman in the world. Most days, it didn't bother her at all when one of her regulars rejected one of her suggestions, or when she didn't click with a new client. That was just the nature of the beast. Today, however, when her third appointment of the day—a newbie—was a total flop, Karleen found herself on the brink of tears as she stuffed a half-dozen outfits back into their vinyl shrouds.

"I'm sorry this didn't work out," the buxom brunette

said, thereby cutting off Karleen's offer to try again. Not that there'd be much point. The woman had hated everything. "Glynelle speaks so highly of you, I guess I just expected…more."

Thinking very un-Christian thoughts, Karleen hefted the bags off the portable rack she carried with her and fixed a smile to her face. "Don't worry about it," she said, laying the slippery bags across the small conference table in the corner and collapsing the rack.

The woman stood. "Well. I have your card." She extended her hand, so Karleen had to awkwardly shift everything to one arm in order to shake it. No offer to pay her for her time, she noticed. Yes, the first consultation was "free," but most clients were courteous enough to at least give her something for her efforts. Karleen briefly clasped the woman's hand—not even wincing when the wonker anniversary ring bit into her palm—then wrestled with bags, purse, rack and door for a good thirty seconds before finally making it out into the hall.

Which is when she realized she had to pee so badly she thought she'd pop. There was a public restroom at the end of the hall, but Glynnie's office was a lot closer. And, thank God, the door to her outer office was open, her secretary apparently at lunch. Karleen dumped everything on the reception-room sofa and rapped on Glynnie's door, nearly knocking the hummingbird-sized woman down when she opened it.

"Too much coffee, dear?" Jo's mother said when Karleen reemerged a minute later.

"Must've been." And damn, she was hungry again. "Sorry I dumped everything outside, this'll just take a sec…."

"Honey…are you okay?"

Karleen busied herself with setting up the rack so Glynnie wouldn't see her reddening face. From the moment Karleen had set foot in the Swanns' comfortable, stable house all those years ago, Glynnie had—to the best of her ability, at least—shouldered at least some of the burden Karleen's own mother had more or less abdicated to lethargy and booze. As busy as Jo's mama had been with her career and all, however, she'd barely had enough scraps left over for her own daughter, let alone some needy little stray Jo'd dragged home. And anyway, Karleen had learned a long time ago that while people might *say* they wanted you to feel you could open up to them, nine times out of ten they didn't really mean it. So while Karleen never doubted for a minute that Glynnie's concern was genuine, neither had she ever felt completely comfortable about dumping her problems on her best friend's mother.

"Yes, ma'am, I'm fine," she said, knowing Glynnie would be rolling her eyes at the *ma'am,* a habit she'd never been able to break Karleen of, even after twenty-five years. "I just…didn't sleep too well last night." *And my aunt is going to drive me insane and, oh, yeah, it's about my new neighbor who I slept with who's now stuck in my brain like a tick on a hound dog?* "And, well, it doesn't look like Doris Montoya's gonna work out."

The bags suspended from the rack, Glynnie had already unzipped one and removed the shell-pink suit from it. Karleen didn't miss the brief frown, but her first and best customer walked out to the middle of the reception area, holding up the suit under her chin to look at her reflection in the large, ornately framed mirror over the butter-colored leather sofa.

"I was afraid of that," Glynnie said on a sigh, masses of straight-from-the-bottle, strawberry-blond corkscrew curls quivering around her cheeks. "Doris isn't exactly known for being easygoing. But when she asked where I got the blue silk suit, and I told her about you, she insisted I give her your number. So I figured, what the hell…" She turned, still frowning, still clutching the suit to her chest. "You really think this color will work on me?"

"I really do. But don't take my word for it. Go try it on."

On a sigh, Glynnie vanished into her private bathroom, not bothering to shut the door all the way while she changed. "So. You and Jo still not talking to each other?" she called out.

Damn. Karleen knew there was a reason why she'd been dreading this meeting. She rubbed at the crease between her eyebrows that was going to become permanent if she wasn't careful. "Glynnie, you know I love you to pieces, but Jo's and my relationship isn't anybody's business but ours."

"Don't be ridiculous," came the disembodied voice, punctuated by the slither of fabric and an occasional soft grunt. "My daughter's been cranky as a witch with piles for the past three weeks. Which is the longest I can ever remember the two of you going without speaking. So the question is, who's going to tell her pride to take a hike first?"

She swung open the door. The suit fit like it had been custom tailored. But Glynnie's pale brows were still dipped over her little button nose.

"You still don't like it?" Karleen asked.

"What? Oh, the suit?" Glynnie gave a dismissive wave. "The suit's perfect. As usual." She glided over to the rack to paw through the offerings, selecting another suit, a dress and a charmeuse pants outfit in an eye-poppingly bright floral print, all of which she hauled back to the bathroom. "Jo misses you."

"I miss her, too, Glynnie," Karleen said softly, leaning against Glynnie's desk with her arms crossed. "But she overstepped the bounds of friendship."

"Meaning what?" floated out from the bathroom. "That

she said how things looked from where she was sitting and you took offense?"

Karleen bristled. "She told you what we talked about?"

"Only that she was worried about you, that she didn't like how you've changed. And I hate to say this," Glynnie said, sticking her head out the door, "but I have to agree with her. It's like you've made this nice, cozy little burrow for yourself where you've decided to spend the rest of your life."

"That is so not true!" Karleen cried as the redhead vanished again and an image of Britney plugged into her tube sprang to mind. "Y'all make it sound like I've become a total recluse! I get out! I do stuff!"

She heard what sounded like a snort. "Such as what? Shopping for a bunch of rich bitches? And don't take this the wrong way, sweetie—" out popped her head again "—but you look like hell on a bad day."

Karleen refused to rise to the bait. "Did you try on the pants outfit yet? I'm dyin' to see how you look in it."

Glynnie was far too shrewd not to know when she'd been purposely nudged—or in this case, shoved—off topic, but she sighed and ducked back inside. A minute later, she came out and did a graceful twirl.

Karleen pressed her hand to her chest. Except her boobs hurt so she removed it. "Oh, wow. It looks even better than I thought it would."

"It's gorgeous." Glynnie patted Karleen's cheek. "I can always count on you to make me look less like the sixty-year-old hag I am."

That, and enough Youth Dew to float a tanker. "Never happen, Glynnie. And never will." As opposed to Karleen's own mother, who before she'd died—at thirty-eight, only a year older than Karleen was now, she realized with a start—

had looked positively used up. In fact, when she'd taken her mother into the hospital that last time, the nurse had actually asked if the birth date on the chart had been a mistake.

"And for that," Glynnie said, disappearing into the washroom again, "I'll take the other suit and the dress, too. I love them all."

"I brought shoes, too."

"Shoes?" Jo's mama shot back into the room, handing the clothes to Karleen to rehang. "Where?"

"In the Dillard's bag."

Her face lit up like a kid's at Christmas, Glynnie sat on the edge of a flame-stitch chair, reverently lifting first a nude-colored, mesh-and-patent pump from its tissue-paper bed, then a pair of coppery sandals. "Ohhhh…I think I'm in love."

"They'd just gotten them in, and you know there's always only one pair of five-and-a-halves. So I grabbed them before anybody else could. I thought the light ones'd look good with the pink suit."

"You, sweetie, are a miracle," Glynnie said, then went behind her desk, pulling her handbag out of a bottom drawer to get her checkbook. Karleen laid the receipts for the clothes and shoes on her desk; after adding them up on her checkbook calculator, Glynnie looked at Karleen over the tops of her reading glasses. "And your hours?"

"Two. I swear," she said at Glynnie's raised brows. "Since I was shoppin' for three other people at the same time."

Glynnie nodded, then wrote out and handed over the check. Karleen frowned. "This is too much—"

"I added something extra to make up for Doris. The woman may be a crackerjack attorney, but she can pinch a penny hard enough to make snot come out of Lincoln's nose. She didn't pay you, did she?"

"Well, no, but…" At the other woman's glare, she tucked the check into her purse. "Thanks," she said, then involuntarily recoiled from the overpowering scent of Glynnie's perfume. Whew. She must have reapplied it after she'd changed back into her own clothes.

"Kar? What is it?"

"Nothing!" Somehow, she didn't think mentioning to her best client—not to mention her best friend's mother—that her Giorgio was about to make her hurl was a good idea. "Is it warm in here?"

Glynnie gave her an odd look, then said, "It is a bit stuffy, now that you mention it. Why don't we get out of here, go have some lunch? My treat."

At the mention of food, Karleen recoiled again, even as she was nearly overcome by the urge to strip a barbecued chicken clean in five seconds flat. Bizarre.

"I'd love to, but I've got more shopping to do for tomorrow's appointments. Maybe next time, okay?"

She gathered up the rack, the leftover dress bags from the Doris Montoya fiasco, her purse, and headed for the door, Glynnie following. When she got there, Jo's mother opened the door for her, then crushed Karleen and all her paraphernalia into a huge hug. Then she held her back, her hazel gaze both stern and kind. "I know it's never been easy for you to let other people worry about you, but there's nothing you can do to stop it. So deal."

At the unexpected expression of affection, Karleen got all choked up. Again. Honest to Pete.

"Thanks," she said, then beat a hasty retreat before she really gave Glynnie something to worry about.

By the time she finished up her shopping at five-thirty, she felt like she hadn't eaten in a week. But here was the weird thing: She'd fully intended on picking up something in the mall's food court, only she couldn't come within twenty feet of it without wanting to puke. How could she be so hungry and not be able to stand the smell of food?

Hopefully she could at least face the grocery store. As long as she stayed away from the deli section and the fried chicken, anyway. Yeah, yeah, shopping when you're hungry was a hugely bad idea, but oddly enough the moment she set foot inside the supermarket, all she wanted was good stuff. Veggies, fruits, whole grain bread. *Brown rice,* for God's sake. Meat, however…uh-uh. It was like that whole side of the store was giving off some sort of weird repelling vibes.

"Kar!"

In the midst of groping a cantaloupe, Karleen looked over to see Joanna rushing toward her, Chance in the cart's kiddie seat, happily gnawing on a bagel. His grin when he saw his "auntie"—not to mention the expression on Jo's face—twisted Karleen up inside. They hadn't been apart this long since Glynnie and Roger had taken Jo to Europe when she was sixteen.

The two women looked at each other for a moment before they both said, "I'm so sorry!" at the same time, then fell into each other's arms, babbling their apologies and earning them more than a few strange looks from other shoppers.

"God," Jo said after they pulled apart. She dug tissues out of her purse, taking one for herself and handing another to Karleen. "Are we the stupidest two women in the world or what?"

Karleen gave a soggy little laugh. "Your mother called you?"

"I'm betting before you'd reached the elevator. Although I'd already decided to put an end to this idiocy." Jo blew her own nose. "And of course I had no idea I'd find you here, I was planning on stopping by later. Or calling, or something."

"Yeah, me, too." Karleen dabbed underneath her eyes. God bless whoever thought up waterproof mascara, was all she had to say. "Sorry about being such a b—" She glanced at Chance, then back at Jo. "Brat."

"You had every right to be, I was totally out of line—"

"You were only bein' a friend. And I overreacted."

"I'm still worried about you."

"I know. But I swear, I'm not…" She swallowed. "I'm not sittin' all alone in the dark every night, gettin' hammered. If that's what you're worried about."

Jo's eyes went wide. "Is *that* what you thought I meant? Oh, God, honey…" She laid a hand on her wrist, shaking her head. "No way." Then, when Karleen nodded in acknowledgment, Joanna's eyes went all big again. This time, at the sight of Karleen's cart.

"Wow. Are you shopping for someone else?"

"No…what makes you say that?"

Jo picked up the rubber-banded bunch of asparagus. "You? Asparagus?"

"It looked good, what can I say?"

But Jo didn't stop there. "Broccoli? Apples? *Spinach?*" Her brow puckered, she lifted her eyes to Karleen. "Okay, spill. What's going on?"

Karleen ripped open the package of multi-grain bread in her cart and broke off a hunk, started to nibble on it. "Nothing's going on. Well, except that I've put on a few pounds so it occurred to me maybe I should start eating food with more nutrition and less calories. Only, you know what's weird? The past few days I've been *constantly* hungry. And yet most cooking smells make me feel icky."

She tore off another hunk of bread and stuffed it into her mouth, mumbling, "What?" around it as she chewed.

Jo was giving her the same weird look her mother had earlier. "Are you peeing like every five minutes?"

"Yeah, now that you mention it. Why?"

One eyebrow lifted.

A second later, Karleen sucked in a breath so hard she nearly choked on her bite of bread. "Oh, cra…er, crud. You don't think…?"

"I've been through it three times, Kar. Add swollen you-know-whats to the mix and I think you got yourself a real *bingo* there."

Feeling the blood drain from her face, Karleen clutched the handle of her cart before her knees gave way. "I can't…I couldn't… That's impossible, we, we used…" Another glance at the kid. "Something."

Joanna gave a short, dry laugh. "You know those twins that live at my house?" While Karleen stood there in total and complete shock, Joanna said gently, "It's been, what? Three weeks?"

"Closer to a month, actually."

"So you're late?"

"You know me, I've never been regular in my life…. Oh, Jo…" She turned what she knew were horrified eyes to her friend. "Do you really think I'm…?" The word lodged in her throat, like a dog not wanting its bath.

"The pharmacy's right over there, honey—"

"Karleeeeeeen!"

Karleen spun around to see Scott and Grady pinballing around the other customers, straight toward her.

Oh, Lord, not now…

Four little arms wrapped around her hips, nearly knocking her off balance. And she could decipher their mixed scents with the unerring accuracy of a parfumier's "nose," a blend of warm little boy and earth and baby shampoo and fabric softener and Play-Doh and Kool-Aid and—oh, yes—their father.

Who, wearing that expression of half-panicked relief common to all parents whose kids have disappeared for more than two seconds, was bearing down on the lot of them, his own cart piled high.

Oh, no. He'd been through this before. Would he be able to tell from her face that she was…you know? If she was, that is. Because maybe it was, well, something else. Some strange virus that made you ravenously hungry and gave you the nose of a bloodhound.

Troy's eyes met hers and panic sank its claws into the scruff of her neck.

"I'll see you later, guys," she said to the boys, peeling them off her legs. Then she took off, trusting Joanna to come up with something she wouldn't have to kill her for later.

Once home (after a quick side trip to Walgreens, since no way in hell was she gonna chance Troy's seeing her in the Smith's pharmacy), she lobbed the cold stuff into the refrigerator, then grabbed the pregnancy test and ran to the nearest bathroom. Her hands were shaking so badly she could hardly get the box open. No need to read the instructions, considering the number of "maybes" she'd had over the course of nine years and three marriages. All those years of *hoping,* of not doing anything to prevent getting pregnant and so much to make it happen. All those *Sorry, try agains….*

Lord, she was like Jell-O in a pair of mules.

She peed…. She held her breath…. She dared to look. *Congratulations!* the little pink line said. *You're a winner!* Karleen sank onto the toilet seat and burst into tears.

Chapter Six

Troy stared at the miserable woman perched on the edge of his sofa until the clanging in his head subsided enough to hear his own voice.

One slip. *One.* A single lousy (okay, not lousy) detour off the boringly straight, obsessively narrow track he'd followed for more than four years…

Why, God? WHY?

"You're sure?" he said. With remarkable calm, considering.

Not looking at him, Karleen smirked. "One test might lie, but I somehow doubt three would." She gave him what she probably thought was a brave smile. "You look like you could use a drink."

"I…no. Believe me, it wouldn't help."

He crossed to the window, although there was nothing to see in the pitch dark. The boys had been sound asleep for an hour. She'd called first to make sure, before she'd come over. And his gut had fisted then, at the tightness in her voice, as though she'd either been crying or was trying not to. The same way it had when she'd booked it out of the supermarket earlier.

"How long have you known?" His voice seemed to come from somewhere else, from some*one* else.

"Since about twenty minutes before I called you."

Troy faced her again, his heart breaking at her expression, even as it slammed against his ribs hard enough to bruise. Man, this sure wasn't anything like when Amy had told him she was pregnant. Not even remotely. He breathed deeply, trying to dilute the sick feeling. "So you didn't know in the store?"

That got a humorless laugh. "Not for sure. Although about a minute before you showed up I had a sudden inkling." Karleen's mouth flattened. It vaguely registered that she must have reapplied her lipstick before coming over. You had to hand it to a woman who had her priorities straight. "I'd been feeling strange for a few days, but I hadn't put two and two together until Jo…" She'd been leaning forward, completely still except for her incessant fidgeting with the stack of magazines on the coffee table in front of her. Now she tightly folded her arms over her middle. "Are you mad?"

He jerked. "*What?* No! Why would I be angry? And who with?"

"Me?"

"That's nuts, Karleen. Yeah, I'm a little poleaxed— okay, a *lot* poleaxed—but sleeping with you was my idea."

Her smile turned rueful. "Not entirely."

"Fine. Then either no one's to blame, or we both are. But getting mad isn't going to solve anything."

She gave him a brief, speculative look before her face disappeared into her palms and she mumbled, "This is freaking unbelievable."

"Guess the condom was faulty," he said, and she laughed again. Except it was about the saddest sound he'd ever heard. She dropped her hands, only to start messing with the magazines again, sorting them into new stacks based on no real method that Troy could see. Then she sighed.

"I tried and tried to get pregnant with each of my husbands," she said dully, "but it never happened. Something to do with my weird cycle. Every doctor I've gone to has said pretty much the same thing, that it wasn't impossible for me to get pregnant, only that it'd be harder for me than for most women. And that as I got older..." Another soft laugh. "Now I know what Sarah in the Bible must've felt like, finding herself pregnant at ninety after all those years of being barren."

Troy pocketed a stray Hot Wheels race car peeking out from the armchair cushion, willing the haze of shock—and extreme chagrin—to dissipate enough to start thinking in terms of *solution*. "Then you'd want to keep the baby?"

Silence jangled between them. "Is that a problem?"

"No. No, of course not."

"And if I didn't? Want to keep it, I mean?"

Troy took a deep breath. "How am I supposed to answer that? If I say it's up to you, it sounds like I don't care. If I say I'd have a hard time with...with the alternative, then you'll think I'm pressuring you into something you might not want."

"Oh, for God's sake, Troy..." Karleen sagged back into the cushions. "I'm here. I asked. Just tell me what you're thinking."

He looked at her steadily for a long moment. "I'm wondering if it's a boy or a girl," he said at last, surprising himself.

She nodded, then pushed herself up off the sofa. Now hugging herself, she walked aimlessly around the room, arranged nearly the way it had been in the old house, their old apartment, to give the boys a sense of continuity.

"Right now," she said, "the inside of my head feels like a tornado went through. To finally get my life to a place where I didn't feel like the rug was gonna get yanked out from underneath me…" Her fingers skimmed the pebbled base of a brass lamp. "I keep telling myself there's a baby growing inside me, and every time I say it the breath gets sucked out of me."

When she fell silent, Troy gently prodded, even though he already knew her answer, "You still haven't answered my question."

"I know." Her fingers hooked the edge of a bookshelf. "All those years I wanted to be a mama so bad I could hardly think about anything else…. You have no idea how long it took me to let go, to finally accept it wasn't meant to be." A smile flickered before she released a long, slow breath. "So, yeah, I want this baby. If it…" Worry shuddered across her features. "If it takes. Only…"

"What?"

"Figures, doesn't it? That I finally get my wish, only to be raising this kid on my own." She finally met his eyes. "Just like my mama and hers before her."

"Who says you have to raise this baby by yourself?"

She made a show of looking around the room before returning her gaze to his. "I sure don't see a husband anywhere around here, do you? And don't even think about going all noble on me by proposing, Troy, because if it wasn't gonna work between us before, it sure as heck isn't gonna work just because there's a baby thrown into the mix. God knows it didn't for my mother."

"I thought you said—"

"Oh, she was married. For about five minutes. My parents got hitched when Mama was six months along with me, but Daddy took off for parts unknown when I was a year old. She was barely nineteen, no education, no skills to speak off…" Her mouth tightened. "All I got out of the deal was his name. All she got was a broken heart and a whole lot of grief, from what I gather. So I sure wouldn't call that *working out,* would you?"

"I'm sorry."

"Why? It had nothing to do with you."

"I can't feel bad for you that you and your mother got screwed over?"

Karleen seemed to consider this for a moment, then shrugged. "Like I said, it's in the past. And I've worked my butt off to move on. But the irony's not sittin' real well, right at the moment."

"I can see that." Troy hesitated, then said, "I have no problem with marrying you, Karleen. And not because it's noble, because it's practical."

"For who?"

"The baby, for one thing. I'm not trying to back you into a corner, but if nothing else, you could go on my health insurance—"

"I don't need it, I've got my own. Look, I appreciate the offer, I really do. And I know I'm probably not makin' any sense, considering everything I just said. But I'm not in anything near the same position my mother was. I've got a house and a job and money put by. I'm feeling a little off balance right now, sure, but I suppose I'll figure it all out.

The same as you did," she added, her mouth curving slightly. "After Amy died. And from everything I can tell, you've done a pretty good job of it, too."

Before he had a chance to recover from the unexpected compliment, a soft, sleepy "Daddy?" caught his attention. Troy pivoted to see a yawning, wild-haired Scotty standing on very unsteady pins at the living-room entrance.

"Hey, squirt—whatcha doing awake?"

Trailing one of the half-shredded, and not particularly well-constructed, quilts Amy had painstakingly made for her babies while pregnant, the little boy trundled over to Troy and lifted his arms to be picked up. "You were talking too loud." He nestled against Troy's collarbone. "How come Karleen's here?"

Troy glanced over at the proud, troubled woman carrying his child, again trying to figure out the odd mixture of yearning and standoffishness in her face whenever she was around the boys. Then it hit him that Karleen was carrying the boys' brother or sister. A thought that had apparently occurred to her at the same moment, judging from her expression.

"Grown-up stuff, cutie," he said. "You need a drink of water or something?"

Scotty shook his head, then wadded up the quilt underneath his cheek and stuck his thumb in his mouth, his eyes already drifting shut again. Troy pointed one finger at Karleen.

"Don't even think about sneaking out while I'm gone."

God knows why she didn't. After all, what else was there to talk about? She'd said her piece, he'd said his, and that was that, far as she could tell.

And yet, here she still was, studying a large embroidered sampler on one wall, full of flowers and hearts and sappy sentiments about home and family.

She heard his footsteps on the stairs, felt him come up behind her. "My mother made that."

"For you and Amy?"

"Yeah," he said on a breath. "When we got married."

Karleen turned, one hand knotted against her unsteady stomach. The hunger had returned, a monster fish gnawing her insides. Her gaze swept the room. "No offense, but your house looks like something out of an L.L.Bean catalog."

"What can I tell you? I don't exactly walk on the wild side."

"So I see." She eyed the pillows on the plaid sofa, each one picking up one of the colors in the fabric. "My place must've given you hives."

"To be honest, I wasn't paying much attention to the decor."

The smile that tried to make an appearance died a quick death as the reality of the situation once again hit her like a blow. To her profound mortification, tears threatened to spill over her lower lashes; when she pressed a hand to her mouth, Troy pulled her into his arms, gently rocking her.

And heaven help her, she simply couldn't find the wherewithal to push him away.

"It's going to be okay, honey," he murmured, and she softly beat his chest.

"How do you figure that?"

Give the guy credit, he didn't have some glib answer in his back pocket. Instead, he simply held her, stroking her hair. Then, finally, he said, "I know you're shaky right now, but maybe you shouldn't reject my proposal out of hand. At least think about it."

As much as she was enjoying the moment, this would never do. Her hands planted on his chest, she reared back to look at him. "Please don't take this personally, Troy, but I do not want or need another husband. I've been down that road three times, and each time ended up in quicksand. So no more talk about marriage, okay?"

Uh-huh. One thing about not having been born yesterday was that she could read the look on a man's face better than she could the Bible. And with a lot less room for personal interpretation. So don't anybody tell her that wasn't relief she saw in those pretty green eyes. At least for a second or two, until that I'm-the-guy-it's-up-to-me-to-solve-the-problem look came back. Honestly.

"Okay," he said, in that tone of a man rethinking his battle plan on the fly, "consider the proposal off the table. But no way in hell are you raising this child *alone*. And I'm not only talking about money, although swear to God, if you even *think* of not letting me help financially—"

"No," she said quickly. What was she, nuts? "No, I don't mean that at all. As long as it's for the baby, fine. It's just the husband thing I have issues with."

Uh-oh. Narrowed eyes. "Well. As long as we're clear on that." Then his finger came up in her face. "But money aside, I'm here for this baby, and I'm here for you. In whatever way either of you need me. Is that understood?"

On a wave of emotional overload, a laugh burst from her throat. "I guess, if I had to get knocked up, at least I picked a decent man."

"Damn straight," Troy said without the slightest hesitation. "If I make a mess, I clean it up. If I screw up, I figure out how to fix it. As curveballs go," he said, his expression killing her, "this is a piker."

Her throat burning, Karleen pulled out of his arms,

digging into her pocket for a tissue. "Still and all, two total strangers, having a baby together..." She blew her nose. "How's that supposed to work?"

There went that look again. "It was never my idea to stay strangers, if you remember."

"I know. But it's probably smartest, in the long run."

"Says who?"

"The person havin' this baby."

"Well, the person who got you in that condition still doesn't agree. Especially now."

"You are one stubborn man, you know that?"

"Pot, meet kettle. Look, I get that we're different, okay? But where is it written we have to be clones of each other in order to get along? Hell, I work with people every day I have nothing in common with, and nobody's come to blows yet. So. When's your first doctor's appointment?"

Karleen actually squawked. "I have no idea, seeing as I found out I was pregnant about five minutes ago! And anyway, you don't have to go with me—"

He glared at her. She blew out a breath.

"Fine. I'll let you know. Can I go now?" she said, feeling like a cranky teenybopper.

Troy gestured toward the door. "Feel free."

She actually got all the way home before she threw up.

The next morning, after AIS's weekly teleconference with all the plant managers, Troy's only hope was to make it back to his office before Blake—who'd been shooting him *what's up?* looks the whole time—got to him.

No such luck. Blake snagged him before he'd barely passed through the conference-room door. He did, at least, wait until assorted VPs and such had dispersed before saying, "Wanna tell me why you look like somebody took apart your brain and then had no clue how to put it back together again? You hardly said two words during the meeting."

Troy glanced up and down the hall before focusing on a spot on the wall behind Blake's shoulder. "Sorry. I was a little...distracted."

"Ya think?" His partner steered Troy toward the elevator. "Let's go. Coffee's on me." When the brushed-steel doors glided open and Troy didn't follow, Blake braced his hand against the open door and glowered. "*Now,* Lindquist. And don't even think about giving me some crap about it being personal. When *personal* infringes on *business,* it becomes my business, too. So move your butt. Time's a wastin'."

Troy got into the elevator, leaning heavily against the paneled interior as it descended, his hands jammed into his chino pockets. "When did you turn into such a big pain in the can?"

"Consider this *payback* for peeling me off that bar stool a million years ago and talkin' me into this gig. You look like crap, man."

The elevator gently bumped to a stop on the ground floor. "And here I thought I was hiding it so well."

"Uh, no."

At ten in the morning, the Wendy's across the street was virtually deserted. Good thing. Not until they'd slid into a booth with their coffees, however, did Troy finally come clean. "You remember that conversation we had a few weeks ago, where you'd asked me if I'd done anything about Karleen?"

Blake's head shot up. "Yeah?"

"I may have left out a detail or two about what exactly happened."

"I thought you said *nothing* happened."

"I lied." Troy sipped his coffee, lifted his eyes to Blake's. Whose brows shot up.

"You *slept* with her?"

"Once. One of those brainless, it's-never-going-to-happen-again things. Going in, we both knew nothing was going to come of it, so there was nothing to talk *about*. Except…" He blew out a long breath. Blake immediately caught on.

"Oh, hell…she's not?"

"Oh, hell, she is. And yes, we took precautions. Such as they weren't."

Blake sagged back in his seat, shaking his head. "And I thought I was having a sucky day when the dog yakked up half a dead bird on the kitchen floor this morning. Hell, in your shoes, I'd be brain-dead, too."

Although Troy hadn't been all that hot on telling anyone—at least not yet—now that Blake knew, his lungs no longer felt as though they'd been sprayed with liquid nitrogen. "This wasn't exactly slotted into my schedule. Or Karleen's, obviously. Although she said she'd always wanted kids, so I don't think she's all that upset about the baby. The circumstances are something else again."

"I can imagine. And you?"

Troy felt his lips stretch into something resembling a smile. "Other than feeling like I'm hanging by two fingers off a cliff?"

Sympathy swam in Blake's deep brown eyes. "You've come through a lot worse."

"I know," he said on a sigh. "And at least this is fixable. If Karleen will ever stop being hardheaded enough to let me fix it."

"Meaning?"

"Meaning, at least I'm in the position to take care of both Karleen and this baby. But she's not having any of it."

"As in, marriage?"

"Well, yes. Except she's insisting we didn't know each other well enough or have enough in common to make a marriage work."

"Not that she has a valid point or anything."

"Especially since she's been married three times already."

"Dude."

"Yeah. And apparently there's some stuff about her mother… I'm still fuzzy on the details, but I'm gathering Karleen's got a real thing about trying to stand on her own two feet."

"There's a lot of that going around these days," Blake said dryly, referring, Troy supposed, to his own wife, Cass, who—despite being broke and, as it happened, also pregnant—had given Blake a similar song-and-dance before finally agreeing to remarry him last year. "In any case," the other man continued, "shotgun weddings went out of style with eight-track players."

"I know, I know. But this just feels so…shaky."

"To you. Obviously not to her."

"But that's what doesn't make sense. The whole thing about being a single mother's got her far more discombobulated than the pregnancy. And yet the more I tried to get across that she doesn't *have* to do this alone, the more she freaked."

"Because you're pressuring her, you numbskull."

"You don't even know her, Blake."

"No. But I know you. And I seriously doubt if this woman even comes close to you in the hardheaded department."

Troy frowned. "How can you say that? If anyone's learned to roll with the punches, it's me."

"Yeah, as long as you can choose which direction to roll. Nobody can ever accuse you of becoming paralyzed when stuff happens, that's for sure. But you do have this thing about taking charge. Being in control."

"And if I hadn't taken charge after Amy's death—"

"Not the same thing," Blake said gently. "You had two babies *depending* on you to take charge. And there's not a person who knows you who doesn't admire you for that. However, even you have to admit you used to be a lot more laid back about, well, everything than you are now. We never used to lock horns over stupid stuff the way we have in the past few years. But anymore…" He scrubbed a hand over his jaw, clearly weighing his words. "If things don't go your way, there is hell to pay."

Troy looked at him, stunned. "That's nuts."

"Unfortunately, it's not." Blake shrugged. "Doesn't bother me, partly because I know how to play you, partly because I understand what's causing it. But the word *micromanage* has come up among the staff, more than once."

"You're not serious."

"Yeah. I am."

When the fizzing inside his head stopped, Troy said, "I had no idea…. Why the hell didn't you say something?"

"Because I kept hoping it would blow over. That the old Troy would eventually kick to the curb this control freak who's taken over your body and we could get back to normal." His mouth thinned. "Unfortunately, it hasn't happened."

"Gee. Thanks for letting me act like a butt-head for four years."

Blake smiled. "It's not that bad. The staff doesn't hate you. They're just…wary of you."

"Yeah, that makes me feel better." Troy took a sip of his

coffee, but it tasted like crap. "Still. What's this got to do with Karleen?"

That apparently merited another several seconds of soul searching, or introspection, or something before Blake leaned forward again and said, "I'd kill for you, you know that. Nobody knows more than me what you've been through, or admired you more for the way you've handled it. Or understands how much of a monkey wrench this is, finding out some woman you barely know is having your kid. The thing is, though…it's not your problem to fix."

"And how exactly do you figure that?"

"Well, obviously you're partially responsible, I'm not saying that. But here's a news flash, buddy—women don't much like being given ultimatums. And they especially don't like feeling like somebody's threatening their autonomy. Doesn't matter what the motive is, or that you're only doing whatever it is 'for their own good.' That doesn't wash anymore. Trust me," he said with a wry smile, "I know whereof I speak."

Troy grunted. Blake downed the rest of his coffee, then said, "You want to regain control of the situation? Then like it or not you're gonna have to cede a lot of that control to her. Otherwise, you're gonna be majorly SOL." He checked his watch, then slid out of the booth. "We need to get back. I've got a conference call coming in from Denver at eleven."

When they got outside, though, Troy nodded toward their building as they headed back. "You think some damage control's in order?"

"Apologizing, you mean?" Blake shook his head. "Nah. Okay, so maybe your selective deafness has put a couple people's noses out of joint from time to time, but I don't think imminent mutiny's an issue. As long as you remember, a lot of these folks have been with us since the beginning. All they want is to be heard. And trusted. To know their opinion counts for something. The way it used to be before."

"Before everything went to hell in a handbasket?"

Blake swung open the heavy glass door leading to the lobby, striding to the elevator and punching the button. "And no matter hard you try, you can't stop those side trips from happening. None of us can."

"You do realize you're preaching to the choir?"

One side of Blake's mouth pulled up as the elevator door slid open. "You and Amy had a great marriage," Blake said as they entered. "I can't see you in some marriage of convenience, buddy, I just can't. Whatever the solution is, I seriously doubt that's it."

As Blake sauntered back to his office and that conference call, and Troy morosely trudged to his, he had to admit he couldn't see himself in some marriage of convenience, either. Which meant that Blake was right.

He hated when that happened.

Chapter Seven

Karleen could feel Troy's glare hot on her back as she handed over the clipboard to the gal behind the reception desk. The middle-aged woman scanned sheet after sheet of Karleen's medical history, then nodded.

"Okay, everything looks fine. How far along do you think you are?"

"Eight weeks and two days." Her face heated. "Exactly."

The woman made a notation on one of the papers. "And…this is your first pregnancy, right?"

"Yes."

"Any problems? Spotting? Nausea? Dizziness?"

"No spotting. I was sick some for a couple of weeks, but nothing too serious. Basically I feel fine. Except for wanting to eat every twenty minutes."

The woman chuckled. "That's about par for the course. And how will you be paying?"

"Oh, just a sec…" Karleen rummaged inside her purse for her wallet, then pulled out her insurance card. The woman entered her information into her computer, then told her to have a seat, they were running a little behind today but one of the midwives would see her shortly.

Karleen turned on her acrylic platform mules and clacked back to Troy. Who was easily the best-looking man in the room. Probably in the whole darn hospital. Any other guy in a sage-green polo and khakis would probably induce a serious yawn-fest. This guy, however…

What a mess, she thought, plopping back into the slightly worn padded chair beside him and shoving her hair behind her ear. *She* was such a mess, no less torn up inside about this—about him—than she'd been when all those sticks had turned pink a few weeks ago. How she could want to bop somebody upside the head who at the same time made her feel all tingly and warm inside, she had no idea. She just knew it wasn't good. Because she'd known plenty of men over the years who'd made her feel all tingly and warm (not to mention want to clobber them one), and it had never turned out well for either party.

Troy was leaning forward, his hands clasped between his knees, intently watching a young couple on the other side of the waiting room. They were giggling softly, the man's hand on the girl's enormous belly. Ohmigosh, she could see their baby kicking from way over here! Then the young man leaned over to kiss the woman on her cheek, and Karleen averted her gaze, embarrassed. Troy cleared his throat, like maybe he was embarrassed, too.

"Did the receptionist say how long it would be before they called you?"

"She didn't know. I got the feeling they were backed up, though, so it might be a bit of a wait."

Her eyes drifted to the couple again. The young man was apparently having an intense conversation with his unborn child. Karleen couldn't decide if it was sweet or silly. She glanced over at Troy, who had shifted his attention to another couple who'd just come in. They were holding hands, too, although the expectant mother didn't look to be any farther along than Karleen. Before she could stop it, a mixture of envy and irritation fisted in the pit of her stomach, at all these couples in love and so thrilled about their baby coming, that for all Troy insisted on being here with her today he might as well have been some stray she'd hauled in off the street.

It was perfectly obvious how uncomfortable he was. He'd insisted on picking her up—even though they could have easily met at the hospital, for heaven's sake—but they'd barely spoken on the way here. Considering the way her life had gone up to that point, didn't it just figure she'd now be sharing the most important event of her life with a virtual stranger?

Because despite getting together for dinner occasionally, or working with the boys in the garden, she couldn't say she felt any closer to him. Of course, having the twins around kinda killed any chance of real conversation. Then again, maybe Troy was doing that on purpose. Maybe, deep down, he wanted to keep his distance as much as she did, no matter what he'd said before. But since he'd clearly put out his own eye rather than go back on his word, here they were. With nothing really to say to each other.

She rearranged her long, ruffly skirt around her thighs, then slammed her purse on top of her lap. "If you need to get back to work, it's okay, I'll understand."

He gave her a funny look, his eyebrows dipped in that way men did when you might as well be speaking a foreign language. "Somehow, I think this takes precedence. And besides, how would you get home if I left?"

"They do have taxis in Albuquerque, you know."

He turned away, shaking his head. Karleen concentrated on breathing in and out, in and out, trying to steady her nerves. Then she crossed her legs, shaking her foot so hard her mule nearly fell off. Another coochie-coo couple came in. Great. She looked at her watch. Hard to believe they'd only been there fifteen minutes.

"They've got magazines," she said.

"Yeah. I see." Troy leaned over, picked up a battered *People* off the pile. Offered it to her. She shook her head.

He started flipping through the pages, still half turned away. Karleen glanced unseeing at the blur of photos, which all seemed to be of pregnant celebrities. She briefly entertained the idea of snatching the mag out of his hands and ripping it into shreds, instead deciding to search for something to talk about that would take their minds off why they were here.

"So. Whatever happened to getting the boys a puppy?"

He tossed the magazine back on the pile, picked up an old *Time* instead. "Turns out I'm getting them a baby brother or sister instead."

So much for steering the conversation into safer waters. "I'm not sure the boys'll be thrilled with the substitution."

To her relief, Troy smiled. A little. "Actually, I thought I'd hold off for a while. Until things settled down."

"And when might that be? When this one's outta college?"

"Good point." He got up, jingling change in his pocket. "I saw a soda machine down the hall. Want something?"

Karleen shook her head again, feeling like they had some game board between them, only one was playing checkers while the other was playing chess.

Two minutes later, he returned, Sprite in hand. He sat, popped off the top. Took a swallow. "So will you come with us? To pick one out?"

"One what?"

"A dog."

She blinked. "Why?"

"Because I thought it would be fun," he said wearily. "And I'm not sure I can handle a pair of excited four-year-olds and a puppy at the same time."

She fingered her purse strap. "Heck, I can't figure out how you handle the twins on your own. How come you don't have a nanny?"

"I did when they were younger. I'd have never survived juggling the business and two babies without help. But the woman I had didn't want to relocate to Albuquerque, and I thought, since the boys were older, anyway, they'd be fine in preschool. And I try to work at least one day a week at home. Still…" He tapped the can against his knee. Someone came out and called the very pregnant lady in for her check-up. Her S.O. helped haul her out of the chair; they both laughed. "I'm thinking seriously of looking for someone again. A housekeeper, at least."

"That makes sense."

Troy took a sip of his soda, then stared at the can like there was a secret code buried in the ingredients list. "Maybe we could work something out."

"About what?"

"To share whoever I end up hiring. You know, maybe you could leave the baby over at my house when you had to be out. Or the whoever could stay at your place while the boys were in preschool. And don't tell me you won't need anyone, not if you expect to keep working after the baby comes. I love my sons, but they definitely wore me to a frazzle during those first few months."

"Of *course* I expect to keep working! I love my job. And my clients count on me. I'd die if I had to give it up."

Although, truth be told, she had wondered how, exactly, she was going to handle that particular situation. How she'd be able to cart a baby and all the baby's stuff around with her when she was working, she had no idea. But neither was she thrilled with the idea of putting a newborn in day care.

"We could split the cost," she said.

She caught the head shake. And the smile. "Whatever."

"In any case, we don't have to make a decision this very minute."

Naturally, he frowned at her. Something he did way too much, far as she was concerned. "You don't want to put it off too long, either."

Somehow, Karleen held in her sigh. And the tears. Sometimes she felt like she was going to go under from all the pressure, to the point where it was beginning to seriously annoy her that she'd hardly had five minutes to even enjoy being pregnant. But the last thing she wanted was for Troy to think she was one of those moody, emotional preggos—never mind that she'd start blubbering these days over absolutely nothing—especially if she was supposed to be convincing him how strong she was. And she *was* strong. She was doing fine. She just cried a lot, was all.

Karleen also couldn't help feeling bad that this pregnancy was obviously contributing to *his* stress. She wouldn't dream of saying that to him, though. He'd jump right down her throat.

She picked up an *American Baby* off the pile on the

table beside her and started doing some aimless leafing of her own, trying to relax. Trying desperately not to dwell on everything that might be wrong, could go wrong still. Or to let her anxiety show. Because she didn't want Troy to think she was a worrywort, either. But she'd sure be a lot happier right now if it was Joanna sitting next to her instead of this man who for sure had to feel trapped.

A pair of midwives started a conversation on the other side of the room. Karleen caught Troy's mild glare. Well, maybe *glare* was too strong a word. A look of skepticism, maybe. Another bone of contention.

"You still mad because I decided to use midwives instead of a doctor?" she said, pretending to be more interested in some article on getting your baby to sleep through the night than his answer.

"I was never mad, Karleen. Just uncomfortable."

"And I told you, it's not like I'm goin' out in the woods by myself to birth this baby. I'm having it right here in the hospital, it's perfectly safe—"

Too late, she heard the words come out of her mouth. Her face on fire, she turned away. "I can't believe I said that, I am *so* sorry."

Troy reached over and took her hand, startling the daylights out of her. Because other than when they'd made this baby, and his holding her when she'd told him *about* the baby, they never touched. Which was fine with her. Things were complicated enough without letting those old hormones loose all over again.

But when his hand tightened around hers, all warm and strong, it suddenly hit her how scared *he* must be. Even more than her, probably. Not for her, she didn't think, since there wasn't any real attachment between them. And anyway, the odds of lightning striking twice were slim to none, which she was sure he knew. Still, it was like flying, she imagined—no matter what people said, the fact was that occasionally planes crashed.

Sympathy rushed through her, so strong she had to resist the impulse to bring their linked hands to her cheek, to kiss his knuckles in a way meant to reassure him that they were in this together. But she didn't, because there would have been no way to explain her actions that would have made sense to anybody. Given their situation, it wouldn't have been appropriate. So all she did was briefly squeeze his hand before extricating her own.

Because sitting around holding hands like they were a real couple wasn't appropriate, either.

Troy glanced over at Karleen as they walked back to his car after the appointment, still undecided about her outfit— a long, gauzy skirt that sat slightly below her waist and a low-cut, stretchy top that ended somewhat above it, both embellished with lots of sparkly stuff. A silver clip held back her hair, all the more to show off the flashing water-falls of silver and copper disks dangling from her ears.

Give the woman a crystal ball and the image would be complete.

"So," he said, opening her door for her, ignoring the eye-roll in response. "That went well, don't you think?"

Karleen gathered up her skirt and slid inside, rearranging everything around her knees. "I guess."

Troy shut the door, went around to his side. Marshaled what few forces he had left. Their conversations reminded him of his first car—the old Chevy would chug along okay for a while, only to give out without warning and at the most inopportune times. He slid in behind the wheel. "Is something wrong?"

She stopped fussing with her skirt and frowned at him. "What are you talking about?"

"You've hardly said a dozen words since we left the clinic."

Over her rhinestone-studded sunglasses, her brows lifted. "Like you've been such a chatterbox."

"I was only taking my cue from you."

Her lips smushed together, she faced forward, plopping her huge coppery purse on her lap. "So maybe I don't feel like talking right now. Don't take it personally."

He put the car in gear and backed out of the parking space. "I'm not sure how else to take it."

"Well, don't. I've just got some stuff to work through in my own head about all of this, that's all. It's got nothing to do with you."

"And if it weren't for me, you wouldn't have 'all of this' to work *through*." He cut his eyes over in time to see one side of her mouth tick. "Right?"

They pulled out into traffic. She cracked open her window. "You decided when you might tell the boys?"

"Is that what's worrying you?"

"Nothing's *worrying* me, Troy, honestly. But no, that's not what I was thinking about. It just occurred to me, is all."

"I haven't decided yet. Probably not until it's a lot closer to…to the due date. Or at least until you're showing. Two weeks is like two years to a four-year-old. Seven months would be incomprehensible." He hesitated. "I will have to tell my parents, though, when they come next month."

"At least that's one thing I don't have to deal with," she said on a sigh. "Only relative I've got is my aunt Inky, and frankly I don't much care what she thinks one way or the other about anything I do."

"Inky?"

"Ingrid. I couldn't say it when I was little and Inky stuck. She's my mother's younger sister. We don't communicate all that often except for when she needs to hit me up for a 'loan.'" She frowned when he went east instead of west. "Where are we going?"

"Shopping. When was the last time you saw your aunt?"

"I don't know," she said irritably, "a few years ago. And what do you mean, shopping? For what?"

"Nursery stuff."

"No, we're not."

"Dammit, Karleen, if this is another one of your I'm-paying-my-own-way deals—"

"No, it's not that." Then he caught her cocking her head. "You're still pissed about me taking care of my own medical bills, aren't you?"

She had him there. Oddly enough, Troy would have thought that four years of butt-, nose- and tear-wiping, of singing tiny boys to sleep or assuaging their fears would be more than sufficient to send Macho Man packing. And yet, damned if watching Karleen make all her own financial arrangements with the hospital didn't send the old male ego into a tailspin.

"I'm The Guy," he said. "I'm supposed to take care of this stuff."

"Says who?"

"Says my DNA encoding."

"Well, tell your DNA encoding to get over it. It's like I told you, I've been paying for health insurance for years. They owe me. And anyway, if this was appendicitis or somethin', you wouldn't be offering to pay, would you?"

"The next time I give someone *else* appendicitis, I'll let

you know. But what if you *hadn't* had insurance? What then?"

A pause. "I suppose that would've been different."

"Why?"

"It just would've, okay? Oh, for heaven's sake—I'm not going to risk my baby's safety for my own pride, if that's what you're worried about. But why should I accept your help if I don't need it…oh, shoot."

The tinny, upbeat tune got louder—and more familiar—when she wrenched open her purse and dug out her cell phone. Troy chuckled. "I don't believe it. 'Hard Headed Woman'?"

"Let me guess," she said, flipping open the phone. "You've got somethin' against Elvis, too…. Hello?"

"Nope. I'm crazy about Elvis."

He caught the brief, shocked look before her whole face lit up. "Hey, Flo! How are you?…" Then her forehead crimped. "Oh, I'm so sorry…. What'd the doctor say? Uh-huh… Well, that doesn't sound too bad. You're taking your meds like he told you?… Good. Of course I can do that…. No, honey, it's no problem at all…. Hold on."

Karleen rummaged in her purse again, pulling out a small pad and a fat red pen. "What do you need? Uh-huh, uh-huh…" She alternately scribbled and "uh-huhed" for another few seconds, then checked her watch. "I'm not sure, I'm not too far away, but somebody else is driving, I'd have to get back to my house first, to get my car…. What?" she said, frowning, when Troy poked her. "Hold on a sec, sugar," she said, then lobbed another "What?" to Troy.

"Emergency?"

She did an "eh" waggle with her free hand. "Flo used to be my neighbor, she's in her eighties, I sometimes run errands for her when her arthritis acts up—"

"Tell her we'll be there soon."

"I can't ask you—"

"Karleen. For God's sake."

She stared at him for a second or two, then said into her phone, "We'll stop by the store, then, and I guess we'll see you in about a half hour?…I swear, it's no problem. You sit tight, honey, and I'll be there in two shakes."

Two (or maybe three) shakes later, they drove up in front of a drab little box of a house—flat roof, chalky stucco, black ornamental shutters—in a neighborhood a half inch away from seedy. Still, early roses bloomed profusely on a handful of hardy bushes standing sentry under a front window, while clusters of happy-faced pansies crowded whiskey-barrel planters bordering the cracked driveway.

"Flo?" Karleen called when they reached the entrance, shifting several Albertsons bags to one hand to rap on the curlicued metal screen door. "It's me, sugar."

"I'm comin', I'm comin'," Troy heard from the other side, seconds before the door swung open to an explosion of vibrant tropical flowers on a loose dress, from which rose a gleaming, beaming face the color of bittersweet chocolate. Even leaning on a four-pronged cane, the thin woman gave Karleen a long, fierce hug, before letting go to smile even more broadly at Troy. "And who is this *fine*-looking young man?"

Karleen did the honors—not surprisingly, Troy was introduced as "my neighbor"—then they carted Flo's groceries inside and back to her bright yellow, excessively tidy kitchen. Cats of all colors, shapes and sizes milled about, watching the proceedings with a detached curiosity.

"Can I offer you folks something to drink? All I have is ice water, I'm afraid."

"Thanks, Flo, but we can't stay—"

"Water would be fine, Mrs. Johnson," Troy said. "But you sit. Just tell me where the glasses are and I'll get them."

"My, my…good-lookin' and a gentleman to boot," the old woman said on a laugh. Her eyes shifted to Karleen, who was busy unloading the groceries and putting them away. "Child, you can leave all that, I'll get aroun' to it eventually. Just bring me my pocketbook from the living room so I can pay you. You got the receipt? And what's that you got in your hand? Now you know I didn't ask for any ice cream."

"No, you didn't," Karleen said, holding out the pint of premium AIS Nutter-Butter Brickle. "But I know this is your favorite flavor, so it's my treat. You want some right now?"

A pleased, little-girl smile stretched the old woman's mouth. "Well, I don't suppose I'd turn it down if it was here in front of me."

Grinning himself, Troy pulled down an ice-cream dish from beside the glasses and handed it to Karleen, who'd already gotten a spoon from the drawer. A big ginger tom hopped up on a vacant kitchen chair, mewing nonstop. Her dish of ice cream clutched protectively to her sunken chest, Flo chuckled, low in her throat. "This isn't for you, you big beggar, and you know it."

Except she held out the ice cream-coated spoon to the cat, anyway.

For the better part of the next twenty minutes, Troy hung back, leaning against the counter as he watched the mutually affectionate exchanges between the two women. From their conversation, he pieced together the essentials, mainly that Flo had been there for Karleen off and on during her teenaged years, and that Karleen clearly adored her for it.

Eventually, though, Karleen stood, making noises about needing to get going. "But if you need me to take you to the doctor or anything…?"

"No, lamb, thank you, I'm fine."

"And what about your swamp cooler? You got it goin' yet?"

Flo chuckled. "You worry too much, you know that? The man across the street said he'd come over on Sunday and turn it on for me, so I'm covered."

Finally satisfied that Flo's needs were all met, at least for the moment, Karleen gave her another big hug—Flo not missing the chance to tell Troy to stop by again, anytime—and then they were back in the car, heading home, and it occurred to Troy that Karleen never had brought the old woman her purse so she could reimburse her.

"I didn't forget," she said. Then, after a couple of beats, she added, "Considering the number of times Flo fed me when my mother 'forgot,' the least I can do is buy the old gal groceries, now and again."

Troy waited out the flush of shame, for his initial—and less than complimentary—snap judgment of the woman sitting beside him. Because maybe Karleen's nails were glued on and her hair was bleached (this, he knew first-hand) and her breasts not really a C-cup, but there was nothing even remotely fake about her heart.

"…But since it about kills her to let me do stuff for her," she was saying, "I have to pull fast ones from time to time." When he chuckled, she squeezed shut her eyes and let her head fall back against the rest. "Don't say it."

"What? That it's okay for you to hoodwink an old woman into letting you help her, but it's not okay for me to help you?"

"It's not the same thing."

Troy released a sigh. "Look, Karleen, I know this whole situation is crazy, but I'm getting really tired of being shut out."

Her chin snapped down. "I am not shutting you out!"

"Then what would you call it?"

"Saving my skin."

"From *what,* for God's sake?"

She faced front again. "You wouldn't understand."

Troy scratched his eyebrow, then dropped his hand back on the steering wheel. "Here's the thing, honey—I can't help being protective, anymore than you can help wanting to help Flo. That's just who I am. That doesn't mean I think you're weak or helpless or incapable of making your own decisions. Obviously you got along fine before you met me, so—"

"See, that's where you're wrong," she said. When he frowned at her, she added, "Yeah, for the past few years, I've been doing okay, but..." She leaned her head in her hand. "It wasn't always like that. *I* wasn't always like that."

"At the risk of being shot down again...care to explain?"

"It's a long, boring story."

"We've got a long, boring ride ahead of us."

Two, three blocks passed before she finally said, "None of the guys I married were bad men. Although the first wasn't a man at all, seeing as he wasn't but nineteen when we drove to Vegas and got married. I was eighteen, Mama had just died, and frankly, I felt like I'd been tossed out of an airplane with no parachute. And Ross caught me. Barely. Hung on for all of six months, too, until we both realized what a dumb thing we'd done.

"Fast forward a couple of years, a few dead-end jobs, a few dead-end relationships, to Jasper. I was twenty-one by then. He was older. A lot older, actually. He was one of the regulars at the restaurant where I was waitressing at the time. His wife had left him a year or so before, and he was lookin' for somebody he could take care of." Her shoulders bumped. "Since I was looking for somebody to take care of me, it looked like a good thing. Except he'd neglected to tell me *why* his wife had left him. And unfortunately, I'm not real big on sharin' my underwear."

"Ouch."

"Not that I'm judgmental or anything—each to his own, I always say—but once you see a guy wearing the Victoria's Secret thong he gave *you* for Valentine's Day…" Karleen shook her head as Troy thought, *Yeah, thanks for the image.* "Anyway, then I met Nate. And I thought, okay, third time's the charm, right? A fellow Texan, owns a couple of restaurants here and up in Santa Fe, not exactly hurting financially. And I tried, I really did, to be a good wife. But there again, it didn't work. We just…I don't know. Got bored with each other or something. I was certainly far better off than I'd ever had before, but something crucial was still missing. Long story short…I couldn't make him happy."

Troy frowned. "Why do you assume it was up to you to make *him* happy?"

"Well, I suppose that's the point, isn't it? That we were askin' something of each other that wasn't fair to ask. However, when *that* marriage failed, I finally took a long, hard look at myself, and I realized that'd been the problem all along, that I'd been looking for fulfillment or whatever you want to call it outside of myself. So I set out to correct that little fault. And here I am, seven years later, an independent woman with a career and a retirement account and my own house—or will be, soon as I finish payin' off Nate—and yes, my own insurance, and at long last I'm proud of who I am." She looked at him. "And that's a *real* good feeling."

Troy remembered the first time the accountant had shown them a P&L statement that showed them in the black, and he smiled. "Yeah. It is." A pause. "You keep in touch with your exes?"

"I still see Nate on occasion. We stayed friends, which is nice. I even went to his wedding a few years back. He got the right woman, this time. The others? No. Don't see much point."

"Did you love any of them?"

"You know, I ask myself that a lot. And the answer is…I don't know. I suppose I thought I did, at the time. I certainly *wanted* to. But looking back, I'm not sure I really knew what my feelings were. Although I will say, when each of my marriages ended? I felt a lot more disappointed than hurt. At the same time, I felt like I'd been sprung from prison. A prison of my own making, to be sure, but a prison all the same.

"It's like…I lose my sense of balance whenever I'm in a relationship. Just like my mama did. Instead of standing on our own two feet, we lean. And then when things go bad, we fall. And things always go bad, Troy. Always."

"Is that a warning?" he said quietly.

"No. It's an explanation. So now you know."

What he knew was that she was shortchanging herself. What he *knew* was that this was a big-hearted woman who'd forgotten to include herself on her to-do list. In the way that most mattered, at least.

"I'm buying the nursery furniture, honey," he said

quietly, earning him a frown. "You can pick out anything you like, but it's gonna be my signature on the credit-card slip."

"Boy, you really do have this thing about being in charge, don't you?"

"I have this thing about carrying my share of the load. Which I can't seem to do with you without bullying you into it. So we're going to do some role playing. I'm you. You're Flo. I'm being the good guy whether you like it or not."

That actually got a little laugh. "I never said you couldn't buy the nursery furniture, Troy." She looked back out the windshield. "Just not today."

Her sudden acquiescence threw him for a second, until his brain caught up to the last three words. "What's wrong with today?"

A long moment of silence preceded "It's bad luck to get everything ready too early."

Yo, her fear said. *Recognize me?*

All too well. Especially considering how close it had come to overwhelming him in the waiting room. Not that he should have been surprised. After all, it had taken nearly two years before he could even watch a movie or TV show about a woman giving birth, another year after that before the sight of a heavily pregnant woman didn't short out his brain. The last thing Karleen needed, however, was to pick up on his residual anxiety.

"Okay, we won't buy anything until you're ready. But…" He smiled over at her. "Is it bad luck to go looking?"

"It's very tempting," she said softly. "Thank you. But I'm not ready yet. Looking at cribs and changing tables and such… It makes it all so *real.*"

"And the sonogram didn't?"

"The peach pit with the heartbeat, you mean?" she said,

but her hand went to her still-flat belly. He got a sudden flash of the kind of clothes she'd wear as the pregnancy progressed. Somehow, he doubted he'd be seeing a bunch of cute little dresses that tied in the back.

Like Amy had worn.

"Could we just go on home?" she asked.

"Sure," he said, nudging aside the slight disappointment at not being able to spend a little more time with her. Especially now that they were actually talking to each other. Like a showy flower, the more she opened up, the richer the color inside and the sweeter the fragrance. "You care if we pick up the boys first?"

"No, of course not. And by the way, bubba... It didn't escape my attention that you didn't let on to Flo that the ice cream was yours."

"I know," he said, and she shook her head.

They rode the rest of the way in silence, Karleen fiddling with one of the stones on her skirt as she stared straight ahead, and it occurred to Troy how dull and staid he was, next to her. How ordinary. Like bologna on white bread.

He picked up the boys, who were beside themselves at being sprung early. After they'd scrambled into their car seats and Troy had buckled them in, he slid behind the wheel, then glanced in the rearview mirror and said, "How'd you guys like to go looking for a dog this weekend?"

"Jeez, *finally*," Grady said, but Scotty said, "C'n Karleen come, too?"

Troy looked over, one eyebrow crooked. She laughed. "I've got a couple of appointments on Saturday morning, but I suppose I could go in the afternoon. Or Sunday. Oh, my God... What landed in your driveway?"

Troy looked up, blinking in the glare of afternoon sun on

the unbelievably vast expanse of white obliterating his house.

"Good Lord," he said, pulling up behind the RV. "It's bigger than my first apartment. What on earth—?"

The door to the thing swung open and out popped his mother, arms outstretched.

"Gramma!" both boys cried, as his mother yelled, "Surprise!"

Indeed.

Chapter Eight

For the most part, Karleen was a big believer in the theory that, if you took the time to scratch beneath the surface, there was more to most folks than was often apparent when you first met them. Like Joanna's mother Glynnie, for instance, who didn't have nearly the rod up her butt you might think.

Troy's mother, however…

The woman had clearly taken one look at Karleen and thought, *I don't think so.* Something about the way the light had gone out of those bright blue eyes, how her smile had gone all hard-edged when Troy had introduced them. Like she knew it wasn't right to judge, but she was doing it anyway.

And under other, normal circumstances, Karleen probably wouldn't have cared one way or the other what some midwestern matron thought of her, having long since accepted the simple fact that, sometimes, people just didn't click. But seeing as how Karleen was carrying the woman's grandchild, it wasn't looking too good for their never having to lay eyes on each other again. So Karleen was willing to do her best to make things work between them.

But honestly. It was everything Karleen could do not to park her hands on her hips and say, "Do I look like a slut, or what?" since clearly Eleanor Lindquist, with her khaki camp shirt neatly tucked into her white cotton pants, her short beige hair and dull coral lipstick and little white Keds, had decided exactly that. Karleen could only imagine what her reaction would be when she discovered the truth. Which, God willing, wouldn't be until after Karleen was safely back in her own house, but she wasn't banking on that.

Naturally, Troy had apologized to Karleen up one side and down the other, as soon as they'd pinched out ten seconds alone when the boys had dragged Gramma and Gampa off to see their room. Karleen's guess was that he was fit to be tied, having his parents show up a month early, without warning, before he'd figured out how to tell them about their new grandchild. Which, she pointed out, wasn't exactly their fault, only then he got miffed at *her,* which she did not take personally. After all, she wasn't the one who'd gone and knocked up a gal from the wrong rung of the ladder.

And anyway, Karleen couldn't really blame Troy's mother for her attitude. In the other woman's shoes, she'd probably assume Karleen was a gold digger, too. In her *own* shoes, she imagined she was going to be every bit as bad with her own child. Maybe even worse, considering some of the boneheaded stunts Karleen herself had pulled over the years.

It wasn't that Eleanor had been rude to her or anything—

in fact, she was the one who'd insisted Karleen stay for dinner, which Karleen figured she'd probably better do, considering the situation. Still, *awkward* didn't even begin to describe the evening. If it hadn't been for the twins being beside themselves with excitement and thus remaining the center of attention all through the meal, Karleen wasn't sure how she—or Troy—would have survived.

So thank God for Troy's daddy—Gus—a gentle soul with a slow grin and kind gray eyes. Eleanor having shooed everybody—except Troy—out of the kitchen, Karleen and Gus now sat out on Troy's back deck, watching the boys playing hide-and-seek with a pair of flashlights in the dying light, like a couple of lightning bugs with Darth Vader complexes. Karleen had kicked off her shoes to sit barefoot on the steps, her back propped against the deck railing; Gus had commandeered a large wooden rocker, nursing a can of diet root beer from the case the Lindquists had brought with them. Not that she'd ever feel like she belonged, or could be a real part of Troy's family, but if it hadn't been for the baby business Karleen might've actually felt comfortable in the tall, slender man's company.

"So. You a native of Albuquerque?" he asked in his broad, flat accent.

"No, sir. I'm from Texas, originally."

"Ah. That would account for the accent."

Gentleness and humor laced the older man's words. Much like his son's, Karleen realized. "I guess, even though I've lived here for nearly twenty-five years. But you know what they say—you can take the tumbleweed out of Texas, but you can't take Texas out of the tumbleweed."

"Karleen, Gampa!" Grady called, his grin barely visible in the waning light. "Look what I can do!"

His cartwheel was executed with a lot more enthusiasm than skill, but Karleen laughed and clapped, anyway. Naturally, Scotty had to try, too, with even more bent elbows and knees than his brother. And Karleen laughed again, which of course spurred the boys to show off their new trick, over and over, tumbling like puppies in the patch of cool, soft grass. For weeks, she'd fought not to let them into her heart, at least not all the way. But this afternoon, when they'd scrambled into the car and thrown their arms around her neck, and it had finally, truly struck her that they were going to be her baby's big brothers, no matter what, she'd taken a deep breath and let go.

Too bad she didn't dare do the same thing with their father.

Gus chuckled softly when the twins cartwheeled right smack into each other, resulting in a tangle of little boys and a chorus of "Ows!" and much head rubbing.

"Y'all okay?" Karleen called out, and Scotty came over to her for a hug, palming his head. She kissed the boo-boo and gave him a squeeze, which she felt all the way to her own heart. Grady, however, was not about to cry, no matter how much his lower lip trembled. So she got up and went over to him, giving him a hug, anyway. Which he duly returned.

"The boys certainly seem to have taken to you," Troy's father said when she returned to the deck. "And you to them."

Seated again, she shrugged, hugging her knees. "I like little boys. It's when they get big that's the problem."

Gus laughed softly. "It's hard on them, not having a mother."

Karleen frowned. "I thought they never knew Amy?"

"I don't mean Amy, specifically. Oh, Troy had that housekeeper for a while, and she was okay, but it's not the same thing."

After a long, somewhat jittery pause, Karleen said,

"Please tell me you're not one of those people hell-bent on fixing up your son for the sake of your grandkids."

A grin preceded "Not just for the sake of the boys, no. Although from what I've seen I think you'd be good for them." He paused. "Troy, too."

Karleen felt her face heat. "Because I like his kids?" she said, playing dumb.

Even in the near dark, she could feel the older man's eyes calmly assessing her. Then he took a swallow of his root beer. None of the family drank, from what she could tell. Well, heck, what was one more nail in the coffin?

"Whoever you think you're fooling about your relationship with my son," he said, "it sure as hell isn't me."

"Sorry to disappoint you," Karleen said. With remarkable calm, she thought, considering how badly her stomach was churning. "But Troy and I are a non-item." Her mouth twisted. "And I think it's pretty safe to assume your wife would blow a gasket if we *weren't.*"

Another chuckle. "Amazing, the way that woman can make her opinions known without saying a single word. But don't let her get to you. Her bark's a lot worse than her bite."

"It's not her bark I'm worried about, it's her growl."

"And the way the hair raises on the back of her neck?"

"That, too."

"So. You don't like Troy?"

Karleen shot a mildly annoyed glance in the older man's direction. "Of course I *like* Troy. What's not to like? But the idea of us together is downright laughable."

"Why? Because you're nothing like his first wife?"

"No, because I'm nothing like *him.* Or any of you, for that matter."

There. She'd said it. Let 'em deal.

"I may not say much," Gus said after a moment, "but I

consider myself a keen observer of my fellow man." He tapped the outer corner of one eye. "You're right, you're not a thing like the twins' mother. Or us, maybe. But Troy looks at you as though he'd happily flatten anyone who dared to hurt you." Gus smiled. "Including his own mother, if necessary."

Now her face positively flamed. "No offense, Gus, but I think maybe you're seein' what you want to see. Not what's really there."

"No offense right back, young lady," Gus said mildly, "but there's not a damn thing wrong with my eyesight. Not these days, at least—"

"Karleen! Karleen!" Flashlight beams darting drunkenly over the lawn as they ran, the boys barreled across the yard, Scotty throwing himself across her thighs. She ruffled his blond waves, releasing the little boy perfume of grass and dirt and the slightest hint of watermelon shampoo. "There's all these little green things in the garden, you c'n see 'em real good with the flashlights! Come look!" he said, pulling her to her feet.

"Gampa, too!" Grady put in, stomping up onto the deck to pull his grandfather out of the chair. "Our punkins are coming up!"

Gus huffed and puffed, pretending to have great difficulty in getting out of the chair, only to then stand so quickly in response to the boys' tugging that they both landed on their butts, and Karleen laughed and her hand went automatically to her tummy, only by the time she realized it she caught Gus's lifted eyebrow.

Oh, hell.

"Why do I get the feeling," Troy's father said in a low voice as they walked across the yard, "that you're growing something this summer besides pumpkins?" When she didn't say anything, he put his arm around her shoulder and gave her a brief hug, and she very nearly dissolved into tears right there and then.

Although he couldn't hear his father's and Karleen's conversation for his mother's virtually nonstop prattle, Troy had been watching Karleen with his children through the kitchen window as he'd loaded the dishwasher, and the thought had come, *You do not want to lose this woman.*

"She's pregnant, isn't she?"

Dishwasher soap squirted everywhere as Troy's head jerked around to his mother. Or rather, his mother's back, since she was shoving leftovers into the refrigerator. Between the boys and Eleanor, Karleen had had virtually no choice about staying for dinner, although she'd looked as though she'd rather trek across Siberia in January— naked—than make small talk with his parents.

Right now, he'd join her. In Siberia, naked, whatever.

"Why on earth would you think that?" he said, stalling.

"Troy. Please. She was in the bathroom constantly, she ate as though she didn't know where her next meal was coming from and her breasts are positively *enormous.* Call it an educated guess."

Neatly dodging the breast comment, Troy shut the dishwasher door and started the cycle, then turned to face the music. And his mother's far-too-astute gaze. Her demeanor wasn't severe, exactly. Just no-nonsense. After everything she'd been through, he couldn't blame her.

"Yes. She is."

"Is it yours?"

He tried a smile. "Got it in one."

Her entire body seemed to sag. "Oh, Troy, honey… What were you *thinking?*"

"What I was thinking is frankly none of your business. Which is pretty much what I'm thinking now, actually."

His mother's mouth tightened. "There's no need to be insolent."

"Then how about not acting like I'm a teenager who knocked up his sixteen-year-old girlfriend?"

"Troy. Honestly." She blew out a breath. "Are you…going to marry her?"

"Not that you're judging her or anything."

Twin coins of color bloomed on his mother's cheeks. "She's nice enough, I'm sure. She's just not…" She waved one hand.

"Amy?"

"Oh, honey." Tears shone in Eleanor's eyes. "Amy was so perfect for you, you know your father and I both loved her from the moment we met her. What on earth could you possibly have in common with this woman?"

"It's okay, Mom. We're not getting married."

"Oh, thank God," his mother said on a gush of air.

"Don't thank God, thank Karleen. Since she turned me down."

Relief turned to renewed horror. "You're not serious. You actually asked her to be your wife?"

"Considering she's carrying my child, it seemed the polite thing to do."

His mother gawked at him. "Don't tell me this pregnancy was actually *planned?*"

"No," Troy said quietly. "It wasn't. And since neither one of us is quite used to the idea yet, either, I'd appreciate it if you'd back off for a minute."

"I'm sorry," his mother said curtly. "I mean, really,

forgive me for being concerned. You lay this bombshell on me and then don't expect me to react? Especially after everything we went through with your father—"

"Mom," he said wearily. "Enough."

She turned back to the island, yanking off a length of plastic wrap to cover the leftover sautéed vegetables. "So when were you planning on telling us?"

"When we were ready. Not my fault you guys got bitten by the RV bug and showed up early."

His mother tossed him a glance over her shoulder, the corners of her mouth barely turned up. "And ruined the surprise?"

"Something like that, yeah."

Once the vegetables had been put away, she said, "I'm surprised Karleen didn't…you know. Take care of things. Nobody has to have a baby they don't want these days."

Troy crossed his arms. "Who says nobody wants this baby?"

After several seconds of locked gazes, his mother looked away. "I can't believe I'm hearing this."

"Well, believe it. And besides, Karleen went through three marriages without getting pregnant—"

"Did you say *three* marriages? Oh, dear God."

"It's okay, I'm thinking the boy right out of high school and the cross-dresser didn't count."

"Oh, dear *God*."

"Mom, I know this is a shock. It was for me, too. And Karleen. But what can I say? Stuff happens. You either cope, or go under. So maybe the situation isn't exactly ideal—"

"Ideal?" his mother practically shrieked. "For God's sake, Troy, this is nothing but some, some romantic *fantasy!* You cannot possibly make a *life* with that woman—!"

"Oh…sorry," Karleen said behind them, and Troy spun around. Her face pale, she glanced from him to his mother and back again. "I was about to ask if you wanted me to get the boys ready for bed. But I can see I'm not needed so I'll just be getting on back to my place—"

"Karleen—"

"It's okay, Troy," she said, backing out of the kitchen, her smile breaking his heart. "She's not sayin' anything I haven't already said. Seems your mother and I are actually on the same side. Right, Mrs. Lindquist?"

"Where are you going?" his mother called after him as he strode to the door.

Troy wheeled on her, his throat working overtime. "Dammit, Mom, I love you, you know that. But right now I don't like you very much. Whether it makes any sense to you or not, I'd like nothing more than to make a life with *that woman!* So if you don't mind, I'm going to see if I can apologize for my mother's brain having apparently fallen out of the RV somewhere along I-25!"

Karleen had barely shut her front door behind her when she heard Troy knocking on it like some kind of fool, calling her name over and over, banging and banging and banging until she feared for his hand.

She yanked the door open, fending off his next blow. "In case you missed it, I had the doorbell fixed weeks ago."

"I'm sorry," he said.

"For putting dents in my door?"

"Better your door than my mother. Which probably isn't the best way to treat someone who was in labor with you for twenty-six hours." When Karleen winced, he said, "I weighed eleven pounds at birth."

"Get *out*."

"No, actually, I'd like to come in."

"I'm really tired, Troy—"

"Just for a minute."

She backed up and let him pass, remaining by her door as he walked into her living room, sinking onto the edge of her sofa. "I apologize," he said.

"For what?"

"My mother being an ass?"

"That's a horrible thing for a son to say about his mama."

"Be that as it may." He shoved his hand through his hair. "There's a reason I went out of state for college. And never went back."

"Don't apologize for your mother. She's only lookin' out for your best interests, like any other mother would. Well, almost any other mother. Mine never quite caught on to that concept. So count your blessings."

Troy blew air through his nose, then said, "She guessed, by the way. That you're pregnant."

"Yeah, I figured that's what must've brought all of that on. I gather she didn't exactly take the news well."

"You could say."

"She's right, Troy. About us. Like I said, she and I are on the same side in this. As opposed to your father," she said on a sigh. "Who guessed, too, by the way. Don't ask me how. No, actually, I take that back—he probably figured there was only one reason why you and I would have anything to do with each other."

Troy frowned up at her. "That's a little harsh, don't you think?"

"Maybe. But it's true. I like your daddy, by the way. You take after him."

"Thank you. But let's get something straight right now—my wanting to hang out with you has a lot less to do with this baby than you might think."

"I wasn't talking about the baby. I was talkin' about sex."

"I know you were," he said. "But it's more than that, too. Which I think would be perfectly clear considering that we only *had* sex once."

"Oh, but what a once it was," she said lightly, only to feel everything freeze inside when his eyes bore into hers.

"News flash, honey—I've moved past *like*. In fact, at the rate I'm going, I'll have zipped right past *have strong feelings for* by next week."

Her ears ringing, Karleen watched Troy intently for several seconds, then pointed toward the kitchen. "I'm about to die of thirst," she said, walking away. "You want anything?"

Even though he said, "No," he followed her to the kitchen, then through to the patio doors looking out over the backyard as she pulled a chilled bottle of fruit juice out of the fridge. She twisted off the bottle cap, taking a sip as she cast a glance at those strong, go-ahead-and-burden-me shoulders.

"That's some dangerous road you're lookin' to go down, buddy," she said to his back. "Which I think your mother just made crystal clear."

She saw one corner of his mouth lift. "My mother wanted me to be a lawyer, but she didn't get her way with that one, either. I think I was in middle school the last time she had a say in who I associated with."

"Or got pregnant?" she said with a small smile.

"That, either." He nodded toward the outside. "Why do you keep the pool lights on if it's covered?"

Karleen frowned at his subject switch, but shrugged. "I feel better with them on, that's all. Somehow knowing there's a great big hole in the ground…" She shuddered.

"Did you ever use it?"

"Oh, all the time. I love to swim. But like I said, it got to be too much of a hassle to keep it up."

"Because you can't afford it."

She stiffened. "That's not—"

"True?" He looked at her, a mixture of annoyance and kindness in his eyes. "Karleen. I'm not blind. Your car is ancient, your stucco's flaking off in places, you don't use your pool. Why won't you just admit that money's an issue?"

Over in her corner, Britney came to; a second later, her wheel started whirring. Karleen took another swallow of her juice, then went over to give the hamster her nightly snack. "Okay, so I'm not rolling in it like *some* people I know. And I know the house needs to be re-stuccoed, I'm workin' up to it. But the pool's a luxury. And the car's still running, so…" Hamster nuggets rained onto the cedar shavings; Britney scurried over to play Stuff the Pouch. "So I'm careful with my money. Since when is that a crime? I could get a new car, or fix the pool…or sock money away for my old age. I choose plan B."

Several beats passed before Troy said, "I'm calling a pool service tomorrow." When she pivoted, her mouth open, he held up a hand, traffic-cop fashion. "It'll be good exercise while you're pregnant, so no argument. And the service will handle all the maintenance so you won't even have to think about it."

Pride warred with gratitude inside her head. Gratitude won out. "Thank you," she said.

"You're welcome. Of course, this means the boys and I will be over here to swim regularly."

"How did I know there'd be a catch?"

"Ah, but there'll also be a pool boy."

Karleen clipped shut the hamster food bag, then brushed the crumbs from her fingers. "Your mother will have a cow."

"This has nothing to do with my mother. A small but crucial point that seems to be eluding you."

"I bet she loved Amy to bits, though, huh?"

Troy looked at her steadily for a long moment. "Let's just say Amy came along at a time when Mom would have been thrilled with anyone who wasn't complicated, or threatened her sense of the Way Things Should Be. It wasn't Amy she loved, I don't think, as much as what Amy represented."

"Looks to me like she hasn't changed her mind on that score."

"And I repeat, what my mother thinks has no bearing on my decisions."

"And if you think I'm fool enough to get involved with a man whose mother hates me, think again. Besides, I thought we'd cleared this up, that nothin' was going to happen between us."

"Something is *already* happening between us, Karleen. And I dare you to look me in the eye and tell me my feelings are one-sided."

It felt like a hot little firecracker went off inside her chest, exciting and painful at the same time. Karleen opened her mouth to do just that—deny it—but the words got all wadded up in her throat. What man had ever looked at her like that, declared his intentions so earnestly? Nobody, that's who. None of her husbands, none of her boyfriends…

Oh, Lord…did this suck or what?

"You're not supposed to have feelings for me, Troy."

"Too bad."

"Too bad is right," she said, trying desperately to keep the shakes at bay, "because spending the evening with your family only confirms what I already knew, which is that I don't fit in with them, or who you are. Anymore than I'd expect you to feel like a part of what's left of my mother's family, back in Texas."

His brows dipped. "I thought you said there wasn't anybody besides your aunt?"

"Not close, true. There's cousins out the wazoo, though, each one more of a hick than the next." She pressed a hand to her heart. "I can be honest about who I am, and what I come from. I don't always like it, and I've worked to change the parts of that legacy, I suppose you'd call it, that don't do me any good. Still and all, I am who I am. And your mama's right, Troy—there's no sense getting all romantic about this."

Troy narrowed his eyes slightly, then unfolded his arms and walked over to her, sliding one hand around the back of her neck and lowering his mouth to hers. She might have made a tiny *mmmph* of protest, only it turned so quickly into a purr of need it hardly counted. The kiss went on and on and on, until everything inside her went all soft and puddly, until hot tears stabbed at her eyes and her heart felt like it would break from the sweetness, the stupidness, of it.

At long last Troy came up for air, even though he kept that hand on her neck, his cheek firmly pressed against her temple. "Still think there's nothing going on here?"

Karleen forced herself to look up at him, into those sweet, foolish eyes. "Since I don't see any magic wands around here, I don't see much point in answering that question, do you?"

Their gazes battled for several seconds before he let her go and walked off, slamming the door shut behind him.

She told herself hormones were the reason she cried for nearly ten minutes afterward.

Chapter Nine

By late June, most days were hot and dry, like a good desert is supposed to be. Karleen was careful, though, to only water her garden in the early morning or after the sun went down, and between that and Troy's biggest cottonwood shading the garden during the hottest part of the day, her tomatoes and cucumbers and cantaloupes—and the pumpkins—were coming along just fine.

So was the baby, praise be.

"Disgustingly healthy," was how the midwife had, with a broad smile, pronounced both Karleen and her little passenger. And now that the first trimester was past, both the exhaustion and barf-fests had eased up. She was still emotional as all get out, but at least the sight of raw chicken no longer sent her racing to the john.

"When c'n we pick the punkins?" Scotty asked, interrupting her thoughts. He was crouched so close she could practically *feel* his breathing as she kneeled in the cool, early morning dirt, yanking out weeds with roots to China. On the other side of the fence, Grady—whose interest in horticulture wasn't anywhere near as pronounced as his twin's—romped with Elmo, the Irish setter/poodle mix (they were guessing) puppy that, in the end, the boys' grandparents, not Karleen, had helped choose from the pound.

The grandparents who had decided to stay for nearly a month, much to Troy's chagrin and Karleen's immense relief, although you would have thought it would've been the other way around. But since their presence put a decided damper on Troy's trying any more funny business—and since Gus had been in hog heaven, what with Troy's house needing so many repairs—their hanging around had truly been a blessing in disguise. However, judging from the worker-ant routine back and forth between the house and the RV over the last day or so, Karleen guessed Troy's parents would be hitting the road fairly soon.

She happened to glance up as Troy came out of his house, dressed in a navy-blue knit shirt and Dockers, looking all handsome and solid and, God bless him, normal, and he looked over and their eyes met, and Karleen—who had gone from feeling perpetually exhausted to feeling perpetually ready to rumble—mused as how a little funny business might not be remiss, right about now.

She let out a mighty sigh.

Small fingers tapped her arm. "Karleen? Whatsa matter?"

"Oh, nothing, sugar," she said, yanking at the next weed.

"So when c'n we pick the punkins?"

The dog stuck his nose through the chicken wire Troy'd nailed along the post-and-rail to keep the mutt in the right yard, then woofed at Scotty, who giggled. Karleen smiled. "Not until they turn orange. It'll be weeks and weeks yet before that happens."

"Will they get real big?"

"Hopefully. We'll have to wait and see."

"Scotty!" their grandmother called, her hand shading her eyes as she stood on the deck. When she noticed he was with Karleen, her mouth tightened. Still, she nodded and said, "Good morning, Karleen."

"Mornin', ma'am. That's a real nice color on you," she said, nodding at Eleanor's crinkly, coral two-piece dress. Karleen had to give the woman points for coming over to apologize, the morning after the Lindquists' arrival. And once reassured that Karleen was, indeed, not out to ensnare her son, Eleanor had relaxed enough that they could at least be cordial with one another, even if Karleen wasn't exactly seeing a huge potential for their ever being bosom buddies.

"Thank you," Eleanor said, a breeze ruffling the hem of her skirt. If not her hair. "It's a lovely day, isn't it?"

"It is that. Gonna be hot, though."

"I imagine so. Still, it's a dry heat."

"Yes, ma'am," Karleen said, although she mentally rolled her eyes. Hot was hot, far as she was concerned. Although there was something to be said for being able to take a shower, dry off and *stay* dry. As opposed to the one time she'd gone back to Texas for a family reunion and basically had dripped the entire three days she'd been there. That had not been fun. But then, neither had the reunion.

Anyway, that was apparently as far as her conversation with Troy's mother was going to go, since Eleanor then said, "Come on, Scotty—you need to eat breakfast and get cleaned up, or we're going to be late for church!"

The little boy made a face, stabbing his kiddie trowel into the dirt. "I don't wanna go to church," he muttered for Karleen's ears only. "I'd rather stay here with you and Elmo."

At least she got first billing over the dog. She looked up to see Troy walking toward them, and all those hormones started panting and wriggling like the stupid dog. Honestly. "Go on, now," she said, giving the boy a hug. "You don't want to keep your grandma waitin'. And anyway, you and Grady are gonna come over and swim later, remember?"

The little boy nodded, then swiveled his head to look up at his father. "You coming, too?"

"Sure am," Troy said, his low voice coursing through her the way it always did. Yep, the man was definitely the full package. In more ways than one, a thought which did nothing to calm down those panting hormones. Troy hauled Scotty up and over the fence, lightly swatting the four-year-old's backside before pushing him toward the house. "So scoot—Grandma made pancakes."

"Grandma always makes pancakes," Scotty grumbled as he trundled off. "I'm bored of pancakes."

Karleen got to her feet, dusting off her knees. As usual, Troy's eyes went straight to her belly, pooching out quite nicely now underneath her stretchy tank top. She supposed she was going to have to do something about maternity clothes before she started to look like a sausage in too-tight casing.

"We're gonna have to tell 'em soon," Karleen said softly, watching the boys troop up onto the deck, the pup tripping them the entire way. "Grady asked me yesterday why I was getting fat."

Troy's eyes shot to hers. "I'm sorry—"

"It's okay, I am." She made a face. "I've already put on

ten pounds, and the midwife said most women only gained around five the first three months."

"So the appointment went okay?"

Some unexpected business thing had prevented his going with her for her last check-up. For all her certainty that she'd wanted it that way, she'd been surprised by how much she'd missed him. Which wasn't how it was supposed to be, not at all.

"Yes, fine. More than fine. But anyway, I was thinkin'…the boys might like to be part of this, you know? Helping me to get the baby's room ready, maybe?" She flushed. "When the time comes, I mean."

"I think that's a great idea," Troy said, obviously pleased. "But that means we either tell them tonight, or not until they come back in August."

"Come back? From where?"

A shadow crossed his features. "My parents offered to take the boys with them for the rest of the summer. They're going to do some sightseeing, then return to Wisconsin for several weeks before driving back down here."

Her jaw dropped. As did her stomach. "And you're actually letting them?"

"I didn't exactly jump at the offer, to be honest. Not at first. But they haven't seen the boys much since they were born. It was hard for me to get away, and my father really hasn't been up to traveling before now. It'll be good for all of them, I think."

"I'm sorry—has Gus been sick?"

Troy looked slightly startled, then smiled. "He's fine now."

Karleen's gaze drifted over to Troy's deck, where his mother was setting out plates of food for the boys. Gus came through the door, Scotty perched high on his shoulders, and Karleen's eyes misted.

"Funny he never mentioned it. We chatted over the fence a lot, late at night," she said in answer to Troy's slight frown. "Your mother and I might have issues, but your daddy's a real sweetheart. I hate to think of him suffering. Still," she said on a rush of air, "I can't believe you're lettin' the boys go for... how long? Six weeks?"

"Closer to seven."

"Wow. And they just got the dog, too."

"Believe it or not, they're taking the dog with them."

"You have got to be kidding."

"It was the only way they could convince the boys to go."

"Well, I'll be," Karleen said softly, crossing her arms. "Hard enough to imagine your mother with a pair of four-year-old boys 24/7—in an RV, no less—let alone a half-grown dog."

"She raised three boys, I suppose she'll survive my sons and a dog for a couple of months."

"Be that as it may, I still don't know how it's not killing you to let them go. It's killing me, and they're not even mine."

His expression softened. "You really mean that?"

She frowned. "That I'll miss the little buggers like crazy? Heck, yeah, I mean it. I love your kids, Troy."

"It's just the concept of loving me you have trouble with, then?"

"Oh, no, you don't—"

"Oh, yes, I do. Karleen..." He reached over the fence and snagged her hand. "I've never been separated from the boys for more than a night since they were born. So, yes, letting them go for this long is the hardest thing I've ever done. I know they'll be fine, and I'm sure we'll talk every day, but how I'm going to get through the summer without them, I have no idea. I only agreed because it will give us more time to get to know each other."

She sucked in a breath. "No."

"Yes."

She sucked in another breath, then let it out saying, "You think there's room for one more person in that RV? I'll sleep with the dog, I don't care—"

Troy's laugh cut her off. "You're not going anywhere, you're staying right here where I can keep an eye on you and our baby." He let go of her hand and backed away. "And we will get to know each other better, honey," he said. "Count on it."

Over the phone to Joanna later that night, Karleen recounted most of the conversation with Troy, ending with "And here I thought I'd be relieved when his folks left!"

"Just goes to show," Joanna said. Only then she didn't say anything more, and Karleen's antennae shot straight up. "What?"

"Oh, nothing. Nothing you want to hear, anyway."

"You think I'm being an idiot, don't you?"

"*Idiot* might be a little strong, but…yeah, basically. I haven't decided if you keep pushing this guy away because you're afraid you'll find out you really don't have anything in common, or because you'll discover you do."

"You're right, that definitely wasn't anything I wanted to hear. And what in tarnation is that supposed to mean, anyway?"

"Okay, think back. To after Bobby's and my divorce, and how you kept after me to put myself out there, start dating again, even though I made it more than clear I'd rather gargle with antifreeze. Finally, I knuckled under, and I hated it with a purple passion. Then Dale came along, and I wasn't interested, but you kept pushing and shoving and trying to shake me awake, because that's what you do. And thank God for it, because eventually all that pushing and shaking opened my eyes and I realized what a good thing I very nearly missed.

"Dale and I aren't a perfect fit, Karleen," Jo said, more gently. "We weren't raised the same way, don't have the same background. But none of that matters. Well, okay, it matters, but we work through it because *we* matter. You forget, Troy's twins and Chance play together at least a couple of times a week, so I've gotten to know Troy over the past couple of months. He's a keeper, Kar. So pardon me if I find your resistance a bit hard to swallow."

"You don't understand, Jo, I—" Wiping tears off her cheeks, Karleen jumped slightly when her doorbell rang. "Somebody's at the door, I've gotta go. I'll talk to you tomorrow, okay?"

Unless she could somehow avoid it, she thought, jumping again when she opened her door to find Troy's mother standing there, in all her permanent-pressed glory.

"Not who you expected, I know," Eleanor said. "May I come in? I won't take up much of your time."

"Oh, um...sure." Karleen stepped aside to let the woman in, remembering her manners enough to ask if she'd like something to drink.

"No. Thank you. The guys think I've gone out for a walk." Her gaze swept the living room, landing for a couple of very telling seconds on the fake leopard throw covering up the worn spot on the couch. Then Britney's personal playground, which Karleen had recently relocated in here. One thing Eleanor couldn't accuse her of, however, Karleen thought smugly, was slovenliness, since Karleen could not abide a messy house. Still, Eleanor shook her head slightly, then met Karleen's eyes.

"I take it everything's okay with the baby?"

Karleen felt a slight frown pinch her forehead. In the entire month Eleanor had been here, she'd never once asked about the pregnancy. "So far, so good."

"And you're feeling well?"

"Fine, thank you."

A brief smile flashed over the older woman's mouth. "Taking your vitamins?"

"Yes, ma'am."

"Well. As long as you and the baby are okay, that's the important thing." She walked over to the hamster's cage; Britney hopped off her wheel and scurried over, sitting up on her haunches and begging. Little hoochie. "I lost track of the number of hamsters, gerbils and guinea pigs the boys went through," Eleanor said. "Troy named his Fred."

"Which one?"

Eleanor chuckled softly. "All of them." She turned, her hands stuffed in the pockets of her wraparound skirt; Britney resumed her race to nowhere. "I suppose you're wondering why Gus and I are taking the boys for the summer?"

Karleen perched against the sofa arm, surreptitiously covering up the spot where she'd practically rubbed the fabric bald trying to remove a nacho-cheese stain. "Actually, I hadn't given it a whole lot of thought. Well, other than thinking that you and Gus must be a whole lot braver than you look." At Eleanor's funny expression, she blushed, then added quickly, "Although Troy said you haven't had much chance to spend a lot of time with them…oh." Her blush deepened. "You're taking them to keep 'em away from me?"

"The thought had occurred to me—at least, it did a few weeks ago—but no. That's not why. I knew, however, if we got the boys out of Troy's hair, he'd undoubtedly use the opportunity to…woo you."

Heavens. When was the last time she'd heard anybody use that expression?

"And don't pretend you don't know what I'm talking about," his mother continued. "I know Troy's smitten with you. And he's always been remarkably single-minded about going after—and getting—what he wants."

"Then he's met his match with me, 'cause I don't lay down and roll over all that easily." At his mother's lifted brows, she gave a dry laugh. "That didn't come out exactly how I meant it. I know how this must look, especially to somebody like you. And I'm not gonna pretend I'm something I'm not. God knows, I've been around the block enough times to wear a groove in the sidewalk. But it had actually been a while for me, too, when your son and I made this baby."

To Eleanor's credit, she didn't flinch. "I believe you."

Karleen shrugged. "Doesn't make any difference to me whether you believe me or not. Just like the…circumstances leading up to this situation make no difference as to the outcome." She tilted her head, frowning slightly. "Troy's actually talked this over with you?"

"No, of course not." Eleanor's mouth quirked at the corners. "But I'm not an idiot."

"So what is it you're doin', exactly? Warnin' me off?"

One eyebrow lifted. "I was given the impression I didn't have to."

"You don't. Which is what I'm not getting. Why you're telling me this. I mean, yeah, you're doing a fair job of pretending you don't hate me—"

"I don't hate you, Karleen! That's just it! I—" To Karleen's shock, Eleanor's eyes got all sparkly before she blew out a breath. "I'll admit, my initial reaction to you was knee-jerk and small-minded. Then finding out you were pregnant, and you're so different from Amy…" She squeezed shut her eyes for a moment. "I'm sorry. That was horribly unfair."

"You got that right. Especially since it's not like I can help it."

"I know that. Which leads me to what I'm trying to say. The thing is…I've been watching you with the boys. They adore you, and with good reason. You're wonderful with them. And you've charmed my husband, too," she said with a fleeting smile. "As well as…as my son. I don't know that you and I could ever be friends, exactly, but I'm not the kind of woman who can't admit when she's wrong. And I was definitely wrong. Not about how different you and Troy are, I still have my reservations about how good you'd be for each other in the long run, but…" Her mouth pinched. "You're a good person, Karleen."

"Did it hurt to say that?"

His mother laughed softly. "More than you know."

Thoroughly confused, Karleen got up to twist closed the living-room verticals, then turned back around. "Then what's the problem?"

"I take it you still feel the same way about Troy? That you don't see this working out between you?"

Ignoring the twinge to her heart—not to mention to other, more intimate areas—Karleen nodded. "Yes."

"Then that's the problem."

"I don't—"

"As I said, Troy doesn't give up easily. *Dogged* doesn't even begin to cover it. He's also responsible to a fault. He's infatuated with you, Karleen. And you're having his baby. Heaven knows, he had plenty of girls after him in high school and college, but he's only been really in love once before in his life and…"

Eleanor hauled in a breath. "It's funny…you hold your baby for the first time, and you think you only have to protect them for so long. Until they finish high school, perhaps. Or college, at the very latest. That there has to be some sort of statute of limitations on wanting to keep them safe. I mean, really," she said on a tight laugh, "Troy's going to be forty next year. He's a hugely successful businessman. He hasn't needed, or wanted, my protection in years. But knowing that doesn't stop a mother from hurting when her child hurts. And after Amy…"

Her hand pressed to her mouth, Eleanor glanced away, then returned her gaze to Karleen, tears sheening her eyes. "If you're as determined that this won't work as he is to *make* it work…I just can't see any good come of this."

Her own eyes burning, Karleen waited for several beats before saying, "I don't want to hurt anybody, Eleanor. Least of all Troy. But I'm not sure what you're asking. Or what you expect me to do."

"I don't know," Troy's mother said on a rush of air. "But I guess…I just thought if I was the obstacle to, you know, you and Troy getting together…"

Karleen's eyes went wide. "You *want* me to marry him?"

"I want him to be happy. And because of that, I won't stand in your way."

"All your *reservations* notwithstanding?" After his mother's curt nod, Karleen breathed out, "Whoa—didn't see that one coming. Still and all…this isn't about you. Going through the motions simply because I'm pregnant might've made sense years ago, but not anymore."

"Then you don't have feelings for my son?"

Karleen waited out the stab of pain. "It's because I do have feelings for him that I'm not taking up his offer. I'm no good at marriage, Eleanor. And your son deserves…" She swallowed. "He deserves somebody who *is*. Like you said, for the long run. So why put all that energy into something that in all likelihood is only going to fall apart, anyway?"

Troy's mother regarded her for several seconds, then released a breath. "That's that, then, I suppose."

"Yes, it is." She paused. "So you can leave the boys here."

"Not on your life."

Karleen laughed, then crossed her arms. "Can I say something?"

A wry smile pulled at the older woman's lips. "As if I could stop you?"

Karleen smiled, too, then said, "If I can be half the mother you are, I'll be doing okay."

Eleanor's brows lifted. "Even though I'm meddling and annoying as hell?"

"If that's what it takes to show you actually give a damn about your kids, then yes, ma'am. You're a good person, too, Eleanor. And I'm a lot less put off by the idea of you being this baby's grandma than I was when I first met you."

Troy's mother laughed, but it didn't escape Karleen's attention that she didn't make any move to hug her or show any sign of affection. "I suppose that's progress, then. Well…I won't keep you any longer," she said, heading toward Karleen's door, only to turn when she got there.

"You don't have to answer this question—I don't expect you to—but assuming you were telling the truth about it having been a long time since you'd…been with somebody else before you and Troy, you know…" She cocked her head. "Why did you? And why him? You don't want his money, you don't obviously want his name or protection. So what *did* you want?"

Then she was gone, giving Karleen something to chew over for the rest of the night.

She was still chewing a week later, on the evening of the Fourth, as she breast-stroked the length of the pool. Guilt, gratitude and sun-warmed water rippled over her as she swam, careful to keep her bleached hair out of the chlorinated water.

Joanna had invited Karleen to a barbecue at her place, but she hadn't felt up to going. Used to be, she never minded being odd man out at one of Jo's shindigs. But today the thought of being around that many happy people in one spot made her want to hurl.

The water sloshed up over her face for a second; when her vision cleared, she saw Troy come out on his deck, dressed in cargo shorts and a loose T-shirt, holding a flat, bright, cellophane-wrapped box under one arm.

Fireworks.

Karleen turned, pushed off the side, headed toward the deep end of the pool.

She'd barely seen him in the week since the boys had left. He'd gone away on business for a couple of days; after his return, his car was gone in the mornings when she got up, the lights in the house rarely on until ten or eleven at night. He'd called a couple of times, to check up on her, but the conversations had been short and almost impersonal, leaving her to wonder if his mother had been overstating a thing or two. If she'd imagined Troy's words, the look in his eyes.

Leaving her to wonder what in the hell was wrong with her that she should find this possibility anything but a profound relief.

From what she could tell in the light spilling across the

deck from inside his kitchen, he seemed to be surveying the yard. After a bit, though, he carried the box back inside, shutting the French doors behind him. Karleen wondered why he hadn't gone to Blake's house or someplace for the holiday—she knew he and his partner were close—but then, she didn't suppose it was any of her business.

She climbed out of the pool, wrapping a Betty Boop beach towel around herself as she trekked back into her house, barefoot and dripping, just in time to hear the telltale *whoosh*-CRACKLE-*pop-pop-pop,* see the disco-esque strobing in her living room. She peered out the front window; Troy stood at the foot of his driveway, his hands in his pockets as the fountain spewed its pyrotechnic confetti ten feet in the air, blindingly bright wisps of red…blue…white…gold.

Still barefoot, Karleen let herself outside, grateful for the blanket of smoke and darkness. Troy pulled another fountain from the box, carried it out to the middle of the road, set it down, lit it, got back. After a second's sizzle, she sucked in her breath when a thousand coppery spiders lit up the night, each airborne for only a moment before plummeting to their graceful, glorious deaths.

"You like fireworks?" Troy asked, startling her. His gaze was fixed on the petering display; she'd had no idea he'd seen her.

She chuckled despite the sudden, tingly sensation in the pit of her stomach. "If it sparkles, glitters or flashes, you know I'm there."

"Right." He tossed the dead fountain into a bucket of water. "I'd bought these for the boys. Before I knew they wouldn't be here." A flashlight beam speared the darkness as he selected another one from the pack, checking for the fuse. "It would have been their first year."

Karleen palmed the mound cushioning the tiny life growing inside her. In the history of humankind, had a father ever missed his children more? She swallowed past the knot in her throat and said, meaning to cheer him up, "It's okay, they'll enjoy 'em just as much next year. Maybe even more."

Troy set the next fountain in place, waiting out a sudden breeze. "Funny how I don't put as much stock in 'next year' as I used to."

He lit the fuse and backed away, but the firey display wasn't anywhere near bright enough to dispel the thick, oily loneliness suddenly swamping the moment. And them, Karleen realized with a sort of grim acceptance. So she tucked the damp towel more tightly around her breasts and crossed the yard, climbing over the low fence to stand beside him. To stand with him, a pair of battered souls against the night and the memories and the loneliness.

"I'm perfectly okay with you staying over there," he said, not watching her.

"I know," she said, not watching him back. "Just don't get any ideas."

"Wouldn't dream of it."

But when she dared to glance over at him, she thought maybe he didn't look quite as miserable as before.

Even if the moment, like the fireworks, was destined to go right up in smoke.

Chapter Ten

"An' we're sleepin' in your room, Daddy!" Grady chirped in Troy's ear. "I got the bed by the window last night, but Scotty gets it tonight. It's so cool! Grandma said we c'n play wif all your cars 'n' trucks, too, if we're real careful."

With a tired chuckle, Troy tugged off the tie Blake had needled him into wearing for the video conference that day as he let himself into his stuffy, silent house. Despite Grady's happy babbling, Troy felt equally as airless and empty, a sensation only heightened whenever he'd talked to his boys over the past four weeks. He was no more used to their absence now than he had been those first few absolutely horrendous days when he'd felt as though his chest would cave in from missing them so much. The only positive was not having to feel guilty about business trips or bringing work home. But, then, he only brought work home as a lame attempt to stanch the seemingly bottom-less hole in his heart.

Troy opened the freshly stripped and stained French doors to let out some of the stuffiness. Although in June the temperature always sank with the sun, by late July, even after 8:00 p.m., the heat often clung stubbornly to the day, leaving plants and psyches limp and enervated.

The grinding squawk of an extension ladder pulled him out onto his deck. He looked over in time to see Karleen brace the ladder against the gutter, then scamper up it and onto her flat roof like a squirrel with a Daisy Duke complex, a Lowe's bag dangling from one wrist. Not her typical jewelry choice.

"Hold on a sec," he muttered into the phone, muting it before he yelled, "And just what the hell do you think you're doing?"

One panel of her swamp cooler already detached, she whirled around. Peachy rays from the setting sun licked at her bare legs, set the glittery fabric stretched over her rounded belly ablaze.

"The pump blew," she said. "Had to wait until it cooled off some before I could get up here and fix it."

"You've done this before, I take it?"

"Yes, Troy, I have done this before. You go on with your phone call, I'll be down in a sec."

After the Fourth, they'd reached what he could only call an uneasy truce: They occasionally had dinner, and some-times she even forgot to look like the heroine tied to the train tracks, hearing the chugga-chugga-CHOO-CHOO! right around the bend.

Didn't stop Troy from wanting to play Dudley Do-Right, however.

"I'm back," he said to his son, keeping an eagle eye on

the daredevil wielding a screwdriver and pliers on the roof next door. "How's Elmo?"

"Fine," Grady said. "He *finally* stopped throwing up so much. Last time it was a mouse or somethin', you shoulda seen it. We could even see the bones, it was really cool! Grandma said it was a good thing, else she was gonna leave 'im on the road somewhere. But I could tell she was only joking…."

"Lemme talk, it's my turn!"

"Uh-uh, I'm not done yet!"

"Yes, you are. Grandma says. Gimme the phone—"

"I said, I'm not finished!"

"Grandma! Grady won't let me talk to Daddy!"

"Let Scotty have a turn, honey," Troy heard his mother say in the background. "Then it's time for your baths."

Both boys went, "Awww…" then Grady said, "I gotta go. Love you."

"Love you back, squirt. Big hug—"

"S'me, Daddy," came Scotty's more gravelly voice. "Do we hafta take a bath every single *night*?"

Karleen hefted the cooler panel back into place, secured it, then gathered up her tools, the box, the bag and started back toward the edge of the roof.

"You have to do whatever Grandma says, buddy."

She turned backward, hooking one foot on the first rung. Troy held his breath.

"That sucks," Scotty said.

"Yeah, I kinda thought so, too, when I was your age."

Delicately gripping the ladder's sides, Karleen shimmied down nearly as quickly as she'd gone up. When she reached terra firma, Troy's breath left his lungs in a *whoosh*. "But the good news is, bathing every night cuts way back on the belly-button lint population."

Scotty giggled, then said, "Whatsa nanny?"

Troy sank into one of the deck chairs. Having shucked her sneakers, Karleen grabbed the hose snaked in the grass to water her garden. Every time she moved, those fake stone rings on her hands flashed in the sun. Oddly, he was getting used to them. "A lady who helps take care of children. Sort of like Mrs. Jensen. You remember her?"

"Uh-huh." Scotty's words kept fading in and out, probably because he was wiggling around. "She made me and Grady take naps when we didn't wanna. Will the new nanny make us take naps?"

Troy snapped his attention back to the conversation. "What new nanny?"

"The one Grandma says we might get when we get back. 'Cause you're gonna have your hands full. Full of what?"

Thank you, Mom.

"Oh, you know. You guys. Work. Taking care of this house. So I'm thinking about hiring somebody to help out."

"Why?"

"Because it would make life easier. We'll talk more when you get home."

"'Kay. S'Karleen there?"

A question posed every night. If Troy had expected their crushes to evaporate within a few days, he'd been sorely mistaken.

"She's over in her yard, watering the pumpkins."

"Are they big yet?"

"Getting there."

"Cool! C'n I talk to her?"

"Well, let's see…" Troy hauled himself out of the chair and headed toward the fence, calling her name. She ignored him. What the—?

Then he noticed the tiny wire running from her ear to the pack-of-gum-sized MP3 player hooked onto the waist-band of her jersey shorts. So he moved into her line of sight, waving the phone until she noticed him.

"It's Scotty!" he said when she unplugged herself.

With a huge smile, she dropped the running hose and tromped across the grass to take the phone. "Hey, sugar! Whatcha up to?"

Not everybody could keep up a phone conversation with a four-year-old, let alone sound as though she actually enjoyed it. But Karleen wasn't faking the way her whole face lit up whenever she talked to the boys.

Or whatever had prompted her to keep him company on the Fourth.

Or still worried his mother enough to sneak over to Karleen's "for a little talk" the day before they'd left. A conversation that Karleen had point-blank told him was between her and his mother and to keep his nose out of it.

Except she hadn't once looked him in the eye.

"…Oh, no!" she now said on a strangled gasp. "He ate a *mouse?*…I bet it was. What a dumb cluck!" She looked over at Troy with laughing eyes, shaking her head. Then she froze, the laughter dying on her lips. "Oh, sugar, that's real sweet of you to ask, but I can't be your nanny…. Well, because I already have a job, for one thing." Then she pressed her fingers against her lips. "I can't do that, either. Of course I love you, honey, I love you and Grady to bits, you know that. But friends can love each other, too…. Okay, I hear your grandma calling you, so you better go on…. I miss you, too, sugar. You be good, okay? And I'll see you real soon."

She handed over the phone, then tramped back to the hose and resumed her watering, and Troy remembered what Blake had said, about ceding control, about not pressuring her. But *damn,* he wanted her so much he thought his brain would melt. Standing beside her on the Fourth without touching her had damn near killed him.

"I asked Karleen if she could be our nanny," Scotty said in his ear, which did nothing to assuage the potential meltdown. Only then—thank God—Troy heard his mother going on about Scotty's needing to come on before the water got cold, and he breathed the sigh of the reprieved.

"Go take your bath, cutie. We'll talk tomorrow, okay?"

"'Kay. Love you."

"Love you, too."

Troy clapped shut the phone and slipped it into his pants pocket, then leaned one hip against the top fence rail. Karleen glanced over, then back, aiming her hose at another part of the garden. Overhead, a cicada began to drone so loudly Troy's skull vibrated.

"Don't even think about giving me grief for gettin' up on the roof," she said.

"Why would I do that? After all, it's not like you're pregnant or anything."

She blew out a sigh, pushing her bangs out of her face with her wrist, and Troy's hormones started humming. In four-part harmony. "The pump needed fixin'. And plumbers charge you a hundred bucks just to set foot on your property."

Troy shook his head, then said, "Garden's looking good."

"It is, isn't it?" she said, radiating pride. "It's been rainin' a bit more'n usual. That always helps. This hard stuff from the aquifer—" she wagged the hose, making the stream do a loop-de-loop "—is the pits."

"Maybe. But you definitely have the touch."

When she didn't say anything, he wondered if he'd

somehow insulted her. Only then she said, "There's something about a garden…I don't know how to explain it." She bent over to pick something off a tomato plant. "It's about putting down roots, I suppose. Not just the plants', but your own as well. That you'll actually be around to see the fruits—or vegetables, in this case—of your labor. Does that make sense?"

"Completely," Troy said softly, feeling a tug. Then he added: "I hear Scotty asked if you'd be their nanny."

Karleen snorted. "It gets worse. He also asked if I could be their mama."

"Did he now?"

Her eyes narrowed. "You put him up to it, didn't you?"

"Nope, he came up with that all on his own. Not that this would be a problem from my end, you understand."

"All too well."

"But just so you know, I'd still get someone else to help out around the house. And with the kids. Although, now that I say this, I'm getting quite an image of you in one of those cute little maid uniforms."

"Lord, you are one sick puppy," she muttered, moving on to the melons. Which were approaching basketball size. Scary. "You're home late. Again."

"You've been keeping track? I'm touched."

"You live next door. It's summer. It's kinda hard not to notice when you come home."

Troy chuckled. "I suppose you already had dinner?"

"I did. At dinnertime, strangely enough."

After a brief pause, he said, "We still on for tomorrow?"

He saw her back tense before she aimed the water farther over. "You know, there's no guarantee they'll be able to tell, if the baby's not turned right—"

"Karleen."

"Fine," she said on a rush of air. "Yes, the appointment's at four-thirty."

"And we really do need to discuss the nanny thing. But you keep putting it off. Or is it me you're putting off?"

Her eyes lifted. "Hallelujah, Lord, he's catching on. However, in the interest of being neighborly and all...how was your day?"

Troy shrugged, even as he noted that these conversations stretched a little further every day, that she opened up a tiny bit more. Not enough yet for him to see completely inside, but he'd take what he could get. "Put out a fire or two, increased my net worth...the usual. You?"

"Pretty good. Talked to Flo, she's going out to California to visit her daughter. With any luck, they'll keep her, she shouldn't be living on her own anymore. Oh, and one of the gals in Glynnie's office is getting married in October, a big shindig at the Country Club, and half the ladies in the firm are beggin' me to help 'em. Why are you looking at me like that?"

"I'm not looking at you—well, okay, I am looking at you, obviously—but I don't get it. Why all these women need help finding something to wear."

"The same reason they *need* ice cream, I s'pose," she said with a is-he-dense-or-what? eyeroll. "And anyway, if they didn't—" Karleen walked over to turn off the hose "—I'd be out of a job." She dumped the trickling hose into the grass. "Out of curiosity, when was the last time you set foot in a department store?"

"Willingly? 1973. And only because Santa was there," he added at her raised brows. Karleen laughed. "Hey, I'm a guy," he said. "I can't go into a mall without shots."

"Well, here's a news flash—lots of women feel the same way. Especially the busy ones. And that's where I

come in. Because what you—and they—see as a jungle,
I see as Six Flags." She grinned, *really* grinned, lighting
up every bit of the darkness inside him. "So it's definitely a win-win situation. Just don't tell anybody I do
most of my own shopping at the flea market, Target or
off eBay."

"Your secret's safe with me."

"Hey, I learned my lesson, after watching my mama and
her sister blow everything they made—which wasn't any
great shakes, believe me—on booze and clothes and stupid
stuff they didn't need, never setting anything aside for a
rainy day. Of which there were more than I want to think
about. So it's bills, then savings, then if there's anything
left over, I treat myself. I may be wearing last year's
designer knockoffs on my feet today, but at least I know
I'll still have a roof over my head when I'm eighty."

"You're a very wise woman, Karleen Almquist."

"Aside from being accidentally pregnant at thirty-seven,
you mean."

Their gazes wrestled for a long moment before Troy
said, "Come over here."

"Why?"

"Just get over here, dammit."

Amazingly enough, she did, although with a look in her
eyes like a dog ready to bolt at the slightest provocation.

"Give me your hand."

After a second or two, she did that, too. And Troy didn't
betray her trust by trying to draw her closer, no matter how
much he ached to do exactly that. Instead he simply kept
her fingers gently, but securely, wrapped in his and said,
"Like I said. You're one smart cookie. Smarter than
probably ninety percent of the human population, frankly.
Yes, you are," he added when she pulled a face. "And if

you can impart half that wisdom to our son or daughter, he or she is going to be one very lucky kid."

Color exploded in her cheeks; she glanced around, as though not sure where to put the compliment. Finally she met his eyes again, her mouth pulled to one side. "Laying it on a little thick, aren'tcha?"

"Only calling it as I see it."

A little snort preceded her snatching her hand from his. "I'll see you tomorrow," she said, then walked away, leaving the air perfumed with her fear.

Monsoon season was in full swing, thick gray clouds clogging the late afternoon sky like blobs of wet cement. Like her mood, Karleen thought as she locked her car in the hospital parking lot and her cell rang, and it was Troy, and her tummy did a series of backflips, and she told her tummy to *cut it out*.

Like that was gonna happen.

"Hey," she said over the wind, "where are you?"

"Stuck in freeway traffic," he grumbled, sounding like the thunder beginning to crank up in the distance. Yeah, they made quite a pair. "Huge backup. On this side, anyway, the other side's moving fine. Short of the car's morphing into a helicopter, I seriously doubt I'm going to make it in time. Are you okay?"

Weaving through the parking lot, she rolled her eyes, even as she pointlessly tried to keep her wind-whipped hair out of them. "Yes, Troy, I'm fine. Maybe you should forget it—"

"Nothing doing. I think we're starting to move, anyway. Don't leave until I get there. And if I miss it, get pictures!"

Oh, for heaven's sake, she thought, silencing her phone before she went inside. It was only another check-up, for goodness' sake.

A delusion she actually held onto until the sonogram technician pointed to the screen and said, "Looks like she's cooperating today," and Karleen—who clearly wasn't firing on all cylinders, said, "She?" and the technician laughed and said, "Your daughter, sweetheart—you're having a little girl," and Karleen stopped breathing. At least, that's what it felt like.

Hands trembling, heart racing, Karleen put her clothes back on in a blur. A thrill of terror spiked through her as she drifted back out into the waiting room, the sonogram photo clutched in her hand.

A baby girl.

A *daughter.*

A chance to get it right, this time.

Or die trying, she thought, touching the tiny image, tasting this and that name on her tongue. Emily, Sarah, Meredith… Strong names. Proud names. The most un-hick names she could think of.

"I'm gonna do right by you, sugar," she whispered, her eyes all prickly. "Swear to God, I'm not gonna let you down."

She sensed Troy sliding into the seat beside her. He gently pried the photo from her fingers; after a moment, he chuckled.

"No pee-pee?" he said, and she choked on her laugh.

"No pee-pee," she affirmed, then leaned against his shoulder, and he wrapped his arm around her and held her close, and Karleen shut her eyes and forgot, for the moment, what, exactly, she was supposed to be fighting.

By the time they left the hospital, giant spears of sunlight pierced the slate-blue clouds, studding everything in tiny amber globes and leaving the air fresh, chilled, invigorating. In a definite what-the-hell mood, Troy took Karleen's hand as they crossed the parking lot to her car, entwining their fingers. She glanced up at him, smiling slightly. Trembling, not so slightly.

"I see rumba ruffles in our immediate future," he said, and she laughed.

And leaned against him. Again. His heart rate spiked. From that, from the news, from pretty much everything, even as terror peeked from behind the euphoria, laughing its nasty, nasal little laugh. *Not now,* Troy thought, and it receded. For the moment, at least.

Oh, dear God—a little girl was going to call him Daddy.

Instantly, images of frilly baby outfits and long, shimmery blond hair and pink doll houses and prom dresses and *wedding* dresses and beating the boys off with sticks flashed through Troy's thoughts. His boys were his buddies, his comrades, his future partners-in-arms. But a daughter…

He sucked in a breath. And smiled.

"You goin' back to work?" Karleen asked when they got to her car.

"Nope." Troy bent slightly at the knees to look into her eyes. Wide. Amazed. Slightly unfocused. "You sure you're okay to drive?"

"Would you *stop* that?" she said, ramming her key into the lock. "I'm fine."

"Liar."

Her mouth twisted. "Okay, I'm not fine. But I'm not in any danger of drivin' off the road, either." She flapped at him. "So go away."

Still, he tailed the 4Runner all the way back to their houses. And when he pulled into his driveway, he noticed she was still sitting in hers, hands clamped on her steering wheel, staring out the windshield.

Troy got out, hopped the fence, walked over. Motioned for her to lower her window.

"Problem?"

"Uh-uh," she said, and burst into tears.

Troy yanked open her car door and hauled her into his arms, and she clung to him, sobbing her heart out, and then she was pleading with him to hold her, to not let her go.

"I can do that," he said, telling himself not to get his hopes—or anything else—up.

Then she lifted her tear-streaked face to his and he kissed her, and she moaned and kissed him back, still clinging, their daughter bumping a little foot or something against his stomach, and hope set all those fenced-in hormones free, and he was a goner. And she looked into his eyes and said, "I need—" and he said, "I know," and led her inside her house, that insanely, wonderfully bizarre house, and slowly, slowly undressed her, peeling away her clothes, her fears, her resistance.

By the time he'd shed his own clothes, sunlight shot through the crystals dangling in her bedroom window, littering her bed, her naked body, with a hundred rainbows. Troy placed a soft, lingering kiss on each one in turn, sometimes forgetting which ones he'd already kissed so he had to start over, which made her laugh through the remnants of her tears.

"I'm sorry," she whispered, her brow knotted, her eyes closed. "So sorry—"

"I'm not," he said. "Roll over."

"I can't, my stomach—"

"Not on your stomach. Trust me," he added, stroking her hip when she frowned up at him.

She got on all fours and Troy curled himself to her spine, shielding her, their unborn child. One hand braced on the mattress, the other weighed first one breast, then the other, before slowly, slowly sliding over her bump, and on down…to tease, and spread, and dip inside, one finger, then two…gently, firmly, gently again, smiling as her breathing went more and more shallow.

She arched back, whimpering, pleading…and he kissed the nape of her neck, tasting her, before carefully, tenderly, filling her.

Claiming her.

She cried out, and he was lost.

And he never, ever wanted to find his way back.

Afterward, they lay spooned together, facing her window, her skin warm under his hand as he stroked her stomach. She hadn't said a single word, but Troy could practically hear her *I can't believe I did it again.* He tugged her closer.

"So tell me about the crystals," he murmured.

"What?"

"The crystals." He reached around to fold his hand over hers. "Why you've got such a thing for sparkly stuff."

"You makin' fun of me?"

The words were teasing, but the vulnerability underlying them pierced his heart. He cupped her shoulder, easing her around to face him. "Hey. You're the most exasperating woman I've ever known. But I would never, ever make fun of you."

Karleen lay on her back, her eyes one with his, for several seconds before pushing herself up and out of the bed and putting on a cotton robe. Then she walked over to the window, palming one of the figurines before coming back to sit cross-legged on the bed.

"This is Kitty," she said, reverently handing him the

piece of cheap glass. "My first. She used to sit on the corner of my second third-grade teacher's desk—"

"Your *second* third-grade teacher?"

"We moved three times that year. Anyway, Kitty'd sat right where the morning sun'd catch her and throw rainbows all over the blackboard. She's not real crystal, just cut glass, but to an eight-year-old, she was magic. When I left, four months after I got there, Mrs. Moon gave her to me. Said that way, I could take my rainbows with me wherever I went."

With a crooked smile, she took the piece of cut glass back from him. "And it was true. Whenever things got rough, I'd look at Miss Kitty and she'd be all shiny and bright and glittery, and she'd make me feel that way inside, even when I didn't want to. And somewhere along the way I decided I wanted to surround myself with glittery things, things that would catch the light and bounce it back to me. Things that make me smile."

"Like the birdhouses?"

She laughed. "And all the junk in the yard. It's crazy, I know." The little figurine flashed as she turned it over and over in her hand. "It's all cheap stuff, collected little by little over nearly thirty years. I know you think it's pretty tacky—"

"As it happens, I'm learning to like tacky."

Karleen twisted to look at him, one eyebrow arched, and Troy groaned, and she laughed. Then he pulled her down beside him, wrapping her in his arms and kissing her for a long, long time.

"As it happens," he murmured, eventually, "I like surrounding myself with things that make me smile, too. That make me feel good. That—what was it you said?—catch the light and bounce it back? Like a certain sassy blonde

I know." When she didn't say anything, he said through a shaky smile, "Of course, if the feeling's not mutual, if you think I'm too staid or predictable or boring or—"

"No!" she said, covering his mouth with her fingers. "Oh, God, no. There is nothing even remotely boring about you, Troy Lindquist. But rainbows aren't real, sugar." Tears crested on her lower lashes. "They're just illusions. And momentary ones, at that."

He gathered her to his chest, his chin in her hair, willing her to relax. To trust. "You're *real,* honey. *This* is real. Whether it lasts for one night or a lifetime. And that's good enough for me."

She didn't reply. No argument, no apology, nothing. Instead she sagged against him, eventually falling asleep. In his arms.

A small victory, Troy thought, but a victory nevertheless.

Crrrrrack *ka-BOOM!*

Troy bolted upright in the bed next to Karleen, willing his brain to process the storm, the hour, his presence in Karleen's bed at the hour. Rain slashed at the windows, pummeled overhead; outside, a waterfall sloshed over a faulty gutter. Another lightning flash seared his retinas, accompanied by more skull-rattling thunder.

And somehow, Karleen—on her side, facing him, the sheet barely grazing her ribs—snoozed through the whole thing.

Resisting the temptation to wake her, Troy got up to relieve himself, only to realize they never had gotten around to dinner and that he was subsequently starved. As Karleen would be, once the storm penetrated her consciousness enough for her stomach—and the baby—to send out "take care of me" signals.

Troy silently pulled on his clothes, then tiptoed out of the bedroom to make sure the rain wasn't coming in any of the windows. In the living room, Britney was doing her best to trim her pudgy little butt on her wheel. Troy clicked on the lamp by the sofa; clearly taking Troy's presence in stride, the hamster waddled down from the wheel to look up hopefully at him, her whiskers twitching. He obliged her by dropping into her cage a few hamster goodies, which she promptly shoved into her cheek pouch. Would that he could feed the humans in the house so efficiently.

As Britney stuffed and munched, Troy took a good look at Karleen's living room, for the first time noticing not only the amazing quantity of dog-eared paperbacks—romances, mysteries, celeb tell-alls—crammed inside the white laminate bookcases, but that they were all in alphabetical order by author. That the cheap prints on the walls were hung perfectly straight. That there wasn't a stray magazine or newspaper anywhere.

That clearly she craved order every bit as much as he did.

"You goose," he whispered, smiling, then headed back to the kitchen, where he flipped the nearest switch, illuminating the god-awful Versailles-wannabe chandelier over the breakfast nook. *Okay, food,* he thought, opening the fridge. A minute into the serious contemplation of the relative merits of eggs over grilled cheese, he thought he heard a bell or something over the storm.

He pulled his head out and listened, frowning.

"What are you doing?" Karleen said from the kitchen door, and he nearly had a heart attack.

"Looking for food. You scared the crap out of me—"

"Shh—was that the doorbell?"

Carton of eggs in hand, Troy looked at Karleen. Who,

he duly noted, looked pretty damned good, even with bed-head and no makeup and cheeks that were looking more and more like Britney's every day.

"You generally have callers at ten at night?"

"Uh-uh," she said, yawning and starting for the door, and Troy said, puffing up, "Like hell. I'll answer it."

"You know," she said to his back as he stomped down the hall, "if you hadn't've been here, I would've answered it, anyway."

Ignoring her, he opened the door to an older, cheaper version of Karleen, like a two-bit drag queen doing Dolly Parton. One long-nailed hand caressed the extended handle of a bruised and battered wheeled suitcase, the other balanced a smoldering cigarette.

"My, my, my," the blonde said, giving Troy a bold once-over. Grinning broadly, she flicked ash onto Karleen's porch. "And who might *you* be, honey?"

Behind him, Karleen muttered the mother of all swear words.

Chapter Eleven

If it hadn' it been for the baby, no way would Karleen have been able to eat. But Troy wasn't taking no for an answer, watching every bite of scrambled eggs disappear into her mouth even as he dispatched his own like he hadn't eaten in a week.

She couldn't imagine a sleeping nightmare worse than the one she was living for real, right now, in her own kitchen. Bad enough she'd slept with Troy again, but then to have her aunt show up, out of the blue…

Well, okay, not so out of the blue. This was Inky, after all. And it wasn't like the signs hadn't been there all along—the phone calls, the pleas for money, the increasingly helpless whinings. But between the pregnancy and Troy, there'd been nothing left over for worrying about what her aunt might be up to.

Yet another example of how ignoring something doesn't make it go away.

Karleen glanced over at Troy, refilling their milk glasses before sitting back down and resuming his meal, and squelched a very heavy sigh. If their earlier hanky-panky had only been about sex, that would've been one thing. Trouble was, she'd already started her free fall long before that; nothing to be done now except wait for the inevitable *thud* when she hit bottom. So at the moment she was far too much of an emotional wreck to play nice. With anybody.

Why was it, she mused as she forced down another bite of eggs, that the more she tried to take charge of her life, the more things seemed determined to spiral out of her control?

"I still can't believe you didn't tell me you were *pregnant*," Inky more or less squealed, her makeup a little desperate-looking in the overhead light. With a slight somebody-walking-over-your-grave shudder, Karleen lifted a hand to her own tangled, mangled hair.

"I didn't figure it was any of your business."

Hurt flooded her aunt's tired blue eyes, weighted with too much mascara, dulled by too many forgotten nights, too many hung-over mornings.

"But I'm this baby's great-aunt, Leenie," she said with a twitching smile in Troy's direction. A scrawny hand reached over to cling like a greedy insect to Karleen's wrist. "And I know how long you've waited for this, how much you always wanted to be a mother!"

"Which is precisely why you can't stay."

Unnaturally thin brows shot up, followed by a breathy, nervous laugh. "Oh, now, I'm only talkin' about a few days, not forever. Just until I pull myself together again."

"You know, it is truly amazing, how after all these years you can still sound so sincere."

Apparently deciding to drum up support from whatever camp she could, Inky now turned to Troy. "It's the pregnancy makin' her talk like this. Maybe you could—"

"Oh, no," he said, holding up one hand. "Whatever's going on here is between you and Karleen. I'm just here for the food."

Inky gawked at him for several beats, then seamlessly started in again with Karleen. "I don't have anyplace else to go, sugar." Ah, yes. Cue the crocodile tears. "I told you, I lost my last job, and there were slim pickings back in Lubbock. So I figured, maybe there'd be something here in Albuquerque. And you and I—well, and this baby," she said, smiling at Karleen's bump, "we're all we've got."

"You are not part of that equation, Inky."

Instantly, all the sweetness and light drained from her aunt's voice. "You can't throw me out, Karleen. We promised your mama that we'd look out for each other."

Karleen nearly laughed out loud. "When did you ever look out for me?" she said, pushing away the uneaten eggs. "It's always been me sending *you* money, making sure *you* were okay."

"Then how is it I can count on the fingers of one hand the number of times you've called me in the last ten years? We used to be so close, baby. Then suddenly it was like you didn't want to have anything to do with me."

"Maybe because I finally got tired of trying to help someone who doesn't really want to be helped." Vaguely, she was aware that Troy had stopped eating to listen intently to every word. "How many times have you sworn you were gonna stop drinking and pull yourself together, stay with one job for longer than a month or two? Ever since I was a child, Inky, it's been one broken promise after another. So excuse me for not wanting to be dragged down anymore. And don't even *think* about smoking in here," she said when her aunt pulled a pack of cigarettes out of her purse.

Inky actually had the nerve to look taken aback, but she tossed a saccharine smile at Troy, then slipped the cigarettes back in her purse. Anybody else would have been too humiliated—or at least ticked off—to stay after Karleen's outburst in front of a total stranger. But not Inky. Oh, not Inky, who had spent so much of her life being humiliated, she'd become immune to it.

And in that moment, Karleen knew she'd lost the battle, a thought that curdled the eggs in her stomach. Because short of calling the cops to physically remove her aunt— and on what charge? Mooching?—she was stuck. With Inky, in her house, until her aunt decided to leave of her own accord.

One trembling hand curved around the baby as a sick feeling of helplessness, of doom, washed over her, that despite all her hard work she'd never be completely free of the genetic taint of bad booze, bad men, bad decisions.

"It's only for a couple of days," Inky said, ever hopeful. Ever delusional. Then she smiled. "I promise."

Regrets tingeing the cool, rain-sweetened air, Troy watched Karleen's face in the light spilling from the open front door as they stood on her porch. Her arms crossed over her belly, Karleen kept her gaze averted, even though her rock-solid jaw said it all.

"You sure you don't want me to stay?"

"Positive."

Still, Troy propped himself against the railing bordering the porch, one leg stretched in front of him. At his back, water dripped steadily from the eaves, splattering around Karleen's plastic roses. "I don't like the idea of your having to handle this all on your own—"

"I can handle Inky. God knows I've been doing it all my life."

God also knew that this was familiar enough territory for Troy to recognize denial when he heard it. "I'm sure you have. But you don't need the stress right now."

"Then please don't add to it," she said quietly, just as Inky yelled her name

from inside the house, only to then appear in the doorway.

"Is it okay to use the towels already hangin' up in the hall bath? And you shouldn't leave the door open like that, honey, there's like a thousand moths in here…. Oh, I'm sorry, Troy!" Flashing him a smile, she pulled her flimsy, floral robe more tightly around her doughy figure. Fingers decorated with chipped red polish clutched a wineglass, clearly filled with her own stash, since he knew Karleen didn't have anything in the house. "I didn't realize you were still here, darlin'. I won't be a sec—far be it from me to be a third wheel! The towels, Leenie?" she redirected to Karleen.

"Yes, those towels are fine," she said, and off her aunt went, humming loudly. Karleen stared after her for a tellingly long moment, then finally returned her gaze to Troy.

"Call me Leenie and you're dead."

"Wouldn't dream of it."

"The crazy thing is," Karleen said softly, almost more to herself than to him, "she's not a bad person. She's just—"

"High maintenance?"

A tiny smile flitted over her mouth. "That's one way of putting it." She paused, then said, "But she's never going to change, anymore than Mama did." Her gaze speared his. "Do you get what I'm saying, Troy?"

He folded his arms over his chest. "You're not your aunt, Karleen."

"No. But she's part of who I am. And nothing's gonna change *that*."

"If you got your act together," he said, "why couldn't Inky?"

"Because I *wanted* something better for myself. Maybe I wasn't an alcoholic, but I could still see the dead-end road in front of me." She shook her head. "Inky can't. Just like Mama couldn't. And even if…" She paused, as though unable to bring herself to say the words. "Even if we did give this a shot, how're you gonna feel the first time she passes out at Thanksgiving, or comes on to one of your relatives? What would your *mother* think?"

Even if we did give this a shot…

Troy stuck his hand underneath the dripping water, relishing the cool against his heated skin. "My father's a recovering alcoholic, Karleen," he said, not looking at her. "Believe me, I've lived through my share of uncomfortable holiday dinners."

Several long moments passed before she said, "Gus? That sweet man?"

"That *sweet man* put us all through holy hell for years. Until my mother left him, about ten years ago. Told him if he didn't get help, they were through."

"Oh my God, Troy…I had no idea."

"Not many people do. So count yourself among the elite few who know the great Lindquist family secret."

"So that was his 'sickness'?"

"Yeah." He twisted to look at her, flicking water from his hand before crossing his arms over his chest. "He's been dry for six or seven years. It wasn't easy, Kar. It still isn't. The temptation never completely goes away. But he was about the same age as your aunt when he finally realized what he stood to lose if he didn't get a handle on his addiction. So it's not too late. It's never too late."

Karleen walked to the other side of the porch, heavily bracing her hands on the railing to look out into her yard. Troy followed her gaze, half watching several of the twirly things spinning slowly in the leftover breeze, gleaming dully. "Then maybe your daddy had a stronger motivation than my aunt's ever had. Because heaven knows, I'm sure not it. I've done everything, said everything I know how, but…" She straightened up again, poking at a wind chime. "You're right, Inky's the last thing I need to be dealing with right now. And I know I gave lip service to throwing her out…" Her arms strangling her middle, she looked at him, anguish—and shame—contorting her features. "But I can't."

"I know, honey. Believe me, I know how hard this is on you. My brothers and I all thought Mom had a screw loose when she walked out on Dad. That's why it kills me to think of you going through this alone."

Her jaw hardened again. "And I'm not about to inflict this mess—*my* mess—on you. Or the boys. Oh, God, especially the boys…" She looked away for a second, then returned her gaze to his. "Thanks, Troy, but I don't need your help."

Troy swallowed back the hot, bitter taste of frustration and said, as gently as he could manage, "You know, there's nothing wrong with being proud of who you are or what you've accomplished. But sometimes there's not much difference between pride and stubbornness."

As he expected, her eyes flashed to his, her brows drawn together. Then she spun on her heel and headed back inside.

"Funny," he said before she reached the door, "the woman I fell in love with would rather put out her right eye than back down from a challenge."

Karleen whipped around. "And you call *me* stubborn? Don't you get it, Troy? The woman you fell in love with doesn't exist!"

"Bull."

Her saw her eyes squeeze shut, her chest rise and fall as she tried to steady her breathing. "This isn't backing down from a challenge, Troy," she said at last, her voice shaking, and he felt like a jerk. "This is refusing to listen to somebody tell me that everything I've fought for is, what? Wrong? Stupid? That I've got no right to determine my own destiny?"

"Dammit, Karleen—I'm not trying to interfere with your choices! Hard as this may be to believe, wanting to help you get where you need to go isn't some kind of threat to your autonomy."

Her hand, and her gaze, flew to her tummy when the baby apparently kicked. After several seconds, she finally lifted her eyes. And in them, past the adamancy, and the determination, Troy saw a yearning that broke his heart.

"My pride is all I've got, Troy. The only thing I can count on. And I spent too many years clawing my way up out of hell to let anybody—not you, not even this baby— take it away from me. I know this doesn't make sense, and I don't expect you to understand…but I simply can't cope with you and Inky at the same time. And anyway, this is family business. So if you care about me, and our child, you'll do whatever makes life easier for me right now. And right now, I need you to go."

Once again shouldering aside his annoyance, Troy stood and walked over to Karleen, palming her belly. The baby stirred, a flutter against his hand. "*This* is family business, too. And if you think I'm going to simply walk away and put you out of my mind, then you don't know what *family* is nearly as well as you think you do."

As he crossed the wet grass, he heard Inky say from the porch, "Oh, Lord, sugar…I hope you two didn't have a fight on my account…."

"You do realize, don't you," Joanna said from the other side of the picnic table in her backyard, "that Karleen would take both of us out without a second's thought if she knew we were talking?"

Troy allowed a tight smile, keeping an eagle eye on Joanna's youngest as he scampered like a curly-headed bug over the enormous wooden fort and swing set on the other side of the yard.

"It's okay, my life insurance policy's up to date."

Joanna chuckled and refilled his lemonade glass, then hugged one knee as she, too, let her gaze drift over to her son. The still-high, late afternoon sun tangled with all those crazy red curls for a moment until she looked back at him, concern swimming in her big gray-green eyes. Naturally, when he'd finally broken down and called her, she'd already known about Inky's return, ten or so days before. Nor did she seem terribly surprised when he'd asked if they could meet after he got off work. But frankly, he was at his wit's end. Wanting to fix the situation and having a clue how to go about that were two different things. From where he was sitting, Joanna was his best, and possibly last, hope.

"I get that she's scared," he said. "I get that she doesn't want to slip back into old destructive patterns. What I don't get is what that has to do with me."

"No," Joanna said, smiling. "You wouldn't."

"What's that supposed to mean?"

She shrugged. "That you're not a woman, mostly. That you're not *that* woman, specifically." She stuck a finger in her lemonade, swirling the ice cubes around. "I know this is a cliché, but Kar's like an abused dog. She could be starving, but the thought of trusting a stranger—even one with food in his hand—is even more terrifying than the possibility of starving to death." When Troy frowned, Joanna blew out a breath.

"I don't know how much Karleen's told you about her life. Knowing her, not a whole lot. But I practically lived it with her. Not that she ever got comfortable with the idea of me coming over to her house when we were kids, but I did anyway. Partly because I was curious, I admit, but mostly because I could tell her home life embarrassed her. And I made it my mission to get her to understand that it didn't matter. Not to me. And anyway," she said, smiling, "my mother was hardly ever around, so I thought any mother at home was better than no mother at home." The ice cubes clinked when she took a sip. "I was wrong."

"Was Karleen abused?"

"Mmm, no," she said, swallowing. "More like neglected. Left to raise herself, for the most part. From what little I saw, I think her mother really did love her. And at least she'd stopped the constant moving by then. But she still had her priorities skewed."

"She was an alcoholic?"

"Yeah."

"Did you ever meet Inky?"

"A few times. She was in and out. I'm not sure how Emmajean—Karleen's mother—managed to keep a roof over their heads, but she did. Which was more than you could say for Inky, who was always out of work, kicked out of her house, whatever. And the men…God. Each one a bigger loser than the next. I know it all sounds very afternoon talk show, but I'm not making any of this up. It's a testament to Kar's character that she came out of it as unscarred as she did."

"Except she didn't. Come out unscarred."

Joanna lifted a hand to fluff her hair off her neck. "Apparently not." A soft, humorless laugh fell from her lips. "And typically, she kept looking for acceptance in all the wrong ways. Not that I have much room to talk—I married too young, and for the wrong reasons, just like she did. The difference is, she *kept* marrying for the wrong reasons. And each time the marriage dissolved, she felt like more of a loser herself."

"She blamed herself for the breakups?"

"Not entirely. But a failed marriage is a failed marriage. She might have never fallen victim to the alcohol, but it took her a lot longer to figure out how to stand on her own two feet."

"So she sees falling in love as a weakness,"

"I think it goes even deeper than that."

"Meaning?"

Her gaze met his, a tiny frown dissecting the space between her brows. "As close as Karleen and I have been all these years, through all the crazy things we did together as kids, all the crying jags we shared when we got older…I always suspected she was holding a piece of herself back. That she never completely felt as though she fit in. As if she was straddling two worlds—the one she grew up in, which she hated, and the one she wanted but never quite felt she deserved." Her mouth flattened. "Not surprising considering how often she'd been let down."

"Like the starving dog."

"Exactly. That's not to say she's not proud of how far she's come. But it's as though she's imposed some sort of personal glass ceiling on herself."

"And now she sees her aunt's return as a threat to whatever progress she's made."

"I wouldn't doubt it." Joanna took a sip of her drink. "I take it you're in love with her?"

Troy stared at his lemonade glass for a long moment. "Hopelessly."

"Oooh, that was more than I'd hoped for." Joanna laughed softly. "Although I don't envy you."

"At the moment, I don't envy me, either."

"You can't let her think you pity her, you know."

"Why would I pity someone who's overcome as much as she has?"

Joanna gave a regal little nod. "Right answer."

"So do I have your blessing?"

That got a loud laugh. "Oh, you had my *blessing* from the first time we met. What you have now is my deepest sympathy." At Troy's grunt, she smiled and asked, "Did this help?"

Troy unfolded himself from the table, downing the rest of his drink. "Actually, it did. Although at this point, this isn't about me, not really. It's about Karleen. And our child. I want more, but…" He shook his head. "Sometimes, I guess the hurt simply goes too deep."

"No hurt goes that deep, Troy. Don't you get it? She wants *more,* too, but nobody's ever given it to her. All Karleen's *ever* wanted is to be won over, by a man more stubborn than she is. Someone willing to actually fight for her instead of shrugging and walking away." Shielding her eyes from the sun, Joanna looked up at him with an enigmatic smile.

"You've gotten this far," she said gently. "Don't give up now."

A towel twisted over her swimsuit after her morning swim, Karleen padded barefoot into her kitchen…where she immediately spotted a filled ashtray on the counter that hadn't been there when she'd gone outside a half hour before.

She picked up the disgusting thing with two fingers and carried it into the living room, holding it out as far from her body as possible.

"You're dripping all over the floor, sugar," Inky said from the sofa, where she sat in her shortie nightgown and robe, her bare feet crossed on Karleen's glass coffee table, watching the *Today Show* while she did her nails.

"And how many times have I told you in the past two weeks—" Karleen set the ashtray on the table in front of her aunt "—that I don't want you smoking in the house?"

Her aunt flicked her a glance. "Sorry, honey. But it was rainin' last night again, and I didn't want to go outside."

"This isn't from last night, it's from this morning. It's bad for the baby, and I won't have it."

"Oh, now, don't go gettin' all high and mighty on me, Karleen. Your mama and I both smoked when she was carryin' you, and you turned out just fine."

"Other than the near constant colds and crap I had all through elementary school? I'm serious, Inky. No. Smoking. Inside. The house."

"Party pooper," her aunt called after Karleen as she stomped back to the kitchen for a glass of orange juice. And maybe a couple pieces of raisin toast while she was at it. In the midst of pouring herself a glass of juice, Inky appeared in her line of vision.

"You want me to fix you some eggs or pancakes or something?"

"No. Thank you." To be fair, her aunt hadn't expected Karleen to wait on her, and often had dinner ready and waiting when Karleen got home from a late appointment. True, Inky was usually already halfway to wasted by then, and true, regularly consumptions of chicken-fried steak and breaded okra and corn bread was wreaking serious havoc on what was left of her figure, but the woman meant well, even so. "I'm fine with toast."

"Now you know that's no kind of breakfast for a pregnant woman," Inky said, clip-clopping in her pink satin Frederick's of Hollywood mules to the fridge. "Sit down, it won't take me but a second to fix you a real breakfast. You enjoy your swim?"

"Mmm," Karleen said, giving up the fight. She felt the bottom of her bikini, making sure it was dry before she sat down. She looked positively ridiculous in the thing with her big old belly front and center, but if all those Hollywood types could let everything hang out—in public, no less!— she supposed she could get away with it in her own backyard.

"Yeah," Inky said, setting Karleen's skillet on the stove and giving it a squirt of PAM, "it's real nice, you having a pool. Although the pool boy leaves a lot be desired. He was here yesterday, did I tell you?" She cracked three eggs into a bowl, then took a whisk to them. "He was sixty if he was a day, with a gut on him that might as well had Budweiser stamped right across it."

"That's just…wrong," Karleen said, trying to keep a straight face as she flicked open the morning paper.

"You're telling me. Got myself all fixed up for nothing."

Inky adjusted the heat under the pan, which sizzled when she poured the eggs into it. "Say what you will about that ex of yours, he did okay by you in the end. Leaving you this great big house and all."

"Nate didn't *leave* me the house. I'm buying it from him."

Inky whipped around, spatula raised. "You are not."

"I am."

"You can afford to do that?"

"He gave me good terms, but yeah. I can afford to do that."

Shaking her head, her aunt turned back to the stove. Neither said anything until Inky set their breakfast in front of them and sat down, at which point Karleen not-so-subtly pushed the classified section across the table.

Inky looked up. "You tryin' to tell me somethin'?"

"It's been two weeks, Inky. Not a couple of days. You can stay as long as you need to, but you've got to get a job. Any job, I don't care. Where are you getting the money for the booze and cigarettes, anyway?"

Her aunt bristled. "I don't suppose that's any of your business."

"Since you're living in my house and eating my food, I suppose it is."

"Food *I* cooked, if I may remind you."

"Inky. Please."

"Okay," her aunt said on a huff, "if you must know, I hocked some of the jewelry Sammy gave me. Not for near as much as I thought I'd get—cheap SOB—but I got enough to tide me over for a while. So—" she waved her fork at the paper "—I have no intention of taking the first job that comes along. And anyway, what are you worried about money for? Isn't Troy supporting you and the baby?"

Karleen's gaze snapped to her aunt's. "*What?* No, he's not supporting me! Why on earth would you think that?"

"But I thought he was one of those rich entre…entrepreters…oh, you know what I mean."

"Entrepreneurs. Yes, he is. But that has nothing to do with me. Of course he'll help support his child, but I'm not part of the package."

Her aunt put down her fork. "Not for want of him trying, if my hunch is correct." When Karleen didn't respond, Inky huffed. "And here I always thought you were the intelligent one in the family. He asked you to marry him, didn't he? And you turned him down."

Karleen met her aunt's gaze dead-on. "I had my reasons."

"What possible reason could there be for you not marrying a good-looking, wealthy man who's obviously crazy about you? And whose child you're carrying, to boot? Have you lost your mind?"

"No, actually for once I'm being completely level-headed about things. Troy and I just aren't a good fit."

One over-plucked brow lifted. "You obviously were at least once."

Karleen stood abruptly, carrying her dishes to the sink. "Being good together in bed isn't enough to sustain a relationship, Inky. Which you of all people should know."

"Oh, now, don't be like this, honey…you know I've only got your best interest at heart—"

"You have never had my best interest at heart!" Karleen said, wheeling on her aunt. "It was always about living for the moment, for both you and Mama! The next drink, the next man, the next night out on the town. I love you, Inky, and I know you love me, in your own strange way. But if you really gave a damn about me, you'd sit down and come up with a plan to sort out your life. Starting with doing something about your drinking problem."

"I do not have a drinking *problem*," Inky said stiffly.

"Yes, I'll admit I like my wine in the evenings, but I never touch a drop before lunch. And I gave up the hard stuff a long time ago. So there's no need to go gettin' your panties in a wad." She smirked. "Or are you worried that'll somehow hurt the baby, too? That she can somehow smell the wine fumes from all the way inside your belly?"

All the old feelings of rage and frustration rose up, stinging Karleen like a thousand jellyfish tentacles. Dammit—she'd turned her back on this life, on everything that had tried so hard to suck her down into the depths with her mother, her aunt, any number of her other family members who, like Inky, would die—literally—before they'd admit they had a problem. But while her back was turned, her life had been waiting for exactly the right moment to find her again.

Except…

Except *now,* she realized, she wasn't the scared little girl, or the confused teenager, or the clueless young woman still waiting for something or somebody to come along and rescue her. So she parked her hands on her rapidly expanding hips and said, "Here's how it's gonna be, Inky—either you pull yourself together, or find someplace else to live. I will change the locks on the doors when you're out, if it comes to that. Because I refuse to raise *my* little girl in a house filled with broken promises and unrealized dreams. You wanna self-destruct, you go do it someplace else."

Horror exploded in her aunt's eyes. "You giving me an ultimatum, Karleen?"

"All tied up in a bow," she said, then stomped down the hall to get dressed for her morning appointment.

Chapter Twelve

"Oh, you didn't have to do that!" Karleen's aunt trilled, taking the white bakery box from Troy. Wearing black shorts and a tank top that revealed far too much wrinkled cleavage and over-tanned leathery skin, she flipped the box open, gasping at the triple chocolate cake inside. "Shoot, boy…if that gal doesn't marry you, I'll have to marry you myself!" She nodded at a second box, still in his hand. "And what's that?"

"For Karleen."

Plucked brows shifted north, but all she said was, "Well, come on in, make yourself comfortable while I finish up in the kitchen. I talked to Karleen a little bit ago, she sounded like she'd be home in a few minutes."

Troy followed Inky back to the kitchen, where the scents of garlic, basil and tomato sauce blessedly overpowered the woman's perfume. Heaven. Which it would not be once Karleen got home and found him there, he was sure.

As fired up as he'd been after his talk with Joanna to *do something,* what that something might have been had yet to present itself. Not good for a man more inclined to take action than mull over a thousand possibilities. He'd checked up on Karleen nearly every day—much to her obvious consternation—but this would be his first opportunity in two weeks to actually get more out of her than a perfunctory "I'm fine."

Should be interesting.

He set the box in the center of the already-set table, chuckling at the gold lamé place mats underneath the Corelle. "I take it she has no idea you invited me over for dinner?"

"Are you kidding? There are a few brain cells left underneath all this," Inky said, pointing to her froth of stiff, pale blond hair. "Those that aren't pickled yet, anyway. You want something to drink?"

Troy lifted an eyebrow, but Inky shook her head.

"I know what you're thinking, but even though a good red Chianti would be perfect with this…" She let out a truly regretful sigh. "I'm watchin' my Ps and Qs these days. So. Water, soda, juice…?"

"Water's fine. Thanks."

Inky pulled a bottle out of the refrigerator, pouring it with great fanfare into a plastic goblet decorated with cartoony tropical fish. Her silvery-blue eye shadow glistening, she handed the glass to him, then opened the oven door to peek inside. "I hope you like chicken parmesan, it's this recipe I got off this Eye-talyan woman who lived in the apartment above me the one winter I lived in Nashville. It's all made from scratch, none of that processed chicken or bottled sauce. Takes the better part of the afternoon, but it's worth it."

Smiling, Troy eased himself up onto a bar stool. "So you like to cook?"

"I sure do. And I'm pretty good at it, if I say so myself. Don't get much opportunity to show off for strangers, though, so this is a treat for me."

"As I'm sure it'll be for me, too. It smells great."

She beamed. "You're a real sweetheart, aren't you? But then, I could tell that right off. Why my niece can't see it is beyond me."

Troy took a sip of his water, meeting the blonde's gaze. "Maybe that's the problem. Being too nice, I mean. I'm seriously considering getting a Harley and not shaving for three days."

Inky laughed. "Don't forget the tattoos. The scarier, the better. Oh, and you gotta work on your sneer. Like this," she said, curling one side of her bright red mouth.

His smile fading, Troy glanced down at the crazy water glass, then back up at Karleen's aunt. "You do realize my being here isn't likely to change her mind?"

"You *not* being here isn't going to change her mind, either. So I figure it couldn't hurt, right?" She reached up to fiddle with one large gold hoop in her ear, her brows pulled together. "Maybe I haven't exactly been a shining example, but I'd do anything to see that gal happy. Which is more than she's clearly willing to do for herself. Oh!" she said at the sound of the garage door opening. "That's her now. Act natural!"

Troy stood just as Karleen came through the door leading from the garage into the kitchen. Her hair was more or less up, her body more or less covered in a leopard-print sundress held in place, as far as he could tell, solely by her breasts and a pair of skinny ties around her neck. An assortment of beads, feathers and metal disks dangled from earlobes to shoulders. And on her feet, matching leopard-print shoes with wedged heels that brought to mind ancient Inca temples.

A look only she could pull off.

She looked from Troy to her aunt, then let out something like a laugh.

"Now, sugar," Inky said, rustling through a bunch of plastic bags on the counter, "don't go making more of this than it is. I just figured it'd probably been a while since Troy'd had a good home-cooked meal. So would you mind fixing the salad while I make the… Oh, come on, I know it's in here somewhere."

"What?" Karleen asked, desultorily pulling out a head of lettuce from the vegetable bin.

"The bread. I know I bought some…." More rummaging, followed by a Look of Extreme Consternation. "Damn. I must've left it at the store."

Karleen dropped the lettuce like it was hot. "I'll go get some—"

"You will do no such thing, missy." Inky grabbed a set of keys and a purse off the end of the counter. "It won't take but two seconds, you stay here and get that salad going."

Karleen stared at the space where her aunt had been a moment before, then started tearing up the lettuce. "Lord, she's even more devious when she's sober."

Troy rubbed his mouth. "So…on a scale of one to ten, how pissed are you?"

Several pieces of shredded iceberg flew into a glass bowl. "About an eight."

"Could be worse."

"Not much."

After what he figured was an appropriate pause, he said, "Any chance of you're looking at me anytime soon?"

"Not if I can help it."

Not being a complete fool, Troy decided against pointing out that her taking out her annoyance with her aunt on him was perhaps a tad irrational. In fact, most other men would have given up by now, got out while the gettin' was good. But since the whole point was to prove to her that he *wasn't* like most men, he dug out his cell phone and flipped it open, clicking the display for several seconds before coming up behind Karleen and holding the phone in front of her. On a soft "Ohhh," she took the phone from him for a closer look.

"Lord, the dog is *huge*. And the boys…" She shook her head, and he could practically see a layer or two of resistance slough off. "I can't wait to see them again."

"Only one more week," he said, clapping shut the phone and slipping it back into his pocket. "I've got something else for you, too."

Clearly intrigued in spite of herself, she looked up at him. "What?"

Troy retrieved the gift-wrapped box from the table and held it out. Karleen's gaze flicked to his as she flushed with obvious pleasure; then she wiped her hands on a dish towel and snatched it from his hands, the box top clattering to the floor in her haste to get it open. The tissue paper batted back, she let out a squeak of laughter.

"I don't believe it," she said as she lifted the tiny pink Onesie with Diva-in-Training written on the front in a flowery, glittery script. "And the *shoes*…" She let out one of those totally female, isn't-this-too-cute-for-words? sounds at the miniature lace-trimmed, satin shoes…and another one for the prissy little headband.

Then she stilled. "You actually went into a department store to buy these, didn't you?"

"I did. And look—" he lifted his arms "—I didn't even get hives."

Laughing softly, Karleen set the box on the counter, neatly tucking everything back into the tissue paper. "Thank you," she said, again not looking at him. She pulled a plump, shiny tomato out of a bowl on the counter, briskly rinsing it off before plunking it onto the cutting board. "They're all adorable."

Troy leaned against the counter, watching her swiftly dice the juicy, glistening fruit. "I've got a couple of possible nannies lined up to interview. Let me know what's good for you and I'll set up the appointments."

She shoved a stray hair behind her ear. "Doesn't matter, just tell me when and I'll be there."

He shifted, watching her earrings tremble as she worked. "So now that we've broken the ice, how about a kiss?"

As he hoped, her head swung around, her mouth open, and Troy swooped down for a nice, long, sweet smooch.

"*Why* do you keep doing that?" she asked the moment he pulled away.

He grinned. "Why do you keep letting me?"

"I don't *let* you," she said, returning her attention to the tomato. "You just go ahead and take what you want. And why are you laughing?"

"So if some guy, say, you never saw before came up and tried to plant one on you, you'd simply let him?"

"No! I'd—" She clamped shut her mouth.

"You'd what?" Troy said, toying with a strand of her hair by her shoulder, making her shiver. When she didn't answer, he chuckled. "Oh, come on, Kar—you like kissing me as much as I like kissing you. Why don't you simply admit it and make life easier for everybody?"

Whack, whack, whack went the knife before she finally said, "Easier for you, maybe. Not for me. Now can we please change the subject?"

"No problem." Still leaning against the counter, Troy let go of her hair, folding his arms. "So how's it going with your aunt?"

Karleen shrugged, scraping the tomato into the bowl. "I told her if she wanted to be around the baby she had to clean up her act."

"Really?"

"Really. And I guess it worked. To some extent, at least. She's definitely cut back on the drinking. And she swears she's looking for a job."

"You don't sound too hopeful."

Karleen went hunting in one of the bags for a cucumber. "Considering how many times she's sworn to change her stripes, only to fall right back into her old habits? And then pulling this little number—" she waved the paring knife between them "—didn't exactly rack her up any points, either."

"Or me?"

"Or you. You could've said no, you know."

"And why would I have done that?" When Karleen snorted softly, Troy pilfered one of the cucumber slices and popped it into his mouth. "You really think she'll still be here when the baby comes?" he said, chewing.

"Who knows?" Karleen said wearily, and Troy took the knife from her.

"Go sit down. You look beat."

"I'm fine—"

"Go," he said, pointing the knife at her, then the kitchen table. "Sit."

"You are *such* a bully."

"That's me, Troy the Terrible."

However, he heard her sigh behind him as she sank onto the chair. "I shouldn't be this tired at five months along."

"Not that you're stressed or anything."

"Says a major contributing factor to that stress."

Troy plunked the knife onto the cutting board and turned around. "Do you want me to leave?"

"God, yes."

"Think of your aunt."

"Believe me," she said with an edge to her voice that warranted taking seriously, "I am."

He wiped his hands on a paper towel and approached her. "You need to keep these up," he said, gently clasping her ankles to set her feet on a second chair. Then he crouched in front of her. "And maybe you should think about ditching the high heels. You could break your neck in those things."

Her eyes met his, glistening with tears. "Lord, if we did live together, one of us would be dead within the week."

"I'll take my chances."

Their gazes tangled for a second before she looked away. "Don't."

"Don't what?"

"I told you—"

"That you couldn't deal with me and your aunt at the same time. I got it. But even you've admitted she seems to be pulling herself together. So that just leaves me." He stroked her shins, refusing to take his eyes off her face. "Why am I so scary, Kar? I'm just a man. A man who's fallen in love—"

"Don't," she said again, the word barely more than a whisper. "Please."

Her apprehension wound around his heart even as he wrapped one hand around both of hers, laced tightly in her lap. Joanna's words shuffled through his brain, about how Karleen had never felt as though she really fit in anywhere, that, no matter how hard she'd worked to distance herself from her past, she still so often felt like an interloper in her present.

That he shouldn't give up.

"Do you have any idea how many days I feel like a total fraud?" he said.

Her eyes shot to his. "What?"

He smiled. "Blake and I worked our butts off to make Ain't It Sweet a success, but we had no idea it would take off the way it did. So I see my name listed as the CEO of a Fortune 500 company and I think, who the hell is this guy? Because deep down I'm the same middle-class schmo from Madison, Wisconsin, still the same chronically broke college kid riding around in the fifteen-year-old Chevy Nova that cost me a whopping two hundred bucks."

After a pause, he added, "Still the same kid who never knew from day to day if his father would be sober enough to even talk to him. So maybe we're not so different after all."

A long moment passed before Karleen said, "Go finish up the salad. If it's not done by the time Inky gets back we'll never hear the end of it."

When he'd been chopping for several seconds, though, she said, "Not one single woman on my mother's side of the family has ever had a relationship that lasted more'n a few years, Troy. Not *one*. We called it the Betsy Curse, in tribute to my great grandmother, who had seven children with four different men. The men in the family all married for life, but the women… Pathetic. We even used to take bets how long somebody or other's new beau or husband was gonna last."

The off-pitch note of her pain vibrated between them. "So you think your marriages were cursed?"

"What would you call it? And what does it matter? A curse, a run of really bad luck, a string of coincidences… The hurt's the same."

He dumped the sliced cucumber into the bowl, then turned. "And the fear?"

Her mouth twisted. "Fear's not a bad thing if it keeps you from making the same stupid mistakes. I don't know, maybe if I had a better handle on what had gone wrong before, I might feel more secure about trying again. But I don't. Yeah, I suppose I can chalk up my first two marriages going bad to being too young, or naïve, or both, to know what I was getting into. But I thought I'd had a few things figured out by my third, and that one didn't work, either. And the very thought of failing again, failing you…"

Ah.

"You won't fail me, Karleen."

Her eyes filled. "Oh, Lord, what *is* it with you? You don't know that! And what's more important, *I* don't know that. You want forever, Troy. And I have no clue how to do that! So you can shower me with pretty talk till the cows come home, but it doesn't change anything. I'm sorry, but this is one battle you're not gonna win."

Irritation spiked through him. "Pretty talk? Is that what you think this is?

When I tell you I love you, you think that's just *words?* Why would I do that, Karleen? Why would I keep putting myself in this position if I wasn't sincere?"

"Because I'm having your baby, for one thing!"

He stared at her, wondering how far he dared push, finally decided it wasn't like he had a whole lot to lose. "Is it so hard for you to believe that somebody could love you, just for you?"

Her eyes widened—*bull's eye*. And in them, he could see the starving dog, petrified to trust, but weakening all the same. Finally, though, she shook her head. "It really kills you not to be in control of the situation, doesn't it?"

"Not any more than it does you," he lobbed back.

He saw her chest rise with her breath as she rubbed her belly. "You are not the boss of me, Troy Lindquist," she said quietly, "and that's that. And why are you laughing?"

Because it was that or hit himself over the head with one of the cast-iron skillets hanging over the stove. But damned if he was going to run. If it was *more* she wanted, then by gum, *more* she would have.

"Because," he said, carting the salad to the table, "I'm getting this image of you going head-to-head with our teenaged daughter. Should be fun."

For the next several minutes at least, he savored the completely flummoxed look on her face.

A week later, Karleen was out back, picking still more tomatoes, when she heard a commotion out front that signaled Troy's parents'—and the twins'—return. She straightened, staring in the direction of all the shouts and laughter, a thick, sticky mixture of dread and anticipation clogging her throat. Not only because she and Troy had to finally come clean about the baby—she was beginning to look like she was trying to smuggle one of the pumpkins underneath her maternity T-shirt—but because the boys' being home again was bound to make things between her and Troy even messier than it already was.

And that was pretty damn messy.

Inky came out onto the back patio, flapping her hands to dry her nails. She'd found a clerical job with a small contractor, but since Inky was still in the stone age when it came to computers, it didn't pay much over minimum wage. So Karleen wasn't holding out much hope that this one would last longer than any of the others. She also had a hunch her aunt had started drinking again. No surprise there. When the inevitable you-know-what would hit the fan, Karleen couldn't predict, but the waiting was about to take her under.

"I take it that's them?" Inky asked. Karleen nodded. "Lord, couldn't you just eat those little boys *up?* His mama sure looks like she thinks she's God's gift, though. Sounds like it, too, bossin' everybody around."

"Oh, Eleanor's not so bad," Karleen said, twisting off another tomato from its caged vine. Since Troy's revelation about his father, Karleen had been inclined to see his mother in a more kindly light. "Bein' protective's not a crime. And she raised a good man. So I suppose she did at least something right."

Inky's gaze on her back was hotter than the mid-August sun, but she apparently decided to let Karleen off the hook this time.

"I'm goin' out tonight, did I tell you? A new guy, we met down at work. Who knows, maybe this'll be the one!"

Oh, Lord. Karleen watched as, still wagging her hands, her aunt clomped back inside, leaving Karleen to her tomatoes and her dread and an inner turmoil that only seemed to increase by the minute.

Troy was a good man, a kind man, a man who made her feel like she mattered, and her refusal to accept what he was offering hardly even made sense to her, at this point. Because the truth was she loved the man with everything she had in her. To have somebody like that actually love her back…

In some ways, she wanted nothing more than to simply let go, to let herself believe in something she hadn't believed in for a long, long time. But for too many years, she'd been the victim of false hope and unrealistic expectations. Men had said they'd loved her before, and changed their minds. They'd pursued her for the challenge, too— Troy's mother's words about his determination to get whatever he wanted never far from her thoughts—only to lose interest once she'd given in.

Add in her own justifiable—in her mind, anyway— fear of failure and the plain fact was she was tired. Tired of being disappointed, partly, but mostly of being that victim. So a big part of her taking charge of her life was learning what to avoid.

Including heartache.

Too bad heartache seemed to happen anyway. Like being It in a dodgeball game with cement blocks tied to your feet—no matter how hard you tried, you just couldn't get out of the way fast enough.

Karleen set another warm, ripe tomato in her basket, then stretched out her back. Damn thing had been giving her five fits, even though she had, in fact, given up wearing such high heels. Not because Troy had bugged her about it, though, but because she'd decided it probably wasn't safe, tromping around on stilts when she was beginning to have trouble seeing those stilts underneath her. Bad enough she had to ask Inky to polish her toenails for her these days.

The basket was getting heavy—how on earth three little plants could produce so many tomatoes was beyond her. She'd give some to Joanna, of course, whose talents did not expand to gardening. And, it occurred to her, some to

Troy's mother. Since the woman was bound to be part of Karleen's life for many years to come, she supposed a little sucking up wouldn't hurt.

Troy's patio door whooshed open; the boys and Elmo came roaring outside, and Karleen got that firecracker feeling in her chest again. Spotting her, the twins let out a whoop and tore across the yard, only to stop dead in their tracks ten or so feet from her fence. Mouth open, Scotty looked at Grady, then back at her.

"Are you gonna have a *baby?*"

Troy stepped out onto his deck, and their eyes met, and five thousand emotions roared through her, not the least of which was that she wished—oh, how she wished!—that she had the courage to take one more chance. That for the children's sake, at least, they could be a real family instead of whatever they'd manage to piece together.

Fixing a smile to her face, she set down the full basket and crossed to the fence, arms wide. "First things first— get over here and give me a hug!" The boys scrambled over the fence, and she plopped down cross-legged on the grass so she could hug them both, kissing first one, then the other, in their damp, messy curls.

"So are you?" Scotty asked.

By this time, Troy had climbed over the fence as well, to squat down beside them. He looked at her, and she nodded. Whatever was or wasn't going on between them, for the next few moments at least, this was about the boys.

"Karleen and I have a little surprise for you guys," he said. "You're going to have a baby sister, sometime around Christmas."

Grady gaped at his father. "No way," he said, so seriously that Karleen couldn't help but laugh. Then she took two grimy little hands and pressed them to her belly, where the baby had launched into her hip-hop number.

"Feel her kick?" she said, and Scotty leaned over to lay his ear against her tummy, and she tenderly stroked his curls, tears burning the backs of her eyes.

As thrilled as Troy was to have his sons home again, the sting of knowing that the woman he loved didn't trust him enough to share that love hadn't abated one whit. Not that he didn't understand her fear, because he did. In spades. After Amy, he'd certainly never figured on falling in love again. Marrying again—for companionship, for sex, for the boys—was one thing. Losing his heart a second time, however… He'd had no idea it was even possible.

Let alone to a woman who couldn't have been less like what he'd thought he was looking for. Falling in love with Karleen was like going to buy a minivan and ending up with a Corvette.

"Daddy?"

Remembering to smile, Troy sat on the edge of Grady's bed; the little boy immediately clambered onto his lap, pulling Troy's arms around him. Elmo flopped across Troy's feet, letting out a huge doggy sigh, as if *very* glad to be home, and Troy hung on tight to his son, reveling in the feel and smell of what he'd missed so terribly all those weeks. The boys were obviously having a hard time wrapping their brains around this new—to them—development. Not that they'd said much yet, but Troy could hear the gears grinding inside both blond heads as they desperately tried to make things add up.

"Yeah, squirt?"

"How do they know the baby's a girl?"

Relieved, he smoothed back his son's hair, as, like a

tropical snake, a skinny arm suddenly dangled from the upper bunk. Troy gently tugged at Scotty's fingers; a giggle floated down from overhead. "They used a special machine to take a picture of the baby inside Karleen. And they could see she's a girl."

Grady's brow puckered. "How? Is she wearing clothes?"

"No, dummy," Scotty put in, hanging over the safety bar. Half the time, both boys ended up in the bottom bunk, but they always started out the night separately. "Girls don't have *peenusses*."

Skeptical blue eyes shot to Troy for confirmation. "Yeah," he said, just waiting for the inevitable *But how does the baby come out?* query. "That's pretty much it."

Grady hugged an orange-haired Wild Thing stuffed toy to his chest. "What's her name?"

"Karleen and I haven't decided yet."

"Is she gonna live with us?" came from the peanut gallery.

Troy waited out the sting, then said, "She'll be here a lot. But mostly she'll live with Karleen. You'll be able to see her all you want, though."

"That's dumb," Grady said, hugging the toy harder. "Why can't we all live together?"

Troy briefly considered pointing out that once the baby became mobile—and insatiably curious about her big brother's things—their not all living in the same house wouldn't necessarily be a bad thing. Still, he'd gladly put up with the inevitable shrieks and bellows and "Why'd we have to have another baby, anyways?" if it meant putting up with Karleen, too.

"Because we can't," he said, thinking, *Yeah, that's smooth.* He maneuvered Grady back onto his pillow, tickling him for a second before tucking a racing car-patterned sheet and summer blanket around assorted skinny limbs. "You guys have had a long day," he said, kissing first Grady, then prodding the dog off his feet before reaching up to hug and kiss Scotty as well. "We'll talk more in the morning."

His father was settled into the sofa in the family room, watching some Civil War documentary on the History Channel. Having enough battles of his own to fight these days, Troy continued on to the kitchen, where his mother was washing out thermoses and things from their trip. Speaking of battles. He would've turned tail there, too, but he was thirsty.

Troy could feel her watching him as he crossed to the refrigerator for a soft drink. He pulled the can's tab and dropped into a kitchen chair, his feet crossed at the ankles.

"Don't start," he said.

Eleanor shook her hands and grabbed a dish towel, then joined him at the table, sinking her chin into her palm. "The boys talked nonstop about her the whole trip. They're completely in love."

"They're four," he pointed out.

"You're not."

Troy took a swallow of his soda, then leaned forward, averting his gaze. "I told her about Dad."

His mother straightened, her hand suspended in midair. "Why on earth did you do that?"

"Because she needed to know that somebody understood."

"Oh, no… She's not—?"

"No, her aunt. And her mother, apparently. Karleen's had it pretty rough." His eyes swung to his mother's. "And you know how it is—it's easier to beat yourself up for something that's not even your fault than to admit that maybe the problem's bigger than you are."

Understanding dawned in his mother's eyes. "She won't let you in."

"Not far enough to do any good. And don't you dare say it's probably for the best."

"Fine, I won't say it. But for goodness' sake, honey… sometimes, all a person can do is say *enough is enough* and move on."

"You didn't with Dad."

"The hell I didn't. When I walked out of that house I was fully aware that I was quite possibly walking out on my marriage, too. I still loved your father, but I'd had it with his refusal to admit he needed help."

"You're talking apples and oranges, Mom—"

"Not as much as you might think. Stubbornness is stubbornness, no matter what form it takes. Honey, Karleen has many good points—a lot more than I'll admit I gave her credit for in the beginning—but trust me, nothing hurts more than being shut out. Except, perhaps, realizing there's nothing you can do to *make* the other person open up. And the harder you try to force open the door," she said, her eyes littered with jagged shards of leftover pain, "the more determined the person on the other side becomes to keep it closed."

Much, much later, as Troy lay awake, listening to the grandfather clock in the living room chime every freaking hour on the hour, he had to admit his mother had a point. Still, he couldn't simply say "Oh, well," and walk away, leaving Karleen to rot inside that damned emotional foxhole she'd dug for herself. Whether that made him weak or strong, he had no idea. But that was who he was. So the world, and his mother, and Karleen, would just have to damn well deal.

Around six or so, he gave up sleep as a lost cause, pulling on jeans and a T-shirt to retrieve the Sunday paper from, natch, the middle of his front yard. He'd no sooner snagged the paper out of the wet grass, however, when a moan from Karleen's yard stopped him in his tracks. He looked over, doing a double take.

Because there, among the pinwheels and whirligigs and cast-stone fauna, Karleen's aunt lay flat on her back, passed out cold.

Chapter Thirteen

Troy tossed the paper onto his porch and started toward the yard, a host of rancid memories leaking into his fresh, hot-off-the-grill fury. Out of the corner of his eye, he saw his father step outside in a white T-shirt and droopy cargoes, his fishing hat plopped on his head.

"Oh, no… Is that Karleen's aunt?"

But Troy didn't stop to answer, sensing the older man following him as he hopped the low fence and strode over to Inky. He loomed over her comatose form, his hands clenched, fighting off the combination of disgust and dismay washing over him.

"It's always worse, seeing it from the other side," his father said in a low voice beside him, then gently squeezed Troy's shoulder. "I know I've already apologized for what I put all of you through, but I'm so sorry, Troy. A thousand times over."

"I know. But right now," he said, considering his options, "I'm only worried about Karleen."

With a soft groan, Inky stirred, opening one eye. Except for her wrinkled dress, raccoon eyes and haystack hair, she didn't look any the worse for wear. A smeared, shaky smile stretched across her face.

"Hey there, sugar," she said, wiggling the fingers of one hand, then trying to sit up. "Guess I didn't quite make it to the front door…. Oh, hell." With another groan, she collapsed bonelessly back onto the grass.

"Inky!" Karleen squealed from the porch, yanking her shortie robe closed as she hustled barefoot down into the yard. Troy caught a glimpse of beet-red face as she skittered past to clumsily drop to her knees beside her aunt, snatching pieces of grass and such out of the woman's hair as she lit into her.

"You promised, dammit!" she said in a low, dangerous voice. "You *promised* we weren't gonna go through this again!"

"I'm sorry, baby," Inky murmured from her prone position, her eyes closed, then clamped limp fingers around her niece's wrist. "But would you mind if we dealt with this later? I don't feel so good."

"I'm sure you don't. But oddly enough, I'm not exactly experiencin' a wellspring of sympathy for you at the moment, either—"

"Karleen…" Troy began, but she shot him a look that froze the words in his throat. Beyond the mortification and the helpless anger—emotions he knew all too well—there was no mistaking the emotional and physical toll her aunt's addiction was taking on her. Especially at this hour. And without her makeup. Her eyes were bloodshot, her skin practically colorless, and exhaustion and worry had begun to seriously erode the early pregnancy plumpness in her cheeks.

That's it, he thought.

Not that he had any idea at the moment what *it* was supposed to be, but before the day was out there was going to be some serious man-action taken or his name wasn't Troy Lindquist.

Grasping her aunt under the arms, Karleen heaved the now-moaning woman into a sitting position. "It's okay, I've got it, you can go now," she grunted.

Right. As if Troy had any intention of letting a pregnant woman—especially this pregnant woman—singlehand-edly haul her larger aunt to her feet.

Troy glanced at his father, then gently lifted Karleen out of the way. "We know the drill," he said, grabbing Inky's arms while his father got her feet.

"Even if I was usually the one playing the part of the drunk," his father said.

They started toward the house, Inky stretched out between them like a felled deer, until she suddenly came to enough to mutter, "I think I'm gonna be sick…."

Ten seconds later, after a cursory glance at her poor plastic roses, Karleen led everyone into the house, direct-ing them to deposit her aunt in the hall bathtub (yes, fully clothed). It was clear, both from her tight-lipped expres-sion and her take-charge attitude, that she, too, knew the drill. All too well.

Inky mumbled something incomprehensible and passed out again, snoring softly.

Karleen ushered both Troy and his father down the hall. "Thank you," she said as graciously as a woman can who's just had a drunken relative delivered to her bathtub, "but I'll take it from here."

When they reached her still-open front door, Troy's father took her by the shoulders. "If there's anything I can do—"

"Thanks, Gus." She stood on tiptoe to kiss him on the cheek. "But I'll be okay."

He gave her a quick hug and Troy a raised eyebrow, then went outside, where he located Karleen's hose and started to wash down her roses.

"Just shoot me now," she mumbled.

Troy stood as close as he dared behind her, haunted by his conversation with his mother. "You know, denial's not only a problem for the person with the addiction."

She pivoted, frowning. "My aunt just passed out in my front yard. I'm not *denyin'* anything, least of all that she needs help."

"No, you're just denying *you* do."

He saw tears gather in her eyes before she looked away, and Troy had to squelch the urge to shake her.

And yet, it wasn't like he didn't understand where she was coming from, didn't remember his own feelings of helplessness and humiliation as a kid. Or the staunch example his mother had set all those years. But then, the downside to pride was that it made you believe even an illusory sense of control was better than nothing. But if pride was all you had, he realized with a rush of tenderness for the woman in front of him, you hung onto it with everything you had in you.

How could he take that away from her?

Very, very carefully, he thought, as something sparked inside his head.

So when she said, quietly, "Please go, I'll be fine," all he said was "If you need anything—"

"I know," she said. "Thank you."

Over the Tetris-like sensation of ideas falling into place

in his brain, Troy heard the door shut behind him as he walked away. The boys were still asleep when he got back to his house, but his parents were both in the kitchen, which smelled of coffee and heated griddle, waiting for the sizzle of pancake batter. They both turned to him, their brows raised expectantly.

"Okay," he said. "Here's the plan…."

Her aunt's announcement left Karleen so stunned, it took her a good half minute to find her voice. "What do you mean, you're moving out?"

"Just what I said." Inky scooped all her underwear out of the top drawer of the bureau in Karleen's guest room and dumped it into her soft-sided bag. "Troy's payin' the deposit and first month's rent on an apartment, on two conditions—that I don't screw up on the job he's offerin' me, and that I stick with AA this time." A bunch of tops joined the underwear in the bag. "I've already been to my first meeting, Troy's daddy went with me before he and Eleanor went back to Wisconsin."

"How…? When…?"

"Troy and his daddy came over to talk to me on Sunday afternoon. Lord, I must've looked like death warmed over. God knows I felt like it. Anyway, you'd gone off with Troy's mama and his boys to the mall. From what I could piece together, that was part of the plan. To get you out of the way so they could deal with me without you gettin' all out of shape."

Karleen watched her aunt scurry around the room, tossing this, that and the next thing into her bag, trying to digest this unexpected—and borderline bizarre—turn of events. And where Troy got off playing God. The creep. And why his doing so was making her heart go pitty-pat in a way it had never done before. Still, being of a sound and realistic nature, she couldn't help but say, "And why is *this time* different from all the other times?"

Her aunt gave her a wounded-to-the-quick look. "You know, I wouldn't mind a little support. If Troy trusts me, why can't you? After all," she said, folding up the grass-stained dress from her little adventure and stuffing it into the bag, "it's not like he doesn't have firsthand experience with the subject. And if his daddy could make it…well, then, so can I."

"In theory, yes." Karleen lowered herself into the wicker chair by the bed. "But you can hardly blame me for being skeptical."

Inky regarded her for a second or two, then let out a rush of air before sitting on the edge of the mattress across from her. Her charm bracelet jingled when she reached for Karleen's hand. "I can't go on the way I have been, honey," she said. And Karleen had to admit, that was a new level of sincerity in her aunt's eyes. "And I can tell you're at the end of your rope with me. And frankly, so am I. Passing out on your lawn like that…" Her head wagged from side to side. "That's just not *right*."

Out of the corner of her mental eye, Karleen could see the angels, huddled in the wings, waiting for their cue to shout "Hallelujah!" But she wasn't ready to give it to them, not yet.

"…Especially since it's because of me you keep putting off Troy."

"Excuse me?"

"Oh, come on, honey—when you said you had your reasons for not accepting his marriage proposal, it doesn't take a genius to figure out I was one of those reasons."

"You weren't-" When her aunt lifted one brow, Karleen

sighed. "So what's this about a job?" she asked, pulling her hand out of her aunt's and leaning back in the chair. "Doing what?"

Inky got up again, this time to get her shoes from the closet. "Cooking, believe it or not. To start, anyway. Something about needing a lunchtime cook for their new cafeteria? But they also have these training classes I could take in the afternoons, using a computer and what-all." She looked at Karleen, her eyes actually sparkling. "And it doesn't pay stupid minimum wage, either."

Underneath Karleen's halter top, the baby shifted. The flutterings were beginning to feel more like real kicks now. She soothed a hand over her belly, then lifted her eyes again to her aunt. "It won't be easy."

"Tell me something I don't know."

"And if you backslide—"

"There will be holy hell to pay. From all sides. I know that, too. I also know it's high time I stop giving lip service to how much I love you and start proving it. And before you jump to any conclusions about Troy only doing this to get in *your* good graces…" She shook her head. "He's not. Said he knew that was a lost cause."

Karleen swallowed past the sudden knot in her throat. "He actually said that?"

"He did. Then again he also said nothing was more important to him than your welfare—and the baby's, of course—so make of that what you will." Inky laughed. "In fact, he said he was *this close* to bodily removing me from your house, he was that worried for you. Now did I get everything out of the bathroom…?"

"Inky, you don't have to leave. Really. You can stay as long as you want—"

"And deny myself the same opportunity to stand on my

own two feet as you? No way. Yes, I'm accepting the leg up Troy's offerin' me, but so what? All he's doing is giving me a chance. I'm the one who has to make something of it."

"But I still don't understand—"

"Why he's helping me? That one's easy. Because you won't let him help *you*. So he figured out how to get around that little obstacle. And let me tell you something else, missy—the day *I'm* too scared to take the chance on a good man like that is the day they'll be saying my eulogy."

"But—"

"And don't even start about *the curse*. That's a lot of hooey and you know it. Whatever curse there was, we all brought on ourselves. If you set your sights low, lowlifes is about all you can expect to attract. But the minute you started to believe you were capable of more than your mama, or me, or Granny, or any of the rest of 'em, you left all of us in the dust. Hell, girl—if you went to all that trouble to pull yourself up out of the mud, why not enjoy what's waitin' for you on the shore?"

As Karleen sat there, blinking at her aunt, Inky went on. "And you know, whether *I* 'make it' or not is beside the point. Not that I don't intend to. But Troy's wanting to protect you, to take care of you, to stand by you, *is*. How you can just throw that away is beyond me."

Inky zipped closed her bag, then hauled it off the bed before tippy-tapping over to kiss Karleen's cheek. "Well, I'm off to start my new life." She smiled. "Maybe you should think about taking the next step in yours?"

Two glasses of ice water in his hands, Troy walked over to Karleen, standing on his deck. Her gaze rested on his yard, deeply shadowed in the late afternoon light, even as her hand rested on her tummy. "So what did you think?"

he asked, handing her one of the glasses, which she took without meeting his eyes.

"The first one, definitely. Mrs. Brooks." She took a sip of the water, hugging herself with one arm. She'd dressed conservatively—for her—in a black tube top maternity pants outfit, her hair pulled back into a ponytail. She still wore at least a half-dozen rings, but she'd toned down the bling by a few thousand kilowatts. "I liked her smile. And her sense of humor."

Smiling himself, Troy took a seat on the glider. "Then I'll call her back, have her come over when the boys are here."

Karleen nodded, but made no move to leave.

Here it comes, he thought, bracing himself. Or rather, re-bracing himself, since for three days he'd been holding his breath, waiting for one pissed-off pregnant woman to land on his doorstep to read him the riot act. That she hadn't, even when he'd called to say he'd set up interviews with a few potential nannies, had rattled him more than he was about to let on.

Then again, perhaps she'd only been marshaling her forces before launching her attack. When she finally turned to him, however, her brows drawn, instead of anger he saw only genuine curiosity.

"The only thing I don't understand," she said, like they'd been having this conversation all along, "is why you'd take such a huge chance on somebody you don't even know."

"I take it we're talking about your aunt and not Mrs. Brooks?"

A smile tugged at her lips. "Sorry. Yes."

"Let's just say I decided to believe her when she said she was ready. Because I saw the same combination of defeat and determination in her eyes that I saw in my father's, when he finally realized what he stood to lose. You're all Inky has, honey. The last thing she wants is for you to hate her."

"If I'd been capable of hating her," Karleen said, "it would've happened long before this."

"I know."

"Still," she said on a breath, "she's stumbled so many times before…."

"So did my father. So do most alcoholics. It's a day-by-day battle, Karleen. But you can't give up. In fact, they're counting on you, to keep being strong when they aren't."

Karleen looked away again. "Inky said you told her it had nothing to do with me."

"No," he said quietly, "what I said was, I didn't step in because of anything I hoped to gain for myself. In fact, considering your oft-stated position on letting me help you, I figured you'd have my head on a platter. But it had everything to do with you."

When she faced him this time, the frown was deeper. "I don't—"

"I did it because I know how hard it is to be someone else's support when you're still trying to get your own act together. And because I love you."

"*Why?*" she choked out. "Why do you love me? I've been nothin' but a pain in the butt the whole time."

"Not the *whole* time," Troy said, smiling. "And when you weren't, I saw flashes of something that had been missing from my life for far too long."

"It can't be that simple."

"Sure it can. If you let it."

Her brow still crumpled, Karleen looked away again, holding her sweating glass to her throat; Labor Day was fast approaching, but fall weather wouldn't happen for a good six weeks yet. "I was mad as hell at you at first. For sticking your big old nose in. I might even be still, a little. But if this takes…" One ringed finger toyed with a thin gold chain resting against her collarbone. "It'd be pretty small of me to resent you for accomplishing something I never could…" Her mouth pressed tight, and, with a pang, Troy realized exactly how much she was laying herself on the line.

"Don't shortchange yourself, honey," he said. "If Inky hadn't been ready, nothing I'd said would have made any difference, either. And she was ready because of you. You'd had years to loosen the lid. All I did was pop it off."

Karleen let out a soft half laugh, then set her glass down on a nearby table, picking up her keys instead. Her flat sandals slapped against the wooden deck as she crossed to him, then leaned over to kiss him on the cheek. "Thank you," she whispered.

Troy grabbed her wrist, fingering her steady, rapid pulse. Her pupils bloomed in her eyes, dark and wary. And he smiled again, oddly at peace. "You deserve everything you want out of life, sweetheart. With someone who gets who you are. And appreciates it."

Then he dropped her hand, lacing his own across his stomach and squinting out over his yard. For several seconds, Karleen didn't move, until at last she whirled around and slip-slapped down the steps and across his yard, through the gate his father had inserted in the fence between their properties.

And Troy watched her, an old song playing in head. Something about wishing her cozy fires and bluebirds and lemonade. But especially, he thought as his heart splintered into a million pieces, he really did wish her love.

Even if it wasn't with him.

And then, on a long, shuddering breath, he set her free.

* * *

When the sun came up the next morning, Karleen was right there to witness it, seeing as she hadn't slept but maybe three hours the entire night. She unfolded herself from the chaise on her patio and went back inside, where Britney was still up, too, running her skinny little paws off on her exercise wheel. Karleen fixed herself a fresh buttered bagel and carried it out to the living room, where she pinched off a plain piece for Britney and dropped it into her cage.

All night long, she kept seeing that look in Troy's eyes. The look that said *he* was the one who "got" her.

Who loved her.

Really, truly loved her, the way no man on earth had ever loved her before. He looked at her like she was everything, made her feel like he'd do anything for her. In fact, he already had, hadn't he?

She chewed her bite of bagel for a while, thinking about that. Underneath her heart, the baby squirmed, like she was trying to get comfortable.

"The thing is, sweetie," she said, rubbing her tummy as she paced back and forth, "maybe I'm goin' about this all wrong. I know, I know…that's the last thing you expected me to say. But then, never let it be said that your mama can't admit her mistakes. Well, here's another one— maybe…maybe your daddy and I aren't so different, after all. I mean, I suppose I could learn to live with Early American. If I absolutely had to."

Her cheek pouch stuffed with fresh bagel, the hamster lifted sharp, beady eyes to Karleen, clearly astounded.

Figuring she may as well take advantage of her audience, Karleen plunked down into a chair close to the cage, twisting her feet around the chair legs the way she used to do when she was little. "So what do you think,

Brit? I mean, I've got a really crappy track record, right?" She pinched off another piece of the bagel, gave it to the hamster. "If I go for it, and it doesn't work… Oh!"

The baby kicked harder than she ever had before, and Karleen laughed. "You tryin' to tell me something, li'l bit?"

And as Karleen sat there, licking butter off her fingers, she thought…why *shouldn't* she have another shot at happiness? So she had a few broken marriages in her past. So what? Troy *wasn't* like the others. But more important, *she* wasn't the same person now she'd been then, either. Like Inky had said, she set her sights a lot higher these days. And if she believed she deserved better in every other aspect of her life, then why in the name of all that was holy shouldn't real, true love be part of that package?

She sucked in a breath. Lord, Inky was right. Everybody was right. Including Troy. She did deserve the best life had to offer.

Or, in this case, what the father of her child had to offer. Which was more than a name, or his protection, or even his money, but the chance to get it right.

"Britney, sugar," she said as she got up, giving the hamster the last little bite of bagel. "Don't take this the wrong way, but you are *not* enough."

Her cheeks stuffed with bagel, Britney waddled back to her sleeping tube. Somehow, Karleen didn't think she'd taken offense.

Suddenly overcome with exhaustion, Karleen lay down on the couch in the living room, almost immediately falling asleep. And when she awoke two hours later, the room was filled with rainbows.

Not illusions. *Promises.*

Hauling herself upright, she caught sight of one of the

child-care books Eleanor had insisted on buying for her when they'd been at the mall. As if pushed, she got up and riffled through the piles of God-knew-what on her desk in the corner of the room until she found the piece of paper she'd written the Lindquists' address and phone numbers on. Then, before she could talk herself out of it, she grabbed the portable phone from the coffee table.

The minute she heard that somewhat imperious voice on the other end of the line, she burst out with, "Eleanor, it's Karleen. Who, if I haven't completely screwed things up with your son, is gonna be your new daughter-in-law. No, you listen to me," she said when Troy's mother tried to interrupt. "I love Troy with everything I have in me, more than I've ever loved anybody in my life, and I know he loves me, too. More than anybody's ever loved *me*. And I know I may not be the classiest thing going, but I swear on the Bible that I will make him the best wife I know how, and your grandsons a good mama, and—"

"Karleen," Eleanor said, chuckling.

"What?"

"Why are you telling *me* all of this?" she said, then Troy's daddy was on the phone, saying, "Please tell me you finally got your head on straight," and she said, "I guess so," and he said, "Good. Now get off the damn phone and go put that poor boy out of his misery."

Since nobody had come up to Troy after the morning conference and given him a concerned, "Is everything okay?" he felt reasonably sure whatever had come out of his mouth had made sense. Once out of the meeting, however, he'd plopped into the chair behind his desk, staring out his window at the vista of city and mountains and sky, replaying a particular fantasy in his head, one where he was Errol Flynn and Karleen was one of those doe-eyed twenties actresses, and he'd swoop down in a manly manner and cart her off to some remote island where he'd lavish riches and attention on her all the rest of her life and she'd shut up and let him lavish, dammit.

Life, he thought, glowering, should be more like a silent movie.

"Troy?" came his secretary Mallory's voice through his intercom, startling him.

Especially, he thought, glowering some more, the silent part.

"There's a Karleen Almquist here to see you?"

He blinked at the phone for two or three seconds before stabbing the answer button. "Send her in. And for God's sake, keep everybody else out."

He came around his desk as she walked through the door. They both froze, he in the middle of the floor, she with one hand behind her, still on the doorknob. She was dressed all in white, some wrinkly, floaty thing that made her look like a pregnant angel, especially with her hair all piled up on top of her head, although the Frisbee-sized earrings and unapologetic cleavage kinda nixed the angel look.

Then she was in his arms, and they were kissing, and even though about five thousand *What the hell?* bells were clanging inside Troy's head, who was he to question having his favorite pair of lips in the world against his? Finally, though, the bells got so loud he had to pay attention to them—which was the annoying thing about bells— so he gently set his hands on her shoulders and put a good quarter inch between them.

"Not that this isn't far superior to your average coffee break…but is there a point to this? Or did you wake up this morning and think, *Let's go torture Troy?*"

Softly giggling, she lowered her head to his chest. And he wrapped her up in his arms, just because he could. And the baby kicked, just because *she* could. And Karleen whispered, "Ask me."

Troy stilled, it taking a minute to summon back enough brain cells from elsewhere to process her question. But when they got there, all out of breath from zipping to and fro like that, they started shouting, *What the hell do you think she's saying, fool?*

He held up one finger. "Hold that thought," he said, then did some zipping of his own, over to a small safe he kept in the office. A minute later, he was on one knee, holding out the small aqua box. Karleen's eyes got huge.

"Is that…?"

"Just a little something I picked up last time I went to Dallas," he said, then flipped it open, and she let out a soft "Oh, my God," and looked as though she'd faint, so he figured he'd done good.

"Will you marry me, Karleen?"

"Sugar, for that ring I'd marry Godzilla."

"Nice to know. Is that a yes?"

One hand clamped onto the edge of his desk, she awkwardly lowered herself to her knees, as well, threading her arms around his neck. "Yes," she said, her eyes watery, her mouth stretched into the brightest smile he'd ever seen. "Yes, yes, yes," she said, kissing him again. "I was only kidding about the Godzilla thing, though."

"I knew that," he said, then took the three-carat Tiffany out of the box, removed the ten-dollar glass monstrosity from her ring finger, tossed it over his shoulder where it clunked off the top of his desk, and slipped on the real deal. "But I know how much you love sparkly things."

She chuckled. Then she said, "I think we both need to get up now before we're stuck here forever."

"Good idea."

He hauled her to her feet, and they kissed some more, after which she went over to the window to watch the ring sparkle in the sunlight. And Troy waited for the penny to drop.

"Troy?"

"Hmm?"

"If I kept saying no..." She turned. "Why'd you have an engagement ring in your safe?"

Smiling, he crossed to her, taking her in his arms again. "I could let you go—I *had* let you go—but somehow, I couldn't give up on you. Not quite yet."

"I see. How long were you plannin' on waiting? Before you did give up?"

"Oh, I don't know." He shrugged. "Forty, fifty years, maybe?"

Her eyes teared again. "You really won't leave me, will you?"

"Not as long as there's breath in my body. Jeez," he said when the baby walloped him. He placed his hand on Karleen's belly, chuckling when Little Miss Diva kicked him again. "What are you doing in there, peanut?"

Laughing, Karleen covered his hand with her own. "A Snoopy dance. That her mama's finally come to her senses."

"You mean, like this?" Troy said, letting her go to launch into an old football victory dance from the dark ages, and Karleen shrieked with laughter, and Troy saw a lifetime of laughter, and tacky lawn ornaments, and making love underneath leopard-print throws, and a four-poster bed flanked by brothel-worthy lampshades.

And filled with their children.

And he danced all the harder.

Epilogue

"Is it time to get her up yet?"

Holding her satin robe closed, Karleen went into the baby's room, her breasts full inside the nursing bra, her feet already cramped inside her white satin bridal sandals. Still in his jeans and T-shirt, five-year-old Scotty stood beside the crib in the dimly lit room, his long fingers wrapped around the rails, peering at his sleeping baby sister. From the kitchen she could hear Inky and Eleanor—Troy's parents were staying in Karleen's old house, which she'd decided to keep for the time being as a guesthouse for relatives—arguing with the caterers. While the sound produced a bubble of contentment in the center of Karleen's embarrassingly full chest, no way in hell was she going anywhere near the kitchen until this wedding was *over*.

"It is," she said, cupping Scotty's head before reaching

in to stroke Meredith's tummy. While both boys adored their baby sister, Scotty still couldn't take his eyes off her, even after four months. And, as the fuzzy-headed baby's eyes fluttered open, her tiny pink mouth stretching into a huge, toothless grin, Karleen could relate. She scooped the baby out of the crib and carried her over to her changing table to change her soggy diaper. "I have to feed her before I get dressed."

Watching the procedure, as he always did, with a combination of fascination and disgust, Scotty said, "Mama?"

"Yes, honey?"

"Why are you and Daddy getting married again if you're *already* married?"

"Well," Karleen said, cuddling the dry baby to her chest and starting out of the room, Scotty trailing behind her, "the first time was about making things neat and tidy and legal. This time, it's about celebrating." Which she sure hadn't felt like doing those last months of the pregnancy when her belly would enter a room five minutes before the rest of her. And wouldn't you know, Little Miss Diva had come two weeks late, to boot.

"And besides that," Troy said, coming up behind them in the hallway and hauling Scotty into his arms, "no way was I going to miss out on seeing this woman in a pretty white dress. Come on, buddy—let's go bug your grandmother and let Mama feed your sister."

Her husband leaned over and gave her a kiss that was a lot longer than it needed to be, and not nearly long enough, then strode back down the hall as Karleen stood there, watching him, pleased to discover that somewhere along the way she'd stopped wondering when she was going to wake up and find out this had all been a dream.

She went back into their bedroom, with the four-poster

bed with its traditional hobnail bedspread, and lowered herself into the plaid wing chair in the corner, where Meredith could get a good look at the rainbows splashed across the wall from all the crystals dangling from the red damask lampshade by the bed, and let out the sigh of a truly contented woman.

An hour later, she walked down the aisle, out in their backyard under a bank of flowering cherry trees (dotted with brightly colored birdhouses), in a designer wedding dress more beautiful than she could have imagined. And Troy stood up there, waiting, his gaze true and sure and calm, and she knew, without a shadow of a doubt, that for the first time—and the last—this man would work at their marriage as much as she would.

Because he was her partner.

Her friend.

The only man who'd ever bothered to see past the surface.

"Hey, there," he whispered when she reached him, cracking everybody up by kissing her before the minister had even started his *We are gathered here todays*. "Yes, ma'am," he said, eyeing the low, crystal-trimmed neckline, "this was *definitely* worth the wait."

She laughed, and gave her bouquet to Joanna—who'd never had a chance to serve as her maid of honor before this—and took Meredith from her aunt, and the three of them stood up there before God and everybody and made promises that Karleen knew deep in her heart would be kept.

Then Troy surprised her with a new wedding ring, this one a ring of diamonds to match her engagement ring, which he slipped over her new acrylic with a wink. And another kiss.

The dress, the ring, her husband's mouth…they all fit perfectly.

And so, at long last, did she.

* * * * *

A sneaky peek at next month...

By Request

RELIVE THE ROMANCE WITH THE BEST OF THE BEST

My wish list for next month's titles...

In stores from 15th June 2012:

❏ Pregnant by the Billionaire – Carole Mortimer, Kim Lawrence & Maggie Cox

❏ Fortunes' Women – Kathie DeNosky, Jan Colley & Heidi Betts

3 stories in each book - only £5.99!

In stores from 6th July 2012:

❏ A Passionate Mission – Marie Ferrarella, Caridad Piñeiro & Nina Bruhns

Available at WHSmith, Tesco, Asda, Eason, Amazon and Apple

Just can't wait?

Visit us Online

You can buy our books online a month before they hit the shops! **www.millsandboon.co.uk**